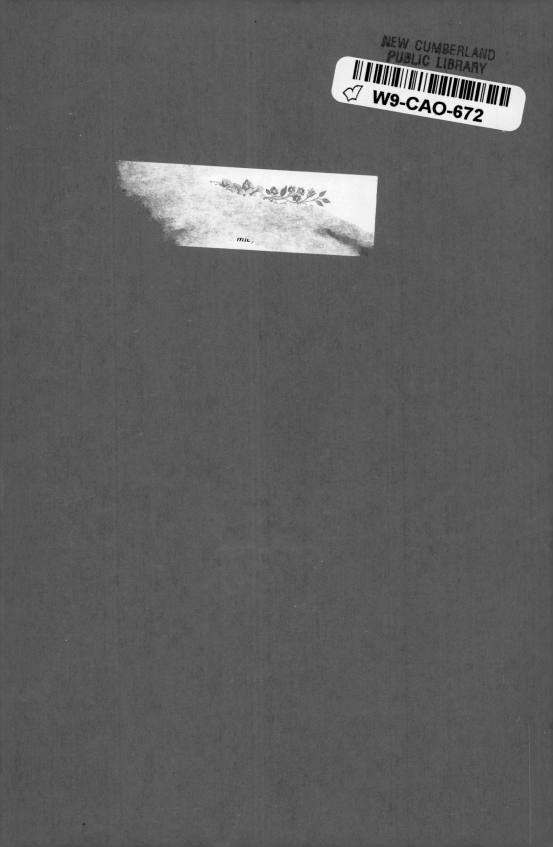

BEACH
MUSIC

NAN A. TALESE
DOUBLEDAY
NEW YORK LONDON TORONTO
SYDNEY AUCKLAND

PAT
CONROY
BEACH
MUSIC

PUBLISHED BY NAN A. TALESE

an imprint of Doubleday
a division of Bantam Doubleday Dell Publishing Group, Inc.
1540 Broadway, New York, New York 10036

DOUBLEDAY is a trademark of Doubleday, a division of
Bantam Doubleday Dell Publishing Group, Inc.

Illustrations by Martie Holmer

Library of Congress Cataloging-in-Publication Data
Conroy, Pat.
  Beach music / Pat Conroy. — 1st ed. in the U.S.A.
    p.   cm.
  I. Title.
PS3553.05198B43   1995
813'.54—dc20   95-13563
                                                CIP

ISBN 0-385-41304-1
ISBN 0-385-47578-0 (large print)
ISBN 0-385-47590-X (limited edition)
Copyright © 1995 by Pat Conroy
All Rights Reserved
Printed in the United States of America
July 1995

10 9 8 7 6 5 4 3 2 1

**This Large Print Book carries the
Seal of Approval of N.A.V.H.**

This book is dedicated to my three
wonderful and irreplaceable brothers:
MICHAEL JOSEPH, JAMES PATRICK,
and TIMOTHY JOHN—
loyalists and life-sharers.

And to THOMAS PATRICK,
our hurt brother and lost boy,
who took his own life on August 31, 1994.

ACKNOWLEDGMENTS

WITH SPECIAL THANKS TO THE FOLLOWING:

SUSANNAH ANSLEY CONROY, my youngest daughter and the great gift of my middle age, whom I love with my heart.

TIM BELK, life-friend, piano man, Southerner in San Francisco.

DOUG MARLETTE, my "Kudzu" friend, who has shown me that the artist works only with fire.

The novelist MICHAEL MENSHAW and LINDA KIRBY MENSHAW, who taught me the meaning of hospitality and made The Roman Years the magic ones.

DR. MARION O'NEILL, lifesaver and Hilton Head Islander.

NAN TALESE, my brilliant and lovely editor. My wish is that every writer could have such a magnificent editing experience.

JULIAN BACH, my agent and the last, great gentleman; and MARLY RUSOFF, my longtime Minnesota friend and one of the great loves of my life.

COL. JOSEPH WESTER JONES, JR., and JEAN GAULDIN JONES of Newbern, Tennessee, for their generosity, courage, and class.

And their son, CAPT. JOSEPH W. JONES III, American hero, KIA Vietnam, the father of my two oldest daughters, who did not live to see the lovely women his girls would become.

AND TO THESE ESSENTIAL ONES:

Lenore and the kids, Jessica, Melissa, Megan, Gregory, and Emily, Melinda and Jackson Marlette, Betty Roberts, Margaret Holly, Dennis Adams, Nuri Lindberg, Jane and Stan Lefco, Eugene Norris, Bill Dufford, Sallie and Dana Sinkler, Sylvia Peto, Sigmund and Frances Graubart, Cliff and Cynthia Graubart, Anne Rivers and Heyward Siddons, Terry and Tommie Kay, Mary Wilson and Gregg Smith, Bill and Trish McCann, Joseph and Kathleen Alioto, Yanek and Mary Chiu,

Henry and Liselle Matheson, Elayne Scott, Brooke Brunson, Carol Tuynman, Joy Hager, Ann Torrago, Bea Belk, Sonny and Katie Rawls, Chris Pavone, Diane Marcus, Sandee Yuen, Jesse Cohen, Stephen Rubin, Bill and Lynne Kovach, Herb and Gert Gurewitz, Steve, Riva, Peter, Ann, and Jonathan Rosenfield, Rachel Resnick, Dick and Patsy Lowry, Morgan and Julia Randels, the people of Fripp Island, the families and teachers of the Convent of the Sacred Heart in San Francisco, the Sobols, the Pollaks, the O'Hearns, the Nisbets, the Harpers of Central Florida, and the Gillespies of Jacksonville, my in-laws, Jean, Janice, Teri, and Bobby, also my niece, Rachel, and my nephews, Willie and Michael. And a fond bow to my first grandchild, Elise Michelle.

NOTE TO THE READER

I am grateful to those who shared their memories and experiences of the Holocaust with me and thus made this book possible:

Martha Popowski Berlin, whose parents, Henry and Paula, were Holocaust survivors, and it was Martha who helped me begin the journey that led to this book. The Atlanta Jewish Community Center, the Children of Holocaust Survivors—Atlanta. The Northern California Holocaust Center, and the Lourie and Friedman families, who welcomed me to their family reunion in Charleston. Thanks also to the many Jewish families in Atlanta who told their stories to me or my researcher, the artist Miriam Karp. I'm grateful to the Old New York Bookshop for publishing the pamphlet *During the Russian Administration: With the Jews of Stanislawow During the Holocaust,* by Abraham Liebesman. The translator from the Hebrew was Sigmund Graubart.

PROLOGUE

In 1980, a year after my wife leapt to her death from the Silas Pearlman Bridge in Charleston, South Carolina, I moved to Italy to begin life anew, taking our small daughter with me. Our sweet Leah was not quite two when my wife, Shyla, stopped her car on the highest point of the bridge and looked over, for the last time, the city she loved so well. She had put on the emergency brake and opened the door of our car, then lifted herself up to the rail of the bridge with the delicacy and enigmatic grace that was always Shyla's catlike gift. She was also quick-witted and funny, but she carried within her a dark side that she hid with bright allusions and an irony as finely wrought as lace. She had so mastered the strategies of camouflage that her own history had seemed a series of well-placed mirrors that kept her hidden from herself.

It was nearly sunset and a tape of the *Drifters' Greatest Hits* poured out of the car's stereo. She had recently had our car serviced and the gasoline tank was full. She had paid all the bills and set up an appointment with Dr. Joseph for my teeth to be cleaned. Even in her final moments, her instincts tended toward the orderly and the functional. She had always prided herself in keeping her madness invisible and at bay; and when she could no longer fend off the voices that grew inside her, their evil set to chaos in a minor key, her breakdown enfolded upon her, like a tarpaulin pulled across that part of her brain where once there had been light. Having served her time in mental hospitals, exhausted the wide range of pharmaceuticals, and submitted herself to the priestly rites of therapists of every theoretic persuasion, she was defenseless when the black music of her subconscious sounded its elegy for her time on earth.

On the rail, all eyewitnesses agreed, Shyla hesitated and looked out toward the sea and shipping lanes that cut past Fort Sumter, trying to compose herself for the last action of her life. Her beauty had always been a disquieting thing about her and as the wind from the sea caught her black hair, lifting it like streamers behind her, no one could understand why any-one so lovely would want to take her own life. But Shyla was tired of feeling ill-made and transitory and she wanted to set the flags of all her tomorrows at half-mast. Three days earlier, she had disappeared from our house in An-sonborough and only later did I discover that she had checked into the Mills-Hyatt House to put her affairs in order. After making appoint-ments, writing schedules, letters, and notes that would allow our household to continue in its predictable harmony, she marked the mirror in her hotel room with an annulling X in bright red lipstick, paid her bill with cash, flirted with the doorman, and gave a large tip to the boy who brought her the car. The staff at the hotel remarked on her cheerfulness and composure during her stay.

As Shyla steadied herself on the rail of the bridge a man approached her from behind, a man coming up from Florida, besotted with cit-rus and Disney World, and said in a low voice so as not to frighten the comely stranger on the bridge, "Are you okay, honey?"

She pirouetted slowly and faced him. Then with tears streaming down her face, she stepped back, and with that step, changed the lives of her family forever. Her death surprised no one who loved her, yet none of us got over it completely. Shyla was that rarest of suicides: no one held her responsible for the act itself; she was forgiven as instantly as she was missed and afterward she was deeply mourned.

For three days I joined the grim-faced crew of volunteers who searched for Shyla's remains. Ceaselessly, we dragged the length and breadth of the harbor, enacting a grotesque form of braille as hooks felt their way along the mud-flats and the pilings of the old bridge that connected Mount Pleasant and Sullivan's Island. Two boys were crabbing when they noticed her body moving toward them beside the marsh grass.

After her funeral, a sadness took over me that seemed permanent, and I lost myself in the details and technicalities connected to death in the South. Great sorrow still needs to be fed and I dealt with my disconsolate emptiness by feeding everyone who gathered around me to offer their support. I felt as though I were providing sustenance for the entire army in the field who had come together to ease the malignant ache I felt every time Shyla's name was mentioned. The word Shyla itself became a land mine. That sweet-sounding word was merciless and I could not bear to hear it.

So I lost myself in the oils and condiments

of my well-stocked kitchen. I fatted up my friends and family, attempted complicated recipes I had always put off making, and even tried my hand at Asian cuisine for the first time. With six gas burners ablaze, I turned out velvety soups and rib-sticking stews. I alternated between cooking and weeping and I prayed for the repose of the soul of my sad, hurt wife. I suffered, I grieved, I broke down, and I cooked fabulous meals for those who came to comfort me.

It was only a short time after we buried Shyla that her parents sued me for custody of my child, Leah, and their lawsuit brought me running back into the real world. I spent a dispiriting year in court trying to prove my fitness as a father. It was a time when I met a series of reptilian lawyers so unscrupulous that I would not have used their marrow to feed wild dogs or their wiry flesh to bait a crab pot. Shyla's mother and father had gone crazy with grief and I learned much about the power of scapegoating by watching their quiet hatred of me as they grimaced through the testimony regarding my sanity, my finances, my reputation in the community, and my sexual life with their eldest child.

Though I have a whole range of faults that piqued the curiosity of the court, few who have ever seen me with my daughter have any doubts about my feelings for her. I get weak at the knees at the very sight of her. She is my certification, my boarding pass into the family of man, and whatever faith in the future I still retain.

But it was not my overriding love of Leah that won the day in court. Before she took her final drive, Shyla had mailed me a letter that was part love letter and part apology for what she had done. When my lawyer had me read that letter aloud to the court, it became clear to Shyla's parents and everyone present that laying her death at my feet was, at best, a miscarriage of justice. Her letter was an act of extraordinary generosity written in the blackest hours of her life. She blew it like a kiss toward me as a final gesture of a rare, exquisite sensibility. Her letter saved Leah for me. But the ferocity of that court battle left me exhausted, bitter, and raw around the edges. It felt as though Shyla had died twice.

I answered my wife's leap from the bridge and the fierceness of that legal battle with a time of disorientation and sadness; and then with Italy. Toward Europe, I looked for respite and hermitage, and the imminence of my secret flight from South Carolina again restored a fighting spirit within me. I had made a good living as a food and travel writer and running away had always been one of the things I did best.

The flight to Europe was my attempt to place the memory of both Shyla and South Carolina permanently in the past. I hoped I would save my life and Leah's from the suffocation I was beginning to feel in the place where Shyla and I had come of age together. For me, the South was carry-on baggage I could not shed no matter how many borders I crossed, but my daughter was still a child and I wanted her to grow into young womanhood as a European, blissfully unaware of that soft ruinous South that had killed her mother in one of its prettiest rivers. My many duties as a father I took with great seriousness, but there was no law that I was aware of that insisted I raise Leah as a Southerner. Certainly, the South had been a mixed blessing for me and I carried some grievous wounds into exile with me. All the way across the Atlantic Leah slept in my lap and when she awoke, I began her transformation by teaching her to count in Italian. And so in Rome we settled and began the long process of refusing to be Southern, even though my mother started a letter-writing campaign to coax me back home. Her letters arrived every Friday: "A Southerner in Rome? A low country boy in Italy? Ridiculous. You've always been restless, Jack, never knew how to be comfortable with your own kind. But mark my words. You'll be back soon. The South's got a lot wrong with it. But it's permanent press and it doesn't wash out."

Though my mother was onto something real, I stuck by my guns. I would tell American tourists who questioned me about my accent that I no longer checked the scores of the Atlanta Braves in the *Herald Tribune* and they could not get me to reread Faulkner or Miss Eudora at gunpoint. I did not realize or care that I was attempting to expunge all that was most authentic about me. I was serious about needing some time to heal and giving my soul a much needed rest. My quest was amnesia; my vehicle was Rome. For five years, my plan worked very well.

But no one walks out of his family without reprisals: a family is too disciplined an army to offer compassion to its deserters. No matter how much they sympathized with all my motives, those who loved me most read a clear text of treason in my action. They thought that by forcing me away from South Carolina, Shyla's leap had succeeded in taking Leah and me over the rail with her.

I understood completely, but I was so burnt out I did not care. I threw myself at the Italian language with gusto and became fluent in the street talk of the shopkeepers and the vendors of our neighborhood. In the first year of our exile, working all the angles of my trade, I completed my third cookbook, a compilation of recipes I had gathered over a ten-year career of dining out in some of the best restaurants in the South. I also wrote a travel book on Rome that became popular with American tourists as soon as it hit the *giornalai.* I urged every American who read it to understand Rome was both sublime and imperishably beautiful, a city that melted into leaf-blown silences and gave a splendid return to any tourist adventurous enough to stray from the main trade routes of tourism. All the pangs and difficulties of my own homesickness went into the writing of that book. The artfully hidden subtext in those first years was that foreign travel was worth every discomfort and foul-up, but took a radical toll on the spirit. Though I could write about the imperishable charms of Rome forever, I could not quiet that pearly ache in my heart that I diagnosed as the cry of home.

I kept that cry to myself, in fact, did not even admit that it was something I heard or felt. I concentrated on the task of raising Leah in a culture alien to me and I hired a maid named Maria Parise from the Umbrian countryside and watched with pleasure as she took over the task of mothering Leah. Maria was a simple, strong-willed woman, God-fearing and superstitious, as only a peasant can be, who brought an undiminishable joy to the raising of this small motherless American.

In a short amount of time Leah became part of the native fauna around the Palazzo Farnese, a beloved *romanina* adopted by the people who lived and plied their trades around the piazza, and she rapidly turned into the first real linguist produced by my family. Her Italian was flawless as she navigated the teeming stalls along the Campo dei Fiori with its wild rivers of fruit and cheese and olives. Very early on, I taught Leah how to tell where we were in the Campo by using her sense of smell. The south side was glazed with the smell of slain fish and no amount of water or broomwork could ever eliminate the tincture of ammonia scenting that part of the piazza. The fish had written their names in those stones. But so had the young lambs and the coffee beans and the torn arugula and the glistening tiers of citrus and the bread baking that produced a golden brown perfume from the great ovens. I whispered to Leah that a sense of smell was better than a yearbook for imprinting the delicate graffiti of time in the memory. I knew that Leah had developed a bloodhound's nose when in the middle of the second year she stopped me as we passed by the Ruggeri brothers' *alimentari* and said, "The truffles have arrived, Daddy, they're here," as I caught that signature odor of pure earth. As a reward, I bought Leah a fraction of that truffle, priced as dearly as uranium, and sliced it into her scrambled eggs the next morning.

The raising of Leah consumed a large portion of my days and made me place my own sorrow over the loss of Shyla in a seldom visited back lot of my life, allowing me no time to devote to my own complex feelings over her death. Leah's happiness superseded everything in my life and I was determined I would not pass our family's infinite capacity for suffering on to her. I knew that Leah, as Shyla's child and my own, would get more than her portion of the genes of grief. Together, our families contained enough sad stories to jump-start a colony of lemmings toward the nearest body of water. I had no idea if the seeds of our madness burned in secret deposits in my beautiful child's bloodstream or not. But I vowed to protect her from those stories, from both sides of her family, that could set in motion the forces that had brought me spiritually bloody and beaten to the Fiumicino airport in the first place. I confess that I became the censor of my daughter's history. The South that I described to Leah at bedtime every night existed only in my imagination. It admitted no signs of danger or nightmare. There was no dark side to the

Southern moon that I recalled to my daughter, and the rivers ran clean and the camellias were always in bloom. It was a South that existed without sting or thorns or heartache.

Because I have inherited my family's gift for storytelling, my well-told lies became Leah's memories. Without realizing it, I made the mistake of turning South Carolina into a lost and secret paradise to my daughter. By carefully editing what I thought would harm her, I turned my childhood into something as glamorous as forbidden fruit. Though Rome would mark her with its most exacting emblems, I did not note the exact moment I touched my child with a lust to see the fierce, rarefied beauty of her birthplace. Even as Leah became part of the secrets that Rome whispered, she was not a native of the city, not indigenous like the flowery lichens that grew along the wall that held back the Tiber.

Almost every night in Rome, when I put Leah to bed, I would tell her a different story about either my or her mother's childhood. But there was one story she had me tell and retell over and over until it took on a fixed, by-the-numbers quality as rote as a catechist's response. Again and again, she would have me repeat the story of the night that Shyla and I first fell in love. Though we had grown up in houses that backed up to each other, had played together as toddlers, had waved back and forth from our bedroom windows, we had rarely thought of ourselves as anything other than best pals. I came from a family of five brothers and Shyla was the closest thing to a sister I ever had. Until the night on the beach in our senior year, when Shyla approached me in a most unsisterly fashion.

"I bet you flirted with Mama first," Leah would say.

"I did not," I said. "I was shy."

"Then why aren't you shy now?" she teased.

"Because your mother helped me make a delightful discovery," I said. "That I had a terrific personality."

"Even in high school?" Leah laughed, knowing the answer.

"I didn't have a personality in high school," I said. "I had pimples."

"But you dated Ledare Ansley, the class goddess, the head cheerleader," Leah said.

"She was shy too, though no one thinks a pretty girl has any right to be bashful. Because we were both afraid of everything, we made a perfect team."

"Her mother didn't like you at all," Leah said.

"She thought Ledare could do a lot better,"

I said. "She had a way of looking at me when I picked up Ledare as though I were a urine sample."

"You are always so crude," said Leah. "But you get mad at me if I'm crude ever."

"I never get mad at you. My job is to adore you. I find it easy."

"Go on with the story. Tell me about you and Mama falling in love. Get to the good part, to the beach party. Get to Mama, Capers Middleton, Mike, and Jordan."

As I spoke, my voice crossing the years and the Atlantic, Leah would always look at the photograph of her lovely, wide-eyed mother that rested on the bedside table. I knew that the story made her love her mother more deeply, feel closer to her in a way nothing else could, and it was just what I intended.

"I first fell in love with Shyla Fox, a girl I had known my whole life, on St. George's Island."

"It was St. Michael's Island," Leah corrected. "It's the island just before the Isle of Orion, where your mama lives now."

"That's right," I said, always pleased by her attention to detail. "A friend of mine was throwing a party at his father's house."

"It was Capers Middleton. His father owned the Coca-Cola bottling company in Waterford. He lived in the nicest mansion on Bay Street."

"Good girl. His father owned the beach house . . ."

"And Mama had dated Capers and a lot of other boys. She was real popular in high school, the sweetheart of Waterford High School. But Capers had brought her to the party."

"You gonna tell this story or you gonna let me?" I asked.

"You. I love the way you tell it," Leah said, her eyes resting again on her mother's picture.

Then I would begin in earnest, going back to St. Michael's Island during that storm-tossed year of northeast winds when the erosion along the barrier islands reached dangerous levels. On the shifting, undermined beach where part of an ancient forest was newly underwater to the north, the baseball team of Waterford High was throwing a party at high tide. It was the night it was predicted the Middleton house would begin to break up and fall into the sea. Four houses, a mile to the south, had been lost during the last spring tides. Though the house was condemned and abandoned, we were giving it a going-away party. Already it had begun to shift seaward, to lean toward the chased silver of the incoming breakers. The surf kept time to our dancing and counted out loud the slipping away of those last hours we would ever be teenagers. All of us had been there at the birth of rock and roll and we had done our part in putting rhythm and desire to music as we danced our way in both wildness and innocence through high school. The authorities had declared the house off-limits and we had broken through the sheriff's lock and liberated the house for one last party at flood tide.

I was almost eighteen and still in possession of that crazy edge of a teenager. Full of bravado and Maker's Mark, I had boasted that I was going to be in that house when it set sail from its anchorage on the old Seaside Road. Ledare Ansley, my date, had too much horse sense to stay in that tilted house illuminated only by the headlights of cars my teammates had driven to the party. On the way to the island, Ledare had told me sweetly that it was time we began seeing other people, that her parents were insisting that we break up soon after graduation. I nodded my head, not in agreement, but because I had not yet found my voice, which lay hidden under a hormonal frenzy that struck me nearly dumb. She also confided in me that she was going to ask Capers Middleton to accompany her to her debut at Charleston's St. Cecelia Society's Ball. My origins were iffy and much rougher than Ledare's, and my mother had warned me for years that this night was coming, but she'd never told me it would hurt as badly as it did.

The whole team and their dates had begun the night dancing to the music of transistor radios; the local station, WBEU, playing all the songs that had accompanied our class through four years of high school. The sea rose invisibly beneath us and the moon shone smooth and bright. A glossy flute of light, like velvet down a bridal aisle, lit the marlin scales and the backs of whales migrating a hundred miles at sea. The tides surged through the marsh and each wave that hit the beach came light-struck and broad-shouldered, with all the raw power the moon could bestow. Magically, an hour passed and we, ocean dancers and tide challengers, found ourselves listening to the sea directly beneath us as the waves began to crash in earnest against the house. Previous tides had already loosened the pilings and foundations pressing the house into the sands. When the noise of the surge and the breakup of concrete and wood grew too loud, many of my teammates and their dates broke prudently and ran for the line of cars and safety, as the water continued to rise beyond all believing. This great tide would eventually rise just over eight feet and it looked as though it meant to overwhelm the whole island. More and more of the dancers broke and ran laughing as the sea began to take the house apart from below. The salt-rusted nails were moaning like cellos in the grain of endangered wood. I was in the middle of doing the shag to "Annie Had a Baby" when a wave tore off the banister of the front porch and I lost my partner, Ledare Ansley, who fled outside with most of the others, squealing with fear and wearing my letterman's jacket.

Left alone, I took my pint of Maker's Mark up to the top floor and went out onto the deck just off the master bedroom. I stood face to face with the moon and the ocean and the future that spread out with all its bewildering immensity before me. It was a time in my life when many things bored me deeply and I hungered for beauty and those realms of pure elation granted to those who had the imagination to know what to look for and how to find it. It was one of the reasons I loved playing right field for the baseball team during that long season as we sparred on the immaculate fields in the sheer beauty of the game's discipline, a law unto itself. Right field was a home place for thinkers if you had the arm to keep the swift boys from going from first to third on a double. I had the arm and the mineral patience of the daydreamer and I roamed the outfield green, lamb happy and nervous when southpaws came to the plate.

A door opened behind me.

"Mama!" Leah squealed.

I looked around to see Shyla Fox in the moonlight. She looked as though she had dressed for this moment with the help of the moon. Bowing deeply, Shyla asked me if she could have the pleasure of this dance.

So we danced toward the central motion of our lives. The winds roared and a strange love rose like a tide between us and rested in the crown of waves that was loosening the frame of the house. Alone we danced beneath the full moon and the battery-powered light of cars as the team and their dates cheered each time they saw the giant shift taking place in the water-damaged foundation. As the Atlantic waters rose in a sanctioned dance of wave and tide, the house began to sway like the first terrible lifting of Noah's Ark. We could hear the other five remaining couples as they screamed with pleasure and terror in that room directly beneath us. I held Shyla closely, dancing with the girl who had taught me how to dance on the veranda of my house. Outside, the players and their dates were begging us to abandon the foundering house and join them at the driftwood fires. They screamed out of worry and honked their car horns out of pure admiration for our daring.

Then the house shuddered as a large wave struck against its cinder-block foundation.

Though I felt that same chilling fear that had sent the others running out of the house, Shyla's eyes held me as we listened to the hammering of the waves beneath us. The cries of our friends now turned to pleas each time a wave washed down over the broken-up road, the salt spray exploding off the beaten-down tarmac that had eroded over time like a cookie half-eaten by a child.

A deck piling snapped outside, loud as a rifle shot. On the radio the Drifters began to sing "Save the Last Dance for Me." Together, as though this scene had long been choreographed in some zodiacal prophecy, we said together and with no hesitation, "My favorite song."

From first note to last, we danced the song that became ours at that very moment. We were silent above the lapping waters as I spun her into the changed shape of a girl who looked at me as none other had. Before her eyes, I felt like a prince fresh-born on the crests of the light-driven waves. She granted me a beauty I did not have and my soul turned proud in the fury of her centered wanting of me. Watching, I felt her ardor creating something glittering and good from my heart. It was then that she led me into the bedroom and I found myself on the torn carpet with Shyla's lips pressed against mine, her tongue against my tongue, and I heard the fierceness and urgency of her whisper: "Fall in love with me, Jack, I dare you to fall in love with me."

Before I could answer, I heard the house shudder once again and push off as it took its first primal step toward the sea. The house tilted, then fell forward as though it were prostrating itself before the power of this once-in-a-lifetime tidal surge. It felt as though a mountain were trying to rise up beneath us.

We left the rug and went out to the newly imbalanced balcony, holding hands to steady ourselves. The moon lit the sea in a freeway of papery light and we watched the boiling white caps feeding on the broken cement scattered beneath the house. We continued to dance while the house kept its appointment with the long tide and I blazed with the love of this young girl.

Our love began and ended with seawater. Later, I would often wish that Shyla and I had entered into a lovers' pact that night and remained in that water-damaged house, enclosed in each other's arms, and had let the ocean pour through the open windows until we rose in some invisible withdrawal and allowed the sea to pull us in a death clench out toward the Gulf Stream and beyond all hurt of history.

When I saw Shyla last I identified her broken body at the city morgue with the Charleston coroner in attendance. He was a man of great compassion and he left me alone as I wept over her all but unrecognizable form. I prayed out Catholic prayers over her because they were the only ones I knew and they came as easily as tears, if only half-remembered. She was bloated from her time in the water, leaving all signs of her prettiness in the shallows of the harbor, and the crabs had done their work. Something caught my eye as I rose to leave her and I bent down and turned her arm. On her left forearm was tattooed the number 36 364 04.

"It was recently done," the coroner said quietly. "Any idea why?"

"Her father was at Auschwitz," I said. "It's his number."

"That's a first," he said. "You think you've seen everything here. But that's certainly a first. Odd. Was she very close to her father?"

"Not at all. They barely spoke."

"You going to tell the daddy about the tattoo?"

"No. It'd kill him," I said, looking at Shyla's body for the last time.

My name is Jack McCall and I fled to Rome to raise my daughter in peace. Now, in 1985, as I went up the spiral staircase that led to my

terrace and a rooftop view of Rome, I took a
music box that Shyla had given me as a present
on our fifth wedding anniversary. Winding it, I
looked over the Roman night. Far off, a bell
struck, sounding much like a lost angel, and a
breeze came off the Tiber. The music box
played Mozart's Piano Concerto No. 21, one of
my favorite pieces of music in the world. The
air was heavy with the dinner smells rising from
Er Giggetto's restaurant below: grilled lamb,
mint leaves, and sage. I closed my eyes and saw
Shyla's face again.

From inside the music box I took the letter
she had mailed to me on the day of her death
and looked at how she had written my name.
Her handwriting was pretty and she took special care whenever she put my name on paper.
I thought about reading it again but instead I
listened to the traffic moving past the Tiber
and lifted the gold necklace from the music
box. It had been a gift from her mother received at her sweet sixteen party and she had
never taken it off until that final day. The necklace had become part of my memory of our
lovemaking. In her will, Shyla made it clear she
wanted Leah to wear it when "she was old
enough to understand the nature of the gift."
Shyla's parents had asked for the return of the
necklace when they sued me for custody of my
child. Because it seemed like such a talisman of

evil and bad luck to me, I had often thought of mailing it to them with no note or return address. It was only a necklace to me that night and I put it back in the music box.

Though I did not know it as I scanned the passersby moving down below, I was in the middle of a year that would change my life forever.

PART I

CHAPTER 1

I AM USUALLY UP WHEN THE PIAZZA
Farnese awakens. In darkness I brew my coffee
and take a cup up to the terrace where I watch
first light come over the deer-colored city.

At six in the morning, the man at the newspaper stand arrives and begins arranging magazines beneath his canopy. Then a truck enters
the piazza from the west carrying bales of *Il
Messaggero* and other morning papers. The two
carabinieri who guard the entrance to the
French Embassy switch on the lights of their
jeep to begin their slow perfunctory circling of
the Palazzo Farnese. Wearing the same expressions, like face cards in a disfigured deck, the

carabinieri seem bored and usually you can see the pale glow of their cigarettes against the dashboards as they sit in their cars during the long Roman night. A van carrying fragrant bags of coffee then arrives in front of the Bon Caffè at the same time the owner of the café rolls up the steel shutters. His first cup of coffee always goes to the driver of the truck, the second to the owner of the newspaper stand. A small boy, the son of the owner, then takes two cups of black coffee to the carabinieri across the piazza just as the nuns in Santa Brigida begin to stir in the convent across from my building.

While it is still dark beneath the annealed stars and low-seated moon a nun opens the small steel gate in front of the Church of Santa Brigida, an act signifying that Mass is about to start. There is solitude in the fatigue of watching such beginnings and I then ritually count the thirteen churches I can see from my terrace. I was still counting them when I spotted a man who had been following us for the last few days enter the piazza from the Campo dei Fiori.

I slipped behind an oleander bush as the man looked up toward my terrace, then entered the Bon Caffè. I continued to count the bell towers and the four great moony clocks whose hands commemorated the exact moment of their death for Rome to see. I listened with pleasure to the music of the fountains in the piazza.

Across the piazza, a nun moved on the church's terrace this Monday morning, heedless as a moth in her mothering of roses. A brindled cat stalked a pigeon into the first slice of sunlight in the piazza, but a bum clapped his hands and shooed them both away. The man who'd been following me came out of the Bon Caffè and looked my way again. He lit a cigarette, then walked to the newspaper stand and bought a copy of *Il Messaggero.*

Below me the piazza began to bloom with life as carts rolled into it and pedestrians entered from the side streets. Pigeons called to each other from the stately rows of fleurs-de-lys that stretched along the entablature of the French Embassy. I love both the regularity and austereness of my piazza.

At 7 A.M. on this day the roofers returned to work on the apartment across the alley, replacing the old rows of ceramic tile with new ones, creating a strange music of nails against tiles that sounded like the playing of xylophones underwater. I finished my coffee and went down to wake up Leah for school.

As I walked over to her window and opened the shutter, Leah asked:

"Is that man still watching for us, Daddy?"

"He's waiting for us in the piazza, just like before."

"Who do you think he is?" she asked.

"I'll find out today, sweetheart."

"What if he's a kidnapper? Maybe he'll sell me to the Gypsies and I'll have to make a living robbing tourists."

"You've been talking to Maria again. Don't listen to her about Gypsies or about Communists. Hurry up, now. Get ready for school. Suor Rosaria always blames me if you're late."

"What if he tries to hurt me, Daddy?"

I lifted my daughter up into the air until we were looking at each other eye to eye.

"I told you before, your daddy may be stupid, but what else am I?"

"Big," she giggled.

"How big?"

"Real big. You're six feet six inches tall."

"What do the kids in your school call me?"

"They call you *Il Gigante,* the giant," she said, laughing again.

"I'm the giant. The guy down there's the little midget who climbs up the beanstalk."

"But the little midget kills the giant by chopping down the beanstalk," she said.

I hugged her and laughed. "You're smarter than hell, Leah. Just like your mama. Don't worry. That was a fairy tale. In real life, giants clean their teeth with the leg bones of guys like that."

"That's disgusting. I'm going to brush my teeth."

I heard Maria let herself in through the front door and call out *"Buon giorno, pic-colina"* to Leah as she passed in the hallway. Maria stored her umbrella in the front closet, then came to the kitchen where I poured her a cup of coffee.

"Buon giorno, Dottore," Maria said.

"I'm not a doctor, Maria," I answered in my own formal Italian. I am unable to master Maria's dialect. It sounds like part chirruping and part speech impediment, but she has never grown impatient when I have trouble understanding her.

"In Italy, you're a doctor," she said in Italian. "So enjoy it and hold your tongue. I love calling you *Dottore* in front of the other maids. They know I work for a man of leisure. By the way, your friend is still there."

"I saw him from the terrace. Does anyone know him?"

"The *portiere* talked to the owner of the Bon Caffè. The stranger says he's a tourist from Milano. But why would a tourist look only at this apartment and ignore the Palazzo Farnese. Bruno, at the newsstand, says that he's sure the man is a policeman and that you must be involved with drugs or the Red Brigades. None of the carabinieri have ever seen him but they're too young to have seen anyone but their mothers. He buys cigarettes in the *cartoleria* from Giannina. The whole piazza is watching him. He does not seem dangerous. They said to tell you not to fear."

"Tell them thanks. I'll try to repay them."

"No need," she answered. "Even though you and *la piccolina* are foreigners, you are part of the piazza. Everyone watches out for his neighbor."

"Marry me, Maria," I said, taking hold of her hand. "Marry me and I'll give you my money and let you raise my child."

"You speak foolishness to me. *Sciocchezze,*" Maria said, giggling madly and jerking her hand away. "*Americano pazzo.* You tease me too much and one day I say yes and what will you do, *Dottore*?"

"Call the Pope and tell him to get his ass over to Santo Pietro for a wedding ceremony."

"You are too big for me, Signor McCall," she said, appraising me. "You would kill me in bed."

"Excuses, excuses," I replied as Leah appeared in the kitchen doorway already dressed for school. She smiled broadly so I could inspect her carefully brushed teeth. I went over her, checked her ears and neck, and nodding approval, I sent her toward Maria, who began to put the child's hair in pigtails. Leah's hair was a dark wave that kindled beneath the electric light. When she shook it, it shimmered, roiled like something half-animal, half-river.

"Bellissima. Bellissima," Maria sang as she twisted Leah's hair into fine braids. "Prettiest little girl in the piazza."

The Piazza Farnese was the central fact of Leah's life. She was blissfully unaware that I was on the run from a past that had put too many hunters in the field against me. She did not remember the flight out of South Carolina to New York or the night flight on Alitalia that brought us to Rome.

She squeezed my hand as we said good morning to the *portiere* and stepped out into the bright light.

The waiting man turned his back and lit another cigarette. Then he pretended to read a historical marker placed just above the door of the *farmacia*.

"You won't fight him, will you, Daddy?" Leah asked.

"You've got my word I won't fight him. You think I'm stupid? After what happened last time."

"It scared me when you went to jail," she said.

"Not half as badly as it scared me. Rome ended your daddy's boxing career."

"All the nuns know you were in prison at Regina Coeli," she said, with great eight-year-old disapproval. "Even Suor Rosaria. It's very embarrassing."

"It was a cultural misunderstanding," I explained as we walked through the crowded piazza. "*Il Gigante* thought he had to kick ass. It was an error in judgment that any American could have made."

"You owe me a thousand lire," Leah said.

"I didn't say a cuss word. I don't owe you a dime."

"You said the 'A' word. That's a thousand lire."

"Ass is not a cuss word. It means a small donkey and it comes from the Bible. Let's see: 'They rode Jesus through the city seated on a small ass.' "

"That's not how you used the word," she said. "If you're fair about it you'll give me a thousand lire."

"I'm an adult," I said. "It's part of my job description to be totally unfair to every child I meet."

"I was in prison with you," Leah said, primly. "Suor Rosaria thinks you ought to be ashamed of yourself."

"I was victimized by a male-dominated society that didn't understand me."

"You were a brute," said Leah.

Anytime I lost my temper, raised my voice, or found myself in a situation that contained the seeds of discord, Leah would remind me of my most contentious encounter with the habits and customs of Italy. It happened in our first months in Rome, when I was still acclimating myself to the myriad responsibilities a man encountered trying to raise a child single-handedly in a foreign city. Every day I found myself overwhelmed by the sheer variety of needs and wants manufactured by this simple child. Leah made me feel as though I required the skills of a city manager to move her through all the mazelike conundrums that Rome could throw up in our paths. Through an act of faith I had discovered the right pediatrician. To get a telephone installed required three trips to city hall, four to the telephone company, three bribes of hard cash, and a case of good wine to the *portiere* who knew the brother of a friend who lived next door to the mayor of Rome. The city prided itself on the extremism of its inefficiency. Its good-natured anarchy left me exhausted at the end of each day.

But I had encountered no trouble in Rome until I relaxed my guard and found myself shopping near midday beneath the canopies that shaded those fabulous fruit and vegetable stands in the Campo dei Fiori. As I led my daughter through that squawking aviary of human commerce, I loved to study the vast tiers of fruit with the wasps sipping the nectar of plums and yellow jackets happy as puppies among the grapes and peaches. Pointing out the wasps to Leah, I admired out loud the accord that existed between the wasps and vendors as if they had signed a treaty of entente to underscore their partnership in the business of selling and eating fruit.

The sheer theater of the street life in the Campo enthralled Leah from our first week in the neighborhood. Each day, we would drift from the north end where we bought bread to our last stop at Fratelli Ruggeri, whose shop smelled of cheese and pork and whose ceiling was hung with fifty legs of prosciutto. Huge wheels of Parmesan cheese as large as truck tires were rolled out from the back. There were five brothers and each brother had a unique and tragic personality as though they had bit parts in five different operas. Each was a law unto himself and they lent a note of improvisation and theater to the selling of their fragrant produce. It was outside of their store that I ran into trouble when I remembered I had forgotten to buy olives.

As Leah and I again walked the length of
the Campo, past the knife-sharpener on his stationary bicycle and the booths that sold lungs
and offal, we ran straight into one of those fire-
breathing marital scraps of the De Angelo couple. Though it took us a while to learn their
names, I had witnessed several fights between
Mimmo and Sophia De Angelo before in the
Piazza Farnese. Mimmo was a laborer and an
alcoholic and could often be seen with a bottle
of grappa drinking alone on the stone bench
that ran for fifty meters across the front of the
palazzo. He was stocky and built low to the
ground with hairy shoulders and thick, powerful arms. When sitting in the piazza drinking
grappa from the bottle, he seemed to grow
dark rather than drunk. Once the darkness
came he began muttering expletives at everything about his life that he found disappointing.
His wife would generally come upon him in this
condition and their screaming at each other
was loud enough to be heard by pedestrians
walking along the Tiber and those coming out
of the Piazza Navona. Whatever protocols the
De Angelos kept in the privacy of their apartment did not apply to their violent public encounters. Leah and I had watched several of
them from our window high over the piazza,
and for sheer volume and quality of invective
this Roman couple were in a class by them-

selves. The quarrels usually ended with a distraught and weeping Sophia breaking into a shameful run back to her home after realizing that the whole piazza was listening to and thoroughly enjoying the couple's histrionics.

"He's mean," Leah had said.

"Italians don't hit," I assured her. "They just yell."

But these domestic quarrels between the De Angelos began to grow in frequency and decibels. Sophia was pretty and theatrical and ten years younger than her hard, inattentive husband. Her legs were beautiful, her figure full, and her eyes brimmed with pain. Each day Mimmo drank more and Sophia wept more and their level of language became more charged with the ancient sorrow of the poor and the hopeless. Maria told me Mimmo was threatening to kill Sophia because she'd shamed him among his neighbors and that a man was nothing if he lost his sense of honor before his friends and countrymen.

None of this should have had the slightest importance in my life. The De Angelos were local color, a troubling coda in the war between the sexes, one I was grateful had nothing to do with me.

But on that particular day our first year in Rome, I was buying olives from the olive vendor, a grumpy, unsunny man whom I was beginning to like for the originality of his sullenness, when I heard Leah scream. I looked up as a punch landed against Sophia's cheek.

It was not the blood that ignited my temper, nor the tears, nor the pleading. It was the deep pity I felt when I saw the terror in Sophia's eyes and the hopelessness I had seen so often as a child. But I was not out of control when I approached Mimmo and was very aware that I was in a foreign country where the customs were unfamiliar and my interference might be fiercely resented.

Mimmo was about to strike again, but I grabbed his arm. Mimmo went berserk when he saw me interfering in his disciplining of his wife. He tried to hit me with his free hand, but I deflected the blow and held both of Mimmo's arms to his side.

"No, signore," I said respectfully in my halting Italian. *"È malo."*

Mimmo let loose with a salvo of Italian profanity that would help clarify the graffiti written on the walls and bridges around Rome when I later was exploring the margins of the old city with Leah. I caught the word *morte,* which made me think that Mimmo was threatening murder, and the word *stronzo,* which was an all-inclusive street term roughly equivalent to "asshole."

Mimmo freed one arm and threw a roundhouse punch at my chin, but I caught the arm again and lifted Mimmo off his feet, slamming him firmly against the wall of the bakery. People had begun screaming and when I looked down I saw Leah's terrified face. Worried for her, I tried to find a way to extricate myself gently from a scene that was assuming the dimensions of grand opera. Then Mimmo spat in my face and for a brief moment I thought about tearing the man's head off, but again, I saw my daughter and knew that I had to disengage and do it quickly before the police came.

I placed Mimmo on the ground near Sophia, who had begun to scream at me to put her husband down. Then I picked up Leah and said *"Mi dispiace"* to Mimmo and his wife several times. A number of the women in the crowd began cheering and clapping as we walked swiftly away. When I heard a police car approaching I was suddenly filled with dread.

I disengaged from the crowd cleanly but then every eye in the Campo was on me as we walked swiftly toward our apartment. We ducked into a café on the Vicolo del Gallo where I often took Leah in the afternoon for ice cream. The proprietress was a motherly, solicitous woman who paid great attention to Leah and gave her a piece of candy every time she learned a new Italian word.

I ordered a cappuccino for myself, and ice

cream for my daughter, and failed to note that I had been followed into the café by Signor De Angelo. The signora fixed Leah an ice cream first, then made my cappuccino in that elaborate hissing ceremony that Italians perform with such style. I did not hear or see Mimmo De Angelo buy a bottle of beer or drink it.

The next thing I knew the base of the bottle had caught me just above the eyebrow and the side of my face went numb as blood poured down it. I caught Mimmo's arm on the second downswing, lifted the much smaller man into the air, and laid him down on the zinc bar flat on his stomach. Leah was screaming and so was the proprietress and so was Sophia and so it seemed was half of Rome as I held Mimmo flat on the bar and watched in the mirror the blood run down my face. Then I ran with Mimmo, sliding him like a sack of laundry down the bar, picking up speed. For ten feet, I ran with Mimmo, knocking off glasses and coffee cups and spoons as I held him by his belt and the back of his shirt. When the bar ended, I let go and Mimmo flew through the air, over a table of surprised customers, and crashed into a pinball machine in a shower of glass and noise and blood.

That night, Leah and I stayed at the Regina Coeli prison on the Tiber River listening to the Roman women on the Janiculum hill calling to their lovers in the prison below. A prison doctor sewed up the cut along my eyebrow with five stitches and argued with the administrator of the prison that Leah was an orphan whose mother had just died and could not be separated from me for any reason. The guard who took Leah and me to a cell asked me what kind of pasta I would like for dinner and did I prefer red wine or white with my meal. Later, I wrote an article for *European Travel and Life* on my stay in prison and awarded the prison restaurant two stars.

Leah and I were minor celebrities when we walked out of Regina Coeli. The short time in prison had improved my skills in Italian immeasurably and I suggested a stay in jail as a surefire way to master the language for any American who was serious about being bilingual in a short amount of time.

But the most durable result of our incarceration was the status and visibility it granted us as citizens of the piazza. Many of the older men who sat on the bench in front of the palazzo thought that much of the greatness of Italy depended on the firmness with which its men handled its women. In a Mediterranean country, especially in the south of Italy and among certain members of the lower classes, wife-beating is a form of family discipline, like the breaking of mules to work in the fields, and certainly not the business of American tourists. But the women of the piazza were unanimous in their contempt for Mimmo and in their boundless admiration for anyone who would shed his blood and spend time in prison in the defense of Italian women.

So it was the whole piazza that watched as the stranger followed us out of the piazza this morning and down the Via di Monserrato.

Leah was wearing a yellow smock and polished brown leather shoes and she studied her image in every window she passed. She felt pretty and her dark hair flashed like a wing in sunlight. Giancarlo, the forty-year-old brain-damaged cripple, called out to us as his exhausted, long-suffering mother wheeled him past the English seminary. No one in the neighborhood knew what would happen to Giancarlo once his mother died, and it was always a relief when they appeared in the streets each morning. The deaf-mute, Antonio, waved to us, and I paused to light one of his cigarettes. English seminarians surrounded us on their way to classes, serious boys who rarely smiled and had an odd pallor as though raised deep inside caves.

"Do you think that man wants to kill us, Daddy?" Leah asked.

"No, I think he just wants to know where

we live and what we do and where you go to school."

"He already knows that. He followed us on Friday."

"It's nothing to worry about, darling," I said, squeezing my daughter's hand. "He's not going to ruin our walk to school."

At 20 Via di Monserrato we stepped into a courtyard of deep, spicy shade and Leah called into the courtyard for the cat, Gerardo, to come out of the garden to receive his morning slice of pepperoni. The cat came to her on the run with tawny movements of leaf and silk. He accepted the meat greedily from Leah, then took it up the formal stairway inlaid with fragments of marble tablets and partially effaced statuary. The man following us was pretending to read the menu in the trattoria in the small piazza.

"If he eats there, I hope he orders mussels," Leah said.

"Shame on you," I said; an American tourist had just gotten hepatitis after eating mussels at another Roman restaurant.

"I bet he's with the Red Brigades," she said.

"How do you know about the Red Brigades?"

"Maria tells me everything. They killed the Italian Prime Minister and dumped him in the trunk of a car. I'll show you where they left him if you want."

"He's not with the Red Brigades. He dresses too well."

"You should dress better. Like an Italian," Leah said.

"I apologize for lacking *bella figura,* you little turd," I said affectionately.

"That's another thousand lire you owe me," she said. "It's not nice to call your own daughter a little turd."

"It's a term of endearment. Another way of saying 'I love you.' All dads in the States say that."

"It's gross. No Italian father would ever say that to his daughter. They love their daughters far too much."

"Is that what Maria says?"

"And Suor Rosaria."

"You're absolutely right. From this moment on, I'm going to concentrate and get me some of that *bella figura.*"

We weaved our way carefully through the morning traffic, for I knew that a Roman never just drives—he aims—and I am always extraordinarily vigilant when we walk to and from school. Once we had seen an English tourist on the Ponte Mazzini throw up his hands in mock surrender and simply stop his car in the middle of the bridge. When I went to see if I could help, the Englishman said, "This isn't driving. I say it's rugby."

"It's going to be a beautiful day, Daddy," Leah said. "No pollution." On some days the pollution level was so high that the Hilton was invisible, and I felt comforted that smog could actually perform a public service.

"St. Peter's head," she said as soon as the dome of St. Peter's came into view above the plane trees along the river. She had confused the words "head" and "dome" when we first had moved to Rome and it was an old joke between us. I looked down at the curve in the Tiber. No river, no matter how polluted or dirty, could quite pull off the trick of being ugly. Few things rivet me like the beauty of moving water.

The man kept his distance and did not even mount the bridge until he saw us walk down the stairs beside the Regina Coeli prison. He was being more cautious now that he knew we were aware he was following us. Perhaps people in the piazza had told him about my throwing Mimmo into the pinball machine.

We entered the courtyard of Sacra Cuore at the end of the long street, the Via di San Francesco di Sales.

Suor Rosaria, a slight but beautiful nun who had a reputation as one of the best teachers of young children in Rome, saw us approaching.

For three years, she had taught Leah and the communication between them was immediate and total. The nuns I had known in South Carolina were rancorous creatures and they had helped poison my odd and tortured Catholic boyhood. Although I knew that it was as impossible to be an ex-Catholic as it was to be an ex-Oriental, I vowed I would never raise Leah as a Catholic. What I had not anticipated was that by living in a Catholic country she would be unable to avoid the Church's magisterial reach.

Suor Rosaria swooped out of the schoolhouse doorway and ran toward Leah, who saw her coming, and they rushed into each other's arms like schoolgirls. I was thrilled by the authenticity of this nun's open and complete love for Leah. Suor Rosaria looked at me with bright flirtatious eyes and said she was glad that we were bringing their guest to school again. With her eyes she made a movement toward the man who had followed us through Rome for the fourth day in a row.

"Chi è?" Suor Rosaria asked.

"He'll let me know," I answered in Italian. "He wants us to know we're being followed. Maybe today he'll let me know why."

"Do you know, Signor McCall," Suor Rosaria said, "that you have the smartest, most beautiful little girl in the city of Rome?"

"*Sì, Suora,*" I answered. "I'm the luckiest man in the world."

"You're the nicest daddy in the world," Leah said, hugging me.

"Now that's how you can earn some real money, tiger. Keeping me from cussing's just small potatoes."

"Be careful of that man," Leah said. "If you die, Daddy, I'll be all alone."

"Nothing's going to happen. I promise." I said good-bye and passed out of the convent grounds, taking a quick survey of the street. Young ballerinas were making their way in those floating ethereal walks of dancers to the studio in the middle of the Via di Francesco di Sales and young art students were slouching and smoking on the art school steps. But there was no trace of the follower. I waited for a full minute, then saw a quick movement of a man's head appear in the doorway of a bar across from the ballet school and just as quickly disappear.

I had put on my running shoes that morning and I broke into a slow trot along one of those straight, comely Roman streets with high walls and no exits, and approached the café.

As I entered, the man gestured to me to join him at the bar.

"I've already ordered you a cappuccino, Signor McCall," he said pleasantly.

"You've been scaring my daughter, Sherlock. I want it to stop."

"You take one sugar in your cappuccino, I believe," the man said. "I think I know your habits."

"Do you know of my tendency to kick ass when I get nervous?"

"Your propensity for violence has been described to me often. But I am a veteran of many self-defense courses. Tai kwon do, jujitsu, karate. I've many black belts in my closet. I've been trained by masters to run from danger.

"But now let us have our coffee, no?" the man continued. "Then we will get up to business."

"I didn't know they had private eyes in Italy," I said as the bartender passed me a cup of cappuccino across the counter.

The man tested his coffee by sipping a spoonful of it and nodding his head appreciatively.

"We are like priests. People only come to us when they are in trouble. My name is Pericle Starraci. I have an office in Milano. But I like to travel around Italy because of my interest in Etruscan art."

"Why are you following me, Pericle?"

"Because I was paid to do so."

"Back to square one. Who sent you?"

"She would like to arrange a meeting with you."

"Who is it?"

"She wants to sign a peace treaty."

"My mother. My goddamn untrustworthy, back-stabbing, pain-in-the-ass mother."

"It's not your mother," Pericle said.

"Then it's my father-in-law."

"No," Pericle said. "It is his daughter."

"Martha," I said, surprised. "Why in the hell would Martha hire you?"

"Because no one would give her your address. Your family would not cooperate with her."

"Good," I said. "That's the first nice thing I've heard about my family in years."

"She needs to talk to you."

"Tell her I wouldn't see her or any member of her family if God himself typed me out a note on his personal computer. Surely she's told you that."

"She told me there was a great misunderstanding that she thinks can be cleared up."

"There's no misunderstanding," I said, getting ready to leave. "I made a vow never to see those people again. It's the easiest promise to keep I've ever made. The second easiest was the promise never to see any of my own family again. I'm very democratic. I don't want to see a fucking soul who ever spoke English to me during my first thirty years on earth."

"Signora Fox understands now that you were not responsible for her sister's death."

"Tell her thanks and that I don't hold her responsible for the depletion of the ozone level or the melting of the polar icecap or the rising price of pepperoni. Nice talking to you, Pericle."

I stood up and walked out into the street.

"She has some information," Pericle said, struggling to keep up. "Something she says you will want to know. It is news of some woman. A woman of coins, I think she calls it."

I stopped when he spoke those words: They went through me like shrapnel.

"Tell Martha I'll meet her tonight for dinner. I'll be at Da Fortunato's, near the Pantheon."

"I already have, Signor McCall," Pericle said smoothly. "See. I told you. I know all your habits."

CHAPTER 2

WHEN FRIENDS COME TO ROME IN early summer to visit me I like to take them to the Pantheon during thunderstorms and stand them beneath the opening of the feathery, perfectly proportioned dome as rain falls through the open roof against the marble floor and lightning scissors through the wild and roiled skies. The emperor Hadrian rebuilt the temple to honor gods no longer worshiped, but you can feel the brute passion in that ardor in the Pantheon's grand and harmonious shape. I think gods have rarely been worshiped so well.

On my first trip to Rome, I spent a whole day studying the interior and exterior architecture of the Pantheon for an article I was writing for *Southern Living*. When the guard ran me out an hour before sunset, I looked around the neighborhood for a good restaurant for dinner that night. Shyla walked from our hotel to join me after spending the day shopping on the Via Condotti. She had bought herself a scarf and a pair of shoes from Ferragamo, for her small, beautiful feet, which were her special vanity. Suddenly, on the Via del Pantheon, the air filled with a strange musky underground perfume that neither of us recognized. Like two bird dogs, we set out on the trail of the scent and found its origin by the entranceway of Da Fortunato. A basket of white truffles exuded the biting, exotic smell that seemed a transubstantiation of some essence of the forest to the garlic-scented, wine-splashed airstreams pillowing through the alley outside the trattoria.

We returned that evening after making love in our hotel room. Afterward, we had held each other tightly, still surprised and shy by how high we could turn up the flame of that tender need we showed for each other's bodies. At certain times in our lives, we crackled in the sheer electricity of our desire to be wonderful in bed. In strange cities, alone, we whispered things we would not tell another soul on earth. We set down feasts for each other and treated our love with tongues of fire. Our bodies were fields of wonder to us.

The waiter, Fernando, but nicknamed Freddie, served us dinner that night. He was heavy-set and deep-voiced and in perfect command of his quadrant of the restaurant. He led us to the small table outside looking out toward the Pantheon, and recommended a bottle of Barolo and a risotto for the pasta course. When he brought the risotto, he produced an elegant, razor-sharp instrument and shaved thin slices of white truffle onto the steaming hot risotto. The marriage of rice and truffle exploded in silent concordat and I shall never forget lifting the bowl to my nose and thanking God for bringing both Freddie and truffles into our life the same night.

The dinner was long and we took our time. We talked about the past and the many things that had gone wrong between us. But quickly we turned to the future and began to talk about children and what we would name them and where we would settle down and how we would raise these ethereal and beautiful McCall children who, though unborn, were already greatly beloved.

Shyla flirted with Freddie every time he came to the table and Freddie responded with a touch of both restraint and Mediterranean charm. He recommended the fresh scampi, grilled briefly, then anointed with olive oil and lemon juice. The olive oil was a deep green and looked as though it had come from a vineyard of emeralds. The scampi tasted sweet like a lobster fed only on honey and it cut into the deep undertone of flavor deposited on the taste buds by the truffles. Shyla poured some olive oil on her fingers and licked it off. Then she poured some on my fingers and sucked the oil off them one at a time as Freddie watched with envy and approval. He honored her performance with an arugula salad, then pulled out a pocketknife, opened it, and began to undress a blood-red orange from Sicily in a patient, sacramental ceremony. The orange peel curled off the deep ruby of the fruit in a long, circular ribbon. I waited for Freddie to misjudge, but he continued to circumnavigate the orange until other patrons began to applaud. When the peel, as long as a garter snake, fell to the floor, Freddie picked it up and presented it to Shyla, who inhaled the sharp smell as Freddie divided the orange and set it before her in an immaculate arrangement, pretty as a rose. He brought glasses impressed with the image of the Pantheon and poured us both a glass of grappa.

A full moon hung over the city, and a Gypsy girl selling long-stemmed flowers moved nimbly through the diners. Three men from Abruzzi sang Neapolitan love songs, then passed the hat for tips, and a fire-eater swallowed his flaming sword and a man with a ukulele sang "I Want to Hold Your Hand" and "Love Me Tender."

"This is just like a Fellini movie, Jack," Shyla said. "Let's never leave this spot."

Crowds of Italian teenagers, insouciant and callow, moved through the streets into the Piazza della Rotonda in ceaseless migrations. Gypsy women appeared in brilliant, gaudy clothing, raucous as parrots, and began working the loungers at the café as waiters tried to intercept them. Carriages drawn by retired racehorses put out into the streets and rolled through the crowds bearing German and Japanese tourists, who were filming everything and seeing nothing.

At the end of the evening, Freddie brought two cups of espresso to the table and asked us always to remember Da Fortunato and the headwaiter, Freddie, who'd been privileged to serve us on a Roman night that he called *"fantastica."* Shyla kissed Freddie in a spontaneous gesture that seemed just right.

As I was studying the bill, Shyla pressed my hand and told me to look up.

What I saw was Freddie leading Federico Fellini and two of the most stunning women I had ever seen to the table next to us. Freddie winked and said, "Always at Da Fortunato."

Then Freddie, who understood the power of gesture, bought a rose from a Gypsy girl and presented it to Shyla along with a wineglass from Da Fortunato.

After Shyla died, I found that glass and that dead rose and the orange peel carefully wrapped and preserved in her safety deposit box. They reminded me that there are nights on earth when a couple can have everything break perfectly for them, nights when the moon is full and Gypsies appear with flowers, and truffles call out to strangers on the street and Fellini takes the next table and Freddie peels a blood-red orange as an act of homage, and on that night in Rome we were in love as no one on earth has any right to hope to be, we conceived our child, Leah, in a union of ineffable and damaged love and a great soaring cry of yes for our future.

Two and a half years later, Shyla went up on the bridge.

On this evening, many years later, Freddie embraced me when I walked into the restaurant and kissed me on both cheeks, European-style.

"*Dov' è* Leah?" Freddie asked.

"She's at home with Maria."

"A beautiful signorina is waiting at your table."

Martha stood up as I approached her. She

extended her hand and I accepted it reluctantly. She did not try to kiss me, nor would I have let her.

"It's nice of you to come, Jack," Martha Fox said.

"It certainly is, Martha."

"I didn't think you'd actually show."

"If I hadn't, you'd have ambushed Leah one day when she was out walking in the piazza."

"You're right. That's exactly what I would've done. What a beautiful young girl she's turned into."

"I don't want to be your friend, Martha," I said. "What in the fuck are you doing here, and why are you trying to reenter my life? I've made it abundantly clear that I didn't want to see you or any of your family again."

"Are you ever going to come back to the South? Are you ever going to show Leah where she really comes from?"

"That's none of your business," I answered.

"I was once your sister-in-law. I admit I never knew you well, but I liked you, Jack. Almost all of us did."

"It seems to me that the last time I saw you, Martha, you were testifying in a court of law that I was unfit to raise Leah."

Martha lowered her eyes and studied the menu for a brief moment. I motioned for Freddie to bring us a bottle of wine, and he arrived a moment later and opened a chilled bottle of Gavi dei Gavi.

"That was a terrible mistake," she said emotionally. "My parents were distraught when Shyla killed herself. Surely you can understand that and have some compassion for them. Leah was their only link with Shyla and the past."

"I'd have had more compassion for them if they'd shown the slightest bit toward me."

"I think my whole family had a breakdown after Shyla's death, Jack," Martha said. "Everybody blamed you for what happened. Myself included. We thought if you'd been a good enough husband, my sister would never have gone off the bridge. No one blames you for anything now . . . except, of course, my father."

"Give me some good news," I said. "Tell me that son of a bitch is dead."

"I love my father very much and I resent you talking about him that way."

"Tough shit."

"My father's a very unhappy man," Martha said, leaning across the table toward me. "But he's got good reasons for his unhappiness and you know that as well as anyone."

"Just for the record. I hate your dutiful daughter routine and you don't have to act like a public relations firm for your parents. Now let's order."

When Freddie came over, he studied Martha's face.

"*Sorella di* Shyla?" Freddie asked me.

"Martha, meet Freddie. He had a crush on your sister."

"Ah, Martha. Your sister was such a beauty. Such sunshine. You look so much like her," Freddie said, bowing deeply.

"I'm pleased to meet you, Freddie. You're very famous in South Carolina."

"We have some nice fat mussels, Jack. Fresh anchovies, very nice. *Calamari fritti.* What would Martha like? Maybe *pasta all'amatriciana*?"

"I'd love to start with the pasta, Freddie," Martha said.

"Anything for the sister of Shyla. Welcome to the trattoria. Come back a thousand times. Mussels for you, Signor Jack. Trust Freddie."

Freddie moved back toward the kitchen checking every table as he passed, and I smiled at his proficiency. Freddie was like a staff sergeant in the army; others enjoy greater status, but without him the whole operation would come to a grinding halt.

I turned and looked at Martha, seeing those soft luminous features she shared with her sister. She had the same doe-eyed self-conscious beauty that in Shyla was edgy and explosive. In Martha, it held its breath, tiptoed into view, took one by surprise whenever she released that tightly coiled spring that controlled the nerve centers of her own quiet uncertainty. Even makeup could not hide the trapped, distracted girl masquerading with pearls and a black dress as a woman of the world.

"My father still blames you for Shyla's death," Martha said. "It's only fair that you know that."

"You know, Martha," I said wearily, "I always thought I'd make a great son-in-law. Fishing trips. Card games. That kind of shit. And I get stuck with that dreary, juiceless, raggedy-assed father of yours. I could never figure him out. But you know all this. You grew up in that hothouse of pain."

"Why do you hate me for loving my father?" she asked.

"Because of your pathetic lack of honesty. The awful and dangerous pretense of loyalty. He's been poison for you just like he was poison for Shyla and your mother. The women in his life cluster around him, protect him, find virtue in his bitterness. You don't love him. You pity him. The way I do. Yet I've rarely met a grander shit on earth."

"Why do you hate him so much?"

"I pity the dreadful son of a bitch."

"He doesn't need your pity."

"Then he's welcome to my hatred."

Freddie arrived with Martha's pasta and my mussels and his arrival was both propitious and welcome. Her dish was sharp, spicy, and even had the forbidden pleasure of containing the flesh of hogs. Though a committed Jew, Martha found no reason to follow the dietary laws handed down in Leviticus. For most of her adult life she had fought border skirmishes with her parents over the pig and the oyster. Judaism was precious to her, but she could not pretend to be observant of its many dietary laws.

"May I try one of your mussels?" she asked.

"Pure *trayf*," I said, passing her one.

"But delicious," she said as she ate it.

"What're you doing here, Martha?" I asked. "You haven't quite answered that very basic question."

"I want to understand why my sister leapt to her death. I want someone to explain to me why her life had become so desperate when she seemed to have so much going for her. Nothing about it makes sense. My parents won't talk about it."

"I can understand that. I haven't told Leah that her mother committed suicide. I just never could quite get my mouth right to tell her about the bridge. It's been hard enough to tell her that her mama's dead."

"Does she know that I'm alive? That she has an aunt and two grandparents who love her?"

"A vague idea," I said. "But I'm encouraging pure amnesia. Please don't look pious. Last time I saw the people you just mentioned was in a South Carolina court of law. If memory serves, each one of you testified I was incompetent to raise my only child. I've raised a beautiful kid. A magical one. I did it without the help of any of you."

"You think it's right that you punish us the rest of our lives by refusing to let us see Leah?" she asked.

"Yes, I think it's right. I think it's justice. Do you remember the generous amount of visitation I'd have been allowed had your parents won their lawsuit?"

"They asked the court that you not be allowed any visitation," Martha said, closing her eyes and inhaling deeply. "They know how wrong they were. They would like another chance."

At that moment Freddie arrived at the table with two grilled sea bream. He prepared the fish for presentation at the table side, removing the head of both fish with a flick of the knife. Then he skinned the bream and lifted the backbone from each one of them as though lifting a violin out of its case. Preparing Martha's first, he placed the white translucent fillet across her plate and moistened it with green olive oil and half a lemon. He performed the same ablutions for mine.

"You will cry," Freddie said, "it is so good."

"Did I order fish?" Martha asked when Freddie left the table.

"You looked like a fish kind of person. He has great intuition and he always likes to surprise me."

As she ate, Martha frequently stared past me and when she talked, she was agitated and kept brushing an imaginary lock of hair from her eyes. Hers was a guileless face, registering every emotion, and I could read it like a page of newsprint. Something was not right with Martha that had nothing to do with the complex emotions aroused by our awkward reunion. The lines in her forehead warned me of trouble on my flanks. Since leaving the South, I had learned the intricacies and tricks of a life on the run and I knew well how to read the secret language of ambush.

"Excuse me for a second," I said, rising and walking to the men's room. I called home and talked to Maria and made her check on Leah. Maria returned to report that Leah was sleeping like an angel, and I breathed easier.

When I came out of the men's room, Freddie motioned for me to come into the kitchen. Among the jostling disciplined movement of cooks and waiters, Freddie whispered: "There's a man eating outside who asks many questions about you, Jack. He asks Emilio if you are bad to Leah. Emilio no like."

"Tell Emilio thanks, Freddie," I said as I moved out of the kitchen and passed down the entranceway of the trattoria, to where Signor Fortunato himself greeted his guests.

Looking outside to the enclosed area where tables were set up, I spotted Pericle Starraci looking into the interior of the restaurant. The private investigator was gesturing to someone on the inside.

When I returned to the table, Martha had almost finished her fish course.

"This is the best fish I've ever eaten anywhere. By far," she said.

"That was Shyla's favorite. That's why Freddie brought it to you."

"Why don't you see anyone from your past, Jack?" she asked.

"Because I'm not fond of my past," I said. "It fills me with horror to think about it, ergo, I don't."

Martha leaned forward. "I see. You've got a love-hate relationship with your family, your friends, even the South."

"No," I answered. "I'm unusual in that re-spect. I have a hate-hate relationship with the South."

"It's dangerous to second-guess where you were born," Martha said, and again I caught her looking over my shoulder to the tables out-side.

"When do you leave Rome, Martha?"

"After I see Leah and after you tell me how my parents can get back in your good graces."

"Talked to a rental agent?" I asked. "You could be here for years."

"I've got every right to see Leah. You can't stop me from that."

"Yes, I can. And instead of threatening me or challenging me, I'd take on a conciliatory note. I've arranged my life so I can leave this city tonight and take up residence in another country with relative ease. I live like a man on the run because I fear encounters such as these. I don't need you in my life and my daughter certainly doesn't need you."

"She's my niece," Martha said.

"She's a lot of people's niece—I'm perfectly consistent—none of my brothers get to see her, either. I'm raising Leah so she can be screwed up by only one single relative. That's me. My family's fucked up and your family's fucked up. But I carefully devised a life so that this condition of perpetual damage will not pass to my kid."

"My parents both cry when they talk about Leah. They cry when they realize it's been so many years since they've seen her."

"Good," I said, smiling. "My heart leaps like a doe in the forest when I think of your parents weeping. They can cry all they want."

"They say not seeing Leah's worse than what happened to them during the war."

"Please," I said, putting my face into my hands, tiring of the effort to be pleasant to my wife's only sister. "In your family, if you talk about mowing the lawn or sewing a button on a shirt or rotating the wheels on a car, you always end up in Auschwitz or Bergen-Belsen. Talk about going out for a burger and a milkshake or catching a movie on TV and the next thing you know, bingo, we're on a cattle car moving through Eastern Europe."

"I'm really sorry, Jack, if my parents over-emphasized the Holocaust in your presence," Martha shot back angrily. "My parents suffered terribly. They suffer to this very day."

"They didn't suffer as much as your sister did," I answered. "As much as my wife did."

"How can you make such comparisons?"

"Because Shyla's dead and your parents are still alive. The way I keep a scorecard, she wins the grand sweepstakes."

"My father thinks Shyla would never have killed herself if she'd married a Jewish man."

"And you still wonder why I don't let my daughter visit your parents?"

"Why do you think Shyla killed herself, Jack?" Martha asked.

"I don't know. She started having hallucinations, I know that, but she wouldn't talk about them. She knew they'd go away eventually. They went away okay. When she went off the bridge."

"Did she ever tell you about the hallucinations she had as a child?"

"No. She didn't say a word about the ones she had while she was married. She kept her craziness private."

"I know what those hallucinations were, Jack."

I looked straight into her eyes. "I don't know how to put this more gently. But so what?"

"My mother wants to see you, Jack," Martha said. "That's why I'm here. She thinks she knows why Shyla did it. She wants to tell you herself."

"Ruth," I said, tasting the word, "Ruth. I used to think she was one of the most beautiful women I'd ever seen."

"She's getting older."

"I was in love with your mother when I was growing up."

"But it was your mother who was the town legend."

"One feels guilt about lusting after one's own mother. I felt none lusting after yours."

"My mother knows they were wrong to try to take Leah away from you. They did it out of grief and fury and fear. My mother knows and my father'll never admit it, but he knows it too."

"Come to dinner tomorrow night, Martha," I said, abruptly. "Come and you can meet your niece."

Martha pulled my head to her and kissed me on the cheek.

"Leave Pericle behind. You don't need the son of a bitch any longer."

Martha blushed as I turned toward the open patio and waved to the private detective cowering below an arrangement of flowers.

"I've got to do a little preliminary work with Leah about her family tree."

"One more thing, Jack."

"Quick, before I change my mind."

"My mother said to tell you that she killed Shyla and she's as guilty as if she'd pulled the trigger herself."

"Why would she say that?" I asked, stunned.

"She wants to tell you herself, Jack. Face to face. Here or back in America."

"Let me think about it," I said. "I'm going to Venice tomorrow. You're welcome to stay in the apartment and get to know Leah. Please don't tell her about Shyla yet. I still have to work out when is the right time to tell her that her mother killed herself."

When I arrived home Maria was already asleep and Leah had fallen asleep in my bed. Her face in repose made me fill up with such amazing tenderness that I wondered if all fathers drank in so hungrily the features of their children. I had memorized every line and contour of her profile; to me it was a secret text of nonpareil beauty. It was beyond my capacity to imagine how to form the words to tell this lovely child that her mother had jumped to her death because she had found life far too agonizing to endure.

The secret of her mother's death lay between us and it was no accident that I had chosen the city of Rome as our place of exile. The pretty walkways over the Tiber were all low and it was a hard city to kill yourself in by jumping off a bridge.

CHAPTER 3

SINCE MOVING TO ITALY, I HAVE written eight articles about the city of Venice for seven different magazines. Venice is a meal ticket for travel writers, and I love it because it is the only city I have ever come to that is more wonderful than my first preconception of it. It transforms me, uplifts me, as I move through the canals and search for those elusive verbal equivalents that will conjure the tremulous magic of the city to readers who will be invisible to me forever.

As I stepped aboard the *taxi acquei,* I inhaled the sea air, a pungent combination of winds from the Adriatic and catastrophic pollution that threatened the very existence of Venice. The varnished mahogany boat began to move along the Grand Canal, and I noted that fever and sewage were still hanging tough in the city. The gondolas we passed moved dreamlike above the water like black, misshapen swans from bouts of whimsy and nightmare. The sun broke out from behind a cloud bank, and I witnessed again the moment when Venice changed for me the nature of light. Light was beautiful everywhere, but only in Venice did it complete itself fully. In the city where the mirror was invented, each palace along the canal preened like snowflakes in their unholdable images of water.

I registered at the Gritti Palace Hotel, one of the finest hotels to grace this capricious, balustraded city. On the Gritti's terrace, I took my position at the best place on the planet to consume a dry martini. Looking out at the river traffic, I lifted my glass and toasted all the heavenly hosts that dwelt beneath the columns of the Maria della Salute across the waterway. I had written a small hymn of praise to the Gritti that had appeared in *Esquire* magazine and the manager of the hotel had always treated me like visiting royalty whenever I came to the city. There is something of the whore in every travel writer and I worried about it everywhere except Venice. The Gritti Palace has that caressed, combed-over, fussed-about quality that is the mark of all great hotels. Its work is done in secret, and its staff, unseen but competent, lives to make you happy.

So, at the point where Byzantium and Europe join hands, I sat alone in the city of masks, holding my drink and waiting for the arrival of two childhood friends. For the second time in less than forty-eight hours I would come face to face with my past. But Venice was enough of an imaginary retreat from the world to make me ready for almost anything. As I sat studying the shapes of flamboyant palaces, the city looked as though a troupe of organ grinders and manic chess players had designed it for the praise of glassblowers. Its celebration of pure whimsy made it a playground and a conundrum, a place where decadence had both a field day and a day off. It always made me wish I was a flashier, less serious man.

"Buon giorno," the concierge of the hotel said, handing me a note. *"Come sta?"*

"Molto bene, Arturo," I answered. "Have Signor Hess and Signora Ansley checked into the hotel?"

"They arrived this morning separately," Arturo said. "Signor Hess left this note for you. He is the famous producer from Hollywood, no?"

"Was it hard to tell?" I asked.

"Mr. Hess is larger than life."

"Been that way since he was a kid," I said.

"The woman is *bellissima*," Arturo said.

"She was born that way," I said. "I was an eyewitness."

I opened Mike's note to me and recognized his almost illegible handwriting, which reminded me of untied shoes.

"Hey, deer-fuck," he began sweetly, "we'll meet for drinks on the terrace at six. Nice joint. Don't beat off on the sheets. Ciao and all that shit. Mike."

High school is a kind of starting gate, I thought as I waited for my friends' arrival above the traffic of the Grand Canal. I had always considered the friends of my childhood special, but it had surprised me to see one of them become world-famous by the time he was thirty. In the darkness of the Breeze Theater, Mike Hess had fallen in love with movies and the world surrounding them. He would watch a movie with the same fastidious passion that an art historian brought to the study of a Titian. His powers of attention and memorization were extraordinary and he could name every actor who appeared in *All About Eve* as well as the fictional characters they portrayed. *Snow White* was the first movie he ever saw and he could take you on a journey from the opening credits to Snow White riding off into the rosy future with her prince, barely missing a single detail. Even his personality had been flamboyant and pixilated, so Mike always seemed destined to make movies.

But I was even more curious to see Ledare Ansley. Mike and I stayed close for a while after college, but I had rarely seen Ledare since our senior year at the University of South Carolina. Though we had dated off and on throughout high school, we'd never seemed to know each other very well. Her beauty had made her unapproachable, apart. She was one of those girls who pass through your life leaving secret wreckage, but no visible wake. You remember her, but for all the wrong reasons. She had written me my first love poem, which she presented to me on my birthday, but she wrote it in code and never felt confident enough to provide me with its key. In high school, for my entire junior year, I walked around school carrying a page of handwritten gibberish, an untranslatable love note I could neither decipher nor enjoy. I thought of that poem now, in Venice, where all images are forgeries stolen from water.

A hand touched my shoulder and I knew that touch.

"Hello, stranger," Ledare Ansley said. "Buy me this hotel and I might blow you a kiss when I go off to bed."

"Hey, Ledare," I said, rising, "I knew you were born to have this place."

"Heaven couldn't be this lovely," Ledare said. We embraced. "How are you, Jack? Everybody's worried about you."

"I'm doing fine," I said. "Leaving South Carolina in the dust has had its rewards."

"I've been in New York for the past five years," she said. "You don't need to sell me on why you left."

"I didn't intend to," I said. "How're your kids?"

"They're fine, I guess," she said and I knew I had struck a sore point. "Both of them live with their father. Capers has convinced them that he needs them when he runs for governor."

"If Capers becomes governor, it means democracy doesn't work."

She laughed and said, "He said to say hello to you. He still thinks very highly of you."

"Since we're passing messages, please tell Capers that I often think of him too. Anytime I ponder viruses or the spores of poisoned mushrooms, I think of him. When my thoughts turn to hemorrhoids or diarrhea cultures . . ."

"I get the point," she said.

"I knew you would," I said. "You were always a quick study."

"*Au contraire,*" Ledare said, "I was the

slowest of all. Remember, I married the charming son of a bitch."

"A slight misdirection. A wrong turn in the road," I said.

"More like modern warfare," she said. "First I blew up the city, tortured all my friends, set the fields afire, salted the earth, then blew up all the bridges that might've gotten me back where I started."

"Didn't work out, huh?" I said, enjoying her.

"You could always read between the lines," she said.

"Uh-oh," I said, looking toward the hotel lobby. "Something oddball this way comes."

Mike Hess moved toward us with his rapid, confident stride. His energy level was high and he always seemed agitated, like a Pepsi bottle shaken before it was opened. Every eye on the terrace locked on to him as Mike approached our table. His grooming was immaculate; his manner efficient and no-nonsense.

Mike grabbed me in a bear hug the moment I stood up and kissed me on both cheeks, more Hollywood than Italy. He kissed Ledare on the lips.

"Hollywood broads still can't hold a candle to you, Ledare. I still get a hard-on when I think of you in your cheerleader uniform."

"You've always known a way to a girl's heart, Mike," said Ledare as we all sat.

"I didn't recognize you without your gold chains," I said to Mike.

"Biggest mistake I ever made," Mike said, laughing at himself. "Wearing those goddamn chains to our tenth reunion. But, hell, everyone wanted to see me play movie producer. My love of my classmates won the day. I gave the public what it wanted. Open silk shirt. Chains glittering in the old chest hair. Who did I take to that?"

"Tiffany Blake," Ledare said. "She was your wife."

"Great woman," Mike said. "Had to drop-kick her right out of my life after my son, Creighton, was born. She had a bad habit of fucking people not married to her."

"You've had that reputation yourself," Ledare observed.

"Hey, careful," Mike said, gesturing toward me. "The last time I saw Jack here, he referred to me as a shallow fuck."

"How rude and ungallant of me," I said, smiling. Then added, "Michael, you shallow fuck."

Mike stood up dramatically and pretended he had been shot in the stomach. He staggered backward, wheeled around, and slumped over the railing above the Grand Canal, feigning death. His performance was real enough to attract the attention of two puzzled waiters, who inquired after Mike's health.

"Get up, Mike," said Ledare. "Try to pretend you know how to act in a good hotel."

"It's a gut shot, *amigos*. No use to call the *medicos,*" Mike said. "Tell Mama I died while saying kaddish for Papa."

Mike snapped suddenly to attention and came back to his seat. He bowed to an elderly Italian woman who certainly had not enjoyed his performance and gave him a look of frosty annoyance. Her contempt seemed to bother Mike.

"There, in a nutshell. See that face," Mike said. "That's why foreign movies suck. There's no life force. No brio here."

"No brio," I said. "In Italy?"

"No life force?" said Ledare. "Anna Magnani, Sophia Loren, these people invented life force."

"Been to a foreign movie lately?" Mike said, ignoring her. "All they do is go in and out of doors. For two endless hours. No one dies. No one gets his ass shot off. No one fucks or laughs. They just go in and out of doors or eat endless dinners. In one door and out the other. Oh, here comes the soup course. They cut their chicken up for a half-hour of screen time. That woman's face. That's all you need to know about why European movies stink."

Ledare nodded her head and said, "She criticized your acting. She didn't fall for your juvenile death scene from *High Noon*."

"Hey," Mike said, "I did the same routine not long ago in the Polo Lounge. Same one. In front of my peers in the industry. And I got a standing ovation from some of the coldest-hearted bastards that ever lived. I speak gospel here."

"You think what works at the Polo Lounge," I said, "will work at the Gritti Palace?"

"Hey, I grew up with you in South Carolina," Mike said, taking my wrist. "There's a palmetto on my birth certificate."

"Admit it, Mike," I said. "Your native land's now Rodeo Drive. That's the real you. Everything else in your life's just affectation."

"Don't you just love it," Mike said, laughing appreciatively. "I could buy and sell this nobody fifty times and still get Grandpa a new set of horseshoes and this guy still gives me shit. You gotta love the guy."

A new waiter came over, shook hands with me, and we exchanged pleasantries in Italian. Then, in English, I ordered a dry Tanqueray martini straight up with a twist. Mike wrinkled his nose.

"Martini. That's like a June Allyson movie. I'm in danger of dying of a Perrier and lime overdose. Only put stuff in the engine that's unleaded. Got to get you two out to L.A. You'd be papaya-breathed in a month."

"I'll translate the Italian," I said to Ledare, "if you explain what Mike's talking about."

"He doesn't drink anymore," she said.

"I've got a personal trainer, the whole nine yards," Mike said. "The cat used to be a cornerback for the Rams, and if you don't think he takes my ass to the well . . ."

"Read any Tolstoy lately, Mike?" I asked as the waiter brought him his drink.

"I like it. I really like it. People shake in their Tinkerbell shoes when I walk into an L.A. meeting and Jack sits here shoveling shit down my throat. Hell, man, I read screenplays non-stop from A.M. to P.M. Non-fucking-stop. If they don't get my attention by the first or second page, the script is airborne, flying the friendly skies out the fucking window . . . time's a precious metal to me, man."

"Translation, please," I asked, looking at Ledare.

"He reads a lot of movie scripts. Doesn't like a lot of them. Busy man," Ledare said.

"Here's to friendship." I lifted my glass to both of them.

The three of us touched glasses.

"There's something about the friends you made as a kid that can never be duplicated," Mike said, and there was a slight catch in his voice.

"Speak for yourself," Ledare answered. "I've made a lot of friends I like better since then."

"Get sentimental and Ledare sends a spear through your heart. She hasn't changed much, has she, Jack?"

"I'm the one who can tell you, Mike. You don't have to ask Jack. Always go to the source," Ledare said before I could answer.

"Why'd you want to meet in Venice?" I asked Mike when I saw that Ledare had hurt him. "You said you had a project."

"Project! I got an idea so fucking ballistic that I could fully arm a nuclear submarine."

"He means he's got a good idea," Ledare explained.

"I won't allow you to dampen my natural enthusiasm, Ledare. So you might as well quit trying. I speak the lingo of my community, just like Jack down here. You want octopus in this burg, you gotta go with the word *calamari*."

"What's the project, Mike?" I asked again.

"Hey, not so fast. This meeting isn't being timed. Let's just sit here and sop up each other's eyes, as the poet said."

"How's Leah, Jack?" Ledare asked.

"Yeah. The mystery kid. The one you Lindberghed out of South Carolina."

"I didn't kidnap her, Mike. She was my kid and I decided we'd move to Italy."

"Hey, I'm sensitive to your sensitivities. That's just the talk around the old gang."

"The old gang," I said softly. "I want to run for cover every time I think about the old gang."

"We had some ups and downs, but we had some great times, too."

"Jack's thinking of the casualties," Ledare said.

"Casualties. I like it. Makes great box office."

"Beautifully phrased," Ledare said. "You add something exotic to Venice. You really do."

"Ledare, I hope this doesn't set our relationship back when I say, from the bottom of my heart, please go fuck yourself. Now maybe you understand why I didn't get around to reading your screenplay."

"You read it," she said coolly. "Because you were in it."

Mike said, "You weren't exactly fair. It hurt me."

"Music to my ears," she said, motioning to the waiter for another drink.

"This is making me nervous," I interrupted. "And it's making me sorry I agreed to come up here for this meeting. I don't enjoy it when people start fighting old wars that they can't win. Especially when I should be getting VA benefits from fighting in the same wars."

"Relax, Jack," Mike said, holding his hands up in a gesture of surrender. "I was warned that you might cut and run anytime. But you need to hear me out. I've thought about doing this for a long time. Worked it out in my head. Tried to position myself in the industry so when the time was ripe I'd be ready to break the melons and spit out the seeds. Everything's in place. I've got a film that's going to be released in the fall that I'm trying to get into the Venice Film Festival. It'll make me some dough as in dough a deer a female deer, and it's a little on the artsy-fartsy side too. Quit nailing my ass in your work, pumpkin, and maybe I can produce one of your screenplays on the silver screen one day," he said, looking at Ledare suddenly.

"Her Southern heart went pitter-patter at the approach of her Beauregard," Ledare said with chill nonchalance as she studied the silhouette of the church across the canal. "I don't care if you make one of my films or not, Mike. That's why you love me."

"I want you two to write a mini-series about the South for me. Based on our town and our families. From the beginning when my grandfather arrived in Waterford to the present time."

"Mini-series," I said unpleasantly. "What an ugly phrase."

"Think of it as many dollars. It'll eradicate any aesthetic problem you might have about writing for television."

Ledare said, "My problem's working with you, Mike. That's what I told you when you first mentioned this to me and it's the same problem I've got now."

"You didn't have a problem accepting a free ticket to Venice, did you?"

"None whatsoever," Ledare said. "I wanted to see Jack again and have him take me to all the secret places of Venice."

"Can you drink the water in this burg, Jack?" Mike asked, lowering his voice. "I mean, from the tap or should I brush my teeth with Perrier? I went to Mexico last year and thought Montezuma had crawled up my ass to take a nap."

"It's Venice, not Tijuana. Water's fine."

Mike seemed happy that one more troublesome aspect of travel had evaporated with my assurance. "What do you think about my concept for the Southern series? Fire away."

"Count me out," Ledare said.

"Wait a minute, sweetgums. Mike here's left out the most important part."

He took a pen and wrote a number down on a piece of paper and held it up for both

Ledare and me to see. A gondolier moved below them, going home for the day, navigating his beautiful boat for himself, not for tourists.

"That's how much money I plan to spend for writers on this series. Let's face it. That's more money than Jack's ever made flipping burgers, and I include paperback and intergalactic sales. Jack sure as hell doesn't make that kind of bread writing about lamb kidneys and *pizza bianca*."

"Thanks for holding my profession in such high regard, Mike," I said irritably.

Ledare studied the figure that Mike had written on the piece of paper, then said, "So this is why everyone in California's so shallow."

"Maybe so," Mike said, his voice rising slightly to meet the challenge of her irony, "but it sure sharpens your aptitude for higher mathematics."

I shook my head as I watched the boat traffic move by them. "I came to Italy to get away from all that."

"Hey, I'm not asking you to write the personal stuff. Nothing about you going to the deep freeze. Nothing about Shyla and the bridge shit. I'm talking about the general history. The big picture. My grandparents. Yours, Jack. Capers' granddad was one of the biggest politicians of his time. I mean, there's a story there. We come from shit, but our families have this burning desire to make it better for their children and grandchildren, and son of a bitch, they pull it off. Look. It's got everything. Two world wars. The civil rights movement. The sixties. Vietnam. Right up to now."

"How long is this mini-series supposed to be?" Ledare asked.

"Hey, a lot of telescoping. Lot of voice-over. We hit the high points and cover the century. I think it's a hell of an exciting idea and if you two don't a lot of writers want to be part of this project."

"Hire them," I suggested.

"None of them were there," Mike said and for the first time I saw the remnants of the old Michael, the boy I grew up with and loved. "Not like we were. They didn't live through what we lived through. I keep waiting for Ledare to write about what we saw in South Carolina as kids, but everything she writes takes place in a tanning salon for feminists in Manhattan."

"Let's not fight," I said.

Mike answered, "Fight, shit. Man, in South Carolina we don't even know how to fight. In L.A. you know you've been in a good fight when your dick falls into the toilet when you take a morning piss."

"I don't want to work with you, Mike," I said. "I came here because I was curious and

wanted to see what it would be like for all of us
to be together again. I get less nostalgic about
the past than you do. But I'm nostalgic about
us and our innocence and what we went
through together and how it might have turned
out if we'd been luckier."

"Then write it like you wish it'd turned
out," Mike said, leaning toward me. "You want
to write it nicer. Great. Make it nice. It'll be
paradise to work with me. I'm a sweetheart to
work with. Here's some numbers I want you to
call. Collect. They'll know you'll be Ma Belling
them."

"Numbers?" I asked.

"People that have worked with me," he
said. "They'll back me up."

"Let me give Jack some other numbers,
Mike," Ledare said. "The people who spit over
their left shoulders when your name's mentioned."

"You make enemies in my business," Mike
said. "That's the nature of the beast."

"Then give Jack the numbers of people
who'd set you on fire just to see if their lighter
worked. Half that town thinks you've always
been a son of a bitch."

"But they didn't know me as a boy," Mike
said. "Not like you guys did. I wasn't this way
when I was growing up."

"I'm sorry, Mike," Ledare said, "I didn't mean for it to sound like that."

"No problem, Ledare. I know where it's coming from. I don't know what happened to me any more than you do. That's why I want you and Jack to do this project. I'd like you to help me find out. I know I'm alive. I just don't know how to feel it anymore. Ciao, *amigos.* I got a meeting. You two, powwow."

As we made our way toward the elevators, Ledare asked, "You're not going to take Mike's offer, are you, Jack?"

"No. The thing I love about the past most is not thinking about it."

CHAPTER 4

THE NEXT AFTERNOON I LED LEDARE through different parts of the city and watched her watch Italian women, exquisitely turned out, moving along the narrow alleys toward their homes. A woman came out of a small boutique and walked toward us, making me step behind Ledare on the narrow walkway just off the Calle del Traghetto.

Ledare stopped and stared at the woman, meeting her eyes, taking in what she was wearing, the high carriage of her walk, the beautiful legs, the thoughtless elegance, everything. She inhaled her scent.

"You'll get used to that," I said.

"I doubt it," Ledare answered. "She is beautiful."

"There's something magic about Italian women."

"She looked like she was spun from pure gold. If I were you, I'd follow that woman to the end of the line and never lose sight of her," Ledare continued.

I laughed and again moved beside her as we crossed through the Campo di Santa Margherita, where a group of small boys were playing soccer beneath the disapproving gaze of an elderly monsignor. An old woman watered a window box full of geraniums and an artist stood at the entrance of the Campo painting the whole scene in the late-afternoon light.

I was deeply aware that I was walking beside one of the lives I had refused to live. Once our pasts were entangled in such complex ways that it seemed we were meant for each other if we allowed ourselves to surrender to the simplest lures of inertia. The friends of our childhood paired us off, almost by fiat. Our temperaments seemed tranquil and complementary from first grade on. Both of us, from the beginning, looked as though we belonged on the same side of the chessboard. It was my mother who first gave me the signifying key that Ledare was bashful to the point of torment. My mother taught me that beauty was often a fine,

untouchable gift, but it almost always belonged
to the world more than the girl. She spotted the
burden and responsibility of Ledare's unasked-
for beauty and recognized that the child was
lonely. Wordlessly, Ledare and I effected a
merger of our solitudes, giving ourselves up to
the main current in our lives. As we walked
beside each other in Venice, both of us felt the
force of a story untold and a journey not taken.
It moved as a third person between us.

I knew that Ledare was hard on herself for
the choices she had made. But she had grown
up in that pampered, baby-talking way that the
South has of making its girls follow the paths of
least resistance. Just when she thought she was
learning to think for herself and make up her
own mind, she found herself in perfect lockstep
with her parents' worst instincts. Though she
knew she had long been immune to her parents' gift-wrapped poison, she found it began to
kill her only when she chose a husband. By a
series of flawless stratagems and carefully
thought-out choices, she managed to marry the
one person who thought she was both worthless and contemptible. She married a man who
was happy to ratify her most negative assump-
tions and sentiments about herself, and who
eventually came to hate everything about her.

When I was a young man I would have
thought this kind of marriage rare. Now I be-

lieve it is as common as grass. I have seen enough loveless marriages to fill up most of the empty spaces in the desert regions of the American West. American mothers teach their sons how to break a girl's spirit without even knowing they are imparting such dangerous knowledge. As boys, we learn to betray our future wives by mastering the subtle ways our mothers can be broken by our petulance and disapproval. My own mother provided me with all the weaponry I will ever need to ruin the life of any woman foolish enough to love me.

Ledare hooked her arm through mine and for a moment we both were happy.

Ledare had married one of those American men who used language and sex without regard to consequence or decency. Her love for him had damaged her confidence in her love for herself. For five years, she had tried to recover a sense of equilibrium after her husband left her for a twenty-year-old woman who was physically a younger, flashier edition of Ledare herself. She told me she had made up a list of the men in her life whom she would trust to fall in love with if she ever felt strong enough to sally forth in those sharply contested fields again. I had been on that list until Ledare remembered that Shyla had committed suicide. When she remembered that, she had crossed me carefully off the list and put in phone calls to the other three men who survived the cut. Like the other women who knew me, Ledare thought I bore much of the responsibility for Shyla's death, even though she knew little or nothing about our life together.

From a bridge overlooking one of the minor canals, I pointed at two elderly craftsmen putting the finishing touches on a gondola. They were employed by the gondola factory that still made the boats by hand.

"I've got a friend named Gino," I said, taking Ledare's arm. "His station's not far from here."

"You figured out a nice way to make a living, Jack. I knew you could roast oysters and cook a pig, but I never dreamed you'd write cookbooks. And it never occurred to me you'd spend your life writing about beautiful cities and great places to eat."

"No one thought you'd write for the movies either."

"I think I did," she said, turning toward me. "But I also think you just might have run away."

"I might have, Ledare. But it's my call and I get to do what I want to do. It's one of the few benefits of growing up."

"I sometimes tell friends in New York about what it was like growing up in Waterford, Jack. I tell about the crowd we ran around with

—all of us—and they can't believe the stories. They say I make it sound like I grew up surrounded by gods and goddesses. They tell me I'm exaggerating. They never believe it. I tell them about Mike first, because they've all heard of him. Tell about you and your family. Shyla and her family. Capers and Jordan. Max, the Great Jew. Mother . . . I can never tone the stories down to make them believable. Was there one of us who didn't seem smart to you, even then?"

"Yeah. *I* didn't seem so smart to me. Even then. Not smart enough to get out of the way."

"Out of the way of what?"

"I didn't know that everything you do is dangerous—everything—the smallest, most inconsequential act can be the thing that brings you crashing to earth."

"Were there any signs or omens? Tea leaves we could have read if we'd been alert?"

"You're not supposed to see the signs. They're invisible and odorless and don't leave tracks. You don't even feel them till you find yourself on your knees weeping over their unbearable weight," I said.

I maneuvered her toward an alley that led past a trattoria and a dry cleaner's with misted windows. The smell of garlic and hanging pork poured out of the trattoria.

"I've never eaten in that trattoria. It must be new."

"How wonderful," Ledare said. "Is that how we turn the subject away from the horror of it all?"

"I've trained myself not to think about South Carolina much, Ledare. Especially those parts that only cause pain. Like Shyla. I hope you understand. If you don't, pardon me, but I don't need to ask your permission about what I get to think about. Nor do you have to ask my permission to write about anything you god-damn feel like. And never, not once, Ledare, have you written a word about what happened to us gods and goddesses of your childhood."

"Why, Jack, it's been years since I've heard the president of my senior class give a speech," she teased, smiling.

"You shitbird, you trapped me."

"It's funny, Jack, South Carolina's always been the forbidden subject to me. I've never written a word about it, alluded to it in the slightest way, and never thought I would until Mike took me to lunch in New York last month. My parents live in absolute terror that I'll reveal secrets of the manor that'll bring shame and disaster to the family name."

"Your family doesn't have secrets, Ledare," I said. "It's just got bones."

"Does it surprise you that Capers is running for governor?"

"Capers is running for governor." I laughed out loud. "It was inevitable. Do you remember how he used to talk about running for governor when we were in first and second grade? Can you believe someone can be that ambitious and single-minded when they're only seven years old?"

"Of course I can believe it. If you remember, Jack, I married him and mothered two of his children," she said and a trace of bitterness put a ragged edge on her voice.

"You know what I think about your ex-husband," I said. "Let's let that subject pass."

"But you don't know what I think about him," she said. "At least not currently. Do you believe he's running as the Republican candidate?"

"A Republican?" I said, genuinely surprised. "I'd rather have a sex-change operation than vote Republican in South Carolina. Even Capers should be ashamed of his ass. No. Not Capers. Shame has no part to play in his buttoned-down theater of the absurd."

"My son and daughter are his greatest fans." She paused and seemed to hold her breath. "They don't like me as much as they like their father. He's a bastard, but charming.

You could put Capers next to a chameleon and Capers would be the one to change colors."

"I can't even think about any of these people without being overwhelmed by a sense of guilt. I feel guilty that I hate Capers, even though I know I've got perfectly legitimate reasons for hating his ass."

"I don't feel a bit guilty for hating him," she said. We stopped for a moment to watch a brindled cat sleeping in a window. "You once tried to explain the relationship of Catholicism and guilt, and I didn't understand a word of it. Your being a Catholic was just one more odd thing about the McCall family."

"Guilt's my mainstream," I explained. "The central theme of my life. The Church laid a foundation of pure guilt inside me. They raised a temple in the soft center of a child. Floors were paved with guilt. Statues of saints were carved out of great blocks of it."

"You're an adult now, Jack. Get on with it. Surely you've figured out how silly and stupid this all is."

"No one agrees with you more. But you were raised an Anglican and Anglicans only feel guilty if they forget to feed their polo ponies or cover their stock margins."

"That's not what I'm talking about. You've always acted like guilt was something real, something you could hold in your hands. You need to let go of it, Jack."

We walked deeper into Venice in silence. As I caught glimpses of Ledare's face, I found her beauty still diffident and withheld. She was so pretty that her comeliness seemed more of a mission than a gift. Ledare had always proved reluctant to accept the responsibilities that beauty asks of women.

I can still remember watching Ledare water skiing in the Waterford River after her mother had bought her a yellow bikini in Charleston. She had always been a show-off on skis, being pulled by a fast boat, doing fancy tricks on her slalom. But on that day, the men of the town lined the banks like crows on a wire to admire the soft, newly sculpted curves that had happened so recently on her thin, girlish body. Her ripening was so sudden and lush that it became a topic of conversation in the pool halls and along the bar stools in town. She had found being pretty trying enough; Ledare found being sexy unbearable. Since nothing discomfitted her more than the unwanted attention of men, Ledare packed the yellow bikini in the same box that held the summer dresses of her childhood days.

I studied Ledare's face, her loveliness, her fine features.

"You promised me a gondola ride," Ledare

said, changing the subject as we began walking
back toward the Grand Canal.

"We're near Gino's spot. The handsomest
of the gondoliers."

"Does he prey on pretty American girls?"

"You're doomed, kid," I said, winking at
her.

As we walked through streets that seemed
too narrow for breathing, we smelled onions
frying in olive oil and heard the sound of voices
carrying, airborne and mysterious, along the
canals. We passed houses where canaries sang
to each other from brightly lit windows, and
inhaled the aroma of fried liver and heard the
slapping of water against the dark, carved hulls
of the gondolas and the scream of male cats.
Ledare paused at a mask shop where grotesque, quasi-human faces stared back at us in
all the mute terror of their eyelessness. We
continued on, listening to the church bells and
squabbles among children, pigeons calling to
each other from rooftops, and the sound of our
own footsteps along the canal.

Gino was waiting at his post near the Ac-
cademia and smiled when he saw us. He bowed
deeply when I introduced him to Ledare. Gino
was short and blond, and had a gondolier's
deeply sculpted body. I noticed that Gino took
Ledare in all at once in a long appreciative
gaze.

The gondola rode high in the Grand Canal, swan-necked and proud as a horse as Ledare sat by me with her arm through mine. Gino moved with strong, perfect motions behind us, a sweet action of wrists and forearms.

Ledare let her hand drift down the side of the gondola as a wave from a vaporetto washed over it while Gino maneuvered the craft expertly through the choppy waters of the canal.

Ledare said, "This city does something to reality. I've felt like a contessa since I arrived. Floating through here, I feel like I'm made of silk."

"You'll wish you were made of money before you leave," I promised. "It's cheaper to live in heaven."

"You think heaven's prettier than Venice?" she asked, looking around us.

"Too much to ask," I said.

I remembered my stay in Venice during Carnevale, after Shyla died, when I had been covering the revelry of Venetians before the long fastings and privations of Lent. During the wildest part of that first night, I had marveled that these people who were celebrating the pleasures of the flesh with such open-ended immoderation could turn so quickly to the darker joys of self-denial.

It had snowed that February, deep drifting snow born in the high passes of the Alps, and I had felt like a child throwing snowballs with other tourists in St. Mark's Square. I had forgotten that Southerners are always made happy by the sight of snow. It always surprises us.

I bought a mask and a costume to blend in with the Venetians in their suddenly disguised city. Running through the streets following various bands of revelers, I joined parties I was not invited to as I let the crowds steer me past the entryways of snow-dusted, candle-lit palazzos. In silence and in costume, I drifted through that white, starry world as strange as those attendant angels who filled up the wall space in unpraised chapels. By not speaking, I lost myself in the lawlessness of Carnevale and felt the power of masks to disfigure the shape of my own superego for the lurid rites of celebration. I thought that Shyla's leap had unmasked me in some profound, unknowable way. But on that night, the mask returned me to myself as I rushed through the city with a sense of rising joy. In the cold of Venice, I felt time burn off me as I danced with anonymous women and drank wine that flowed easily in this greenhouse of pleasure where I felt myself recovering something lost in a playing field of masks. I watched a young priest scurry into a safe passageway, as though the air itself was contaminated. He looked around once, taking it all in, and we bowed to each other before he

disappeared. He was right to flee this unloos-
ened night, religious only at the fringes, and he
crossed himself as he entered his hermitage.
The priest had escaped the one licensed whirl
that centered around lust's shining eloquence.

Then I ran down slippery, half-lit streets,
going deeper and deeper into the unknown
Venice, wishing I could weep, at last, for poor
lost Shyla. I thought the tears would come easily behind a mask, but I was wrong again. After
her death, I had no time to cry for Shyla and I
covered my grief with the excuse that Leah
needed my strength far more than any breakdown. So I made an appointment for myself at
Carnevale and as I wandered farther into Venice covered with chasubles of snow, I wanted to
make time for all the tears I carried in me.
None came, not a one, because the spirit of the
city lifted me along with the fog that rose up
along the waterways as ice began to erase the
current in the smaller canals.

Another party of ten to twenty people sped
past on a narrow and treacherous path and a
woman reached out and grabbed my hand. I
followed her as fireworks exploded high above
the Grand Canal and a siren went off deep in
the unsleeping city. She led me up stairs to an
apartment where we slow-danced to a Frank
Sinatra album of love songs at a party so

crowded that we simply swayed against the other bodies in the smoke-filled room.

The woman was masked but my imagination filled in every detail of her features. In their masks, all the women turned into famous beauties and all the men dazzled with their handsomeness and the woman I danced with began to ask me questions in Italian. I could not speak a word of Italian without letting the entire country in on the fact that I was an American.

"Ah!" the woman said in her rich, musical voice. "I was hoping you were Chinese."

"Then I am Chinese," I said in Italian.

"I am a contessa," she said proudly. "I can trace my family's origins all the way back to the twelfth doge."

"This is true?" I asked.

"On this night, everything is true," she said. "All women are contessas at Carnevale."

My Italian had come to its farthest border and I asked in English, "Does the mask make it easy to lie?"

"The mask makes it necessary to lie."

"Then you are not a contessa," I said.

"I am a contessa on the same night every year. And I expect the whole world to pay me the homage I am due."

I stepped back and bowed deeply. "My adored contessa."

"My servant," she said, curtsied, then disappeared into the crowd.

Back outside, I walked westward through the deepening snow and my feet began to freeze in my silly costume shoes. Pretty women hidden behind lacquered masks laughed and ran away at my approach. The Venetian alleyways, claustrophobic and narrow, exaggerated my height and my shadow thrown across courtyards seemed vast and ecclesiastical. Near the baroque facade of the Church of the Gesuiti, a woman appeared in the snow, alone. She giggled when she saw me, half-frozen and ridiculous in my cheap costume, but she did not run away. We both laughed when we realized we were the only two people out in this obscure part of the city.

The masked woman, dressed virginally in white, took my hand as I tried to speak, but she put a silencing finger to my lips. Returning her touch, I traced her full bottom lip with my finger until she bit it roughly. She then took my hand and hurried me through passages and beneath arches until we came to a part of the city where I had never walked.

When we entered an alleyway too narrow for two people to walk side by side, she turned and wrapped a scarf around my eyes, laughing as she made sure the blindfold covered my mask completely. Convinced I could see noth-

ing, she led me down the alley, leading me like
an aerialist beckoning on the high wire. Far off
in the city, I could hear the voices of the cele-
brants sounding distant and abstracted.

I followed her blindly and trusted her as she
led me through a doorway and up four flights
of narrow stairs. We entered a room and she
removed the scarf from my eyes; the room was
so dark that I could see nothing clearly in the
perfect warm darkness and heard only the slapping of water against the sides of unseen boats
tied up outside.

Then I felt her naked against me and her
mouth found my mouth and her tongue hunted
for my tongue and drove it back deep against
my throat. Her mouth tasted like wine and seawater, like womanhood distilled. I licked her
throat and breasts as she moved me toward a
bed, laid me down on freshly laundered cotton
sheets, then unbuttoned each button of my costume. She licked my chest in her purring descent down my body. When her mouth reached
my penis, she took it down her throat and back
up in a swift purling motion like a fire-eater
and pushed the limits of both burlesque and
desire. The scrimmage of her tongue took me
to the high ledges of orgasm, then she released
me suddenly and rolled me over her. We kissed
again and I tasted myself and the taste of her
mouth was a different flavor as I entered her. I

knew in that moment that she would choose to remain anonymous. There would be no ceremony of unmasking. As I moved inside her and rode her with abandon I surrendered myself to the night, a night when sex bloomed like a wildflower in a secret alcove of the imagination, when lust roared and bawled and allowed itself to be primal, animal, unnamable as it was in the caves and forests and the light of fires when fire was not yet a word and the body still was a being without a name.

Now as the gondola moved through the lights playing in the Grand Canal, I tried to remember her long, unseen limbs, to conjure her every movement in the deciduous empire of touch, every pressure of her breasts and response of her legs and heels, all shivers and sighs in the bright résumé of her passion. She had spoken no words to me nor I to her, and the mere fact of our wordlessness had excited me further.

When I came, my scream met her scream and our tongues bruised against the sound. Then, exhausted and sweating, we fell off each other and again we heard the splash of water, of boats drumming against their moorings and straining against ropes and tides accompanied by our own heavy panting as our lovemaking cooled slowly. Her hair fell against my chest as we lay together in the blackened room.

Ledare touched me on the cheek, her fingers wet from letting them drift in the currents. "A penny for your thoughts."

"I was thinking about the place of existentialism in modern literature," I said.

"Liar," she said, flicking her fingers and spraying me playfully with canal water. "Whatever it was, I could tell it was nice."

"Life-changing," I said.

"They built this city so you'd never want to leave it, didn't they, Jack?" Ledare said.

"No," I said. "I think they are nicer than that. They built it so you'd always have something to dream about."

"It breaks my heart how pretty it all is," she said.

"Venice travels well," I said. "She won't leave you."

In the room, I'd heard footsteps moving through the snow, light and muffled. The woman left the bed quickly, but again she put a finger to my lips. She returned with my costume, my soaked shoes, which she must have had warmed on some kind of heater. When I'd dressed she led me to the doorway and ran my hands over her unseen face like a blind man reading his favorite poem in braille. Then she put on her mask, then mine, and once more blindfolded me with a scarf and led me down the stairway and into the snow.

I followed her through the bitterly cold night toward the noise and the crowds and the beginning of Lent. I attempted to talk to her in my Berlitz Italian, begged her for her name, explained that I wanted to see her again, to take her to dinner.

She laughed when I spoke and her laughter revealed that she knew her mystery and her silence were the essential erotica of our time together.

We crossed a bridge and her hand left mine suddenly as I was asking her if Venice was her hometown. I tried to call out to her but realized there was no name to call. Removing the scarf from around my mask, I found myself disoriented at an intersection of four Venetian alleys. I listened for sounds of running or flight, but her escape was silent. I spun in a circle but only saw other masked figures like myself coming over bridges, some carrying bottles of wine, some candles or flashlights. The flashlights crisscrossed through the snowy air. Voices rose everywhere, but it was her silence I longed for.

I tried to retrace my steps, but this was Venice and the woman had given me all the time she was willing to give.

Before I left the city, I wandered over it, especially in that obscure neighborhood by the Gesuiti where I guessed my secret lover had taken me. I wanted to thank and praise her and cry her name aloud. I had not made love to a woman since Shyla's death. My body had been shut down until that night of snow in Venice and the woman of the mask, the woman who understood the mystery of remaining unnamed, the woman who did not utter a single word.

Much later, I suspected that the woman might have been Shyla herself, telling me it was time to get on with my life and to forget about her. Dressing up and playing make-believe were two of the things that Shyla loved best.

When Ledare and I arrived at the Gritti Palace, I paid Gino with a fifty-thousand-lire note. Gino kissed Ledare's hand and offered to take her on a tour of the smaller canals for free the next day. Then we went up to dress for dinner.

Mike was already seated when we walked into the Taverna La Fenice later that evening.

"Have a seat. You look beautiful, Ledare. You could get arrested in that dress," Mike said. "Nice place here, Jack. No pizza joint for the three mouseketeers, huh?"

"It's an old favorite of mine," I said. "I thought you two would like it."

When the waiter came to take our order, I was explaining the menu.

"The pastas are terrific here. The *bigoli con*

granzeola is made with a crab sauce. They don't taste much like our blue crabs, but they taste great anyway. The veal dishes are all good. If you like liver, Venice is the place."

"Just tell the guy I'll have a hamburger and a green salad with Roquefort cheese dressing," Mike said.

"They don't have hamburgers here. And they don't have Roquefort cheese dressing in Italy."

"No hamburgers. It's a restaurant, isn't it? The fucking Four Seasons in New York serves hamburgers."

"I'd trust Jack on this one," Ledare said. "He covers this territory."

"I don't believe the Roquefort cheese dressing either," Mike added. "Where do they make Roquefort cheese? Answer me that one?"

"In France," Ledare said.

"Right. France. Next fucking country, yes? Bet it's not three hundred miles from here. I don't eat salad without Roquefort."

"You will tonight," I said.

"Italy's still the Third World, man. You'd think they'd get the picture and sign up for the twentieth century. Get me some veggies and some of that thin veal. What's that real skinny veal called? Starts with an *s*?"

"Scallopini."

"You order for me, Jack," Ledare said.

I smiled and said, "Smart girl," and proceeded to order them a Venetian feast that began with carpaccio and was followed by a risotto brimming with fresh green spears of asparagus. We finished with the leg of lamb, eggplant, and spinach and, too sated for dessert, we ordered espresso and a glass of grappa.

Mike's salad arrived, but he did not touch it when he found it was dressed with olive oil. So I instructed the waiter, in Italian, to bring us some ingredients from the kitchen. When they arrived he mixed some yogurt and mayonnaise in a bowl, then added Worcestershire sauce and Tabasco before he crumbled a wedge of Gorgonzola into the mixture. The waiter tossed a fresh salad with the newly made dressing and could not hide his contempt for the result.

"Great stuff," Mike said happily as he tasted it. "I told you they had Roquefort cheese stashed around here somewhere."

It was only a few moments later that Mike brought up the subject he was in Venice to pursue. "Let's talk a minute about the project. What do you two think? The greatest change in the South since World War II?"

After thinking about it a moment, Ledare said, "The invention of instant grits. No, that's not it. That you can buy a taco, a *taco,* in almost any small town in the South."

Mike frowned and said, "You're not being serious. How about you, Jack?"

"I'm not going to work on your project and I personally don't care what the biggest or the smallest change has been in the South."

"This is big money, Jack. More money than you've ever made. I've done some checking. This is a personal favor from me to you. I had to do some fast talking to get you approved. Ledare's got a couple of credits, a little name recognition. Your Julia Child imitation doesn't bring shit to the project."

"I'm out of it, Mike."

"Will you work as a consultant?"

"No."

"Why?"

"Because you'll want us to write about Shyla and I'm not going to do that."

"We won't have to say she jumped off the bridge. Or we can just do that off-screen."

"Count me out. You're also going to want to write about Jordan and the sixties."

"No. Wait a sec," Mike said, holding his hand in the air. "You're getting ahead of the game. See, I want it in a context. Don't you see? It's not just about us. It's about this century. My grandfather coming to Waterford not speaking but ten words of English. He meets your grandfather, Jack. It changes both their lives forever. We're here at this table in Venice right now because of a pogrom that took place in Russia in 1921. Isn't that true?"

"Yes," I agreed, "that's true."

"Look, that past defined us, like it or not. And then we lived through some shit. You asked about Jordan. Hell yeah, we deal with Jordan. Who changed us more than Jordan Elliott? Do you know where he is, Jack?"

"Rumor has it he died. We all went to his memorial service."

"Rumor has it that he's alive, that you know where he is. Rumor has it that he's in Italy."

"If he is, he's never gotten in touch with me," I said.

"If he had, would you tell me?" Mike asked.

"No, I wouldn't tell you."

"I don't agree with what the son of a bitch did in the war, but God damn, it's great drama. Especially if we learn how he got away."

"You could make that part up, couldn't you?" Ledare asked Mike. "Maybe Jack's right. Maybe he died while trying to escape or hide."

"I want to get at the truth," Mike said. "It's a matter of principle that we be as factual as we can. I'm gonna find that son of a bitch and pay him a ton of money to tell his story."

"Did he say 'principle'?" Ledare asked me in mock surprise. "Did Mike just say 'principle'?"

"Another point of business," Mike said, ignoring Ledare. "I want you both to hear me out on this before you start screaming. I know what you're going to say, but what I say might surprise you."

"Fire away," Ledare said, shrugging her shoulders.

"I've joined Capers Middleton's campaign committee in his run for governor of South Carolina. I'm his executive chairman in charge of finance. We'd like very much to put both your names on his election committee."

Ledare looked perfectly stunned and said, "How do you say 'fuck you' in Italian, Jack?"

"You don't need to know. Just say 'fuck you' in English and double it for me."

"I know where both of you're coming from. But you're both wrong. The cat's changed. I talked with him in New York before I flew over here, and this is one forward-looking son of a bitch. He's got some real radical ideas about how to finance education and industry clear into the next century."

"Yoo-hoo, Mike," Ledare purred murderously. "You forget I was married to the forward-looking son of a bitch. He had some real radical ideas about how to pay child support, too. He preferred not to."

"His divorce from you is causing a little

trouble in his campaign. I won't lie to you,"
Mike said.

"Good," she said. "He's a coldhearted,
ruthless bastard, Mike. I fell in love with him
once, married him, had two children by him,
and learned to hate him slowly and over time.
He's poison in all the right places and all the
wrong ones, too."

"He feels bad about you, Ledare. He told
me that himself. He admits he was an asshole."

"The University of South Carolina," I interrupted, "1970, Mike. Very big year. You may
remember we learned something very significant about our boy, Capers Middleton, that
year."

"Not all of us," Ledare said. "Some of us
didn't learn a thing about Capers' nature or
sense of integrity from that telling moment.
One of us went from that amazing existential
moment and married him."

Mike breathed deeply and waited for our
anger to pass before he resumed speaking. "No
one hated Capers for that more than I did. But
he stands by what he did and still thinks of it as
an act of patriotism. He wants to tell us everything that led up to that night at the draft
board. That'll be part of the mini-series."

"I'm sorry, Mike, I'm off the project,"
Ledare said.

"For God's sake. What's the big deal?"

Mike said. "Besides, I know you both could use the cash."

"Is that it, Mike?" I asked. "Do you think you can buy us, that we're for sale for the right price?"

"I'm not talking about buying anyone, Jack," Mike said, and now his tone changed. "I'm talking about doing good work and telling a great story and getting to know each other again. The money's just gravy. You know, all the chocolate ice cream you can eat?"

"And your friend Capers wants to tell us all about his heroic role at the university? Come clean as an American hero?"

"He was a hero to a great many people. I'd say ninety-five percent of the people of South Carolina supported what he did."

"Those same people all supported the Vietnam War."

"The sixties. That's tired old shit, Jack. Lousy box office," Mike said, still uncomfortable as the object of Ledare's uncompromising gaze.

"I want to go on record with you, Mike. Right now. Say it up front. Everything I believed in the sixties, I still believe with all my heart. I've repudiated nothing," I said.

"A lot of it was self-righteous bullshit. Admit it," Mike said.

"I admit it. And I still believe it."

"Okay," Mike said, "what Capers did is open for debate. I've got an open mind on the subject. But it didn't hurt anyone. You got arrested, Jack, but you didn't do hard time."

"No, it hurt all of us. It was a killing blow, Mike. See? We loved Capers and believed in him and followed him." I smiled.

"But you've gotten over it. Everyone has."

"Not the guy you're looking for. I bet Jordan hasn't gotten over it," Ledare said. "If he proves to be alive, I mean."

"You do know where he is?" Mike asked me again.

"No, Mike. We went to his memorial service, remember? Because of Capers Middleton, none of us has seen Jordan since 1970."

Mike removed a checkbook from his breast pocket and wrote out a check for ten thousand dollars. He handed it to me.

"That's a down payment. Take me to Jordan . . . and there's another ten thousand where that came from."

I looked at the check and laughed. I lit the end of it with a candle on the table that had burned nearly to the end of its taper. I watched as the check made a splendid blaze and then I dropped it into Mike's espresso cup.

"Mike, I want you to study me. Bone up for final exams. You need to learn how to be a human being again. You were a good one once. You just forgot the steps."

Mike leaned forward and his eyes blazed at me with rancor. "I got news for you, Jack. You ain't the captain of all the teams anymore. High school's over and let's face it, little Mike's doing better than anybody. From *People* magazine to *Who's Who* to Oscar night, Michael Hess is someone to be reckoned with in the world of film. All of us at this table've done damn well. Ledare writes her celebrated screenplays. You write cookbooks for fat tourists and a couple of travel books to tell assholes how to get to the Sistine Chapel. But I win the sweepstakes."

"Please shut up, Mike," Ledare said. "Listen to yourself. Bragging about being in *People* magazine for God's sake. It's too pathetic."

"I'll say what I want to say. Look at Jack. So self-righteous and smug. For what, Jack? For what goddamn reason? You burn the check up like you're Francis of fucking Assisi. But here's what I've learned, pal. I make that check large enough, I keep adding the figures, and eventually I'll hit the price when you go to your knees and give me a blow job."

"You're gonna be writing a long time before you hit that number, Mike," I replied, smiling in an attempt to defuse the tension at

the table. But Mike seemed hell-bent to continue the frontal assault.

"You sneer at me. You sneer at Capers
Middleton, whose only sin is trying to make
South Carolina a better place to live. We may
not live up to your high fucking standards,
Jack, but none of our wives ever went up on the
bridge. All of our girls are still walking around
with their Gucci bags and credit cards. None of
them had to be fished out of the river. Sorry to
be so blunt, ol' pal. But those are the facts."

I closed my eyes and did not open them
until I felt under control. I wanted to lunge
across the table at Mike and beat his face in
until my fist ran with his blood. Then I thought
about Leah and Shyla and did not respond to
Mike's attack.

"Go ahead, Jack," Ledare said calmly. "Kill
him. He deserves it."

"I'm sorry," Mike said suddenly. "Jesus,
I'm sorry, Jack. That wasn't me that said that.
Open your eyes. You can see remorse written
all over me. R-E-M-O-R-S-E. Remorse. As
pure as it comes. I swear to you, Jack. That
wasn't me talking. No one loved Shyla more
than I did. You gotta give me that."

I opened my eyes and said, "I give you that.
You loved Shyla and that's the only reason I'm
not drowning your sorry ass in the Grand Canal."

"Let me drown his ass," said Ledare. "Boys get to have all the fun."

"Great line," Mike said. "Write it down and I'll get it typed up in the morning. That'll go in the screenplay."

The evening ended. As we walked back to the Gritti Palace, Mike tried to undo the damage and was perfectly charming and even made me laugh a little.

I said nothing and contented myself with listening to Mike. I knew him well enough to understand that jokes and laughter were part of his elaborate ritual of apology. But beneath my laughter, my mind was spinning. I had to return to Rome to warn Jordan Elliott that Mike Hess was hot on his trail.

CHAPTER 5

I DROVE MARTHA TO THE ROME AIR-
port, and once there she checked and
rechecked her tickets to South Carolina as
soldiers from the Italian Army walked by her
carrying machine guns.

"I'll never get used to all these machine
guns in airports," she said.

"It cuts down on shoplifting," I said. "Let
me buy you a cappuccino here. They won't let
me go to the gate with you."

"Because of terrorism."

"I guess. The Red Brigade's about petered
out. But the PLO's still frisky. Libya's making

noise. The IRA's around. Even a liberation movement in Corsica."

"Why do you live here with all this going on?"

"Wasn't Atlanta the murder capital of the U.S. last year?"

"Yes, but the airport's perfectly safe," she said.

We bought cappuccinos and watched a group of brilliantly clad Saudis enter the building and pass a large contingent from Ghana swathed in their native finery. It seemed a citizen from every country would pass you by if you only stood in the Rome airport long enough, and this connection to the whole world never failed to thrill me. I could smell the love of travel here and feel that rush of adrenaline in travelers as they glanced up at departure boards and studied the small numbers on their neatly inscribed tickets. An airport was a place where I could actually see time move. People sifted through doors and gates like sand through an hourglass.

"I don't have to tell you this, Jack. Leah's a magnificent child. You're doing a splendid job."

"I'm just watching, Martha. She's raising herself."

"I wish you'd bring her back home."

"I don't think so," I said, as softly as I could. "I'm sorry, Martha."

"I can promise there'll be no scenes."

"How can you promise that? Not with your father."

"Did you always hate him?" she asked gently. "Even when you were a child? Our houses backed up to each other."

"No, I only got to hate him after I really got to know the guy. I think it started when he sat shiva when Shyla married me."

"My mother begged him not to."

"And so when he sat shiva for a second time after Shyla's death my high regard for him only increased."

"He's a good Jew. He was right to sit shiva then."

"And he was dead fucking wrong to do it after she married me," I exploded.

"Again, he thought he was being a good Jew."

"And a bad human being. Do you like your father, Martha? Shyla sure didn't."

Martha was thoughtful for a moment.

"I respect him, Jack. Pity him. For all he's been through."

"Whatever he went through, he's sure as hell paid the world back in spades."

"He says that your keeping him away from

his granddaughter's the cruelest thing he's faced," Martha said.

"Good. Jack McCall surges past World War II in a nose-to-nose race to see who can make George Fox suffer most."

"He can't help who he is or what makes him suffer," Martha said.

"Neither can I, Martha. Now it's time to get you through security."

At the security gate, we embraced and held each other for a long moment.

"I appreciate your doing this, Martha. It was a grand gesture. You took a chance, and I appreciate it."

"I hope it's only the start. We'd like Leah to be part of our life, Jack. My mother wants to see you badly."

"Tell her thanks. I'll think about it."

"You and Shyla, Jack," Martha said wonderingly. "I never knew what made it work."

"Neither did anyone else," I said as Martha turned toward the opaque gazes of five heavily armed airport guards.

I returned to my apartment and spent the rest of the day working on the article about Venice and the Gritti Palace. I like writing about strange cities and cuisines because it keeps me at arm's length from the subjects that are too close to me.

To capture the sense of place in each country I visit, I work hard at turning homesickness into a kind of scripture as I describe what the native-born cherish most about their own countries. Writing about Venice always presents a challenge. The city is a peacock tail unfurled in the Adriatic and the sheer infinity of its water-dazzled charms makes you long for a new secret language brimming with untried words that can only be used when describing Venice to strangers. Venice has always brought me face to face with the insufficiency of language when confronted by such timeless beauty. I've put in the hours trying to make the overvisited city mine and mine alone. I've tried to notice things that would surprise even Venetians.

When I finished, I typed out four recipes I had received from different Venetian chefs, then addressed the article to the editor of *The Sophisticated Traveler* at the *New York Times*. Having given the package to the *portiere* I walked across the Tiber to the shul Leah attended once a week.

Leah came out surrounded by other children, the boys all wearing delicate little yarmulkes, small as mittens. She ran toward me when she saw me and I picked her up and spun us both around in the street.

"Did Aunt Martha catch her plane?" Leah asked. "I just love her, Daddy. We had so much to talk about."

"She worships you, sweetheart. But so does everyone else."

"She asked me a question I couldn't answer," she said as we began to walk.

"What was it?"

"Am I Jewish, Daddy?" Leah asked. "Martha asked me that and the rabbi asks it all the time. The rabbi doesn't like it that I go to a Catholic school."

"Suor Rosaria doesn't like it that you go to shul. But according to Jewish law, you're Jewish."

"But you?" she asked. "According to you, what am I?"

"I don't know, Leah," I admitted as we walked through the noisy streets of Trastevere toward the river. "Religion's strange to me. I grew up Catholic, yet the Church hurt me. It damaged me and made me afraid of the world. But it also filled me with wonder. Your mother was a Jew and proud of it. She'd want you raised as a Jew, so that's why I send you to shul."

"What do you want me to be?"

"What I want is not important. You can choose for yourself. What I'd like is for you to study both and reject both."

"Do they worship different gods?" she asked.

"No, honey. I think it's the same cat. Look,

I know I'm going to pay for this in the future. You'll grow up without religious roots and when you're eighteen I'll find you dressed in saffron Hare Krishna robes with your head shaved, chanting Hindi, and playing a tambourine in the Atlanta airport."

"I just want to know if I'm a Jew or a Catholic."

"You pick, darling." And I squeezed her hand.

"Martha says that I'm a Jew."

"If that's what you want to be, then that's what you are. I'd love for you to be Jewish. Nothing would irritate my family more."

"What's South Carolina like?" Leah asked, changing the subject.

"Horrible. Very ugly and depressing to look at. It smells bad all the time and the ground's covered with rattlesnakes. It has laws making all children slaves from the time they're born until they're eighteen. The state doesn't allow ice cream or candy to be sold inside the state line and requires all kids to eat five pounds of brussels sprouts a day."

"I hate brussels sprouts."

"That's only the start. All kittens and puppy dogs are drowned as soon as they're born. Stuff like that. You never want to go there. Trust me."

"Aunt Martha said it was beautiful and that

she wanted me to come visit her next summer. May I go?" We walked on without my responding.

"What kind of ice cream do you want?" I asked as we walked into the bar near the Piazza Trilussa. *"Limone o fragola?"*

"Fragola," she said, "but that didn't answer my question."

"You want to eat five pounds of brussels sprouts a day and be sold into slavery?"

"You just say those things so I won't ask about Mama."

We ate our cones in silence. Mine was hazelnut, which reminds me of smoke and ice and darkness. Leah had chosen the strawberry ice cream today. Each day, she alternated between the taste of lemons and strawberries; it was one way she brought a sense of order and structure to her motherless life.

On the Ponte Sisto, we stopped and looked down at the Tiber, its flow quickening as it neared the rapids close to the Isola Tiberina. Two elderly fishermen were casting their lines into the river, but I knew I lacked the raw physical courage required to eat a fish caught in those impure waters. Even in the softest light, the Tiber looked rheumy and colicky.

"I know all about Mama," Leah said, licking her cone.

"If Martha said one word . . ."

"She didn't," Leah jumped in quickly. "I've known for a long time now."

"How'd you find out?" I said, careful not to look at her, keeping my eyes on the fishermen.

"I heard Maria talking to the *portiere,*" she said. "They didn't know I was listening."

"What did they say?"

"That Mama killed herself by jumping off a bridge," Leah said, and as the words came out of my pretty, over-serious daughter, I could feel the ruthless slipping of my heart. She tried to say it matter-of-factly, but the words resonated with the awful authority of Shyla's act. At that very moment, I knew that by treating her as an equal, I had robbed her of any chance of being a child. Worse, I had allowed Leah to mother me, stealing from a generous, eager child what my own mother had rarely been known to offer me. I had let Leah carry my implacable sorrow, and turned her childhood into a duty.

"Maria said my mother was burning in hell. That's what happens to people who kill themselves."

"No," I said, kneeling beside her and gathering her to me. I tried to see if she was crying, but could see nothing through my own tears.

"Your mother was the sweetest, finest woman I've ever met, Leah. No God would ever hurt a woman that decent and good. No

God would say a word to a woman who suffered so much. If a God like that exists, I spit on that God. Do you understand?"

"No," she said.

"Your mother had periods of great sadness," I whispered. "She would feel them coming and warn me that she was going away for a while. But she'd be back. There were doctors, hospitals. They gave her pills, did everything they could; and she'd always come back. Except the last time."

"She must have been very sad, Daddy," Leah said, crying openly now.

"She was."

"Couldn't you help her?"

"I tried to help her, Leah. You can be sure of that."

"Was it me? Was she unhappy when I was born?" Leah asked.

I knelt and held her close again, letting her cry long and hard, and waited for her to slow down before I spoke.

"There never was a baby loved like your mother loved you. Her eyes filled up with love whenever she looked at you. She couldn't keep her hands off you, wanted to breast-feed you forever. Shyla loved every single thing about you."

"Then why, Daddy? Why?"

"I don't know, darling. But I'll try to tell

you everything I understand. I promise if you'll remove the strawberry ice cream cone from the back of my neck."

We both laughed and dried each other's tears with the napkins that had come with the cones. I knelt down on one knee and let Leah wipe the ice cream from my shirt and neck. Two diminutive nuns approached us on the bridge, and when I made eye contact with one of them, she looked to the ground, shy as a whelk.

"Do you think it hurt?" Leah asked. "When she hit the water?"

"I don't think she was feeling much. She'd taken a bunch of pills before driving to the bridge."

"The bridge, Daddy," she said. "Was it higher than this?"

"Much higher."

"Do you think she was thinking of the night at the beach? When the house fell into the sea? When she fell in love with you?"

"No, darling. She had just come to a time in her life when she couldn't go on."

"It's too sad. It's just too sad," Leah said.

"That's why I couldn't tell you. That's why I never wanted this day to come. Why didn't you ask me all this when you found out?"

"I knew you'd cry, Daddy. I didn't want to make you unhappy."

"It's my job to be unhappy," I said, stroking her dark hair. "You don't have to worry about me. Tell me everything you're thinking."

"That's not what you said. You said our job was to worry about each other."

I picked my precious child up in my arms, squeezed her tightly, then hoisted her onto my broad shoulders.

"Now you know, kid. You'll be learning to live with your mama's death for the rest of your life. But me and you are a team and we're gonna have a hell of a good time. Got it?"

"Got it," Leah said, still crying.

"Did you say any of this to Aunt Martha?"

"No, I thought you'd get mad at her. I want to visit her. I want to meet the rest of my family, Daddy," she said, with all the equanimity of a stubbornly precocious child.

CHAPTER 6

BEFORE DAWN THE NEXT MORNING, Leah crawled into my bed and snuggled up to me, her form curving against my back, deft and supple as a kitten. She stroked my hair with her hand until we both fell asleep again. No words needed to be said and I marveled at the very strength of this child.

When we finally awoke, I realized how late it was and gently shook Leah.

"You've got to get ready. Maria's taking you to visit her family in the country today."

"Why don't you come with us?" she said as she jumped out of bed after giving me a big hug.

"I'll come later," I promised. "I've got some business in Rome to take care of first."

"Maria's already here," Leah said. "Smell the coffee."

After I put them on a bus to Maria's village, I walked down the Via dei Giubbonari still feeling bruised and shaken by the reality of what Leah now knew.

I walked through the Jewish Ghetto, past the theater of Marcellus, where a homeless man was living beneath a black arch among a nation of cats. The man was schizophrenic and harmless and I had seen old women in the neighborhood feeding leftover pasta from the same bowls to both the man and the cats.

I cut over to the Via di San Teodoro, then across the Circus Maximus, and strolled the length of the rose garden at the beginning of the Aventine hill. The garden offered a panoramic view of both the Circus Maximus and the Palatine hill with its earth-colored broken palaces stretching along the ridge of the hill like a ruined alphabet.

I turned and surveyed the part of the city I'd just walked through, picking a spot among the roses where I could see if anyone had followed me. At times I felt foolish doing this, but the sudden appearance of Pericle Starraci in the piazza and Mike's plan for the film seemed to confirm the rightness of my caution.

I left the rose garden and walked past the orangerie, where mothers entertained their small children and tourists took pictures of themselves with the Vatican captured in miniature far up the Tiber. When I passed Santa Sabina, I ducked into the courtyard and pretended to study the fragmentary mosaic over the nave of the church while looking again for a merciless stranger who might discover the whereabouts of Jordan Elliott because of my own lack of prudence.

It was because of Jordan, not Leah, that I had spotted the surveillance by Pericle Starraci the first day he had identified me in the Campo dei Fiori. "Paranoia has a sharper taste if the danger is real," I once wrote to Jordan in a postcard from Bergen, Norway.

I walked quickly through the Piazza dei Cavalieri di Malta, where a tour bus brimming with Americans was unloading its bovine cargo.

When I was sure I was not being followed, I slipped into the Benedictine Church of Sant' Anselmo. Mass was in progress and I heard the monks lifting their voices in ancient plainsong as I made my way to the third confessional on the left-hand side of the church. A sign announced that its confessor spoke German, Italian, French, and English. After two Italian women came out making the sign of the cross, I entered the confessional and knelt down. The priest within turned off the light, indicating that he was done with absolving crimes against God on that day.

"Father Jordan," I said immediately.

"Jack," Jordan answered. "I've been waiting for you. Four people have already come to me for confession this morning. A record, I believe."

"Word's out," I whispered. "A holy man's on the loose at Sant' Anselmo's."

"Hardly. Would you like me to hear your confession, Jack?"

"No, I don't think so. I'm not ready for that yet."

The voices of the monks lifted up in their serene chant to God.

"God's patient, Jack. He'll wait."

"No, he won't. He doesn't exist. At least, not for me, he doesn't."

"That's not true. He exists for all of us in different ways."

"Prove to me there's a God."

"Prove to me there's not one," the priest said softly.

"That's not much of an answer."

"It's not much of a question, either," said Jordan.

"At least try," I urged. "Tell me about the beauty of the sunsets or the grand designs of snowflakes. Tell me in words, no matter how stupid or silly, why you believe in God."

Jordan sighed. I knew his own faith had stalked him through days and nights of despair, and when it finally chose to pounce, he was ready for it and let himself be devoured like a lamb. Readiness is the opening God needs, I thought, as I listened to my friend in the dark, Latinized air.

"Jack," said Jordan, "the wing of a fly is proof enough of the existence of God for me."

"I've lost the gift of faith. I used to have it, but I lost it and can't seem to get it back. I don't even know if I want it back. I've forgotten how to pray."

"You're praying now, Jack. You're on a quest. It takes different forms with all of us." Jordan paused. "How'd the trip to Venice go? How's Mike? How's pretty Ledare?"

"They're both fine, although Mike has taken the Hollywood stuff to the extreme. He dresses in suits that look like they were made from the foreskins of llamas."

"What is the movie that Mike wants to make?" he asked, ignoring my comments.

"The kind that tells the story of Jordan Elliott, who disappeared in 1971 and hasn't been heard from since."

The chanting had stopped and the church gave off a strong odor of incense and melting tallow. Without the chant, the church seemed suspended in midair, and I was aware that Jordan was strangely still.

"What does Mike want to tell about Jordan Elliott?"

"He wants to tell our story. The sixties included. It's a hell of a story."

"It ends with Jordan's death."

"That's the conventional ending," I said. "But it sure as hell isn't the one that Mike believes. I implied that Mike's become a trifle shallow. I didn't say he'd become stupid."

I tried to study Jordan's face through the confessional screen but, as always, he kept his cowl pulled down around his head. Jordan was now only a voice to me, as he'd always tried to be since that amazing day when Jordan Elliott's mother came to Rome to tell me that her son was living there in secret. Because he was a hunted man, Jordan agreed to meet with me if I would agree not to see him face to face.

"How did Mike hear the rumors that I was still alive?" the priest asked, and there was an exhaustion in his voice, something damaged that I had not heard in him before.

"The same source. Always the same source. When Mrs. McEachern went to confession at the Vatican several years ago and someone she taught English to in eleventh grade was her confessor."

"Mistaken identity," Jordan said. "That's what I told her that day."

"She's also the voice teacher at Waterford High. Claims she never forgets a voice."

Jordan scoffed, but he was shaken by what I had told him. "What are the chances of hearing in Italy the confession of a South Carolina English teacher who once taught you *Life on the Mississippi* in high school?"

"Not good," I admitted. "The rumors started in earnest when she got back to town. But they had been floating around Waterford since the day of your untimely death."

"I was so overwhelmed then. I didn't have time to think it through."

"You didn't do badly. I read your obituary and I went to the memorial ceremony as an honorary pallbearer."

"So did Mike."

"He has interviewed Mrs. McEachern. A lot of folks think her story had a lot of credibility. She is neither a quiet nor a flaky woman. What better place to hide in the modern world than the priesthood?"

"No, Jack," the priest said. "You've never understood that either. The priesthood's the worst place to hide. You become a priest to remove the mask, to come out from under the rock."

"You became a priest because you were

good at running away, not because you were good at facing things. You and I are blood brothers when it comes to that."

"I became a priest to better worship my God," Jordan said angrily, "you low-life son of a bitch."

I tapped on the thin membrane that separated me from my confessor's ear. "Excuse me, Lord. My confessor just called me a foul name."

"Only under extreme provocation."

"I brought you some mail from your mother."

"She's planning a trip over here next spring."

"I didn't tell you. Shyla's sister came to town. Tracked me down with a private eye. It surprised me that I was pleased to see her. She's trying to find out everything about her sister."

"Then you should help her."

"I might."

"Tell her what I think about Shyla, Jack. Tell her that I think that Shyla is the only saint I've ever met, the only holy woman."

"Too bad she didn't marry a saint," I said, getting ready to leave.

"You're not even close," Jordan agreed. "But she married a hell of a friend."

In the darkness of the confessional, Jordan

quietly prayed the words and made the sign of the cross.

"Go now and sin no more, Jack," Jordan said. "You're absolved of sin."

"This was no sacrament," I said. "I delivered the mail."

"So it's not a conventional absolution," the priest said, "but you're not a conventional man."

"Lay low for a while," I advised. "Mike's got enough money to find Jimmy Hoffa."

As I left the confessional booth, I turned toward the chanting monks standing in their pews and walked to the altar where a priest was just finishing Mass. The Italian vernacular reminded me of the Latin responses I used to say during the Common of the Mass during my childhood. A painting in a side altar caught my attention and I studied it, wondering if this painting of the Annunciation was the work of Raphael or someone who had studied the techniques of the master with great precision. In Rome, masterpieces were as common as Easter eggs and you never knew when you would stumble across one in your wanderings. Since I knew enough about the history of art to know that the answer to the painting's provenance would not come from me, I made a note to look up the artist the next time I had business at the Vatican library.

Crossing the nave of the church, I knelt beside an older Roman woman, put five hundred lire through a coin slot, and lit a single candle for the repose of Shyla's soul. Impatient with the flame and the gesture, I rose too quickly and started the long walk down the aisle. On the other side of the church, I watched as Jordan left the confessional and made his way to the side door leading to the interior of the monastery.

Jordan had rarely let me get a good look at him since we had resumed our long-interrupted friendship in Rome. He felt that the less I knew about his life as a priest the more protection I would have if someone blew his cover. I knew he went by another name during his daily rounds in his order, but he had never revealed that name to either his mother or me. As I watched him move quickly toward that netherworld of prayer and fasting that now sustained him, I could still spot the swagger of the athlete beneath his habit. His head was shaved and he was bearded, but any woman with an appreciative eye would have turned to admire his handsomeness and physicality. Of all the boys I ever played ball with, Jordan Elliott was the only one I feared when we took the field together. The hardships of the monastery had only made a hard body more formidable. He did not seem to possess the interior governors on his reserves of physical courage that the rest of us did. On the playing fields of Waterford, that gentle priest I watched moving gracefully toward some modest cell deep in the city would kick the country ass of any boy who got in his way and all of us knew it. In a full-contact scrimmage before the Bishop England game, Jordan once nearly tore my head off when I went out to receive a swing pass from Capers Middleton. It was the day I learned what smelling salts were.

As I resumed my way out, I saw something that looked vaguely like a firearm sticking out of a confessional in front of me, pointing at Jordan. I had worked side by side with photographers for much of my career, knew many of them were fanatical about getting the perfect shot, but never knew one who would occupy a confessor's seat during a Mass no matter how much money he was earning from the shoot. I heard the Nikon's rapid-fire clicking as the telephoto lens recorded every step of Jordan's departure. Then I watched the camera withdraw inside the confessional as the monks began to sing again.

Stepping into another side chapel, I waited for the unseen photographer of the departing monk to make his appearance. For five minutes, there was not even the quiver of a curtain around the confessional, then I saw a well-dressed man carrying a leather bag step out, make the sign of the cross, and genuflect before he turned and left the church. Though the man did not see me, I know it would have surprised him if he had discovered I was still in the church. In my mind, I retraced my steps going backward, wondering where I had let my guard down, when I took the rituals of security and watchfulness so seriously whenever I paid Jordan a visit.

But as I watched the private investigator Pericle Starraci pause at the holy water font and bless himself, I caught a look of preening self-satisfaction on his face and was quite sure that he thought he had solved the disappearance of Jordan Elliott once and for all and had the photographs to prove it.

CHAPTER 7

I WAS IN THE MIDDLE OF A DREAM
about Shyla when gunfire in the piazza awoke
me at three in the morning. The sound of a
motorino racing down the side street just below
my bedroom window made me think of the
drone of June bugs tied to a string and let loose
in the false freedom of circles. The dream
washed itself out when I turned on my night-
light and made my way down a dark hallway
toward the living room. In the piazza, I heard
the sound of people running and screaming,
and far off on a hill above Trastevere, a siren
howled its way down a curving street, the sound
echoing back on itself. Leah was already at one

of the windows watching the policeman bleed to death.

The man was nearly dead, and it was hard to believe a man's body could hold so much blood. It would prove to be a last-gasp action of the Red Brigades, and this poor, dying policeman would be the final fatality the city of Rome would suffer due to the extreme views of that group.

"He's so young," Leah said.

"A kid," I agreed, looking down at the man as a crowd began to form, shouting prayers and imprecations as the carabinieri who guarded the French Embassy tried to keep order. A doctor from the next building checked his pulse, and nodded his head sadly.

"Why did they kill him?" Leah asked.

"His uniform. He represents the government. He stands for Rome," I said.

"There should be a better reason," she said. "Think of how his parents will feel."

"It's politics, sugarpeeps," I said. "It makes everybody stupid. When you grow up, you'll know what I mean."

"Don't tell Ledare this when you pick her up today," Leah said as I carried her back to her bedroom. "We want her to like Rome, don't we, Daddy?"

"That we do."

"Will they clean up the blood before she gets here?"

"That's one thing Europeans do great," I said, laying her back down in bed. "In this century, they've had a lot of practice cleaning up blood. No one's better at it."

"If the Great Dog Chippie were here," Leah said, starting to fall asleep as I watched her, "the men who did that would be in big trouble, right, Daddy?"

"They'd be lying in the piazza," I said quietly, "covered with dog bites. Chippie was always there when you needed her."

"A great dog," Leah said, then slept.

After I got Ledare Ansley settled in the guest room, I told her about the early-morning killing and invited her to go along with me on a typical day of an American living in Rome. She had spent two weeks in Venice and Paris often listening to Mike talk about all the memories he carried with him of his family and town, and still trying to convince her to come aboard on the project. I began to lead her through the winding pathways of Rome, knowing it would make her drop the subject. It only takes Rome about ten minutes to make you forget you have ever been anywhere else on earth. With Ledare, I had the pleasure of watching the wizardry of stones and broken columns take her by surprise. In Rome, every step you take has been taken by a Caesar, a pope, or a barbarian before you. We floated above the history of the West as Ledare related the tales of Waterford to me. Each step I took with Ledare carried us over a dozen civilizations, layered like shirts in a drawer.

At the top of the hill we paused to watch an elegant young couple coming out of the chapel of the Palazzo dei Conservatori to the applause of relatives, friends, and passersby like us.

Making my way through the crowd with Ledare, I ducked inside the courtyard of the museum and walked past the outsized monuments of the statue of Constantine, distributed in gigantic, unsettling fragments around the courtyard. We passed by a huge veiny hand, large as a caboose, and an index finger taller than I am.

"Because you write, Ledare, and because you write in English, there is one holy shrine here that you must see," I said as I pointed to some Latin words on an entablature.

"I don't do Latin," Ledare said. "What does it mean?"

"An elderly Englishwoman showed me this tablet when I was up here with Leah. She told me that the emperor Claudius had taken his legions across the English Channel. She asked me to consider the amazement of our forebears as they watched war elephants disembarking on the beaches of Dover."

"Probably like we felt when we first saw television," Ledare said, smiling.

"Quiet," I ordered. "No jokes. When Claudius returned victorious from his campaign in England, he had this inscription carved on a page of pure Luna marble. Look carefully at these four broken-off letters that spell B-R-I-T."

"Okay, I give up. I surrender," Ledare said.

"This is the first mention of Britannia, the isle of England, in all of history. Our mother tongue began at this spot, Southern girl."

"I can't take all this in. It gives me a headache," Ledare said.

"We should fall to our knees in gratitude at this spot," I suggested.

Ledare said, "You go ahead, darling, I'm wearing panty hose."

"Ha! I see you're no romantic," I said.

"I'm romantic about people, Jack," Ledare said. "I've got real self-control when it comes to rocks."

As we moved southward away from the museum and toward the Forum we walked onto the Belvedere Tarpeo, where a cluster of Japanese tourists huddled close to a tour guide pointing toward the Temple of Saturn. The air filled with the snapping shutters of Minoltas and Nikons, sounding like some parliamentary debate of extinct insects. I jumped when a handsome young couple who stood apart from the group called to me to take their picture. I took their camera, advanced the film, set the light meter, then after Ledare gestured for the couple to move several steps to their right, I managed to photograph them with both the Temple of Castor and Pollux and the Colosseum in the background. We took turns bowing to each other, then Ledare and I continued down the hill secretly replenished by that meeting of strangers.

On the Via di San Teodoro, we took turns drinking out of the fountain in front of the Belgian Embassy. The water was pure and cold and came out of the Apennines tasting like snow melted in the hands of a pretty girl. I led Ledare down the long street to the antique store where I came to pay my rent once a month.

Savo Raskovic was looking through a large leatherbound volume when we walked through the door. Savo took one look at Ledare and said to me, "Finally, you have gotten yourself a girlfriend. It is unnatural to be without a woman so long. I am Savo Raskovic."

"Pleased to meet you, Savo," Ledare said

as this tall elegant man took her hand and kissed it. "My name is Ledare Ansley."

"Ah, Jack. My friend," Savo said, "I have such beautiful things to sell you. You have such good taste, but you have no money."

I put my hand on the shoulder of a Venetian gentleman made of wood and exactly my height who guarded the entrance to the antique shop.

"Let me buy the Venetian. For all the rent I have paid you, the price should be nominal."

"For you, a special price," Savo said, winking at Ledare. "Twelve thousand dollars."

"I could buy a real Venetian for less than that," I said. "The price is outrageous."

"Yes, but it is better to be robbed by a friend than an enemy, no?"

His brother, Spiro, came out from the back of the store, where he had been doing the accounts. Spiro was far more demonstrative than his brother and he embraced me and kissed me on both cheeks.

"Do not kiss him, Spiro," said Savo, "until after he pays his rent."

"My brother is only joking. Do not take him seriously," Spiro said. "Americans are very sensitive, my brother. They do not understand Balkan humor."

"That was Balkan humor?" I said. "No wonder you immigrated to Italy."

"This beauty, this *bell'americana*," Spiro said, kissing Ledare's hand. "You have answered our prayers. You plan to marry my poor tenant."

"You boys have to work on him," Ledare said. "He hasn't even asked me for a date yet."

"We're childhood friends," I said. "The Raskovic brothers are handsome thieves who call themselves landlords."

"Ah, Jack," Spiro said, pointing to a photograph taken in the early fifties of the brothers standing in a group of beautiful men and women including Gloria Swanson. "We were beautiful when young."

"Once we were part of a salon, signore," Savo said, "where the only ticket for admittance was attractiveness."

Spiro said, "The mirror used to be my best friend. Now it is an assassin."

"Here is my rent for the next three months," I said.

"Ah, music," Savo said, smiling at his brother. "The sound of a check being written."

"Ah, a symphony," Spiro agreed. "May the *bella donna* always find her way back to our doorstep."

"The streets of Rome are far more beautiful when you walk upon them, signora," said Savo.

"Marry him," Spiro said. "Take him off our hands."

"Gentlemen," I protested.

"You nauseate me," Savo said as we moved toward the door of the store. "American men know nothing of romance. Women need praise, poetry . . ."

"Sounds good to me," Ledare said and both men kissed her hand as we departed. "You boys keep working on Jack here."

On the Via dei Foraggi, I showed Ledare the second-floor apartment where we had spent our first year in Italy and the small piazza on the Via dei Fienili where the neighborhood first took us in and made us welcome. It was in this piazza that I had begun to feel taken care of in the Roman way. When I brought Leah shopping, the bread lady, Martina, would cut her a piece of *pizza bianca;* Roberto, who ran the *alimentari,* would slice her a hunk of Parmesan cheese; and Adele, who sold the freshest, most carefully selected vegetables, would carve a piece of snow-white fennel for Leah to chew on when she had finished the cheese. It was these Romans who had taught Leah to speak the Italian language with the most authentic Roman dialect and they had done it by committee. And so they had thought it was an act of treachery and snobbery when I moved with Leah to the Piazza Farnese. Adele, the vegetable lady, had wept when we came to make our farewells. But now Adele called out my name when she saw me. As she asked about Leah, I saw her rough hands were still stained with chlorophyll from trimming the stalks of artichokes, and she told Ledare all about Leah's love of wild strawberries and raspberries in season. I finished shopping for our evening meal and was about to leave the piazza to go to lunch with Ledare when I saw Natasha, the girl with the white dog. She was taller and prettier than the last time I had seen her. When I rented the place on the Via dei Foraggi, the girl with the white dog, as Leah called her then, was the first person we had met in the neighborhood. I was looking for a place to shop when Natasha had stepped out of her apartment house to walk her dog, a well-groomed terrier that had the bearing of an old aristocrat and the paranoia of a small animal that spent his life avoiding crowds.

I tried to talk to her in my elementary Italian, made, no doubt, even stranger by my South Carolina accent. I said good afternoon, explaining I was an American and was new in the neighborhood, that my child was three years old, and her name was Leah, and that I would like some information about shopping. After this long soliloquy, I had exhausted both myself and my rudimentary knowledge of the language. The girl with the white dog had thrown her head back and laughed.

"The hell with it," I had said. "I'll find the goddamn stores myself."

"I speak English," the girl had replied. "My mother is Italian and my father works for UPI."

"Please never tell him what I just said to you. I beg your pardon. My name is Jack Mc-Call."

"Natasha Jones," the girl had said. "Let me take you around to all the shops and introduce you. People are very charming here once they get to know you."

Quietly I approached Natasha.

"Excuse me," I said. "Aren't you Sophia Loren?"

Natasha spun around, saw me, and laughed. "Signor McCall, you never come back to the piazza to visit," Natasha said. "Leah will be an old woman when I see her next."

"This is Ledare Ansley, a friend of mine from the States," I said.

Natasha curtsied nicely and said, "Did you know Leah's mother?"

"Very well. All of us grew up together."

"Did Signor McCall always tell jokes?" she said, not looking at me.

"Always," Ledare answered.

"And they were never funny at all."

"Not once," said Ledare.

"Then he has not changed," Natasha said, giving me a sly grin.

"Natasha is in love with me," I explained to Ledare. "It often happens with young girls when they meet handsome, dashing adult men."

"Do not believe a word he says, signora," Natasha said.

"Never have," said Ledare.

"You miss me, don't you, Natasha?" I asked.

"Not at all. Bianco misses you," she said, gesturing toward her dog.

"Just Bianco?" I asked.

"Yes, just Bianco. Of that I am certain," she said.

"Come over and listen to the new Bruce Springsteen tapes Leah got," I said. "She'd love to see you."

"Perhaps I will," Natasha said, walking away with her dog toward the Via di San Teodoro.

A motorcycle backfired in the next street and an old man fell to the ground, covering the back of his neck with his arms. The shopkeepers came out slowly to see if there was trouble and the motorcyclist appeared in the piazza, his engine backfiring irregularly. Everyone laughed at the old man, but after having seen the dead policeman, I fully understood his anxiety.

Natasha turned back. "An American tourist was killed near Salerno today," Natasha said. "My father told me."

"Terrorists?" I asked.

"Who knows," she said. "But it is always good for Americans to be careful. Please explain it to your friend."

"How do I explain it?"

"Tell her that Italy is complicated," Natasha said, and as she said it I saw Jordan Elliott watching us from an alleyway.

At first, I turned away from him, since I had never seen him outside in public. When I turned back around as I led Ledare down the stairs that led into the piazza on the back side of the Capitoline hill, he had vanished from sight. In Rome, nothing was more invisible than a priest or a nun. Every day you could run across geeselike flocks of them from all the nations of the world.

I wondered if it was a bout of pure homesickness that had brought him out into the sunlight of Rome. As we walked toward the theater of Marcellus, we crossed a busy street lined with buildings from the fascist period. Then I spotted Jordan with his back to us sitting on top of a bench-sized marble fragment of a broken column. To run ahead of us the way he did, I realized that my friend knew the streets of Rome and all its shortcuts much better than I had imagined. Perhaps he just wanted to see what Ledare looked like after all these years. Circumstance had stolen Jordan's youth away from him, and perhaps he had an uncontrollable desire to watch some of those lost years from a distance.

He kept twenty-five yards ahead of us, never looking back, as I maintained my role of tour guide and pointed out the sites of historical note as we passed through the main street of the Jewish Ghetto. I stole glances at Jordan and led Ledare through the maze of lightless streets. It was a perfect place to stage an assassination, or arrange an affair, but you had to know the streets by heart.

With Jordan in the lead, our path took us by the Tortoise Fountain with its handsome boys helping turtles crawl up to a higher fountain. I watched as he walked past the outside tables of the Vecchia Roma restaurant, spoke to a waiter, then disappeared inside.

"Let's have lunch outside," I suggested. "Here in the sunlight."

"Is this the most beautiful restaurant in the world or what?" Ledare said as she took her seat. I saw that I had exhausted her in the walk. Rome exhausts the human eye quickly and too much beauty too quickly offered is wasted. After ordering us a bottle of *acqua minerale,* I excused myself and went to try to find out where Jordan had gone. He was waiting for me in a stall in the men's room. He began speaking to me as soon as I entered.

"These were left in the confessional at Sant' Anselmo," he said, sliding a manila envelope beneath the stall. I opened the envelope and took out a series of blown-up photographs showing me entering the confessional and Jordan emerging from it.

"You look good," I said.

"I look so much older," he replied. "Trappists are never photographed. I was shocked by my appearance."

"I saw the private eye when I left the church," I said. "He was the same guy that Martha Fox hired to follow me and Leah around Rome."

"I was glad to see you look even older than I do," Jordan teased.

"You're a monk," I said, speaking toward his voice. "You don't get up with kids in the middle of the night, don't worry about bills to be paid, or where the next buck is coming from. And you guys've discovered the true fountain of youth, the real secret of staying perpetually young."

"What's that?"

"You don't have anything at all to do with women," I said.

"So women age you?" Jordan said and I could feel his smile behind the closed door.

"No, women kill you from the inside out. It's the liquor you drink in order to live with women that ages you."

"My abbot has moved me to another monastery, Jack," Jordan said. "He won't let me tell even you where it is."

"He's right," I said. "I let you down. I brought the outside world to you."

"Mike Hess wrote me a letter saying he wants to meet with me. He mentioned the movie. I called my mother as soon as I got the letter and told her to be extra careful."

"Does your father know you're alive, Jordan?" I asked. "Has Celestine ever let on to him?"

"She knows my father would turn me in to the authorities," Jordan said. "His whole life's been a one-way street. He can't change."

"These photos," I said, looking at them again. "It's me and my confessor whom I've never seen. You don't look much like the Jordan Elliott we grew up with."

"I've got to disappear for a while, Jack. Even from you," the priest said.

"I understand," I said. "I'll miss you, Jordan. Don't make it too long."

"That Ledare. Still a looker, isn't she?" Jordan said. "I'd do anything to spend a couple of days talking to her."

"Maybe someday," I said.

"It can't be, Jack," Jordan Elliott said. "I'll always be dead for people like Ledare."

"There's got to be a statute of limitations on all this," I said.

"Perhaps," the priest said as I readied myself to leave. "But there is no such statute for murder."

CHAPTER 8

FROM WATCHING MY OWN DAUGHTER, I had learned that motherlessness caused one of the great thirsts of the human condition. Leah could not look at a woman without sizing her up as a wife for me and a mother for her. She never gave up hope that I would one day bring home that special woman who would give a sense of harmony to our unbalanced lives. When I introduced Ledare to Leah, I spotted the exact moment when Leah made the silent selection of my old friend as the leading candidate to take over the running of our household. Leah made a bad habit out of hero-worshiping any woman I brought home to dinner, but

Ledare had the added attraction of being one of those mythical creations who populated those tales I told her about my childhood.

"I never thought I'd get to meet Ledare Ansley in my life. You were the homecoming queen at Waterford High School, the president of the National Honor Society, and the head cheerleader."

"How on earth do you know all that?" asked Ledare.

"The yearbook is a sacred text to Leah," I answered as we settled in the kitchen and I began to prepare the evening meal.

"My mother edited the yearbook," Leah said. "She wrote to you that she'd never forget the good times you both shared in Mr. Moseley's economics class. It was fifth period. You told each other a million secrets. That's what she wrote."

"Ah, the shallow years," Ledare said, smiling. "How I adored them."

"You went with my father to the house on St. Michael's Island," Leah said. "That's the night you broke up with Daddy and made out with Capers Middleton in Daddy's car."

"Not my best career move," said Ledare.

"I've always thought Capers must be very nice," Leah said. "My mama dated him in college and you married him. He's very handsome."

"It was like growing up with a movie star," I said as I lit the stove and started the water for the pasta, salting it and turning the heat on high. Leah rushed out of the room and returned with that well-thumbed copy of her mother's yearbook. She flipped through it expertly and turned to the picture of the cheerleaders.

"My mama was very cute, wasn't she?" Leah asked.

"She was just precious, darling," Ledare said. "You've got your mother's eyes, her pretty hair, and her smile."

"Did you have a favorite cheer?" Leah asked. "Daddy claims he does not remember a single one of them."

"He never taught you the 'Waterford High Fight Song'?" Ledare said in mock surprise. "Now that's just dereliction of duty."

"I didn't even know there was a fight song," said Leah.

"Look at your mother. Here in this picture. On top of the human pyramid," Ledare said, pointing to the nine-girl squad stacked precariously at half court. "Once we got out of the pyramid, the student body knew the fight song was coming."

"What a lousy song," I said. "I challenge you to think of a lower form of music than fight songs in the American South."

"Quiet, Jack. You're not part of this," Ledare said. "Stand beside me, Leah. Now, lift up your arms, just like this. That gets the student body off their feet. Now we're going to spin three times and face the flag of Waterford High."

Ledare spun and Leah followed her example clumsily, but watching every movement.

"Now we lift our pompons in the air and shake them steadily as the marching band plays our fight song. Shake 'em, honey."

Both of them stood in the middle of the kitchen shaking imaginary pompons as I rolled fresh pasta through a pasta machine until the dough held a bright, lineny shine. Then I began cutting it into long strips as Ledare and I sang a song I had left far behind me years ago.

"Fight on, fight on, brave Dolphins,
Fight for our lovely town.
We'll strive to beat each team we meet,
Not one will keep us down.

Strive on, strive on, brave Dolphins,
Seize for our school this day.
When victory comes, we'll hear those
  drums
On fields where our teams play."

"It's still the worst song ever written," I said.

"Your father always lacked real school spirit," Ledare explained. "But your mother more than made up for it."

"Even then," I said as I opened a bottle of Barolo and let the wine breathe. "My burning honesty caused me to stand out among my feckless peers."

"Is that true?" Leah asked.

"It's all hindsight," Ledare said. "Your father was just as ridiculous a teenager as all the rest of us."

"Did you go to my mama's funeral?" Leah asked suddenly.

Ledare answered, "I sure did. Saddest thing I ever saw, sugar."

"Everybody really loved Mama, didn't they?"

"We adored that girl," said Ledare.

"I'm dropping the pasta," I said. "Get ready to eat like kings and queens."

"Anytime Daddy wants to change the subject, he drops the pasta," Leah explained.

I could smell the red wine imparting some of its silken character to the aromas rising out of the skillet, where it blended and bound the congruent personalities of the tomato and garlic with the happy green smile of basil.

After we finished the pasta, I assembled a

large army of greens and arranged them deftly until they took on a disheveled order. The olive oil was extra-virgin and recently pressed in Lucca and the vinegar was balsamic, black from its careful aging in rimmed barrels, and soon the smells of the kitchen coalesced to make me dizzy as I kissed the two women in my life and poured the wine to toast the health of the three of us.

"Let me taste the wine, Daddy," Leah said.

"Just a sip. Italian authorities get suspicious when little girls die of cirrhosis of the liver."

"Too much wine taste," Leah said, wrinkling her pretty nose.

It was a windless night, and the air smelled of rosemary as Ledare lit eight candles around the terrace and I laid out the dessert. We sat beneath a trellis of yellow roses and I cut off roses for Leah and Ledare. When I smelled the flowers I thought of South Carolina and quickly put them away. The yellow jackets had already retired for the evening, and the pigeons moaned in their invisible nests on the rooftops and an ambulance raced along the streets beside the river with its siren caroling its eerie two-note melody.

"Oh, Daddy," Leah said suddenly, bringing both hands to her mouth. "I forgot. You got a telegram. Antonio brought it up to Maria, and Maria gave it to me before she went home."

"I'm glad you forgot it. Nothing good can come from a telegram. Whatever it says will ruin this meal and give us indigestion. I can't think of a single reason why we should stop eating to read something which can only mean trouble."

"Jack," said Ledare. "It could be urgent."

Leah had already darted out of her chair and was in headlong flight through the next room. By the time I called out to her, she had descended the first five steps of the circular staircase. We could hear her running through the long hallway to her bedroom. Then her footsteps ran back toward us as a violinist played "Für Elise" for the early diners at Er Giggetto.

"There," Leah said, laying the telegram beside my place. "Special delivery."

I had a premonition as I studied the yellow envelope with its opaque cataract window. I smelled the yellow roses in the trellis again.

"I'll open it after we finish."

"How can you eat when something important might have happened?" Ledare asked.

"Someone might have left you a million dollars," said Leah.

"Too much television for you, my dear."

"This isn't a television show," Ledare said. "This is real life. That's a real telegram. Read it."

Carefully, I opened the envelope. The telegram read: "Come home. Mom's dying of cancer. Dupree."

I rose and walked to the edge of the terrace and stared out to the dark strip that was the river and at the lights on the hill above Trastevere. Ledare took the telegram and read it with a gasp.

Then to my surprise, I laughed, an idiot's chuckle that I couldn't suppress. It broke loose all the inhibitions that clustered about those seven words, arranged like forbidden fruit in the telegram. I howled with laughter that was both helpless and pain-filled.

"Jack," Ledare said. "Please let me in on the joke. I can think of lots of ways one might react to a telegram like that. But laughter's not one of them."

"My mother's not even sick," I said. "She's just after something. Something big. Lucy's a great strategist."

"How do you know, Daddy?" Leah said, taking the telegram from Ledare. When she read it she broke into tears and went to Ledare for comfort. The telegram had opened up an old family wound that I had long forgotten. I did not know how to begin to explain to either Ledare or my daughter the scenes from my life with my mother where she had used the imminence of her own demise.

"Mom does this to get attention," I said, realizing I was convincing no one. "This is an old story between us."

"Don't you think you should call your brother and find out?" Ledare suggested.

"If you sent me a telegram saying you were sick, Daddy," Leah said, sobbing, "I'd go to you."

"Laughter," Ledare said. "That's the last thing I'd expect out of you. Lucy may not be perfect, but she's certainly worth a tear or two."

"I'm telling you, she's not dying of cancer. I look bad to you right now, but if you place this moment in time, my reaction's perfectly reasonable, even predictable."

"Why are you laughing when my grandmother is dying? What would you think if I laughed when I heard you were dying?" said Leah.

She began to weep quietly again and Ledare took her into her arms.

I looked at them both for a moment, then finally said, "I didn't prepare you very well for this moment, Leah, because I never thought it would happen. I thought my parents would die and get buried and none of my family would bother me about it. My express wishes were that none of my brothers, parents, or any member of my family would ever bother my sorry ass again. But I guess I was wrong."

"It's my family too, Daddy."

"Only in the abstract. You haven't made eye contact with any of them in years, and you don't remember a single thing about them. My mother's not dying. She's acting out. She's got something spectacular up her sleeve."

"Cancer's not spectacular enough, Jack?" Ledare said, still stroking Leah's long dark hair.

"She *says* she has cancer. If my mother claimed it was a nice day, I wouldn't believe it unless she took a lie detector test and had a notarized letter of confirmation from the weatherman. Look. Mom's told us she was dying of cancer before. This is an old trick of hers. She's the type of woman who thinks that cancer'll elicit sympathy from her callous and ungrateful children."

"None of you will care if this poor woman is dying?" Ledare asked in amazement.

"You're not listening to what I just told you. She did this same thing fifteen years ago. I've seen this play before, and so have all my brothers. Look, I'll prove it. Come down to the living room and I'll put in a call to my meddling brother Dupree, and I'll let you listen in on the other line, Leah. You can interpolate how the conversation's going, Ledare, by listening to my side of the good-natured family banter. The McCalls of Waterford—we're known for the high hilarity of our family brouhahas, the nuclear potential of our rapier-like wit . . .."

"What means this word 'brouhaha'?" Leah said.

" 'What means this word, "brouhaha"?' " I repeated. "Do you think I've kept this poor child in Italy too long? She's losing all the natural rhythms of her native tongue."

Leah lay down on my bed next to the telephone and I went to the other phone and dialed my brother's number in Columbia, six time zones away in a pretty house near the university.

After the telephone began to ring, I asked Leah, "You there, sweetheart?"

"I'm lying on your bed, Daddy. I'll be listening to every word."

"Did I ever tell you that you were the greatest little girl who ever lived on the planet Earth?"

"About a hundred times. But you're prejudiced. You're my father."

Then Dupree McCall picked up the phone and said "Hello?" in an accent and intonation that I would have recognized had I been gone from South Carolina for a hundred years.

"Hello?" Dupree said again.

"Dupree, it's me, Jack. Jack McCall. Your brother."

There was a long silence.

"I'm sorry, but I don't have a brother named Jack. The name's familiar, and I've heard legends about the boy's existence, but, sorry, pal, I can't help you. As far as I know, there's no brother named Jack in my family."

"Very funny, Dupree. I'll accept some good-natured ribbing about my disappearance from the family circle, but not much."

"Oh, did it appear I was being good-natured? Excuse me, you rotten son of a bitch. I'm mad as hell and I plan to beat the shit out of you as soon as I see your sorry ass . . ."

"Say hello to Uncle Dupree, Leah," I said.

"Hello, Uncle Dupree. This is your niece, Leah. I can't wait to meet you."

"Leah, sweetheart," said Dupree, nonplused. "Forget what I just said to your daddy. I was just joking with that good-for-nothing scoundrel. How are you, baby?"

"I'm just fine, Uncle Dupree. I'm going to be nine my next birthday."

"I got a boy that's nine, name of Priolieu."

"What a pretty name. I've never heard of it."

"I married a Charleston girl. They name all their kids last names. It's an odd habit, ask your old man."

"I got your telegram, Dupree. That's why I'm calling."

"Could I talk to your father alone, honey?" Dupree said. "I know why he wanted you on the phone, but he'll explain everything to you after we've finished talking. I want to talk to him brother-to-brother. Is that all right, Leah?"

"Of course, Uncle Dupree. Is it okay, Daddy?"

"It's fine, darling. I'll tell you everything after we hang up."

"Hey, Leah," Dupree said. "You got lots of people over here who love you. We don't know you very well, but we're waiting for the chance."

Leah hung up the phone.

"The telegram, Dupree."

"You're calling to see if it's bullshit, right?"

"You're getting warm. I roared laughing when I read it. My daughter and Ledare Ansley, who's here in Rome, seem to think it denotes a certain shallowness in my makeup."

"Every one of the brothers who got the news laughed."

"All my brothers laughed too," I said to Ledare, who was watching as I talked. Leah went and sat beside her on the sofa. They looked to me like a gathering of a grand jury.

"Listen, Jack, I know you're wondering,"

Dupree said, "if I'm lying about Mom and her condition. Let me put it this way, Tiger. Do you think I would gather together in one room the four biggest assholes I've ever met just to satisfy a lifetime of white lies?"

"No, it seems out of the question," I admitted. "What kind of cancer does she have?"

"I'm not answering that question," Dupree said. "I've still got rights."

"You're not going to tell me . . ." I said, knowing instantly what he was going to say.

"Go to the head of the class," Dupree said. "You're the first one to guess. If you think about it, God does have a certain wry sense of the absurd. Mom's got leukemia."

I shouted and began laughing again as Leah and Ledare looked at each other with expressions of horror.

"Is this another lie?" I said, getting control of myself again.

"It's the living truth," Dupree said. "It's what's going to kill our mother." He started to say more, then stopped, and I could hear his tone change.

"She's in a coma, Jack. She may not come out of it. She wants you to come," Dupree continued. "She asked me earlier to call you. I told her I had enough problems without eating your ration of shit."

"What's that sound?" I asked.

"What sound?"

"Are you crying, Dupree?"

"Just a bit. So fucking what?"

"I've never heard you cry before."

"Get used to it, pal. Mom's dying. You can laugh all you want to, but I've been in there to see her. It's bad, Jack, and I'm not sure there's much time."

I looked at my watch and thought about plane schedules, reservations, and when the Alitalia office opened the next morning.

"I'll be in Savannah tomorrow evening. Can you pick me up at the airport?"

"Dallas wants to get you. I've already called Shyla's parents and told them you were coming."

"Why the hell did you do that?"

"The papers you signed said the grandparents had visitation rights."

"Not in Italy, they don't."

"You've proven that. They want to have a peace parley. I think it's a good idea."

"Did they tell you Martha was over here?"

"She called to tell me she was going."

"Thanks for the warning."

"You haven't talked to me in years, Jack."

"I'll call you tomorrow and let you know when I'm arriving."

"Are you bringing Leah?"

"Not this trip. Good-bye, Dupree."

I hung up the phone, walked to the window, and stared down to the traffic of our austerely beautiful piazza.

"I've got to go to South Carolina, Leah," I said. "I'll only stay a few days. If my mother dies, I'll fly you over for the funeral. If she doesn't, we'll go back next summer. It's time you were reunited with Frankenstein's family."

"You were wrong to laugh, weren't you, Daddy?" Leah asked.

"It appears I was very wrong."

"Are you sad about your mama?" she said.

I looked at my daughter and felt the mortal tenderness I always felt for this child who had given me most of what passes for meaning in my life.

"I've always been sad about my mother," I said. "But now, I'd better call Maria and tell her to pack a suitcase tonight."

"Go pack," Ledare ordered. "Leah and I have things to talk about."

I was breaking a solemn vow I had made after Shyla had leapt from a bridge in Charleston. I was going home.

PART II

CHAPTER 9

NOT HAVING A DAUGHTER WAS THE
great sadness of my mother's life. She had produced a houseful of boys to raise and the noise
level was always too high and the rooms over-
heated with testosterone and the sheer energy
of roughhousing and life lived by the seat of the
pants. All her life she added to her doll collection, which she planned to pass on to the
daughter who was never born. Lucy McCall
had always appeared too breakable and
glasslike to have produced such a tall and boisterous tribe. My mother carried an ache inside
her always that I am sure the birth of a daughter would have done much to alleviate. We had

made her life boy-haunted, son-possessed. If there was such a thing as being too male, we McCall brothers embodied it.

I saw my brother Dallas before he saw me. He was the third son and the only one who had followed my father's footsteps into the practice of law. Dallas had long ago become expert at hiding the rough edges of himself and keeping his darkness undercover.

We shook hands and exchanged pleasantries in the most formal manner.

"You never said good-bye to any of us," Dallas said as we walked to the baggage claim.

"I was in a hurry," I said, shaking his hand. "Good-bye."

"Joking about it's just going to make it worse," Dallas said. "You've got a lot of answering to do."

"I've got no answering to do, Dallas."

"You can't just walk back into a family's life after five years just like nothing happened . . ."

"Yes, I can. I'm an American and a free man and I was born into a democratic society and there's no goddamn law in the world that says I have to have a fucking thing to do with my weird-ass family."

"Only laws of decency apply," Dallas said as we waited for the luggage. "You should have brought Leah—we need to get to know her and she deserves to know the other members of her family."

"Leah doesn't know what the word 'family' means," I said. "I admit it might screw her up in the long run. But it also might make her the healthiest human being on earth."

"Sounds like a test tube baby to me," said Dallas.

"Would you rather have been a test tube baby or be raised by Mom and Dad, just like we were?"

"He's leading the witness, Your Honor," Dallas said to an imaginary judge.

"How are you raising your boys, Dallas?" I asked.

"I tell them that the only thing they've got to look out for is . . . everything. Be careful of everything. Hide your head and cover your ass and always make sure you carry a flashlight and dry matches."

"McCalls," I laughed. "You're raising them to be McCalls."

"No, that's what I'm raising them to watch out for," Dallas said. "You haven't asked how Mom's doing."

"How's Mom doing?" I said.

"She's worse today."

"Which hospital's she in?"

"She insisted on staying in Waterford."

"You didn't take her to Charleston or Savannah? You put her in the goddamn Waterford hospital? Why don't you just put a gun to her temple and blow her brains out? She's got leukemia, Dallas. You go to the Waterford hospital for hangovers and blood blisters and cold sores, but never for anything serious. Would *you* go to the goddamn local hospital if you had leukemia?"

"Hell no," he admitted. "But Mom insisted on Waterford. A lot of new talent's come to town. We even got our own surgeon."

"Our mother's dead meat," I said. "She'll be killed by her own stupidity. Serious diseases require serious doctors and serious doctors go to serious cities to make serious money. Loser doctors go to loser towns the same way that shit floats downstream. There's my baggage."

"Do I have to listen to grief from you about the lousy medical care we're giving to the mother you've ignored for five years?" he said. "Dupree's cabling you was not universally applauded."

"I wish he hadn't," I snapped as I removed my bag from the conveyor belt and started following the crowd out toward the parking lot.

"Call us old-fashioned," he said, taking my briefcase. "We come from that school of thought that thinks it's proper to cable a son when his mother has made that particular request."

"You should've done it after she was dead."

"Mom's changed a lot in the last five years. Too bad you didn't get to see any of those changes. Her new husband's been good for her."

"Do I have to meet her new husband?" I asked. The thought of adding any more emotional weight to my coming home seemed unbearable. I had completely forgotten that I might have to meet my new stepfather for the first time.

"I haven't even begun to figure out my own father," I protested. "I see no reason to muddy up the waters and try to begin a relationship with a man who's only committed a single crime."

"What crime has poor Jim Pitts committed?"

"He married the woman who ruined my life and made it impossible for me to find happiness during this lifetime."

Dallas laughed and said, "She was a rookie when she raised you. Just getting started. It was the youngest kids who felt the full flowering of her genius."

"Lucky me," I said. "Funny about Mom. I think I've been mad at her my whole life, yet I adore her. I can't bear to think of her hurting or in trouble."

"She's a paradox," Dallas said. "The last thing you want your mother to be."

"How's your law practice?"

"So many clients I have to give out numbers in the waiting room," said Dallas. "I've had to hire armed guards to control the crowds."

I laughed and said, "Going into practice with Dad hasn't turned out so well."

"People in small towns like their attorney of record to be sober when he draws up their will or checks a title," Dallas said. "Dad passed out on the conference table last week while we were conducting a deposition."

"Didn't you tell me he was on the wagon?" I remarked.

"His liver must look like a distillery," Dallas said. "Let us say it hasn't done the practice much good."

"Do you still hero-worship me and consider me a god among men?" I asked. "Like you did when I was a kid."

"I've missed you, Jack," Dallas said. "I don't make friends easily. We're brothers and don't have any choice in the matter. I take my family seriously because it's all I've got."

"I had to heal myself, Dallas," I said. "I didn't do it so well, but it came naturally. It felt right to go to Rome."

"You can leave," he said, "I've got no problem about that. But where's the rule against visiting. What about letter writing?"

"When I first left," I said, "I wanted to disappear out of my own life. You ever felt that way?"

"No," he answered. "Not once in my life."

"We're different people."

"I like guys like me a lot better than I like guys like you," Dallas said.

"So do I," I answered and my brother laughed. Though my whole family was bruised and tested, it had found solace in the healing unctions of laughter. This dark humor had preserved us from both sanctimony and despair.

"How's your darling wife and family?" I asked.

"Fine. Thanks for asking," he answered.

"Don't worry. I won't call her Miss Scarlett when I see her."

"Thanks for nothing," Dallas said.

"You tell her Lincoln freed the slaves yet?" I asked.

"I don't care that you hate my wife."

"I don't hate your wife, Dallas," I said, delighting in his defensiveness. "She kind of floats into view like a Portuguese man-o'-war . . . or a jellyfish. I distrust women who float."

"She just has good posture. We're very happy together."

"Anytime I hear a husband pathetically say,

unasked, that he's very happy with his wife, I smell the divorce courts, mistresses, and midnight flights to the Dominican Republic for quickie separations. Happy husbands never mention the fact. They just live in pure ether and grin a lot."

"A positive attitude takes you a long way," he said. "Something you haven't had for a long time."

"Nothing phonier than a good attitude," I responded. "It's so American."

"Great to have you back," Dallas said, shaking his head. He started the car and eased out of his parking space. "It seems like only yesterday that I used to think you were a fabulous guy."

"Time flies."

"I'm glad you came, Jack. Mama might be dead by the time we get there."

"That old positive attitude," I said, then caught myself.

When Dallas said nothing, I attempted safer territory.

"Where am I staying?"

"You can stay with us if you like, but Dad really wants you to stay with him. He says you can have your old room."

"Great—just what I long for," I said sarcastically.

"He's gotten kind of lonely, Jack. You'll

see. It's hard to hate someone who's so needy and eager to please."

"It'll be a snap for me."

"Do you ever get tired of having all the answers?"

"No," I snapped back. "Do you ever get tired of asking none of the right questions?"

"Can you ever forgive Mom and Dad for being exactly who they were born to be?" Dallas' eyes were focused on the dark band of roadway leading from Garden City to the small bridge that crossed the Savannah River west of the city.

"No, that's the one thing I can't forgive them for."

"Fine," he replied grimly. "Half your problems with the world are about to be solved, big fella."

"Watch the road, counselor," I said. "We're passing into our home state."

Because it serves as a borderline between two states, the Savannah River holds a prominence in my mind that other rivers lack. A sign bid us farewell to Georgia and another welcomed us into the state where all the McCall children had been born, raised, and touched by the routines and dialects of our homeland.

But some invisible river also runs among the members of my family, marking off separate realms of the spirit that render our brotherhood both inscrutable and promissory. People have always made the mistake of thinking we are closer than we really are. We resemble each other in some ill-made, unthought-out way, like cheap copies, but in most things we relate to the world in opposing styles.

Dallas is comfortable being a Southerner and has never aspired to being anything else. What makes him feel complete and centered in the world can all be found in a hundred-mile radius of our birthplace. He carries himself with a seriousness missing from the nervous systems of the rest of us. Of all my brothers, it is Dallas who has chosen the most conventional path, one with built-in safety features. Throughout his life, he admired the men who became church elders in Waterford, or served on the city council, or headed up the funding drives for United Way. People trust him because he avoids extremes. His is the voice of reason in our passionate, breakneck family, where screaming is considered a higher form of discourse and a shouting match the upside of dialogue.

I reached across the car and squeezed the back of my brother's neck. His muscles were taut and he winced with pain at my touch. Though Dallas had a reputation for being gifted at arranging treaties of armistice and missions to the interior, I knew that was only a trick of the trade the lawyer's art had taught him. He had forged a reputation for levelheadedness that he had paid a steep price for in bulk purchases of antacids. His calm exterior had been won with the chalky help of Maalox. Though Dallas faked his way through his professional life by assuming an air of self-possession and presence of mind, he knew there was not the slightest chance I would be fooled by the charade. Though he longed to take his place among the cooler heads in our town, a working knowledge of fire was the way to his heart.

I breathed in the low country air as each mile took us farther away from the industrial effluents that distilled in the bright sunshine of Savannah.

The shinier, silk-tender air came streaming over me with each mile we traveled and I could smell my own boyhood sneaking up in a slow, purloined dream as I closed my eyes and let the chemistry of time allow me to repossess those chased-off, ghostly scents of my lost youth. I found my whole body leaning forward in anticipation as the car crossed over the pine barrens of Garbade Island and I saw the long graceful bridge that spanned the mile-long Broad Plum River. On its own, my spirit seemed to relax, like a folding chair let out by a pool. Because even beauty has its limits, I shall always remain a prisoner of war to this fragrant, voluptuous latitude of the planet, fringed with palms and green marshes running beside rivers for thirty miles at a time, and emptying out on low-lying archipelagoes running north and south along the coast before the Atlantic's grand appearance. The low country had laid its imprint on me like the head of some ancient king incised on a coin of pressed copper. The whole earth smelled as though a fleet of shrimp boats had returned for a day's work on tides of rosewater and eelgrass.

"Miss that smell?" Dallas asked. "You could live in Rome for a thousand years, but I bet you'd still miss the smell of those tidal flats."

"Rome's got its own smells."

"You gotten the itch out of your system yet?" Dallas asked. "It's hard to make your life's work packing a bag."

"My life's taking place in another part of the world," I said. "No sin in that."

"You raising Leah to be an Italian?"

"Yep. I sure as hell am."

"Better get that girl on over here. We'll give her a couple of weeks of basic training. Bring out the redneck in her."

"You know, you sound like an idiot when you play 'Southern boy' with me," I said.

Dallas punched me playfully on the shoulder. "That's why I do it. See if you still get pissed off when I go into one of my routines."

"It's not a routine anymore, Dallas. I suspect, by now, it's a life."

"I'm Southern to the bone," Dallas said, glancing at me. "Unlike you, I don't hang my head when I say it out loud."

"You know better than that," I said, then changed the subject. "What does Mama look like?"

"Like road kill," he said through tight lips.

"How's everybody taking it?"

"Great," Dallas said sarcastically. "Mom's dying of cancer. Things couldn't be rosier."

The hospital was prettily situated on the banks of the Waterford River, but once inside, it gave off that institutional antiseptic smell that was uniquely American. The hallways were lined with drawings by schoolchildren, octogenarians, and lunatics who had excelled with crayons and fingerpaints during occupational therapy. For the last twenty-four hours I had made a grand effort to think of everything except my mother's condition. The past was one country where I tried to limit the number of free trips. When we came to the waiting room where the family had gathered together in mute, rough-hewn vigil, I felt as if I were walking into a mine field.

"Hello, everybody," I said, trying not to

make eye contact with anyone in the room. "Long time, no see."

"I'm Jim Pitts," an unfamiliar man's voice said. "Your mother's husband. We haven't had the pleasure."

I shook hands with my new stepfather and felt light-headed, as though I were walking through the atmosphere of a planet so dense that songbirds could neither fly nor sing.

"How are you, Dr. Pitts?" I said. "You have nice taste in women."

"Your mother will be very grateful that you came," said the doctor.

"How is she?" I asked.

Dr. Pitts looked perplexed, then frightened, and I saw that this tall, white-haired stranger with his baritone voice was close to tears. When he tried to speak and no words followed, he could not have given me a more accurate or devastating portrait of my mother's condition. In appearance, the doctor was a much softer, toned-down version of my father, but when I mentioned this later to my brothers, none of them had made this connection. Like teen-agers, the doctor and my mother had eloped two years before, when the ink was barely dry on our parents' divorce decree. My brothers had kept Dr. Pitts at arm's distance and still treated him as an unlikely addition to the fam-ily circle. He looked like a man who valued constancy and recited maxims about birds in the hand.

"The other kids call me Doctor," he said. "Please call me Jim."

Except for my youngest brother, John Hardin, the other "kids" were in their early thirties, but I said, "Glad to, Jim."

"The face is familiar," my brother Tee said out loud to the room. "But I can't place the name."

"You from around these parts, stranger?" Dupree said, winking at Dallas.

I told them both to get laid in Italian and Dallas broke out laughing. Dupree rose out of his chair first and gave me a hug. He was the only person I knew who could embrace you and keep his distance at the same time. Being the smallest of the brothers, he had a natural gift for arbitration, for those delicate negotiations which bind families together or send them into scattered and ungatherable fragments.

"It's good to see you, Jack," said Dupree. "Any chance of us getting to meet Leah again?"

"Seems like there's a chance for anything," I said, returning his embrace, then accepting the full-fledged bear hug of my brother Tee, the second youngest of five boys. Tee's emotions were always out front, running over the banks. My mother considered him the softest version of the McCall male and by far the best shoulder to cry on among the McCall brothers. But Tee also held the biggest grudge against our mother. He was the only one who would say, out loud, that she had crimes of incompetence and inattention to answer for . . . Because of this, her coma had hit him particularly hard.

"Brace yourself, Jack," Tee said. "Mom looks like shit. I don't know what Dallas told you but it's worse than you imagine."

"He'll see soon enough," Dallas said.

"I thought it was an act," Tee said. "You know, our mother's not above putting on an act to get her way. I tried to figure out what she wanted. The doctor here bought her a Cadillac, so I knew it wasn't a car. He got her a ring big enough so a gorilla couldn't lift his arm. So I knew it wasn't a diamond. But she's a master planner. Right? We know she's got something up her sleeve. Right?"

"I resent what you're implying about my wife," Dr. Pitts said.

"Relax, Doctor," Dupree said. "Tee's just thinking out loud."

"Hey, Doc. Trust me," Tee said. "You don't know the broad. You're brand-new at the game. I'm not criticizing Mom. Really. I admire this about her. Just because it happened to screw up my life. Hey, I'm not one to hold grudges."

"Could you write me a prescription for an animal tranquilizer, Doctor," Dupree said. "I need to put Tee down for the night."

"Your mother's the most wonderful woman in the world," Dr. Pitts said, rising to leave the waiting room. "What a shame her sons can't see it."

When he had left I said, "I go away for a little while and you guys go to seed. I thought I'd trained you better than that."

Dallas shook his head and said, "Dr. Pitts has had some trouble adjusting to us. He lacks wit, irony, sarcasm, all the necessary cruelty that makes life possible in this family."

"He thinks Mom's perfect," Dupree said. "Nothing wrong with that. It's how a husband's supposed to think."

"Dupree hasn't changed," Tee said. "Still the biggest phony in the world."

"Go see Mom, Jack," Dallas said. "Get ready for the shock of your life."

Then I walked down the corridor with Dallas and entered the intensive care unit. Once the door shut behind us I closed my eyes, took a deep breath, and leaned against a wall to regain whatever equilibrium I could before looking at my mother.

"Tough, huh?" Dallas said. "I should have warned you that the brothers had all gathered."

A nurse in a gauze mask motioned us

toward a bed and signaled five minutes with her left hand as I approached a bed where a woman unrecognizable as my mother lay. The name tag read "Lucy Pitts" and for a moment my heart swelled thinking a terrible mistake had been made, that this broken woman was masquerading as the beautiful mother who had borne five sons and could still fit into her wedding dress. Her body was frail and covered with bruises.

I touched my mother's face; it was hot to the touch and her hair was wet and unkempt. I leaned down to kiss her and saw my own tears fall on her face.

"Jesus, Dallas," I said. "She's not faking. Who would've ever thought that Mom was mortal."

"Be careful. The doctor tells us she might be able to hear us, even in the coma."

"Really?" I wiped my tears away. Then I leaned over again and said, "Your son Jack loved you the most. Your other children resented you and thought you were horseshit. It was Jack who was always your biggest fan, your number-one cheerleader. Jack, Jack, Jack. That's the only name you must remember with love and adoration when you wake up from all this."

I took my mother's hand, pressing it softly

against my cheek, and said, "I keep expecting her to open her eyes and scream 'Surprise.' "

"Not this time," Dallas said.

"The guy she married," I said. "He seems all right."

"A nice guy. Further right than Attila the Hun, but a decent sort."

"She deserves a decent sort. She always has."

"Mom thinks you hate her," Dallas said.

"I've had my days."

"Dad thinks you hate him too."

"He's on the right track. How's his drinking?"

"Not bad lately," Dallas said. "He got drunk for a month when Mom married Dr. Pitts, but then he sobered up and started dating teenagers."

"Has he been to see Mom yet?"

"You've been out of the loop for a while, Jack. After Mom's honeymoon with Dr. Pitts, they returned to their house on the Isle of Orion and found Dad sitting in their living room. He had drunk all the doctor's booze and he had a shotgun pointed at Dr. Pitts' heart. He had a plan worked out to kill Dr. Pitts, kill Mom, then kill himself."

"Should you be talking like this?" I asked, pointing to the bed.

"She knows all about this," Dallas said.

"She even got where she could laugh about it, but it took a while. Dad had been drunk a month, and the whole week that Mom and Dr. Pitts were in Jamaica. His scheme was foolproof except he had not planned on being drunk when the happy couple returned from their travels. Nor did he expect that Dr. Pitts would have such a well-stocked liquor cabinet. Dad had drunk every drop of liquor the man owned, but it had taken him the full week to do it. He was too drunk to lift the gun to fire when the honeymooners returned. By the time he got organized, Mom and Jim Pitts had run screaming into the night."

"Did they press charges?"

"Yes. They certainly did."

"You got them to drop the charges."

"Yes. But it took some work. Dr. Pitts is terrified of the man who graciously gave of his own sperm to bring us into this world. All my considerable legal skills were brought into play. It was a mess."

"Why didn't anyone tell me?"

"You don't get to play it both ways, pal. You leave the family—the family isn't required to tell you every Dear Abby story that comes up."

"You just told me that my old man threatened to murder my mother and her new husband. Someone should have told me," I insisted.

"No, no. It seems to me a great man once wrote a letter to all the members of his family . . ." Dallas began with bitter irony.

"The letter was a mistake."

"Quite possibly it was a mistake, but it still arrived safely in all the mailboxes of all us Mc-Calls. The man stated quite unequivocally that he never wanted to hear from any members of his immediate family ever again. Nor did he wish to correspond or communicate with anyone who had ever known him as a child or adult in Waterford. He wanted to see no one from his hometown, his college, or his family. The great man was starting life anew, afresh, and this time he was going to get it right."

"When I wrote the letter, I thought I knew what I was doing."

"We did too," Dallas said. "We adhered to your wishes and most of us did not try to contact you during those years."

"Shyla," I stammered. "I didn't know what to do."

"Neither did we," Dallas said. "We loved her too."

I knelt down beside my mother and tried to pray, but none of the old words seemed adequate. I listened to her hard, rasping breathing and laid my head against her chest. Her valiant heart sounded strong and certain and that heartbeat alone gave me reason to hope.

There was suddenly a slight change in her breathing and something must have registered on a machine where the nurses were, for an efficient black nurse came and took Lucy's pulse and adjusted the flow of the intravenous into her veins.

Then another nurse came over and pointed disapprovingly at her watch like a teacher circling a misspelled word in red ink.

"She's not gonna die," I whispered to Dallas.

"If she doesn't do it in the next few days, they think she's got a pretty good shot."

I leaned over and kissed my mother's cheek, then took her hand and pressed it against my own cheek.

"Say good-bye, Jack," Dallas advised. "In case she can really hear you."

"Listen to me, Mama. It was your son Jack who loved you the most. Your other children resented you and called you terrible names behind your back. It was always Jack who was your biggest fan, your number-one cheerleader. Remember that nasty Dallas. He was always spiteful and hateful toward you."

Dallas laughed as the nurse hustled us out of the intensive care unit.

Outside in the hallway, I felt hammered, flattened out.

"Your old room's made up for you," Dallas said. "Dad's real excited about you coming."

"He gonna be there?"

"Not tonight," Dallas said. "We had to put him in the drunk tank at the jail. Just to dry out. He's taken the news about Mom real hard. Odd, Jack. He still loves her and seems lost without her."

"Take me home," I said. "The scene of the crime."

CHAPTER 10

NO STORY IS A STRAIGHT LINE. THE geometry of a human life is too imperfect and complex, too distorted by the laughter of time and the bewildering intricacies of fate to admit the straight line into its system of laws.

The next morning the family gathered slowly again as the ruined cells skirmished in the silent lanes of Lucy's bloodstream. This gathering was irregular and off-center. None of us wanted to be here. In her coma, attached to all the machines of measurement and warning, Lucy could not hear the house of McCall rallying to her side. No one loved theater or spectacle more than my mother, but this coming together contained no aspects of whim and it was not a joke. She had taught her sons to laugh, but not to grieve. And so, with nothing to do, we sat around and waited, trying to learn the laws and courtesies of dying. Under such extreme pressure, we got to know each other again. We had come to a meeting place in our lives that would be part summing up and part winking to the gods of darkness. The waiting room filled up with strange openings, disorders, and slanted windows facing out to the past. But all exits were barred and there seemed to be no way out as we groped for common ground, as we looked for a straight line to share.

Though we thought we were learning the protocols of dying, we did not know which ones applied to our mother. I had gotten to the hospital at seven that morning and had visited her amid those humming machines that were monitoring her vital signs. The nurses told me there was no change and I was soon banished to the waiting room, where I would learn the arts of vegetating and stillness as I awaited news. I sat surrounded by piles of bad magazines. I observed the decor and the furnishings and thought it took a sensibility of remarkably piddling genius to design a room this jarring. From a machine, I bought a cup of coffee so mediocre as to encourage the writing of an article pleading with the coffee-growing nations not to export coffee to this country until Americans learned to do it right.

My brother Tee arrived next, unshaven and unkempt. It looked as though he had found all his clothes at the bottom of a laundry hamper. He taught autistic children in Georgetown County and when asked about why he chose such a profession he would say, "After growing up in this family, I found autism refreshing." Tee always found himself in the dead center of family battles and was always being caught in acts of unsure and ambiguous diplomacy, though no one ever doubted his good will.

"I'm not sure if I'm glad to see you or not," Tee said to me.

"You've got about a week to figure it out," I said. "Then I'm back to Rome."

"What if Mom dies?" he asked, then said quickly, "Don't answer that. Forget I even asked the question. I feel guilty enough as it is. I read that leukemia is the only cancer that's strictly affected by the emotions. Remember that time I flunked biology? Or the time I shoplifted a bag of M&M's when I was five? It made her emotional. A leukemia cell could've formed right then when she was spanking my fanny."

"Good thinking," I said.

"You're tired of me already, aren't you?" Tee asked.

"No, Tee. I'm worried about Mom," I said. "I'd hate to come to this hospital with bad breath. This place thinks a tongue depressor's a major breakthrough in science."

"It's gotten better," Tee said. "By the way, brace yourself, big one. John Hardin's on his way to town."

"How's he doing?" I asked.

"Staying out of the mental hospital," Tee said. "Dupree watches over him and rides herd on him pretty close. Mom still refuses to think anything's wrong with him. But that's her baby. She's always cared most for John Hardin."

"Does he know she's sick?" I asked.

"I told him yesterday," Tee said. "But he laughed too, once he heard it was leukemia. Thought I was pulling his leg. Be careful of John Hardin. He can be sweet but his temper is hair-trigger. He offends easily."

"Thanks for the warning," I said as Dupree and Dallas made their way down the long hospital corridor toward us.

"No change, huh!" Dallas said as he threw himself heavily into a couch. "You've been in to see her, Tee?"

Tee shook his head and said, "My value to the family lies in my waiting room manner. When you guys fall apart, you'll need Tee, the Rock of Gibraltar, to steady you out and get you on course. I haven't been in that room yet.

The thought of Mom's dying gets to me bad enough. I'm keeping clear of the real thing."

"Makes sense to me," Dupree said as he walked toward the door leading to the intensive care unit. "By the way, Jack, an early warning signal. John Hardin's left his island house and is on his way here. Dad's due to be released from jail right about now."

"It's a Norman Rockwell painting in the making," I said.

"Forgot to tell you, Jack," Dallas said. "Life in Waterford's still interesting. Fucked up, but interesting."

"Bad movie," Tee added. "Lousy script. Poor location. Ham actors. Hack directors. But melodrama up the old wazoo."

Jim Pitts, our stepfather, approached us from the other corridor, his step military and even spritely despite a noticeable limp in his right leg. He lifted his hand to stop Dupree from going in to check on Mom, indicating that he would like to talk to all of us. I found myself resenting Dr. Pitts for the single crime of having married my mother, yet I had rejoiced in Rome when she wrote me she was leaving my father. It was obvious he felt natural as Lucy's sons gathered in a semicircle around him. My mother's condition had forced us into an alliance none of us wanted. He was a measured, soft-spoken man whose sentences took time in the saying. When he was nervous, a slight stammer caused an even greater logjam of words.

He said, "I went to see your father and gave him a full report on Lucy's condition. Even though your mother didn't wish to see him, the fact that she's in a coma changes things. I did what I felt to be right. I asked him to visit her this morning."

"That was nice of you, Doctor," I said.

"Too nice," Tee said. "Kindness gets my guard up. Makes me suspicious."

"I never had children of my own . . ." Dr. Pitts began.

"You didn't miss a thing," Dallas said.

"What I mean is, if I can do anything for you boys . . ." he said. "I will always keep your wishes uppermost in my mind. If I make you uncomfortable, or if you wish to talk privately, I can always go outside and smoke a cigarette. I understand how a stranger could make you ill at ease at such a time."

"You're our stepfather, Doc," Dupree said. "You're Mom's husband. You've got more right to be here than we do."

"That's very kind," the doctor said. "But I'm aware of the discomfort I may cause."

"You?" Tee said. "Cause discomfort? Wait till you see us around our real father."

"We make you nervous, Doctor," said Dallas. "But don't take it personally. The McCall brothers have that effect on everyone."

"Speak for yourself, bro," Tee said.

Dupree said, "You've been nice to my mother. We appreciate that, Doctor."

"Let me go check on my sweetheart," Dr. Pitts said, moving toward the door at the end of the room.

"Nice guy," Dupree said.

"If you like the type," Dallas answered. "He's too dull for me. No balls. No juice. No pizzazz."

"I like it when a guy marries my mom and lacks balls," said Tee.

"I don't need pizzazz after Dad," I said.

"Or juice," Dupree said. "A perfect day for me is when nothing out of the ordinary happens, where I never lose my temper, or get mad at my boss. I'd like the temperature always to be seventy degrees, the sky clear, and my car always to start. I'd like to stay this age always, never get sick, and have baseball played all year round. I don't like surprises. I like routine. Patterns make me happy."

"You sound like a dope," Dallas said.

"He sounds just like you," Tee said. "You're a lawyer, the scum of the planet. You want peace and quiet in your life, but you want the rest of the world to blow up around you. If three hundred passengers die in a flaming plane crash in Atlanta, three hundred lawyers go to bed happy knowing a big paycheck's coming up."

"It feeds the family," Dallas said, grinning.

"Human suffering feeds your family," Tee corrected.

"Oh, cut the wordplay," Dallas said. "Ah, what's that lovely sound?"

"A siren," Dupree said. "Mozart to Dallas."

"A payday coming home to papa," Dallas said, and none of us saw our father coming down the corridor in his classical mode of unsteadiness.

When our father entered the waiting room every one of us knew immediately that he'd been drinking.

"Ah! The source of all joy," Tee whispered as the sons observed the father's long entrance in silence.

"How did he get liquor this early in the morning?" Dupree asked Dallas. "He must bury liquor bottles all over town, then dig them up like a dog when he needs them."

Dallas said, "I'm lucky enough to be his law partner. I've found a pint of liquor in a law book he hollowed out. Found another in the tank behind the toilet in the women's bathroom downstairs. Another in a rain gutter outside his office window. If hiding things paid well, he'd be a millionaire."

While my father was entering the room, I tried to see him with new eyes, not as the boy who grew up ashamed that his father was the town drunk. He still made an effort to carry himself with dignity and he still possessed that strange handsomeness that makes aging easy for some men. His hair was thick and silver, as though it were made from a tarnished tea service. His body had softened, gone to seed in the usual places, but you could tell that this had once been a powerful man. I waited to hear the voice, that finely tuned baritone instrument that lent weight to every word he ever uttered. His bloodshot eyes fixed us to the spot and he stared at us as though he were waiting for someone to introduce him to strangers. His specialty, long since perfected, was to make every moment difficult.

"I guess you think I should hire a marching band to welcome you back," my father, Judge Johnson Hagood McCall, said to me.

"It's great to see you too, Dad," I said.

"Don't look at me that way," my father ordered. "I refuse to accept your pity."

"Jesus Christ," Tee whispered.

"Say hi to Jack, Dad," Dupree suggested. "It's a question of manners."

"Hi, Jack," my father said, mugging, his

words soft around the edges. "Great to have you back, Jack. Thanks for not calling, Jack. For not keeping in touch."

"I tried to call you a couple of times, Dad," I said. "But it's hard talking to a man after he's passed out."

"Are you implying that I have a drinking problem?" the judge said, rising up to his full length, his head thrown back.

"An outrage," Tee said happily.

Dallas said, "Like saying Noah had a problem with the weather, Pop."

"Drink some coffee," Dupree offered. "Sober up before you go see Mom."

My father looked at me, then sat down on a chair, falling the last several inches.

"You heard that your mother deserted me for a much younger man, I suppose," he said to me.

Dallas said, "The doc's a whole year younger than Pop here."

"There's no need for your editorial comments, Dallas," the judge said. "I am merely stating the facts. His money blinded her. Your mother always had a weakness for material things and ill-gotten pelf."

"Pelf?" Tee said. "Mom likes pelf? I don't even know what it is."

"That's why you're only a public school teacher in the state that ranks last educationally in this great nation," the judge said. "They allow you to teach other idiots, I am told."

"My kids are autistic, Dad," said Tee.

"Aren't you glad Dad's drinking again?" Dupree asked me, trying to divert attention away from Tee. "I never feel closer to the old boy than when he's going through delirium tremens."

"I'm not drunk," the judge said, "I'm on medication."

"Dr. Jim Beam," Dallas said. "Still practicing after all these years."

"I have an inner-ear infection," the judge insisted. "The medicine affects my sense of balance."

"That infection must be hell," Tee said. "It's been around for thirty years or more."

"All of you were in league with your mother against me," said the judge, closing his eyes.

"Got that right," Tee said.

"God help me ignore the whimpering of this pack of craven dogs," the judge prayed.

Tee began barking and Dupree turned to me and said, "*Moi,* a craven dog."

"Shape up, Dad," Dallas said. "Don't embarrass us in front of Dr. Pitts. It was nice of him to invite you down."

"He is a home wrecker," the judge said. "Nothing in the world could keep me from my wife's bedside when she faces the Maker. The

Lord will be very hard on Miss Lucy, I'm afraid. The good Lord is harsh with those women who abandon their poor husbands at the time of greatest need. Mark my words."

"Time of greatest need?" Tee asked.

"Ear infection," Dupree said, helping him out.

"Bulletin just in," said Dallas, going over to brush dandruff off our father's wrinkled suit. "She's no longer your wife. You'll need that information fresh when you go see her."

"She only divorced me because she went through a midlife crisis," the judge said, more to himself than to us. "It's far more common than you might think. It usually occurs when a woman goes through the change of life—when she can no longer bear fruit."

"We're fruit," Tee said to me, pointing to himself.

"Get hold of yourself, Dad," Dupree said, bringing back a cup of hot coffee in a paper cup. "We're gonna need you before this is over."

"Where is John Hardin?" the judge asked. "He is the only one in this family who has remained constant to his father. Through all of this, he and he alone still loves me, still respects the institution of fatherhood. Can you believe it?"

"Tough," Dupree said.

"Hard to swallow," Tee said.

"Jack," my father said to me. "There's plenty of room at the house. Please feel free to stay with me."

"I'm already there, Dad," I said. "I slept there last night."

"Where was I?" my father said and I saw the fear in his eyes as he tried to remember.

"Drying out," Dallas said. "In your pied-à-terre over at the county jail."

"Then tonight we'll talk," the judge said to me. "Just like old times. All of you boys come over. I'll barbecue steaks in the backyard just like I used to do when you were kids."

"That'd be nice, Dad," Dupree said. "Thanks."

"Sounds great," Tee agreed.

"Tell them, Jack," my father said, his eyes changing, glistening. "Tell them what I was like in the early days. I used to walk down the street and everyone used to step aside out of respect. I was a man of substance then, someone to be reckoned with, wasn't I, Jack? Tell them what people used to say. The boys were all young then, they might not remember."

"They said you were the best legal mind in the state," I said. "The best lawyer before a jury. The fairest judge."

"It got away from me, boys. A good reputation goes only so far. Mine was a vanishing act I didn't see coming. It didn't fight fair . . . came up behind me. Ambushed me. Tell them, Jack. You were proud to be my son."

"Proudest thing about me, Dad," I said truthfully.

"I've quit drinking three times this year, Jack," the judge said. "But life wounds me in the places only hope can reach. This thing about Lucy. Lucy. My Lucy."

"Not yours anymore," Dallas said. "Get that straight before Dr. Pitts takes you in to see Mom."

Tee was looking out the window, watching something closely, when Dr. Pitts came out of the intensive care unit and made his way to where my father was sitting. We heard the sound of a boat's motor droning in a high-pitched whine on the river.

"No change," Dr. Pitts informed us all, then said to my father, "Thank you for coming, Judge. Her doctor told me the next day or two are critical. If she can make it through them, he believes she has a fighting chance."

"C'mon, Mom," Tee yelled by the window. "Give 'em hell, girl."

"You're in a hospital," Dallas said, "not a sports bar."

"Thanks for that timely bulletin, bro," Tee said. "And get ready for a full-contact scrimmage. John Hardin's tying up his boat down at the dock."

"Help us, Jesus," Dallas said.

"Worse than it used to be?" I asked Dupree.

"Still a bit off," Dupree said. "But he's become a little dangerous. He spooks easily."

"Now, for the enjoyment of our live audience, ladies and gentlemen, we present madness," Dallas said.

"First death," Tee said, "then drunkenness."

"Calm down, Tee," Dupree suggested. "Don't let him see that you're nervous."

"I'm not nervous," Tee said. "I'm scared shitless."

"He hasn't had his shot this month," Dupree said. "He's fine after he's had his shot."

There was a tap on the window and John Hardin made a motion for Tee to unlock it. Tee made a motion with his arm that John Hardin go around to one of the doorways and John Hardin answered him by selecting a brick that formed the border of a flower garden near a memorial fountain. When it looked as though he was going to hurl the brick through the window, Tee unlocked it quickly and John Hardin pulled himself up into the waiting room with catlike ease.

"You ever heard of doors, John Hardin?" said Dallas.

"Yeah, I heard of them," my youngest brother said, "I just don't like them."

His eyes surveyed the room until they rested on me.

"Mr. Pizza," he said.

"Hey, John Hardin," I said. "Yep. I still live in Italy."

"I looked up Italy in an atlas recently," he said. "It's not anywhere near America. What's the sense of living in a place that's not even near America?"

"Folks're different," I said. "That's why Baskin-Robbins has thirty-one different flavors to choose from."

"South Carolina is all the flavor I need," he said.

"It's nice to see Jack, isn't it, John Hardin?" Dupree said.

"Speak for yourself," John Hardin said. "How's Mom?"

"Bad," Dallas said. "Real bad."

"What's that supposed to mean, Dallas?" John Hardin said.

"She's terrific," Dallas corrected himself. "She'll be back soon after she finishes her ten-thousand-meter run."

"Relax, bro," Tee said. "Let me get you a cup of coffee."

"Caffeine makes me crazy," John Hardin said.

"Hold the coffee," Dupree said.

"I guess you think we should bow down to hail the conquering hero," John Hardin said to me.

"Put it off for a day or two," I said. "Don't feel you have to rush it."

"I hardly knew you were gone," my youngest brother said, then went to take a seat as far away from us as he could get. He lit his first cigarette and began smoking it seriously.

"Ever hear of lung cancer?" Dupree asked.

"Ever hear of diarrhea of the mouth?" John Hardin answered and we backed away from him.

We turned our attention to him, but secretly. He was tall, thin, and sunburned in an unhealthy way. There was something about John Hardin's eyes that carried the terror of suddenly freed birds in them. Though each of us recognized that we had survived a spectacularly rocky childhood and thus carried a portion of impairment and breakdown, none had been as grievously harmed as John Hardin McCall. Even as an infant, John Hardin carried sensibilities primed and calibrated to register the slightest disturbances. Always he seemed too openhearted and innocent to survive the battle that was our parents' infamous love affair with each other.

He was the baby of the family, the best-loved child of all of us, and he was not tough enough to endure the long years watching our world go corrupt around the edges, our father drink enough hard liquor to fill up an averaged-size mobile home, and our mother grow weary of even faking the art of mothering.

Tee, the brother nearest John Hardin in age, watched him in alarm. "Tell Jack about your tree house, John Hardin."

"Tree house?" I asked.

"Grandpa gave John Hardin an acre of land on the water," Dupree whispered. "John Hardin's become something of a hermit. He's spent the last year building this tree house in an oak tree that hangs out over Yemassee Creek."

Dallas said, "It's nice but it'll never make the tour of homes."

Dupree whispered to me, "The elevator never made it to the top floor in that boy."

John Hardin said, "Why can't this family shut up? Is there anything wrong with everybody just shutting up?"

"Have you had your shot this month?" Dupree asked John Hardin.

"Every time I get upset you ask me if I've had my goddamn shot," John Hardin answered, flushing with rage, and punching the palm of his hand to keep his hands from trembling.

"Your doctor called me," Dupree said, walking up to his brother. "You skipped your appointment. You know you get agitated when you don't get your shot."

"I get agitated when you get on my ass for not getting a shot."

"You ought to quit eating red meat for a while, bro," Tee suggested to John Hardin. "Try a little Zen meditation. I don't believe in medication."

"A guru is born," Dallas said acidly. "Quit sounding like you were born in California."

"I hate California and everything that comes from there," Dupree agreed. "It makes me sorry we won the Mexican war."

John Hardin ended all talk of nutrition and geography by saying, "Fourteen medical doctors went on trial last year for murdering their patients. That's a fact. Put that in your pipe, losers."

"So what?" Dupree asked after a silence that waited too long.

"You don't get it. It doesn't reach out and slap you in the face. What do you guys need to face the truth? Skywriting? Wake up. It's perfectly clear."

"You're scaring Jack," Dupree warned.

"He's never seen you since you turned into Quasimodo."

"I'm going to tell your boss, Dupree," John Hardin said. "I'm going to report you to the proper authorities. Bet your ass, I am. You work as a government employee for the state mental hospital. On the scale of one to ten, that's a minus three. No status, no pay, the bottom rung of society."

Tee threw a newspaper over to Dupree and said, "You might want to check the want ads, bro."

"I'm happy in my job," Dupree said. "I get to work with neat guys like John Hardin all day long."

"One day, you assholes are gonna go too far with me. You'll get to me because I know what you're saying. I've got ways of knowing everything you think about me, what you're planning."

"C'mon, John Hardin," said Dallas. "That's just the red meat talking."

"Do you want to go in and see your mother, John Hardin?" Dr. Pitts asked. "Your father's upset and maybe you could help him by joining him."

"I know what you're trying to do," John Hardin said. His face twisted as the howling winds of paranoia rose out of deep uncharted canyons within him. "Don't think I don't know what you're trying to do. I'm on to you. I'm on to all of you."

"I just wanted you to have a chance to see your mother," Dr. Pitts tried to explain. "I didn't mean to upset you."

"You know she's dead," John Hardin cried out, but there was a rising fury in his voice, not grief. "You want me to be the one who discovers she's dead when it's you who killed her. You. She didn't have cancer when she was married to my father. Ever think of that? You're a doctor. A goddamn doctor. You could've given her a physical exam every goddamn day. But no. You ignore all the signs of cancer. The seven deadly warning signs. Every doctor on earth knows about the seven deadly signs."

"Jesus Christ," I said.

Dupree said, "Let's go together to get your shot."

John Hardin's eyes blazed as he spoke. "I hate you the most, Dupree. You're number one on my list. Then comes Jack. Precious Jack, the firstborn son who thinks he was born in a manger. Then comes Dallas, who thinks he's some kind of genius when he actually doesn't know shit . . ."

"Let me buy you a drink, son," my father said, hearing the commotion as he came out of the intensive care unit shaken.

"That's the last thing he needs, Dad," Dupree said. "Liquor makes it worse."

"It don't do a lot for Dad either," Dallas observed. "Why don't you try one of those shots on Dad?"

"I'll go with you," Tee said to John Hardin. "You and I'll go with Dupree to get that shot."

"The only cure that'd help me at all is for everyone in this room to get cancer and for my sweet mother to walk out of here with me."

Dupree rose and approached his brother cautiously. "Please, John Hardin. We know how this ends. You'll get disoriented and do something stupid. You won't even mean to do it or know you're doing it. But it's in your hands. Get a shot or the cops'll put out a bulletin to pick you up."

"If I needed a fortune-teller, asshole, I'd go order a Chinese meal," John Hardin screamed. "You want me to get that shot so you can be part of the cover-up. Right? You know that they're killing Mom right now. They're poisoning her bloodstream. It destroys her liver, her kidney—everything. Know anything about science, losers? Any of you guys pay attention in Mr. Gnann's chemistry class? Mom's not coming out of that room. She's not. She's not."

"Just what we need," Dallas whispered to no one in particular. "An optimist at a death watch."

"I'm the nicest of the brothers," John Hardin said. "Mom said that, not me. I'm just reporting the facts. She said I was her favorite. The pick of the litter."

"You were the baby," I said. "She always loved you the best."

"How you like them apples?" John Hardin gloated, pointing at my other brothers. "Even the precious one, the oldest, sides with me."

"Son, why don't you sit here with me and we'll talk about the good old days," the judge suggested.

"The good ol' days? What a laugh that is. You want something funny, losers? Want something to laugh about? How's that for a punch line? The good ol' days."

John Hardin moved quickly to the open window and let himself out. We watched him sprint to the boat dock and gun the boat out toward the main channel, heading away from town.

"It may take time," the judge said, "but this'll make us closer as a family."

"I can feel it working already," said Dallas as he watched John Hardin's boat in the distance.

Late in the afternoon I took my fifteen-minute turn at my mother's bedside, holding her hand and kissing her cheek and softly telling her everything I could about her granddaughter. I also told her that her face was still pretty by any measure or at any age, but I knew that she would hate to be studied without her makeup on or her hair combed as I was doing now. Small lines radiated out from her eyes in a dozen cutting streams. Similar lines flowed from the edges of her lips, but her forehead was as smooth as a child's. My mother had used her beauty as a razor in this town; it was the only weapon she had brought to a luckless life. There were other women in Waterford more beautiful than she but none more sensual, or indeed, more overtly sexual. I have never seen a sexier woman than my own mother and for as long as I could remember, she had attracted men in droves. Her figure was still full yet slim and was the envy of her peers and the wonder of her sons. Her feet, which she took great pride in, were beautiful, her ankles shapely and perfect. "Your mother's a package," the judge used to say in admiration. "She's a real package."

I looked at the silver bag of chemotherapy dripping its poisons into my mother's veins. It seemed pure as spring water, the color of expensive gin, and I imagined the malignant engagement of cells that was being joined in the underglooms of her bloodstream. The chemotherapy smelled acrid and corrupt, and I thought again of the warning that Lucy was in

as much danger of being killed by the chemotherapy as by the leukemia.

Dupree relieved me after my fifteen minutes were up and I noticed that we were instinctively obeying an innate chronology, taking
turns from oldest to youngest in the exact order
of our birth.

The weight of my brothers' gaze was almost
too much for me when I returned to the waiting room. My exile had changed their understanding of me and I could feel their morbid
curiosity. I was leading a life none of them
knew anything about, with a child none would
recognize if she walked into the room that very
moment. I wrote about places they had not
seen, of food none had tasted, of people who
spoke languages few of my family had heard.
My clothes were different and they no longer
felt easy in my presence, nor I in theirs. In
some way we all felt measured, discarded and
dismissed. And I was found guilty because I
proclaimed by my absence that the South was
not a good enough place for me to live and
raise my daughter.

Flowers kept arriving for Lucy that were forbidden in the intensive care unit, so my brothers and I fanned out through the hospital dropping off bouquets to patients who lacked

flowers. Dallas' wife, Janice, came by with their two kids and I watched young Jimmy and Michael look at me with suspicion as they climbed easily into the laps of their other uncles.

"Serves you right for being a stranger so long," Dallas said and I laughed in agreement.

At five o'clock, Lucy's young doctor, Steve Peyton, gathered us together for the grim yet hopeful prognosis. My mother had let the symptoms go on far too long before she sought medical help. The doctor told us again that the next forty-eight hours were critical, but if she could make it through that time period, she would have a chance of surviving this episode. We stood uncomfortably before him like prisoners before a judge famous for his harshness. Though his words frightened us, we tried to make the best of a bad situation. As soon as he left, Dr. Pitts went back in to be with his wife.

My brothers and I sat together in silence.

Then Dallas said, "Anyone seen Dad?"

"You took him home to change," Tee said.

"And I brought him back here."

"He went to smoke a cigarette a couple of hours ago," I said.

"Uh-oh," Dupree said. "I'll take the West Wing."

Dallas found him passed out in an empty room on the second floor. He had drunk a whole bottle of Absolut Vodka. My father thought that no one could smell vodka on his breath and he often drank it when he made long appearances in society. It was unconsciousness that betrayed his secret drinking, not bad breath. Dupree and I carried him out of that hospital room and down the stairway as Tee and Dallas ran ahead, opening doors. We laid him in the backseat of Dupree's car and Tee got in and let our father's head rest on his lap. Dallas and I jumped in the front seat with Dupree, who drove us to my father's house. Because I had been gone so long the town's loveliness ambushed me as I listened to my brothers' small talk.

Dupree went slowly along the oak-lined avenue that ran beside the Waterford River. Twelve mansions, immemorial and speechless as chess queens, lined the other side of the road. The mansions and the water oaks stood in exquisite counterpoint and one could feel the urge of long-dead architects to build splendid houses, asylums from the long summers, houses without artifice or whimsy that would last a thousand years and not dishonor the water oaks, so lordly and fine on the green altar that rose from the salt river.

I heard my father stir in the backseat. For a moment, it seemed as if he had quit breathing, then a soft, childlike snoring began again and I relaxed.

"I thought he'd stopped drinking," I said.

"He had," Dupree said, checking his father in the rearview mirror. "He blamed the liquor for the divorce. Like he was some kind of prince when he wasn't drinking."

"When did he start back?"

"Immediately," Dallas said. "Dad claimed liquor was the only thing that could get him through his grief over his lost mate. His words —lost mate—not mine. He's an old-fashioned kind of guy."

"Hey, you think I don't have ears, you little bastard," the judge said from the backseat.

"Oh good," Tee said. "Dad's up."

"You think I don't have feelings?"

Dupree looked at me and we both shrugged our shoulders.

"Those aren't feelings you're experiencing, Dad," I said. "Those are delirium tremens."

My father roared back, "How do you say 'fuck you' in Italian, Jack?"

"*Va fanculo.*"

"Well you can *va fanculo* yourself all night. I'm glad you're keeping your fat ass in Europe and I'm only sorry you came home to take advantage of my hospitality."

"You, Tee, and I are staying with Dad," Dupree explained. "We'll have our old rooms. Be good to take a trip down memory lane to the place we were tortured as children."

"Boo-hoo. Boo-hoo," my father mocked. "You kids don't know what a bad childhood's like. You wouldn't have lasted five minutes during the Depression."

Dupree and I both repeated the last sentence at the same time and with the exact didactic intonation of our father.

"Depression must've been hell," said Tee.

"Gets worse every year," Dupree said. "No one survived the son of a bitch. America was wiped out except a few strong men like Dad. His pussy sons wouldn't've lasted a day."

Dupree eased the car through Dolphin Street, which cut through the two blocks of downtown. The shapes of the stores were characteristic of the town's distinction. Each store was different, but seen together, they gave the street an undisclosed unity, the look of some perfectly lit marina with a full consignment of interesting yachts tied up at night. I always wondered how a town so pretty could produce people so mean.

"Why didn't Mom keep the house?" I asked Dupree. "I never thought she'd give that house up in a million years."

"Your mother makes the whore of Babylon look pure as the wind-driven snow." A voice came from the backseat—he was keeping up his end of the conversation. "I surrendered my seed to Delilah after she bestowed upon me the kiss of Judas."

"He goes biblical when he discusses Mom," Dallas explained. "Thinks it puts him on a high moral plain."

"But the house," I persisted. "I think she loved it more than she loved us."

"Way she explained it was this," said Dupree. "The house was so full of bad memories for her that an exorcist wouldn't do her any good."

"It's a house full of beautiful memories. Beautiful memories," Father wailed sadly.

"What's a beautiful memory, Dupree?" I asked.

"Don't know. Heard of 'em. Just never had one."

My brothers and I laughed, but the laughter had a cutting and bitter edge. Dupree reached across the seat past Dallas and squeezed my hand. That secret gesture was his welcome home. He was assuring me that I could always find rescue in the country of brothers. The friendship of my brothers burned in a soft fire and my absence had not quite made the fire go out.

The house where we were born was lit by the last light of day and the tide was high in the river as Dupree pulled the car into the driveway. Looking at the house was like looking at a secret part of myself, a place that revealed the scars and craters from the dark side of the soul, the side where suffering and agony and hurt too great to bear lumber off to lick their wounds. It was also adjacent to where Shyla had lived.

"Help me out of this damn car," our father shouted.

Dupree and I helped him out of the car and through the garden, repeating once more the scene we had been part of hundreds of times in our childhoods. It had helped mark those childhoods and I was sure it had gone a long way to damage what lives we had made for ourselves as adults.

"You know," Dupree said, "I wouldn't mind if Dad was a drunk, if he wasn't so mean."

"Can't have everything," I said.

"See why I live in Columbia?" Dupree asked.

"Any questions about Rome?"

"Not a one. Always made sense to me."

"I'm tired of this shit," our father said. "I'm gonna whip both your asses."

"There's four of us, Dad," Tee reminded him.

"Face it, Pop. You're old and weak and over the hill. We're all in our prime and we don't like you very much."

"I set him up in practice, Lord," the judge wailed at Dallas. "I handed him a million-dollar law firm."

"My clients buy track shoes after they meet Dad," Dallas said to us. "That's how fast they want to get away from our firm."

"God, it's good to be home," I said. "The old homeplace. Family albums. Home-cooked meals. Church picnics. Sly old Dad doing magic tricks for the grandkids."

"I don't have to take this shit."

"Yeah you do, Dad," I said. "You can't walk without our help. And yes. Thanks. Think nothing of it. A pleasure to be of service. Don't mention it."

"Thanks for nothing, losers," my father said.

Dupree and I began to maneuver the judge into the house. Waterford is still one of those American towns where doors are locked only by the friendless or the paranoid. The two of us performed a flawless pas de deux as we pivoted in the doorway and brought the judge into the entrance hallway without once having brushed the doorjamb. It is a small skill perfected by the sons of drunkards, one of many learned by girls and boys whose parents live out their lives feeding rivers of gin or bourbon to the interior seas of their addiction.

But our father balked at going up the stairs,

so we walked him into the living room in a clumsy finishing gait that made us look like contestants in a three-legged race. We laid him down softly and he was asleep before we brought his feet up under a pillow and removed his shoes.

"There," said Dupree. "Wasn't that fun? God, that McCall family knows how to have a good time."

I looked at my father and a sudden pity came over me. What a sullen voyage fathering had been for this complicated and overbearing man.

"I hate to say this," Dallas said, "but after that, I need a drink. Go on into the den and I'll make us one."

In the den, I looked over the library and felt that slight pleasure I always felt when I realized my parents were so broadly read. I moved my hands along the worn set of Tolstoy and thought again about the irony of a father who loved Tolstoy but could not quite bring himself to love his own family.

I smelled the books and in so smelling realized that I was breathing the smell of myself, the familiar incense of the past coming to me in an envelope of aromas: woodsmoke, law books, floor wax, sea air and a thousand other lesser scents that went into the making of this strange wine of air and memory.

Behind the desk were all the family photographs, beautifully framed in long chronologically ordered rows. The first photo was of me as a baby, blond and sweet. My parents were so handsome that they looked like the children of royalty sworn to secrecy. They shone with a radiant health. Dad hard and muscled and home from the war; Mama's generous beauty as voluptuous and lush as a field of flowers in the rain. I wondered about the joy they must have taken in each other's bodies, the fires and passions that must have lit the way to my conception.

The pictures, all of them, broke my heart. In photographs, like most children, we always smiled and our parents were laughing. All the images that hung on the wall spoke a fluid, happy language of a comely man and woman who had produced a line of light-haired children sleek as otters, shining with vigor, robust and green and hard to hold back. "What a lovely, wonderful family we all were," I said to myself as I studied the photographs that framed the flood tide of egregious lying.

In one photograph, there was a picture of me standing in the background, not smiling. I looked at it and tried to fathom what I had been thinking. It was taken the week I had gone to the hospital because my father had broken my nose. I had told the doctor it had happened at football practice and had cried when the doctor reset it. My father had hit me again on the way home for crying.

Who wouldn't have loved to have a boy like me? I thought as I studied the shy boy I once was. And I was handsome. Why didn't anyone ever think to tell me that?

Dupree walked into the den and handed me a gin and tonic. "You look awful. Jet lag getting you?"

"I'm exhausted, but I don't think I could sleep if I tried. I need to talk to Leah, but it's too late, she's asleep."

"Got any pictures?"

"Yep." I handed an envelope to Dupree, and my other two brothers came in and looked over his shoulders.

They took their time looking at the photographs of this niece they did not know. They smiled and laughed as they perused each one carefully.

"She's the spitting image of Shyla," Dupree said. "But she's got Mom's eyes. I know some women who'd kill to have Mom's eyes."

"A magic kid, Dupree. Nothing I'm doing. I'm just keeping out of the way."

"You look at Shyla's house when we came in?" Tee asked.

"No, I don't plan to look at that house ever

again in my life. Of course, all that could change in the next thirty seconds."

"You've already got problems building over there," Dallas said. "Ruth Fox called my office yesterday to see when you were getting in. We heard about Martha tracking you down in Rome."

"A lot of people included me in their travel plans this spring."

"Ruth wants to see you badly. She's suffered more than anyone since Shyla died," Dallas said.

"I didn't know there was a sweepstakes," I answered.

"She's a wonderful woman, Jack. I hope you haven't forgotten that," Dallas said.

"The last time I saw her was in court. She testified that I'd been an unfit husband to her daughter and an unfit father to Leah."

"Go out on the veranda and look over at her house," Dupree said.

I rose heavily, more fatigued than I knew I could be and still be awake. I walked through the familiar rooms of this lovely but neglected house and out the front door between the pure white columns that symbolized both the elegance and simplicity that was known in South Carolina as the Waterford Style. It was dark now and I looked out toward the river and the starry sky rinsed with the tin enamel light of a flickered, early moon. Then I turned and walked to the other side of the veranda and looked toward the large house contiguous to the vast grounds where I had spent my childhood years. When she was a girl, I had spotted her beauty before the ripening had begun and had studied the house where such mystical transformations were taking place while stars and Waterford slept. I had recognized Shyla's loveliness long before we felt any stirrings in our bloodstreams toward each other. I glimpsed Shyla's mother on the second-story veranda, Ruth Fox still slim as a flame, as she stood watch, dressed in a white robe. She was standing in the exact spot where Shyla used to stand throwing me kisses that had once sweetened the whole world for me.

Ruth waved to me, a gesture of sadness and silence.

I nodded. All I could manage was a nod and I thought it would kill me.

CHAPTER 11

FROM THE SMOKE OF A DREAM TOO dark to remember, I woke in the bedroom with my boyhood locked in a fixed position around me as a timber-laden barge sounded its horn on the river, trying vainly to rouse the sleeping bridge tender. I had grown up encircled by rivers. A river could not make a sound without seeming to call out my name. In darkness I rose fearing for my mother's life, carrying that fever within me, as natural as hunger now. I listened and heard other sounds in the house as my brothers began to stir in the same bedrooms that had remained untouched since the day we marched out to encounter our own

lives. The movement of brothers made a delicate, sustaining noise in this newly resurrected
household. I smelled the coffee brewing as I
shaved and Dupree fed me and Tee a good
breakfast before we drove to the hospital to
renew our vigil.

When we entered the waiting room again,
Dallas was already there trying to start up a
conversation with a very groggy and un-
forthcoming John Hardin.

"No change," Dallas said as we walked in
and staked out our own territory around the
room. John Hardin's face was so guarded when
he looked at me that he reminded me of a secret ballot. Tee went up to him and put his arm
around his shoulder and said, "You all right,
bro? You should've been with us last night . . .
it was a powwow among the brothers. It was
something. We were so funny that the lions
couldn't sleep."

"I wasn't invited," John Hardin said, slapping his brother's hand and throwing it off his
shoulder. "Get your hands off the merchandise. I know all of you think I'm a homo because I'm not married."

"No we don't," Dallas said. "We think
you're smart."

"We don't care what you are, bro," Tee
said. "We just wish you felt more comfortable
being around us."

"Careful what you ask Santa for," Dupree warned.

"Dupree isn't happy unless he sees me in a straitjacket," John Hardin said, eyeing his brother with wariness. "That always gives him a cheap thrill. Right, Dupree?"

"I'd rather watch Johnny Carson," Dupree said.

"Hush, bro," Tee admonished Dupree.

"Dupree sees John Hardin in difficult situations that none of us know about, Tee," Dallas said. "He's gotta be there at show time."

"What's show time?" I asked.

"You'll find out if he doesn't go ahead and get his shot," said Dupree, thumbing through the morning sports section. As Dupree said this, I thought that he was an anomaly to me; part of Dupree seemed as tightly wound as a watch and another part as if some coolant kept the main engine of his psyche from overheating. The tension between him and John Hardin hung like a power line between us.

"You treat me like I'm still the baby of the family," said John Hardin.

"You'll always be my baby brother," Dupree said to the newspaper.

"See, it's all unfair," John Hardin said, as if he were tasting pure lemon juice. He fought to articulate his feelings. "I can't grow up in your eyes. Because I have these spells, these problems, you never can believe I actually've grown up. When I get crazy, it's got nothing to do with being young. It's all its own thing. It's outside of me. It does what it does and takes me along with it. Does that make sense?"

"Nope," Dupree said.

"Yeah. It does," I said. "I know exactly what you're saying."

"Me too," said Tee.

"It all makes sense until something bad happens, John Hardin," Dallas said. "Then it's hard to remember that you can't help it."

"Getting a shot's the easiest thing in the world," Dupree said. "Get a shot, nothing happens. Don't get one, the race is on."

Tee said, "He's old enough to decide whether to get a shot or not."

"Thanks, Tee," John Hardin said. "I really appreciate that."

"Tee's never around when the flag goes up," Dupree said.

"Tee's right," I said. "It's up to John Hardin."

"It's easy to have theories when you live in Rome, Jack," Dallas said.

After this exchange John Hardin separated himself from the rest of us and was smoking cigarettes nonstop as he watched the sparse river traffic pass by the hospital. He gave off an impenetrable aura of solitude and danger, though he listened to every word spoken in the room and processed the language through a filter that was haphazard, imperfect. Dallas explained the problem for me when we walked in the hospital garden. For John Hardin, the English language was an instrument of disharmony, bedlam, and obfuscation. Words spoken in innocence by one of his brothers could take on an aggravated significance in John Hardin's mind. Every conversation with him had the possibility of turning wrong in an instant. He had a great many interests and was extremely well read, but the slightest change of emphasis or shift of intonation could disorient him and send him spinning wildly out of control. One had to cross an eerie demilitarized zone, heavily booby-trapped and bristling with observation points and eccentric, variable passwords to gain access to those stationary realms where John Hardin felt safe. His equilibrium was movable and adrift.

"Has anyone thought about Mom?" John Hardin asked, framed in smoke. "You talk about everything else. Does anyone know whether she's going to live or die?"

"Dr. Pitts is with her now, John Hardin," Dupree said, rising and moving across the room toward his brother. "He's conferring with the doctor."

"He's not our real father, you know," our

youngest brother continued. "If you look on my birth certificate you won't find any mention at all of any Dr. James Pitts. How do we know he's telling us the truth about Mom? He could be injecting her full of drugs. Killing her slowly so he can steal all our rightful inheritance."

"Mom doesn't have much," Dallas said, approaching his brother cautiously. "Believe me, I'm the executor of her will."

"There's a lot that's rightfully ours," John Hardin said. "You guys may wash your hands of material things our mother spent her whole life working for. But I'm made of tougher fiber."

"Fiber," Dallas whispered. "He thinks he's a throw rug."

"Dr. Pitts likes us," Tee said. "He won't try to cheat us."

"He's got a burglar's eyes," John Hardin said. "He's the type of guy who's always looking at the second story of houses, hoping to see an unlocked window."

"He's got penetrating eyes," Dallas said. "He's a surgeon for God's sake."

"No, John Hardin's right," Tee said quickly. "There's something wrong with the doc's eyes."

Tee's irresolution made him sometimes both the ally and the enemy of both sides. It never occurred to Tee that vacillation was a form of taking sides that betrayed all parties.

Dallas began to move about the waiting room, jangling his keys in his pocket so loudly that all eyes turned suddenly on him. He had thought that by earning a law degree, marrying a woman from a good family, and conducting both his business and private affairs with restraint and dignity he would be spared the more baroque and unbridled excesses of his family's behavior. His family embarrassed him and always had and he sought immunity from its extravagances and its lack of all caution or reserve. Dallas longed for dignity and thought that precious little to ask, especially when his mother was dying. But he knew if he brought it up or laid this request on the table, anything could happen. He knew that this group was capable of anything. In despair, he sat down next to me and said, "This isn't a family. It's a nation."

"Once we find out about Mom, I'm outta here," I said.

"It's not like this usually," Dallas said. "But when we're trapped . . . all in one room."

"Dante couldn't have described hell more vividly," I said.

"Never read the cat," Dallas said. Then looking around the room, he whispered, "Do you know I told my wife not to come here today. Not because I didn't want her to be here, but because I'm worried about the unknown. I never know what's going to happen or who's gonna blow. Humiliation takes so many forms here. I don't know what to look out for."

"In our family that's easy," I said. "Look out for this: all men, all women, and life in general."

"Oh God," Dallas groaned. "Just when I thought it was safe to go back into the water, here comes Dad. Will it be the drunk Dad or the sober Dad?"

My father knew all the nuances and protocols of the grand entrance, especially when he was sober. He appeared at the door clean-shaven and impeccably dressed. He stood erect, like the infantryman he once was, his eyes sweeping the room like a raptor surveying an acre of hunting ground for prey.

I counted to four and then inhaled; the smell of English Leather cologne stormed my nostrils and brought back everything that was wrong about my childhood. English Leather was an unmistakable sign that my father was going to try to clean up his act and not drink for the next several days. He seemed to have an internal barometer that registered when he had crossed some line of conduct or self-regulation that required fine tuning. He was not just an alcoholic, he was a complicated alcoholic. He used sobriety as a weapon of surprise. All during my childhood he would suddenly stop drinking, splash himself with cologne, and give those who loved him great reason to hope that life would be better. That was the meanest thing about him. But we all eventually learned never to fall in love with our father sober.

"English Leather," I said. "The smell of pain."

"I get physically sick when I smell that stuff. I swear I do. I buy him a new kind of aftershave lotion. Think he ever wears it? Hell, no," said Dallas. "That's what my office smells like."

"Boys, I'd like to thank you for taking care of your father last night," the judge said, his voice avuncular, intimate. "I tried to take a brief catnap in a room not in use. I've been so worried over Lucy, I didn't realize how exhausted I was."

"No problem, Pop," Tee said.

"I woke up with a grand feeling this morning," the judge said.

"Only person I ever knew who liked hangovers," Dupree deadpanned.

My father continued, "I think her leukemia's on the run as I speak, routed from the field, and I think we'll all be laughing about this in a month or two. Look at you guys, down in the mouth, hangdog. Where's the pep?"

"We don't need a cheerleader, Dad," Dallas said. "Try being a father. That might help."

"A good attitude can carry you a long way

in this life," the judge said. "I suggest you boys start working on one."

"Good attitude's tough, Dad," Dupree said, "when your mother's dying of cancer."

"C'mon, bro," Tee said, "you're not letting something that small get to you."

"I confess," Dupree said, "it bothers me."

"Relax, boys," our father said, trying to comfort us. "I know that woman in there better than anyone else alive. Her toughness is going to get her through this. She's pretty as a picture and that sometimes makes people underestimate her. But that's a Trojan warrior that gave birth to you. You could stick her hand in a fire and she wouldn't give you the password to Troy."

"Our dad," Tee said. "Homer."

"Sit down, Dad," Dallas suggested. "Her doctor'll be here soon to give us a report."

"No cancer's tough enough to kill Lucy McCall," the judge said. "She's one tough nut. I need to go in there and let her know I'm at her side. I could always comfort Lucy when the world was going to hell around us. I was her rock, her safe harbor in the storm. During my career on the bench many people used to come before me to plead their cases. I'm a student of the law and have been my whole life. I know the law inside out. I know its majesty and its coldheartedness."

"Hey, Dad," Dallas said. "Does this look like a jury? We're your sons. Don't make speeches to us."

"When the law failed, as it sometimes does, I would often fall back on the power of prayer."

The talk irritated Tee, who said to us, "I like him better when he's drinking."

"No one likes him when he's drinking," Dallas corrected. "You like him when he's passed out."

"Let's you and me take a ride," Dupree said to John Hardin, who had begun pacing in great agitation, like a leopard in a new wing of a zoo.

"Drop it, Dad," I said, not liking what I saw in John Hardin's eyes. Something was closing in on him from the inside out. His eyes looked as if they belonged in a runaway horse.

"Let me get you some coffee, bro," Tee said to John Hardin.

"Caffeine makes it worse," Dupree said.

"Who hired you to be my watchdog?" John Hardin said to Dupree through clenched teeth. "Did you answer a want ad? Who gave you the job of overseer? Who told you to run my life?"

"Fell in my lap," Dupree said, flipping through a magazine, but not reading a single word, tense, ready for action. "Just blind good luck."

"He baits me. You're witnesses to how he drives me crazy. It's subtle. An undertone you can barely hear. But he's like an echo. I say something and his voice follows a couple of seconds later. It's always a slight disapproval. An editorial. A commentary that makes me look like some nut on the loose. What you see is what you get. All of you can see that I'm perfectly okay. There's nothing wrong with me that a little peace and quiet couldn't cure. Of course, I'm worried about Mom. They're lying about her. But lies don't work with me. I see them for what they are. I'm not saying Mom's not sick. Maybe she's got the flu. But leukemia's out. Leukemia, guys. Remember Mom and leukemia? It couldn't be. Law of averages, man. Remember."

"We remember Mom and leukemia," I said. "Trust me."

"It's a joke," John Hardin said.

My father's hands began to tremble as he started to speak again. "I couldn't sleep last night . . ." he began.

"He was out cold," Dallas whispered and moved toward the window, which he opened, letting in the smell of the river.

"So I prayed to our Lord for a miracle last night and when I saw the sun rise over the Atlantic this morning, I took it as a sign that he'd heard my prayers and that he'd deliver poor

Lucy from her appointment with the Black Angel of Death."

"I didn't know death was a Negro," Dupree said, but he was not looking at his father now, he was watching every movement of his brother John Hardin.

"Shut up, Dad," John Hardin screamed. "Don't you ever know when to shut up? There are satellites up there. Miles up there. The Russians put them there. The angels listen to us from up there. They use the satellites. The satellites are connected to these light fixtures. Everybody can hear everything we say or think. So will you shut up?"

"Come with me, John Hardin," Dupree said, his voice friendly but firm.

"Leave my boy alone," the judge said. "He's upset about his mother."

Dallas looked over at me and said in surprise, "This is why you live in Italy. You're the smartest one of all of us."

"Plenty of room over there," I said, watching as Dupree moved in on John Hardin.

"Two things I ain't worried about, bro," Tee said, trying to calm John Hardin down. "Satellites and angels."

"You've never seen the big picture," John Hardin explained.

The door opened at the end of the room and Lucy's doctor, Steve Peyton, walked in with

James Pitts. Dr. Pitts had tears in his eyes and as Dr. Peyton tried to comfort him John Hardin started to scream.

"Quiet, son," the judge ordered. "This is a hospital zone. You could get a citation."

It was his stepfather's tears that got John Hardin started. Tears were few among McCall males; they were as rare as pearls in that severe treasury where grief was stored.

"No change," Dr. Peyton said. "No good news to report except that she's hanging in there."

"Get hold of yourself, boy," the judge said to his screaming son, who had lowered his voice to a moan as the doctor spoke.

"No shot," Dupree said. "The bats in his head are all busting loose."

John Hardin looked to that part of the room where his brothers were. He shut his eyes, trying to clear his head of extraneous noise and disturbance, but all was humming and in uproar there, and neither world, the one inside or the one he opened his eyes to face, was safe for him now.

John Hardin's voice broke as he said, "They're killing our mother in that room and none of us care. We should go in there and help her. She protected us from him when we were just little babies . . . There's the bastard who's killing our mother."

"Meet John Hardin, Doc," Tee said. "Bet you didn't learn about him in med school, did you?"

John Hardin began to walk toward Dr. Peyton in a menacing but mechanical way.

"Let's move, Jack," Dupree said, both of us rising to intercept John Hardin's unsteady passage across the room toward the doctor. Expertly, we altered his path and moved him toward the soft drink machine, where Dupree put in three quarters and got his brother a Coca-Cola.

"I'd rather have a diet Coke," John Hardin said. "I'm trying to lose weight. Everyone in this town's fat as pigs and I want a diet Coke."

"I'll take the Coke," Dallas said.

I fished three quarters from my pocket, separating them from a handful of Italian change.

"What's that stuff?" John Hardin said, taking an Italian coin from my palm and holding it up to the light.

I said, "A thousand-lire piece," I said. "Coin from Italy."

"What a stupid country," he said. "Can't even make quarters."

John Hardin put it in the machine and the Italian quarter slid all the way through the system without a hitch. "Worthless. Even the machine won't take it."

But the coin had diverted John Hardin's attention.

The doctor surveyed the room and it was clear from his eyes that he was ill at ease among our brawling, quicksilver McCall clan. Our high-spirited unpredictability was unnerving him.

"Mrs. Pitts has a temperature of one hundred and five degrees," Dr. Peyton said and his announcement silenced the room. "John Hardin's technically right when he says that I'm killing his mother. I've put her on the most powerful chemotherapy we can. Her white cell count is alarmingly high. She's in terrible danger. Lucy could die at any time. I'm trying to prevent that. I don't know if I can."

John Hardin screamed, "Ha!" and began a threatening walk toward the young doctor, wagging an index finger menacingly. "All of you heard him. He admitted he isn't worth a shit. He just admitted he's killing her. Follow me, brothers. We've got to save our mother's life."

"Calm down, John Hardin, or I'll be driving you to Bull Street myself," Dupree said, mentioning the location of the state mental hospital.

"But you heard him, Dupree," John Hardin said, his arms outstretched now. "He's killing our mother. He just said it."

"He's trying to save our mother," Dupree said. "Let's not make it any harder on the doctor."

The judge cleared his throat from across the room and the court of venue changed again in that emotionally charged room.

"This is God's way of punishing Lucy for leaving me," the judge said in the silence that followed. "This is just desserts. Nothing more or less."

I had promised myself I would keep calm and be inconspicuous, but Dad's remark flushed me out into the open. "Hey, Dad, how 'bout shutting up. Nothing more or less."

"You don't frighten me, son," he said. "Free speech is a protected right in America the last time I was in a law library. Add that to the fact that I'm armed."

Dr. Pitts and Dr. Peyton were wordless as they both stared at Judge McCall, who returned their stare without malice and with perfect equanimity.

"He's just kidding, Dr. Peyton," Tee assured him. "Pops doesn't have a gun."

With this challenge, Dad lifted a pistol from an ankle holster and began spinning it on his finger, a parody of old gunslingers. Dallas walked across the room, took the gun away, and returned with it, opening the cylinder, revealing that the gun was not loaded.

"No guns in the waiting room, Judge Mc-Call," Dr. Peyton said, relieved.

"I got a deputy sheriff's badge right here." The judge held up his billfold. "Says I can carry a gun anywhere in Waterford County. Bring that firearm back to its rightful owner, son."

"Give it to you later, Dad," Dallas said. "It makes me nervous when you flash it when you're sober."

"I'm glad we don't have gun control in this country," Dallas said. "So drunks like Dad can walk around practicing their draw."

"It keeps the Indians away." The Judge tried to joke, but his sons were angry with him.

I began to feel the roots of exhaustion curling into the deepest tissues of my body. I had written over ten articles on the perils of jet lag and considered myself something of an expert on how a precipitous change of time zones can exact a terrible price from a traveler. And now, deep inside myself, I felt my body preparing for sundown in Italy, even though the day was young in South Carolina. I was used to the night sounds of the piazza, of police sirens far off in the city of Rome, musicians playing mandolins for tourists, and the sound of Leah's bare feet coming down the hall to have me read her a story.

Leah. Her name cut into me and I checked my watch and promised myself to call her at three in the afternoon, which would coincide nicely with her bedtime. I looked at those surrounding me in the waiting room and realized Leah would not recognize a single person in this room besides myself. And I couldn't decide if I had rendered her a great service or cut her off from those powerful forces that were one half her legacy of blood and cunning and folly, the legacy that was gathered in a dark vigil to protest the death of our mother. Though I had differences of opinion with almost everyone in the room and though dissonance was what my family did best, there was an inalienable beauty and affirmation in this drawing together and it moved me. Five years ago I had declared myself a man without a family. Now, I could not decide if that was a cardinal sin or merely wishful thinking.

I got up, restless, eager to move around.

Walking down the corridor to be alone, I was followed by Dr. Pitts and we continued until we found ourselves standing outside the main entrance. Though he was still uncomfortable with me, his solicitude and obvious concern for my mother moved me.

"Jack, may I have a word with you?" Dr. Pitts asked.

"Sure."

"Your mother wants to receive the last rites."

"How do you know?"

"I know everything about her," Dr. Pitts said. "I know she would want me to get in touch with Father Jude at Mepkin Abbey. You know him."

"The Trappist," I said. "Mom used to take us up to visit him a lot when we were kids. He even lived with us for a while in the fifties."

I walked back to the telephone and called the abbey, and then returned to the waiting room and led my stepfather to an open window, away from the family crossfire.

"Have you called Father Jude?" he asked.

"I talked to his abbot. I'll drive up for him now."

"Take your mother's car, it's still in the lot," Dr. Pitts said. He then broke down and with those tears, he proved again that his love for her was, at least, a match for our own.

CHAPTER 12

I COULD SMELL MY MOTHER'S PER-
fume, White Shoulders, in the airways and
crannies of her Cadillac. Part showboat and
part gas hog, the car in its imperial spacious-
ness fitted the image my mother had constructed for herself since she'd become a doctor's wife. A judge's wife is always
shortchanged by the need for judiciousness and
caution. Though Lucy had led a spectacularly
injudicious life, she'd always felt the pressure
of those strict injunctions. As a doctor's wife,
she'd blossomed into the sweet vanity of her
natural flashiness. Leukemia is her reward for
such behavior, I thought.

Taking back roads all the way, I drove from Waterford toward Mepkin Abbey, a small city of prayer hidden deep in a semitropical forest thirty miles from Charleston, South Carolina. Its isolation was intentional. In the hazes of the backwater of the Cooper River, quiet men with their heads shaved retreated from the world to dedicate their lives to solitude and spiritual rigor.

Here, silence was one of the lesser gods and fasting one of its adherents. They raised their voices in song each day, some of the men, old and frail and lovely as hourglasses. They sold their eggs and their honey to local middlemen, Baptists and Methodists, who distributed the produce throughout the state. I had always thought these were the oddest men, despite the fact that Mepkin Abbey had been a place of refuge for my mother and the rest of us when the judge had been drinking heavily. We used to come to Mepkin Abbey to escape and heal our broken spirits. We would stay in the guest houses and go to Mass each day with the monks and my mother would walk the woods with Father Jude for hours. I grew up believing that my mother was in love with this baffling and quiescent man.

As I drove down the long driveway leading up to the monastery, a small red fox, a saucy and fresh-faced pup, ran out of the forest and stopped. I slowed down and watched the pup, which showed not a trace of fear. I whistled and he cocked his head, his stare steady and inquisitive. Then his mother rushed out of the woods and grabbed her errant pup by the nape of his neck and carried him swiftly back to her lair.

Wildness, I thought, that's what I've missed in Italy, that intimate connection with the inhuman and untamable.

Father Jude was waiting for me beside the bell that divided the strictly accounted-for hours in the lives of monks. He was a tall man, built like a heron and with the face of a spooked herbivore, and vaguely off-balance. In human relationships he had always seemed maladroit and overly cautious. To my mother, Jude was indisputably a holy man, but to me he made faith seem like melancholia. When I was a child, I thought he was afraid of me, as though my bones were made of the most fragile porcelains. As an adult, he avoided all eye contact with me. I headed the car toward the same highway that had brought me to him. He was so jumpy you would have thought I was driving him to a whorehouse.

On the ride back to Waterford he spoke very little and was oblivious to the cypress swamps and ink-black rivers of the Edisto and Ashepoo and Combahee. But as we crossed the

first of a series of bridges that marked the beginning of the saltwater zone, where the
marshes of Waterford assumed dominion over
the cottonwood and tupelo forests, he found
his voice:

"Do you miss God?" the priest asked. The
pure simplicity of the question startled me.

"Why do you ask, Father?"

"You were a very religious boy once," the
priest said.

"I believed in the tooth fairy then, too," I
said. "That dime underneath my pillow. I like
solid proof."

"Your mother told me you were a fallen-
away Catholic," he said.

"That's right," I said, annoyed by the statement, but trying to catch myself. "That doesn't
mean I don't enjoy a little bingo game every
now and then."

"That's all the Church meant to you?" the
priest said. "Bingo?"

"No," I answered. "It also means the Inqui-
sition. Franco. The Pope's silence during the
Holocaust. Abortion. Birth control. The celi-
bacy of priests."

"I see," the priest said.

"Just the tip of the iceberg," I said.

"But God," he said, "what of him?"

"We're having a lovers' quarrel," I said.

"Why?"

"He helped kill my wife," I answered. "Not really, of course. But I find it easier to blame him than me."

"An odd take," he said.

I looked over at the thin-faced man with his profile of a minor saint. His gauntness gave him a fierceness his soft voice lacked.

"We thought Mom was having an affair with you when we were younger. We all were sure of it."

The priest smiled but did not look shaken by the revelation.

"You were too close," I continued. "There was always something strange and unspoken when you two got together. Whispers and touching of hands. Going off together in the woods. My father was jealous as hell. He's always hated you."

"Ah. The judge," the priest said. "Yes. But he didn't understand either. He once confronted me about your mother and said he had proof we were lovers. He even claimed that he'd written the Pope."

"Were you lovers?" I asked.

"No, but we loved each other," Father Jude said.

"But why? What was the attraction?"

"It was not attraction," the priest said. "It was history."

"History?"

"I knew her before she met your father."

"Keep going," I encouraged him.

"Our souls take comfort in each other," the priest said. "Secrets bind us. Early ones."

"Why don't you just speak in Latin? You'd make more sense," I said.

"Do you know anything about your mother's childhood?" he asked.

"Sure."

"What?"

"She was born in the mountains of North Carolina. She was raised in Atlanta. She met my father in Charleston."

"You know nothing. Just as I thought," he said.

"I know more than you do," I said, then added, "pal."

We rode for a minute in complete silence before he answered, "No, you don't . . . ." He waited for a full ten seconds before he completed his sentence.

". . . pal," he said.

As soon as I parked my mother's car, we hurriedly but silently entered the hospital and went straight to my mother's bedside. I waved to my brothers as we passed them, but the priest moved through the waiting room as though they were invisible. Already, his lips were moving in prayer as he laid his case at the foot of her bed and began to prepare himself for administering the last rites. But before he began, Father Jude knelt beside my mother, took her hand in his, kissed the center of her palm, closed her hand, then quietly wept.

Finding his behavior odd and unbecoming, I walked over to the window. I looked out the blinds toward the river, trying to make my presence disappear. This priest was a difficult man to warm up to, ice cold in the center, blizzardly at the edges. My mother's friendship with him always seemed like a rejection of me.

Then I heard him say, "They don't know what we went through, Lucy. They don't know how we got here."

The words surprised me as much as his tears. Here I was judging this gaunt priest for his remoteness, yet I stood before my unconscious mother without allowing myself to feel a thing. My own tears seemed landlocked and frozen in a glacier I could not reach or touch within me. What kind of man was I who could not even bring himself to weep at the bedside of his dying mother? I thought. My mother had raised her sons to be hard and stoical and it cost her that portion of tears we should have shed for her in this hospital. I turned back toward Father Jude, who was now preparing himself to administer Extreme Unction.

Extreme Unction, I said to myself, as the priest lit candles and handed them to me. In-

troit and compline, I said, eucharist and conse-
cration, kyrie and confiteor. Was there ever a
boy who loved the soaring language of his
church more than I? In the language of my
church I could approach the altar of God with
words like flung roses sustaining me. Without
faith so long, I could hear my church singing
me love songs as the priest stepped closer to
my mother: The words were winged and feathered, drifting like Paracletes around me. This
mother, this holy earth, this basilica that once
had housed me.

Vested in a violet stole, Father Jude put a
crucifix to Lucy's mouth for her to kiss. Because she was unconscious and in danger of
death he forgave Lucy all of her sins and, according to the faith, Lucy's immortal soul
blazed like a newly formed coin. It was now
pure white.

Father Jude made the sign of the cross and
addressed me. "Will you please say the responses?"

I nodded. "Been a long time. English or
Latin?"

He did not answer, but simply began: *"Pax
huic domui,"* and the altar boy in me leapt back
into existence. Silently, I translated the words I
found so beautiful. "Peace be unto this house."
Then answered, *"Et omnibus habitantibus in
ea."*

And unto all who dwell therein.

I watched Father Jude perform the asperges, sprinkling holy water over my mother's body, across her bed, then sprinkling me. He handed me a small black book and opened it to page 484 and pointed. My eyes fell upon the words, "May the devils fear to approach this place, may the angels of peace be present therein, and may all wicked strife depart from this house. Magnify, O Lord." The beads of holy water flowed down my face.

I remembered how often in my life I had prayed for my own father to die after one of his binges and this thought overwhelmed me as I recited the Latin responses. Father Jude was calm now, lost in the formalities of the sacrament, subsumed by function.

We worked well together, as we had years ago when I would serve Mass for him at Mepkin Abbey. He dipped his thumb in a vial of holy oil and anointed Lucy's eyes in the form of a cross. I read the English as he recited the Latin. "Through this holy unction and of his most tender mercy, may the Lord pardon thee whatsoever sins thou has committed by sight."

He then anointed her ears in the sign of the cross, then her nostrils, her lips, her hands, and her feet.

"*Kyrie eleison,*" he said. Lord have mercy.

"*Christe eleison,*" I responded. Christ have mercy.

Lastly, he prayed to put to flight all the temptations of the Evil One and asked Jesus to take Lucy up in his loving arms after the sufferings and tribulations of this transitory and sinful life.

I looked at my mother as my mother for the first time since I had returned home. I had once lived inside that woman, I marveled, my bloodstream comingling with hers. When she had eaten, it had nourished me. I tried to imagine her before I was born, dreaming of the child inside her, forming me into the boy she needed me to be, the one who would grow up much too close to her, much too in love with her, dazzled by her fierce health, her famous beauty. Can a boy love a mother too much? What happens to a soul when that love wanders as mine had, and turns to other pursuits? How can all that happen in one lifetime and how on earth did it happen to me?

The last rites ended and Father Jude removed his violet stole.

He turned to me and said, "You owe the Church again."

"Why?"

"Because your mother's going to live."

"How do you know?"

"I was heard," the priest said.

"What mumbo jumbo," I said. "What arrogance."

The priest grabbed my wrist and cut the blood flow. He said fiercely, "No, Jack. Faith. It's faith."

Leaving the hospital early, I went shopping at the Piggly Wiggly for a dinner I wanted to fix for my father and brothers. After the endless bounty of the Campo dei Fiori, I had not sufficiently prepared myself for the barrenness of the produce department of a small-town Southern supermarket. But I am a flexible man, especially when it comes to my kitchen, and I bought beans and vegetables and spareribs, then hurried off to my father's house to get it ready.

My brothers also tired of the ambiance in the waiting room and I soon found them sitting around me in the kitchen as I started the evening meal. My father was continuing his sober vigil at the hospital in the company of Dr. Pitts and Father Jude. I was peeling potatoes when I remembered that I had not spoken to Leah since my return. Twice I had called her, but it was long after her bedtime. I checked the clock on the wall and realized it would soon be midnight in Rome.

"Did you guys invite John Hardin for dinner?" I asked as I used the phone in the kitchen.

"Sure did, bro," Tee said, taking a sip of his beer. "He said I could tell Jack to kiss his ass and he didn't need to eat any of your fancy food."

"His loss," I said as I spoke with an overseas operator and gave her my credit card number, the code for Italy, the city of Rome, and finally my apartment in the Piazza Farnese.

The phone rang twice before I heard Leah answer it, and I responded.

"Daddy?" she said.

"Hey, kiddo." I felt my throat tighten with my love for this child. "I'm here with some of my brothers and all of them send their love to you."

"How's Grandma Lucy, Daddy? Is she going to be all right?"

"They don't know. They hope she's going to live, but they're just not sure right now."

"If she dies, can I go to the funeral, Daddy?"

"You'll be on the next plane, I promise. Is Maria taking real good care of you?"

"Of course, Daddy. But she makes me eat too much. She feeds me too much. She dresses me too warmly. She thinks all my dolls have germs. She makes me pray for you a lot. We lit three candles in three different churches for your mother yesterday."

"Good for her. How is school? How is Suor Rosaria? How is everyone on the piazza?"

"Everyone's fine, Daddy," Leah said, then her voice dropped a register.

"Momma's parents called me last night. We talked a long time."

My heart froze. "What did they say?"

"Grandpa hardly said anything. He just cried when he heard my voice. Then Grandma Fox took the phone away from him. She was *so* nice. So sweet. She said she hoped they'd see you while you were home. Are you going to see them?"

"If I have time, sugarpeeps," I said. "It's hard, Leah. Grandpa Fox doesn't like me very much. He never has."

"He told me that they have every right to see me," Leah said.

"There's a lot I haven't told you, darling," I said.

"But you'll start telling me?"

"As soon as we're back together. As soon as I know something about Mom."

"I found a photograph album in the library. There are two people standing beside a river. Are those my mother's parents? Are those my grandparents?"

"I know the picture," I said. "Yes."

"They look so kind."

"Yes, that's how they look."

"Martha called earlier tonight," Leah said. "She was afraid you might get mad that she'd given our number to her parents."

"It doesn't make me the happiest man on earth," I said, "but we seem to be swept along by family events this month. Something's up, Leah. And when something's up, you can't fight the flood tide."

"Does everyone ask about me? Do they want to meet me?"

"They're *mad* to meet you," I said, "and I'm mad to be with you again." I looked up and saw Dupree, Dallas, and Tee walking toward me.

"Can we say hello to our niece?" Dupree asked. "We won't be long. Just want to welcome her into the family."

Dupree took the phone and said, "Hello, Leah. This is your uncle Dupree and you don't know this yet but I'm going to fall in love with you and you're gonna fall in love with me. In fact, I'm already in love with you just hearing your daddy talk."

Winking at me, Dupree listened to Leah's response and the delight in his face told me how the conversation was going. Dallas reached out for the phone, but Dupree slapped his hand away, then he said, "Your uncle Dallas wants to say a word to you, darling. But remember, it's your uncle Dupree who's the pick of this sorry litter."

Dallas took the phone and said, "Don't you listen to a word he says, Leah. This is your favorite uncle Dallas. You'll like me a lot better than Dupree because I'm funnier, handsomer, and I've got a lot more money. I've got two kids of my own for you to play with and I'll give you all the ice cream you can eat every day. Now, my brother Tee is reaching for the phone . . . Yes, we'll have a great time. Okay, here's Uncle Tee. He weighs four hundred pounds, never takes a bath, and tells dirty jokes even to little girls. No one likes Tee, so we can't expect you to be any different."

He handed the phone to Tee, who said hello, then was the first of the uncles to listen to Leah and see what was on her mind. Tee laughed again and again, then said, "God, you get here and we'll have a blast. I'll teach you how to go crabbing and toss the shrimp net. We'll catch us some fish off the dock, and I'll even take you deep-sea fishing if you're good. If you're bad, I'll teach you how to smoke and buy you your first pair of high heels. Now, here's your daddy. People say we look alike, but I'm twice as good-looking."

I said good night to Leah, then Maria commandeered the phone and demanded to speak to me. Whenever she spoke long-distance, Maria was overaware of money wasted, so she spoke rapidly, lapsing into the almost unintelligible patois of her village.

"*Lentamente,* Maria," I said.

Maria talked on, complaining about the prices she was paying for food, repeating the gossip of the piazza, and assuring me that Leah was as smart and beautiful as she was when I left. She ended her part of the conversation by hoping she had not wasted much money, and urging me not to forget the irresistible charms of Rome.

Then Leah got back on the phone and said, "Daddy, will you do something for me?"

"Anything, kiddo. You know that."

"Don't be mad at Mama's parents for calling me. Promise."

"I promise," I said.

"And one more thing," she asked.

"It's yours," I answered.

"Tell me a story," she said.

"I'll never forget the year of the flood and the time the Great Dog Chippie . . ." I began.

CHAPTER 13

WE LEARNED TO MEASURE TIME BY the drip of the chemo through the plastic tube that led to a needle in my mother's arm. Her heart rate wrote its signature across a graph paper as it beat steadily under the watchful gaze of nurses. Her doctor delivered reports twice a day in a dry, uninflected voice. Tee brought a football and my brothers and I went out to toss the ball around the parking lot several times the next day. My mother's temperature had gone down a full degree. For the first time we felt cautious optimism.

After leaving the hospital the next evening, I went home, slept for a while, and then drove my mother's car to Mike Hess' recently purchased retreat in the low country.

Pale light still held Waterford in the hot palm of the backsliding day. Late April is that time of year when light seems to melt into the river and touch the blossoms of the transfigured trees; it made the town seem tenderly kissed with regret as the river moved away from the fading sun.

Slowly, I drove out toward the island country east of town. The bridge went up and stopped me when a snowbird heading south came through. I turned on the country music station out of Savannah so I could feel completely Southern again. The music acted as a marinade in my weary spirit.

Mike's house sat on a hundred fragrant, breathtaking acres on the inland waterway, that winding, storied channel of navigation that ran between buoys and markers for a thousand miles between Miami and Maine. I had always known that if you were skilled enough, you could set sail from the Waterford River to any port in the world. You could go anywhere, could do anything. You could cast yourself on a flood tide and escape the terrors of your own life.

Mike's house was itself a grotesquerie, although it was surrounded by an exquisite garden laid out in painted groupings of lily of the valley, narcissus, alyssum, and forget-me-not. Banks of azaleas leaned against it and dogwood lit up the side yard in white fire.

The house had been built in that faux-Southern style that is both main attraction and main affliction of Southern suburbs. All are ghastly imitations of Tara, or Tara-inspired. One may safely subtract five points from any Southerner's IQ for each column in the front of his or her house. White columns are often the metaphorical bars of the Southern prison from which there is no parole or escape.

I walked through the fussed-over garden wary of entering the house. I passed a gardenia bush on my way to the dock and felt a sudden wounding at my leaving my mother on this night. There across the river in the distance was the hospital where she lay comatose.

I was startled by Ledare's voice: "Hello. Welcome home."

Turning, I looked at the pretty woman who stood before me, and kissed her lightly on the lips, as brothers and sisters do.

I turned into the breeze. "Is the house prettier on the inside?"

"Mike used a Hollywood decorator," Ledare answered. "Flew him out here and gave him a blank check. It's like Monticello meets *A Thousand and One Nights*. It's unique."

We walked along a brick path to the front

door of the house. The interior design looked hasty; everything appeared bought, nothing collected, each room being more antiseptic than the last. Several English hunting prints hung on the sitting room walls: pale, attenuated Englishmen riding to the hounds on the South Carolina sheetrock. In the South, those emblematic hunting prints populate the walnut-paneled walls of meretricious and second-rate law firms.

As though reading my mind, Ledare said, "Mike's sensitive about his hunting prints. His home in L.A. is awash with them."

"I see," I said. "Where is the host?"

"He called from the airport on his portable phone," she answered. "He should be arriving any minute. I should warn you. He said he had mystery guests coming for drinks after dinner."

"How'd you get here? I didn't see another car."

"I took my father's boat across the river," Ledare said.

"You still know the river," I said with admiration.

She smiled.

I said, "Can I help with dinner?"

"I didn't tell you?" she said. "You're cooking it."

"Wonderful."

"You write cookbooks. I write screenplays.

It wasn't hard to figure. My father gave us a washtub full of shrimp."

"Let's peel them together. Did you get any pasta?"

"I got everything," Ledare said. "Mike told me to stock up, so I bought everything edible they had in Charleston."

It is an unwritten law that people who don't cook and who do not savor food own the finest and most fabulously equipped kitchens, and Mike was no exception. Standing side by side before an immaculate counter, Ledare and I peeled shrimp that had been swimming in Waterford creeks two hours earlier. We headed the shrimp, then disrobed the white flesh of their pale, translucent shells. With a sharp knife, I removed the long, inky vein that ran from head to tail. Outside, the sun lay down on the river and the tides blushed in rosy gold. Even the kitchen had a view of the river. As we worked, the spiny crowns of the shrimp piled up in the bottom of the sink.

"Are you working on Mike's project?" I asked.

Ledare nodded and answered, "It's not an accident we're here now. Mike heard about your mother and called me right away in New York. He's not given up on you participating in some way. How's your mother? Not getting better, I understand?"

"She's hanging in there," I said. And then, changing the subject as tactfully as I could: "Are you staying at your parents' house?"

"Just for a while," she said. "I figure there'll be six months of research before I write a single line. There's still room for you on this project. I'd love it if you'd do it."

"It's not for me, Ledare."

"Think about it. Mike's taking this seriously. It'd be the longest mini-series in history if he can pull it off."

I checked the water in the pasta pot. "Not enough happened in this town to do a mini-series. Not enough happened in this town to do a sixty-second commercial."

She looked at me.

"You and I are two of the main characters . . . in the later episodes of course. Names'll be changed, everything fictionalized, but we're in it."

"Mike, of course, didn't tell me that."

"He would have told you, but you showed no sign of being interested in the project."

"The project. Sounds like NASA. I don't know this version of Mike. I don't like what he's become." I turned the knob on the electric stove to high, then switched it off. I hate electric stoves, and love the sight of flame on a stove top.

"Mike's become a producer in all the full

horror of the breed," Ledare started to explain when we heard a car pull up the driveway. "It's the lowest form of human life and he's the nicest one I know. Smile, Jack. The shallowness comes with the territory."

Mike entered the house on the run.

"Sorry about your mama, Jack," he said as he hugged me. "I got about a thousand people in Hollywood I'd pay good money to get leukemia and God has to give it to someone sweet as her."

"That's nice, Mike," I said. "I think."

"Ciao, sweetheart," Mike said, kissing Ledare on the cheek. "It's heaven to see you both. I'm starting not even to recognize myself in L.A. I yelled at a kid, a nineteen-year-old intern, yesterday. Made her cry. Felt like shit."

"You're famous for yelling at people," Ledare said.

"But I don't like it. It's not the real me."

"It is if you keep doing it," I said. "You want a drink?"

"I sure do, and not club soda," Mike said. "Fix me a margarita."

"I can't," I said, "I'm an American."

"Bourbon, then," he said.

"Me too, Jack."

I got the drinks and we sat on the screened porch, letting the perfume of the garden, the smells of our town, flow over us. I was grateful for a respite from the hospital.

"Jack," Mike said, "I want to apologize to you for how I acted in Venice. That wasn't the real me you met in that city. That's the asshole I've become, to my shame. I act like that because that's how I get things done in the industry. Kindness is laughed at . . . goodness met with contempt. I'm embarrassed and I only hope you'll forgive me."

"We were babies together," I said.

"All of us were," Ledare added. "We love you for life, Mike."

"We know who you are and where you come from," I said. "It's hard to be famous, isn't it?"

Mike looked up suddenly, his eyes shining. "There's not one good thing about it. Except the money. And sometimes I think that's the worst of it."

"Assuage the guilt," Ledare said. "Share the money with your pals."

"I've made shitty films," Mike said. "I've been a perfect prick and all I've got to show for it is money."

"I've been a perfect prick too and all I've got to show for it is I know how to make pasta," I said, leaning over and squeezing Mike's shoulder. "Come on, let's get dinner."

"I'll help," said Ledare.

Grudgingly turning back to the electric stove, I assembled the ingredients and soon the smell of garlic frying in a rich green olive oil wafted out onto the porch, where Mike remained staring out toward the garden and the river. I was aware of how Ledare and I suddenly seemed more comfortable with each other. She began to tell me what she had learned of Mike's life since I had been gone. For five years, Mike had been seeing the most prominent psychiatrist in Beverly Hills and he was having fugitive moments of perception that had brought him to the idea of the Waterford film.

The action adventure movie had become his stock-in-trade and all of them played off the lionhearted fantasy life of teenage boys. His films had more need of plasma units than the Red Cross did after an earthquake. They also had more need of ammunition than an Israeli battalion staring down at Syria from the Golan Heights. But the films were not sleazy, just unimportant. They entertained "with a capital *E*," as Mike would tell his investors, men who trusted Mike's unerring sense of bad taste. Market research was apparently the vehicle Mike depended on to instruct him in the secret capriciousness of public taste. In one movie, the hero died in an apocalyptic shootout with a local gang, until a poll after the preview screening demonstrated that the audience preferred to exit into the night with a grinning, triumphant hero in their collective consciousness rather than a corpse. Reshooting took place on a back lot, a modern resurrection ensued, and *voilà,* the hero walked slowly into the alphabet of the closing credits, all limbs intact and all villains inert and harmless on the battleground of his last stand. Because of market research, Mike no longer had to depend on the hunches of directors or the artistry of screenwriters. The public knew exactly what it wanted and Mike was bright enough to feed it to them raw.

Like many powerful men in Hollywood who had made too much money too fast, Mike was now in a strange, illusory time where he wanted to make films of stature and substance. He was beginning to want Hollywood's respect as well as its fear and envy. He also acknowledged to Ledare that there was no more dangerous time in the life of a producer. Nothing was more pathetic or superficial than a movie producer who wished to make a statement with a film. Sentimentality appalled him, yet he could hear it sounding in himself, far off, like wind chimes. Desperately, he now wanted to tell the world about the courage of his own family and the small Southern town that had embraced and taken that family into its safekeeping and shelter.

Ledare and I were crucial to his plans.

Over dinner, Mike unfolded for me in detail his ideas for the series. He wanted it to begin with his grandfather, Max Rusoff, who was a butcher in a Russian shtetl when a pogrom led by a regiment of Cossacks broke out. The film would follow Max out of Russia to Charleston and his life as a peddler who walked Highway 17 between Charleston and Waterford. One of Max Rusoff's first customers in Waterford had been my grandfather, and their friendship had not wavered for over fifty years.

"I know all the stories," I said to Mike. "I grew up hearing them."

"I want to tell my family's story because other Jews don't even believe that Jews live down South."

"Let me ask you this, Mike, and I'd like an honest answer," I said. "Are you planning to have my wife, Shyla, leaping off that bridge in Charleston?"

Silence and restraint broke the energy of conversation and my words seemed to hang in the air. Ledare looked to Mike.

"We're changing all the names," Mike said. "The story will be definitely fictionalized."

"But a Jewish woman will kill herself by jumping off a bridge?"

Ledare took my hand. "Shyla's part of all of our stories, Jack. Not just yours."

"Shyla was my cousin," Mike said. "She's just as much a part of my family's history as she is yours."

"Good," I said. "Glad you feel that way about your family. How do you feel about your other cousin, my daughter, when she watches your TV program and sees a fictionalized version of her mother leaping off a bridge? And Mike and Ledare, how do you think I'm going to feel about it and how dare you two even think I'd participate in a project like that?"

"The suicide takes place off-screen," Mike said quickly. "Jack, I have to have you on this one. I'm going to need your help. I need it badly and so does Ledare."

"The suicide of Shyla does not have any part of this goddamn screenplay," I shouted.

"A deal," Mike said, "if you agree to help us with the rest of the story."

"You know the rest of the story," I said. "We all lived through the same things. We danced to the same music. We went to the same movies. We even dated the same people."

"He's talking about Jordan," Ledare said, her voice registering neutrality.

"We went to Jordan's memorial service together," I said evenly. "We sat together and we cried together, because Jordan was our first friend to die."

"You're lying," Mike said. "Hate to be so brutally frank, pal. But you're lying through your teeth."

Reaching into his breast pocket, he pulled out a packet of photographs and threw them across the table at me. They were snapshots taken of Jordan coming out of the confessional at Sant' Anselmo, of Jordan entering the cloistered garden. I saw several of myself looking around to see if I was being followed.

"A nice snapshot of my confessor in Rome," I said, examining the photographs one by one. "And here's a nice picture of me walking up the Aventine. And another of me going into the confessional. And what do you know, here I am coming out again, free of sin and beloved by the Lord."

"I've had those photographs blown up out at Warner Brothers and compared to pictures of Jordan in high school. Jordan Elliott is your confessor in Italy. You pass him messages and letters from his mother. I've got a tape of one of your so-called confessions."

I turned to Ledare, and for a long moment, I could not find my voice.

"Did you know anything about this, Ledare?" I asked.

"Leave melodramatics out of it," Mike said.

"I'll pay you for Jordan's story and I'll pay you to tell everything that happened between you and Capers Middleton at the University of South Carolina."

"One question, Mike," I asked. "Who's gonna pay me to kick your ass? I don't much like being followed. I don't much like being photographed in secret. And I sure as hell don't like having my confessions taped."

"They're not confessions," Mike said. "There's nothing religious about it. I want this story to cover my family, from Russia, through the Holocaust, all of our friendships—and goddamn they were friendships, Jack. It's gonna end with Capers Middleton's election as governor of the State of South Carolina."

"If Capers Middleton is elected governor of South Carolina, then I don't believe in democracy anymore," I said, trying to compose myself and calm my voice, which was shaking. "This state has already made me distrust democracy by continuing to elect Strom Thurmond year after year."

"You were his campus campaign manager when he ran for president of the freshman class at the university."

"Don't hold that against him," Ledare said. "Capers was different then. And I was Capers' first wife. The mother of his two children."

"He admits he was a lousy husband to you,

Ledare," Mike said. "Who hasn't been? I've been married four times. Shyla swan-dived off the bridge."

My control broke and before Mike knew what was happening I lifted him off his chair by his tie and pulled him toward me until our noses almost touched.

"I like to think, Mike, that the reason Shyla killed herself didn't totally have to do with my being a rotten husband. I was a rotten husband for your information, but I pray to God not rotten enough to send my very nice and very tormented wife to that bridge over the Cooper River. Do you understand, Mike? Or do I have to break your nose as a small reminder?"

"Put Mike down, Jack," Ledare ordered.

"I apologize, Jack. That was a terrible thing to say. I'm truly sorry. That wasn't the real me speaking . . ."

Ledare finished the line by saying, "It's the asshole I've become in Hollywood."

I gently returned Mike to his chair and adjusted his tie with a quiet tenderness.

"I'm very sorry, Mike," I said.

"I deserved it. You should have broken my whole face in. I say things all the time that I can't believe I say," Mike said and his voice was soft, chastened. "Do you know my mother hates me? She does. No, don't look at me that way, but I'm telling you, she hates everything

I've become. I disgust my own mother. She looks at me and says, 'What's wrong with just being happy? Where's the sin?' "

Suddenly the lights of an automobile illuminated the living room, and a car pulled in front of the house.

"The mystery guests have arrived," Mike said brightly, quickly moving toward the door.

"Do you have a clue?" I asked Ledare.

Ledare said, "Not the slightest."

Then I saw a surprise and an agony register in Ledare's eyes that even her well-known composure could not hide. There was heroism in the way she brought herself under control and I turned around to see her ex-husband and my ex-friend Capers Middleton walking in with his second wife, Betsy.

"Hello, Capers," Ledare said, shaken. "Hello, Betsy."

Betsy said to Ledare, "We were going to bring the kids, but they both have tests tomorrow and it'll be late when we get back to Charleston."

"I'm coming to see them this weekend," Ledare said stiffly.

"You were right, Mike," Capers said in appreciation. "I think this is a complete surprise."

"Man," Mike said, pleased with himself. "Bingo!"

"Hello, Jack," Capers said. "It's been a very long time. I've told Betsy all about us."

"Take a good look at me, Betsy," I said, "because you're never going to see me again."

"He told me you'd be like that," Betsy said, giving her husband an appreciative glance.

Capers Middleton was one of those Southern boys who had a perfect, polished, glittering look to him with no anomalies of expression or carriage. His handsomeness was an extension of his impeccable breeding. Once, I had loved looking at his face as much as girls did. It was the same face that taught me that good looks were the last things to be trusted.

Capers put out his hand to shake mine, but I refused.

"I'm not over it, Capers. I never will be."

"It's all in the past," Capers said. "I'm sorry about what happened. I wanted to tell you that to your face."

"You've told me," I said. "Now get out of my sight."

"He's here for a purpose," Mike said. "I invited him and I want you to act nice to our future governor and his wife. Let's go into the den for a drink. Capers has a proposal that I think you should listen to, Jack."

"I'm going home, Mike," Ledare said.

"Please stay, Ledare," Betsy said. "We can

talk about the kids while the men talk about business."

Ledare looked at Capers with an expression that was startled, birdlike. "I can't believe she said that to me."

"Betsy has this old-fashioned idea that you might like to hear about the progress of our mutual children."

"Everybody into the den," Mike ordered. "I'll pour the cognac."

The tension in the room made the air strange and electric. While Mike poured the cognac, I tried to guess at Betsy's age, then remembered she was twenty-five. I knew I had seen her before, but could not place where. Then it came to me and I laughed out loud.

"I was thinking of doing several things, Jack," Ledare said. "Laughing was not one of them."

I pointed at Betsy, barely able to speak. "Betsy was Miss South Carolina. Capers dumped you for a Miss South Carolina. Betsy Singleton of Spartanburg."

"I was very proud to serve my state for an entire year," Betsy said and I liked her scrappiness. "And to represent South Carolina at Atlantic City before the whole world was my happiest moment before my wedding day."

"I've been living in Europe too long, Betsy. I forgot girls like you existed. You might win this governor's thing, Capers. South Carolina might just buy this shit."

"Give her a break," Mike said. "She's just a kid."

"She's been wonderful to our children," Capers said. "Ledare will be glad to tell you that."

"Betsy has been very kind to me also," Ledare said.

"That's so sweet of you to say," Betsy said.

"Ledare didn't mean a word of it," I said. "It reeked of insincerity."

"Let me be the judge of that, please," Ledare shot back icily.

"You gave up Ledare Ansley for Betsy," I said to Capers. "What a shallow fuck you are, Capers."

"Jack, please, please control it, man," Mike said.

"Kiss my ass, Mike." And I turned to him. "I'll never forget what Capers Middleton did if I live to be a thousand and I'll never forgive the son of a bitch either. What the hell did you think was going to happen when you brought us together? That we were going to go out to a blind and shoot ducks together tomorrow?"

"This was a very cruel idea, Mike," Ledare said, suddenly rising and taking her snifter and pouring her cognac into Mike's glass. "You shouldn't have done it to Jack or me. You shouldn't have done it to Capers or Betsy."

"How else can I get us all back together?" Mike said. "It's for the project. Remember who's producing this project. Please stay."

But Ledare was already striding with her pretty long legs out the back door. Mike followed her, trying to talk her into returning, but I heard the motor crank and knew the boat was moving toward Waterford.

I turned to study Capers' yearling wife, Betsy.

She was one of those Southern girls too pretty for me by half. Betsy looked like a poster child for an ad extolling the virtues of drinking milk. Everything about her struck me as overdone and combed out and thought through. Her perkiness was of that dreamy, mechanical sort that often wins beauty queens Miss Congeniality trophies. She possessed the kind of looks that inspires praise but not lust. Her smile made me want to ask for her dentist's name.

"You're twenty-five, aren't you, Betsy?" I asked.

"Are you running a census?" Betsy fired back.

"Yes, she's twenty-five," Capers said.

"Let me guess. A Tri Delt at South Carolina."

"Bingo," Mike said, coming into the room again.

"Junior League."

"Bingo," Mike said again.

"How did you know that?" Betsy asked.

"You've got the Junior League squint. All sorority girls in college learn to squint that way to make their husbands feel properly adored when they utter some inanity."

"You're stereotyping me, Jack," Betsy said and I saw real fire in her.

"The South stereotyped you, Betsy. I'm just testing the limits of the stereotype."

Capers put his arm around his wife and said, "Betsy was raised to be a Southern belle. No harm in that."

"I'm proud of it," Betsy said.

"Southern belle," I said. "It's a mark of shame in the South now, Betsy. Smart women don't call themselves that anymore. If a woman calls herself that, it usually means she's dumb as a pinto bean. You're obviously very bright, even though you have deplorable taste in men."

"I'm still a Southern belle and I think I have the best taste in men of any woman in South Carolina."

"I married Betsy because of her loyalty, Jack."

"Wrong. There's only one real crime a man can commit that is unforgivable."

"What's that?" Capers asked as Mike resumed his seat.

"It's unforgivable for a man of any generation—any generation—to betray and humiliate the women of his own generation by marrying a much younger woman. You didn't marry Betsy for her loyalty, pal. You married her for her youth."

"There are unexpected pleasures in betrayal," Capers said and Mike laughed in agreement. "I always liked your piety, Jack."

"I'm a lot cuter than the women of your generation," Betsy said, playing up to Capers and Mike.

"Wrong, Junior Leaguer." I could feel myself turning mean. The cognac was doing its work and I felt the thrilling disquiet that had come into the room. I took Betsy's measure, and went for her throat. "The women of my generation were the smartest, sexiest, most fascinating women ever to grow up in America. They started the women's liberation movement, took to the streets in the sixties to stop the unbearably stupid Vietnam War. They fought their asses off for equal rights in the workplace, went to law school, became doctors, fought the corporate fight, and managed to raise children in a much nicer way than our mothers did."

"Chill out, Jack," Mike said. "Betsy's a kid."

"She's a dimwit," I said. I turned to Betsy. "The women of my generation make men like me and Mike and your chicken-hearted husband look puny and uninteresting by comparison. Don't talk about those women, Betsy, unless you're on your fucking knees genuflecting out of admiration."

"He was in love with Ledare once, Betsy," Capers said with his elegant composure intact. "She broke up with him just before the St. Cecelia's ball in Charleston. Jack's always been bitter that he comes from the lower classes."

"Betsy, you aren't worthy to kiss Ledare Ansley's panty hose," I shot back.

"But she married Capers, and dumped you," Betsy said. "I do have to say she's gone up in my estimation."

"I thought I could count on you to have good manners," Mike said to me, trying to defuse the rapid escalation of the repartee. "Betsy's a great chick. She and Capers have been out to my place in Beverly Hills a couple of times this year."

"I'm only trying to hurt Capers," I said. "Because Capers knows I can write Betsy's life story right here, this moment, in this room. I've met a thousand women like poor Betsy. It bothers Capers that he has married a living, breathing Southern cliché. I can tell Capers who Betsy'll vote for in the next fifty years, how many children she'll have, and what she'll name them. I can tell Betsy her silver pattern, her china pattern, her father's profession, her mother's maiden name, and the Confederate regiment her great-great-grandfather served in at the Second Battle of Bull Run."

"My great-great-great-grandfather was killed at Antietam."

"So sorry, Betsy. These details sometimes trip me up."

Betsy took a sip of cognac and said, "Where'd I get my master's, asshole?"

"I wish you wouldn't use language like that, darling," Capers said.

But I was thrilled and surprised by the comeback and said, "Not bad, Betsy. *Complimenti.* I never would've guessed. Every time I think I know everything there is to know about Southern women, they send me a curve ball I could never hit. That was simply terrific."

"I only marry smart, savvy, and beautiful women, Jack," Capers said. "I should have proven that to you by now."

"Shut up, Capers," I said. "I need to insult your wife a little more so she'll run off in a huff."

"I'm thinking about kicking you out of my house, Jack," Mike said.

"Unfortunately, Mike, there's a size problem," I said. "You shut up, too, because you and I are going to have a long talk about why you set up this evening."

"Hey, Jack," Betsy said. "Now I understand why your wife jumped off the bridge. I'm just amazed it took her so long."

"Ever say that again, Betsy, and I'll beat up your husband. I'll beat his face in so badly that he'll be working in a freak show instead of the governor's office."

Betsy turned toward Capers, who remained unflappable. "My husband doesn't look scared."

"He's scared. He just doesn't show it."

"He went to Vietnam. You were a draft dodger."

"That's right, Miss South Carolina. Funny part is, I can still kick his ass. If guys like me had gone to Vietnam, we would've won the war. Ponder that the next time you're making cheese biscuits or deviled eggs."

"Liberals are all the same," Betsy spat out, and she was uncomfortable on center stage. "I heard your wife was a raging feminist."

"We both were," I said. "I'm raising my daughter to be one too."

"What good will that do her?"

"She won't be a fucking thing like you, Betsy," I said, "because I'd throw my daughter off the Cooper River bridge if she was anything like you or married to someone like Capers Middleton."

Betsy Middleton rose with great dignity and turned to her husband. "Let's go, Capers. We can spend the night at your mother's. I'll call the maid."

"Night, night, Betsy," I said, hearing my voice mocking and cruel. "I remember the talent portion of your Miss America number. You twirled fire batons. I was embarrassed for my whole state and every woman in it."

Betsy was in tears as she left and I felt a sickening sadness overwhelm me.

"Nice, Jack," Mike said, shaking his head. "What a sweetheart."

"Call Betsy tomorrow for me, Mike," I said. "Tell her I'm sorry and that I'm usually not such a perfect shit. It's her husband I loathe, not her."

Capers Middleton seemed unruffled by my attack on his wife. His eyes were clear and blue. In this light and time, I thought he looked like a man hatched from an egg near the arctic circle.

"If you ever did that to a woman I loved," I said, "you'd be calling your dentist to set up a surgical appointment."

"Exaggeration," said Mike, stepping between us. "It's always limited you."

I looked at Mike. "A guy from Hollywood should never get into a discussion about exaggeration."

Capers cleared his throat as if about to speak, then looked directly at me.

"I need your help, Jack, and I've missed our friendship."

"Listen to him, Jack," Mike said. "Please listen to Capers. If Capers gets to be governor he plans to run for president of the United States."

"If he gets it I swear to God as my witness that I'll apply for Italian citizenship," I said.

"I would like you to become a part of my campaign team, Jack," Capers said.

I looked at Mike, amazed. "Am I having trouble making myself understood to this asshole? I hate you, Capers, and besides you're a Republican. I hate Republicans."

"I used to hate 'em too," Mike admitted. "Then I got rich."

"Our breakup is well known in the state and that might present me some problems in the campaign."

"I certainly hope it presents you with a million problems and you fully deserve all of them," I said.

"Next month, the state newspaper is doing

a long in-depth profile of me and a local TV show is almost finished with a documentary that follows my entire career through South Carolina politics."

"Do they do the part at the university?" I asked.

"Both go into it," Capers said, and there was an evenness to his voice that seemed uncanny. "Most South Carolinians think it proves my love of my country. But the downside is that others think I betrayed the trust of my closest friends. It could become a character issue and we think the Democrats are going to try to play it up."

"*Viva* le downside. If Judas Iscariot had mated with Benedict Arnold, you'd have inherited the earth."

"Capers has shared his vision of the state with me and if he gets elected there won't be a more forward-looking governor in the country."

"Stop it, Mike. I'm getting dewy-eyed."

Capers continued, "What happened to us in college wouldn't have happened at any other time except for the Vietnam War. But I was standing up for what I believed in. I thought my country was in trouble."

"The tears. They still come. Drivel does that to me," I said.

"Those were heavy times," Mike said.

"Even you have to admit that, Jack. I dodged the draft then because I thought it was the right thing to do and I didn't want to get my ass shot off in a country I couldn't even spell."

Capers added, "All of us made mistakes during the Vietnam War."

"I didn't," I said. "I didn't make one fucking mistake during that entire war. I honored myself by being against that silly-ass war."

"The tide's turning in favor of Vietnam vets," Capers said.

"Not with me. I'm tired of hearing Vietnam vets whine. Has there ever been a group of vets in this country who were such crybabies, who shouted 'poor me' so loud and so often? They seem to have absolutely no respect for themselves."

"A lot of us were spit on when we came back to this country," said Capers.

"Bullshit," I said. "A lie. An urban myth. I've heard it a thousand times and I don't believe a word of it. And it always happens in the airport."

"That's where it happened to me," said Capers.

"If it happened as much as Vietnam vets claim it happened, no one during those years could have stood up in the airports of America with all that spittle on the floor. You're lying, Capers, and if it happened you should have

rammed the teeth down the asshole's throat
that did it. That's what I can't believe. A million Vietnam vets get spit on and no one loses a
tooth. No wonder you lost the fucking war."

"Always loved this about Jack," Mike said
to Capers. "Still do. Some people may not like
it, but Jack takes it to the hoop."

"It's what I've never liked about him," Capers said, staring at me. "In his world there's
no room for compromise, for shadings of
meanings, for elbow room, for maneuvering.
Yours, Jack, is a world of either-or, all or nothing. It's a world of extremes played outside of
all known margins. It always sounds sincere,
but it has nothing to do with life on earth."

"Eloquent shit," Mike said in admiration.
"Very eloquent shit, that."

"I'm a flexible man," Capers said. "It's what
brought me this far."

"You're an amoral man," I said. "That's
what's brought you this far."

I walked toward the front door without saying good-bye and heard Capers' voice behind
me say, "You'll be calling me, Jack. Because
one thing I know about you. You love Jordan
Elliott. That's your weakness."

In a blind rage, I drove away from Mike's
place fast, spinning my mother's tires on the

dirt road that ran through the center of his property. My hands were shaking on the steering wheel and I felt cold all over, even though the April air was warm and flower-scented. I was mad enough to run over a person or a highway sign, but nothing got in my way when I hit the main highway going west back toward the town.

I drove straight to Ledare's house, where she was waiting for me in a white wicker chair on the veranda. On the wicker table was a bottle of Maker's Mark and a bucket of ice.

I was still trembling from my confrontation with Capers and spilled some bourbon as I poured myself a drink, and then threw myself into a chair.

"I knew you'd come. Practically dreamt it," Ledare said. "How'd you like your encounter with the Prince of Darkness?"

"Do you mind if I break this bottle and sever every artery and blood vessel in my body?" I said.

Ledare kicked off her sandals and brought her feet up beneath her. I took a swallow of the bourbon.

"I hate this town, this state, this night, those people, my past, my present, my future . . . The only thing I absolutely look forward to is my death. This makes me very rare among human beings, who seem to fear death above all things—but I look upon it as a long, paid vacation where I'll never have to think about South Carolina or Capers Middleton again."

Ledare laughed and said, "In the movies, now's the time for the heroine to utter a meaningful, life-affirming line. Like 'I know that was hard, darling, but don't you find me cute?' You'd then look at me, desire me passionately, then realize the night was young and life is long."

"That's how it works in the movies?" I asked.

"That's how it works in real life too," she said.

"So I'm supposed to find you 'cute.' "

"I'd prefer 'darling,' " she said.

I looked at her, and as always, liked what I saw.

"I went after Betsy," I said, moaning. "That poor woman's never done a single thing to harm me and I went straight for her jugular. All because I wanted to get Capers."

"I couldn't be more delighted," Ledare answered. "You know, there's nothing more humiliating than having your own children being raised by a child herself."

"You and I have both been sued for the custody of our children. How did Capers win? I thought I had a great chance of losing Leah and I understand why, but I bet you're a good mother."

"Good, but not smart. I gained a lot of weight after the birth of Sarah. I made a mistake by not losing it right away. I didn't know that Capers was repulsed by overweight women. Not that he's different from other men in this country. None of you men will be satisfied until bulimia becomes part of the wedding vows. So Mr. Capers began a series of affairs that ended with the lovely Betsy."

"But the kids?"

"It took me about a year to lose the weight that lost Capers," she said to the darkness. "By then, he had spread the word that my screen writing was more important than my marriage. We separated and I moved to New York with the kids. Started going out with most anyone who asked me. Wasn't too picky. Or too careful. Bad time, Jack. And I'm ashamed of every minute of it. It helped take off the edge of my own hatred of Capers. Being married to him was like being buried under ice. He did to me what he did to you. Private eye. Photographs. One of the men was a black man, a writer I'd met on a book tour. Couple of the guys were married. That's how he stole my kids from me."

"You want me to drive back and beat him up?"

"Do you always talk about beating people up?"

"I prefer to look at it as the heroic mode. Also, Ledare, I'm a guy. I know what worries and bothers other guys. Getting beaten up ranks real high on the list. Besides, you know I was just trying to make you feel better."

"If you want to make me feel better," she said, "talk about killing him. Just beating him up isn't enough."

Ledare took my left hand and held it up to what small amount of light the veranda could coax from the river. Twice she twisted my wedding ring in circles around my finger. My hands are small and look as if they belong on a man a half foot shorter than I am.

"Why do you still wear your wedding ring?"

"Because I never got a divorce. And I haven't remarried. It reminds me of Shyla."

"Sweet Jack. Behind all that thunder, you're just pure honey."

"No I'm not, but I would have been if I'd have had a different father."

"I just had a small run-in with my mother," Ledare said. "Every time I hear my mother's voice I get orphan-envy."

"You think it's weird I still wear my wedding ring?"

"No. I told you I thought it was sweet."

"But a little odd."

"A little. Do you take it off when you go out on dates?"

"I don't date much."

"Why not?"

"When a woman you love kills herself, you worry about yourself, Ledare. Even though you know that complex forces—forces I don't even know about and could never understand—contributed to her death, the fact is that I contributed my part. I think about that every time I call a woman to go out for dinner."

"You think the woman you take to dinner might commit suicide?"

I laughed at her joke. "No. You think that if you like the woman and she likes you and there are many dinners and then many kisses and then wedding bells, that then you may be looking at another body in the morgue . . ."

"I'm sorry I said that, Jack. Please forgive me."

"Every night of my life, I see Shyla leap in my dreams. It injects itself somehow. I could be kayaking in a river in Alaska and she would come out of the woods above me and hurl herself off a cliff. Or I can be walking down a street in Amsterdam, and find myself walking beside a canal, hear a scream, and Shyla will be plummeting from the heights of those great houses that press in on all the canals and I'll leap in to save her. I'll open my eyes underwater and there'll be a thousand of her floating by me, all dead."

"You must really look forward to going to bed."

"Sleeping's not my favorite part of the day."

There was silence for a while. "How'd you get to keep Leah?" Ledare asked quietly.

"What happened to your oak tree?" I said, sitting up, and changing the subject. "You had the most beautiful oak tree of all of them."

"Capers," she said. "All during our marriage, he thought that oak blocked the view of the sunset over the river. In the year it all fell apart, he would walk out to that tree with all of his office staff. They'd carry what looked like cups of beer and pretend to admire the sunset."

"It's not making any sense."

"They were really carrying a very powerful weed killer in those cups. While admiring the sunset, each person would surreptitiously pour the weed killer into the ground. It took about six months before the poor tree began dying. Everybody in Waterford was furious, but Capers denied everything."

"Did you know about it?" I asked.

"No, of course not," she said. "A member of his staff told me about it years later. But my father suspected Capers right away."

"Funny, I've come to a point in my life when I prefer an oak tree to a human being. Hell, I prefer crabgrass to Capers Middleton."

"He still thinks you two'll be friends before it's all over."

"Not after tonight he doesn't," I said.

"Back to Leah," she said. "Let's go back to your custody trial."

"Shyla's parents, naturally enough, thought I was responsible for Shyla's death. After the funeral, I had one of those small hideous depressions. My brothers checked me into the hospital in Columbia and they began treating me for depression. It took a while for the drugs to make me chipper and to want to play horseshoes with the other inmates."

"Where was Leah at this time?"

"She was staying with the Foxes, who, of course, were grieving over their loss of Shyla. Leah was a magical kid even then. The idea came upon them, and I'm sure innocently enough, that Leah could replace Shyla. They sued for custody while I was still in Columbia."

"How did you win while you were in a mental hospital?"

"My brother Dupree works at the hospital. He came to tell me what the Foxes had done. Rage is a major antidote for depression. My agony over Shyla's death was replaced with my fury over her parents trying to steal our child.

Her father testified during the trial that I had beaten Shyla repeatedly—the list of atrocities went on and on. He was lying, but they were desperate to keep Leah, to keep something of Shyla."

"No wonder you moved to Italy."

"My family rallied around me. Brother Dallas took the case for nothing. The Foxes fell apart on cross-examination. Shyla had written a suicide note. Then my family testified for me as a father. I never suspected my family had this kind of dignity . . . a greatness of soul despite everything that's happened to us. I saw a family I didn't know I had and that's why they were so hurt when I left for Italy soon after the trial with no plans ever to see them again."

"I don't blame them either."

"I did it all wrong," I admitted. "But I can't change it now."

"Shyla wouldn't have liked it that you left the South forever."

Hearing in her voice a hint of gentle reproval, I looked at her.

"I needed a rest from the South," I said finally. "I find it exhausting to think about and overstimulating to live in and maddening to try to analyze."

"If Mike doesn't do this project, I'd like to write about all of us," said Ledare.

"Make me a Charlestonian," I said. "Then

your mother wouldn't have to disinfect the porch every time I come to the front door."

"She doesn't do it *every* time," Ledare said. "She just wishes you'd learn to use the back door."

"How you getting along with your parents?"

"Daddy looks at me and thinks, 'Bad seed.' Mama gets teary-eyed and thinks, 'Bad egg.' They both get nauseous when they think their girl lost a chance to be the governor's wife."

"If that guy becomes governor, birds won't even fly south over this state for the winter."

"Sign on for this movie, Jack," Ledare said suddenly.

"Why?" I asked. "It all seems so wrong to me. Too many danger signals."

"We can get to know each other as grown-ups," she said. "You'd like me as a grown-up."

Ledare reached out and took my hand. "Biggest danger of all," I said.

CHAPTER 14

THE NEXT MORNING I DROVE OUT IN sweet sunshine, taking the two-lane road through the marshes and forests and over the tidal creeks that gave way to the Atlantic Ocean ahead. A black man was throwing his shrimp net from a bridge at low tide. It webbed out, spinning like a ballerina's skirt, a flawless circle of hemp, hitting the water and sinking rapidly to the bottom. I imagined its weights sinking to the silty floor, trapping every mullet, shrimp, or crab passing through that circle's arc, and wondered where my own cast net was, if I still had the patience to fill a beer cooler with shrimp when they were running strong and fast in the spring.

Crossing the small bridge over Bazemore Creek, I thought of the map hanging in the study at Dad's house. It was a Mercator projection of Gaston Sound that included the Waterford River and Waterford itself. It marked the limits of the territorial sea and the contiguous zone and it was on that map that I had learned there could be beauty in the sheer collection of useful information. The town was located at latitude 32° 15′ and the average mean high tide rose 7.5 feet in the Waterford River. Small but valuable numbers covered the channels and rivers in a meticulously arranged graffiti, each number telling the depth of the channel at mean low tide. I had loved studying the map because it was a printed explanation of where I had been placed on earth. It was a love song to location, a psalm of praise to both measurement and extent. I drove from island to island, moving past salt marshes that changed the way a man thought about the color green, and past black beauty parlors and closed-down gas stations. I saw every detail of that map, while my senses blazed with the almost animal smell of the marsh.

At the Isle of Orion, I stopped at the security gate and gave my name to the guard. She eyed me fiercely, as though I had come to plunder all the silver and china on the island. Begrudgingly, she gave me a temporary pass and directions to the Elliotts' house.

"Don't feed the alligators," the woman ordered.

"What'll I do with the dead dog in the trunk?" I asked as I quickly pulled away from the gate.

The Elliotts lived in a beautiful two-story house on the oceanfront. Knocking on the door, I waited only a few moments before Celestine Elliott opened the door and threw herself into my arms.

"You're still big," she said.

"You're still pretty," I said.

"I am not. I'll be sixty-eight years old next month," Celestine said, but she was wrong. Her face contained a natural prettiness that time could work on but never completely eradicate.

Celestine Elliott had always been called the perfect military wife, the handmaiden of her husband's extraordinary rise through the ranks of the Marine Corps. She was a woman who dazzled without effort and who made her husband look far superior than he actually was simply because he had attracted such an uncommon woman to his side. She possessed the gift of total attention, especially when speaking to men who could advance her husband's career.

Many people, including Celestine, thought that General Rembert Elliott would have made Commandant of the Marine Corps if he'd never had any children. His only child, Jordan, had done more damage to his career than the Japanese bullet that had almost killed him at the Battle of Tarawa.

Celestine led me into the living room and poured us two cups of coffee as I looked out toward the Atlantic at a ship making its way north toward Charleston.

We sat and exchanged pleasantries before I handed her an elegant Fendi bag containing two letters and several gifts from her son.

"There's trouble, Celestine," I said quietly.

A deep voice echoed before she could utter a word. "More trouble than you've ever known, my dear."

Rembert Elliott, every inch the Marine general, stared at his wife with a blue-eyed look that was as pure and uncomplicated as sea air. He stood in the doorway that led to the back door of the house. All color drained from Celestine's face and I calmly reached over and took the two letters she was holding.

"Hand me those letters, Jack," the general ordered.

"They're mine. I wrote them," I said, standing.

"You're a liar. You and my wife are both

liars," the man said, his rage so visible that it almost made his face indecent. "You're a traitor, Celestine. My own wife, a traitor."

"What happened to your golf game on Hilton Head, General?" I asked. I had not expected him to be at home.

"It was a ruse to catch you two in the act," the general said.

"I call it a lie," I said. "Welcome to our little club."

"Capers Middleton gave me these photographs taken in Rome," the general said. He started to hand them to his wife, then thought better of it and threw them violently to the floor. Celestine said nothing as she picked up the photographs. Tidiness was second nature to her even during the most savage of her husband's assaults. She paused to look at one of the photographs of her pale, ascetic son.

Then Rembert Elliott did something that surprised both his wife and myself. He stepped back as Celestine retrieved the scattered photos, unsure of his next move, transfixed by doubt. The assault of fortified beaches was his specialty but the beachhead he now faced seemed much too dangerous for storming. It required strategies that demanded the subtleties of veils, ruses, and secret envelopment. The general had attended no war college that made his encounter with his own small family more easeful and less subject to discord. Even his wife, as she now stared at him defiantly, looked like an enemy scout who had slipped into his house beneath concertina wire to booby-trap his kitchen.

When this man of action found himself unable to act, I took advantage of his uncharacteristic fixity. Leaving him posed in a standstill, I walked to a bathroom on the first floor and tore Jordan's letters into fragments and flushed them down the toilet. When I returned, both Celestine and the general were sitting in chairs measuring their reborn distrust of each other.

"You made me sit through a memorial service for a son who'd disgraced me when you knew he was alive?" the general asked.

"I thought he was dead," she answered.

"Why didn't you tell me when you found out?"

I answered, "Because you hated him, General. You always hated him and Jordan knew it, Celestine knew it, I knew it, and you knew it. That's why she didn't tell you."

"I had a right to know," the general said. "It was your duty to tell me."

"I'm not a Marine, darling. A fact you have some difficulty remembering."

"Your duty as a wife," the general corrected himself.

"Let's talk about your duty as a father," she fired back angrily. "Let's talk about how you treated your son from the day he was born. How I sat by and watched you bully and torment that wonderful, sweet boy of ours."

"He was effeminate when he was a child," the general said. "You know I can tolerate anything but that."

"He wasn't effeminate," she shot back. "He was nice and you can't tell the difference."

"He'd have grown up as one of them if I left his raising to you," her husband said, his voice accusatory and contemptuous.

"One of *them*?" I asked.

"A homosexual," Celestine explained.

"Ah! The horror of horrors," I said. "The fate worse than death."

"Exactly," she said.

"I wouldn't've put so much pressure on Jordan," the general said, "if you'd been able to bear other children."

"Of course, how convenient it's all my fault."

"A lone wolf makes the worst kind of soldier," General Elliott said. "They're a danger to any unit. They can't tailor their egos for the good of the group."

"Sort of like you, dear," Celestine said. "When it comes to family."

"You've never understood the military."

She laughed and said, "I've understood it all too well."

"For fourteen years, I've thought my son dead," the general said, turning to me. "How do you expect me to feel?"

"Glad," I suggested.

"I've already notified the proper authorities," the general said.

"What did you tell them?" Celestine said.

"The name of the church where these photographs were taken," he said. "And the possibility that he committed a crime. You've got a lot of questions to answer, Jack."

"And few answers to give, General," I said.

"You destroyed those letters, I presume," he said.

"Just notes I wrote to Ledare Ansley," I said.

"Tell her I'd love to see her," Celestine said. "I heard she was in town."

"Jack," the general said, "I could have you arrested for hiding a fugitive."

"You certainly could," I answered. "Except no one's been accused of a crime. And the criminal you suspect seems to be dead."

"Are you denying that my son is in those pictures?" the general said.

"In Italy, I'm limited to those confessors who speak English," I said.

"It's Jordan, isn't it, Jack?" the general asked, his voice straining, incautious.

"I can't tell you that," I said.

"You mean, you won't," he said. "Celestine?"

"Darling, I've no idea what you're talking about," she said.

"All those trips to Italy," the general said. "I thought it was your passion for art."

"The art's always one of the highlights of the trip," Celestine said.

"I hate art museums," General Elliott said to me. "That's where she meets with Jordan. I see it clearly now."

I studied the general's face and for a moment felt a chord of sympathy for this emotionally limited and tightly wound man. His mouth was as thin as the blade of a knife. He was short but powerfully built, in his late sixties, and his eyes burned with a simmering blue that could terrify men and charm women. All his life, people had been afraid of Rembert Elliott and this knowledge had given him great pleasure. He was the kind of man America needed during wartime but did not know where to put when the armistice was signed.

Like other men who've spent much of their lives training to kill enemy soldiers, Rembert Elliott had made a perfectly appalling husband and father. Throughout his marriage, he had treated his wife like an adjutant who'd received a bad fitness report. Jordan had been raised by his mother's kisses and his father's fists.

The general rose heavily and went over to study the photographs again.

"That priest. That's my son, isn't it?" he said to me.

"How the hell would I know?" I said. "It's my confessor. You ought to get to church more, General. You'll notice this little screen separating the priest from the poor sinner. It's there for a reason. So you can't see each other clearly enough to make an identification."

"You're claiming this isn't my son?" the general said.

"It's my confessor," I said again. "No court of law can make my confessor testify against me or vice versa."

"I think this is my son."

"Great. Congratulations. Together at last. Don't you love happy endings?"

Celestine walked over and stood in front of her husband, looking directly into his eyes.

"It is Jordan, Rembert," she said. "Every time we've been to Rome, I've gone to see him. I tell you I'm shopping."

"Liar. Liar," the general whispered.

"No, darling," she said softly. "Mother. Mother."

The general turned to me. "So you've been the courier."

"That's one way of putting it," I answered.

"I was raising him to be a Marine officer," the general said.

"Looked like the Gulag Archipelago to me," I said.

"Jordan came of age in the sixties," he said. "That's what destroyed him. What would any of you know about fidelity or patriotism or a sense of values or ethics?"

I shot back, "Ask us what we know about child abuse."

"You were a generation of liars and cowards. You shirked your duty to your country when America needed you."

"I just had this same stupid conversation with Capers Middleton," I said. "Let me sum up: bad war, started by bad politicians, fought by bad generals, and fifty thousand guys were flushed down the toilet for no reason whatsoever."

"Freedom's as good as any reason to die."

"Vietnam's or America's?" I asked.

"Both," he said.

Then I went over and embraced Celestine. "He moved to another monastery in another part of Rome. He's safe," I told her. "I'm sorry I had to destroy his letters." And I walked out of the house.

As I was getting into my mother's car, General Elliott appeared at the door and shouted down to me, "McCall."

"Yes, General."

"I want to see my son," he said.

"I'll tell him, General. He's never had a father before. He might like it."

"Will you help arrange it?" General Elliott asked.

"No, I won't."

"May I ask why?"

"I don't trust you, General," I answered.

"What do you suggest I do?" he asked.

"Wait," I answered.

"You don't think it's possible for a man to change, do you?" he asked.

I looked at the straight-backed, unspontaneous man and said, "No, I don't."

"That's smart," the general said. "I don't either."

Celestine hurried out onto the porch. "Jack, go straight to the hospital. Tee just called. Your mother's out of her coma."

All my brothers except John Hardin were waiting for me outside the main entrance of the hospital when I arrived. I jumped out of the car and found myself surrounded by my brothers, who tossed me back and forth embracing me.

"Mama," Tee screamed aloud, "she did it."

"Is she tough or what?" Dupree said.

"It'll take more than cancer to take that old girl out," said Dallas.

"I couldn't help but think she was pretending to be dying," Tee said, "just to make me feel guilty."

Dupree hit Tee playfully on the shoulder. "Mom's got more important things to do than make you feel guilty."

"Yeah," Tee challenged. "Like what?"

"Yeah. Like what?" Dallas agreed.

"Only Dr. Pitts has seen her. He thought it would be a great idea if you went in to see her first," Dupree said.

"Mama," I said. "Mama."

We whooped and hollered again and Tee reached over and held my hand briefly just as he used to do when he was a very small child and I was the largest, gentlest brother in the world to him.

The nurses had moved Lucy from intensive care and the family had gathered in a different, happier waiting room.

A spirit of euphoria seized us all and even the saturnine Father Jude looked relieved by the turn of events. We gathered around Dr. Pitts and listened to him repeat what the doctor had told him. As he told us of the fever's lowering, the stabilizing blood pressure, and

the slow return to consciousness, my brothers
and I felt like inmates listening to a proclamation of amnesty. Since we had been jittery and
downcast for so long, the elation felt odd, the
sense of ebullience, foreign.

"Why don't you go in to see your mother,
Jack?" Dr. Pitts said.

"Tell her a few jokes," Tee said. "Belly
laughs are what she needs now."

"I hardly think so," Dr. Pitts said.

"Thinking's never been Tee's long suit,"
Dallas said.

They were still talking among themselves
when I left them and walked down to my
mother's private room.

Her eyes were closed, but her face was still
remarkably pretty for a woman fifty-eight years
old. I had not spoken to her in five years and
that knowledge tore at me as I approached the
bed. I had gone to Rome to save my life and
had never once considered the thoughtless cruelty of just walking out of the lives of so many
people. Lucy opened her eyes and her blue-
eyed gaze took me in. Without question, Lucy
was the most maddening, enthralling, contrary,
and dangerous woman I have ever met. She
claimed to know everything there was to know
about men and I believed her. Her powers of
description were vivid and refined. Her imagination was extraordinary and could not be

reined in. She was a liar of prodigious gifts and saw no particular virtue in telling the truth anyway. She could walk into a roomful of men and stir them up faster than if someone had thrown a rattlesnake among them. She was also the sexiest woman I had ever seen in my life. One thing my brothers and I had learned the hard way was that it wasn't easy being the son of the sexiest, most flirtatious, most legendary woman in your town. My mother never saw a marriage she didn't think she couldn't break up. She boasted that she had met few women in her league.

I waited for her first words.

"Get me some makeup," Lucy said.

"Hi, Jack," I said. "It's wonderful to see you, son. Gosh it's been a long time."

"I must look like a crone," she said. "Do I, do I look like a crone?"

"You look beautiful."

"I hate it when you're insincere."

"You look like a crone," I said.

"That's why I want the makeup," Lucy said.

"You must be tired," I said, trying to say something neutral.

"Tired?" she said. "You're not serious. I've been in a coma. I've never been so rested in my life."

"Then you're feeling good?" I tried again.

"Good?" she said. "I've never felt worse. They're pumping me full of chemotherapy."

"I've got it now, I think. You feel rotten, but very well rested," I said.

"Did you bring Leah with you?" she asked.

"No, but she sends her love."

"That's not enough. I want to hold that girl and tell her some things," Lucy said. "You, too. I have to explain my life to you."

"You don't have to tell me anything," I said. "You've already managed to ruin my life. There's nothing to add."

"A little humor, right?" she asked.

"Right."

"Just checking. Coming out of a coma's odd. It's like digging yourself out of your own grave. Am I still cute?"

"A doll. I already told you."

"Get Dupree's wife over here. Tell Jean I need makeup and plenty of it. She knows my brands."

"A coma doesn't seem to do much for vanity," I said, teasing her.

"But it's the ticket for weight loss," she said. "I bet I've dropped five pounds since I've been here."

"You had us worried."

"The leukemia's gonna kill me, Jack," she said. "It's incurable for a woman my age.

Sooner or later it's going to come back and kill me. The doctor thinks I have just over a year."

"It terrifies me to hear you say that."

"I had to tell someone. I'll lie to the others," she said, and I could see her weakening. "I want to visit you and Leah in Rome."

"We'd love to have you," I said.

"I need to see you over there. I don't know what it's like. I need to have you love me again. I need it more than anything in the world."

I was not looking at my mother, but her words spoke deeply to me. She was quiet and when I looked up she was asleep. Lucy McCall Pitts going to Rome, I thought, and then thought that if Italy could survive the Huns, it could surely survive a simple visit by my fire-eating, cunning mother. She was sleeping deeply now and I, her oldest son, thought she looked eternal, unkillable, and the center of this earth. Dallas came in and motioned that it was time for me to go.

"What did she say?" Dallas asked me as we walked down the corridor.

"Not much. She told me that she loves me the best and would've had her tubes tied if she'd known the other sons would turn out to be such bitter disappointments."

"Uh, that again," he said. "Anything else?"

"She called for makeup."

"She's back," Dallas said excitedly. "She's really back."

Tee and Dupree met us in the hallway. Tee whispered so he could not be heard by the others in the waiting room.

"Good news," Tee said. "More family problems."

Dallas groaned but Tee continued, "Grandpa just called. Ginny Penn's missing from the nursing home."

"Not again," Dallas said.

"No problem," Dupree said, always the pragmatist. "She's in a wheelchair. It's not like we've got to alert the highway patrol."

"Her third breakout," Tee said. "I'm getting the idea she's not adjusting well."

"Grandpa can't lift her," Dallas said. "It's a temporary arrangement. Until her hip heals."

"She thinks we've abandoned her," Dupree said.

We left the hospital and piled into our mother's car, and as I drove quickly through town, Dallas thought aloud, "Only three roads she could've taken and she couldn't have gotten very far on any of them. She has not taken the rest home experience with much aplomb."

"I talked to her on the phone," I said. "She's hated it."

Ten minutes later I took a left down the long paved road that led to the river and the

home. Immediately, we could see our grandmother, working the two wheels of her wheelchair, grimly resolute. I passed by her, turned
the car around in a driveway, then pulled up
beside her.

Ginny Penn did not pay any attention to the
car, but kept stroking those two wheels in time,
like an oarsman navigating up a difficult stretch
of river. Though she was sweating and red-
faced, she was exhilarated by her escape and
had put far more distance between herself and
the nursing home than seemed possible. She
looked to the side, saw us moving slowly beside
her, and burst into tears. She looked at us
again, then she pressed herself harder, her
shoulders straining, until finally she stopped
and began sobbing into her hands, reddened
with oncoming blisters.

"You want a ride, Ginny Penn?" Dallas
asked softly.

"Get away from me," she said, through
tears.

"Your doctor called," Dallas said. "He's
worried about you."

"I've fired that old coot. I need to be rescued, boys. Someone has to help me or I'm
going to die in there. No one listens to you
when you get old. No one listens and no one
cares."

"We'll try to help you any way we can," I said from the driver's side.

"Then walk right back to that hospital and say, 'We're rescuing our grandmother from this hell hole.' Gather up my belongings. And if you really want to help old people in this town, you should shoot the cook. She can't even serve a raw carrot without mucking it up."

Dallas looked at me and shrugged. "We were looking for a more diplomatic approach."

"You boys just leave me alone," Ginny Penn wailed. "I'm on my way to a friend's home. I'm going to go calling."

"What friend?" Dallas asked.

"I haven't decided. I've got friends up and down the county and all of them would consider it an honor to entertain a lady like me. I'm not trash like your grandfather. My people were somebody."

"Come on, Grandma," I said. "Get in the car with us and we'll entertain you."

"You," she said and her gaze at us was imperious and overbearing. "You were raised to be common. Your poor mother's nothing but dirt and your father's certainly nothing to write home about."

"You raised Dad," Dallas pointed out. "You've got to take some of the old credit there."

"I take full responsibility," our grandmother declared. "I married your grandfather with my eyes wide open and I knew what I was getting into. I married for all the wrong reasons."

"Give us one," I asked.

"He was an eyeful," Ginny Penn said at last. "Oh, boy. I used to sweat just looking at him."

"Enough of this trashy talk, Ginny Penn," Dupree said, opening the door and walking toward his grandmother. Tee and I lifted her gently out of the wheelchair and placed her in the backseat of the car. It was like lifting a cageful of small birds and she seemed more husk than fruit as we placed her lying down on her back. She was now too weak to sit up.

"We'll make a deal with you, Ginny Penn," I said. "We'll try to get you out of the home, but you've got to go back now. We've got to do it right."

But Ginny Penn was already asleep when I spoke these words. We drove her back and turned her over to her nurses, who woke her and chastised her for her behavior.

"Traitors," she hissed as a nurse pushed her and the wheelchair back to her room, her cell, her abandonment.

As I drove Dallas back to his law offices, all of us were silent and thoughtful.

"It must be terrible to get old," Dallas finally said. "I wonder if Ginny Penn wakes up each day and thinks it's her last day on earth."

"I think she wakes up and hopes it's her last day," I said.

"We didn't tell her Mom was out of her coma," Tee said.

"Why make her feel any worse than she does now?" Dupree said and we all laughed.

"She's tried her whole life to make the world think she was an aristocrat."

Dallas said, "I think we should simply genuflect whenever we approach her and it'd cut down on the bullshit."

"She's a blue blood and we're something a dog pulled off the road," Tee said.

"Do you remember her telling us about the plantation where she grew up?" Dupree asked. "We always thought she was lying because she never took us there for a visit."

"Burnside," I said. "The famous Burnside Plantation."

"She wasn't lying," Dupree said. "It really existed and that's where she was raised."

"Then where is it?"

"Under water," Dallas said.

"Under water?" I echoed.

"It was located outside of Charleston, near Pinopolis. When they dammed the river to make Lake Moultrie, Burnside was covered by the rising waters caused by the building of the dam. Ginny Penn was a Sinkler on her mother's side and Burnside was the Sinkler plantation."

"Now I get it," I said. "Ginny Penn was so distressed after losing her ancestral home, she went out and married a Puerto Rican, our grandfather."

"She could never tell how the story ended," Dupree said. "She evidently saw the flooding of her home as a terrible sign from God. An omen of some kind."

"How'd you find this out?" Tee asked.

"My wife, Jean, commutes to Charleston twice a week. She's working on her master's degree in history. She was fooling around over at the Charleston Library on King Street and came upon a memoir of the Sinkler family. Ginny Penn's mentioned twice. The house was as pretty as Ginny Penn's always claimed."

"It's a relief to know royal blood does flow through these tired veins," I said.

"I like being a redneck," Tee said. "It suits me."

Dallas looked at his younger brother and said, "It sure does."

"You don't have to agree that fast," Tee cautioned.

"It's Tee's friends you got to worry about," Dupree said to me.

"I'll second that," Dallas added.

"Hey, I love my friends. Great guys, great gals," Tee said.

"A shrimper'd look like a Rockefeller walking into Tee's front door," Dallas said.

"He's drawn to the lower class," Dupree said. "I've always wanted him to attract a higher type of scum."

"Better brothers are all I need," Tee said. "Ha. Good line. Huh? You guys used to maul me when I was a kid. But Lil' Tee's coming into his own. No longer can his brothers take him lightly."

When we got home we watched the sunset from the upper veranda, where we had once played together as boys. I could remember sitting in this same wicker chair more than twenty years before feeding Tee a bottle while my mother, eight months' pregnant with John Hardin, got dinner ready, my father working late at the office, and Dupree on the front lawn teaching Dallas how to throw a football. Except for memory, time would have no meaning at all. Yet we sat together where the light was best and the last seen light best of all. It was here we gathered to say farewell to the sunburned, dark-complexioned days which finger-painted the river in the tenderness of its insomniac retreat.

From my father's poorly stocked kitchen, I brought up cold beer that we had stopped to buy at Ma Miller's, along with peanuts, dill pickles, and a rectangle of sharp Cheddar cheese, which I sliced and placed on saltines with slivers of red onion. My brothers ate for fuel, not pleasure, and there were few things I could serve that they would not put in their mouths. The phone rang deep inside the house and Dallas went in to answer it.

When he came out Dallas said, "Mom ate some solid food."

We cheered and offered a toast to the river and our mother, who could look out at the same body of water from her hospital window a mile downriver.

"That's one tough broad," Dupree said, taking a swallow of beer.

"Not tough enough for leukemia," Dallas said. "It'll get her next time."

"How can you say that?" Tee said, jumping up and walking to the railing, his eyes turned from us.

"Sorry," Dallas said. "Reality helps me make it through the bad times . . . and the good ones."

I could see that Tee was wiping tears away from his eyes as soon as he shed them. His emotion made the rest of us edgy and I said, "It was my love that brought her through the crisis. My heroic flight across the Atlantic to be with my mother in her time of need."

Dallas smiled, then said, "No, it was the quiet love of her often-ignored, often-ridiculed third son, Dallas, that rescued her from the crypt."

"Crypt," Tee said. "Our family doesn't have a damn crypt."

"I reserve the right to be literary," said Dallas. "That was a literary flourish."

"I didn't know you were a literary man," I said.

"I'm not," said Dallas, "but I like to nurse a few pretensions now and then."

"A few," Dupree said. "You had any more a CPA couldn't keep up with them."

"Quit crying, Tee," Dallas said. "It makes me feel I don't love Mom enough."

Tee said, sniffling, "You don't. You never have."

"Not true," Dallas said. "I was a little kid once and thought there was no one like her. Then I grew up and started to learn all about her. Naturally, I was horrified. I'd never been face to face with such powers of deceit. I couldn't handle it. So I ignored her. No sin in that."

"I love her ass," Tee said. "Even though she's screwed up my whole life and ran off every girlfriend I ever had."

"Can't hold that against her," Dupree said. "Your girlfriends were all natural disasters."

"You didn't know them like I did."

"Thank God," Dallas and Dupree said together.

"You're lucky you can cry," I said to Tee. "It's a gift."

"You cried since Mom's been sick?" Dallas asked Dupree.

"Nope. Don't intend to," Dupree said.

"Why?" I asked.

"Who wants to be a pansy like Tee?" he asked.

Darkness came up on us and stars lit up one by one in the eastern sky. I thought about my own tears, the ones I had never cried over Shyla. In the days after her death I waited for them to come in floods, but none appeared. Her death dried me out and I found more desert land in my spirit than rain forest. My lack of tears worried, then frightened me.

So I began to study other men and was comforted to find I was not alone. I tried to come up with a theory that would explain my extreme stoicism in the face of my wife's suicide. Each explanation became an excuse, because Shyla Fox McCall deserved my tears if anyone on earth ever did. I could feel the tears within me, undiscovered and untouched in their inland sea. Those tears had been with me always. I thought that, at birth, American men are allotted just as many tears as American women. But because we are forbidden to shed them, we die long before women do, with our hearts exploding or our blood pressure rising or our livers eaten away by alcohol because that lake of grief inside us has no outlet. We, men, die because our faces were not watered enough.

"Have another beer, Tee," Dallas said. "It'll help."

"Don't need help, bro," Tee answered. "I'm crying because I'm happy."

"No," I said. "Because you can."

"Let's call Leah again," Dallas suggested.

"Great idea," I said, getting up and walking to the screen door.

"Something's up," I heard Dupree say.

"What's that?" Dallas asked.

"No one's seen John Hardin," Dupree said. "Grandpa checked his house and there's no sign of him anywhere."

"He'll turn up," Tee said.

"That's what I'm afraid of," Dupree said, looking out into the darkness. We could see the lights of the hospital now, downriver.

CHAPTER 15

I DO NOT KNOW WHY IT IS THAT I HAVE always been happier thinking of somewhere I have been or wanted to go, than where I am at the time. I find it difficult to be happy in the present.

During long evenings in Rome, at dinner parties full of pretty countesses, the scent of Pinot Grigio on their breaths, their laughter infectious and bright, I could find my mind drifting westward despite my promise that I would never return to my native state. But I carried Waterford around with me the way a box turtle conveys its own burdensome shell. Tender cries of homesickness would lightly echo through me until I found myself closing my eyes and walking the airy streets of Waterford made weightless by the buoyancy of my nostalgia.

Now, walking down Blue Heron Drive toward my father's and brother's law office, I found myself longing for the rough disharmony and noise of Rome. I mounted the steps quickly and made my way to the second-floor offices, which gave the appearance of the second-rate and the down-at-the-heels.

Dallas was writing on a legal pad and finished his thought before he looked up to see me.

"Hey, Jack," Dallas said. "Welcome to my money machine. Let me finish this and I'll be right with you."

Dallas wrote a bit more and then stabbed a period with great flourish. "I lost two more clients today. Clients react badly when they see the firm founder throwing up in a gutter."

"Is the law firm making money, Dallas?"

"*Money* magazine's doing an interview with me today," Dallas said and there was a dark cynical edge to his voice. "*Fortune* magazine wants to erect a statue of me outside this building because of my cash flow."

"Bad, huh?"

"Not good."

"Dad any help at all?"

"When he's sober. He dries out a couple of

times a year," said Dallas. "It's sad because then I get to see what a brilliant legal mind he really has. He's been really bad since Mom got sick."

"He's been really bad for over thirty years," I said. "Jesus, he gives liquor a bad name."

"He still loves Mom."

"I thought the new husband would make him see the light," I said.

I looked at Dallas, straight and handsome behind his desk.

"Why don't you go out on your own?" I asked.

"He needs me, Jack. This is all he's got," Dallas said. "He doesn't have anyplace else to go. You may not've noticed, but our father's a tragic man."

"What does he contribute to all of this?" I asked.

"Because he was a very respected judge," Dallas said, "that's something. He makes a good appearance in a courtroom when his brain isn't marinating in a quart of bourbon."

"How's Grandpa?" I asked. "Can he still handle it when the Yankees come down to hunt deer?"

"He can still field strip a deer faster than you can tie your shoelaces," Dallas said with pride in his voice. "Before you go back, we all ought to go over there and have an oyster roast."

"Sounds good. But it depends on Mom getting on her feet," I said.

"Any new word?"

"Haven't been down there yet today," I said. "The sheer psychic weight of the family's wearing me down. Dupree and Tee are already over there. I'll get down there this afternoon.

"I've got to see Max," I said. "He's been leaving messages all over town for me."

"He's still a client of this firm," Dallas said. "Max is a rock."

I started to leave, then paused and looked back at my brother, and said, "If you ever need any money, Dallas, would you let me know?"

"No, I wouldn't, Jack," Dallas said. "But thanks for offering."

Back in the street, I made my way past the familiar stores whose very existence was threatened by the opening of shopping centers and Wal-Marts. I nodded to people I had known all my life, but I knew there was an aloofness in my greeting that registered with those who greeted me back. I did not want to linger and catch up on old news. The best thing about a small town is that you grow up knowing everyone. It is also the worst thing.

I crossed the street and entered Max Rusoff's department store. I went straight up the stairs and into the office where Max was going over accounts with a pencil. That pencil, in the age of computers, was the key image in any assessment of Max Rusoff.

"The Great Jew," I said and Max rose up to greet me.

He hugged me and I felt the extraordinary power of his arms and body even though his head only came to my chest.

"So, Jack. Where have you been? Max is now last on your list. I should have been among the first," Max admonished.

I stepped back and put out my hand. "Shake, old man. See if you still got it, Max."

Max smiled and said, "My hands aren't old, Jack. Not my hands."

Before me stood a squat, powerful man, built low to the ground and shaped like a fire hydrant. His neck, by itself, always looked strong enough to harness a plow to and I had seen him toss hundred-pound feed bags to my grandfather as though they were hotel pillows. He seemed deeply rooted and spread out. When I was smaller, shaking hands with Max seemed as painful as getting my hand caught in the door of a Buick. It was like being bitten by something mechanical, larger than life.

From the time I was a teenager, I had tried to put Max on the floor when we shook hands. I thought my manhood would be assured on the day I made Max beg for mercy beneath the power of my grip. But that day had never come. It was always me who ended up on my knees begging for Max to desist as the bones of my right hand were crushed together in agony.

We shook hands and Max played with me for a couple of seconds before he brought me yelping to my knees. Rubbing my hand, I took a seat in the bright, well-appointed office with its breathtaking view of the river.

"Making any money?" I asked, knowing how much delight Max took in the poor-mouthing language of the American salesman.

"Paying the bills," Max said, "but barely. Things could not be worse."

"I hear you're making millions," I teased.

"If we have a roof over our heads next year, it will be a miracle," Max intoned. "But I understand the cookbook business has not made you the banker's worst enemy either."

"It didn't sell enough copies to buy my daughter a pair of shoes," I complained.

"It sold over ninety thousand copies and went through fourteen printings," Max said. "Do you think I do not keep up with you? Even though you hide yourself like a bandit in Italy? I understand the tax man smiles every time you write him a check."

"He doesn't have a bad day when you pay your taxes either, Max," I said.

"Speaking of money," Max said, "Mike told me he saw you. They throw money at my grandson in Hollywood. Did he tell you he got married for the fourth time? Another Christian girl. Beautiful like all the rest. But you would think after four times he could marry at least one Jewish girl and make his parents happy."

"Mike's trying to make himself happy," I said, defending my friend.

Max shook his head and said, "Then that is Mike's greatest failure of all. He's out there with the *meshuganahs*. He works with only crazy people. He hires only crazy people. Or he makes them crazy. I do not know which is which. I visited him with my wife out in this Tinseltown. His children, they all have blond hair. They have never heard of such a thing as a synagogue. He lives in such a house as you have never seen. Big as this town this house seems to me. I tell you the truth. His wives get younger and younger and I'm afraid he will next marry a twelve-year-old. His swimming pool is so big, he could raise whales in it."

I laughed and said, "He's done very well."

"Tell me. How is your mother? How is Lucy?"

"Doing better, but we are afraid to count on it," I said.

"I am very sad for you all," Max said, "but happy for me. It brings you back to Waterford when nothing else can. Why did you not bring Leah?"

"You know why, Max," I said, looking away from him at a pattern in the oriental carpet.

"I want you to talk to Ruth and George while you're here." I shrugged. "Do not shrug your shoulders so at Max. Who gave you your first job? That I ask you."

"Max Rusoff," I answered.

"Your second."

"Max."

"Your third, fourth, fifth . . ."

"Max, Max, Max," I said, smiling at Max's strategy.

"Was Max good to Jack?"

"The best."

"Then make Max happy and go see Ruth and George. They have suffered too much already. They made a mistake. They know it now. You will see."

"It was a real big mistake, Max," I said.

"Talk to them. I will set it up. I know what is best. You are just a boy and what does a boy know."

"I haven't been a boy for a long time."

"You will always be a boy to me," Max said.

As I rose to leave I said, "Good-bye, Max. I tell everyone I meet in Italy about the Great Jew. I tell them about the Cossacks and the pogrom, about your coming to America."

"Do not call me this Great Jew thing," Max ordered and his voice was pained and flummoxed. "This name. It's embarrassing."

"I call you this because that's what everyone calls you," I said.

"This name it follows me wherever I go," Max said. "It is like a tick I got in the forest . . . easy to pick up but hard to get rid of."

"It comes from your story in the Ukraine."

"You know nothing about the Ukraine or what it was like," Max protested. "Everything gets exaggerated."

"And it comes from your life in Waterford," I said. "My grandfather told me that part and Silas doesn't exaggerate."

"You've not been to see your grandfather," Max said. "He's hurt."

"I've been chasing his wife around the city streets," I said. "Ginny Penn made another break for it yesterday."

"Still, he wants to see you."

"My time's limited, Max." Max shook his head. "Show me what you used, Max," I said, changing the subject. "Show me your weapon."

"It is a tool," he said. "It's not a weapon."

"But you used it as a weapon once," I said. "I know the story."

"Only once was it a weapon."

"It's the only thing you brought from the old country."

Max walked over to the corner of his office and began to turn the numbers of a safe he had kept since I first knew him as a child. Reaching in the safe once it had clicked open, he pulled out a homemade box. He took off the top and unwrapped a velvet cloth and pulled out a meat cleaver that he still kept sharp. The cleaver's blade caught the light and looked like a slim mouth.

"It was from my home, Kironittska," Max said. "I was a butcher's apprentice."

"I want to hear the story, Max," I said. "I want to hear it again."

"One does not know where love will take you," Max said, beginning the story I had heard a dozen times as a boy growing up in Waterford.

Max had been born in the Ukraine, at a time when all Jews were forced by decree of the Tsar to live their lives out in the Pale of Settlement. There they led lives of desperate poverty in the twenty-five western regions that made up the Pale.

He was born on March 31, 1903, in the small city of Kironittska, the fourth of four children. The last thing the family needed was another mouth to feed, for this was a world that could barely sustain those who already existed. Poverty ennobles nothing but marks everything and it touched Max with an indelible imprint, made even more horrible by the fact that his father was a professional beggar who made his uncertain living by begging for alms each day, except the Sabbath, along the winding merchant streets in the Jewish Quarter. No one was ever glad to see the unctuous approach of Berl, the Schnorrer, who would fill the air with his high-pitched cries and entreaties. He often took his children with him on these humiliating forays to ask for money from people who had worked hard to earn it. While Jews tolerated their beggars more than people of most religions, one could not sink lower than to be Berl, the Schnorrer.

The family lived in a hovel in the poorest section of the already poor town where hunger was the only companion that many families could count on to be at their table. Max's mother, Peshke, sold eggs at the open market in the town square every day of the year and the weather had marked her plain face with the harsh graffiti of Russian winters. Early in the morning, before sunrise, she would go out to buy eggs from the peasants; then she would take her place in the square where she had a legal permit to carry out her trade. The tax she paid for that permit gave them the only legitimacy her family knew. It was a difficult trick to sell enough eggs to buy food for dinner each night, and so it was with great bitterness that she watched her husband slink into the square, his loud, flapping presence causing her to think that Berl was put on earth solely to cause her shame.

For the first years of his life, Max was raised and nurtured by his sister Sarah, who was ten years old when he was born, and was given the entire responsibility of taking care of both Max and his older sister, Tabel, who was seven.

When Max was three, Tabel was sent to work at a button factory and so his father took Max on his rounds of begging through the alleyways of the city. Berl had taught Max how to walk up to rich people with a small box and ask for alms at the same time displaying his irresistible smile. Berl had been amazed by how much a handsome little boy like Max could entice from the purse of a manufacturer. Max suddenly seemed like a good-luck charm for the whole family.

Peshke heard the first screams coming from the street leading to the river, screams accompanied by the hoofbeats of the Cossacks' horses and cries of alarm. The peddlers scooped up as much merchandise as they could carry and ran in utter pandemonium as six Cossacks entered Mullenplatz with their swords drawn and already bloody.

Berl watched the scene from a stone wall where he sat with Max. Seeing an extraordinary opportunity, he moved along the safety of the wall carrying his child and crept under one of the stalls recovering four oranges, five apples, and two ripe bananas. Seeing further that he was unobserved, he recovered a jar of honey, six fat sugar beets, and a whole cauliflower—all of which he deposited in the deep pockets of his tattered, unwashed gown.

He stayed hidden beneath one of the stalls until he heard the hoofbeats moving away from him. Gathering courage, he made a break for the street leading to his home, not knowing that two of the Cossacks were helping themselves to the produce just as he had done. He saw the largest of the Cossacks, a great blond statue of a man, leap for his stallion, and instantly horse and man moved as one animal toward him. Berl ran, but he had no chance, so he turned and lifted his young son up toward the Cossack in supplication, appealing to the love of all men for children. Max screamed as he saw the Cossack's bloodthirsty charge. The Cossack's sword went under Max's bare feet, and with a sword thrust as expert as it was deadly, disemboweled Berl, the Schnorrer, without harming his young son.

Max fell down on top of his father who grabbed him and hugged him close with his arthritic fingers.

"Say kaddish for me" were his father's last

words on earth. Berl died with his son hysterical upon him and covered with his father's
blood.

The magnificent charge of a Cossack horse-
man with saber drawn would be the first thing
that Max Rusoff would remember from his
childhood. That murderous instant would mark
his birth into the light of consciousness in this
world.

The death of Berl began the long, slow unraveling of Max's mother, Peshke. Poverty is its
own dementia, but something loosened around
the fringes of Peshke's mind after the murder
of her husband and his humiliating burial in a
pauper's grave. The tragedy of Berl's death was
diminished in the eyes of most of Kironittska's
Jews because of the stolen food found in his
pockets. To be a beggar was one thing, but to
steal from peddlers who had fled before an advance of *pogromcyks* was quite another.
Though his mother never mentioned the word
to him, Max learned that shame could do more
damage to a human being than any pogrom.

When Max was eight, he was sent to be an
apprentice to the blacksmith, Arel, the Muscle.
For five years, Max helped Arel in his shop,
tending the horses, carrying tools and heavy
buckets of steel ingots, and working in the
household for Arel's demanding and unhappy
wife, Iris. Arel was a gentle, long-suffering man

who helped the boy in his study of Hebrew and the Torah.

When he was thirteen, he received his bar mitzvah in a ceremony involving other boys as poor as he was. The ceremony was brief, eloquent, and simple and the next day Max wore his father's tefillin for the first time at morning prayers.

It was the same year that Arel, the Muscle, dropped dead in his blacksmith shop and his wife, Iris, told Max that to her he was just an extra mouth to feed and as a widow she had more troubles than a pomegranate had seeds. And so Mottele, the Blade, reluctantly took Max on as his apprentice. Mottele had a terrible temper, but a decent business. Some of the *shayner Yid* or honored Jews were his customers and he had as great a reputation for honesty as he did for his explosive rages. Though all knew about Max's willingness to work hard for small recompense, few realized that after his days in the blacksmith shop and those in the butcher shop hauling carcasses and breaking the bones of cattle and sheep with the sharp blades of his new profession, Max was ripening into a strapping and powerful young man.

A year after his sister Sarah and brother-in-law Chaim moved to a new life in Warsaw, Max was called to the Mullenplatz and told his mother had gone mad when a gang of Christian ruffians had rushed her stall and crushed every egg she had for sale.

When Max reached the marketplace, he could hear his mother's wailing high above the other noises of the market. He led her home, but he could not quiet or reconcile her. Like one of the eggs she spent her whole life selling, something in Peshke was broken beyond repair in this trivial incident.

Peshke never went back to the Mullenplatz to sell eggs; all light had gone out of her and Max became her sole caretaker. For a year he did everything for her, fed her, cleaned up after her, took her for long walks along the river whenever he had a free moment.

But one night in the deep of winter, he woke up when he felt cold air hit his face. He rose quickly, lit a candle, and saw that his mother was not in her bed. He also noticed that her clothes were all in their usual places. At the doorway, he cried out when he saw the bare footprints in deep snow and that a blizzard had come in over the mountains that night. Hurriedly, he dressed himself and mumbled prayers to the Master of the Universe to have mercy on his mother. He ran out calling for his mother, but he had entered a silent frozen world that was both all white and all black. He followed her footprints until they disappeared in the snow. He walked through the city in despair, cursing God's name and cursing him especially for making people hopeless before he graciously allowed them to die.

In the Mullenplatz he found his dead and naked mother sitting in the same spot where she had sold eggs her whole life. He covered Peshke's face with kisses, then lifted her and carried her through the silent city. Max could sling a side of beef up to a wagon now and his mother seemed light in the carrying. His sorrow was devastating and complete. While he sat shiva, the butcher, Mottele, the Blade, and his family took care of Max and Mottele's customers brought Max food during the seven days he mourned for his unlucky mother. His siblings had all drifted to the west, all lost to Poland.

For the first time in his short life, Max saw every sunrise and every sunset as he said the beautiful kaddish prayer.

The war years from 1914 to 1918 were difficult and terrifying for the Jews of Kironittska. Even as the armistice was signed, civil war began to rage in Russia after the assassination of the Tsar and his family. As Mottele said during one of the early sieges, "Good times are bad for the Jews. Bad times are simply unspeakable for the Jews."

When the Whites held the city the Jews suffered a great deal more than with the Bolsheviks. Pogroms were frequent and many Jews were murdered by mobs of roving undisciplined soldiers. No one slept easily in the Jewish Quarter and the Angel of Death held the city in its palm like a fly.

But Mottele warned Max about the Bolsheviks. "*Nu,* Max. The ones who smile and call you 'Comrade,' those are the real murderers, the real swineherds. *Nu,* listen to me, Max, I have thought about these things. Communism is a way for the government to steal from everybody. Capitalism? Communism? All rubbish and one is no different than the other. No matter who is in power, it's always bad for the Jews."

Mottele had just finished this harangue when Rachel Singer and her sixteen-year-old daughter, Anna, came into the shop to get their roast beef for a Sabbath meal. Abraham Singer owned a tile factory that employed seven hundred workers and he was, by far, the richest Jew in Kironittska. Mottele noticed that his assistant, Max, rushed to the counter to serve the Singers, even though Max knew that the proper protocol was to allow Mottele, the Blade, the privilege of serving his most distinguished customers.

"Keep hacking away at that bull," Mottele said, elbowing Max aside, and it was then that he saw Max staring in open-faced wonderment at the unadorned beauty of Anna Singer. Anna was known to be the most beautiful girl to come out of the Jewish Quarter of Kironittska since Rabbi Kushman's daughter of a century before. Even the *goyim* admitted that she was the loveliest young woman in the city. Her face was like a magnet for the eyes of men and women alike. Her figure was lovely and her disposition gentle.

When Rachel and Anna Singer left the store, Max ran to the entryway and watched Anna walk through the admiring crowds with her mother. Mottele laughed when he saw how smitten Max was and how innocent the boy was about the impossibly strict social lines that bound all Jewish life in Kironittska.

"*Nu,* Max," he said. "The world is set up by the Great One in such a way that the Anna Singers of the world never look at the poor schlemiels like Max Rusoff. There are things meant to be opposites in the world. There are apples and oranges, Russians and Jews, Poles and Russians, kosher and unclean, pigs and cattle, rabbis and apostates, and so on. Anna has walked on oriental rugs her whole life while you wallowed in the mud. She had a private tutor who taught her French and Russian and math besides Hebrew. She plays the piano like an angel. She is the pride of all Jews in Kironittska."

"She is like a flower," Max said, sighing, and returning to his work among the bones and blood of slain animals.

"But one for someone else to smell," Mottele said, but softly because every man has felt the way young Max was feeling.

"Is Anna betrothed yet?" Max asked.

"All the *shayner Yid* have come to seek the hand of Anna Singer. Now get to work. Get your mind back to the loins of cows, not women. Do not repeat to anyone else this foolishness about Anna Singer. You would be the laughingstock of the Mullenplatz. Tell only Mottele. Mottele you can trust."

On May 4, 1919, the city awoke to an eerie, unnatural silence and the citizens of Kironittska realized that the Bolsheviks had withdrawn their forces for the third time during the course of the civil war. For two days, no Jew stirred from his home as all hid and waited for the Whites or the Cossacks or one of the other killer bands to attack. After a while people began to emerge and a certain cheer and optimism was felt in all the war-beleaguered quarters of the city.

A week later, the marketplace was full and bustling with commerce again and the hagglers were reunited with the sellers and roosters crowed and geese honked in sadness and young girls bought pretty combs for their hair and the peasants staggered through the streets, vodka-sotted and with pockets full of kopecks after the sale of poultry and livestock. The smell of yeast and bread bloomed out from Bakers' Row, a tank of live carp was for sale at the fishmonger's, and the man selling umbrellas prayed for rain.

Then suddenly, everyone was silent as a hundred Cossacks crossed the Kironittska bridge, their sabers drawn and their horses moving at a quick gait. Their mission was terror and terrorizing. They were an attachment of a Cossack regiment in pursuit of the Red Army, which had pulled out a week earlier. Kironittska was to be punished for the crime of having been occupied by the enemy troops.

The Cossacks tore through the Mullenplatz like a whirlwind. An eighty-year-old Jewish woman who sold raisins and grapes was trampled to death by two Cossack horsemen riding in tandem. Eight Jews and five Christians lay dead before the Cossacks began chasing the fleeing townsmen down side streets. Ten more Jews died trying to make it to the Grand Synagogue where they were sure God would protect them from the wrath of the enemies. But God was silent as they were struck down and silent as the Cossacks set the Grand Synagogue on fire. Then the Cossacks began to gallop out of the city to rejoin their regiment. They left seven fires burning behind them, twenty-six dead, hundreds wounded, and the city agonized in its every stone. Screaming was heard in distant streets as straggling Cossacks made last slashing runs against the people.

Max had closed the shutters of the shop as soon as he heard the disarray and the screaming. This is what Mottele taught him to do in case of danger. Outside, he heard the panic of his neighbors and although he wanted to run out and help his fellow Jews, he remembered the massive Cossack who had killed his own father and the thought of those unsmiling horsemen filled him with terror.

Then he heard Mottele beating against the shutters of the butcher shop and when Max opened them Mottele fell through the doorway, a glancing saber slash torn across his back. Max pulled him through the door and lifted Mottele up on top of the counter where meat was sold to the customers.

Tordes, the Bean, the barber from across the street, had watched Max pull Mottele into the butcher shop and had come to help. Though cutting hair was his trade, Tordes also pulled teeth, applied leeches, and was well known for his expertise with pharmaceuticals and medicines.

"The bastards. The bastards," Mottele screamed over and over.

Tordes, the Bean, had brought a jar of alcohol with him. "This will hurt, Mottele, but it will disinfect the wound. He could have been slicing his bacon with that sword last night, the cutthroat."

Max had never heard anyone scream so loud as Mottele did when the alcohol hit the open wound. "That hurt worse than the sword," Mottele screamed.

"The Grand Synagogue," Tordes said to Max as he cleansed Mottele's wounds. "It is on fire, may their names be written on the buttocks of Satan."

Suddenly, there was a softer, though more urgent beating against the tin shutters and when Max opened them a bleeding, devastated Rachel Singer came through the door, blood dripping down her face from a head wound.

"My husband," she said. "My daughter, Anna. Please someone help."

And Max Rusoff—the one afraid of Cossacks, the one whose mother died insane and naked in the snow, Berl, the Schnorrer's son, Max who was insignificant and unknown in the life of the Jews of Kironittska, Max who was secretly in love with the beautiful and unobtainable Anna Singer—that same, poverty-stricken but God-fearing Max bowed to this bleeding, distinguished woman, reached for his cleaver, and ran toward the house of Anna Singer.

The house was ten blocks through a twisting narrow alleyway and Max did not pass a soul during his madcap sprint toward the Singer home. The Jews of Kironittska had withdrawn as Cossacks were firing their rifles down near the river. With every step he took, Max went further into the privileged world of the *shayner Yid,* those prosperous Jews who lived in fine homes and whose achievements gave pride to the whole Jewish community. As he ran, he did not think of being frightened, only that harm might come to Anna Singer. At the open gate to the Singer house, Max paused and summoned his courage and got his breathing under control. He prayed to the God who had made Samson to grant him the strength to do battle with the Philistines as he heard the screams of Anna Singer. In a paroxysm of cowardice and doubt he rushed into the courtyard.

Abraham Singer lay on the cobblestones shot through the heart. Two servants lay dead beside him. There was a Cossack rider atop his mount watching another Cossack raping a screaming Anna Singer just inside the open door of the house. The Cossack on the horse was laughing and did not see the approach of the apprentice butcher until Max was beneath him. The Cossack looked down and said one word, "Yid." Yes, Jew he was and a butcher he was. Max had never killed a human being and everything about his life and sensibility as a Jew shouted out against the possibility, but as a butcher he brought an awesome knowledge of arteries and soft places and killing points to the task at hand. The Cossacks were an old story among Jews but they had made one egregious error when they had ridden in to Kironittska: they had chosen to rape the young girl that Max Rusoff secretly loved.

The Cossack looked down from his great horse and saw a squarely built and short Jew, but he could not know that Max could lift a full-grown steer to the meat hooks in the back of the butcher shop with a single, graceful movement. The Cossack laughed out loud, surprised to find a pious Jew who would fight back, but the laughing Cossack had no way of knowing that Max was famous among the other butchers for keeping his blades sharp. The Cossack's saber was half out of its scabbard when Max struck the first blow and removed the Cossack's arm cleanly at the elbow and ended his laughter forever. So swift and so shocking was the attack, that the young Cossack simply lifted the bleeding stump into the night air, puzzled and disbelieving, and missed the terrible second stroke as the butcher, holding on to the pommel, leapt into the air and buried the cleaver in the Cossack's throat, severing a scream in mid-cry.

The witnesses to this scene, and there were two cowering servants hiding in the garden, both agreed later that it was the savagery of the butcher's attack that had so alarmed them. After they watched the sandy-haired head of the Cossack fall onto the cobblestones in this most amazing redress of grievance between Jew and Cossack, they were overcome with a profound terror.

Anna Singer screamed again from the house and her cry broke Max's heart. He charged through the open door, his face spattered with Russian blood and his fury risen to a perfect, murderous pitch as he found the second Cossack with his pants down to his ankles driving himself hard into the prone body of Anna, who lay screaming and fighting beneath him.

Max Rusoff grabbed the Cossack by the hair and yanked backward so viciously that he almost tore the man's scalp off. The Russian screamed and lunged in rage but he did not lunge quickly enough as the cleaver slashed through the Ukrainian darkness one more time. The cleaver whistled through the air again and the Cossack's penis landed beneath a chair in the dining room. Then with two hands and murderous aim, Max drove the cleaver into the brain of the black-haired Cossack with a single, perfectly placed stroke and the war of Max and the Cossacks was over.

Anna Singer was weeping and had turned toward the staircase to hide her nakedness. Picking the remains of her dress off the floor, Max covered her as best he could. Then he removed a cloth from the table and placed it over her body. He tried to speak to her, to console the beautiful but violated young girl whose father lay murdered outside the door. But he could not coax a single word out of his mouth.

He went to the door and saw that a peasant had abandoned a vegetable cart near the gate of the Singer house. He ran to it and pushed it through the gates and into the courtyard. The Cossack horses were nervous and confused with the smell of their masters' blood fresh in their nostrils. Then stealthily the two Jewish servants emerged from their hiding place in the garden. Max called out to them.

"Take these horses to Mottele's butcher shop," he ordered.

Then Max lifted the bodies of the two Cossacks and threw them like sacks of potatoes into the cart. He gathered up the missing body parts, an arm and a head in the courtyard and a penis underneath the chair. Anna had disappeared upstairs and Max tore a curtain in the drawing room and took it outside and covered the bodies of the Cossacks. He then walked calmly through the darkened alleyway that led to the Street of the Butchers and Mottele's shop.

When Rabbi Avram Shorr entered Mottele's butcher shop, he almost fainted at the sight of the bodies of the two Cossacks stacked like cordwood against the wall, their mutilated corpses eerie and unsettling in the light of a single candle.

"Who is responsible for this abomination?" the rabbi asked.

"I am. Max Rusoff."

"When the Cossacks discover this atrocity, they will bring a thousand riding into this city to avenge their deaths."

"Great Rabbi," Mottele said, bowing low in fealty to the distinguished visitor. "It is a great honor to welcome you to my humble shop. Max has some questions he wishes to ask that only a rabbi can answer."

"He has put the entire Jewish community in great peril," the rabbi said. "What are your questions, butcher?"

"If the Reb please," Max began. "Would it be possible to suspend the laws of kashruth for a single night?"

"Jews do not suspend their dietary laws just

because of a pogrom," the Reb answered. "Now is the time that we keep the laws even more steadfastly. God allows the pogrom because the Jews have drifted from the laws."

"Just for one night, Reb?" Max asked.

"These horses of the Cossacks," the rabbi said, looking at the two great steeds that took up much of the back part of the butcher shop. "Who would believe such horses belong to Jews? When the Cossacks find these horses they will begin the slaughter of Jews."

"You are our witness, Reb," Max said. "There was no cruelty in the death of these two horses."

"I do not understand you," the rabbi said.

At that moment the legs of the horse nearest the rabbi buckled and it sank to its knees, making a slight, desperate noise of strangulation. Max had cut the throat of one horse and Mottele the other, but they had done it so swiftly and expertly that the horses felt something slight, much less irritating than the bite of a horsefly, as their jugulars were severed by the most carefully honed blades.

"Move, Reb," Max said quietly.

The rabbi moved back toward the door and the horses collapsed and gasped their dying breaths.

"Why did you do this to these poor creatures?" the rabbi said, for he was a great scholar and teacher who had never witnessed the slaughter of so large an animal before.

"Because the Cossacks will not find these horses," Max answered. "If the Reb could suspend the laws for a night, we could feed all the poor Jews of the city on horseflesh."

"Absolutely not. Horse meat is *trayf,* unclean, and Leviticus forbids Jews to eat the flesh of an animal that does not chew its cud."

"Just for one night, Reb," Mottele said. "We could send steaks to the poorest homes."

"Not for one night. Not for one second. One does not suspend the dietary laws because a butcher from Kironittska went crazy. You are thinking that I am too strict, but it is the Torah that is strict."

"Another question, Reb," Max asked shyly.

"Ask it," the rabbi said. "I suppose now you will want me to give my permission to eat the Cossacks."

"It concerns the Cossacks, Reb," Max said. "When the Jews bury the dead tomorrow at the Jewish cemetery, could we also bury the Cossacks?"

"You would bury such garbage with the sacred saints of our people?" Rabbi Avram Shorr said. "You would defile the bones of our ancestors by burying such filth, such *trayf* beside them? This is out of the question."

"Then what should we do with the Cossacks, Reb?" Mottele asked.

"Why should I care what happens to the
Cossacks?" the rabbi said.

"Because the rabbi himself said that these
two Cossacks could bring a thousand Cossacks
to this city."

"I see your point, butcher. Let Matchulat,
the Coffin Maker, fit these two for a coffin.
Once the coffin is nailed shut, they become
corpses, not Cossacks. Let me ponder this
problem through the night and I will come up
with a solution to this dilemma. Tell me,
butcher," the rabbi said, staring at Max, "did
you know you had this great beast of violence
beating inside you?"

Max, in shame, said, "No, Reb."

"You are as cruel as a Pole or a Litvak," the
rabbi said, surveying the carnage around him.
"You are an animal, like the worst of the *goyim*.
I feel shame for all Jews when I look about this
room. We are a peace-loving, gentle people
and it causes me to shudder to think that we
Jews have produced such a savage, such a muti-
lator."

"My father was killed by a Cossack," Max
said.

"Max is a pious Jew, Reb," Mottele said.

"You should talk sense into this Jew," the
rabbi said. "What did you say to this warrior-

like Jew when he brought these two dead Cossacks into your store? I can see he respects you,
Mottele. What did you say to him? How did
you upbraid him?"

Mottele looked around at Max, then back
to the rabbi, and spoke. "The first thing I said
to Max when I saw the Cossacks, Reb, forgive
me, but I said '*Mazel tov.*' "

As Rabbi Shorr was leaving, five of the
other butchers who had shops on the street entered Mottele's shop carrying the long knives
and cleavers of their trade. All had come when
they heard the task that Mottele and Max had
set for themselves that night and they came in
the brotherhood of their stained, melancholy
profession, the quiet solidarity of men who
make their living dividing up animals into cuts
of meat. They were wearing white aprons and
all were strong, hardworking men who understood the necessity of getting rid of all the evidence of the Cossacks and their horses. Three
of the men went to the horse that Max had
killed and the other two went to help Mottele.

The beautiful horses began to disappear as
the butchers plied their trade. They worked
hard, diligently, purposefully eviscerating and
dismembering the horses with astonishing skill
and speed.

Max spotted a cringing, scurvy black dog
that hung around the market begging for scraps

at the same time Mottele spotted him. He was about to shoo the skeletal animal away until Max stopped him.

"Tonight, we can feed him," Max said. And so the stray dogs and cats of the city dined on horse meat—the butcher's art is one of reduction and the butchers of Kironittska enjoyed their finest hour as the two horses left that shop in chops and steaks. There was free offal to feed family pets for days. By the time they had finished their labors and cleaned the shop of its great quantities of horse blood, there was no way anyone could tell that two horses from the Cossacks' cavalry had ever been tethered in Mottele's butcher shop. A new pride could be felt by all in the butchers' shul.

The next day, hundreds of mourning Jews massed in procession for the two-mile walk to the Jewish cemetery. Twenty-six Jews had been killed in the outbreak, but twenty-eight coffins made their way to the cemetery on the shoulders of Jewish men. Rabbi Avram Shorr had considered the problem of how to dispose of the bodies of the two Cossacks and had come up with a most functional solution.

In the middle of the wailing and sorrowing crowd, the butchers of Kironittska carried two of the coffins and moved along with the procession of over five hundred mourners across the bridge and out toward the poppy-rich fields of the countryside.

The crowd poured into the cemetery, but its numbers were so great that many had to watch the burials from outside the sacred grounds. As the Jews buried their own dead in the cemetery, outside the wall Max and the butchers buried the two Cossacks and smoothed the dirt flat over their graves. The throng of black-dressed mourners hid their work from the eyes of strangers. When the ceremony was over, every Jew walked over the Cossacks' graves on the way back to the city and every Jew spit as he passed over them. They had shed Jewish blood the day before, but they went to their Creator awash in Jewish spittle.

The Red Army took back Kironittska a month later. It was a time when many people were swallowed up in the baleful incoherence that grips a country when brother is set against brother. Russia lost thousands of unknown soldiers during that time and the two nameless Cossacks registered themselves in that anonymous roster of lost combatants.

But the life of Max Rusoff had been changed forever. From that day forward the Jews spoke of him with a combination of fear, revulsion, and awe. No one was sorry the Cossacks were dead, yet most were deeply troubled by the manner of their deaths. In the mind of his *landsleit,* the image of Max leaping into the night air to bury his cleaver in the throat of a Cossack was a transfiguring, indelible one.

And so the Jews of the city began to withdraw from Max, and Mottele's business was severely diminished by this withdrawal. Rachel Singer never came back to Mottele's shop in her lifetime. Max tried to visit Anna several weeks after her father's funeral to inquire about her health but was turned away from the house with great unnecessary rudeness by a family servant who made it clear that Max would never be a welcome guest in that house. "Only during pogroms," Max said to himself as he returned to the butcher shop. Six months later Anna Singer's engagement was announced to a wealthy fur trader from Odessa and Anna Singer passed out of Max Rusoff's life forever.

Soon after Anna's wedding, Rabbi Avram Shorr summoned Max.

"I understand that you have ruined Mottele's business," the rabbi said.

"People are staying away from the shop. It is true, Reb."

"You are bad for the Jews of Kironittska, Max," the rabbi said. "You are like some dybbuk that has entered the body of all Jews, an evil spirit that inhabits us all. A woman found her sons playing in the streets the other day.

One had a knife and was pretending to stab his younger brother. After she beat the boy, she asked him what kind of game he was playing. The boy replied that he was pretending to be Max the Butcher's Apprentice and his little brother was playing the role of the Cossack."

"I am sorry, Reb," Max said.

"Even our children are infected. Still I would like to know, Max, where did this hideous reservoir of violence come from?"

"I was in love with Anna Singer. It was a secret," Max said.

The rabbi's laughter thundered through the hall of the Eastern Shul.

"A butcher's assistant in love with the daughter of Abraham Singer?" the rabbi said, disbelievingly.

"I didn't aspire to marry her, Reb," Max explained. "I simply loved her. Mottele told me that was not possible."

"Abraham would have thrown you out of the house if you had even dared to ask," the rabbi said.

"Not on the night of the pogrom," Max said. "That night, Abraham Singer would have welcomed me like a rabbi."

"You witnessed the violation of his daughter," the rabbi said. "Abraham would not have liked that."

"I killed the violator of his daughter," Max

said. "Abraham would have liked that very much."

"You were a savage that night," the rabbi spat at Max.

"I was a Jew that night," Max said.

"A Jew more cruel than the *goyim*," the rabbi said.

"A Jew who does not allow Jewish girls to be violated," Max said.

"You do not belong in Kironittska, butcher. You have unsettled the Jews of the city."

"I will do what the rabbi says," Max said.

"I would like you to leave Kironittska forever. Go to Poland. Go anywhere. Go to America."

"I do not have enough money for the passage," said Max.

"The mother of Anna Singer has come to me," the rabbi said. "She will give you the money for your passage. The Singer family is uncomfortable that you are still in the city. Abraham had many powerful brothers. They are all afraid you will talk about what you saw that night."

"I have talked with no one," Max said.

The rabbi answered, "The Singer brothers do not trust a butcher's assistant to keep his mouth shut for long. Peasants are known for their loose tongues."

"I did not see the Singer brothers on the night of the pogrom," Max said.

"They were home praying for the deliverance of our people like all pious Jews were," the rabbi said.

"I too was praying," Max said. "My prayers took a different form."

"Blasphemer. Murder is never prayer," the rabbi said.

"I am sorry, Reb. I am not an educated man."

And so Max Rusoff left Kironittska for the long and dangerous journey to the Polish border, and from there he booked passage on a freighter sailing for America. During the voyage in the overcrowded steerage section, Max met a language teacher from Cracow by the name of Moishe Zuckerman. It was Zuckerman who gave Max his first English lessons, and to the surprise of both of them Max showed a natural aptitude for languages.

At night, Max would stand on the deck of the ship studying the stars and practicing the strange new language that he would soon have to speak. Max had no one to meet him at Ellis Island and that made him different from most other Jews he met on the freighter. But Moishe Zuckerman understood that Max could not just land in America with nowhere to go. And so Moishe Zuckerman made all the bewildering arrangements, found a temporary room for Max in the home of a cousin, and finally put him on a train at Pennsylvania Station to South Carolina, where he told Max there was beautiful land and no ghettos. Riding all night through the states of the Eastern seaboard, Max tried to control his fears for he knew there was no possibility of return. The farther south the train went the less of the new English he had learned did he understand. By the time he reached Charleston at ten in the morning, all the words had been softened and moistened and stretched out by the purring elisions of Southern speech.

He was met by Henry Rittenberg, who approached him immaculately dressed and surprised Max by addressing him in Yiddish. Because of his dress and the elegance of his manner, Max had mistaken him for an American. The Jews of Charleston were extraordinarily generous to the strange Jews who wandered into their midst and Henry Rittenberg called his friend Jacob Popowski, who had just lost a salesman in a territory that ran south to the Georgia border.

A week later, Max was walking out of Charleston laden down like a beast of burden with two packs.

For the first year, Max walked the lonesome highways and forests of the sparsely populated roads. He was an exotic, outlandish presence to these Southerners he visited unbidden as they plowed fields behind mules or tended their scrabbly poultry in grassless farmyards. At first his English was primal and comic and Max would spread his wares out for a housewife and let her finger the baubles and brushes he offered before her. "You like. You buy," he said in his heavily accented voice that frightened some of the women, especially the black ones. But there was something about Max's face that many of the women along Highway 17 found reassuring. As his grasp of English improved and he became a familiar sight entering the range of vision of these hardworking and lonely people, the visits of Max Rusoff gradually came to be anticipated and even cherished. The children of the farms adored him from the very beginning. He always brought something in the pack that he gave to the children for free. A ribbon here, a piece of candy there.

On the road Max would exchange merchandise for a place to sleep in the barn and eggs for a meal. In fact, the housewives along his route began to call him "the egg man" because of his refusal to eat any food they prepared for him except for hard-boiled eggs. The hard-boiled egg was the only way he could nourish himself, yet still remain a pious and kosher Jew. He had cut his earlocks and shaved his beard when he saw how much he stood out among the other citizens and even the Jews of Charleston. But the business of becoming an American in the South would require more laxness than even Max had figured.

By the end of the first year, Max bought himself a horse and wagon and his operation got much larger, as did the scope of his ambition.

It was with this horse and wagon that he extended the range of his travels and in the second year he arrived at the small river town of Waterford and ventured farther into the sea islands that made their way into the Atlantic. In Waterford he drove his horse slowly through the streets of the town and took note of the kinds of stores the town had and the kinds it lacked. He questioned the townspeople who treated him in the courteous but offhanded way that Southerners have always regarded strangers. His accent caused some of them to laugh, but Max did not mind.

In his second year in South Carolina, Max was driving his wagon down the farthest road of St. Michael's when he heard a man shouting at him across a narrow saltwater creek.

"Hey," the man said, a young, strong-shouldered man with a pleasant, sunburned face. "Are you the Jew?"

"I am," Max shouted back.

"Been hearing about you. I need some things," he said, "but wait a few minutes so I can row over."

"Be my guest," Max said, proud of the American lingo he was daily adding to his vocabulary. "I've got all the time in the world."

Max watched as the stranger rowed himself across the small creek in a wooden bateau.

The man got out and shook Max's hand.

"My name is Max Rusoff."

"And mine is Silas McCall. My wife is Ginny Penn and we'd like you to stay the night with us. We've never met a Jew, one of the people of the Book."

"I won't be much trouble," Max smiled.

"Ginny Penn's already boiled up a dozen eggs," Silas said, helping with the horse. "You ought to start up a store and stay put," Silas said. "Aren't you tired of peddling door to door?"

"Yes," said Max.

This was the way that Max Rusoff met his best friend in the New World and how the destiny of one Jewish family became intricately bound with a Christian one. The lines of fate operate with a dark knowledge all their own and their accidental encounter would change the lives of all around them. Both men knew much about solitude and had been waiting for the other's appearance for their whole lives. In less than a year, Max had opened his first small store in Waterford and had brought Esther, daughter of Mottele, the Butcher, over to America to be his bride. Their wedding party was given by Silas and Ginny Penn McCall. Many of the best people in Waterford attended.

In 1968, Max and his wife Esther took a trip to Israel and in Yad Vashem, the memorial to the slain Jews of the Shoah, Max found the married name of Anna Singer among the slaughtered. She had been with the Jews of Kironittska who had been taken to a huge pit and machine-gunned by SS gunners. For an hour, Max stayed at Yad Vashem and wept over the impossibility and innocence of his love for Anna Singer. There was something about the purity of his love for that beautiful girl that represented the best part of himself. Though he was sixty-five years old then, he still felt like that sixteen-year-old boy struck dumb by the comeliness and charm of that pretty, flashing-eyed Jewish girl. He could not bear the thought of her kneeling in her nakedness and shame, of Anna dying unpraised and unhonored and buried in an unmarked pit. He never told Esther that he had found Anna's name. Max had a dream on the same night he read her name on the list of the dead.

In this dream, he saw Anna Singer and her

husband and children rousted out of their homes by the Nazi beasts. He watched the fear on Anna's face, the same fear he had briefly glimpsed on the night she had been ravished in her own home as her father lay dead in the courtyard. On her face, Max saw that Anna knew that she was about to die for the crime of being the chosen of God. Her hair looked like dark fire that ran down her shoulders. As she approached the pit, holding hands with her children, she walked between a jeering line of Nazi soldiers.

In this dream, Anna began suddenly to dance, but the dance was invisible to the soldiers and to the other doomed Jews around her. It took Max several numbed and bedazzled moments to realize that Anna Singer was dancing for him, acknowledging through memory and time that lonely, dishonored Jewish boy who had loved her from afar, but had loved her with a fury that burned brightly all the years of his life. She danced and the birds began to sing and the air smelled of mint and clover as the line of Jews kept being pushed forward to kneel a last time and die.

Suddenly, Max saw what had inspired the graceful dance of Anna Singer. On one side of the pit, there was a butcher shop on a narrow street of Kironittska and a strong sixteen-year-old butcher had come out to see what the commotion was all about. He came out muscled and shy into the sunlight. The young Max stopped when he saw Anna dancing and he bowed deeply and would have joined the dance but there was great work to do.

Before he began he looked at her and saw that Anna had transfigured herself into the girl who had once come into his shop with her mother. She knew that Max loved her, and being a girl with choices to make, this time she would make the correct choice. She shouted across the pit, yes, yes to Max, yes always to Max, my avenger, my protector, my love.

Max Rusoff went up to the two remorseless and cowardly Germans firing bullets into the helpless throng of women, children, and rabbis, and he cleaved their heads like the ribs of sheep with two powerful blows. Then he went along the stiff line of Nazis and leaping in the sun and putting his cleaver through their brainpans, sinking as deep as the eyeballs, cut them down one by one as he made his slow, bloody way to his love. His strong arms were covered with the blood of Germans when he finally stood before her and bowed his head to her and offered a battalion of slain Nazis as her dowry.

Then the blood was gone and only sunlight remained and Anna kissed Max tenderly and invited Max to the dance at last. They waltzed toward the butcher shop and whatever life there is on the far side of time. In each other's arms they danced toward the field of paradise where the stars shone like a love letter from a generous God.

Max awoke to machine gun fire and the sight of Anna Singer's bullet-riddled body tumbling with her children into the pit.

When he returned to Waterford, Max went to the synagogue he had helped build with his own hands to say kaddish for Anna Singer.

In the American South, he prayed for her soul. By this time, the townspeople referred to him as "the Great Jew," not for anything he had done in the universe, but for what they had seen him do in their town. When he traveled to Israel that first time, he went as mayor of Waterford.

CHAPTER 16

I SPENT THE REST OF THE MORNING running errands for my mother. Dupree and I went back to Rusoff's Department Store to buy her a new nightgown and makeup. We also bought her three wigs she could wear in the coming weeks when her hair would fall out due to the chemotherapy. We bought her the best wigs available in Waterford and Dupree wore one of them all the way back to the hospital as he told me about his days among mental patients at the state hospital. He worked well with manic depressives and had an inordinate empathy "for schizophrenics of all flavors" as he described it.

In the early afternoon, the nurse helped my mother get into the nightgown we had bought her and she was wearing one of the wigs when I came in for my daily ten-minute visit.

"The wig must've cost a fortune," my mother said.

"Ten thousand dollars," I said. "But Dupree helped. He pitched in five bucks."

"The gown's lovely," she said.

"Makes you look like a movie star."

"Where's John Hardin, Jack?" my mother said.

"I haven't seen him for a couple of days."

"Would you keep your eye peeled?" she asked me. "He can be a handful, that boy."

"That's what I hear," I said.

"I called Leah today," my mother said, surprising me.

"What did she say?"

"She invited me to Rome," Lucy said. "I promised to visit her as soon as I am strong enough. I also invited her to come home for a long visit. I'd like her to be with me when the loggerheads come in to lay their eggs, from May to August."

"The turtles'll lay whether she's home or not," I said.

Lucy said, "I'm in charge of the program over on the Isle of Orion. We monitor the beach. Count the turtles. Make sure their eggs are unmolested."

"Leah would love that. Look, a whole crowd wants to come in now. Grandpa's out there. Everyone wants to see you, Mama. I'll come back later. I have to leave on Sunday."

"You can't. That's not fair," she said.

"It's not fair to Leah for me to be away this long."

"Who's keeping her?"

"Charles Manson just got paroled," I said. "He really needed the work."

"Get on, you. Come see me tomorrow. Please look out for John Hardin."

When I arrived back home it was not yet three in the afternoon; I saw Ruth Fox sitting on the veranda of my father's house. I turned off the motor and laid my forehead against the steering wheel of the car. I felt bruised and exhausted to the point of insensibility. Closing my eyes, I did not think I could bear one more confrontation or ghost from my complicated past. I especially had no desire to exchange harsh words with the mother of the woman I had most adored. I thought of Leah in Rome and how much I missed her. How much more had Ruth Fox suffered, I thought, by losing both Shyla and Leah in the space of a single year? I looked up at the silhouette sitting motionless and patient in the white wicker chair.

Wearily, I got out of the car and walked toward my mother-in-law.

Even in the harsh sunlight, Ruth's beauty touched me and I thought how uncommon it was for one town to have produced this generation of beautiful women. In a sudden revelation, I saw what Shyla would have looked like in her sixties.

Ruth was trim as a girl and silver-haired. As I approached her, that long shock of hair looked like something stolen from the night sky. Her eyes, in shadows, were dark even in broad daylight, so I could not read what she was thinking as I drew near her chair.

The marsh behind the house with the tide rushing into the creeks took on a darker smell, like a beast in hiding, as I faced a damaged part of myself and my past. Though I tried to think of opening words, no gambit presented itself. I stepped onto the veranda. In silence we studied each other. We had been dead to each other for too many years. Finally, Ruth spoke.

"How is our Leah?" she said, her accent a gentle echo of the Pale of Settlement, the shifting borders of Eastern Europe.

"So," she spoke again, "I ask you, Jack, how is our Leah?"

"My Leah is fine," I answered.

"She is a beautiful girl," Ruth said.

"Martha brought us pictures. She even made a nice video of Leah talking to us."

"Leah's a great kid, Ruth," I said.

"We need to talk."

"We're talking right now," I said and I heard more coldness in my voice than I had intended. I saw in her face Shyla's face, and there was also Leah's face, and the connection startled me.

Ruth said, "We need to review our relationship from A to Z."

"Start with this," I said. "We have no relationship. Our relationship ended the day you and your husband took the stand and tried to take my child away from me. Everyone understands the nature of the mistake now, but only because I won. If you had won, I would never have seen Leah again."

"You have every right to hate us," she said.

"I don't hate you, Ruth," I said evenly. "I hate your husband. I've never hated you. You didn't tell the judge that I beat Shyla and Leah. Your husband did."

"He is the most sorry," Ruth said. "He knows he wronged you. He would like to explain some things to you, Jack," she said. "I would also very much like to explain some things."

"You can start with 'the lady of the coins.' "

"I have to end with 'the lady of the coins.' I

cannot begin there," Ruth said, her face pale and fragile in the stark light.

"Those were her last words," I said. "They make no sense to me. Martha says you know what they mean. Tell me."

"Those words will make no sense until I tell you the whole story, dear Jack."

"Please don't call me 'dear Jack.' "

"Did we not love each other, Jack?"

"You loved me until I married your daughter."

"We are Orthodox Jews. You cannot blame us for being upset when our daughter marries a Gentile. Your parents were equally upset that you married a Jewish girl."

"I'm merely keeping the record straight," I said, and I sat down in the porch swing and began to rock gently back and forth. "You treated me badly."

"If I had explained to you the meaning of 'the lady of the coins . . .' " She stopped as she fought to compose herself. Then she continued, but each word was hard-earned. "Then I could not have blamed you for Shyla's death. By blaming you, Jack, I could take an action. I blamed you so that I would not plunge into despair."

"So you let me plunge into despair instead."

Ruth Fox looked at me. "Jack, you know nothing of despair."

I leaned toward her and whispered fiercely, "I've got a working acquaintance with it."

"You know nothing of it. You know its edges. I know its heart," Ruth said firmly, quietly, and convincingly.

"Here we go again," I said, irritated. "The Holocaust trump card."

"Yes," she said. "That is the card I choose to play. I earned my right to play it. So did my husband."

"And play it you have," I said. "If Shyla didn't eat everything on her plate, your husband would scream 'Auschwitz.' "

"Will you see my husband, Jack?" Ruth asked. "He very much would like to see you."

"No. Tell that sorry son of a bitch I never want to see him again."

Ruth stood up and walked over to me, but I refused to meet her gaze. She took my hands and kissed them softly. Her tears fell until my hands were covered by tears and kisses and the touch of her hair.

"I ask you to see my husband. I ask it for me."

"No," I said, emphatically.

"I ask you to see my husband," she repeated. "I ask it in the name of Shyla. The little girl that we conceived. The one you loved. The one who bore Leah. I ask it in Shyla's name."

I looked at Ruth Fox and saw the woman who was my wife's first hermitage. I thought of Shyla inside Ruth's body and Ruth's enormous love of her troubled daughter and wondered how I could possibly survive if Leah ever killed herself. It was Leah, not Shyla, who made me rise.

"I'm going back to Rome, and Mom's going to try to visit us if she gets enough strength back by December. Leah and I'll fly back with her after Christmas. Mom wants to go to Mass at the Vatican on Christmas Eve."

"Leah, here in Waterford," Ruth said.

"I loved Shyla. Anyone who ever saw us together knew I loved your daughter. I'm sorry I was Catholic. I'm sorry she was Jewish. But love works that way sometimes."

"We know you loved her, Jack," Ruth said. "And Martha told us that you're bringing Leah up as a Jew. Martha says you take her to the oldest synagogue in Rome each Sabbath."

"I promised Shyla if anything happened to her, I wouldn't let Leah forget that she was Jewish," I said. "I like to keep promises."

"Leah," Ruth said. "Will you let us see her?"

"I'll let you see Leah as much as you'd like, but on one condition."

"Anything," Ruth Fox said.

"I'd like to know what you and George knew about Shyla's death. We don't have to blame each other for anything. I can tell you what she said and was thinking in those days leading up to the leap. I have no idea what she knew about your past. She was always sad, Ruth, but I'm sad and that was one of the things that brought us together. We could make each other laugh. I thought I knew everything about her. But I didn't know the important things, the ones that'd save her."

"My husband is waiting to see you."

"Tell George I can't now," I said. "But when I return with Leah . . . Then we'll start."

"Have you visited Shyla's grave since you returned?"

"No, I haven't," I said, almost angrily.

"It is a nice stone. Very pretty. You would like it," she said.

"Leah and I will go together."

Back at the hospital, I watched as Dr. Pitts walked my grandfather, Silas, and my father in to see my mother. The brothers were again comfortable with me around them and when Dallas came in from the law firm we went over the day's activities together. My mother's doctor was talking about releasing her to her own bed in less than a week's time. In the distance, we heard the honking of horns far down the river. Dallas began to tell us about a divorce case he was working on, when Dupree went to the window and looked out.

"The bridge is open," Dupree said. "Tee, get those binoculars."

"I've got them in my briefcase," Dallas said. "There's an osprey with chicks nesting on a telephone pole near my office."

The horns grew louder in the distance.

"Slow boat at rush hour," Dallas said. "Nothing worse."

"Rush hour in Waterford," I said.

"Town's grown," said Tee.

"There's no boat," Dupree said, looking through the binoculars.

We joined Tee at the window and looked downriver at the open bridge.

"Has to be, bro," Tee said. "They don't open the bridge for exercise."

"I'm telling you. No boat," Dupree repeated.

"John Hardin knows the bridge tender, Johnson," Tee said. "Keeps the guy company sometimes."

"Why did my heart just stop?" Dallas said.

My father came up behind us and said, "What're you boys looking at?"

"Where's John Hardin, Dad?" I asked.

"He's fine. I just told your mother. I saw

him at the house this morning. He looked like a million bucks. All he wanted was to borrow a gun."

Dupree lowered the binoculars and looked at our father with a baleful gaze. Lifting the binoculars, Dupree studied the bridge again and said, "Jesus, I see John Hardin. He's holding something. Yeah. Congratulations, Dad. It's your gun."

"You lent a gun to a paranoid schizophrenic?" Dallas said.

"No, I lent one to John Hardin," the judge said. "The boy told me he wanted to do a little target shooting."

As we looked back out the window a man appeared on the span in the center of the open bridge, running full speed. He did not break stride and we watched in fascination as he dove headfirst into the channel of the Waterford River.

"That's Johnson," guessed Tee, and the four of us took off, sprinting together down the hospital hallway toward the parking lot.

In Dupree's car, with Dupree driving fast through the tree-lined streets, we could see the flashing blue lights of three squad cars spinning in unison at the edge of the town side of the bridge.

"They take maritime traffic very seriously, boys," Dallas said. "This ain't local law he's breaking. The feds'll be all over this one. They also don't like motorized traffic disrupted at this time of day. And they sure don't like guys with pistols taking over the only bridge to the sea islands. They could hurt John Hardin."

Dupree drove taking the back streets, avoiding the traffic that was backed up from Anchorage Lane to Lafayette Street, but he had to force his way between a line of cars that was backed up on Calhoun Street, which led directly to the bridge.

"These drivers are highly pissed," Dallas said as Dupree bullied an elderly woman into backing up until her bumper touched the Toyota Corolla behind her.

Dupree honked his horn loudly and forced his way into the empty lane going in the opposite direction from the bridge. He raced past the stalled line of cars and disbelieving drivers and gunned it until he reached the two squad cars also parked in the wrong lane. The four of us jumped out and joined the line of police officers who stood facing a defiant John Hardin across an expanse of water. John Hardin, alone at last, confronted the rest of the world.

When we reached the bridge's edge, we saw Sheriff Arby Vandiver trying to negotiate with John Hardin. But all of us knew John Hardin had entered that untenable zone where the voices inside him and the buzzing confusion on

the bridge made him obedient only to the au-
thenticated world of his own interior. He had
long ago created his own island and he was his
own bully pulpit when the extraordinary and
unruly flash of madness overcame him.

"Hey, Waterford," John Hardin was
screaming. "Fuck you. That's what I think of
the town and everyone who lives in it. What a
rotten little excuse for a town. Everyone who
grows up here, or is forced to live here even for
a small amount of time, becomes a complete,
worthless asshole. It's not your fault, Waterford. You can't help it that you're rotten to the
core. But it's time. You're just not worth a shit
and it shows."

"Makes you proud to be a McCall," Dallas
whispered.

"Okay, John Hardin," Sheriff Vandiver ordered through a bullhorn. "Hit the switch and
let the bridge swing back. You got traffic
backed up for miles."

"They should never've allowed this bridge
to be built, Sheriff. You know better than anyone. Remember how pretty these islands used
to be before they built this bridge? You could
walk for miles without ever seeing a house.
Wild turkeys were all over the place. You
couldn't throw out a baited line without catching a fish. But now? Hell no. A thousand generals live out here by their stupid golf courses.

One million retired colonels and their stupid wives built their tacky retirement homes. There are seven golf courses between here and the beach. How many golf courses do these assholes need?"

"He's got a point," someone said in the crowd beginning to swell on the bridge behind us. Another crowd was forming on the ocean side of the bridge.

"I got to get my bridge back, kid," the sheriff said.

"This used to be a fabulous town," John Hardin shouted, appealing to what he supposed to be the sheriff's shared sense of nostalgia.

"Yeah, kid, it was heaven on earth," the sheriff said wearily, his voice oddly distorted by the volcano-shaped instrument. "Hit the switch and bring Daddy's bridge back to him or I might have to hurt you, John Hardin."

When he heard this, Dupree moved in to take over the negotiations by saying to the sheriff, "Hey, Vandiver, get this straight. You ain't hurting John Hardin."

"Won't be me," the sheriff said. "Regulations say I got to call the SWAT team from Charleston during a siege situation. They're on their way by helicopter."

"What'll they do to John Hardin?" Jack asked.

"They'll kill him," the sheriff said. "Especially since he's armed."

"Call the SWAT team off, Sheriff," Dallas said. "Tell them to turn back. We'll get John Hardin to close the bridge."

"It don't work that way," the sheriff said.

"Then tell them his brothers are here and are going to talk him out of it," Dupree said.

"I'll tell 'em that," the sheriff said, walking back to his car.

John Hardin was watching us carefully as this discussion went on, and he followed the sheriff with his eyes.

"I know what you're saying, Dupree," he shouted. "You're telling everyone I need my shot and then I'll settle down. The world may think I'm crazy, but I think the world's crazy—so who's to say who's right? I'm never letting another car cross this goddamn bridge. Fuck you, Waterford. Fuck you, little town. There's a reason small towns are small. You're small 'cause you're not worth a damn. A boat should never have to wait for a car. A car's an inferior mode of transportation. I've liberated the Waterford River for all the boats in the world."

Dupree stepped forward, the one who loved John Hardin the best and the one John Hardin hated the most.

"Close the bridge, John Hardin," Dupree demanded.

"Eat a big hairy one, Dupree," John Hardin answered, using his middle finger to give his words fuller effect. "This town is so shitty it gave my poor mother leukemia. When I was a kid, nobody died of cancer. Now everybody's got it. Explain that, would you, you stupid sons of bitches. None of you grinning idiots care about how you're screwing up this town. It started with this bridge. Too many assholes crossed this bridge with their golf clubs. They didn't know what matters. Beauty matters . . ."

"I'm going to lose every client in this town tomorrow morning," Dallas whispered to me. "There won't be one left."

"That's all," John Hardin screamed. "Just beauty. You people been to Hilton Head lately? They're gonna sink that poor fucking island with concrete."

"Close the damn bridge, John Hardin," Dupree said, just loud enough for John Hardin to hear him. Commuters began beating their horns in frustration until the noise was too loud for anyone to hear anything else. John Hardin fired a shot into the air and then the sheriff and his deputies began ordering the protesting horns rendered silent.

"That's my brother Dupree," John Hardin screamed from his island of steel. "If they had a contest to find the biggest asshole in the world, I guarantee he'd be a finalist."

"Nevertheless," I shouted back, taking up for Dupree, "please close the bridge, John Hardin. It's me, Jack, talking and asking you to please close that bridge."

"My brother Jack left Waterford and his family to go to a country that only eats lasagna and pizza pie and that kind of shit. So how does he expect to understand I'm not closing the bridge because beauty matters. It really matters."

"Fuck beauty," Tee screamed, exasperated and embarrassed by the ordeal.

"Easy, Tee," Dallas said. "We are face to face with pure madness."

"Great diagnosis," Tee whispered sarcastically.

"When I was a kid there wasn't one new house built on the Isle of Orion. Now there's not a vacant lot on the front beach. Erosion everywhere. Loggerhead turtles can hardly come up on land to lay their eggs. Just imagine what these poor mother turtles think," John Hardin said.

"Turtles don't think. They're just turtles," Dupree said. "You're talking like a dope, John Hardin."

"I never understood why you lived in Europe," Dallas said, "till this very moment."

"Lots of rentals," I said.

"What a loser," Dupree screamed back at John Hardin. "You've been a loser and a phony since the day you were born. Mama just told me that. She's out of her coma."

"Mama's out of her coma?" John Hardin said. "You're lying. Fuck you, Dupree McCall." John Hardin's voice was as poignant as a train whistle now. "I won't close this bridge until everyone shouts, 'Fuck you, Dupree McCall.'"

"Organize the cheer, brothers," Dupree said. "He means it. And if the SWAT team gets here, they'll kill our brother. They don't play."

We ran down a line of cars and enlisted volunteers from the crowd to pass the word from driver to driver. The sheriff shouted instructions to the large gathering on the other side of the bridge as the tension surrounding the siege began to mount and the very air felt dangerous to breathe.

The sheriff took his bullhorn and said, "On three. One. Two. Three . . ."

The town chanted, "Fuck you, Dupree McCall."

"Louder," John Hardin demanded.

"Louder."

"Fuck you, Dupree McCall," the crowd thundered.

"Now close the bridge," Dupree shouted. "Before I come over there and whip your ass."

"You gonna pole-vault, asshole?" John Hardin shouted.

"There are ladies present on the bridge," Dallas said, changing tactics.

"I apologize to all the ladies I might've offended," John Hardin said, and there was true contrition in his voice. "But my mother has leukemia and I'm really not myself today."

"Mama's out of the coma," Dupree shouted again. "She wants to talk to you. She won't see the rest of us until she talks to you. Close the bridge."

"I will under one condition," John Hardin said.

"This'll be good," Dupree said to us, his lips as still as a ventriloquist's. "I've never seen him this bad."

"I want all of my brothers to get stark, buck naked and jump into the river," screamed John Hardin, and there was some laughter in the crowd.

"I'm an attorney in this town," Dallas said. "People don't take their problems to a man seen naked on a bridge."

"We got to do it," Dupree said.

"Fuck you, Dupree McCall," Tee said. "I'm a public school teacher in this state. I can't do it. I just can't."

"If we don't, the SWAT team'll shoot John Hardin."

Dupree had started walking toward the opening of the bridge and was already removing his clothing. The rest of us followed him, also removing our own clothing.

"We get naked," Dupree said, "then you throw the gun in the water. We jump in the water. You close the bridge. Deal?"

John Hardin thought a moment, then said, "Deal."

Dupree stepped out of his underwear, followed by Tee, then me, and finally a very reluctant and grumbling Dallas.

John Hardin grinned happily as he savored the sight of us, his naked and humiliated brothers. "All of you've got little dicks."

Laughter erupted from those within earshot. Even the sheriff and his deputies laughed.

"Are there reporters here?" Dallas asked.

I turned around and saw a photographer with several cameras around his neck and another with a camcorder.

"Photographers too," I reported.

"My career's dead," said Dallas, his despair deepening.

"This news'll go statewide in a flash," Tee said.

Dupree looked up and surveyed the sky, then shouted, "Throw the gun in the water. That was part of the deal."

John Hardin hesitated, then threw the pistol into the saltwater river.

"We're going to jump in," Dallas said. "Then you close the bridge. Deal?"

"The drinking water in this dump of a town gave my mother leukemia. You get your water from the Savannah River, you dumb bastards. It's got nuclear waste, garbage from paper mills . . ."

"Is it a deal?" Dupree repeated. "Mama's out of the coma. She asked about you first. She really wants to see you."

"Mama. Mama," John Hardin cried out.

"A deal?" Dupree said once more.

John Hardin looked back at us. Suddenly his eyes filled with malice, then he screamed, "Jump, you naked bastards, jump. And I hope the sharks eat your tiny little peckers right off. Jump and then I'll close the bridge."

"I'm afraid of heights," Tee said.

"Then I'll help you," Dupree said, as he pushed him off the bridge.

Tee screamed in pure terror all the way down until he hit the water. When he surfaced, the rest of us jumped off the Waterford Bridge together and I think we did it with a fine sense of style.

I hit the April-cool water and went deeper underwater than I'd ever gone in my life, so deep that when I opened my eyes I had to swim blindly upward toward the light. The water was opaque and cloudy with the rich nutrients that grow so abundantly in the jade-bright marsh. When I burst out of the surface of the water, my three brothers' eyes were fixed on the steel girders of the bridge above us and as I looked up the bridge began its ponderous, inanimate swing as John Hardin kept his part of the bargain. The sheriff waved down to us and shouted out his thanks.

The tide was incoming and powerful and we were already a hundred yards upstream when we saw the sheriff and his men put John Hardin in handcuffs and place him in the police car.

"What now?" Tee asked.

"Let's let the tide take us to Dad's house," I said.

"My career's finished," Dallas moaned.

"Go into something new, bro," Tee said. "Like synchronized swimming. Naked."

We laughed and Tee and Dupree immediately dove underwater and their two hairy legs came out side by side with their toes pointed and they kicked in unison a time or two before emerging coughing and blowing water out of their nostrils. But still laughing.

"We do have little dicks," Tee said.

"Speak for yourself, son," Dallas said.

"I can see your dick. We're all hung like

chipmunks," Tee said, floating on his back, sadly examining his barely sufficient genitalia.

"Question," I said, dog-paddling and relieved that the siege was over. "How often does John Hardin go off like that?"

"Two or three times a year," Dupree said. "But this is new. He's never used a gun before and he's never gone up on a bridge. I give him an 'A' for creativity on this one."

"It's sad. So pathetic," Dallas said, floating on his back.

"Yeh, it is," Dupree admitted. "But it's also funny."

"Tell me the funny part," said Dallas. "Our brother's being taken to an insane asylum in handcuffs."

Dupree said, "You ever think you'd jump off a bridge stark naked with the whole town watching?"

I roared with laughter and with love of my brothers as I began to backstroke through the water. For a few moments we swam in silence, and I was lost in thoughts of both exhilaration and sadness. We were low country boys, strong swimmers, good fishermen, who had grown to manhood in a household of secret terrors that had marked each of us in different ways. We carried a strange darkness about us composed of mistrust and distortion. We used laughter as both a weapon and a vaccine.

As we moved, the water felt like cold silk on my body and I had never known such a clean, animal nakedness. I listened to the small talk of my brothers and drew closer to them with every word they spoke. Through them, I could study some of the flaws I brought to bear in my own life. Like me, they had scratchy, muffled temperaments, but were courteous to everyone they met almost to a fault. All were no-nonsense and rough around the edges, but they could look me in the eye, express affection with their laughter, and never appear eager to make it to the nearest door or the next assignment when I was in their company.

We waved to people on the riverbank, and as the tide moved us, I could tell my brothers did not want this day to end any more than I did. Taking turns, we told stories to each other, and my brothers, like me, mark time by cherishing the details that stud the layers of each great story. They were Southern boys and they knew how to make a story sizzle when it hit the fat. Their voices bloomed around me and I loved the sound of my native tongue as it came out of Southern mouths. My brothers talked all at once, shouted each other down, as we floated through the heart of our river, the one that had sung to us as boys. Like evening smoke, I listened to my brothers' speech, their sugary accent with its soft kittenish purr of consonants, its hissing, cottonmouth sibilants, the tenderness of all words passed through the dewdrop illusions of my native tongue.

In a small armada of brothers, I stroked through the waters that led to my father's house aware that I would be on a plane headed for Europe and my daughter the next day and that I had just lived through a week that would change the course of my entire life. I felt ties to this river, to this town, to this open indwelling sky, to everything around me.

My daughter knew none of this or none of what made this so inexpressibly vital to me. Tomorrow, I would return home, tell Leah everything I saw and heard and felt, then trust her openhearted, hungering, and motherless spirit to forgive me. I had taken her away from what we both were. I had given her everything except the South. I had stolen her calling card.

Mike Hess and Ledare drove me to the airport in Savannah the next day and I signed on to do the movie project. Mike had caught me in a weak moment when I found myself fully in love with my own story all over again.

CHAPTER 17

IN THE DERANGED BUT HONORED light that shone down on those years I call my childhood, I grew up in a three-storied, many-roomed house that made me fall in love with impractical architects who conjured alcoves and oddly shaped rooms large enough to spread out in during the most deadly quarrels of my parents. I was a nervous boy and a secret staircase was my favorite room. Because of his love of the law and good bourbon, our father took the house for granted. But my mother breathed the house in through the pores of her skin, knew every inch of it by heart, and would even talk to the house on occasion when lost in her own thoughts during the labors of spring cleaning. To my father, the house was a place to hang his hat and his clothes and store his collection of books, but my mother treated it as a prayer answered by a generous world.

It had been constructed in 1818 in what became known as the Waterford Style; its solid foundations were of stucco over tabby and its two stories of verandas faced east to catch the cool breezes that lifted off the river even during the hottest summer days.

The rooms were spacious and high-ceilinged and there was an attic that smelled of mothballs and cedar and was crammed with enough discarded furniture and chests and piles of drapery to hide a small city of children in peril. But the house had come into the hands of Johnson Hagood and Lucy McCall out of controversy and by accident.

From the beginning of their marriage, we were told that our parents acted like two storm fronts moving against each other. There was something mismatched and synthetic about their union. My source for this disturbing information was my voluble grandmother, Ginny Penn, who always let me believe that my mother had fallen off the back of a cabbage truck and had somehow lured my callow father to the altar. Perhaps reacting to this snobbery of his mother, my dad had brought my mother,

Lucy, to Waterford as his lawfully wedded wife before he had mentioned her name to his parents. No one knew her and not a single citizen of Waterford had ever heard a thing about her people. Nothing is more important to a Southerner than origins and Lucy's were counterfeit the moment she met my father in an Atlanta burlesque club. My father had been drinking and did not know that Lucy was a stripper off duty. Johnson Hagood had just returned from fighting in the European Theater during World War II and had seen enough carnage for a dozen lifetimes. He was looking for a fresh start and Lucy was looking for a way out when they stumbled across each other. Their marriage took place in the office of a justice of the peace near Fort McClellan, my father in his dress uniform, Lucy in a loose, high-necked white dress. I was born five months after their wedding ceremony and my mother used to refer to me as her "love child" until Ginny Penn broke her of the habit. I liked being called a "love child" by my mom.

I knew little of this when I was growing up and learned it piecemeal, in fits and starts, during that time after my mother's first hospitalization for leukemia. The sources were varied and surprising, but the main one became my mother herself. Cancer enabled her to confront a past shockingly bereft of moments of grace.

To Lucy, my father looked high-born and pretty. He appeared to be her best chance to escape a predestined and dreary life and she took it without giving it much thought. Since she had no background at all, Lucy turned all her bright powers of imagination to the task and made one up. When she had to, she invented her own autobiography and when it proved good enough for Johnson Hagood, she incorporated it, word for word, into the story she always told about herself.

My father took Lucy O'Neill at her word and told his parents he had married a dancer from Atlanta who was perfecting her art as a member of the corps de ballet. In 1947, Atlanta did not have a ballet company functioning within the city limits, but our father would have had no way of knowing that particular cultural fact. Lucy O'Neill had an offbeat nuanced kind of beauty that had sprung naturally out of a weedy gene pool heavily posted with warning signs. But it was her figure that drew men to her, those surprising curves that make words like "voluptuous" explode on the tongue with the sweetness of tropical fruit. I have always suspected that my father married the shape of a woman and had not a clue about the nature of that woman herself. He knew she was raw and unschooled, but had no idea she was illiterate. What captivated him was that he thought he saw in her a brightness of pure spirit. But, in fact, he was marrying Lucy O'Neill to hurt his mother and had succeeded beyond his wildest capacity for vengeance. Ginny Penn Sinkler McCall pronounced Lucy "pure trash" the moment she laid eyes on her.

But a burlesque show is not a bad university for a sixteen-year-old girl who has never been to school to earn a degree in the behavior of men. In her world, a woman had to understand the alphabet and text of lust and the lines were easily learned and put to use. Lucy always had an advantage over those combed and pampered women she would later meet in Waterford because her knowledge of men came from the bottom and not from the top. She knew the boys, beer-sodden and screaming in the sawdust for her to take off her bustier and sticking dollar bills in her garters, and did not know the ones in their tuxedos talking about the poems of Sidney Lanier at fraternity parties during the spring. Her view of men was one-dimensional, but not inaccurate: men were prisoners of their genitalia and women were the keepers of the keys to paradise. Her theories about the relationship between men and women were brutally frank and animalistic, and she never changed them during her whole life. At parties, when she moved toward the lines of conversant men, every woman in the room fastened eyes upon her with malignancy and wonder. Though she lacked all polish and refinement, no one understood the basics any better than Lucy McCall.

On the first day she met him, Lucy created for Johnson Hagood her past as an only child in a respected Atlanta family. She had grown up in a Tudor-style house on 17 Palisades Road in the Brookwood Hills section of Atlanta. Her father had been a member of the King and Spaulding law firm, which was known as the only Catholic law firm in the city, and he specialized in trust funds. Her mother, Catherine, had been related to the Atlanta Spauldings on her mother's side and both her parents were members of Sacred Heart Church and her mother had been the first Catholic member of the Atlanta Junior League. Both had been killed in a train wreck in nearby Austell when Garner O'Neill tried to race a train to a crossing.

Lucy was sent to live with a maiden aunt in Albany, Georgia, whom she hated. She had run away from home when she was sixteen and hitched a ride to Atlanta from a farmer delivering eggs to the farmer's market. From 1947 to 1986, this was the official version of Lucy's history and not a word of it was altered for any reason.

• • •

The story was a real one told to her by an older stripper who had been Garner O'Neill's mistress for years, before a train accident took his life and his wife's. Whenever her husband or children asked Lucy questions about her parents, she wept so copiously and spontaneously that all lines of scrutiny or inquiry were cut off at the source. From this, my mother learned the power of both stories and tears. The tragic death of the O'Neills formed the outline of the story she claimed to have lived, but had not. She remained faithful to this story, which gave her more than a passing acquaintance with the soundness of the contrived and made up, the irresistibility of fiction.

Ginny Penn McCall, who had grown up among the Charleston Sinklers and who knew in her bones the subtle secrets of breeding and refinement, spotted Lucy for the phony she was at first sight. By listening to her accent, Ginny Penn could tell that Lucy had not been raised in Atlanta, much less born into a distinguished family. Ginny Penn declared that first evening to her husband that Lucy "was nothing but trash, pure white trash, and I don't believe a single word about her parents or any train wreck at the Austell Crossing." Lucy, knowing she had not fooled Ginny Penn, then set about

to win the affection of her father-in-law, Silas
Claiborne McCall.

He was famous as a hunter and fisherman
in the county, and Lucy soon learned that
Ginny Penn had never fired a rifle in her life.
Leaving her string of sons with Ginny Penn as
the seasons passed, Lucy took to the woods
with Silas when deer season began and was
there in the boat when the shad and the cobia
made their runs upstream during the spring to
lay their eggs in fresh water. During the winters, they sat together in duck blinds waiting for
the flocks of pintails, greenheads, and mallards
to land in flooded rice fields. Because she knew
the secret passwords that accrued around the
selection of tackle and ammunition, Lucy
found the gradual seduction of Silas McCall
child's play. Though Ginny Penn complained
from day one that Lucy did not know the difference between Grecian sterling and Rogers
silverplate, Silas bragged that his daughter-in-
law could cast a line as far as a man and could
track a wild boar through a black water swamp.
Ginny Penn's complaints about Lucy were similar to the ones she had once made about Silas.
When Silas set about measuring the character
of a stranger, Ginny Penn would check the
china cabinet for theft. Silas pronounced to the
town that he thought his daughter-in-law was a
"good ol' girl." That was the highest recom-

mendation among a certain order of Southern men and the thing that Ginny Penn would always hate most about my mother.

In the fall of 1948, after marrying Lucy, Johnson Hagood McCall entered the freshman class of the law school at the University of South Carolina in Columbia through the good offices of the GI Bill. He commuted from Waterford, staying in a boardinghouse three days a week, then returning to his wife and hometown for the rest of the week. The war had raised the level of his ambition and he found the study of law easy. He was well structured, rational, and just, and he discovered he had a gift for argument and wordplay. Law school also gave him a chance to mingle with women who had put off their college educations to work in war-related industries. The company of intelligent women was a forgotten pleasure to him, and that first year it made him critical toward Lucy, whose commonness was highlighted by her vivacity and freshness. An early bitterness set in as Johnson Hagood regretted his impulsive marriage and recognized how little an asset Lucy was going to be. He discovered quite by accident that she had never heard of Mozart or Milton or the Holy Roman Empire. Not only was she unlettered, she seemed to possess almost no natural curiosity at all about his study of jurisprudence.

Each day she listened to the radio and he never saw her reading a book or a magazine and she seemed utterly bored whenever he tried to discuss a thorny problem in contract law with her. When he told her he wanted her to enroll in some college courses to broaden herself, Lucy told him straight out that all her energies and attention would be devoted to the care of her children. If he wanted a college-educated woman, he should have thought about that before he married her. Lucy's happiness with her pregnancy was so touching to Johnson Hagood that he let himself be carried away with the childlike sense of mystery she brought to the task. His capitulation sealed a lifelong pattern between them. The child in Lucy seemed always to reign over the man in my father. "Watch out for vulnerable women," my father would later tell us. "Vulnerable will get you every time."

The pregnancy forced Ginny Penn to action. She practically abducted Lucy to Charleston for a month and conducted a crash course in the customs and courtesies of Southern life. Admonishing Lucy to observe and not to speak, Ginny Penn imparted a basic knowledge of silver, china patterns, table manners, small talk, and codes of conduct during those four weeks of intensive training. In that period, Ginny Penn learned to her dismay that Lucy came from even lower orders of the white South than she had intuited.

At Henry's Restaurant on Market Street, Lucy had studied the menu with care and concentration and then had ordered the same thing Ginny Penn did each and every meal. Ginny Penn thought this showed little imagination or spunk, but it did show a willingness to learn and Lucy's gift for mimicry approached the heroic.

To Ginny Penn's surprise, she found that Lucy was a quick study. When they returned to Waterford, Lucy could hold a fork properly and cut a piece of meat on a Wedgewood plate without drawing attention to herself. She could set a table for ten and knew what to do with a salad fork as well as a fish knife, and understood the difference between a red wine glass and one for white wine. Ginny Penn also taught Lucy how to prepare seven different meals for each day of the week, since Johnson Hagood had complained that Lucy couldn't boil crabgrass. Though not renowned for her own cooking, Ginny Penn had been well schooled in the basics and she had been taught to cook in the distinctive and serious Charleston way. She even imparted to Lucy with great ceremony her secret recipe for crab pilau, a low country dish pronounced with a Huguenot inflection as "purr-low." Cooking, she taught Lucy, was one sure way to discern refinement in a woman. To take cooking too seriously was a sign of discontent, but to have mastered seven unassailable meals that impressed both the palate and the eye was the mark of a serious woman who knew how to get by with just enough.

Soon after she returned to Waterford, Lucy McCall and her husband rented a charming but shabbily renovated slave quarters behind the house of Harriet Varnadoe Cotesworth. Johnson Hagood had to use every ounce of grace and eloquence he possessed to rate an interview with the reclusive Miss Cotesworth, who was one of a long line of oddballs, a species indigenous to the small-town South. She was a rancorous woman with a strong cast toward paranoia who had long been feared in town. Her house had not been painted since the 1920s, and to earn money, she sold off pieces of her family's antique furniture one at a time to Herman Schindler, an antique dealer from Charleston. She agreed to rent to Johnson Hagood because she desperately needed the money and knew that he was related to the Sinklers of Charleston. She made the deal through a half-opened back door and without looking at the face of the man she had rented to nor asking the name of his bride.

Left alone for much of the week as her husband attended law school in Columbia, Lucy began a long slow courtship of Harriet Varnadoe Cotesworth and she used all the tricks she had learned in her in-service training in Charleston. She picked flowers, both wild and cultivated, and arranged them in simple glass vases, then left them on Harriet's back doorstep. Whenever Lucy shopped, she made sure that she bought extra tomatoes or cucumbers or whatever was in season for her landlady. Whenever she made biscuits or baked bread, she made extra for Harriet. There was no guile to this and no motive, but Lucy was as lonely and cut-off in Waterford as Harriet Cotesworth.

While Harriet did not allow Lucy to see her in the first month of the McCalls' residence in the slave quarters, Harriet accepted the gifts of flowers and food. She fastidiously penned thank-you notes on thirty-year-old stationery that Lucy cherished, but could not read. Johnson Hagood would read them aloud for her when he returned home for weekends and Lucy would claim she loved the sound of his voice reading words so delicately strung together. Soon Lucy began to set tasks for Johnson to perform around Harriet's house. One weekend she had him repair Harriet's dangerously undermined front steps. On another, he talked Harriet into letting him up on the roof where he spent two days patching a leak. He was skilled with tools and Harriet soon emerged from her solitude and began to depend on him as a handyman. But it was to Lucy that she lost her heart.

Once, after seeing no sign of life or movement at Harriet's for several days running, Lucy pushed open the back door and entered the mildewed, decaying wreck of a house. Furniture was piled to the ceiling in some of the rooms, but Lucy followed a path through the furniture that led from room to room until she came to a beautifully carved circular stairway.

The house felt as if it were underwater and the mildew had an iodine smell like a bed of kelp. A bit of flowered wallpaper came off in her hand as she began to climb the stairs calling, "Miss Cotesworth, Miss Cotesworth." When she finally got to the master bedroom, she pushed open the door and saw Harriet Cotesworth passed out on her bedroom floor lying in a pool of her own urine.

When Harriet awoke in her bedroom that night, Lucy was with her and she told the older woman that she had double pneumonia, but that old Dr. Lawrence had given her a huge dose of penicillin and thought they had caught the disease in time. Lucy had cleaned up the bedroom and had placed fresh flowers everywhere. She had disinfected the bathroom and changed the linen and thrown open the curtains to sunlight for the first time in years. But Harriet was far too weak and disoriented to complain about anything. Though her blue eyes were suspicious and fearful, she was not conscious long enough to make a scene. When she awoke again, Lucy spoon-fed Harriet homemade vegetable soup.

Lucy nursed Harriet through her bout with pneumonia and did it with grace and good cheer. In those two weeks the Waterford-maligned Miss Cotesworth found the daughter she never bore and in the last two years of Harriet's lifetime Lucy learned how a daughter is supposed to act when a mother figure lies dying before her. Both brought sufficient wounds from their own pasts to make up for the extraordinary abyss that separated them socially.

Harriet continued the process that Ginny Penn had begun in Charleston and began to teach Lucy some of the traps and perils she would encounter during her life in Waterford. The older woman told Lucy of the secrets and scandals that had disfigured the histories of the old families of Waterford. There was nothing like a scandal to demythologize the sheen and vigor of a grand old South Carolina name. She proved this by telling Lucy about the fall of a dozen distinguished families whose patriarchs and sons could not keep their hands off girls from the lower classes. Though Harriet was

telling the same story that had befallen Johnson Hagood, she did not seem to make the connection, for her growing affection for Lucy had
blinded her.

On November 5, 1948, I was born in an upstairs bedroom of the Varnadoe Cotesworth
house in the four-poster bed where generations
of both Varnadoes and Cotesworths had been
born. I was christened Johnson Varnadoe
Cotesworth McCall at Harriet's insistent
urging, and Lucy was delighted to comply since
the name infuriated Ginny Penn. All Waterford
laughed when Lucy bestowed this honorable,
tongue-twisting name on her firstborn son, but
Harriet Varnadoe Cotesworth wept with happiness. It had been her intention to name a son
after her beloved father and she'd finally lived
to see this wish consummated.

The Varnadoe Cotesworth in the central
nervous system of my baptismal name caused
me great discomfort during my childhood because the whole town knew that I was no
Cotesworth and had never laid eyes on a natural-born Varnadoe. My passport and driver's license identified me always as John V. C. Mc-
Call and during the Vietnam War I claimed to
campus activists at the university that my parents had named me for the Viet Cong.
Throughout my life, it was only with a rare
friend or deep in the middle of a drunken eve-

ning when I would reveal, with shame and apology, the pretentious midlands of my given name.

For six months Waterford laughed at Lucy's grandiosity until Harriet died suddenly in her sleep. The laughter stopped forever when Harriet's will was read and everything she owned, including the Varnadoe Cotesworth house, went to Johnson Hagood and Lucy McCall.

Ownership transfigured Lucy. She loved the size and shape and simple grandeur of the house where she would raise her children. The house imparted to my mother a passion for beautiful architecture, an uncanny eye for antiques, the habits of a gardener, the compulsiveness of a birdwatcher, and a love of the sound of rainwater tap-dancing on an oxidized tin roof during a summer storm. Both she and my father restored the rundown overload of antiques they found in the rooms and halls and attics throughout the house. The house brought them together in a way nothing else had done, not even my birth.

The Varnadoe Cotesworth house was a valediction of my parents' queer union, but the story behind their unexpected inheritance transfigured my mother and made her feel that she might be in the middle of living out a lucky life despite everything. Lucy called it the greatest story ever to come out of the South and told it to those reverential clusters of tourists who would traipse through our house each year in the Spring Tour. My mother would dress up in Southern crinolines, her bare shoulders pretty in the candlelight, and give the visitors a brief history of her house before she blew their socks off and changed the Spring Tours forever by relating the story that Harriet Cotesworth had told her in the days leading up to my birth.

Each year my brothers and I would gather to hear my mother describe the lovely Elizabeth Barnwell Cotesworth, Harriet's great-aunt, who once walked the wide board pine floors where we played as rough and tumble boys. She would tell her story with such passionate conviction that we, her worshipful sons, would think she was narrating the tale of her own maidenhood, when we thought she must have appeared as lovely and magical to young men as she did to us.

"Her name was Elizabeth Barnwell Cotesworth," my mother would begin, "and she was born in the bedroom where my own son Jack was born well over one hundred years later. Her beauty was legendary by the time her parents sent her to a finishing school in Charleston. While attending a dance South of Broad, Elizabeth first met a presentable young lieutenant stationed at Fort Moultrie by the name of William Tecumseh Sherman. One dance with her put this West Point graduate under her spell."

Whenever Lucy mentioned the name of the Anti-Christ, Sherman, a gasp would go up from the assemblage who were mostly southern and had grown up with their relatives passing down stories of Sherman's rape and despoliation of the South. No Southerner, no matter how liberal of spirit, could ever forgive Sherman's prodigious March to the Sea when he broke the back of the Confederacy forever. My mother played the crowd's abhorrence of Sherman for all it was worth. We would stand above her, lined along the banisters in our pajamas, and my mother would wink at us and we would wink back as her voice continued to weave the spell of Elizabeth and her suitor. Though the crowd never saw us, we kept in Lucy's line of sight and her story thrilled us every time we heard her tell it. Each year, we heard the story grow and change as she added details of her own. Because the story of Sherman and Elizabeth belonged to my mother and to her alone, it marked the beginning of her transfiguration in Waterford society. All through my childhood, she met those well-dressed crowds on the Spring Tour who moved from street to street led by guides who carried silver candelabras to light their paths. Since she had been onstage before, Lucy found that playing her part of a

Southern lady of breeding and leisure was easy. When she greeted the hushed, shuffling throngs who approached these old houses as though they were private chapels, Lucy could hear the in-drawn breath of the entire group as she made her appearance on her own veranda wearing a dress that Ginny Penn had given her. Through the years, as my mother gained confidence in herself and in her position in the town, she became famous in the neighborhood for her storytelling gift. My mother gave credit where credit was due and claimed she owed it all to General Sherman. My poor brother Tee, who grew up mortified by his given name, Tecumseh, was christened in honor of the soldier, not the great chieftain.

When I was a senior in high school, one of my Christmas gifts was my own ticket to the annual Spring Tour of homes. Many of the parents of my classmates went in together and got a special group rate, thinking it was high time that their graduating seniors learned about the architectural glories of our town. That night, in 1966, I approached the house I grew up in as a tourist for the first time and I shared the crowd's wonder when my mother stepped out in her Southern plantation dress, her hair done in ringlets, her face aglow in the soft, falling light of candles. I looked upstairs and saw my younger brothers positioning themselves between the spaces of the dowels on the upstairs veranda. In the early years my mother was callow and got many of her facts wrong but she told the story of the house on this night with an air of solid professionalism. Her voice was lovely as she welcomed the group that gathered in a semicircle before her front steps. When she welcomed the ten seniors from Waterford High, we let out a great cheer.

I was holding hands with Ledare Ansley and we were coming to the end of our high school romance. Jordan was dating Shyla and Mike and Capers had brought the sassy McGhee twins whose parents sat on the Board of the Historic Foundation. I had always heard the Sherman story hidden away in shadows, catching snatches of it as my mother led the crowd from room to room.

I cannot tell you how proud I was that night when I listened to my mother's voice begin to tell the story of Harriet Varnadoe Cotesworth, which led to the story of Harriet's great-aunt Elizabeth. She had been born in a rare Waterford snowstorm and some of Elizabeth's extraordinary charm was attributed to the six inches of snow that blanketed the town on the night of her birth. As I heard Lucy list all the delicious details of Elizabeth's life proclaiming the former occupant's specialness and all-absorbing rarity, once again I fell under her spell.

Making a motion for all of us to follow, my mother led the visitors into the living room where she waited patiently for all to settle in before she continued. Shyla held onto Jordan's arm, saw me watching them, and blew me an exaggerated kiss that I pretended to catch in midair. Mike Hess carried a passion for history even then and he hung on every word my mother spoke. Capers lifted up a serving dish from a secretary in the hallway, turned it over, and read the word "Spode" to himself. Capers knew well my mother was an upstart and a pretender and he hoped to catch her in an error of taste. But Lucy had a seventeen-year-head start on him and she long ago had perfected her game plan. What was inauthentic in our house, and there was much, was kept well out of sight during these azalea-rich days of the Spring Tour. In the early years, she had made such missteps, but social humiliation was a fast cure for either oversight or ignorance. She covered her traces well and never made the same mistake twice.

"After that first dance, Lieutenant Sherman wrote to Elizabeth in the raw, honest prose style he would use in his memoirs. He told her that his dance with her had changed his life forever."

"Do I have that same effect on you, Jordan?" I heard Shyla whisper near me.

"The same," Jordan whispered in her ear.

"And you, Jack?" she said, winking at me.

"Elizabeth," I whispered to her. "Oh, Elizabeth." And Shyla curtsied and an older lady put her finger to her lips.

"Sherman told her that it was the first time in his life that he consciously wished for a band to play on forever and for a waltz to never end," my mother said. "But he had to join a veritable army of low country gentlemen who knew that Elizabeth was the one exceptional prize of that season. All the Charleston boys were mad for our Elizabeth.

"But it was Sherman who intrigued her, Sherman she wrote home about to her mother and father, who read these letters in this very room. She described the walks that she and her lieutenant took in the long afternoons. The walks were slow and intimate and they told each other secrets about themselves they had never told anyone else."

Capers raised his hand and Lucy said, "Yes, Capers, do you have a question?"

"Was Sherman handsome?" he asked. "I always thought he was ugly as homemade sin."

The members of the group laughed demurely.

"Was Sherman as good-looking as Capers?" Mike said. "That's all Capers really cares about, Mrs. McCall."

Again there was good-natured laughing and Lucy said, "He was not considered a handsome man by his contemporaries. But as many of the women in this room could tell you, looks are not always the main thing. There is the matter of character, ambition, and passion. People speak of his intensity. There was even rumor of a Charleston boy from a good family who wanted to challenge Sherman to a duel because of Elizabeth. But it was Sherman's look that made him think Sherman might be the wrong man to challenge.

"Sherman kissed Elizabeth, at least once, and there is proof of this in a letter that Elizabeth wrote to her young niece, Harriet Cotesworth's mother. After that kiss, both felt themselves betrothed to each other forever. It was then that Sherman came to this house to meet Elizabeth's parents. It was in this room that Sherman asked to have a word with Elizabeth's father alone. He asked Mr. Cotesworth for his daughter's hand in marriage. When Elizabeth and her mother returned from a nervous walk in the garden, both women broke into tears when they smelled cigar smoke. Let us go into the library and I'll tell you what happened."

My mother led the way, slim-waisted and girlish, and I felt myself about to burst with pride for her bravura performance. She had turned herself, through years of dedication and hard work, into a woman worthy to live in this house. A fierce antodidact, she had remade herself into something she had not been born to be. I felt like carrying a sign saying that it was my mother conducting this tour and telling this story. Already, I could feel the group hooked by the unlikely romance of Sherman and Elizabeth.

"What happened?" Mike Hess said as the tour settled about the library with its leatherbound sets of books.

"Whatever it was, it sure wasn't good for the South," an elderly man said. "She's talking about the devil incarnate."

"The Sherman boy sounds kind of sweet to me," the man's wife said, teasing him.

"On May 13, 1846, Congress declared war on Mexico," my mother said, "and the following week Lieutenant Sherman received orders that his battalion would join the Army of the West before moving out to the territory of New Mexico to defend Santa Fe."

"What about Elizabeth?" Shyla asked.

"Did she get married, Mrs. McCall?" Jordan asked.

My mother played the crowd perfectly, then said, "William Tecumseh Sherman and Elizabeth Barnwell Cotesworth never laid eyes on each other again."

There was an audible gasp and Lucy waited

a moment before resuming her narrative. But now she had them all in the palm of her hand and I learned much about how to hold the attention of strangers by observing my mother closely that evening. Her voice began again, rising up above the breathless, ingathered group who strained to hear her every word.

After a full year passed, they broke off their engagement with great regret on both sides and six months later Elizabeth married Tanner Prioleau Sams, a merchant from Charleston with an impeccable family line and possessor of all the effortless grace of the Southern manner that Sherman, with his chilly Midwestern reserve, had lacked. Tanner Sams had been the spurned suitor who had talked of challenging the young Sherman to a duel because of his courtship of Elizabeth. Patience and the outbreak of a strange war won the heart of Elizabeth for Tanner Sams, who remained grateful to the armies of Santa Anna until his dying days.

So Elizabeth faded into her role of wife and mother and hostess and, by all accounts, brought a great dignity to every aspect of her life. Her character was true and her beauty deepened with the years and even Mary Chesnut cited her attendance at three balls in her Civil War diary and each citation was more glittering than the last.

After the Civil War began, Sherman did not come South again until he came to set it on fire. He made the South suffer and burn in the high octane of its own passionate codes. More than any other Northern general, Sherman loved the South because he understood both its pride and contradictions, but this knowledge did not keep him from moving through its mountains and river valleys with a cold and unstinting fury. He had come with his men from the Mississippi to the city limits of Atlanta and he had watched his armies choking on their own blood and leaving the corpses of tens of thousands of Illinois and Ohio boys planted forever in Southern earth his men had made holy by their sacrifices. Cutting his supply lines, Sherman laid waste to Atlanta and taught his soldiers the value of matches when you wanted an enemy whimpering and on his knees. Sherman remembered his elegiac time in Charleston and the extraordinary love that Southerners exhibited toward their fragrant land and comely houses. For five hundred miles, he ravished that pretty South and burned every house his armies approached. From Chickamauga to the Atlantic, he rode out the seasons, moved his men with relentless and inexorable cunning, and wrote his name in fire and blood across the sacrificial body of Georgia.

Sherman made the boys of the South shed

their blood and their lives in a hundred Southern streams and fields and roadsides. He made
Southern women scream out for their dead and
wounded and he found out that the suffering of
bereaved and hungry women could be as effective as a fresh regiment in bringing a war to its
close. He cut through Georgia as if the state
were made of butter and he taught the state
some unalterable lessons about the horror of
warfare. Through the long cool autumn of
1864, he rode with his army loose in the field,
moving unappeasably through the smoke of
burning plantations as the South's first con-
queror.

Sherman's name became the vilest two-syllable word in the South. Beautiful women with
the manners of countesses spat in the dirt after
pronouncing his name aloud.

Sherman was leading his men toward Savannah and the trading lanes of the Atlantic
and the history of military strategy. He was riding toward Elizabeth. My mother continued,
"When General Sherman took Savannah after
his pillage of Georgia, it was greatly feared that
he would aim his armies at Charleston, the city
and the populace that had begun the hostilities
in the War Between the States. Charleston had
endured a bitter siege and all were preparing to
evacuate the city before the onslaught of Sherman's army. The citizens of Charleston had al-

ready decided to burn Charleston to the ground by their own hand and not to allow the hordes of Sherman to put the holy city to the torch. Those who loved Charleston would burn it. The Yankees were not worthy of such distinction.

"Rumors abounded that Sherman had moved his armies across the Savannah River and those rumors proved true. The entire South and the entire nation waited to hear that Sherman had turned the fury of his forces on the city that had begun the terrible conflict. But as he reached Pocotaligo, Sherman turned his armies on a surprise advance and drove them toward Columbia, where he wreaked great havoc and burned that city to the ground.

"After Sherman made his surprise move and razed that city, he wrote a letter to Elizabeth's mother, who still lived in this house. When the Yankees had taken over Waterford early in the war, her mother had refused to flee and spent the entire war under Yankee domination. They accorded her great respect. This is the letter that General Sherman wrote to Elizabeth's mother," she said.

My mother walked the length of the library as the crowd parted to let her pass. She flicked on an electric switch lighting a Chinese vase lamp that illuminated a framed, handwritten letter hanging on the wall.

"Since all of you can't get close enough, I'll read this aloud if you don't mind."

But my mother did not have to read the letter on the wall; she had long ago committed it to memory and there was not a sound in the house as we listened to my mother's voice.

Dear Mrs. Cotesworth,

I remember my evening in your house with great pleasure and much sadness. I heard about the death of your husband at Chancellorsville and that news caused me much grief. I noted that the cavalry charge he was leading at the time broke the Union line and inflicted heavy casualties on the Union forces. There was honor in his death and I hope that brings you solace.

By now, you have heard that I am leading my army against the Confederate forces defending Columbia. The South is broken and the war will soon be over. I would like you to extend my greetings to your daughter, Elizabeth, and to tell her that I still hold her in the highest regard. I have never been sure if the war against Mexico and the great victories won by the American forces there were worth the loss of Elizabeth. I have thought of her many times as my army has moved through the South and inexorably approached that part of the world that Elizabeth once made magic for me by her simply being alive.

I would like you to pass a message to your daughter. Tell Elizabeth that I present her the city of Charleston, as a gift.

Very Sincerely,
Wm. T. Sherman
General of the Army

No tour group in history ever got more bang for their buck than those lucky house-lovers who were led through the Varnadoe Cotesworth house by my mother. I knew that every time she told that story she was trying to regain something for herself. My mother wanted someone to feel about her the way Sherman did about Elizabeth and she knew that my father would never be that man. I used to stand on our dock looking back at that sun-struck house of my childhood and tell myself that I would one day love a woman the way Sherman did. I wanted to walk the whole world until I found a girl I could write letters to that her descendants would hang up on library walls. I would march to the sea with that girl's name on my lips, and I would write her name in the sands until the tides washed over it. The story marked me. But it changed my mother's life.

She had made the story hers and hers alone. It struck a chord of abundance and resonance deep within her. It could not mask the limitless hurt she had suffered as a child, but it could give her a rich faith in the future, in all the negotiable currency of pure possibility. This great story made the truth bearable for my mother. Against all odds, Lucy was the keeper of Elizabeth's house, the owner of General Sherman's pure cry of human loss and love.

As the crowd moved down the steps away from the house, my brothers called out to me and I turned around to wave good-bye to them. I would be leaving the house forever in several months and my sweet brothers would be left to their own devices.

"Hey, good-looking," my mother called out, "you're not getting away without kissing your mother good night."

I blushed but ran up the stairs and my mother hugged me tightly to her. Mike and Capers and Jordan applauded loudly and I blushed again.

My mother rubbed the lipstick from my cheek and we looked at each other suddenly and all the swiftness and cruelty of time came over me in a rush and almost brought me to my knees. My mother saw it too and felt it. Her eyes fastened on me and her hand touched my cheek.

"General Sherman, General Sherman," a girl's voice cried out. "We're leaving now."

The voice was exaggerated and Southern and my mother laughed and said, "He's coming, Elizabeth."

I ran toward the voice and the outstretched hand and was surprised to see it was Shyla.

PART III

CHAPTER 18

AS A TRAVEL WRITER, I KNOW MY AIR-
ports and I know every square foot of the Leonardo da Vinci airport in Rome by heart. But
on the day my mother touched down for her
first visit to Italy the following December, the
airport itself seemed transformed and magni-
fied by the significance of my mother's arrival.
We had nearly lost her in that first week when
she had been in the coma and her recovery had
assumed magic proportions for all of us. It had
brought me back into the family circle after a
long intermezzo of sadness and lost time when
I tried to heal a spirit badly damaged by Shyla's
death. I had reconnected with something of the

highest consequence and the repercussions of that visit rang in the deepest channels with an echoing richness that amazed me. Going back to see my stricken mother, it never occurred to me that I would encounter my lost self waiting for me at her bedside.

As the passengers began to make their way out of the double doors, past the customs inspectors and the unsmiling soldiers armed to the teeth, I pointed out my mother to Leah and said, "Go give that woman a hug. That's your grandmother, Leah."

Leah moved easily through the crowd and I trailed behind her. As Lucy searched for us, Leah approached her and said, "Ciao, Grandma. I'm Leah McCall, your granddaughter."

Lucy looked down at her dark-eyed, lovely grandchild and said, "Where you been all my life, darling?" then knelt down on the floor and folded Leah into her arms. Then she rose and kissed me. We collected her bags and Lucy, holding Leah's hand, followed me out of the Rome airport and into a Roman taxicab.

My mother's recovery was remarkable and her face shone with a ruddy good health that seemed impossible after the no-holds-barred assault her body had just withstood. Her hair had grown back though it was very short; her step was light, and I saw more than one middle-aged Italian man give her the once-over with their languorous, appreciative glances. She had written me that she was walking five miles a day and had only missed a single month of checking the beach each summer morning for the signs of a nesting loggerhead turtle. Even in December, my mother had the best suntan in the airport.

Lucy looked out at the throngs pressing forward to meet travelers and shook her head at the noise and congestion. "Gives new meaning to the phrase 'Chinese fire drill,'" she said.

"I'm trying to raise Leah not to be a racist, Mom," I said good-naturedly.

"That's not racist. I've never seen a Chinese fire drill in my life," Lucy said, "until just now."

She took out her Italian money, which she had acquired in Savannah for the trip, and showed it to Leah. Holding a thousand-lire note, she said, "I don't know whether that's worth a nickel or a billion dollars."

"Think of that as a one-dollar bill, Grandma," Leah said.

"What a smart little girl," Lucy said. "A girl with a head for figures doesn't need to worry about hers."

"You look great, Mama," I said. "Remission becomes you."

"I was bald as a pig for a couple of months," she said. "If you've got any extra money lying around, invest in wigs, son. You've got beautiful hair, Leah. Just like your mother had."

"Thank you, Grandma," Leah responded.

"I've got more presents for you in my bags than I have clothes," Lucy said. "Everybody in Waterford sent you a present, because they want you to know how badly we want you to come home."

"December 27," Leah said. "We're going back to Waterford with you. You're going to love Christmas in Rome, Grandma."

"Do you remember how much I loved you as a baby, Leah?" Lucy asked, hugging the child to her.

"I can't remember anything about South Carolina," Leah said. "I've tried, but I just can't."

"Next summer I'm going to have you work in my turtle program on the Isle of Orion. We're saving the great loggerhead turtle from extinction."

"Wow. And I can see all this?" Leah said happily.

"See it?" Lucy said. "I'm going to train you to be a turtle lady."

"Waterford must be so wonderful," Leah said. "Do you know, Grandma, you're the first person I've ever met who knew the Great Dog Chippie besides Daddy."

"Chippie?" Lucy said glancing sideways and oddly at her son. "A great dog."

"I tell stories about Chippie to Leah," I explained.

"What's to tell," my mother said, puzzled. "Chippie was a mutt. A stray."

"No, Mama," I said and she caught the slight disapproval in my voice. "Chippie was a magnificent beast. Fearless, brilliant, and a great protector of the McCall family."

"He sure saved the McCall family a bunch of times, didn't he, Grandma?" Leah said.

Lucy finally got it. "Oh yes," she said. "I don't think any of us would be here today if it wasn't for Chippie. . . . That great, great dog."

That night, when I was putting Leah to bed, she hugged me tightly and thanked me for allowing her grandmother's visit.

"I love your mother, Daddy," Leah said. "She is so sweet to me and you're exactly like her."

"Please," I cautioned. "Don't go overboard."

"It's true," Leah said, "and she said I'm the spitting image of Mama. What does that mean?"

"Spitting image?" I said. "It means you look exactly like your mother. Would you like me to tell you a story? How about the time that

Shyla and I fell in love at the beach? Or any of the others?"

"Was your mother a good storyteller, Daddy?"

"She was the best," I conceded. "No one could lie like my mother."

"Is a story always a lie?"

I thought carefully before I answered. "No, a story is never a lie," I said. "A story gives only pleasure. A lie gives mostly pain."

"Then I want my grandmother to tell me a story," Leah said. "That won't make you feel bad, will it, Daddy?"

"Let me go get her," I said.

"Good night," Leah said, kissing me. "I only like Great Dog Chippie stories when I'm feeling sad. Tonight, I feel happier than ever."

In the living room, I looked out on the Piazza Farnese and watched the Romans hurrying through the cold, shut-down streets. I could see both the pedestrians and my own anonymous image in the reflected, back-lit window. In the same pane of glass, I could have an unseen surveillance of unknown Romans or the luxury of self-study. The travel writer was looking inward and I examined myself.

I had just turned thirty-seven years old but the slouching figure I saw squinting back at me in light and glass high above the piazza had felt inanimate and peripheral to the main flow of action for too long now. The figures below me seemed charged with purpose as they made their way across the piazza and disappeared into one of the seven streets that led into the heart of Renaissance Rome. They strode with purpose, armed with resolution, whereas everything I did seemed insubstantial and forced. I longed for engagement, intrusion, and a little more Mardi Gras than Lent in my life. Perhaps because of my mother's arrival and her surprising vigor, I realized that I had satisfied myself with observer status in the human race for too long. Caution had wounded me. Fear had gotten too tight a hold on me; it had slowed my step, eclipsed my spontaneity, my willingness to take a corner on two wheels. I saw myself as I was, framed in that window—a man afraid of women, of love, of passions, and the staying power of friends. At this crossroads of my life, all ways looked appealing and I knew that was exactly what was wrong with me.

I heard my mother enter the room behind me: "It's cold as Alaska in here. Don't they believe in heat in this country?"

"I'll turn it up. These old buildings are drafty," I said.

"Also be a darling and get your sweet mama a Chivas Regal on the rocks," Lucy murmured. "They do have ice in this country, don't they?"

I fixed her a drink, made myself one, turned up the heat, and walked back toward the living room. Lucy was standing in front of the long glass windows that I had just left, watching the movement of people below.

"What are those folks doing?" she asked.

She turned to receive her drink and said, "Thank you, darling. I feel perfectly dreadful, like a herd of bison just trampled me down-wind."

"It's jet lag. You probably should get to bed."

"I've got dozens of letters to give to you," Lucy said. "And messages galore, but they can wait. What's this rumor about you and Jordan Elliott?"

"Just a rumor," I said. "There's nothing to it."

"There's nothing more tacky than a son telling lies to his dying mother," Lucy said.

"You're not dying," I said. "Don't talk like that."

"I'm officially dying," Lucy said proudly. "I've got a letter from my doctor to prove it. Tell Jordan this is my last chance to see him."

"I don't know what you're talking about," I lied, feeling trapped by the woman who had both taught me to hate lies and to use them when necessary.

"He would adore seeing me," she said, for

it was impossible for Lucy to believe that any man would deny himself the pleasure of her company.

"Is there anything you'd like to see especially during your time in Rome?" I asked, changing the subject.

"Lourdes," she said.

"Lourdes?" I asked.

"Yes. Lourdes," Lucy answered.

"That's in France, Mama," I said. "This is Italy."

"Isn't that just up the road?" she asked.

I laughed and said, "No. It's not just up the road."

"Well, if my life is so unimportant to you, I guess we can just skip Lourdes," Lucy said, pouting.

"Mama," I said, "I've been to Lourdes. It's all bullshit and it's a thousand miles from here."

My mother answered, "It is not."

"Mama, I'm a travel writer. I know how far it is from fucking Rome to Lourdes."

"You don't have to resort to vulgarity," Lucy admonished.

"The miracle business is in a slump," I said.

"Well, I heard there were some churches in Rome where miracles've occurred," Lucy continued.

I snapped my fingers. "Why didn't I think

of that? Of course, Mama. You want miracles. This city's loaded with miracles. There's the church with a piece of the true cross and the one with the crown of thorns. We'll have a ball. We'll go to every miracle-working church in the city and I haven't even mentioned St. Peter's."

"I must go to the Vatican," Lucy said.

"I've gotten you an audience with the Pope," I said, "and we're all going to Midnight Mass at St. Peter's."

"An audience with the Pope," Lucy exclaimed breathlessly. "What dress should I wear? Thank God I have my real hair back. I look kind of trampy in my wig."

"Get some sleep now, Mama," I said. "You'll need to get rested before you can start enjoying Rome."

"I'm enjoying it already," she said. Then she paused. "Is there any special lady friend you might want me to meet?"

"No," I said. "There is no special lady friend I'd like you to meet."

"That little girl deserves a mother," Lucy said. "It may not be my place to say it, but Leah's simply starved for feminine affection. She's got those funny eyes that a motherless child always gets."

"She does not," I said, irritated.

"You can't see it," Lucy said, "because you don't want to see it. You need to be out beating the bushes, flushing out that poor girl a mama."

"She doesn't need a mother," I said, angry that I could not purge the defensiveness from my voice. "Maria loves her as much as any mother could."

"Maria doesn't speak English," Lucy said. "How can Leah learn about maternal love from someone who can't even speak the language."

"I'd be better off if you hadn't been able to speak English," I said.

Her laughter was a shiny thing, like pewter flung high in the air, and she laughed all the way down the long hall to her bedroom.

We visited the churches, chapels, and basilicas of Rome seeking the saint that would intercede for Lucy. And while we did I taught her to appreciate the coffee of Rome, stopping often for a quick espresso or cappuccino. Each day we had lunch at Da Fortunato and Freddie would wait on us with his impeccable manners and fractured English. Freddie doted on Lucy and lunch became both a feast of antipasti and pastas and a time for Lucy at the age of fifty-eight to practice the art of innocent seduction in a city that honored food and seduction far more than innocence.

Altogether we visited twenty-one tombs of exalted individuals lucky enough to have made it into the Calendar of Saints. Lucy kept a meticulous list of the tombs she had prayed before. She revealed that she was certain that a delegation of these saints would be there to greet her if her prayers went unanswered and she happened to die. I would roll my eyes, but my mother was unflappable and tireless as I escorted her through those dark, ornamental streets whose buildings blushed with the harmonious rouges of time, some ocher, some tinted with cinnamon, some with a brushed, uncertain gold.

In each church, as we were leaving, Lucy would take handfuls of holy water and scoop it up and douse her lymph nodes where the killer cells of her leukemia had clustered. Then she would walk gamely out of the church dripping holy water off her winter coat for half a block. This baptismal ceremony seemed ludicrous to me, to say nothing of embarrassing.

"It comforts me," Lucy would say, sensing my displeasure. "Just put up with it."

"Why don't I just have a priest bless the water in the Trevi Fountain," I asked, "and you can swim a couple of laps in it every day?"

"You always fail when you try to be witty," she said.

"We're going to be the first people ever arrested for excessive use of holy water," I said.

"The Church can afford it, son," Lucy said.

"Finally, we've reached an area of theological agreement," I said.

Since I give one of the great tours of the Forum, I thought I would trick my mother into some real sight-seeing by taking her down into the ruins of that unburied city. But nothing I told her about the workings of the Roman Senate or the rise and fall of Caesars interested her in the slightest. She was single-minded in her unswayable desire to win sympathy and medical intercession from some minor saint and had no curiosity about pre-Christian Rome at all.

"These are just rocks," my mother said as I explained why the Arch of Titus was erected. "If I wanted to see rocks, I'd take a ride up to the Smokies."

"This is one of the places Western civilization sprang out of," I intoned.

"You sound like a brochure," she said, looking at the guidebook I had written. "Your books are hard to follow."

"You don't have to look at the book, Mother dear," I said. "You're with me."

She said, "You just go on and on so. Just summarize. Wrap it up."

"Oh," I said, barely containing myself. "That's the Forum, Mom. Now let me take you to other piles of rock. But before we go, let me show you the Temple of Saturn. Ask this God to cure your leukemia."

"What God?" my mother asked.

"Saturn," I said happily. "Top of the line Roman God. It can't hurt."

"I'll not have strange gods before me," she said proudly.

"Picky, picky," I said, turning toward the eight columns. "Saturn, please cure my poor mama of cancer."

"Don't listen to him, Saturn," Lucy said, "The boy's cutting the fool."

"Just covering all the bets," I said, leading my mother up toward the Campidoglio.

The day before Christmas, I took Lucy to the Church of Santa Maria della Pace so she could cleanse her soul of all sin before she received Communion at Midnight Mass on Christmas. We ambled through the Piazza Navona, stopping at booth after booth so Lucy could buy figurines of the Holy Family, gaudily decorated wise men, and placid-faced shepherds for her manger back in Waterford. The piazza shimmered with a seasonal carnality and hustlers moved with the ease of lynxes among the tourists. An elegant woman in a fur argued with a shrill peasant from the Apennines over the price of a recumbent Christ Child. A street artist without a smidgen of talent chalked a portrait of a Japanese woman who complained that the artist had made her look Korean.

Entering the church, I pointed out the

graceful expressive sibyls painted by Raphael, but once again, my mother was uninterested in art when there was work to be done on her soul. She looked around at the dark line of confessionals and said, "How do I confess when I don't know a word of Italian?"

"Here's an Italian dictionary," I said, handing her a small book.

"Very funny," Lucy said. "This is one dilemma for pilgrims that never occurred to me."

"But it occurred to Mother Church," I said, pointing to a confessional at the rear of the church. "There's an English-speaking priest in there. What are your sins? It's hard to commit a sin on chemotherapy."

"I despaired a few times, son," Lucy said, not understanding that I was trying to joke with her.

"That's not a sin, Mama," I said. "That's modern life tapping you on the shoulder and saying 'hi.' "

"I shouldn't be long," my mother said as she entered the brown-curtained confessional and I heard the priest's screen slide back with a click.

I listened to the murmur of my mother's voice behind the velvet curtain and the lower register of the priest's voice in response. Kneeling, I tried to pray, but I could not feel much action in the regions where the soul most frequently moved about looking for comfort. So often when I came to a church I would find myself considering the floor plans of nothingness instead of trying to strike up a conversation with God. As a child I spoke easily with him, but I had a gentler gift for small talk then and took myself less seriously.

My mother suddenly stuck her head out the curtain and stared at me. "Are you playing a trick on me?"

"Took you a while," I said.

"For penance, this priest gave me five Our Fathers, five Hail Marys, and said I had to bake him a dozen chocolate chip cookies."

"These modern priests," I said. "They're going too far."

"Jordan loved my cookies," she said, then turned back to the confessional.

"This is a church, madam," I heard Jordan say. "I find your behavior appalling."

Both came out of the confessional at the same time and I watched as my mother jumped up into Jordan's arms and he held her, rocking her, with her feet dangling off the ground.

"This means, Jordan, that some prayers are truly answered," she said.

"For me too," he said.

"Since the day you disappeared, I've prayed that you were alive and well," Lucy said.

"Your prayers helped. I felt them," Jordan said, putting her down on the marble floor.

"Please. I just had lunch," I said.

"Ignore him," said Lucy.

"I always have," Jordan laughed.

"Are you a real priest?"

"That's what they tell me," he said. "I just made your soul shiny for God. You're all set for Midnight Mass at St. Peter's."

"Does Jack go to confession?"

"Never," Jordan said. "He's incorrigible."

"Make him," my mother said.

"Unfortunately, Jack has free will just like the rest of us," he said.

"You look wonderful. Just like a priest."

"You're still one of the prettiest women on earth, Lucy," Jordan said.

"Your order needs to spend more money on optometrists," she said. "But thanks."

"See you at the Vatican," Jordan said. "Bye, Lucy. Bye, Jack."

That night the three of us took great care in dressing for a Christmas party before we went off to Mass at St. Peter's. I took my time putting on my tuxedo and Leah came in to insert my cuff links and admire me. Leah wore a long white dress with a scooped neckline that showed off both her fragility and comeliness. Taking a string of pearls from Shyla's jewel box,

I placed them around Leah's neck as we both stared in pleasure into the antique mirror.

"Daddy, I'd like to get my ears pierced," Leah said to me, the girl in the mirror speaking in the same precise voice as the child below me.

"Aren't you too young for that?" I asked her.

"Three girls in my class have their ears pierced," Leah said. "I'd like to wear Mama's earrings. They're so pretty."

"We'll see," I said, looking at Leah. Her eyes were palace brown, like Rome.

"May I wear lipstick tonight?" Leah asked.

"Yes. If you'd like."

"I would very much."

"Do you know how to put it on?" I asked.
"I don't."

"Of course," Leah said. "I practice whenever I spend the night at Natasha's house."

Leah unfastened an evening purse that had belonged to Shyla and took out a tube of lipstick. She pursed her lips and expertly applied the lipstick to her curving pretty bottom lip. Then she mated her lips together and moved them back and forth until the top lip had reddened congruently with the lower one. This gesture of Leah's, this application of lipstick in all its simplicity and innocence, I realized, was one of the first of those unrecallable milestones passed by every child in her inexorable passage out of her parents' lives. Her body was a time-piece and Leah, not I, was its contented owner.

Lucy walked straight into this rite of passage and said loudly, "Oh no you don't, young lady."

She marched over to the mirror and took the lipstick out of Leah's hand.

"You're far too young for lipstick, Leah. And you can march right to your bedroom and take off those pearls too. It's vulgar to put pearls on a little girl. Now, run along and wash your face off good."

Leah looked up at me in astonishment and I realized that she had never been treated like this in her life. I had never been anything but quietly insistent when we discussed some issue of importance between us. Leah knew very little about the natural humiliation of being a child and how grown people regularly trample on the feelings of the little people so helpless under their care.

"Go to the living room, Leah," I said. "You look perfectly wonderful."

Leah avoided meeting her grandmother's eyes as, furious, she exited the room. Yes, she's a McCall, I thought as I watched her proud retreat.

"You hurt Leah's feelings," I said. "Don't ever do it again."

"Someone needs to look out for the best interests of that child," Lucy said. "You've dressed her up like a whore."

"Mama," I said, trying to be patient, but feeling my own darkness rising within me. "Paris and Linda Shaw are throwing a party for you. He's a wonderful novelist and she's an elegant hostess and they live in a beautiful apartment. All of our friends in Rome will be there. They want to show me and Leah that they love us. They want to show you that they're very happy you're alive and that you've come to visit and that I'm getting back together with my family after years of separation. But I knew you'd find some way to ruin this evening. All during my life, you always worked hard to mess up a happy occasion. Happiness seems to enrage you. Celebration pisses you off."

"You don't know what you're talking about," Lucy said, backing away. "I've always loved parties."

"You do. And you'll have a good time at the one tonight. But you're an engineer of discord," I said. "What you just did was ruin the party for Leah, and because Leah's going to be unhappy, you just ruined it for me."

"It's not my fault if you don't understand what's appropriate for a little girl and what's not."

"I'm going into the living room, Mama," I

said and I heard the coldness in my voice. "And I'm going to tell Leah that she looks lovely and what she's wearing is fine. You just gave me a small glimpse of why I hate America and why I always felt ugly as a child."

"Your childhood was pure happiness," Lucy sneered. "You don't even know what a bad childhood looks like. And you're raising Leah to think she's the Queen of Sheba or something."

"Get control of yourself, Mother," I said. "I'm going to talk to Leah."

"You'd better back me up, Jack," Lucy whispered hotly. "Otherwise that child'll have no respect for me at all."

I found Leah on the terrace, shivering in the cold and crying hard. I led her into the living room where we sat on the couch and she, heartbroken, cried. When her sobbing began to slow down, I chose my words with great care.

"Lucy was completely and totally and undeniably wrong in saying what she did, Leah," I said, hugging her to me.

"Then why did she say it?" Leah asked, wiping her tears with her hand.

"Because she's nervous about the party," I said. "There's no one my mother's ever met that she didn't feel inferior to. It's easier to be mean to you and me than to face the fact that she's terrified to meet our friends in Rome."

"I thought I looked pretty," Leah said.

I kissed her and said, "No one's ever looked better. Since the beginning of time. At least to me."

Leah's composure was returning slowly. "Should I put Mama's pearls back in her box?"

"You look perfect with them. Except now your eyes are swollen and red."

"I couldn't help crying, Daddy," Leah said. "I've never had anyone talk to me like that."

"She's jealous of you and all the things you have," I said. "My mother always told us that her childhood had been bad, but she wouldn't say how. I now think that it was more than bad, that it was truly terrible."

"If she had a bad childhood, Daddy, why would she want to hurt me?" Leah asked.

"Because when you have been hurt you lose your trust in the world," I said. "If the world's mean to you when you're a child, you spend the rest of your life being mean back."

"I don't think I like your mother, Daddy," Leah said.

I laughed. "You don't have to. You can choose to like any human being you feel like liking. That's your decision and in that, Leah, you're a sovereign nation unto yourself. But what you don't know about my mother is coming up for your inspection."

"What do you mean, Daddy?" Leah asked.

"My mother is a great undiscovered actress," I said as we heard Lucy's high heels clicking rapidly down the marble hall.

She made a grand entrance with a loud rattling of gold chains and bracelets. She looked at Leah and exclaimed, "You look absolutely heavenly, darling. Just ravishing. A rare statement of impeccable taste. Are those Shyla's pearls? They look as beautiful on you as they did on her. Here, let me wash your lips with this cloth. I want you to wear some of my own lipstick. It's far more chic and grownup than the kind you're wearing. I bought you a tube of your own just today."

As Lucy very carefully removed the lipstick from Leah's mouth and began applying her own, she noticed that Leah had been crying.

"Did your father say something to hurt your feelings?" Lucy said, turning a furious eye on me. "Men! They're not much good for anything except breaking your heart and letting out the hogs."

"Letting out the hogs?" Leah asked.

"Just an expression, honey," Lucy said happily. "Growing up in the South, I learned lots of country expressions. You be nice to Leah, Jack. You don't understand what a treasure you have here. And enjoy this girl while you can. You won't have her forever."

Within a few minutes we left for the party

in Trastevere, in order to arrive exactly an hour after the invitation said the party would start. Time is an elusive and foreign concept in Rome and no Roman worth his salt or his lineage would feel anything other than keen embarrassment over arriving at a party at the suggested hour. When I first came to the city, I had arrived at eight o'clock for dinner parties, only to find hostess after hostess in the shower. It takes a while for Americans, noted by the Romans for their hilarious punctuality, to adjust, but adjust I did.

I stood by the door, introducing Lucy to my Roman friends. Lucy looked lovely, and was her most charming and gracious self.

"Who's this?" she whispered as a handsome man with a lionesque head stormed through the front door.

"Mother, I'd like you to meet Gore Vidal," I said. "Gore, this is my mother, the predatory Lucy McCall Pitts."

"Go on," Lucy said. "You're not Gore Vidal."

"I beg your pardon, madam," Gore said, arching his eyebrows like a misplaced king.

"Mom, don't play Eliza Doolittle with me," I said, nervous because I knew of Gore's massive contempt for his native unwashed.

"You're the writer Gore Vidal," she said. "I've read all your books."

"I rather doubt it, madam," Gore said. "I've written far too many. I've had trouble calling them all to mind myself."

"No," Lucy insisted. "At the library in Waterford, I've won the award for the citizen who reads the most books more times than anyone in the history of the town."

"Jack. This is a play and I'm being set up as a fool. Such egregious provincialism makes me long for an insulin shot."

"It's just my mother being herself," I shrugged.

"It's nice that you can visit your son, Miss Lucy," Gore said. "My mother was a perfect monster."

"I'm sure she just didn't have much to work with, Gore," Lucy said and Gore bellowed with laughter and swept on into the party.

My mother moved among my Roman friends for the next two hours and she made her brand of Southern charm seem contagious. She moved from group to group and I could hear her accent all night, followed by the laughter and appreciation of my friends.

As Leah and I made our way through the ranks of the party-goers, it seemed only minutes before the bells of Rome were warming up in a dozen belfries near us and the soft hands of clocks were inching their way toward the midnight hour. Thanking Linda and Paris for

the party my mother paused to bid farewell to
Gore Vidal, whom she had taken a shine to.

"Gore," my mother said, "come visit us in
South Carolina."

"Lucy, darling," he answered, "why on
earth would I do that to myself?" and both of
them laughed as he kissed my mother's hand,
then Leah's.

Gore said, as he studied Leah's curtsey to
him, "This child is lovely. She looks as though
she were born in pearls."

"The pearls were my idea," Lucy said, walking out into the Roman night as Leah and I
shared a look.

A cab let us off near the Tiber and we
joined that great, splendidly dressed crowd that
made its way between the two encircling colon-
nades that led to St. Peter's. It was a slow-mov-
ing, reflective congregation, like some grazing
flock of herbivores who fed on prayer and incense and unleavened bread. Being so near a
church again reminded Lucy that she had cancer and she said a rosary as we waited in the
prodigious lines that formed around every entryway. In all of its exuberant excess, St. Peter's
had always prompted me to remember that the
simplicity of the Protestants had sprung quite
naturally from the exorbitance of churches like
this. Baptist friends from the South had to fight
off a gag reflex when I brought them face to

face with the Roman Church's inflation of taste. But I liked the excess of it all, the sumptuousness, and I tried to explain to visitors that this is what the artists of the Middle Ages thought that heaven might look like. The incense recalled my boyhood days as an altar boy, the smell of prayer put to the torch.

When we got to our places and kneeled, Leah whispered to me and said, "Grandma doesn't like it that I'm Jewish."

"I don't care," I said. "Do you?"

"She says it'll only confuse me spiritually."

"I was raised Catholic," I whispered. "I'm totally confused spiritually."

"Grandma said you don't know the first thing about raising a Jewish girl," she said.

"She's right," I said. "I'm winging it, kid. Doing the best I can."

"I told her you were doing a great job."

"Thanks. You won't later."

"Why?" she asked.

"Growing up," I explained. "In a couple of years, everything I say'll strike you as silly or ridiculous. Even the sound of my voice'll irritate you."

"I don't think so. Are you certain? *Certo*?" she asked.

"*Certo*," I said. "Part of natural law. I used to think everything my mother said was absolutely wonderful and that she was the smartest person in the world."

"No," Leah said.

"Yes," I said. "Then I became a teenager and realized she was a complete idiot. And so was everyone around me."

"It must be interesting," Leah said, eyeing my mother. "This becoming a teenager."

"One finds it so," I said as the basilica continued to fill up with the hushed vast throngs.

When I sat back, I felt a tap on my shoulder and I heard Jordan's voice directly behind me. This surprised me, but then I remembered that it was Jordan who had gotten me tickets for the Midnight Mass.

"Leah's a doll baby. It's like watching Shyla," Jordan said to me. My mother began to teach Leah to use the rosary and both of them were concentrating on the row of white beads Leah held in her hands.

"One of the letters you brought today, Jack. My father wants to come to Rome to meet me after the New Year."

"I'm glad only if you are," I said. "Your dad's never been one of my favorites." I stood up to let some late arrivals push by me for their seats in the center of the row.

Jordan said, "You've always had this silly prejudice against sadism. What do you make of it?"

"The science project you did in high school," I said in a low voice, "the one on coral snakes. They rarely bite anyone, but the ones they do almost never survive. Your dad's like that."

"Mom claims it's a peace mission," said Jordan. "He wants to extend an olive branch."

"Or beat you to death with it," I said.

"He's coming. Whether I agree or not," Jordan said. "What shall I do?"

"A transfer to Patagonia."

"Hush, son," my mother said in her most commanding voice. "The Pope's coming up the center aisle."

"Later," Jordan said and disappeared into the Christmas night.

A choir of nuns sang birdlike in a distant eyrie as the Pope moved down the main aisle blessing all as he passed. I watched as my mother received the Papal blessing and took it in with the gratitude of an outfielder shagging a long fly ball. The Pope was surrounded by a whole civilization of cardinals and monsignors who escorted him with the same patience I had seen with cowbirds in the low country following the footsteps of a prize bull.

At Communion time I followed my mother up to the rail where we both received the Eucharist from Pope John Paul II. As we lined up with the surging crowds around us, I watched as priests appeared in every side altar and dozens appeared at the main altar to distribute the body and blood of God in a sacrament of mass production. But my mother looked radiant and hopeful as she prayed for a long time on her knees when we returned to our seats. Looking toward the back of the church, I saw uniformed men with machine guns vigilantly appraising the crowd's behavior. The Pope looked thin and gaunt and I remembered that he had been shot by a young Turkish assassin in the piazza outside. I felt the Mass going through me, but not touching me. I was part of what was wrong with my century.

Later, I would say that it was at this moment in the Vatican that I began the terrible countdown toward the unknown. In the days to come I would try to reassemble all those random thoughts that coalesced when I looked toward the rear of St. Peter's and watched those men with their silent coverage of the Pope's flanks. I had an appointment with darkness that I was walking toward with wide-eyed innocence and a placid sense of well-being. Time itself had spotted me in an open field. I had been singled out by hooded, peregrine eyes when all I was feeling was an utter buoyancy and joy that my life was filling itself in, repairing all the cracks and damage. But first I had to endure the terror-haunted void of forgetfulness. I had to wait for my cue, for the lights to shine on me, for my unutterable time to call out my given name as a casting call for evil itself.

Two days later, on December 27, 1985, I could feel no change in the barometric pressure as I paid the taxi driver who helped me unload the luggage at the Rome airport. As far as I could tell, no star shifted a single magnitude of candlepower as Lucy, Leah, and I entered through the middle door, past the armed carabinieri, and made our way to the Pan Am check-in booth. Nothing was different on this trip than on any of the other thousand I had taken in a lifetime of send-offs and journeys.

I do not remember handing in all the tickets and passports at the Pan Am check-in place nor do I remember looking at my new watch to tell my mother it was two minutes after nine o'clock. We had ten pieces of luggage among us and the ticket man and I had a brief skirmish about whether I should pay for extra baggage. Across from Pan Am, an El Al flight was taking off at the same time and an enormous crowd jostled against each other as they moved through the security checkpoint that led to the flight gates. Above us, armed guards patrolled a steel runway with machine guns and the bored, disinterested faces of guards were everywhere. Leah would reconstruct all of this much later.

I took our boarding passes and looked over toward the gates when I saw four strangely dressed men walking toward us. Two wore elegant gray suits, two were dressed in blue jeans, and all wore scarves that partially concealed their faces. The men began opening duffel bags they carried and one of them pulled the pin of a grenade and tossed it. Then all four men pulled out machine guns and in a blind, heedless fury turned their deadly fire on those in the eight-hundred-twenty-foot-long terminal. I reached for Leah and threw her over the ticket counter on top of the man who'd just issued our boarding passes. "Stay down, Leah," I screamed and I then moved toward my frightened, disoriented mother who had drifted out toward the center as security forces began returning a murderous fire and Italian guards closed in fast on the four Palestinian terrorists who were there to kill as many people as possible before being cut down themselves.

Lucy was standing straight up, openmouthed, when I reached her and tackled her and lay my body on top of hers. It was then that I felt two bullets from an AK-47 automatic rifle, one to my head and one to my shoulder. I heard my mother scream once, then I was overwhelmed by the pandemonium of gunfire and grenades exploding near us and the screaming of those unharmed but paralyzed with terror. "Are you okay, Mama? You okay?" I asked as I watched blood spotting her winter coat; then I lost consciousness. A man and a woman lying beside us were dead.

What I tell you next I learned later.

When the shooting stopped, sixteen people lay dead and seventy-four wounded and the airport looked like a sheep's abattoir. Leah rushed from body to body in a desperate search for her father and grandmother. My great weight had pinned my mother to the floor and Leah had to enlist the aid of an El Al attendant to roll me off her. I would not regain consciousness for three days. Blood covered my head and eyes and Leah began screaming when she thought I had died. But this would be the day she would learn about the strength of grandmothers.

"Jack's still breathing. He's alive. Let's make sure we get him on one of those first ambulances. We're gonna need your Italian, darling," my mother said.

Leah and Lucy raced toward the main door as the sounds of ambulances lifted all over Rome and they streaked along with camera crews and journalists toward Fiumicino. When the first ambulance team burst into the stricken airport Leah began screaming, *"Mio papà, Mio papà, Non è morto. Sangue, signori, il sangue è terribile. Per favore, mio papà, signori."*

The two men followed the pretty young child they thought was Italian and I was the first one taken out of the airport and into an ambulance and the first victim to appear on Italian television as a camera crew began filming. My head and upper torso were covered in blood and Lucy's winter coat looked like it had been dipped in the blood of her son as she held onto me. It was an image that was being broadcast all over Italy.

At that very moment Jordan Elliott was coming out of the class he taught on the limits of dogma at the North American College, near the Trevi Fountain. As he entered the teachers' lounge, he saw a cluster of his brother priests huddled around a television set.

"There's been a massacre at the Rome airport," Father Regis, a Latin scholar, said. "It looks very bad."

"They're bringing someone out now," another voice said.

Jordan did not recognize me because of the blood, but he cried out when he saw Leah and Lucy hurrying to keep pace with the stretcher-bearers. In a daze, he heard the announcer report the location of the hospital near the Vatican where surgeons were already gathering from all over Rome to receive the wounded.

Jordan sprinted out of the room without explanation in a headlong dash to a taxi stand. He
had been right halfback in the same backfield
at Waterford High where I had played fullback,
Mike Hess had been the left half, and Capers
Middleton had called signals at quarterback. It
was well known around the state in 1965 as the
Middleton backfield and when the team
needed short yardage they went to their huge,
pug-nosed fullback, me. But when they needed
the long yardage, they went to their big-play
back, the one who could turn it upfield, the guy
who ran the hundred in ten flat, the swift and
elusive Jordan Elliott. No Roman who passed
Jordan as he raced toward the taxi stand in the
Piazza Venezia ever forgot the speed of that
priest, or at least that is what he told me. When
he reached the first waiting taxi he jumped in
the front seat screaming, *"Al pronto soccorso.
All'ospedale. Al pronto soccorso."*

When they unloaded me at Santo Spirito
Hospital, Jordan was waiting for us.

"Go to the waiting room, Leah and Lucy,"
he commanded. "I'll meet you down there
later. Trust in the Lord."

As the stretcher-bearers began their long
run toward the clear hallways, Father Jordan
ran beside me making the sign of the cross and
giving me the short form of absolution used
only in cases of extraordinary urgency. He said

it in Latin because he knew I was one of those irritating fallen-away Catholics who retained a strong nostalgia for the Latin service.

"Ego te absolvo ab omnibus censuris, et peccatis, in nomine Patris, et Filii, et Spiritus Sancti. Amen."

This performance of Extreme Unction led off the evening news in Italy. As Jordan began making the sign of the cross over my two grievous wounds, he said while holding one of my hands, "If you are sorry for all your sins, please squeeze my hand if you can hear me, Jack." There was a small pressure from me, he said later, and Jordan went on, "You are absolved of all your sins, Jack. Go into this operation with no fear for your soul. But remember who you are, Jack. You're Jack McCall from Waterford, South Carolina, the strongest man or boy I ever knew. Use the strength now, Jack. Use every ounce of it. Fight this thing with everything you've got. Leah, your mom, and I are waiting for you. Use your strength for us. Fight this one for us. The ones that love you, need you."

The door burst open into the brightly lit operating room, but before they took me away, he said, I squeezed his hand one more time and this time harder.

"Into God's hands I commend you, Jack McCall," said Jordan, making a final sign of the cross at the door where the surgeons began to work on the two bullet wounds.

Much later, when I began to piece together the fragments of any memory I had of the incident, I remembered some of the wild ride from the airport into Rome. Leah was crying and saying, "Daddy, Daddy, Daddy," over and over again and I tried to reach out for her, but a sleeping numbness spread through me like a drug and there was silence and darkness again. The next thing I remember is the ambulance taking a corner fast and Lucy shouting to the driver, "Slow down," and the heartbreaking sound again of Leah crying and my frustration at not being able to comfort her.

I was in the operating room for six hours. The surgeons managed to save my left eye. The bullet that entered my shoulder lodged near the lung and that was the bullet that almost killed me. I had already bled profusely when I reached the operating room table and my heart stopped twice during the course of the operation. But the strength that Jordan talked about prevailed and I, because of fate and luck and perhaps because of the prayers of those who loved me, survived the airport massacre in Rome.

For six days, mirroring my mother's own recent stillness, I lay in a coma. Later, I could resurrect no dreams from that period of dor-

mancy and stillness. Though I had some sense
that it had been a time of vivid, transfiguring
dreaming, nothing of it remained that I could
hold on to, except a phantasmagoria of bright
colors. The assault of colors was the only thing
I brought back from my voyage in timelessness
as my body concentrated on its task of survival.

Finally, I awoke slowly to bells. It was as
though I was rising like a bird from a cavern in
the center of the earth. I could feel that thing
called "self" reconstructing in my bloodstream
while I formed my first conscious thought since
being wounded. I listened to the Eternal City
call out my name. For an hour, I listened and
wondered where I was and why I could not see.
But this was all done calmly and without panic.
Then I heard voices talking quietly in the room
around me. I concentrated hard on recognizing
the voices, but they were low-pitched so as not
to bother or awake me. Then I heard one voice
and that voice made me struggle to recover my
own from wherever it had gone to hide. For
another hour, I concentrated on coming to the
surface, coming out to the light, to the world of
bells and voices, to that world abandoned
where I could laugh and talk. For a long time I
thought about the first word I would say and
struggled fiercely to say it in my blindness and
in the pain I was beginning to feel for the first

time. Finally, I heard the word forming like a gemstone in my chest. "Leah!"

"Daddy," I heard Leah scream back, then I felt my child kissing the side of my face that was not covered with bandages.

"Daddy, thank God, Daddy, thank God, Daddy, Daddy, Daddy," Leah said over and over again. "I was so afraid you were going to die, Daddy."

"No such luck," I said slowly and the full measure of my disorientation was becoming clear to me.

"Hello, Jack," Lucy said to me. "Welcome back. You've been gone a long time."

"Did we catch that plane?" I asked, and the whole room exploded into laughter.

"Don't you remember, Daddy?" Leah said.

"Help me," I said. "First, why can't I see any of you?"

"Your eyes are bandaged," Lucy said.

"Am I blind?" I asked.

"You almost were," my mother said.

"Nice word 'almost,' " I said. "I feel like I've been run over by a rhinoceros."

"You were shot twice," a third voice said.

"Who else is here? Ledare, is that you?" I said, lifting an arm up toward her.

Ledare took my hand and sat beside me. "Hey, Jack, I came as soon as I heard."

"Ledare, that's so nice," I said.

"Leah hasn't left your side once," Ledare said. "Your mother and I have taken turns going to your apartment to get some rest and clean up. Leah's been here the whole time. What an extraordinary child you've raised, Jack."

With those words of praise, Leah broke down and wept as hard as it was possible for a child to weep. Ledare moved off the bed and Leah crawled up against me. She cried for ten minutes and I let her cry and did nothing to stop it but pressed her tightly to me. I let the sobs run down and the tears dry and I did not speak until she lay silent beside me.

"Want me to tell you a story?" I asked.

"Yes, Daddy. Tell me a great story," Leah said, exhausted.

"I only know one great subject," I said.

"The Great Dog Chippie," Leah said, brightening. "Did you know the Great Dog Chippie, Ledare?"

"Yes," Ledare laughed. "I knew Chippie."

"She was a mutt, for God's sake," Lucy said, but I pointed a warning finger at her.

"I want to hear a Great Dog Chippie story, Daddy," Leah said.

"You've got to pick the subject," I said.

"Okay," Leah said, and she grew curiously quiet and thoughtful. Then she said, "I know the story I want to hear."

"You've got to tell me," I said, puzzled.

"You may not want to tell it, Daddy," Leah said.

"I'll tell anything," I said. "It's only a story."

Leah began crying again, then got control of herself and said, "I want to hear about the Great Dog Chippie and the Rome airport."

"That's the silliest thing I've ever heard of," Lucy said.

But Leah was crying again and I said, "No, Mama. I know what Leah's after."

"I just think it's nonsense to dredge up bad memories," Lucy said. "We've all been through enough. I'm so upset I forgot I had leukemia with the commotion and all."

"Listen, Lucy," I heard Ledare say as I began my story.

"On December 27, 1985, Jack McCall and his lovely daughter, Leah, were packing for their trip to South Carolina. Jack's wicked mother, Lucy, was bawling out the maid, Maria, in English even though Maria only could speak Italian."

"I resent that," Lucy muttered.

"It's only a story, Mama," I said, then continued. "All of Leah's friends from school had come to wish her a *buon viaggio!* and they lined up along the piazza singing to Leah as her taxi pulled away into the Rome traffic. I heard something I hadn't heard for years. It was a familiar bark and I looked behind me and saw a small black dog with a white cross on its throat running after the cab . . ."

"It's the Great Dog Chippie," Leah said.

"I thought Chippie was dead because she'd disappeared years before in Waterford and my mother, the evil-hearted Lucy, told me that Chippie had gone off in the woods to die."

"I used to have to feed that dumb dog," Lucy protested.

"Every story needs a villain," I explained.

"Believe me," Lucy said, "this story's gonna have some."

"I told the cabdriver to stop and then opened the back door. The Great Dog Chippie jumped into the back of the cab and licked me on the face for a full five minutes. Then I introduced the Great Dog Chippie to the Great Girl Leah and Chippie licked her face for the next five minutes. Then Chippie saw Lucy and the hair on the back of her spine bristled and the Great Dog went '*Gggg-rrrr.*' "

"I'll admit that ratty dog didn't like me," Lucy said, "but she sure warmed up to me at mealtime."

"Why didn't she like you, Grandma?" Leah asked.

"I used to wop her on the butt with a broom when I caught her sleeping on the couch," said Lucy. "Of course, that was about five times a day. You couldn't teach that dog doodly."

"The Great Dog Chippie was too busy performing heroic acts to learn silly animal tricks. So Chippie rode with us all the way to the Rome airport and I made plans to buy a special cage, so that we could bring the Great Dog Chippie back to South Carolina with us. The taxi pulled up to the main entrance and Leah, the Great Dog Chippie, and the wicked Lucy walked happily with me into the terminal. The first person they saw was Natasha Jones, with her wonderful white dog, Bianco. Leah went over to introduce the Great Dog Chippie to Bianco and it was decided that the two dogs would share the same cage for the trip back to the States . . ."

I sensed the room tense and I didn't know why until I heard Ledare say, "Natasha Jones was killed during the massacre, Jack. Her father and brother were wounded."

"Jesus Christ," I said. "I don't even remember seeing Natasha and her parents that day."

"I didn't go to her funeral because I wanted to be with you, Daddy," Leah said, her voice fragile.

"You did right, Leah," I said. "I needed you more than Natasha did. Could someone tell me what happened? I'm going to need some help if

I'm going to finish this Great Dog Chippie story. I don't remember another thing. Nothing."

Ledare began talking because she saw that neither Lucy nor Leah could speak. "Four gunmen entered the airport with their weapons concealed. They carried thirteen hand grenades and four AK-47 automatic rifles. You were at the ticket counter when the shooting broke out," Ledare continued. "You picked Leah up and threw her behind the counter where she lay flat on the ground until the shooting stopped. Then you ran and knocked your mother to the ground and shielded her from the bullets. That's when you were hit. Once in the head just above the left eye. The bullet missed the brain by a centimeter. Once in the shoulder that lodged in your chest, piercing the left lung."

"I don't remember a single thing that happened," I said.

"A man in Málaga, Spain, called up a radio station and took credit for the airport attacks for the Abu Nidal Group and the PLO. There was another massacre in Vienna at the same time. Can you imagine the nerve?" Lucy said.

"Long live Israel," I said. "Okay. Let's get back to the story. As Chippie was getting to know Bianco, the Great Dog's eye started roving around the airport. Chippie had an amazing ability to judge people's characters just by looking at them. It was an instinct that Chippie was born with. Just like bird dogs have an incredible sense of smell, Chippie had a great sense of sniffing out good from evil. She looked around and saw happy people getting ready to take wonderful trips, until her eyes rested on four men she didn't like. In fact, we can be brutally honest and say the Great Dog Chippie didn't like these four losers at all."

"Uh oh," Leah said. "Those four guys are gonna get it now."

"The Great Dog Chippie walked over to take a peek at what was going on. The nearer she got to those four the more cunning and wolflike the Great Dog Chippie became. In fact, she seemed to grow stockier and more muscular and her fangs sharpened as she caught a scent of evil like she'd never smelled before. She leapt up on the counter of the bar and moved like a great cat, stepping gingerly over coffee cups so that she didn't spill anybody's cappuccino. By the time she reached the end of that counter, the Great Dog Chippie had transformed herself into a dog of war, a dog of blood. The city where a wolf had once suckled Romulus and Remus had need of wolves again, fiercer and more bloodthirsty than the one who had mothered Rome's founders. Rome called for a wolf . . ."

"And the Great Dog Chippie answered," Leah cried out.

"The Great Dog Chippie answered, all right," I said. "The four men began to take out their AK-47's and their hand grenades. They then turned toward a crowd of people who had gathered at the Pan Am and El Al ticket counters. One of them pointed at sweet and wonderful Natasha Jones and another man pointed his rifle at the delightful and beautiful Leah McCall and just before they began firing, the four men heard something that froze the roots of their souls with fear."

"Ggg-rrr," Leah snarled fiercely.

"Ggg-rrr," I snarled along with her.

"They had forgotten about one thing," I said.

Leah said, "They'd forgotten about the Great Dog Chippie."

"The Great Dog went for the first terrorist's throat and her fangs severed the carotid artery as they tore through the neck of a man who'd never hurt anyone else again. His rifle went off, harmlessly spraying bullets into the ceiling. The second terrorist shot at the Great Dog Chippie but that dog had already sunk her fangs into that man's genitalia and the scream from that man brought security police running from everywhere. Then Chippie whirled and ran through a hail of bullets as the remaining two men standing knew who their true enemy was now. The Great Dog Chippie was hit by one of the bullets, but one bullet isn't enough to stop the Great Dog Chippie."

"No way," Leah said happily. "One bullet's nothing to the Great Dog Chippie."

"I sure as hell didn't see that damn dog," Lucy said.

"The third man had a knife scar that went the length of his face. The Great Dog Chippie went for that scar. Her fangs ripped into the man's face and as the man hit the ground the dog leapt toward the throat of the last man standing. The last man stood his ground and fired all his bullets into the Great Dog Chippie. Chippie, the Great Dog, staggered toward the last man, but did not have the strength to make it. She turned to Jack and Leah and Lucy and gave them a last affectionate bark of farewell. Then the Great Dog Chippie put her head between her paws and died a sweet and peaceful death. An El Al security guard shot the man who killed the Great Dog Chippie and killed him on the spot."

"No, Daddy," Leah said. "The Great Dog Chippie can't die. It's not fair."

"Chippie died when I was eighteen, sweetheart," I said. "Because your mama died, I never wanted to tell you that Chippie'd died too."

"Chippie's grave's in the backyard," Lucy said. "It's kind of pretty. Jack made the tombstone himself."

"I've been waiting for that story since you were hurt, Daddy," Leah said. "I wish it were true."

"Stories don't have to be true. They just have to help," I said. "Now, darling, I'm exhausted."

"Let him get some rest, Leah," Lucy said. "I'll take you home and feed you."

"I'm staying here," Leah said.

"You'll do what I say, young lady," Lucy insisted and I could hear the fear and the relief in my mother's voice.

"Leah and I are a team, Mama," I said. "Let her be."

"Are we still going back to Waterford when you get well?" Leah asked.

"Yeh, kid. I didn't do this right. You don't know any of the stories that made you who you are."

"The movie's on, Jack," Ledare said. "Mike sent me the first check when he heard you were shot. You're hired whether you want to be or not."

"Some of the stories Mike wants," I said, "are the ones I need to tell Leah."

"You tell the ones you know," Ledare said. "I'll fill in where I can."

"Ledare?" I asked. "Did you come here because of the movie?"

"Sorry to disappoint you," Ledare answered. "I came because you needed me."

"You're welcome to Italy and everything in it," my mother said. "I'll be getting back to Waterford day after tomorrow. Need to get out of this crazy country. Course, I'm gonna hire an armored car to ride to the airport. I won't feel safe again till I smell collard greens cooking."

"We'll follow you when we can, Mama," I said.

"Jordan was on television," Ledare said, "giving you the last rites. Mike has the tapes. So does General Elliott."

"The plot thickens."

"Why is Jordan hiding, Daddy?" Leah said. "He's been here to the hospital a bunch of times. But always in the middle of the night."

As I tried to answer, I felt myself falling away from all of them and sleep felt like a black hole where all time fell in an endless cascade that began with lost words at the touch of Leah's hand against mine and ended in a sleep too soon in the coming.

CHAPTER 19

I LEFT THE HOSPITAL DAYS LATER with a plum-tinged wound of entry that Leah touched tenderly as my bandages were removed for the last time. Dr. Guido Guccioli, who had saved my sight, gave me last pointers about the necessity of resting my eyes and the dangers of strain. He explained how the rods and cones clustered like colorless grapes along retinal nerves and how the operation he performed was much like tuning a piano the size of a quail's egg. The doctor and three of the nurses came down into the street as Ledare and Leah helped me into the taxi that would take me home.

"Hey, Guido. Can I French-kiss you?" I asked.

"No, of course not, it would be undignified and unsanitary," the doctor said as he kissed me on both cheeks. "But with Signora Ledare, it would be a different story."

On the taxi ride home, I rolled the window down and let the soft, pillowed air flow over and through me. It was smooth as new linen across my face. Even the Tiber smelled rich and dark when we passed above it as it divided itself into two congruent fragments of river and embraced the sharp prow of the Isola Tiberina.

In the Piazza Farnese, a small group from the neighborhood had gathered outside of my building. Maria, her fingers entwined with her rosary, was there, as were a few neighbors; two nuns wearing gardening gloves emerged from their jewel-box cloister, the Ruggeri brothers ran over from the *alimentari*, their hands smelling of cheese; there was Freddie in his white waiter's coat, the olive man and two of the fruit ladies from the Campo, the chicken-and-egg lady, the beautiful blonde from the office-supply store, Edoardo the master of coffee and *cornetti*, Aldo the newsman, and the owner of the piazza's single restaurant.

A small cheer went up among the assembled friends when I emerged from the taxi and made my way unsteadily toward the front door.

Because of my being wounded, the massacre had touched this piazza in a direct and personal way. The merchants sent over fruit and vegetables from the Campo dei Fiori and would not take Ledare's money during the first week of my return. The fishwives sent up mussels and cod. The chicken man brought up freshly killed hens. My generous neighbors took care of everything during the first weeks of my convalescence at home.

Each day, I walked among them through the narrow streets, building my strength.

Though I have traveled on almost every continent and spent time among scores of nationalities, I have never quite fathomed or understood the gruffness and originality that Romans bring to tenderness. Their instinct for the small gestures of friendship is unerring. The proficiency they bring to the task of embracing the acceptable stranger is a form of municipal cunning. My neighbors welcomed me back to the piazza, and rejoiced in my recovery. Romans, Romans, I thought. They cannot crook their little fingers without teaching the rest of the world inimitable lessons about pageantry and hospitality.

Watching my return, I later learned, through a pair of high-powered Nikon binoculars, was Jordan Elliott, clean-shaven and dressed in jeans, worker boots, and a well-cut

Armani dress shirt. He watched as Ledare and I entered the building, me leaning more on her than on the tubular rubber-tipped walking cane they had given me at the hospital. The bureaucratic process for checking out of the hospital had just about finished me and the emotional homecoming so touched me that it took away the last bit of strength I could muster. The *portiere* held the door as though a prince were returning and I smiled my thanks to him. A photographer from *Il Messaggero* captured the authentic note of cordiality and nostalgia in the homecoming. The flower ladies pressed bouquets of anemones and zinnias into Leah's arms.

But there was little sentimentality in Jordan's surveillance of the scene. His binoculars were trained on the crowd, not on me, as I disappeared into my apartment building, its huge black doors closing behind me like the wings of an archangel. Only when the crowd broke up did Jordan isolate the object of his patient oversight. The man was trim and soldierly in bearing and Jordan figured that he must have watched my return from the safety of the simple café on the piazza and emerged only when the crowd had begun its wordy dispersal. When he reached the fountain nearest my apartment, Jordan shivered as he reflected how odd it was to be studying in all the intimacy of magnification the robust figure of his own father. General Elliott moved with an infantryman's attention and grace, studying each face as it passed by him. He was clearly looking for Jordan and Jordan could imagine his father's impatience as he failed to see him in the crowd.

Soon after I had been brought to the hospital, Jordan had appeared on television sets all over the nation as the ambulance doors opened and I was wheeled into the emergency room. As a Trappist priest who had spent much of his adult life in a monastery, the one thing Jordan little understood was the power and rapidity of modern communication. The expression of grief and horror on Jordan's face when he caught sight of me became famous the moment it was flashed by satellite into all the newsrooms of the world. As he took my hand and leaned down to whisper the words of the last rites in my ear while I was wheeled from a ramp down the corridors of the alerted hospital, the lines of worry and compassion on his angular face came to define the dynamic, rugged symmetry of Italy's own communal agony. His face became famous on the peninsula within a twenty-four-hour period. By accident, the conferral of Jordan's anguish became an eloquent gift to Italy. His face expressed everything that Italy felt about the slaughter of the holiday travelers. Italian journalists began to

search for the mysterious priest. But Jordan
sank back into the hidden depths of the priest-
haunted city as photographs of him began to
appear on the front pages of American newspapers.

On the Isle of Orion, General Elliott recognized his son immediately. When the same tape
rolled again fifteen minutes later on CNN, he
copied it so he could return to it at his leisure.
General Elliott's face was unreadable, but his
son's face had always been a book open for all
the world's inspection. The well-trimmed beard
hid the dimple he had inherited from his
mother. But the handiwork of fifteen years had
not changed his son's face, only deepened it,
made it more recognizable. Jordan's eyes were
unforgettable and his father had certainly not
forgotten. He told his wife Celestine nothing
and she did not hear about my misfortune until
late the next day. By then, as we later learned,
the general had already gotten in touch with
Mike Hess and Capers Middleton. That night,
they all compared the photographs of the priest
coming out of the confessional on the Aventine
hill with the priest who met my ambulance at
the hospital in Trastevere. In a secret phone
conference the next day, all agreed they had
found their man.

His being captured by the camera's eye for
just that split second had brought on a wave of

visitors Jordan never would have wanted, but immediately after, Jordan vanished into the terra-cotta silences of monastic Rome. Before the surgeons had returned me to my hospital room, Jordan had moved from an obscure monastery located in one of the more un-celebrated abbeys in the Caelian hill to a half-way house in Trastevere that cared for priests who had problems with drug addiction. A bar-ber had shaved his beard and he was issued a pair of tortoiseshell glasses.

An underground machine had gone into operation as soon as Interpol in Rome head-quarters had received a photograph of young Jordan Elliott and myself after a baseball game our senior year in high school. It was accompa-nied by a blowup of the photograph of Jordan looking tenderly down at my body as it was be-ing wheeled hastily up the emergency ramp. A fingerprinter's assistant at Interpol had copied the information and sent it to her brother who worked for a monsignor who oversaw a com-mittee to reform the system of accounting at the Vatican Bank. Jordan Elliott was wanted for questioning in the death of a young Marine corporal and his girlfriend that had taken place in 1971. The bulletin indicated that Jordan might have changed his name and was believed to be masquerading as a Catholic priest of an unknown order. Jordan Elliott was described as being very intelligent, physically powerful, and perhaps armed as well. General Elliott had secretly notified Naval Intelligence, who got in touch with their connections in Interpol and Italy.

This was the first time since he had escaped to Europe that Jordan knew for sure that he was a hunted man. Though he had long suspected it, he had withdrawn from his life in South Carolina with such finality—there had even been a funeral service—that he had thought any pursuit of him had long since miscarried through lack of evidence or a fresh trail. Only his mother and I were partners in his conspiracy. Jordan had lulled himself into a feeling of invisibility and now, as he watched his father, he realized that his concern for me had put both of us in a dangerous situation.

The general positioned himself in the shadows of the fountain's splashing sarcophagus, made of Egyptian granite, surrounded by illegally parked cars.

He was still uncommonly handsome, Jordan thought, as he studied his father's regular features with his weather-beaten golfer's face and tanned, muscled arms. Jordan also noticed the first signs of wattles erupting beneath his father's chin. He doubted a son had ever feared a father as Jordan had feared his and the word "father," so sacred and primal in world religions, so central to the harmonic mystery of Catholicism, had always sent a shivering down his spine. It came to Jordan not as a two-syllable sound of a sweet-breathed, comfortable man armed only with rattles and lullabies, but as an army in the field with blood on its hands.

"Father." Jordan said the word out loud. Your father is home, your father is home, your father's home. . . . The four most feared words of his boyhood coming from his sweet-lipped mother's mouth. Jordan's fear and hatred of his father had always been the purest and most unclassifiable thing about him. The power of that hatred had shaken the composure of every confessor that Jordan had gone to for the forgiveness of his sins in his career as a priest. His abbot had told him as recently as a year ago that the kingdom of heaven would be denied to him if he could not find it in his heart to forgive his father. As he studied his father he realized that he was no nearer to that heavenly kingdom than he had been as a ten-year-old boy weeping after still another beating and dreaming of the day he would kill his father with his bare hands.

His mother had written to Jordan—his father wanted a reconciliation, and Jordan was preparing for that rendezvous when his youthful photograph arrived in the Rome offices of Interpol and made its secret way through the labyrinthine alleyways and courtyards of the Vatican to his abbot's small office. Jordan thought his father had betrayed him. But he also thought it was possible that Capers Middleton had sold out his old friend as a dramatic setpiece for his governor's campaign in South Carolina. His abbot agreed. The abbot possessed an Italian's scrupulous mistrust of politicians, and also a sweet but starchy sentimentality about fatherhood.

A few days after I returned home, Maria answered the doorbell and escorted Mike and Capers into the living room where I was with Ledare. Mike's impatience was a palpable force in the room and he paced beside the windows, a motor on overdrive somewhere in his central nervous system. But Capers was unflappable and controlled and seemed interested in taking a careful inventory of all my antiques and paintings. As his eyes wandered among my possessions, he said, "You have nice things. What a surprise, Jack."

"Take a quick inventory, then get the hell out of my house," I said.

Mike interrupted quickly. "This is a business call. About our movie. You don't have to fall in love with Capers. Just listen to him."

"I don't like Capers," I said. "I tried to make that clear in Waterford."

"You were clear, but wrong," Mike said.

"Mike," Ledare said, "you shouldn't've done this to either one of us."

"You're under contract, darling," Mike said. "I'm not required to run things by you. Ask the Writers Guild."

"Capers is a lit match with us," Ledare said to Mike. "We're the gasoline. You know it well."

"We both wanted to see if Jack's all right. We were worried," Mike said.

"I've been praying for you," Capers said, at last.

"Mike," I said. "There's a Bible on my night table. Turn to the New Testament and start reading the story about Judas Iscariot. Capers'll find it eerily autobiographical."

"The cat's never at a loss for words," Mike said in admiration.

"Ol' Jack," Capers said. "Always comparing himself to Jesus."

"Only when I'm with the man who once crucified me and all my friends," I said, feeling cold and angry. "Normally I model myself after Julia Child."

"Your shooting was headline news in South Carolina," Capers said, his voice even and eerily controlled. "As soon as I heard, I made plans to fly to Rome to visit you in the hospital. In fact, there'll be an article about our visit in the state newspaper next Sunday."

"Accompanied by photographs?" I guessed.

"How much will it cost me?" said Capers.

"More than you've got," I said.

"You didn't find Jordan," Ledare said. "That's why you're here."

"We didn't even get corroboration that Jordan Elliott's alive," Capers said. "We tried the Franciscans. The Jesuits. The Paulists. The Trappists. The Benedictines. I had the help of the Bishop of Charleston. Mike was in constant contact with the Cardinal of Los Angeles. Something has gone wrong and the whole system has shut down on us.

"We circulated all the photographs taken by the detective. Not one Franciscan in this city can make a positive identification of this bearded American priest. Every Franciscan we talked to was sure this man was not a member of their order. Yet he wears their habit and he heard confessions in one of their most important churches."

"Tell Jack the weird part," Mike said.

"I was getting to that," Capers said. "We got an interview with the head honcho of the Franciscans. The main man. The guy was a born leader, carried himself like a prince. He gives us some of the same old, same old. Looks at the photographs. Never seen the guy. But then he said something interesting. He told us point-blank that the Franciscans as an order and this abbot in particular don't take kindly to pressure from Americans trying to track down a member of their or any other order wanted for war crimes in America. Then he asked us to leave his office. But, Jack," Capers continued, leaning forward, "we never told anyone about any war crimes. We were just looking for Jordan. We never told anyone why."

"So what?" I said. "You think the Franciscans aren't going to do some checking on their own? They've been around since the thirteenth century."

"Did you tip Jordan off?" Capers asked.

"Listen good, Capers. I don't want to have to go over this again. I was in the hospital with all the lights out," I said. "But I would have warned him if I'd known you two were coming. I'd have suggested he do exactly what he's done . . . go underground until you guys go away."

"If there's no Jordan, there's no television deal," Mike said. "There's no movie."

Ledare looked at Mike. "Why would Jack care about that?"

"Because if there's no movie, there's no presidential pardon for Jordan Elliott," Mike said. "This is all part of a big plan, Jack."

"I see," Ledare said. "The mini-series ends with Capers Middleton getting a presidential pardon for his old friend Jordan Elliott. Then at the governor's inauguration in Columbia, the Middleton backfield will be united at last, a symbol of Governor Middleton's ability to heal the wounds that have torn his generation asunder."

"No, baby. Fine as far as it goes," Mike said. "But take it further. Take it six years down the road at the Republican National Convention. Or wait a full ten, when Capers drops his hat in the ring for president of the United States."

"Be still, my passport," I said, shaking my head sadly. "If I truly loved my country, I'd throw you right out that open window, Capers, and let you free fall five stories to the piazza below. But alas, my patriotism is all talk."

"Whoever your opponent is," Ledare said, "I'll write speeches for him. I'll work for free and grant interviews to every tabloid in the country. I'll give them the names and measurements of every bimbo you slept with during our hellish years of marriage."

"You won't do anything because of the kids," Capers said matter-of-factly.

"They'll be old enough then and I won't care what they think."

"Your weakness, dear, is that you'll always care too much what they think," said Capers, going for the kill. "You're very much aware that Mother's Day is not at the top of their list of favorite holidays."

"Let's cut to the chase," Mike said. "Are you going to help us find Jordan or not, Jack? You signed a contract, too."

"Cup your hand to your ear, Mike," I said. "Please listen to me this time. We have already had one painful meeting about this and I don't look forward to another. I won't help you at all because I hate your good buddy Capers. Is that clear enough?"

"You'd describe your feelings toward me as hatred?" Capers asked.

"Yes," I said, "that would eloquently sum it all up."

"Is there nothing I can do to change the way you feel?" Capers asked.

"I'm afraid not, Capers. Sorry old chum."

"Let me level with you, Jack," Mike said, looking at Capers who nodded at him.

"The movie needs Jordan because none of us knows his whole story. He's the key to it all. I need to sign him up or I don't think I can sell it to one of the networks. Got it? That's my professional interest. Now, Capers: The Democrats are going to try to highlight what Capers did to his friends in college. They've collected photographs of Capers surfing with Jordan, and of all of us triumphant after we won the state championship in football. Get the picture? I've seen the ads they're writing up. The stuff is catastrophic."

"So this has nothing to do with friendships or nostalgia or simple regret," I said.

"Nothing," Ledare answered. "It has only to do with Capers' favorite topic . . . Capers Middleton."

"You're not as pretty when you're cynical," Capers said.

"But I'm a lot smarter, aren't I?" she shot back.

"It's a mean world you're a part of, isn't it, Capers?" I said.

Capers answered, "It's mean for all of us. Style is what we mean by how we manage it."

"Style, you know about," said Ledare. "But, darling, substance is where you draw a blank."

"Tell Jordan we'd like to meet with him," Mike said. "We're in contact with his father. We've got a win-win proposition for him."

"I get it," I said. "Capers is the hero of our movie."

Capers said, rising to leave, "I've always been the hero, Jack. You had a minor role from the beginning—the sidekick, the chum, the good buddy."

"Be nice to the writers, Capers," Ledare said, "before we put you in high heels."

"That's why I got to the producer first," Capers said. "Funny line, Ledare. But don't you dare tell me how to walk the waterfront. We're at the Hassler."

After they had left, I slept for a while, and when I awakened, the night had turned cold and there was a blue, dewy texture to the darkness. The wind that rushed off the Tiber brought a smell of leaves and paper. Pages of *Il Messaggero* with its day-old news scudded across the piazza like clothes blown off a line. I walked to the far window of the apartment, checked the clock again, and saw that it was 9 P.M. on the nose. Turning on a light in a little-used hallway behind me, I stood centered in the frame of a huge rectangular window and I could see the graceful dome of St. Peter's light up the modest Roman skyline. Then I saw a light wink on and off in the darkness. Hello, the light said in Morse Code. I waved and asked Ledare to come join me by the window. I pointed toward the bell tower of St. Thomas of Canterbury and she saw a column of light winking on and off.

"That's Jordan," I said. "That's how we now have to communicate."

"What does he want?" she asked.

A lingering flash of light shot toward us, followed by a short flicker, then another long beam of light followed by darkness.

"Kilo, in Morse Code. It means 'I want to meet with you.' "

"How will you know where to meet?"

I scratched the back of my head, the signal

that I had received the message. Three short beams of light were followed by three long ones. Then the same exact message was sent several moments later.

"Number thirty-three, Ledare," I said. "Get the *Blue Guide to Rome and Its Environs*; it's on the table there. Turn to the index, page 399. There's a list of churches in the far right-hand column, starting with Sant'Adriano. That is church number one. Count to thirty-three for me."

"The thirty-third church listed is St. Cecilia in Trastevere," said Ledare.

"Good," I said. "That's a big church."

I scratched my head again and there was a final flash of light. "Jordan says good night. We meet two days from now in Trastevere."

"Is that where he lives?"

"I don't think so," I said. "Although I have no idea where he lives. He thinks it's safer for me to know as little about his life as possible."

Ledare, looking down toward the wind-swept piazza at one lone man crossing it swiftly, said, "Do you think Jordan's lonely, Jack?"

"I think loneliness is the central fact of his life," I said.

We took a long taxi ride through the winding alleyways of Rome, and once we were sure we were not being followed I told the driver to take us to the restaurant Galeassi in Trastevere. We got out of the cab quickly and walked toward the huge, brooding presence of the Church of Santa Cecilia. I walked Ledare to the right side of the church beneath a painting of the Assumption of the Virgin Mary on the ceiling above us. We crossed the ancient paved floor toward a bank of confessionals that stood in a soldierly file on the opposite end of the church.

Two of the confessionals had lights on, indicating the presence of a confessor within, but only one bore a discreet sign marked "English." Motioning for Ledare to wait for me in a pew, I entered one side of the confessional and drew the curtain. Out of habit, I opened the curtain slightly to see if someone had followed us to Trastevere. I heard Jordan's muffled voice rendering absolution in flawless Italian to an elderly Roman woman whose deafness made her confession an open book to any within shouting distance.

The panel slid and I saw the shrouded profile of Jordan through the screen that separated confessor from sinner.

"Hey, Jordan," I said.

"Hey, big fella," Jordan said. "I'm glad to know you're all right."

He then told me that his superiors had been

questioned by representatives of Interpol regarding a fugitive priest wanted for questioning about a crime that took place in 1971.

"The report could have come from several places, but the two most likely are my father or Capers Middleton."

"Your mother'd kill your father," I said. "And Capers practically convinced me that he needs you worse than you need him."

"Trusting Capers presents a small dilemma," Jordan said crisply.

"Where else could this've come from?" I asked.

"Mike could've told friends in Hollywood about his hiring the private investigator. Your mother could've told members of your family. My father could easily have confided in some of his oldest friends. There are a million scenarios."

"What now?"

"My abbot wants me to go away from Rome for a while," Jordan said. "Until the weather clears."

"Will you tell me where you're going?" I asked.

"No, you know I can't do that, Jack," Jordan said. "But I'd like you to do me a favor. I'd like you to set up a meeting for me with my father. But use extreme caution, be very careful."

"I will," I said. "Ledare is with me and she could help."

"Good. Ask her to come to the other side of the confessional and let's plan how the meeting with my father should take place."

"When are you going to see your mother?" I asked.

"I already have. She understands why I need to see him. I've always wanted to have a father, Jack. You know that. I've never had one in my life."

"You overrate it," I said.

"No," he said. "I just need one."

CHAPTER 20

TWO DAYS LATER I AWAITED THE AR-
rival of General Elliott in the bar of the Hotel
Raphael.

When he finally appeared, his eyes swept
the room in a hard, predatory gaze. Looking to
his right and left, he marched toward my table
and put out his hand. I stood up and we shook
hands perfunctorily.

"Your wounds are healing well?" the general said.

"I'm feeling much better, thank you," I replied.

"You're taking me to see my son, is that
understood?" the general said.

"No, that's not understood at all," I said. "I'm going to take you on a walk through Rome. Jordan'll decide if he'll see you or not."

"But he knows how I want to see this all resolved in his favor," the general said. "He must know that I wouldn't have come all this way if I didn't still love him."

"First, he wants to see if anyone's followed you," I said.

"That sounds a bit like paranoia to me," the general said.

"General," I asked, "don't you think paranoia's appropriate in this instance?"

"I would never do anything to hurt my son," the general said.

"You already have," I answered. "We'll know if you want to reverse that by the end of the day."

"What do you mean by that?" the general snapped.

"We'll see how it plays out."

The two of us left the Raphael and proceeded to walk to the Santa Maria della Pace where we approached a side door on which I knocked loudly three times. Three knocks were heard in reply, the door swung open, and I led the general through the doorway beneath the semicircular porch and into the interior where we passed the graceful sibyls of Raphael himself as we made our way toward a beautiful marble altar and out through a sacristy door that led to the cloisters where shy nuns watched our passage without comment or interest. Another *portiere* awaited us with an open door and I passed along ten thousand lire for the services of both men.

We were now loose in the alleyways of Rome, the secret part of the city that I loved best. It was like walking through fields of rust and burnt-siena in this many-warrened section of Rome with its deep, one-roomed shops whose proprietors sat behind antique desks patient as stalagmites. I could not restrain myself from pointing out shops of historical or architectural merit as we wound through the streets that cut off suddenly from the Via dei Coronari. Twice, we doubled back on ourselves, then took a cab at a taxi stand near the Corso Vittorio Emanuele. I ordered the driver to take us to the Pincio, near the Borghese Gardens.

"This is amateur hour, Jack," the general said. "I worked for Navy Intelligence for two years and you can't shake a good tail just by playing tag."

"We are just amateurs, General," I said. "Please bear with us."

"Who's making sure we're not being followed?" the general asked.

"Jordan," I answered.

"We passed by him?"

"Twice," I said. "How've you liked Rome?"

"I haven't. Too chaotic. The city has no sense of order," the general said.

I disagreed and said, "It has a perfect sense of order. But it's a Roman sense of order and not necessarily understood by outsiders."

We were dropped off at the Pincio and I led the general along its promenade, which overlooks all of Rome. From there everything looked different; from the height and the angle of the walkway were revealed thousands of scrupulously kept terraces hidden on the rooftops of the city.

We walked on until we came to the Spanish Steps, which we went down, with me holding on to the general's arm for balance. It was as hard and sinewy as a young wrestler's and I could not help but notice what a fine figure of a man he was and I well understood how a young soldier could follow such a detached, unreachable man into battle. If he had any soft places, they were well hidden.

The general grew impatient with the game-playing and I was beginning to grow exhausted and irritable, but by the time we reached Dal Bolognese on the Piazza del Popolo, I was positive we were not being followed. However, the coiled intensity of the general alarmed me. He clearly had no capacity for lightheartedness or small talk, and nothing about Rome seemed to interest him.

We entered the bar Rosati and I paid the cashier for two *cappuccini.* Though the general looked agitated, he saw he had no choice but to continue his participation in this long, enervating diversion. The bar was filling up with businessmen who needed their *aperitivi* before wandering out to their favorite restaurants for lunch.

The general watched me closely as we both heard the sound of a helicopter overhead but he kept his equanimity and his demeanor calm. There was little to be said between us that would not open old wounds and the silence was wearing on me. Under normal circumstances, the general did not mind spending time with people he knew disliked him. It made the other person extremely self-conscious and prone to error and he tried to use this to his own advantage.

"What's the next step?" the general asked.

"I don't know," I answered, looking out toward the Piazza del Popolo. "We must be patient."

"I've been patient, and all we've done is go around in circles."

Then I saw Ledare walking in swift steps out of the Via del Babuino toward the monumental gate, Porta del Popolo. She did not look in our direction as the general studied her well-rehearsed promenade across the length of the piazza. A blue Volvo station wagon came through the Porta del Popolo and drove toward Ledare, stopping beside her. Four men, all Franciscan priests, emerged from the car and each began to move off in different directions from the obelisk in the center. One of the priests stopped and Ledare kissed him lightly on the cheek and pointed to the place where I was with the general.

"Where's his beard?" the general said.

"Shaved it after he was on television," I answered. "You saw that in the photographs."

"He's heavier," the general said.

The priest walked toward us with the sun behind him, a diffident, disinterested walk that lacked all resolution.

"Is it him?" the general said. "It's been so long. And the sun's in my eyes. I can't tell if it's really him or not."

"Do you want to be alone with him?" I asked.

"Not yet," the general said. "Please stay. At least until we get the matter of introductions over with."

"You don't need any introduction," I said. "It's your son."

As the priest approached us, he pulled back his cowl revealing a head of thick dark curls.

The general reached out to shake hands with his son and there was a sudden movement in the bar behind us as three men burst out of the interior of Dal Bolognese. The general held his son's hand fiercely as an undercover agent from Interpol expertly placed handcuffs on the priest. Every entrance into the Piazza del Popolo was suddenly blocked by blue Fiats with their swirling azure lights and their irritating sirens.

"I told you it was amateur hour, Jack," the general said. "They fitted me with a device. They've followed us every step of the way."

"Jordan wanted me to give you a message if it turned out this way, General," I said, watching as two agents roughly dragged Ledare toward us. "He made it simple. You didn't surprise him at all."

"Let him deliver the message himself," the general said, staring at his son.

"Now will you tell me my part in this silly charade, Jack, me boy?" the priest said to me in an Irish accent so thick that even the Italian policemen knew this was no American. He also removed a pair of dark sunglasses.

"Where is my son, Jordan Elliott?" the general demanded of the Irish priest.

"I don't know what you're talking about," the priest said affably, enjoying the excitement and the crowd that had gathered around them.

•   •   •

For hours they questioned me at Interpol's headquarters about my relationship with Jordan Elliott and I answered all their questions forthrightly. I could tell them nothing about this priest's daily existence in Rome. I had no idea what order Jordan belonged to or where he slept at night or where he celebrated Mass. But I gladly provided a list of churches in which we had passed letters to each other and I offered the detail that he wore the habits of several different orders.

Celestine Elliott also underwent a grueling interrogation about her knowledge of her son's underground activities, but Jordan had protected her with the same shroud of ignorance he had me. Celestine answered her interrogators with a blind unclassifiable fury, but offered no information not required by the questions.

Ledare was released after being questioned for less than an hour. She was a minor player by her own admission, had not seen Jordan since she was in college, and only talked to someone claiming to be Jordan through a confessional screen. When released, she went back to my apartment on the Piazza Farnese and with the help of Maria began to pack Leah's bags for a long stay in America.

Jordan later reported to me that while his father stood in the Piazza del Popolo watching the Irish Franciscan coming toward him, Jordan himself stood on a terrace above the Red Lion Bookshop observing his father's exercise in bad faith unfold. Treachery and misunderstanding had been the only constants in their lives together. He could forgive his father for venality, but not for treachery, not again. Jordan had stayed long enough to see his father's confusion the moment he realized that his trap had been avoided and he had fallen prey, instead, to one set for him. But there was such anguish on his father's face that Jordan had felt for a moment a dormant pity. Jordan had watched as his father spun in a circle looking at doorways and rooftops and the ramparts of the Borghese Gardens, knowing that Jordan was watching him and realizing that he had been outmaneuvered and outsoldiered by a son who had never led men into battle. By this action, the general also knew he had driven a stake through the heart of his marriage.

That night after I was released and was back home I stood at the far window looking out toward the bell tower of St. Thomas of Canterbury and saw only blackness. Ledare and I had gone over the events of the past day. Since the scene in the Piazza del Popolo, neither of us had heard from Jordan, Celestine, or the general. That evening, when she went to bed, I told Leah the whole story of my friendship with Jordan Elliott. All life connects, I told Leah. Nothing happens that is meaningless.

After turning out Leah's light, I returned to the living room and poured both Ledare and myself a glass of Gavi dei Gavi, which I had chilled in a bucket of ice. We toasted each other halfheartedly and drank in silence before Ledare said, "How're you feeling, Jack? You're still recovering, and must be exhausted."

I put my hand to my head and then to my chest.

"In all the excitement, I forgot that I was hurt," I said.

"Has your eye cleared up?" she asked. "Is it still blurry?"

I put my hand over my right eye and stared at her with my left, then said, "The guy in the projection room still needs to adjust the knob . . . but just a little bit. It's getting better."

"I called Mike and told him that the general had issued the warning to Interpol," Ledare said. "He was relieved. I think he suspected that Capers might have done it."

"The project limps on," I said.

"Mike liked this part," she said. "He liked the general betraying the son a second time. He said it was biblical."

I said, "It's scary. Nothing bad can happen

to any of us that won't be great for Mike's film."

I looked up at the window, saw something, then rushed into the vestibule of the front hall, flicked on the light, and stood framed in the window that had the apartment's only view of St. Peter's. Someone was sending signals from the bell tower but if it was Jordan it was an hour after our appointed time. Whoever was handling the flashlight was an amateur at Morse Code and it took three times before I could decipher any message at all.

"Jordan is safe," the first message said.

"God bless you," said the second.

"Where do you think Jordan is tonight?" Ledare asked.

"I don't know, Ledare. I've never known."

"How'll he get back in touch with you?"

I was about to answer when I saw a figure making its way across the piazza and heading straight for my apartment. "Jesus Christ," I said. "Tell me my shot-out eye is deceiving me."

Down below, General Elliott was moving toward my building as though he were being reeled in by a line.

"Do you have a rifle?" Ledare said. "The kindest thing to do would be to shoot him before he reached the door."

The buzzer sounded its ugly raspberry

cheer, and Ledare kissed me on the cheek and said good night. She had endured all the psychodrama of which she was capable in a twenty-four-hour period.

I walked to the speakerphone in an unlit hallway and then picked up the receiver.

"*Chi è?*" I asked.

"Jack," the general said. "It's me. General Elliott. I'd like to see you. Please, Jack."

I thought about it for almost a full minute before I pressed the button that unlocked the two immense doors that led into the palazzo. I waited for the elevator to make its slow, whirring ascent to the fifth floor and I led General Elliott into the living room, and without asking, poured him a drink, mixing a martini of Bombay gin and a twist of lemon straight up in a flaring, bird-bath-shaped glass. As I handed the general the martini, he said, "If I were you, I'd never have let me into your apartment."

"I considered that tack. But my natural-born saintliness always takes precedence over my darker, more uncharitable habits," I said, not even attempting to hide the mockery in my voice. "Also, I'm curious about why you are here. I thought I'd never see you again and I cherished the thought."

"My wife was not at the hotel when I returned," the general said, and I could tell it was a painful admission for him. "She'd checked out of the room and left me a note. She's leaving me."

"Imagine. Celestine coming to her senses after all these years," I said.

"She left me without resources. Little money. No passport. No ticket. No clothes," the general said, taking a tentative sip from his glass.

"Use your credit card to buy tickets and clothes," I told him. "Go to the embassy tomorrow to arrange for a new passport."

"I don't have a credit card," the general said, embarrassed. "Celestine took care of all the details of our lives. I don't carry a wallet. The lump it made in the back of the trousers always seemed unmilitary to me."

"I'll help you get back to the States, General," I said.

"I'm afraid I trusted her for all the details of the marriage," the man said. "But I think I lost her today."

"You took me by surprise," I admitted. "I certainly thought Jordan was erring on the side of caution."

"I made a mistake with my son. I thought he had no gift for strategy or thinking on his feet. He surprised me. First in college. Then today."

"By surprising you, he ruined his life," I said.

"And my wife's, and my own."

I tried to take the measure of the man sitting before me, but his tenseness made any casual study uncomfortable. Though controlled and disciplined even now, something rumbled just below the surface, bottled like a mean-spirited genie, ready for a turn toward malevolence. Even though he was dressed in civilian clothes, a general's face shone hard as a diamond above his Brooks Brothers shirt. I knew that generalship was an art and a calling and an incurable illness. Arrogance is its natural resource and its favorite vacation is a fifteen-minute retreat to a full-length mirror.

"About today," the general said.

"Yes. Start with today."

"Capers came to me some time ago with the plan for a presidential pardon for Jordan," the general said. "This surprised me because, despite the rumors, I had thought Jordan had died. I believed in his suicide, or I convinced myself I did. But Capers showed me the pictures of Jordan leaving the confessional.

"Those were unbearable times for all of us. I've never hated a generation of young men and women as I hated yours and Jordan's. Nor was I alone in my feelings."

"You weren't uppermost in our prayers either."

"A Marine was killed by Jordan. So was a

daughter of a Marine. As a man of honor, my complete fealty belongs with the murdered Marine. I can't help that, Jack. That's the kind of man I am."

"You've been true to your nature," I said. "You've nothing to apologize for."

"I can't change. I'm a Marine before I'm a father, a husband, or even an American. If the Commandant of the Marine Corps ever decided that the President was a threat to our nation, I'd lead a battalion of Marines across Memorial Bridge for an open assault on the White House."

I could detect no bravado in this boast and the words stood out strong, in relief.

"How far would you and your Marines get?" I asked, out of curiosity.

"With the element of surprise and the right Marines and a half-hour head start, I'd hand you the head of that President that night."

"Like a chocolate mint on my pillow," I said.

"I chose the profession of arms," he said. "I chose a difficult century in which to practice it."

"General, you do understand that the young Marine in question and the Marine's daughter he was with . . . they were killed by accident."

"That is what my wife claims to be true. If we'd taken Jordan today, he'd have been put on trial and the truth could've finally come out. The legal people I talked to assured me that with Jordan becoming a priest and his sense of remorse, there was a chance that Jordan wouldn't serve a single day of a prison sentence. But I owed that Marine and his girlfriend that trial of my son. If they could die, then he could take the witness stand and explain his actions that led up to their deaths."

"He might've agreed with you," I said. "But you didn't have the decency to wait and ask him yourself."

"Decency," the general said. "I think my son committed treason during the Vietnam War."

"I think he probably did too."

"But my wife tells me you helped him to escape."

"He committed treason on purpose," I said, bothered that Celestine had confided such incriminating evidence to her husband. "He didn't mean to commit murder."

"You'd help a person who betrayed his country," the general sneered. "What kind of an American are you?"

"The kind who wouldn't hand you the head of my President," I responded sharply. "But back to your son: I'd help Jordan anytime he needed help and I've proven that."

"Even if it trampled on your country's flag," the general said, rising out of his seat and pacing across the marble floor. Before I answered, I carefully considered the question in all its troubling parts. During my whole life, I had been too quick with my answers. Glibness was simply a method to fend people off when they came too close.

"For the love of your son," I answered, finally. "Yes, sir. I'd trample on my flag."

"You and my son do not have the stuff that made our nation great," the general shouted, his voice echoing down the wide hallways.

"Not all of it, general," I agreed. "But we've got some of it."

"You didn't fight for your country," he sneered at me.

"Yeh, we did," I said. "That's the part you're not getting."

"How dare you even imply that?" the general said. "I saw a lot of the finest young men who ever lived die over there, fighting in my division."

"They were wonderful young men," I agreed. "War always kills terrific young men. This is a fairly well known fact, General."

The general said, "There's a beauty in dying for one's country that you'll never know."

I replied, "Neither will you, General. I hate to bring this up, but you survived all your country's wars."

"What do you believe in, Jack?" the general asked, tauntingly. "Is there some belief so sacred you carry around inside you that you'd let no force on earth defile it?"

Again I thought before I answered. Several moments passed before I said, "Yes. One. I'd never betray my child."

General Elliott stepped back as though I had thrown carbolic acid in his face. *"Semper Fidelis,"* the general whispered. "They're the two strongest words in my heart. They just are. Nothing else explains today. The loss of my wife. My son. *Semper Fidelis."*

"This is the city where those two words were coined, General," I said. "Do you have any money? A place to stay? You eaten anything?"

The general shook his head.

I put my arm around his shoulders and led him out toward the hallway. "General, I never led a squad of Marines in a raid in Cambodia. But I can cook like a son of a bitch. I have got a wallet full of money, and a spare room with a view. It may not last long, but tonight you're going to like me better than you like Chesty Puller."

"Why are you doing this?" the general asked suspiciously. "You should hate me more than anyone."

I laughed as I led him to the kitchen and then said as I rummaged in the pantry for a box of dried pasta, "I cheerfully loathe you, General. But you're my best friend's father and I don't want you sleeping on a bench near the Tiber. Also, this gives me a chance to prove the natural superiority of liberals to Nazis. Those chances come rarely during one lifetime."

So, on a cold Roman night, General Elliott sat on a stool in my kitchen as a wind roared out of the Apennines and rimmed the lips of the smallest fountains with a thin windowing of ice and we two enemies talked to each other man to man for the first time in our bristling, ungiving history together. My coming so close to death had opened something up in me that I thought had closed forever. The general had spent a day in agony. The sheer loneliness of the words *Semper Fidelis* withered on his tongue when he considered the trap he had set for his son with all the brightest intentions.

We talked carefully, avoiding the center of things, all the explosive subjects that both trapped and entwined us and had led us to the dispiriting events of the day. For me the South had taken the general prisoner at birth, secured the cells of his character, and never granted him furlough or early release. He also had the easy flow of charm that was indispensable to any man who wished to rise fast in the military service. The general displayed this charm as I cooked for him and refreshed his drink. He told stories about his own childhood, stories about my grandfather and the Great Jew, the coming of Shyla's parents, and the general's own years attending the Citadel.

By the time I showed him to his room, each of us had seen the other in a way we never had before. We had conversed as gentlemen. The abundance of our grievances and fury lay between us like mines, but we stepped gingerly over and around them, choosing dignity to get us through the difficult evening.

And I admired the courage it took for Elliott to present himself at the doorway of his enemy, and the general seemed grateful that I had opened that door.

When I had given the general his towels and a spare toothbrush, he asked me, "Is Jordan a good priest? Or is it just part of his disguise? A game he's playing?"

I thought about it and said, "Your son's a man of God."

The general shook his head in disbelief and said, "Doesn't that surprise you? Was I so wrong about my son? Wasn't he a little bit on the wild side?"

I laughed quietly, remembering, then said, "Jordan Elliott was the wildest son of a bitch I ever met in my life—bar none."

CHAPTER 21

FROM THE DAY HE ARRIVED IN WA-
terford, Jordan Elliott was known as the "California boy." To South Carolinians, California
was the point where the American dream had
started to turn in the sun and go terribly wrong.
It was a forbidden country where all human
passions were venerated to excess and all restraint pushed to its ineffable limits.

The time was known as the Jordan Summer. No one had ever seen anything like him.
His blond hair grew down to his shoulders and
he glowed with a radiant, God-given health.
Though not conventionally handsome, he wore
the hard-cast face of a long-distance runner.

He had fearless but broken eyes, and they were breathtaking. Waterford would discover immediately that Jordan Elliott lived life as though it were a free fall from a high-flying plane. He brought revolutionary ideas with him from California and dispensed them freely.

In that summer, I would remember my friends and their souls, light and air-streamed as mallards, set loose among the vast table linen of the great salt marshes, happy among the green riches of a land so full with life that the rivers smelled like some perfect distillate made of spartina and the albumen of eggs. The boys of the low country were accustomed to taking their pleasure from the rivers around Waterford: fishing trips that lasted for days, floating through a dozen tide changes, rubbing baby oil and Mercurochrome on their sunburned shoulders as the game fish of those moon-leavened waters fought for permission to take their hooks—the sheepshead, the migrating cobia, the spottail bass, the sweet-tasting trout—all those fresh fillets would turn golden in their frying pans and fill their bellies and brighten all the generous upright days of their boyhood. The marsh country satisfied all five senses of a boy a hundred times over. I could close my eyes while throwing my cast net for bait in a tidal creek at low tide, and the summer air would fill my lungs. I could believe that

I was a sailor, a merchant marine, a sea-born creature of water and marshes. The black mud of the creeks squirted between my toes and I could hear a porpoise driving the mullet toward a sandbar in the river.

Jordan's effect on Waterford was cataclysmic, though it would take years to assess either the damage or the benefits of his bold passage through the life of the town. For his contemporaries, he opened up the windows of time, he brought news of the great wide world to their door. Life was fable and theater and myth because Jordan willed it to be so.

Jordan was a military brat, the son of a lieutenant colonel, and one of those migratory, interchangeable, and ultimately invisible children who drifted in and out of the colorless housing of the two Marine bases in town and the naval hospital. The lives of these children were so transient that there was little reason for a native Waterfordian to waste time getting to know them well. They simply passed through the town and its schools each decade, mostly unnoticed and unpraised.

Capers, Mike, and I first saw Jordan on Dolphin Street as we were slowly making our way to an American Legion baseball game at the high school field. We were in no hurry and moved slowly down the main shopping street during one of those fragrant Southern days when the pavement was hot to the touch and all the plants seemed about to burst into spontaneous combustion. The heat lay inside of things. Blasts of cold air came from within the stores whenever a shop door opened and hit the three of us with a welcome coolness. Sailboats were stalled in the windless bay like dragonflies trapped in the amber of a weatherless high noon that would last forever. Time stood still and babies in their carriages squalled from discomfort and heat rash and the impatient lassitude of their mothers. The summer wrote its name on the sizzling asphalt and there was not a dog in sight.

"What in the hell is that all about?" Mike said, the first of the group to spot Jordan flying down Dolphin Street on a skateboard, weaving expertly and dazzlingly between cars in the stalled traffic.

"Damned if I know and damned if I care," Capers said, feigning indifference, but there was an edge of uncertainty that both Mike and I caught. Capers was the arbiter of fashion and trends among our group. He welcomed acolytes, but didn't cotton well to rivals.

"That's the new kid," I said. "The one from California."

I never forgot that first sighting of Jordan Elliott, his palomino-colored hair floating above him as he shot down the street on the

first skateboard ever to make it across the borders of South Carolina. I watched in awe as
Jordan navigated between Buicks and
Studebakers while all the eyes on that Southern
street turned their collective, disapproving gaze
on the stranger. Jordan wore a bathing suit, a
torn-up tee shirt, and cut-off tennis shoes, and
he moved down that street noisily and showily,
making hairpin turns and reverses that seemed
impossible and superhuman. His sunglasses
were wrapped around his head and appeared
more like a mask of defiance and outlawry than
anything to do with the laws of optics. Store
owners and customers ran out into the shim-
mering wall of heat to watch the performance.

Deputy Cooter Rivers was issuing a parking
citation to a tourist from Ohio when he noticed
the commotion and whistled Jordan to a stop
in the middle of the street.

Deputy Rivers was an amply built, dull-wit-
ted man who had an amateur actor's love of
crowds and he was delighted by the attention
he drew from his townsmen as he approached
the long-haired boy. Deputy Rivers said, "Well,
well, Little Eagle. What have we here?"

"What'd you want? I'm in a hurry," Jordan
said behind his sunglasses, and he seemed
oblivious to the commotion he was causing.

"Put a 'sir' on the end of that sentence,
boy," the deputy thundered.

"Which one?"

"What?" the deputy said, confused. "All of 'em, boy. Every goddamn one of them if you know what's good for you."

"I'm sorry, sir," Jordan answered, "but I don't understand a word you're saying. Could you please speak English?"

Mike and I joined several members of the crowd as we burst out laughing.

"Boy," the deputy replied angrily, "I don't know if you're considered funny where you hail from, but you try to rattle my cage with your brand of crap and I'm liable to shut your runnin' gums in a hurry."

Jordan stared out from behind his sunglasses, unreadable, foreign, in perfect control. "What did this guy say?" he asked the crowd and again there was laughter.

Cooter Rivers' accent was indeed thick and difficult even for a fellow South Carolinian to decipher. And when provoked, the deputy talked faster than normal and this accentuated a slight speech impediment that the public schools of Waterford never quite got around to correcting. His gutturals were lazy and his labials floated toward incomprehensibility. Agitated, his words ran together in an untranslatable stream. Cussing beneath his breath, Cooter wrote up a ticket and handed it to Jordan. A few men in the crowd clapped as Jordan studied the ticket.

Jordan then said, "Did you finish high school?"

A flustered Rivers answered, "I almost did."

"You misspelled 'violation,' " Jordan said. "You misspelled 'moving.' "

"I got my point across," the deputy said.

"What do I do with this ticket, man?" Jordan asked.

As Deputy Rivers made his way through the crowd, he shouted back, "You can eat it for lunch for all I care, Little Eagle."

The crowd began to disperse and most of them missed the moment when Jordan ate his traffic ticket as easily and deliberately as a carriage horse eating a carrot. He munched on it, then swallowed the last of the ticket with a slight gagging sound.

"You play baseball?" I asked.

"I play everything," Jordan said, taking his first look at the tall, rangy, flat-nosed boy I was in those years.

"Any good?" Mike asked.

"I can play a little bit." And in the secret language of athletes Jordan was letting us know that we were in the presence of a player. "My name's Jordan Elliott."

"I know who you are," Capers answered.

"We're second cousins. I'm Capers Middleton."

"My mother said you would be too ashamed to come meet me," Jordan said, amused. There was something both charming and off-putting about his self-assurance.

"I heard you were weird," Capers said. "You just proved it."

"Capers! What a name. A caper's a little berry in Europe they put on fish and salads. It tastes like shit."

"It's a family name," Capers said, thornily, defensive. "It's very important in South Carolina history."

"Oh gag," Mike said, pretending to throw up on the curb.

"My father thinks the Elliotts back here are hot shit," Jordan confessed.

"It's a fine South Carolina name," Capers agreed. "Very fine."

"I knew I should've taken that vomit bag the last time I flew Delta," Mike said and Jordan laughed.

"I'm Jack McCall," I said extending my hand. "A McCall's next to nothing in this town."

"Mike Hess," Mike said, bowing. "Capers lets us hang around to polish his coat of arms."

"They both come from very good families," Capers said.

"Capers thinks we come from white trash," I said. "But he'd die of loneliness if we weren't around."

"You shouldn't've eaten that ticket," Capers said. "It showed a disrespect for the law."

"Let's bring him to practice," I said. "We've got three guys hurt."

"How're we gonna explain his hair to Coach Langford?" Capers asked.

"He's from California," Mike said. "That explains everything."

If we had walked on to the baseball field with a Mau Mau chieftain or a Tibetan basketweaver, Coach Langford's reaction could not have been more incredulous.

"Well, what do we got here?" Coach Langford said.

"Military brat, Coach," I said. "Came from California."

"He looks like a Russian Communist," Langford whispered.

"He's Capers' cousin," said Mike.

"A distant cousin," Capers quickly said.

"California, you say," Coach Langford said. "We've got a spare uniform, son," Coach Langford said. "You ever play this game?"

"A little," Jordan said.

"You ever pitched?"

"A time or two."

"Put a sir on the end of that," Coach Langford demanded.

"Sir," Jordan said and he said it with the exact same inflection and feeling as though he had uttered the word "shit." He had a genius for making an adult feel uncomfortable without resorting to overt discourtesy. Jordan Elliott was the first rebel I knew to enter the precincts of Waterford since the firing on Fort Sumter, the first who treated men in authority as aliens, as interlopers whose job it was to depress the natural joy and ebullience of youth.

As we watched him put on the uniform, Capers said to us, "I think we made a big mistake bringing him to practice."

"I like him," Mike said. "He takes no shit. He acts just like I would if I had an ounce of courage. Which I proudly do not."

"He's an athlete. That's for sure," I said, studying the skateboard. "How'd you like to try to ride that thing?"

"My mother told me all about him. They should've put him in reform school years ago," said Capers.

"Let's see if he can pitch," I said.

"He's just a poor Marine brat. They move every year. Give him a chance," Mike added.

"None of them fit in when you come right down to it," Capers said. "They don't know who they are. Got no place to call their own. I feel sorry for them."

"He's an Elliott. A South Carolina Elliott," I teased.

"From a *fine* family. *Very* fine," Mike added happily.

Capers smiled as he watched Jordan walk onto the field.

"Pitch, new boy," Coach Langford said, tossing Jordan his own glove and a baseball. "Where's your hat?"

"The hat didn't fit."

"All that damn California hair," the coach said. "We gotta do something about that situation. Otis, you bat, son. The rest of you boys spread out in the field."

The catcher, Benny Michaels, finished fastening his gear, then crouched behind the batter's box and started taking warm-up pitches from Jordan. Jordan warmed up slowly, but you could tell it wasn't his first time on a pitcher's mound. There was nothing fancy in his delivery; it was workmanlike and competent. Then Otis Creed began to run his mouth.

Otis was the first boy in Pony League to chew tobacco on a regular basis without throwing up. His father ran the marina on the inland waterway and Otis carried with him that freckled, sunburned look of someone who had grown up around boats and the good mechanical smell of small engines being repaired. He could tear down a boat's engine as easily as a recruit could assemble a field-stripped M-1 rifle. Otis could not diagram a declarative sentence or find the value of X in the simplest algebraic equation. Waterford was a town famous for its street fighters, and Otis Creed moved with the slack-jawed swagger of the natural bully.

"I never batted against no girl before," Otis said loud enough for even the outfielders to hear. "She's kind of purty too."

The laughter spread through the ranks of the team, but it was nervous reflexive laughter.

Jordan started his windup and threw his first pitch straight at the fillings in the upper part of Otis Creed's mouth. It was with that pitch that the boys of Waterford learned about the speed that Jordan brought to the task of hurling a baseball. Benny never came close to catching that first one. It hit the chicken wire backstop with a solid twang as though a string had broken on an overtuned guitar.

"She tried to hit me. That was intentional," Otis said, rising and dusting off his pants and pointing his bat menacingly at Jordan. But Jordan paid Otis no attention at all, just received the toss from the catcher, then walked back to the rosin bag, tossed it up and down a couple of times, the dust exploding between his fingers like a dandelion going to seed.

"Throw strikes, new kid," the coach ordered.

The second pitch was thrown just as hard. It missed Otis' throat by a millimeter and sent Otis spinning out of control once again, falling backward toward the visiting team's dugout.

"Otis, you look a bit tense in the batting cage," Coach Langford said.

"He's wild as a billy goat, Coach," Otis shouted.

Jordan said, "I still remind you of a girl?"

"You sure as hell do, Goldilocks."

The next pitch hit Otis high on the rib cage, making a sound like a watermelon hit by a throwing knife.

I was standing next to Mike in the outfield and said, "Otis could never read the handwriting on the wall."

"Looks like we found us a damn pitcher," Mike said.

"The question is: Can he throw it over the plate?" I said.

Otis rose painfully to his feet, roared once, then started out toward the mound, brandishing his bat. The long-haired boy did not appear to be cowed and took several steps forward to meet Otis' charge. Coach Langford got between them first and kept them separated with his spavined, meaty hands.

"Not smart to make fun of a boy who throws that hard," Coach Langford said to Otis. "Can you get that ball over the plate, son?"

Jordan turned his blue eyes at that drawling, overweight coach who ran a gas station for a living and brought an irrepressible love of sport and young boys to the task of coaching. Even then, Jordan could take a quick read of anyone, and was as clear-sighted as he was mercurial and moody, and Jordan saw the goodness of the man below that primitive, fascist exterior that is the general rule among the Southern fraternity of coaches. It was the man's basic and abiding sweetness that Jordan felt as Coach Langford put the ball back into Jordan's glove and said, "Son, now I'd like to see you strike him out."

In four pitches, Jordan struck Otis out swinging. There was an audible murmur from the boys in the field as they admired the speed of Jordan's pitch and the explosive, satisfying pop it made in Benny's glove.

For Capers, Mike, and myself, the addition of Jordan completed our group in some elemental way. In our junior and senior years of high school, Jordan was the right halfback in what became known as the Middleton backfield and we lost only two games in those final two years. On the basketball team, Jordan was a tremendous leaper, a scrapper under the boards, and he hit the jump shot from the corner that won the lower state championship game against North Augusta High. His pitching improved every year as he grew into his formidable manhood and his fastball was timed in the high eighties by the end of his senior year when he took his team to the brink of the championship.

But it was Capers who recognized Jordan's potential that day: Beneath the flowing mane of blond hair, he saw both the attractiveness and the danger in Jordan's rare smile, rare in its openness and candor, hidden by the rebellious, unhappy boy who seemed at war with the entire adult world. Capers recognized the sexual aura that Jordan wore in his insolent, thin-lipped assurance. Sensing a potential rival, he sought to befriend Jordan before the stranger proved dangerous.

No protest ever arose from me or Mike because we had learned from our early boyhood to follow Capers' lead in everything. Capers expected it as one of his natural rights in a friendship that had been imbalanced from the beginning. Because Capers grew up in a household that revered politics, he understood the strategies that involved silence and indirection. He would plant an idea in Mike that would cause an argument with me and both of us would turn gratefully to him for relief or intercession. Often, he simply became the tie-breaking vote called to intervene between his bickering friends. His tyranny was encased in velvet and appreciated. Capers admired the horseplay and mischief that Mike and I brought to his strait-laced life; he rarely made any demands of his own and Mike and I never realized that Capers always got his way. We were the instruments of a superior political instinct who was ruthless in the sweetest, most generous way. In the South, the cotillion of Machiavelli is always played as a soft-shoe, in three-quarter time.

But it was Skeeter Spinks who really bonded the friendship of the four of us. Skeeter came out of the lowest echelons of the white South and he came out mean. His time in high school had been a reign of terror for Waterford's teenage boys because Skeeter liked to brag that he'd beaten every boy in school at least once. Smart boys especially dreaded his approach, for he took special pleasure in humiliating them. His frame was enormous and he combined an overworked farm boy's strength with a lifetime of bad manners. He was volatile, thick-necked, and the possessor of a both razor-blade and hair-trigger temper. Skeeter was one of those boys of nightmare that make having a penis during an American childhood almost unendurable.

In the summer of 1962, Skeeter had chosen me as his special project for the season. The advent of school integration had aroused Skeeter's virulent hatred of black people and Skeeter's daddy personally blamed my father, Judge McCall, for the coming of integration to Waterford. As a rising ninth-grader, I was a little too young for Skeeter to beat senseless, but I could never pass by without Skeeter putting me into a headlock and playfully humiliating me in front of a crowd of girls. He had taken to slapping me lightly and playfully in the face, but as the summer wore on there was a slight but constant escalation in the vigor of the slaps. I tried to avoid all the places where Skeeter hung out, but Skeeter noticed this and part of his pleasure was crossing the streets to find the places where I went to avoid him.

During Pony League that summer, I had nowhere to hide because Skeeter never missed a baseball game. I had just reached the height of six feet and the weight of one hundred fifty pounds, and I was gangly and not yet comfortable with my size. I felt soft and comic, like a Great Dane puppy, but Skeeter decided my size was a new threat coming up through the ranks. He had been out of high school for a year and working as an auto mechanic at the

Chevrolet dealership when he heard that I had referred to him as that "zit-faced jerk-off."

It was true. I was guilty of sullying Skeeter's reputation with those exact words, but I had said it among friends, never dreaming it would get back to Skeeter. Walking one day with Capers, Mike, and Jordan, I was talking about a terrific game we had just lost to Summerville 1–0. We were replaying every pitch of the game when two carloads of last year's football linemen screeched to a halt and Skeeter and five of his friends jumped out and faced us. We were still wearing our gloves and sweating from the game. Jordan was carrying a thirty-four-inch Louisville Slugger that I had broken with a foul tip and Jordan had repaired with masking tape.

Skeeter went right to work and slapped me across the mouth with a swift backhand that sent me to my knees, tasting blood in my mouth.

"I heard a rumor you called me something bad, McCall," Skeeter crowed. "I wanted to see if you had the guts to call me that to my face."

"Jack told me he thought you were a prince among men and a credit to the white race," Mike said, trying to help me rise.

"Shut up, Jew boy," Skeeter ordered.

"Get lost, Skeeter," Capers said. "We weren't bothering anyone."

"Button your lip, pretty boy, before I tear

both your lips off and feed 'em to the crabs for dinner," Skeeter said and rabbit-punched me on the back of the neck and sent me sprawling to the ground again.

That's when Jordan hit the bat against the sidewalk, just to let Skeeter know there was a new kid in town.

"Hey, booger-face," Jordan said. "You look like the Clearasil poster child. You got any cheeks beneath those pimples?"

Mike closed his eyes sadly and later would admit that he thought that Jordan had just uttered his last words on earth and that Skeeter, with his IQ of an Ice Age vegetarian, would think up new and gruesome ways for the California boy to die a grisly death.

"He called you booger-face," Henry Outlaw, the punt snapper on the football team, said.

"Henry picked right up on that," Mike said.

"Shut up, Hess," Henry said, "or I'll cut your butt and eat it raw."

"I ain't believing I heard that right," Skeeter said, moving slowly toward Jordan, who simply held the bat more tightly. "Could you repeat it, pretty please?"

"No, penis-breath," Jordan said. "I won't repeat it you ugly, Dumbo-eared, gapped-tooth, hyena-faced redneck. And don't take another step toward me, or you'll be shitting out the splinters of this bat all night long."

"O-o-o-h," Skeeter's crowd said in mock terror as Skeeter laughed out loud and pretended to shrink back.

"You some of that Marine shit they get in at Pollock Island every year?"

"Yep, I'm some of that Marine shit," Jordan said. "But I happen to be Marine shit that's carrying a baseball bat."

"I'm gonna take that bat away from you, then kick your ass all over this town," Skeeter said and his voice was a hiss, something mean of spirit and snakelike. "Then I'm gonna shave your head bald."

"The bat's your first problem, dick-head," Jordan said.

"Don't piss him off any worse than he already is," I said quietly to Jordan.

Henry Outlaw said, "This shitbird's dead meat, McCall."

"You ain't got enough guts to hit me with that bat," Skeeter boasted.

"You better pray that's true," Jordan said and then surprised everyone by smiling at Skeeter.

It seemed unnatural that Jordan was not the tiniest bit cowed or intimidated by Skeeter. The fight was obviously a mismatch, a pure case of a full-grown man picking a fight with a boy. Jordan simply held on to the bat and stared Skeeter down as Jordan awaited the coming charge, balanced and composed. None of the boys on the street that day knew that Jordan Elliott had spent a lifetime being torn up by a full-grown Marine. Though he feared that Marine with all his heart, he did not fear young hoodlums and punks.

Skeeter removed his tee shirt, sweat-stained and fouled with oil, and threw it at one of his friends. He spit on his hands and rubbed them together and stood facing Jordan, bare-chested, his muscles deeply defined and cruel in their elegant arrangement.

"Jesus," Henry Outlaw said in pure admiration of that honed, keenly developed body.

"Tell your friend about me," Skeeter said beginning to make feints toward Jordan. "He's fairly new in town and don't realize he's about to die."

Mike said, "Jordan, I'd like to introduce you to our real good friend, Skeeter Spinks. We're all real proud of Skeeter. He's our town bully."

Capers and I laughed and for a moment it looked as if Skeeter was considering changing his line of attack.

"Me first, Skeeter," Jordan said, getting Skeeter's attention back to the business at hand. "Skeeter? You're named for that little bitty insect that sucks blood out of babies asses? The guy we used to be afraid of in California was a surfer named Turk. We California boys don't worry too much about dopes named after insects."

"Oh God," Henry Outlaw said. "This boy's asking for it so bad."

"It'd take a real chicken-shit to hit a man with a baseball bat instead of using his fists," Skeeter growled.

"Yeh," Jordan said. "It's a shame you aren't fighting a real brave son of a bitch."

"Use your fists," Skeeter ordered. "Fight like a man."

"I'd be glad to Skeeter," Jordan said. "But we're not the same size. And we're not the same age. You're bigger than me. Just like you're bigger than Jack. So what this baseball bat does is even up the fight a little bit."

"My guess is that you ain't got the guts to use that thing," Skeeter said, charging Jordan suddenly and without warning.

That night, as Skeeter Spinks lay in the intensive care unit of the hospital, all of Waterford knew that Skeeter had guessed wrong.

Later, the town would learn about Jordan's extraordinary sense of balance and his unflappable poise. His movements were lightning fast and that day I saw Jordan react with the speed of an Eastern diamondback when Skeeter made his ill-advised charge. What was also clear was that Jordan had been ready for the fight the moment he tapped the bat on the cement. And once he had primed himself, he glowed with a concentration that was nearly a state of prayer. What we had witnessed was not simply courage, but a form of recklessness that came from deep within Jordan's spirit. He almost killed Skeeter Spinks with that baseball bat.

Jordan stepped aside and avoided Skeeter's first headlong rush. Skeeter's plan was a good one and he tried to sweep Jordan off his feet the same way he had brought down small halfbacks who slashed off tackles during high school games. The plan fell apart when Jordan avoided the tackle and brought the bat down solidly against the back of Skeeter's head. That first blow caused a concussion to the rear of his brain. The sound was like a hand ax cleaving through a chicken carcass. Instead of staying down, Skeeter staggered to his feet, humiliated and furious, and made another, though far less certain dive for Jordan, whose faith in wielding the bat had not been misplaced. The second swing of the bat broke three of Skeeter's ribs and one of the splintered bones punctured his right lung. That's why he was vomiting blood when the ambulance arrived.

Skeeter still did not get the point and made

one last fruitless lunge toward Jordan, who stood his ground with that same chilling, imperturbable air of calm. That's when Jordan broke Skeeter's jaw. The broken jaw ended Skeeter's career as the town bully. Never again did he provoke the nightmare of a young Waterford boy and there wasn't a single young boy in town who didn't know Jordan Elliott's name the next day. No arrest was made and there were never any legal repercussions against Jordan.

I was later to discover that love and pain were synonymous in the life of Jordan Elliott. As our friendship grew closer and Jordan witnessed on several occasions my humiliation at the sight of my father's drunken ravings, he told me about the time he had run away during seventh grade. His mother had hunted the surfing beaches of Southern California until she found him out in the Pacific looking toward Asia for the next wave to ride. It was soon after that Mrs. Elliott forced Jordan into the psychiatric office of a Captain Jacob Brill. Over and over again, Jordan repeated this story to me, word for word.

Jordan did not shake hands with Captain Brill, nor acknowledge his presence as he walked into his office and studied the decor of the room. The doctor and the boy sat in silence for a minute before Dr. Brill cleared his throat and said, "So."

But Jordan was comfortable with silence and didn't answer a word. He could sit for hours without uttering a sound.

"So," Dr. Brill said again.

Still, Jordan did not speak, but turned his full attention to the psychiatrist. All his life Jordan had stared directly and inquisitively at adults and few of them could bear the silent weight of his scrutiny. "So why do you think your mother sent you here?" Dr. Brill said, trying to jump-start some kind of interaction.

Jordan shrugged his shoulders and just looked at the pale-skinned unprepossessing man who sat before him.

"She must have had a good reason," the doctor continued. "She seems like a very nice woman."

The boy nodded.

"Why are you looking at me that way?" the doctor asked. "You're here to talk. I'm paid good money by Uncle Sam to listen."

Looking away from the doctor, Jordan turned his attention to a modern painting of a square and a circle and a triangle, interposed on each other in different colors.

"What do you see when you look at that painting?"

"Bad taste," Jordan answered, turning his gaze back to the doctor.

"Are you an art critic?"

"No," Jordan answered, "but for my age, I'm something of an aficionado."

"Aficionado?" the doctor said, rolling the word. "You are something of a show-off too."

"I speak Spanish, so it's not showing off, Doctor. I also speak French and Italian. I've lived in Rome, Paris, and Madrid when my father was stationed at the embassies. My mother loved art and got her master's in art history from the University of Rome. She passed her love of art on to me. Believe me, she'd hate that painting of yours a lot more than I do."

"You're not here to talk about my taste in art," Dr. Brill said. "We're here to talk about you."

"I don't need you, Doc," Jordan said. "I'm doing as well as can be expected."

"That's not what your parents or teachers think."

"It's what I think."

"They all think you're a very disturbed young man. They think you're unhappy. So do I, Jordan. I'd love to help," Dr. Brill said, and his voice was soft and Jordan could not find a false note in it.

Jordan hesitated, then spoke, "I'm upset. True. But not for what they think . . . I deserve better parents. God made a terrible mistake. He delivered me to the wrong people."

"He often does that," Dr. Brill agreed. "But your parents have impeccable reputations. Your reputation's anything but. They say you have no friends."

"I choose to be alone."

"Loners are often misfits," Dr. Brill said.

But Jordan was ready for him and fired back, "So are shrinks."

"Pardon me?"

"Shrinks are some of the biggest losers in the world. I've heard my father say it a million times. He said it today."

"What did he say today, exactly?" asked Dr. Brill.

"He said you become shrinks because you're so incredibly fucked-up yourselves."

Dr. Brill nodded his head and said, "In my case, your father is absolutely right. I endured a perfectly miserable childhood. It made me want to fix up the world."

"You can't fix my world."

"I can try, if you'll let me, Jordan."

"I'm here under false pretenses. My parents don't like who I am. But they don't know me. They don't know anything about me."

"They know you only make C's and D's on your report card."

"I'm passing," the boy said. "My teachers

could stop clocks from ticking. That's how boring they are. Boredom should be one of the seven deadly sins."

"What bores you?"

"Everything," Jordan said.

"Do I bore you?" Dr. Brill asked good-naturedly.

"Brill," Jordan said, fixing the doctor with his blue-eyed gaze, "people like you are death. You'll never understand one thing about me."

"I'm the fifth psychiatrist you've been referred to," Dr. Brill said, consulting his notes on a clipboard. "They all take note of your hostility and your unwillingness to conform to the therapeutic process."

"I don't need a shrink, Doctor," Jordan said. "Thanks for your time, but I've got something that helps me where none of you guys can."

"Could you tell me what it is?" the older man asked. "I'd like to know."

"I'm religious," Jordan said.

"What?"

"I'm very religious. I'm a Catholic."

"I don't quite understand."

"Of course not," Jordan said. "You're Jewish. A lot of shrinks are Jewish. At least the ones I've met."

"I think it's a positive sign you have deep religious feelings."

"Thanks," Jordan said, rising to his feet. "Can I go now?"

"You certainly cannot," the doctor ordered, motioning for the boy to sit back down. "Your mother tells me you have some anxiety about your father's new duty station."

"I've no anxiety at all. I'm just not going with them."

"You're twelve years old. You've no choice in the matter. I think it would behoove us to work on strategies to make the transition easier."

"Yeh, I'm twelve," Jordan said. "Do you know how many schools I've been to? Ten. I've been to ten schools, Doc. Do you know what it's like walking into a new school every year? It's awful. Nothing good about it. Not one thing. That's why military brats are so fucked up. They're either a hundred percent ass kissers or they pull duty at the funny farm."

"You learn to make friends easily," Dr. Brill continued, his voice still charged with an undercurrent of irony. "It teaches self-reliance and flexibility. You learn about organizing your time and it prepares you to deal with crisis."

"It teaches you how to be lonely," Jordan said in a harsh whisper. "That's all it teaches you. You don't know anybody. You learn how to live your life without friends. Then I get to come into an office like this and someone like

you starts asking me why I don't have any goddamn friends."

"Your father's received orders to Pollock Island, South Carolina," the doctor said, again
reading from his notes.

"South Carolina," Jordan said contemptu-
ously. "Now there's a dream assignment."

"Your father's pleased with it. You should
feel okay because it's good for your father's career. A big step up."

"My father hates me," Jordan said looking
at the bad painting again.

"Why do you think that?" the doctor asked
softly.

"Observation," the boy replied.

"Your mother told me that your father
loves you very much. She says he has a tough
time expressing that love."

"He's good with hate. He expresses that
very well."

"Has your father ever struck you, Jordan?"
the doctor asked, and he could feel the shutting
of all the gates around this boy, the closing
down.

"No," Jordan lied, worthy son of a Marine
officer.

"Has he ever struck your mother?" asked
Dr. Brill.

"No," Jordan lied again, secret warrior of
the Corps.

"Does he pick on you?" the doctor asked.

"Yes."

"Does he scream at you and make your life a living nightmare?"

"Yes."

"Then let's figure out a strategy for you in South Carolina. Let's outflank and outmaneuver the military man. Your mother told me that your father might be at Pollock Island for all four years of your high school."

"So what?"

"You'll have time to make friends. Try to make some fast. Look for some boys you'd like to hang around. Some nice boys."

"In South Carolina?" Jordan asked. "Get off it, Doc. I'll be lucky if the kids there have teeth."

"Play all the sports. Get a girlfriend. Spend the night out with your friends. Go on fishing trips. Your father's going to have a lot of responsibility in his new job. He'll be under a lot of pressure. Keep away from him, Jordan. Figure out ways to avoid him at all costs."

"I'm his hobby," Jordan said. "He wants me to be exactly like he is and I'd . . . rather be dead."

"Why do you surf?" the doctor asked. "Why do you wear your hair long? Just to make him mad."

Jordan smiled and said, "It drives him

crazy. It *is* why I wear my hair long. It's not why I surf."

"Why, then? I'd like to know."

"Because surfing makes me feel like I'm in the presence of God. The ocean. The sun. The waves. The beach. The sky. I can't explain it, Doc. It's like praying without any words."

"Do your parents have any idea about your religious nature?"

"They don't know one thing about me."

"Have you always felt this way about your church?"

"It's the only thing in my life that's stayed the same," Jordan answered. "It was comforting when I was a kid. It's comforting to me now. Prayer's the one thing that makes me feel I'm not alone."

"You're lucky you have your faith, Jordan. Very lucky."

"You're Jewish. What do you believe?"

"I'm Jewish," the doctor said, quietly, wiping his glasses with his tie. "And I believe in nothing."

"I'm sorry. That must be terrible," Jordan said.

"You're a fine boy. A very fine boy."

"I tried to make you hate me when I first came in."

The doctor laughed. "You did an excellent job," he said. "I like your fighting spirit. I like everything about you, except for the fact you're a liar."

"How did I lie?" Jordan asked.

"You said your father never hit you. You said he didn't beat your mother," the doctor said in such a tone that Jordan was certain that the man knew everything.

"He's never touched either one of us in his life," Jordan said, but there was no spirit or conviction in the words.

The doctor applauded, clapping his hands together not in mockery, but in appreciation. "Well done. You and I both know his career might be over if you spoke the truth. I understand why you have to lie. Keep out of his way, Jordan. I've seen lots of men like him. They grow more dangerous as their sons grow older. You're smart enough to learn how to avoid his fists. Outsmart him."

"I'll try," Jordan said.

"You haven't had much fun in your life, have you?" the doctor asked.

"Not very much."

"What's the worst thing that ever happened to you? I know, you can't tell me about your old man. But in school."

Jordan thought about his short life and how he had never received a single letter from a friend he had met in school. He had never been asked to spend the night with a classmate and he had never danced with a girl.

"In third grade," Jordan finally said, "I transferred into a school in February. It was my third school that year. On Valentine's Day, my class had a big party and the teacher had put out boxes with the names of all the kids in the class. In the morning, the kids put all the Valentine's cards in the boxes of their friends and kids they liked. The teacher then read your name out and you'd go up and get all your Valentines. One girl named Janet Tetu received over sixty Valentines. She was so nice and pretty some of the boys sent her four or five."

"And you didn't get any," the doctor said softly.

"I still've never gotten one," the boy said. "My father doesn't believe in Valentine's Day. He thinks it's a sissy holiday."

"I wish we'd met sooner, Jordan. Play sports again when you get to your new school. It'll make your father happy and it'll keep you out of his way," the doctor advised.

Jordan shook his head and answered, "No. He picks me up after practice. That's when I'm trapped. Those are the worst times. When I'm alone with him."

"Your mother'll pick you up. I promise that."

"The Colonel makes the rules in our house."

"I'll make this rule," Dr. Brill said. "Your mother picks you up or you don't play sports. No exceptions."

Later, Jordan told me he couldn't believe the conviction of the doctor, but said, "A deal."

"I've been seeing your mother all this year, Jordan," the doctor said.

Jordan was surprised. "I didn't know that."

"She's very worried about you. She's very worried about herself."

"So what's new?"

"She told me what your father does. No, don't be alarmed. She swore me to secrecy. She's forbidden me to report it to the military authorities and all of us know they wouldn't do anything anyway. Your mother believes your father loves you very much but . . . she also thinks he might one day kill you."

Jordan told me he broke down when he heard those words spoken aloud, the ones he always believed in his heart to be true. He felt himself break open in a deep undiscovered place, one of the dark spaces he had created for himself as a boy. He had wept enough in his life to keep a small aquarium of saltwater fish alive, but the tears had been fierce and private. In front of this small, kind doctor he felt them run down his face in hot spillings. The tears came fast because the secret was out and this odd-shaped, unassuming man had gotten his mother to admit their mutual nightmare at last. During his childhood, he had often awakened in the middle of the night when he had rolled over and his cheek felt the cool wetness where the tears had fallen. It was as if someone had thrown a glass of water on his pillow.

"I talked with your father about this," Dr. Brill said quietly when Jordan regained control of himself.

"Oh no," Jordan said, his eyes fearful, despairing.

"He denied it all. I showed him this medical report from last September when you were admitted to the naval hospital with a hairline fracture of the jaw."

"I got it playing football," Jordan said.

"So you told the admitting physician," Dr. Brill said, handing the manila folder to Jordan. "But you didn't even go out for football this year. Coach McCann corroborated that."

"It was a touch football game with some enlisted guys," Jordan said, trying to think ahead of the doctor.

"Your father did it, Jordan," the man said. "You don't have to lie anymore to protect him."

"What did my father say?"

"He denied it completely. He was very cool

and polished at first. Then he got angry as he continued to deny it. After he convinced himself that I'd totally made the whole thing up he got furious. It must be terrifying to face his fury as a wife or a son."

"Did he ever admit it?" Jordan asked.

"Never did. I told him I didn't admire officers and gentlemen who made a habit out of lying."

"You said that to my father?"

"Yes," the doctor said. "He, of course, threatened to kick my fat naval ass."

"He could do it too, Doc," Jordan said.

"He most assuredly could, but I suggested that the ensuing court-martial might be somewhat detrimental to his career. I made a deal with him. I'd keep quiet if he stopped the abuse."

"Do you think it'll work?"

"No. But your mother does. I want you to do your part by keeping out of your father's way. Be polite. Play his game. Your tough-guy, wise-ass role pisses him off. Get rid of it when he's around. I'll check in with your mother periodically. Could you cut your hair?"

"No. I can't give him that satisfaction yet. I'll cut it before I start high school though. I promise."

"That seems fair to me. Good luck. I'll write you sometimes."

"I've never heard from a single shrink I saw before. You're not gonna write me, so don't say it," Jordan said.

"Yeh, I am," Dr. Brill said. "Every year you're gonna hear from me."

Jordan shrugged and asked, "When?"

"On Valentine's Day," the man said.

That was the summer that, on the tree-shaded streets of Waterford and the sun-sifted beaches of the Isle of Orion, Jordan Elliott entered our lives.

In Pony League, we batted in the first four positions. Mike batted first and led the league in hitting. Capers batted second and led the league in doubles and triples. Jordan batted third and pitched the team into the state finals. I was the biggest boy in the league and hit twelve home runs that summer.

In the championship game against Greer, we were beaten 1–0 when I lost a fly ball in the lights while playing right field. The loss was devastating to me, but Coach Langford reminded us that no Waterford Pony League team had even made it to the state finals before. He told me that there would be lots of championship games to come and that I should learn about losing young so I could savor the joy of winning when I got older.

Spontaneously, Jordan asked me and Capers and Mike to spend the night with him at his house on Pollock Island after the game. We could sleep late, he said, then play basketball at the base gym, or go swimming at the Officer's Club pool. I cleared it with my mother, then walked across the parking lot and joined Mike and Capers in the back of Colonel Elliott's car. Jordan was in the front seat, his blond hair still wet from the sweat and exhaustion of pitching the game. The loss sat heavily on us and we were unusually quiet as we watched Colonel Elliott discussing the game with Coach Langford.

"Did you ask your father if it was okay if we spent the night?" Mike asked.

"I asked Mom before the game," Jordan answered. "He wouldn't notice if I asked the Harlem Globetrotters to spend the night."

Colonel Elliott approached the darkened car still dressed in his Marine uniform. Even his demeanor looked as though he had ordered it through Supply. His carriage was erect and he moved with pantherish grace. When he reached the car, he fumbled for his keys, opened the door, closed it, then put the key into the ignition.

"Dad," Jordan said in the darkness.

Colonel Elliott did not answer. Instead, he backhanded Jordan so hard that his head snapped back against the seat and his baseball cap flew into Capers' lap in the backseat.

"You walked five batters. Five goddamn batters. I told you not to try to throw that sinker until you've mastered it. Didn't I tell you that, mama's boy? Didn't I tell you that?"

"Dad," Jordan said, trying to warn his father of our presence hidden by darkness in the backseat.

Another backhand silenced Jordan as the colonel continued, "You walked the goddamn kid that scored. If you hadn't given that little bastard a free ride, then that error wouldn't have cost us the ball game."

"But I made the error, Colonel," I said from the backseat as the surprised Marine turned around to see the three of us staring at him in shock.

"Boys, I didn't know you were here. Hey, good game, you three guys, and what a hell of a season this has been. I'll tell you one damn thing, we've got ourselves a nucleus of athletes in this car that's gonna shake this town up. I'm the only one in this town that knows just how good you guys are going to play together. Let's stop for a milkshake. How about a milkshake, son?" the colonel said looking over at Jordan who was staring out of the open window toward the still-lit field.

Jordan nodded his head and I knew it was because Jordan dared not speak. Colonel Elliott bought us all a "victory" milkshake and was most charming on the ride home. But a secret link had been forged between Jordan and me. We were members of the same sorrowing, broken-faced tribe. There is no stronger brotherhood than between two boys who discover that both were born to fathers who waged war on their sons. That night, I told Jordan about my own father and the luminous disaster that bourbon had played in the unhappy history of my family. We traded stories until sunrise, as Capers and Mike slept soundly in the guest room—Capers and Mike who had lived the lucky life of children who had never even been spanked by their parents.

After the Pony League season ended, the four of us spent two weeks on the Isle of Orion under the supervision of my grandparents, Silas and Ginny Penn McCall. We surf-fished in the breakers catching spottail bass and flounder for dinner. I discovered that summer that I loved to cook and feed my friends, and I enjoyed the sound of their praise as they purred with pleasure at the meals I fixed over glowing iron and fire. I had the run of my grandparents' garden and I would put ears of sweet corn in aluminum foil after washing them in seawater and slathering them with butter and salt and pepper. Beneath the stars we would eat the beefsteak tomatoes and okra and the field peas flavored with salt pork and jalapeño peppers. I would walk through the disciplined rows that brimmed with purple eggplants and watermelons and cucumbers, gathering vegetables. My grandfather, Silas, told us that summer that low country earth was so fertile you could drop a dime into it and grow a money tree.

Each night, I would make a campfire on the beach from piles of twisted driftwood as the other boys cleaned the catch of the day. The wood fire smelled of sargassum and salt air, attar of the Gulf Stream, and its perfume would lightly touch the trout and bass fillets as I sautéed them in butter.

At low tide, we would go with our cast nets to the smaller creeks at the rear of the island. The three of us took turns showing Jordan how to hurl the net. Capers gave the first demonstration, looping the rope around his left wrist, then placing part of the weighted net between his teeth, and grabbing two other sections of the net with his hands. It took both hands, your mouth, and your wrist to execute a throw properly. It also took rhythm and practice and good eye-hand coordination. Jordan had all the prerequisites, and on his fifth toss the net bloomed in a perfect circle before him, as lovely and gossamer as a spiderweb. With that toss, Jordan caught his first white shrimp and his first blue crab. We filled an ice chest with shrimp that low tide and I fed them shrimp dishes for the next four meals. When the shrimp were gone, we went crabbing and caught enough crabs to feed ourselves for a week. I stuffed a four-pound flounder with a mixture of crab and shrimp and baked it in my grandmother's oven, flavoring it with lemon juice and garlic, experimenting with cayenne and paprika and soy sauce and olive oil. Thus I began to take the first steps toward what would become a career.

After these meals, we would lie on our backs in the sands and moan with the pleasures of overeating. We were surprised when we discovered Jordan could call almost the entire night sky by name. Venus was the lamplighter in the Western sky that started the whole show each night. We stared up at the sky and talked about our lives, telling stories that didn't matter because those are the only stories American boys can tell.

The single disappointment Jordan had that summer was when he discovered the quality of the surf in his new home. He had no idea one could be disappointed with an entire ocean, but he felt completely let down by the Atlantic. Standing with his surfboard beside him, he first looked at the waves coming in at low tide with complete disbelief.

"What a pussy ocean," Jordan said.

"What do you mean 'pussy ocean'?" Capers said, as though Jordan had insulted the entire state. "It's *the* ocean, man. The Atlantic Ocean."

"It just won't do," Jordan said. "It's just not big enough."

"Not big enough?" Mike said. "How much bigger can it be? It's the ocean, for God's sake."

"The Pacific's a real ocean," Jordan said. "This is something else entirely."

Jordan could activate Capers' Southern chauvinism even in those early days of their friendship. Capers said, "Is everything in California better than anything we've got in South Carolina?"

"Yep. Everything's better in California. This is a Third World state, boys," said Jordan, sadly watching the puny waves as they puttered into shore.

"What's that supposed to mean?" I asked.

Jordan explained, "Let me put it this way. South Carolina is the Oklahoma of the South. That's about as low as you can get."

"But you're an Elliott," Capers said. "A South Carolina Elliott. That's one of the most distinguished names in South Carolina history."

"Can't help that," Jordan said. "It's still a loser state."

"You come from something special," Capers said. "No one's taken the time to explain to you about your ancestors. I'm also an Elliott on my mother's side. We're second cousins once removed. There are books written about the Elliott family."

"There are many books written about my family too," Mike said.

"Name one," Capers said, not quite sneering.

"Genesis, Exodus, the Book of Kings, Deuteronomy . . ." Mike reeled off.

"Those don't count," Capers said.

"They do to me," Mike said.

"You said that. Not me."

And then one day in the middle of July when a failed hurricane from the Caribbean struck the South Carolina coast and the Atlantic finally produced some waves that even a California boy could admire, Jordan taught us how to surf. He was a patient teacher and taught Mike how to get up on the board first, then brought Capers out where the big waves were breaking and got him up on the board on the third wave he rode. The storm increased in ferocity as I started out to meet Jordan who sat on his surfboard while thunder roared over us in a deep-throated howl and lightning cut through the black, boiling clouds.

To avoid being swept back to shore, I had to dive under the waves, as they came at me with the force of a small building collapsing. The sky was dark and the rain hurt my cheeks and eyes as I struggled to reach that dead zone in deep water where Jordan awaited me. When I reached Jordan, I held tightly to his board and rested for a few minutes before I tried for my learner's permit as a surfer. We floated on the ingathering swells that came rolling from behind us without pause. On land, I could see the palm trees, supple as ballerinas, bend their heads toward the ground in gestures of shy submission.

"What about the lightning?" I asked, as terrible bolts cut through the sky.

"Lightning doesn't hit guys like us," Jordan answered confidently.

"Why?" I asked.

"We're out here to surf, Jack," Jordan admonished. "This isn't a class in electricity. So pay attention. Watch me. Choose a wave that seems right for you. One you can be part of. I like that third one. Now watch. Timing's everything."

I watched as Jordan's eyes measured that third wave as it began its supple rise behind us. As it gathered height and strength, Jordan started to paddle confidently until the board was cutting through the water at the identical speed as the wave which caught the board and lifted it. As the board rose, Jordan lifted himself to his feet, crouched yet relaxed, and guided the board down the face of the wave like a careful man taking an escalator for the first time. The board cut the water like a knife cutting linen and Jordan rose high in the air, then dropped straight down as the wave sent him hurtling toward the beach. It looked as though Jordan were riding the back of a lioness onto the sand.

His posture remained low and balanced and I could hear Mike and Capers cheering for him on the shore as a plane of furious white water chased him, carried him, and brought him all the way to the white sands where he stepped off the board as easily and daintily as a woman stepping into her box at the opera.

As Jordan swam back to me, he would guide the board up over each wave, the board pointing straight up as Jordan was lifted almost completely out of the water. The waves seemed endless.

"Are these as good as California waves?" I shouted as Jordan paddled up beside me and I grabbed on to the board.

"These are California waves," Jordan shouted back. "These waves got lost. They belong in the Pacific. They must be exchange students or something."

"That last South Carolina wave gave you all you could handle," I said.

"There's no order to these waves. Califor-

nia waves come in sets of seven. You choose
the third or fourth wave because they're the
largest of the cycle. This is chaos."

"The Pacific sounds too predictable," I
yelled over the winds and waves. "Simple-
minded."

"The Atlantic is a cheesy, second-rate
ocean," Jordan shouted back, but he was starting to judge the incoming waves again. "It
would be okay if it had a hurricane come up
the coast every day. But it'll never be the Pacific. Now, you ride, Jack. See that fourth wave
forming? Don't be afraid when the bottom
drops out of it. That's the board entering the
heart of the wave. Just rise to your knees on
the first one. Remember, it's all about surfaces."

"Surfaces?" I asked.

"Think about it," Jordan said, sending me
off into the wave with a strong push. "It'll get
clear to you."

That summer, we became known as the
boys who rode the storm, the hurricane riders
who learned to surf on some of the largest
waves to come ashore that year. I caught five
waves that afternoon and it changed the way I
felt about water. I fell three times and one of
those times changed the way I felt about falling. I was sucked beneath a massive wave,
flipped over, struck on the head by the surf-

board, and then somersaulted out of control through waters so disorienting that I lost all sense of direction. I panicked as I swallowed water, tumbling wildly, then suddenly popping out of the water standing straight up, surprised, and then flattened by the next wave crashing over my shoulders. The sea on that day was terrifying. But Jordan taught us that if a sea could be ridden, it could not be untamable. He kept emphasizing that one had to honor the surfaces of both the wave and the board. All sports, he insisted, reduced to their simplest physics became easy.

Jordan's gift was both madcap and daredevil, and while Capers came to distrust Jordan's recklessness, Mike and I prized it. Jordan's love of daring and his rash need to live on the edges of things, his reaching for experiences that went unnoticed by other people gave us adventures that summer that previously would have been unimaginable. Throughout his life, Jordan's greatest fear was that he would be buried alive in that American topsoil of despair and senselessness where one felt nothing, where being alive was simply a provable fact instead of a ticket to a magic show. It was not that Jordan was a thrill-seeker, but that he found an elegance in action that he found nowhere else.

That summer, the four of us climbed the

water tower in the center of the town because Jordan wanted to get a bird's-eye view of Waterford. We hopped a freight train and rode it all the way to Charleston, then hitched a ride back on a watermelon truck, laden with the summer-swollen fruit. Jordan loved long-distance swims and surprised Silas McCall by twice swimming from Pollock Island all the way to the Isle of Orion, a distance of eight miles and directly across a shipping channel. But Jordan moved through the water with otter-like grace and playfulness. He was as strong a swimmer as anyone that Silas had ever seen and Jordan had no fear of depths or tides or sharks. When he swam he seemed like part of that same mystery that made the tides move. He seemed moonstruck and water-born as he swam between the islands.

One midnight, when we all were spending the night at Mike's house, Jordan got us to pretend we were members of the French Resistance who were sent by Charles de Gaulle on a suicidal mission. Our job was to blow up the Pont Neuf in Paris just at the moment that Hitler would cross it to visit his victorious Armies of the Reich. Jordan had made up fake but realistic-looking bombs that he assigned each of us to attach to the stanchions of the Waterford Bridge with waterproof tape. Into the midnight water we jumped feet first, each of us carrying packets of dummy flares wrapped expertly and looking like sticks of dynamite. Before Jordan let us swim back toward the city marina, he swam to each of us to inspect the job and, not satisfied with any of our performances, he retaped the fake explosives below the waterline to his exacting, perfectionist standards. Finally we watched him set an alarm clock and a fake fuse and then he signaled us to release ourselves into the outgoing tides, which funneled back past the town where we had hidden towels and clothes on the deck of a dry-docked yacht. Jordan planned his joint operations down to the last detail. As we floated back toward the town and our life, Jordan checked his watch and said, "Now," and we all looked back knowing that the bridge had exploded and that the torn body of the Führer lay on the bottom of the Seine.

Jordan's fascination with both anarchy and the fugitive stance caused some dissension too, particularly in Capers' view of the world. For Capers, Jordan was the only boy he'd met who signaled danger from every pore of his body. Capers had never seen a rebellious nature manifest itself before in his large tribe of cousins. His fascination with Jordan became as scientific as it was personal, for he knew no Elliott or Middleton who was not conservative and gentlemanly to the core of his being. But Jordan pointed out to Capers that their ancestors had once helped get rid of an English king and some had fought with Francis Marion against the Redcoats in the malarial swamps north of Charleston.

"We began as rebels, as men who went against the grain," Jordan told Capers. "Our ancestors helped man the cannons when the South fired on Fort Sumter. I'm much truer to the spirit of our ancestors than you are, Capers."

"Only time will tell that," Capers answered, not believing a word of what Jordan said.

When the full moon came at the end of August, the four of us decided that we would swim out to meet it, going deeper than we ever had before. Jordan paddled his surfboard past the breakers into the black waters a quarter of a mile off-shore. We swam slowly beside him, sometimes grabbing the board and hitching a ride the way a remora does to a shark.

"This is deep enough," Capers warned.

"A little bit further," Jordan urged.

"We're in shark city, U.S.A.," Mike said.

"Not part of their food chain," Jordan said.

In twenty feet of water, Jordan slipped off the board and the four of us watched the moonlight play on the surface of the water. It enclosed us in its laceries as we watched the moon spill across the Atlantic like wine from an overturned glass. The tides rushed through our legs as we dangled, innocent as bait. Far away, we could see the light of the caretaker's house where my grandfather would be sitting reading a book and listening to a country music station. We were so far out that the house looked like a ship that had run aground. With the light all around us, we felt secreted in that moon-infused water like pearls forming in the soft tissues of oysters. Our four heartbeats stirred the curiosity of the black drum, the pompano, and the whiting that hunted for food beneath us.

A porpoise sounded twenty yards away from us in an explosion of breath, startling us.

"Porpoise," I said. "Thank God it's not a Great White."

Then another porpoise broke the water and rolled toward us. A third and a fourth porpoise neared the board and we could feel great secret shapes eyeing us from below. I reached out to touch the back of one, its skin the color of jade, but as I reached the porpoise dove and my hand touched moonlight where the dorsal fin had been cutting through the silken waters. The dolphins had obviously smelled the flood tide of boyhood in the sea and heard the hormones singing in the boy-scented waters. None of us spoke as the porpoises circled us. The visitation was something so rare and perfect that we knew by instinct not to speak—and then, as quickly as they had come, the porpoises moved away from us, moved south where there were fish to be hunted.

Each of us would remember that night floating on the waves all during our lives. It was the year before we went to high school when we were poised on the slippery brink between childhood and adulthood, admiring our own daring as we floated free from the vigilance and approval of adult eyes, ruled only by the indifference of stars and fate. It was the purest moment of freedom and headlong exhilaration that I had ever felt. A wordless covenant was set among us the night of the porpoises. Each of us would go back to that surfboard again and again in our imaginations, return to that night where happiness seemed so easy to touch.

For over an hour we drifted in our own private Gulf Stream, talking of our unlived-in lives, telling jokes and stories that are both the source of intimacy and evasion among teenage boys.

In his preliminary talks with Ledare and me about the Southern mini-series, Mike would come back over and over again to that night.

"Who asked the question that night about suicide?" Mike asked me.

"Capers asked it," I said, remembering. "He wanted to know how each of us would kill ourselves if we had the choice."

"What did I say?" Mike asked. "My memory is shit."

"Liquor and pills," I said. "You said you'd steal a bottle of your father's favorite bourbon and a bottle of your mother's sleeping pills."

"That'd still be my first choice," Mike said.

"I said that I'd put a bullet through my brain. But Jordan had his suicide all planned out."

"That's what I remember," Mike said.

"He said he would steal a boat at the Pollock Island marina. He would've already mailed his mother and father a letter stating how much he loved his mother and how much he hated his father. He would hold his father responsible for the suicide. After stealing the boat, he would drive out to sea as far as the gasoline would carry him. Then, he would begin slitting his wrists and arteries very carefully and methodically. He would leave his blood all over the boat, because he wanted his father to see his son's blood. When he began to weaken, he would slip over the side of the boat and offer his body to Kahuna, the god of surf. He knew it would drive his father crazy that there wasn't any body to bury."

Ledare had asked, "He knew all of this in

eighth grade? How did Capers say he was going to kill himself?"

"Easy. Capers said he wouldn't ever consider suicide. It was the coward's way out and he preferred to stay and fight through whatever problems he faced."

"Oh, noble man," Ledare said.

"You're prejudiced," Mike said.

"It's true," she said. "Poor Jordan. He must've been far more miserable than we ever knew."

"It'll make a great scene," Mike said.

But I knew that Capers was the central figure of all of us who had drifted on the surfboard that night. Capers lived perfectly contained within his own deep dream of himself as a work in progress. He was the only one of us who actually observed himself in the various stages as he made his way through life. Self-doubt was unknown to him. He always knew exactly where he was going and he was a master of all the fine points of coastal navigation.

We would discover that later when we accidentally got in Capers' way. We came out of that summer with our friendship sealed. But the story of our friendship would bear bitter fruit and would one day bring tears to the eyes of all those who loved us well.

PART IV

CHAPTER 22

FANTASY IS ONE OF THE SOUL'S brightest porcelains. As the day rapidly approached when I would take Leah into the forsaken realms of my past, I felt the floodgates of recall open up in a ceaseless flow. As a travel writer I had specialized in the artistry of my own escape from what was most intimately mine. I had kept my eye on the horizon and fled all calls for the careful study of my own nest. My entire professional existence depended on the sincerity of my clean break with the past. The world was my subject and my hometown was the stimulant that drove me out to seek the world. In my head shimmered the

lights of a thousand strange cities and towns
which I could recall in glamorous detail and I
could speak easily of ports where peppers and
tangerines arrived in open-air markets piled in
black boats or of smoky bazaars where young
girls were sold as prostitutes and monkeys for
meat, or of places where men told stories over
tarot cards in languages that seemed to have no
vowels.

But Waterford lay buried and many of its
stories moved through my subconscious. Deep
within myself, I could hear the distant oratorio
forming as I pieced the fragments of my past
together like a piece of music and shared them
with Leah. Leah had cherished the few stories
of Waterford I had told her perhaps because
she instinctively knew that they were opening
up a history where one day Leah would discover herself. I had always told her that there
was nothing more beautiful in the world than a
story, yet it is I who had reigned as the chief
censor in the text of her imagination.

In the three months before our flight to
America, I tried to tell Leah everything that
might help her understand and survive the trial
by family she would now endure. And as the
stories unfolded, Leah would often seek out
Ledare and listen to Ledare's version of the
same remembrance. Ledare's memory was
often harsher and more piercingly focused.

With Ledare, Waterford sounded like the county seat of an all-suffocating decorum. My Waterford loomed as a masked ball with the twin themes of lunacy and surprise. Taken together, a two-steepled skyline began to form in Leah's mind.

On the trans-Atlantic flight to Atlanta, I took a leather photograph album out of my briefcase, a special one that I had kept under lock and key during those years I kept her past hidden from her. I opened it and showed her pictures of my grandmother and grandfather in front of their caretaker's house on the Isle of Orion, photographs of her uncles, and I gave small, intimate biographies of each as our plane sailed through a brilliant aquamarine sky.

A careful, dutiful child, Leah memorized the names and faces of all her relatives, near and far.

"Who is this, Daddy?" Leah asked, looking at a faded Kodachrome.

"That's me and Mike Hess and Capers Middleton in first grade."

"You're littler than I am now," she said.

"That's the way time works," I said as I studied the image of myself taken over thirty years before. I could remember the moment that Capers' mother had taken the photograph and I could remember the taste of the Pecan

Sandies my mother packed in my lunch box every day that year.

"Who's that?" I asked.

"A pretty little dog," Leah said.

"Not just any pretty little dog."

"*That's* the Great Dog Chippie," Leah cried out. "But Daddy, she's so small and cute. I thought Chippie must be the size of a St. Bernard."

"No," I said. "She slept with me, on my pillow, every night. My mother would come in, kick her out, and banish her to the downstairs, but Chippie'd always be there when I woke up in the morning."

"Is that Mama?" Leah said pointing to a sad-eyed, overly dressed girl.

I nodded. "It sure is. That's third grade and she'd come over to show my mother her new pair of saddle oxfords. That's why she's pointing at her feet."

"Daddy, I'm so excited," Leah said, squeezing my arm. "I never dreamed I'd meet my family. Do you think they'll like me?"

"They'll eat you up with a spoon."

"Is that a good thing?" Leah asked.

"They'll love your little Roman ass."

"Bad word. That's a thousand lire."

"Not now," I said. "We're going to land soon. Now, it's a buck."

"Is Ledare meeting us here?"

"No," I said. "We go through customs in Atlanta and she'll be waiting for us in Savannah."

"Are you excited about going back to live in Waterford, Daddy?" my daughter asked.

"I'm terrified," I admitted, and then added, "But, at least, it's quiet in Waterford. Nothing much happens there."

"Everything happens in Waterford," Leah said and I saw that she was speaking directly to the photo album.

Before landing, I looked down at the green hills and hidden lakes of Georgia and tried to address my anxiety.

Then I watched my daughter move back and forth among the photographs of my past and realized that I had raised a child with a longing for any rumor of home, and that I would have to put aside my own fear.

Ledare met us at the Savannah airport and drove us straight to Elizabeth on Thirty-seventh for a dinner that I had arranged before I left Rome. I had already begun to worry about how to make my living as a travel writer when my travel was going to be limited to day trips from Waterford, but my editor at *Food and Wine* had told me about a new generation of Southern cooks who were both classically trained and dedicated to revolutionizing the fundamentals of Southern cuisine. I was told they all preserved their fondness for grits and barbecue despite their desire to sneak goat cheese into the tossed salad.

In the handsome, high-ceilinged Victorian outside of the historic district, I went back into the kitchen to interview Elizabeth Terry and her staff as they prepared redolent and beautifully constructed meals for tables of conservatively dressed customers. She told me the names of all the leading chefs who were most intimately connected with the new transformation of Southern cooking. That first evening back in America we ate a light, superb meal that would have been impossible to find anywhere in the South except New Orleans during the seventies. Leah dined on pasta Amatriciana, which she pronounced delicious and wondered aloud why her father told her she would never again eat good pasta until they returned to Rome. I admitted my error and described the years I had labored as a food critic tasting ghastly combinations of pasta and sauce in Italian restaurants from Texas to Virginia that all deserved shutting down by the health department at best, a fire bombing at worst.

Later, we spent our first night beneath a South Carolina sky at the house on the Isle of Orion that Lucy had rented for us. Ledare had gotten the keys earlier and had done a preliminary inspection of the premises and found the house far more than adequate. It was built on a high bank overlooking a saltwater lagoon.

As I walked through the house for the first time, I was pleased to see that the owners, a Mr. and Mrs. Bonner, had selected their furniture and paintings with great care. They were people of good taste, people I would like to know, I thought, as I studied a wall of family photographs where the Bonners strutted their children's blond good health and their straight toothy smiles that spoke so eloquently of the orthodontist's art. The kitchen was adequate and Lucy had already stocked it with food. In the master bedroom, I found a writing table and a four-poster bed that I would have bet was a Bonner family heirloom.

Upstairs, I heard Leah squeal with pleasure as she discovered a bedroom to her liking. I unpacked her suitcases as Leah took a shower. Taking care not to wrinkle the clothes that Maria had so sadly and lovingly folded, I filled up an antique dresser and laughed out loud when I discovered the three boxes of pasta and the whole salami Maria had packed in case the Americans failed to feed Leah in the proper manner. I made a mental note to call Maria in the morning to let her know we had landed safely and that Leah had eaten pasta that had met with her approval. Leah walked out of her newly claimed room in her pajamas, sleepy-eyed and smelling of powder. She was asleep before I got past the first sentences of a story.

I found Ledare downstairs lighting a fire she had already laid in the fireplace. She had fixed me a drink and handed it to me as I watched the flame consuming the dry oak.

"To your homecoming," Ledare said.

"This could turn out to be hell but it's decorated nicely," I said, looking around.

"Why don't you use a radical approach and try to enjoy your time here?" Ledare suggested.

"Please," I said. "You must try to humor my existential anguish."

"You'll have plenty of time for that," Ledare said. "Mike called, and he'd like us to write an outline of the mini-series in a month. He told me to tell you no more excuses and he wants a note from your doctor saying you actually got shot in the head by a terrorist."

"I still feel uneasy about the project," I said to Ledare. "How can we write for Mike without hopping into bed with Capers."

Ledare said, "The subject's fascinating and I think we can learn things about ourselves we don't know. We can recapture some of the magic of the good, lost times."

"It's dangerous to write about what you don't know," I said.

Ledare got up to go and said, "It's dangerous *not* to."

I woke much too early the next day, and when
Lucy came by the house she found us watching
a televangelist warning his audience that Arma-
geddon was almost here due to the licentious-
ness and evil of mankind. Lucy cooked a large
breakfast for Leah and lied to her when the
child asked her the meaning of the word "licen-
tiousness." I clearly corrected my mother's error. After breakfast, Lucy made sure that Leah
was dressed warmly enough, then took us both
for a first long walk on the Isle of Orion's four-
mile beach. The tide was out and the water flat
as we walked on the beach gathering shells and
examining the barnacle-covered driftwood that
had washed up during the previous night's
tides. The day was windless and even the
seagulls had to stroke their great wings to keep
aloft. The ocean mirrored the sky and few
swells or ridges disturbed the brown pelican
floating twenty yards away from us.

As we walked, Lucy showed Leah all the
safe spots for swimming and where the water
grew treacherous and riptides moved in fierce
turbulence. She explained to Leah that if she
were ever caught in the undertow's grip that

Leah must allow herself to submit to the undertow rather than fight against it.

"Allow the undertow to take you out to deeper water, darling," Lucy said. "The undertow's weak out there, and it will let you go. Then you can just swim slowly back toward shore and catch a wave all the way in."

Together, woman and girl studied the detritus tossed in random piles near tide-pools. Lifting the broken shell of an Atlantic blue crab, Lucy pointed out the deep blue coloring along the torn claw, "the most beautiful blue in all of nature."

Leah was so filled with delight and curiosity that the walk continued for hours as Lucy shared all the knowledge of the littoral she carried with her. They collected what shells they could find but only the coquina clams were plentiful on the beach. Lucy promised a cornucopia of them when the spring tides began and the ocean really began to warm up.

"Shells. We'll gather the most beautiful shells the Atlantic has to offer. The rarest too. But we've got to be vigilant. We've got to work hard. We've got to commit ourselves to coming out here after every high tide."

"We can do it, Grandma," Leah said. "Daddy told me you could teach me everything there was to know about the sea."

"He knows some things himself," Lucy said

modestly, but pleased. "Of course, I'm sure he's forgotten most of it since he took it on himself to become a European. Come over here, child. Let me show you how erosion is eating up this beach."

On the seashore, Lucy had found the text of all creation imprinted daily on the sands of the Isle of Orion. By walking the beach each morning, Lucy had strengthened her belief in God and come to understand that she was no more important to the planet than the smallest plankton that floated in the invisible broth that served the softest orders of the food chain. It had helped Lucy when she could think of her own bloodstream as an inland sea not much different from the one that she and Leah walked beside. Her leukemia was similar to the virulence of red tides that attacked Southern beaches during the summer, causing fish kills that made the seabirds crazy with gluttony. A beach was a fine place to come to grips with all the cycles of the universe. It eased her fear of dying.

She watched Leah's pretty run down the beach toward the carcass of a small shark. The crabs and gulls had already done their small-scale butchery. The shark's eyes had been picked out and a larger predator had removed part of the dorsal fin. As her granddaughter ran, Lucy told me that she would teach this child everything and tie her to the South so completely that I could never take her back to Italy. I gave her a look, then let it go.

After we came in from the beach, I drove Leah the eighteen miles on Seaside Road in the oversized Chrysler Le Baron that Lucy had encouraged my landlord to leave for me.

We touched five sea islands before we crossed the J. Eugene Norris Bridge into Waterford proper. Even when I was recuperating in Rome I had imagined making this tour with Leah and had practiced the itinerary in my mind, choosing with care which streets I would drive her down and at which houses I would stop to reveal their histories.

I took a right after the bridge and drove slowly past the mansions of the planter class who had built their houses facing east toward the sun and Africa. Spanish moss hung from the water oaks in such smoky profusion that the houses looked like chapels seen through veils. Labrador retrievers slept on marble steps. Brick walls, inked with pearly lichen, hid carefully tended gardens from the common view. It was the neighborhood where both Shyla and I had grown up and its streets seemed to disappear into a field of lost time and drift like childhood itself.

We drove down Porpoise Avenue past the stores of the main shopping street with their eighteenth- and nineteenth-century facades crowding both sides of the street. Once I could close my eyes and name all the shops and their owners on both sides of the street, but modern times had brought an influx of strangers to town who had opened up health-food stores, office-supply shops, and banks with unfamiliar names that had merged with giant financial institutions from Charlotte. I also noticed that the names of the oldest, most honored law firms had changed their aristocratic shingles to reflect the death of managing partners and the rise of feisty young attorneys who wanted their own names engraved on the signage of Porpoise Avenue. When we passed the Lafayette House I pointed out the shingle of my father and brother: McCall and McCall, Attorneys-at-Law. Luther's Pharmacy had closed, the Huddle twins had given up their barbershop, and the Breeze Theater was now a fashionable men's shop. Lipsitz's shoe store was where it always was and its mere survival seemed a necessary corrective amid the change.

When we came to Rusoff's Department Store I told Leah that was where we would find Max, the Great Jew. Then we drove to a poorer section of town and I showed her a small brick two-story building that had been the store that the Great Jew had opened when he first moved to Waterford. We drove past Waterford High

School and the football field where I had
played fullback and both Shyla and Ledare had
been cheerleaders in that long-ago world where
innocence was at least an illusion that young
Southerners could cling to until the world
brought them up short. Every street contained
vivid transparencies of my past, and Shyla's
face began to appear to me in every billboard
and stop sign. And I understood that I had
come back to go face-to-face with Shyla for the
first time since she died.

As we drove down De Marlette Road,
named for the French explorer who had first
landed at Waterford in 1562, I pointed out the
Waterford River, caught in bright glimpses between the houses built along the high bluff. I
once had been able to name every family and
the children who had lived in each house we
passed, but death and mobility had scrambled
the deck and made the certainty of my memories suspect. Finally we drove up to the entrance of the small but well-cared-for Jewish
cemetery, a half mile from the town's center.

It was surrounded by a vine-covered brick
wall and oak and cottonwood trees provided
shade and comfort as I swung open the iron
gate decorated with the Star of David. I led
Leah by the hand, walking through long rows
of tombstones decorated with Hebrew letters

that were a roll call of all the Jewish names that had followed Max Rusoff to Waterford.

I stopped before one of the graves, and when I read Shyla's name it took my breath away. I had not returned to this graveyard since we buried Shyla, and seeing "Shyla Fox Mc-Call" made me cover my eyes with my left hand. The word McCall looked out of place in this acre of Scheins and Steinbergs and Keyserlings.

"Oh, Daddy," Leah said. "It's Mama, isn't it?"

I had expected to comfort my daughter but I fell speechless. The shock of Shyla's death had quickly turned to its details, then to a trial to decide the fate of our child. That pain had rendered me tearless, insensate. Though I felt thunderstruck, I still could not cry, but only stare. I stroked Leah's hair as she wept.

Finally, I said, "This is the wrong cemetery."

Leah answered me, "I knew you'd make a joke."

"I'm that predictable?" I asked.

"Yes. You always make jokes when you're sad," she said. "Tell me a story about Mama," Leah said finally, kneeling down to pull weeds out of the pale winter grass that covered the grave.

"What's your favorite?" I asked.

"Tell me one you haven't told me before," Leah said. "I can never really see Mama, she never seems real."

"Have I ever told you a story about how your mother used to drive me crazy? How she could make me angrier than hell?"

"No," Leah said.

So I told Leah the story of the black woman in Charleston who Shyla had found in an alley near Henry's Furniture Store. Shyla had the heart of a socialist and the soul of a missionary and she spent a lifetime unreconciled to human or animal suffering of any kind. Shortly after we were married Shyla was shopping when she came upon an unconscious black woman covered with sores lying in an alley.

Shyla walked into Henry Popowski's store and asked that Henry call her a cab, which he gladly did. Then she had to cajole a most reluctant cabdriver into helping her lift the prone body of the anonymous black woman into the backseat of his cab. At the end of the cab ride she again coaxed the driver into helping her carry the woman into the one-bedroom carriage house we had rented behind a Church Street mansion.

When I arrived home from my job as restaurant and movie critic for the *News and Courier*, we had one of the bitterest arguments of our marriage. Shyla contended that no human being would leave a poor helpless black woman passed out in an alley surrounded by a racist white society. I argued that I would be more than happy to pass up such an opportunity. If that were the case, Shyla screamed, she had certainly married the wrong man and she would soon be looking for a husband who was far more humane and compassionate than I was. But I thought compassion had nothing to do with the fact that a black drug addict covered with sores and smelling like a billy goat was lying in the only bed in a one-bedroom apartment. I also contended that we'd be evicted as soon as our racist landlords found out that they had added a black hooker to their roster of tenants. Shyla shouted that she would not conduct her life to conform to the wishes of racists nor would she have married me had she known I was a secret Nazi. Nazi, I had yelled. I complain when you bring an unconscious heroin addict and put her into my goddamn bed and suddenly I'm in charge of all the crematoriums at Bergen-Belsen. Every time I argue with you, I start out on King Street in Charleston and end up at the Brandenburg Gate in Berlin leading my Nazi youth boys in a spirited rendition of the "Horst Wessel Song." If the shoe fits, Shyla fired back, wear it, and neither one of us had noticed that our guest had awakened until we heard her say, "Where the fuck I be?"

"You be in my fucking house," I said to her.

"And you're welcome to stay for as long as it takes to get back on your feet," Shyla said sweetly.

"I'll be damned if that's so."

"My husband is a racist bastard," Shyla explained. "Don't pay attention to him."

The black woman, disoriented, said, "You people kidnap my ass?"

"Yeh," I said, irritated. "We left a ransom note in your grandma's outhouse."

"Racist to the core," Shyla shouted, beating her fists against my chest. "Racist scum. I go to bed each night with the chief Cyclops of the Ku Klux Klan."

"Good," I said. "That's a step up. From Auschwitz to Selma in a single goddamn leap."

"You're the fucking Klan, man?" the black woman asked.

"No, ma'am," I explained, trying to control myself. "I'm not in the Klan. I'm just a poor, godforsaken white man, underpaid and underappreciated, who'd like you to remove your pus-covered body from my bed."

"Racist pig," Shyla screamed. "You're what gives white Southern males, masters of oppression, a bad name."

"Got that right, honey," the black woman said, nodding her head.

"Our guest agrees," Shyla said triumphantly.

"She's not our guest," I said.

"If I ain't your guest, what the fuck am I doing here?" the black woman said.

"Sisterly togetherness," Shyla said. "What a beautiful thing."

"Can I take a bath?" the black woman asked.

"Of course," Shyla said at the same time I said, "Certainly not."

"Did you forget we were invited for drinks by my publisher?" I asked.

"I certainly did not," Shyla said sweetly. "And I'm ready to accompany you to that Neanderthal's house."

"Do you mind if we don't take your new friend, Harriet Tubman?" I asked faking civility.

"I have to go to a party with my soon-to-be-former husband," Shyla said. "You take a bath and pretty yourself up. Here's ten dollars for a cab. Leave your name and address and I'll take you to lunch next week."

"I personally am not leaving this house until this woman is out of it," I said.

"Yes, you are," Shyla announced, "or I file for divorce tomorrow. The first divorce in

South Carolina history caused by white racism."

Shyla rushed out of the carriage house and I, eyeing the black woman suspiciously, followed her out the door.

When we returned from Mr. Manigault's party, the black woman had bathed, fixed herself a meal, then stolen all of Shyla's clothes, shoes, and makeup. She packed it all up in the leather luggage Shyla had bought me for my birthday. On her way out, she lifted the sterling silver from the secretary near the doorway. Then she called a cab and cheerfully reentered the underworld of black Charleston.

I chuckled at the memory as I stood over Shyla's grave with Leah.

"We laughed at that story more than anything that ever happened," I said. "We'd go to some new, strange town in Europe and your mother would whisper, 'Where the fuck I be?' "

"Did the police ever catch the woman?" Leah asked.

"Your mama would not let me call the police," I said. "She claimed that the woman needed all that stuff more than we did. She was glad the woman took it. I wanted the woman to be enrolled in leather-tooling classes at the state pen."

"Mama didn't care that the woman stole her clothes?" Leah asked.

"I used to see the woman sometimes walking around in Shyla's clothes," I said. "I'd be off covering a story with a photographer and I'd see her working a stretch of territory near the Cooper River bridge and I'd have the photographer take a picture. Shyla used to love it that I kept those photographs in an album."

"Did she get new clothes?"

"She drove straight to Waterford, went to the Great Jew, told him what happened, and came back to Charleston with a whole new wardrobe. She could always depend on Max."

"Were you mad at Mama?" Leah asked.

"At first, I was furious. Naturally. But everything that happened was in perfect character for Shyla. I could've married a hundred South Carolina girls who'd've walked over that woman in the alley. But I married the only South Carolina woman who'd've brought her home."

Leah stared at her mother's name for a long time before saying, "Mama was a nice person, wasn't she, Daddy?"

"A sweetheart," I said.

"It's so sad, Daddy," Leah said in a whisper. "It's the saddest thing in the world. She doesn't know anything about me. She doesn't know what I'm like or how I could've loved her. Do you think she's in heaven?"

I knelt down beside my daughter and the earth was hard and cold against my knee. I kissed her cheek and brushed the hair back from her face.

"I know what I'm supposed to say to make you feel better," I said. "But I've told you. Religion confuses me. It always has. I don't know if Jews even believe in heaven. Ask your rabbi. Ask Suor Rosaria."

"I think Mama's in heaven," Leah said.

"Then so do I," I said and we walked hand in hand out of the cemetery, pausing to look back at Shyla's grave, once, before we got in the car.

I would always remember that visit to Shyla's grave as one of the hardest things I had ever done in my life. I grew angry with Shyla again but kept that anger to myself. When she leapt from the bridge, Shyla never considered the day when I would have to bring our daughter to mourn her loss at graveside. There were so many things that Shyla hadn't thought of.

From the cemetery, we drove back down Perimeter Road, past Williford Curve, took a left at the eyesore of a community college, and went four long blocks before turning into the driveway of my childhood home.

"This is where I grew up," I told Leah.

"It's so beautiful. And so big," she said.

We walked out to the dock and I pointed back toward the town where the river dog-legged left toward the sea. Carefully, I tried to acclimate her to where she stood and pointed toward the sea islands where we had spent the night in our rented house and then pointed in the general direction of Italy. Leah seemed un-interested in this geography lesson so I quickly took her back down the dock past the spartina grass of the marsh that had that wintered-in look of depletion. In the cold months, the marsh slept invisibly, beneath the mud, as the shoots of new grass, sharp as cut glass, began to form. The new marsh was beginning to make its move.

The back door of the house was unlocked and as we entered the kitchen I breathed in the smell that elucidated the complex issues of my childhood. The salt marsh was part of that smell, but so was my mother's laughter, coffee grounds, the frying of chicken, sweaty uniforms thrown in heaps by the laundry room, cigarette smoke, cleaning detergent . . . all of them I remembered as I led Leah by the hand.

We moved out through the dark hallway and into the dining room, where I took a crys-tal salt shaker and tried to shake some salt in my hand, but the humidity had long ago turned the contents of that shaker into a small imita-

tion of Lot's wife. I sniffed the pepper but it
was so old it could not even make me sneeze.

Upstairs, I showed Leah my bedroom,
which still contained pennants I had put up
when I was a kid. A dusty scrapbook, long un-
read, told the story of my small-town athletic
career from Little League to college.

Leah pointed to a door that led to a half-
hidden top-floor attic. Like all children, she
gravitated toward the roomful of old trunks
and discarded furniture. She discovered a bag
full of roller skates and piles of strange-looking
keys. Going deeper into the attic, she found an
album of photographs of me taken when I was
a baby. There was a clarinet and a sailboat and
a box full of outdated life jackets.

I let her rummage around as I sat going
through old scrapbooks in a desultory fashion.
The newspaper clippings had aged as I had,
and when I came across a picture of Shyla con-
gratulating Capers after a game, leaping into
his arms in classic cheerleading fashion, I felt
unbearably sad and replaced the scrapbook on
its dusty shelf.

Then I turned my attention to the paperback books and it seemed that not a single one
had been moved from its place. This room had
long served as a retreat from the disharmony
and sadness of the first floor, and it was here I
had fallen in love with these books and authors

in a way that only lifelong readers know and understand. A good movie had never once affected me in the same life-changing way a good book could. Books had the power to alter my view of the world forever. A great movie could change my perceptions for a day.

I had always kept these books in alphabetical order from Agee to Zola, and I had read for the way words sounded, not for the ideas they espoused.

"Hello, Holden Caulfield," I said, taking the book from its shelf. "Meet you at the Waldorf under the clock. Say hey to Phoebe. You're a prince, Holden. A real goddamn prince."

Taking out *Look Homeward, Angel,* I read the magnificent first page and remembered when I had been a sixteen-year-old boy and those same words had set me ablaze with the sheer inhuman beauty of the language as a cry for mercy, incantation, and a great river roaring through the darkness.

"Hello, Eugene. Hello, Ben Gant," I said quietly, for I knew these characters as well as I knew anyone in the world. Literature was where the world made sense for me.

"Greetings, Jane Eyre. Hello, David Copperfield. Jake, the fishing is good in Spain. Beware of Osmond, Isabel Archer. Be careful, Natasha. Fight well, Prince André. The snows,

Ethan Frome. The green light, Gatsby. Be careful of the large boys, Piggy. I do give a damn, Miss Scarlett. The woods of Birnam are moving, Lady Macbeth."

My reverie was broken by Leah's voice. "Who are you talking to, Daddy?"

"My books," I said. "They're all still here, Leah. I'm going to pack them all up and take them back to Rome for you." And I walked down the stairs, went back into my bedroom, and raised the window that looked out to the roof and the garden. The wood was warped and it took me several minutes before I could remove the screen. Then I climbed out to a flat part of the roof that gave me a view of the river and the garden.

"You ever climbed a tree?" I asked.

"Not one this big," Leah said. "Is it dangerous?"

"I didn't think so when I was a kid," I admitted. "But now that I think about you climbing around in it, I feel faint and dizzy—like I'm going to have a heart attack."

"Is this your and Mama's tree?" she asked.

"The same one," I said. "Now the branches are so broad you can walk upright on some of them, but I want us on our hands and knees most of the time. Let's be careful."

"Were you and Mama careful?"

"No, we were nuts."

I stepped out onto a limb that touched the roof and lowered myself to another huge branch, thick as a sidewalk. I reached back and helped Leah onto the branch and the two of us crept slowly to the center of the tree. The oak was the only thing from my childhood that never appeared smaller than I had remembered it. We made our way to a well in the trunk of the tree where the remnants of a tree house still provided a comfortable observation post. Leah was thrilled.

I pointed toward a smaller white house that sat at the very end of the garden. An older woman was sweeping the steps of her modest porch. "That's Shyla's mama. That's your grandmother, Leah."

"Can I speak to her?" Leah whispered.

"Yell down to her," I said. "Ask if we can come over."

"What do I call her?" she asked.

"Try Grandma," I advised.

"Grandma," Leah said, her voice bell-like in the great tree. "Grandma."

Ruth Fox looked up, surprised. She took her broom and walked into the garden where she had heard a child's voice.

"Up here, Grandma. It's me, Leah," Leah said, waving down at her grandmother.

"Leah. Leah. My Leah," Ruth said, stammering. "Are you crazy? Get down from that tree. Jack, are you trying to kill my only grandchild with your foolishness?"

We climbed down from the great oak tree and Leah jumped into the arms of her grandmother. Ruth fell apart when she took Leah into her arms. I felt like an eavesdropper as I turned my back and saw something I had forgotten near the fish pond in the garden. Walking away from Leah, I noticed that the small stone epitaph was in bad repair. Coi and goldfish floated like chrysanthemums in the dark pond. I rubbed the worn lettering on the flat stone and made out the words, "The Great Dog Chippie."

I decided that I would show Leah Chippie's grave some other day. Turning back, I saw Ruth saying something to Leah that was making her smile with pleasure. I wondered if George Fox knew that his granddaughter had come home.

Then I heard music coming from the Fox house, Rachmaninoff's Rhapsody on a Theme by Paganini. The choice of homecoming music surprised me because I knew that George Fox held that particular composition in contempt and thought it banal and sentimental. But I also knew that it was Shyla's favorite piece of classical music and George was playing it with such passion and conviction out of homage to Shyla and an act of gratitude to me for the return of their granddaughter to his house.

The music ended and George Fox appeared at his window and we looked at each other. We sized each other up and a great hatred ran like a stream between us.

"Granddad," I heard Leah say as Ruth pointed to her husband. Our mutual love of Leah softened both of us and brought us back into our better selves. As Leah ran up the stairs into the Foxes' house, George Fox and I bowed to each other. He mouthed the words "Thank you," then disappeared from view.

CHAPTER 23

AS A SEASONED TRAVEL WRITER, I HAD
returned to the embarkation point, entered the
forbidden city of Waterford as though permitted voyage at last, to a severe wonderland that
had killed my wife outright and that had left
me estranged from my own family and friends.
In my eyes, the town was a dangerous place,
riddled with cul de sacs and dead ends, and you
could not turn your back on it for a single instant.

It was my daughter, Leah, who returned my
town to me as a favor and an endowment. She
found magic in it because all my stories began
and ended here, and because each day she ran

into Shyla's childhood by accident. At school, she sat at the same desk near the window where she was told her own mother had sat during elementary school. After school, she would go to the Foxes' house where her grandfather gave her piano lessons and Ruth Fox took great pride in spoiling her rotten. Leah found it odd that I had spent so much time away from a town so comfortable. Rome could tuck Waterford into a small pocket of its coat and never even notice a change in its clangorous, teeming environment. For Leah, it was like living life in miniature. Intimacy came with the territory. By removing Leah from her birthplace, I had only proved that exile was the surest way to sanctify the path that led toward home.

Though I had told no one how long I was staying, I had based my whole return on my mother's health. Ledare and I worked on the movie project for Mike because the pay was good; we got to study the past at our leisure and kept learning new details that surprised us, and it offered a time each day when we could be together. I had never spent time with a woman so easy to be with for such long periods. The story we worked on was partially our own, but the more direction we received from Mike Hess the more we realized that the disappearance of Jordan Elliott from our lives was piv-

otal to the success of the project. Mike seemed
to think that he could fix all of our lives, if only
we could make sense out of the series of catastrophic events that had divided us down the
middle at so early an age. Mike carried around
with him a nostalgia for a time and a set of
friendships that was irreparable. Ledare and I
conducted hundreds of interviews and wove together a narrative that cast light on both the
mini-series and the high points of all of our
lives. By asking about others, we learned thousands of things about ourselves. Yet those
things we could not answer made the other
half-completed and inert. Jordan had disappeared completely into the underworld of
Catholic Europe. Neither his mother nor I had
heard from him since the day his father betrayed him in the Piazza del Popolo. Jordan's
war with his father and Shyla's leap from the
bridge were the two bookends of our conflicted
time together in the South. Ledare and I spent
the last of winter and the first months of spring
making up a timeline of all the incidents that
had brought us to this state of preparation and
watchfulness. We waited for something to happen that would cleanse us of all that was unknowable or ambiguous about our pasts. What
we lacked was resolution, an ending. I could
tell myself I had come back to write the script,
show my daughter the country and the people

from which she had sprung, and maybe fall in love with Ledare just a little bit. Only my mother knew, because of her instinctive and complete mastery of every nuance of my behavior, that I had come home for reasons I could not admit even to myself and that I would not leave until she had died. The movie became my excuse.

Each morning at six-thirty, before school, Lucy would meet Leah and take her for a long walk on the beach. Here, Lucy made the shoreline a text of great beauty. On early-morning walks Lucy taught Leah to recognize the eggshell of a skate, the dark triangle of a shark's tooth, the differences between starfish, and the aesthetics of shell collecting in general. Lucy's favorites were the angel wings, with their folded, ethereal flamboyance, the olive shell, in all its modesty, the channeled whelk, and the oyster drill for the intricacy of its seemingly accidental architecture. She had retained her girlish love of sand dollars even though this beach was a Comstock Lode of these doubloonshaped relatives of sea urchins. Their prevalence along the shell-strung beach soon cheapened them even to Leah, but like all shells their value lay in the symmetry of their form. To Lucy, the whole coastline of South Carolina was a love letter written by God as a literal translation of his abundant love for the beachcombers of the world. She also tutored Leah in how to recognize the signs that the mother loggerheads made in the sand when they began to lay their eggs in May.

After their walks, they would hose their feet off, dry them with large towels left on the deck, and Lucy would drive Leah into town for school. Because of her illness, Lucy demanded that I surrender all mornings to her, and because of that same illness, I complied. It was another warning from my mother that her days were numbered and that she wished to tie up all the loose ends of her life and needed some forbearance from her children to accomplish all these soft duties with a certain amount of grace.

Each day after school, George and Ruth Fox were waiting for Leah as she emerged from her classroom in town. They would walk her to their house on the Point where Ruth would fix her cookies and milk, and George would give her piano lessons three times a week. She played with vivacity for a girl her age and the only thing she lacked to keep her from being great was obsession. The piano required monogamy, and Leah had far too many other interests and hobbies for her to surrender her life to the keyboard. But George was a patient teacher and her training in Italy had been impeccable. Leah's natural ebullience was more than a match for George's attraction to darkness. The music they made together gave great pleasure to both of them. After each lesson, George would play for Leah, trying to show her what beauty could be coaxed out of a piano if someone took the time to be the instrument's servant and devotee.

Every Friday, Leah spent the Sabbath with her grandparents. Ruth would light the Sabbath candles, then serve the Sabbath meal. Though I had promised Shyla that I would raise our daughter as a Jew, I fully expected the brunt of that responsibility to fall on Shyla's shoulders. There were few questions about Judaism I could answer easily, and no matter how many books I read, no text could illuminate the theological rain forest where the tenets of that complex and hairsplitting faith luxuriated and multiplied like papayas. I had tried to raise her to be a good Jew, but I did not exactly apprehend what constituted such a notable creation. Together, we had learned the simplest Hebrew prayers, but I felt like an impostor whenever I mouthed the beautiful, mysterious words. I was as uncomfortable with a language that read from right to left as I was with rivers that flowed north. It was outside the natural order of things as I knew it, even though I was fully aware that Hebrew predated English by nearly two thousand years. I was relieved that George and Ruth took over Leah's religious instruction without a word ever passing between us. Friday and Saturday belonged to them from sunset to sunset. Though they were grateful to me, the Foxes never invited me to share one of these Sabbath meals. The history between us was still on fire. We were courteous around each other to the point of parody. Actors in the same drama, we played our parts with a certain stiffness and dissonance. All the words were pleasant and all rang false. Ruth tried to hide the tension with her volubility and high-pitched laughter and she fluttered like a songbird on the days when I arrived at five-thirty in the afternoon to pick up Leah. George hovered always in the background, hands folded primly. Solemnly, he would bow to me and I would reply with my own terribly formal nod of the head. Though both of us were glad of the armistice, neither of us knew what strategies would lead us around the impasse of distrust and hatred that we both felt whenever our eyes met. For Leah's sake, we were cordial; for Shyla's sake, we were no more than that.

In the first month of our return, I introduced Leah to everyone who had importance to Shyla's and my lives and showed her everything about the world we had grown up in. We pored over high school yearbooks that had been left behind in the Foxes' attic when Shyla and I had gotten married.

Pressed between the pages were mementos of Shyla's high school life: orchids from proms fell out in tough, withered petals like lost gloves of elves. She had kept the ticket stubs of movies she attended with the names of the movies carefully inscribed along with her date for that night. I smiled as I came across stub after stub with Jordan Elliott's name written out in Shyla's clear hand. There were programs from school plays and football games and events at the synagogue. Notes that had been passed to her in class were also dated and annotated. An essay she had written about Lady Macbeth in Advanced English with its A+ grade and its rapturous note of congratulations written by her teacher, John Loring, were preserved in the advertisements at the end of the book.

"Let's see what you wrote," Leah said, flipping through the yearbook.

"Oh my God, I'm praying I didn't sign the stupid thing."

"Of course you signed it, Daddy. You married Mama."

"Yeh, but I didn't know I was going to marry her then."

"Here it is. Look, Daddy. Read it to me."

"This is worse than I thought. This is horrible. I can't possibly read this when I'm sober."

On a page marked "reserved," the word itself penned in by an emphatic parenthesis, I in my stupid embryonic manhood had written, "Dear Shyla, Just little ole me getting in line to write some 'sweet nothings' to one of the sweetest girls in the world. Never forget fifth-period English class and the way Mr. Loring's face turned red every time you called him 'stud.' We sure have been through a lot together, but I can honestly say it was worth every minute of it and it was all done in the spirit of good, clean fun. (Well, not that clean!) When you get tired of that nasty sex maniac, Jordan, you know you can crawl up the tree to my window anytime. (Ha! Ha! That's a joke!) Don't forget who put the 'bop in the bop-she-bop' and who put 'the ram in the ram-a-lang-a-ding-dong.' Always remember the Senior Trip and the time that Crazy Mike put the rattle-snake in Mrs. Barlow's car. Try not to get into too much trouble this summer and let's get drunk together every night at the university next year. To a girl who's 2 sweet 2 B 4 Got-10. Jack."

Looking up from the yearbook, I was more embarrassed than moved by what I had written at the end of senior year.

"I was an idiot. A perfect jackass. Now I

can understand why the Foxes hated my guts,"
I said. "Why your mother ever married me'll
remain one of life's mysteries."

"I think it's very nice," Leah said.

Force of habit was not one of my major virtues, but I had tried to cultivate at least the
camouflage of certainty with Leah. Like most
children, regularity appeased some primitive
urge in her. Leah was used to having a sched-
ule and it gave her an inherent sense of order
and time and the correctness of things. Without
the presence of Leah I feared that my travels
would all begin at midnight and that all my
meals would be completed beneath the silence
and star shine of three in the morning. My
child ensured a certain normality and provided
the antidote to my natural disconnectedness.

Several days a week we met my mother and
Dr. Pitts for drinks at their beachfront house at
six. I wanted to spend as much time as I possibly could with my mother, and though it bothered me that I had to share this time with a
relative stranger, I realized that Dr. Pitts was
part of the package. For her entire life, Lucy
had been searching for a man who would hang
on every word she said and who would take
with utter seriousness her most flippant and

random thoughts. She had found that man in Jim Pitts. He adored her.

I did not wish to pass my knowledge of cold inarticulateness on to Leah. Deep in my heart, I thought that it may have killed Shyla. By coming home to be with my mother, I hoped that the glacier inside me would finally calve and break off and seek the warmth of the Gulf Stream waters that were also my heritage.

Lucy had done exceptionally well in remission; her complexion was rosy again and her health improving. We all knew this flowering as a false spring, but Lucy was inspirational in her desire to live and her enthusiasm was catching. She was not about to surrender without a fight.

I was sitting in the living room of my mother's house and watching Dr. Pitts as he made his stiff, ritualized approach that took place at six every evening.

"Choose your poison," he said to me.

"A Bombay Gin martini. Straight up. With a twist," I said.

"And you, mademoiselle?" the doctor asked Leah.

"Lemonade, please, Doctor Jim," she said.

Lucy walked in from the garden and came over to kiss both of us. Her kisses were indifferent, given so casually as to appear thoughtless. She smelled like wild sage and earth.

"The usual, dear?" Dr. Pitts said, from the

antique bar where he hovered over a row of cut-glass decanters. "Love Potion Number Nine?"

"Sounds divine, darling," Lucy said, winking at Leah. "You think it's time to feed the Four Horsemen of the Apocalypse, Leah?"

Leah checked the grandfather clock at the end of the room and said, "Yes, look."

Sitting down opposite me, Lucy began singing a country song from her vast repertoire. This time she chose Johnny Cash's "I Walk the Line."

She had a deep, good voice and she loved to show it off. Dr. Pitts smiled with affection as she sang and he mixed.

There was a slight movement beneath a chair at the far end of the long sitting room and another near the drapery along the windows facing south. It took less than a minute for the four box turtles that Lucy kept as pets in the house to begin their slow stately walks away from their secret hiding places. Their appearance seemed enchanted to Leah no matter how often she had witnessed Lucy's singing invitation to them to join the rest of the family for cocktails. Their shells were etched and delicate, porcelains made from foxfire and chocolate. They looked like pond flowers moving across the room. When all had arrived, surrounded her feet, and looked up at her with that ethereal patience that seems to be the hallmark of cold-blooded animals, Lucy passed two bowls over to Leah and watched as her granddaughter fed the turtles raw hamburger and lettuce. The turtles were mannerly and each waited its turn. When they finished, they turned and moved with liturgical grace back to the underworld of the house as Dr. Pitts timed their exits to his appearance with the drinks.

"I tried to sing rock and roll to them once, Leah," Lucy said, taking her vodka tonic from her husband, their eyes meeting quickly.

"It'll put hair on your chest," Dr. Pitts said, moving from Lucy to Leah, who took her lemonade with thanks.

"But the turtles didn't budge with rock and roll," Lucy swore. "Then I tried Christmas carols. Nothing. Because of Doctor Jim, I sang the Navy hymn. No turtles. Then I sang 'The Wabash Cannonball' and those turtles came out of the gates like racehorses. These are pure country turtles and they respond to country rhythms. Nothing else moves them."

"It's true, Leah," Dr. Pitts said. "I'm the chief witness for the defense. Wouldn't mind signing an affidavit to that effect. A man's got his word and that's the most precious thing, don't you know?"

He handed me my martini and like all ex-military men that I had ever met Dr. Pitts fixed a perfect one.

"Here's blood in your eye," Dr. Pitts toasted, lifting his glass, "and fire in your belly."

I had noticed in my time home that most of what Dr. Pitts had to say was either ritualistic or purely social in nature. He was gentlemanly enough to know he was required to speak on occasion, but sensible enough to know that his best strategy during cocktail hour was his deference to his wife. He liked to say of himself that he was a man of few surprises, but what he meant was that he thought of himself as boring.

"Finally, there's going to be some activity around here," Lucy said to Leah. "Not a thing of consequence has happened since you arrived on the island. But that's all about to change."

"What's going to happen, Grandma?" Leah said, walking over and sitting in her grandmother's lap. I watched as my mother's fingers ran easily through Leah's black hair.

"Big doin's." Lucy said, "Ginny Penn's coming home from the hospital tomorrow. All my boys'll be here for the weekend."

"John Hardin too?" Leah asked.

"I got a phone call from John Hardin today," Lucy said. "He was in marvelous spirits. He's getting out of the hospital and is coming down to Waterford Sunday to be with all of us." Then she turned to me. "John Hardin wants to show Leah his tree house. I'd like to go when you do. I hear it's just marvelous what he's done."

"Is John Hardin really okay, Mama?" I said. "The last time I saw him he was holding the whole town at bay at gunpoint, and he seemed a bit overwrought to me."

"You've always been insensitive to John Hardin," Lucy said. "You've never taken the time to see the world as he sees it."

"If I could see the world as he sees it, I'd be handcuffed to the same cot at the state hospital, Mother dear."

"Sometimes your humor is in execrable taste, son."

"That wasn't humor, Mother."

"What's wrong with John Hardin?" Leah asked.

"He's got headaches," Lucy said.

"He's got bats in his head," I said.

It was almost seven and there was still light in the western horizon. As we looked out to the sea a wind lifted off the crests of the incoming waves creating a dialogue between the palms and bearing an iodine taste. The ocean air was heavy and sacred to Lucy, who had come to know what life felt like when it was lived in completely. Her senses blazed like five Lenten candles when she stared out into that portion of the ocean that extended beyond their land. I knew she believed the salt air and saltwater could save her.

The raccoons had already gathered in her backyard garden, clamoring loudly and jockeying for position. In their rowdy banditry, they looked like a pack of miscast hounds with their arched backs and clownish faces. But they were formidable animals. The back door slammed and Leah came out with the bag of dried cat food and the leftovers that Lucy had designated for that night's feeding. For five minutes, the raccoons chattered and hissed and chased each other until the food was finished and the animals slipped out of the backyard and into the line of trees of an empty lot. When they disappeared it was like the memory of smoke that had gone.

"When I first came to the low country, your great-grandfather told me something I've never forgotten."

"Grandpa Silas?" Leah asked.

"He was my first teacher down here. He shared everything he knew about these islands."

"He wants to teach me how to shoot a deer," Leah said. "But Daddy says Great-grandpa's got better things to teach me."

"Silas told me *this* the first day I met him," Lucy said. "He told me that when the white man first came to these islands, a squirrel could climb a tree on this beach, head west, and not have to touch the ground until it reached the Mississippi River. That's how thick the forests used to be in this country."

"What about the marsh?" Leah asked. "How could the squirrels get across the marsh?"

"Smart girl," Lucy said. "Never take anything at face value."

Dr. Pitts and I had watched the evening feeding from a picture window in the den. There was an odd imbalance between us, as if the generation that separated us was a river of such treachery that no harbor pilot could promise safe steerage through its wreck-filled channels. I could tell that my mother's husband desperately wanted me to like him and his inarticulate efforts at small talk were the doctor's way of bridging the gap between us.

"Isn't she beautiful?" Dr. Pitts said.

"She certainly is," I agreed and it took me a moment to realize that the doctor was not talking about Leah.

"She's interested in everything. Got the raw enthusiasm of a girl. Never seen anything to match it. Her energy level is off the charts. I, for one, can't keep up with her. You're damn lucky to have such a mother. Quite a girl. Quite a girl."

I knew that Dr. Pitts was rambling because he was uncomfortable with me. No matter how hard I tried I could not think of a single thing to say to put the doctor at ease. I let my mind drift through a series of safe subjects—fishing, golf, gardening, inflation, taxes—but nothing rose up spontaneously to break the silence between us. The effort left me exhausted, but no words took flight.

"Your brothers, Jack? Do they talk about me? Do they like me? Any information you could give on this subject would be much appreciated. Also treated with strictest confidentiality."

"All of us know you love our mother, Doctor," I said. "We're very grateful to you."

"So they're not resentful of my taking command, so to speak," the doctor said as both of us fixed our eyes on the women in our lives.

"Dad's an alcoholic, Doctor," I said. "I think that beneath the lake of booze he's consumed since the early sixties, there's a fairly decent man there. But I think he'd've been better off if he'd started drinking gasoline instead of bourbon. It would've killed him faster and we'd've hated him less."

"Your father called today," Dr. Pitts said. "Again, I'm afraid."

"Why's he calling here?"

"He gets a little tight, then calls to harass

your poor mother," he said. "I guess I should step in and put an end to it, but she says she can handle it. She needs all her strength, you know. It doesn't do her much good to spread it around too thinly. Especially on nonsense."

"I don't understand leukemia," I said. "Mom seems healthier than she's ever been. She walks five miles a day after she wakes up. Her coloring's back. Can she beat this thing?"

"Anything's possible. The body's a funny thing. It's so full of surprises that it makes conventional wisdom seem silly."

"So you think Mom might beat it?" I asked, and I realized that this was the first time I had dared to have any hope at all.

"I prefer to think that your mother'll live forever," Dr. Pitts said, choosing his words carefully. "I simply don't think I could live without her. I have great hope for her because I've got no choice."

"What kind of leukemia does Mom have?"

"The worst," he said.

"Is her doctor any good?" I asked.

"It doesn't make any difference how good he is," Dr. Pitts said, clearing his throat uneasily.

Dr. Pitts walked off to refresh the drinks and I noticed a slight misstriding as though my stepfather were trying to conceal a limp. Taking our drinks out, we joined Lucy's attendance to the warming springtime air. Plovers had begun to arrive from South America, rumoring the green tumult that would follow them.

We sat on the deck listening to the sea come in at its own pace. The waves moved, rhythmically and as if ordained, like the sands of a moon-brightened hourglass. It was so peaceful and orderly and I looked fondly at my mother, who had always longed for such rituals of domestic tranquillity. The theatrics of pure normality moved her enormously.

Lucy was the first to see him coming. She did not give a sign that anything was amiss, but stood up and smoothed out the wrinkles of her dress with her hands.

"Jim, darling," she said. "Could you run me quick back to T. T. Bones before the store closes? I forgot to buy the pasta and the bread for dinner."

"Of course," Dr. Pitts said, setting down his drink. "You entertain our guests."

"Let me and Leah ride with you," Lucy said and I saw her worried glance down the beach. I looked in the direction she was looking and understood everything without a word passing between us.

"Could you pick up a jar of Hellmann's mayonnaise for me, Mama?" I said.

"I'll be more than happy to," she said. "Please start the water for the pasta."

I looked at the figure of the man drawing nearer and said, "I'll do that right now. Leah, pick up a dessert that looks good for your lunch."

As they went through the house, I walked down the steps that led to the beach. The tide was coming in by inches as I watched my father drawing near, holding on to a pint bottle as though it were filled to the brim with semiprecious stones. His gait was unsteady as he headed directly toward the house and found me blocking his path. We took each other's measure in the half-light of dusk.

"Taking up body surfing?" I asked. "Or just out speed walking to lose weight?"

"I need to speak with your mother," Johnson Hagood said to me without affection. "I need to inquire about the state of her health."

"Her health's lousy," I said. "She's dying. Now beat it, Dad. You scare Mom every time you do this."

He looked up toward the house, then back at me. "I haven't been drinking," he said, lifting the almost full bottle. "I brought this for show."

"Sure."

"My children have all turned, like rabid dogs, against me."

"Not soon enough," I said.

"You haven't brought your daughter to see

me yet," he said in a wounded, self-pitying voice. "I guess you two've gotten too big for your britches living in Europe and being entertained by royalty."

"Yeh, we're in one Hapsburg palace after another," I said, shaking my head sadly. "We've been to see you twice, Dad. You were comatose both times."

"I've been under a lot of pressure lately," Johnson Hagood said, checking the level of bourbon against the half-lit sky.

"What kind?"

"To quit drinking," he said without irony, but I laughed out loud. "You've always hated me, Jack. You were always the leader of those who conspired against me."

"Not always," I corrected him. "For a couple of years, I just pitied you. But hatred came easily after that."

"You take Leah to see Shyla's parents every day. The Foxes treated you worse than I ever did."

"The Foxes tried to take my child away from me," I said. "You tried to take my childhood. The Foxes failed. You succeeded."

My father looked past me toward the house where he thought Lucy was watching the scene. He screamed out to her, "Lucy! Lucy! Flag of Truce. I need to talk to you."

"You're going to embarrass her in front of all her neighbors."

"That's always been her weak spot," my father chuckled. "She actually cares what her neighbors think. It's given me great tactical advantage over the years. Look, get out of my way. There's a doctor on Hilton Head who can cure your mother. He uses that medicine made out of apricot pits that you can only buy in Mexico."

"Yeh," I said. "Nobody dies of cancer in Mexico. Mom's already got a doctor. He'll do just as good a job killing her as anyone else."

He unscrewed the cap of the bottle and took one quick swallow of the Old Grand-Dad. I had seen my father consume a whole pint of bourbon without coming up once for air. He studied me.

"You were the weirdest of all my children and that's saying something," he said at last. "That's a sweepstakes you should take pride in winning. What a happy nest of losers."

And then he said, unscrewing the bottle cap again, "You were born ugly, son. Even I can't be blamed for that, although you and the rest of them would like to blame me for the ocean having too much salt. No, I had people tell me you were the ugliest baby ever born in Waterford, all red-faced and colicky and runty. Your face has always looked like roadkill to me."

My father's capacity for meanness could always take my breath away. Woe to the child born with freckles, astigmatism, birthmarks, or red hair. He could always find his adversaries' softest flanks and there was nothing he would not say to damage the people he loved most on the earth.

"Mom's not here, Dad," I said. "She got Leah and Jim out of harm's way when she saw you coming. She sent me out here to get rid of you."

"You and what army?" he said.

I shook my head and said, "Dad. Mom's married now. She's got a new life. You don't need to embarrass her or humiliate her in front of her new husband."

"We took vows before almighty God," he said grandly. "The King of Kings. The Lord God of Hosts. The Maker of All Things Great and Small."

"She dissolved the vows," I said. "With the help of a lawyer. You heard of lawyers?"

"She deserted me in my time of greatest need. I was helpless, vomiting in every gutter, lifting my arms into the night for an angel of mercy. Alcoholism's a disease, son. Your mother deserted her post like a nurse forsaking a leper. That's why God struck her down with cancer."

"I'll tell her. She'll be glad to hear it," I

said. "Clear out, Dad. Let me walk you back to Grandpa's."

"I don't tolerate assholes and degenerates for escorts. I consider you both. I've taken a look at all your pansy cookbooks. I'd like you to know that I wouldn't touch any of that shit during a famine."

"I'll write a cookbook just for you, Dad. One chapter'll be 'Dry Martinis.' The next could be 'Margaritas,' then 'Scotch and Soda,' then 'Bloody Marys.' "

My father said proudly, "I drink my liquor straight."

"Then I'll simplify my cookbook. The recipe could read: 'Buy a bottle of liquor. Open it up. Drink that sucker down. Throw up in the sand. Pass out at your leisure.' We could call that recipe: 'Breakfast.' "

"Have some respect," Johnson Hagood said. "I already told you it was a disease. I need compassion, not censure."

"Get out of Mom's front yard," I said, my temper fraying slightly.

"I'm not in her front yard. The piece of land on which I'm standing belongs to the littoral of the great state of South Carolina. No man or woman can purchase or lay claim to the beach itself, which belongs to the state and the people in perpetuity. Don't argue law with me, idiot child. I'm the best goddamn lawyer you've ever seen and I've forgotten more about South Carolina law than you'll ever dream about."

"You threw your law career away in a bottle of Jim Beam."

"I'm a deeper man than you'll ever be, Jack. I drink because of despair, disillusionment, and emptiness of the soul. Things you know nothing about."

"Because of you, I could give a course at Harvard on all those subjects," I shot back. "But let's be clear: you drink because you love to get drunk."

"Why should I listen to what you say?" my father answered and there was a new venom in his voice. "You're nothing but a faggot who writes cookbooks. A mama's boy who mastered the arts of the kitchen and hearth because he couldn't tear himself away from his mother's skirts. You were always easy to shop for. I'd just think about a nice present for Lucy and buy it for you instead."

I tried to get control of myself again and said, "I've heard it all before, Dad. You forget everything you say because you're drunk. All of us remember everything because we're sober. The only part you'll remember is me kicking your ass up and down the beach. We've been in this dance for too long. Let's look for another way."

"I like this way. I need it to express my contempt for you. My utter loathing. Dear boy, you can always pretend you don't care what I say. But you're like the rest of your siblings. You care far too much. I look for things that'll hurt you the most, then I use them for pleasure. It's a sport I invented. It's my favorite recreation. I call it kid-fucking. You find out where they're weakest. You work away at that spot like a dentist probing at a small area of decay. Go deep enough and you hit a nerve. Probe a millimeter deeper and you can put them screaming on their knees."

"Don't do it, Dad," I whispered. "I'm warning you."

"Ladies and gentlemen, help me welcome to our center stage, the lovely and ethereal Shyla Fox."

I rushed at my father and grabbed him by his throat, lifting him up in the air on his tiptoes. He struggled and tried to hit me in the face with the pint bottle but I grabbed it and threw it far out into the raging surf.

"Your sorrow about Shyla's all an act," he spat at me. "Everything about you's fake. I've watched you walk with your little girl out of the Foxes' house. It's so sweet. The loving father. The grieving widower. Yet it's all play-acting. If Daddy makes believe long enough then the whole world'll think he loves his little daughter.

All I see is your coldness, Jack. I see the Iceman Cometh. Because I've lived with that cold inside me and it's ruined my whole life."

"I'm not anything like you."

"You got me written all over you," he boasted, laughing. "All my sons wear that mark of ice that I've been fighting my whole life. Look at poor Dallas. My law partner. He's got a nice wife and a couple of kids, but it's not enough for him. So he goes looking for the first girl who'll spread her legs for free and he thinks he's discovered the mother lode. All of you'll be looking for love your whole lives and you'll never even know when it's sleeping right beside you."

"You don't know anything about us," I whispered savagely.

"Look up there," Johnson Hagood said, looking toward Lucy's house. Lucy had returned with Jim and Leah from the store. I watched as she walked up to the picture window framed in the false light and peered out into the real darkness. We could see her perfectly and she could not see us at all.

"That's what I lost," my father said to me. "Because I didn't know what I had. I'll bet you didn't have a clue how much you loved Shyla until you saw her in the morgue. Did you, Jack?"

He looked at his ex-wife one last time, then screamed out, "I love you, Lucy. I still love you."

As Lucy fled from the window he added, "I love you, you monstrous cunt."

CHAPTER 24

MAX AND ESTHER RUSOFF TOOK GREAT pleasure in the conduct of their business pursuits in Waterford. Max was a wizard at selling and Esther kept the account books with an infallible accuracy and a penmanship as pretty as a row of tulips. To them, business was an extension of the arts of courtesy and welcome, and anyone who entered their store came as an honored guest. Max was the greeter, the kibitzer, and the joke teller, while Esther worked behind the scenes in accounts and monitoring the stock.

They prospered. Their small food store became the town's first supermarket and they opened Rusoff's Department Store in the spring of 1937. The department store quickly became famous for its fashions and the fairness of its prices. The first woman to drive from Charleston to Waterford to shop received a free purse and got her picture in the next week's edition of the local paper. To the Rusoffs' surprise, they discovered they were good at marketing and advertising. Everything they touched turned golden and they could not believe their good fortune or the blessings that God had showered upon them.

In 1939, the God of the Jews went into hiding. For years letters had arrived at Max and Esther's house from relatives scattered through Russia and Poland. Esther had been religious about corresponding with everyone who was family and from the very first days of his residence in Waterford, Max had always sent money back to his family in Europe.

In 1939, the letters from Poland stopped forever. The mails grew quiet and the Yiddish language died for Esther Rusoff that year.

When Silas McCall learned of the Rusoffs' fears for their relatives, he arranged a meeting with the Honorable Barnwell Middleton, the representative from their district in the United States Congress. Hard-nosed and aristocratic, Middleton sat in Harry's Restaurant in Waterford in October of 1941 and stared at the weathered face and enormous arms of Max Rusoff. Silas McCall sat beside him as Max told of the disappearance of his and Esther's families when the German Army entered Poland and then invaded Russia. When Max had finished speaking, he handed the congressman a list of all their relatives, their names and addresses. There were sixty-eight people on the list, including four infants.

Middleton cleared his throat and took a sip of black coffee before he spoke. "It's a bad time, Max."

"What do you know?" Max asked.

"That it's bad. That it's worse than you think. That it's worse than anybody thinks."

Silas interrupted angrily, "Goddamn it, Barnwell. The man's worried sick. Don't make it worse until you know something for sure."

"It'll be bad news, Max, whatever I find out."

"We are Jews," Max said. "We have had bad news before."

Over a year passed and the Rusoffs heard not a single word from Barnwell Middleton. By then the United States was fully engaged in the war. Max had heard no news at all of Kironittska's Jews and the silence that had first fallen on Poland now fell on Russia. It was the year that their two sons, Mark and Henry, enlisted in the United States Army. Sending their sons off to fight the Germans made Max and Esther Rusoff feel like Americans as nothing else ever had. Max had given both boys miniature replicas of the Statue of Liberty when they were shipped overseas and they kept the small statues on their persons for the entire war. They fought as American soldiers with great fierceness and resolve, and as the sons of the Great Jew they were unafraid of Cossacks. They fought north toward the Europe where the collective voices of all the Rusoffs on both sides of the family had fallen silent.

In the middle of 1943 Barnwell Middleton met Max and Silas for lunch for the first time since he had promised Max he would try to find out the fates of his and Esther's families. For the first fifteen minutes of the meal, Barnwell talked about the progress of the war, the victories and defeats of the Allies, and the somber mood in Washington.

Silas listened impatiently, then said, "Get to the point, Barnwell."

"Have you been able to check on our families?" Max asked.

"Yes," Middleton answered, his voice grave. "I wish I hadn't received any answers. But I have."

Then Barnwell leaned across the table and took Max by the hand and held it fiercely as he delivered the news from Eastern Europe in a

South Carolina café known for its bad coffee and good pie.

"Max," he whispered. "All the names you gave me. All of them . . . All dead, Max. Every one of them is dead."

Max said nothing. He neither tried to speak, nor thought he could utter a sound if asked a direct question.

"There's no way for you to know that," Silas said. "It's wartime. There's confusion. Armies in the field. You can't know for sure."

"You're right, Silas," Barnwell conceded. "Some of these people could've escaped or been overlooked. Some could've hidden. The information was a long time in coming. I'm not even sure where it came from or who retrieved it. The source is in Switzerland and I know he's German. That's all I know. He says that all your family is dead, Max. All of Esther's family is dead. There are no Jews in any of the towns or cities you gave me with the list of names."

"*Judenrein*," Max said, at last.

"They're killing every Jew they can find," Barnwell said. "Except the ones they're forcing into slave labor. Your family was mostly slaughtered in fields. The Jews were forced to dig their own pits, then were machine-gunned en masse."

"There were four infants. Babies," Max said.

"The Germans aren't particular," Barnwell said.

"They machine-gun babies?" Silas asked.

"Or bury them alive after they kill their mothers," Barnwell said. "There was one teenage girl they thought was Esther's niece. She's in hiding in Poland. But it turns out she only has the same name as a girl on Esther's list, Ruth Graubart. A shame. It turns out she is no relation at all."

"What happened to this child's family?" Max asked.

Barnwell shrugged his shoulders and said, "I suppose the same thing that happened to yours. They said the Polish underground could smuggle her out."

"Then you should do it," Silas said.

"The price was a tad high," Barnwell said, his voice ironic and detached. "They were asking for fifty thousand dollars cash."

Silas whistled and Barnwell released Max's hand at last. Twirling his finger, Barnwell gestured to the waitress for another round of coffee.

"Nice world," Silas said. "Tell me one nice thing about the human race."

"That girl," Max said.

"What girl?" Barnwell asked.

"The one in hiding. The one you thought was Esther's niece," he said.

"No relation at all. She's from another part of Poland entirely."

"Still. She is a Jewish girl in trouble."

"Yes," Barnwell said.

"Esther and I would like to bring that girl to America," Max said.

Both men looked at Max as though they had both misheard him.

"She's not yours, Max. And she's not Esther's," Silas said, "and she comes with a fifty-thousand-dollar price tag."

"She's a Jewish girl in trouble. That makes her mine. It makes her Esther's. You say her family is probably dead. Like my family. If we do not help her, who will?"

"The life of one girl doesn't make much difference in a war this big," Barnwell answered.

"I think it does," Max answered.

"But you don't have fifty thousand dollars cash," the congressman said, with finality, rising from the table with the air of a man who has spent enough time on a disagreeable subject. "Nobody in this town has that kind of cash."

"Except you," Silas said. "Elect a man to Congress in this state and he's a millionaire in four years. Tell me how it works, Barnwell."

"God smiles on lambs and fools," Barnwell answered.

That night Max took Esther out on the veranda overlooking the Waterford River and together they watched the sun gild a low-lying herd of clouds with an unearthly, brokered gold. They drank schnapps from small crystal glasses. It was a ritual that celebrated their prosperity and their need to relax after the endless labors of their first years in the town.

Max could not figure out a way to tell the woman he loved best in the world that she had lost her entire family. Esther came from a family of enormous intimacy and affection, and he did not know how to tell her that her Europe had died.

Max had a second schnapps and then told her in Yiddish.

For six days, Esther Rusoff mourned and then a young rabbi conducted Sabbath services in their house. Max and Esther pledged to build a synagogue in Waterford to honor their families.

When shiva was over, Esther lay in Max's arms again and whispered to him before they went to sleep.

"That girl, Max. The one that Barnwell mentioned to you."

"I have been thinking of her too," Max said.

"What can we do?"

"Sell everything," Max replied. "This

house. The department store. The supermarket. Start again."

"Can we get fifty thousand dollars? It is a lot. Too much maybe."

"The bank will lend us the difference," Max said. "I am sure of it."

"Then this is what we will do," Esther said.

"Yes," Max said.

"You would do it whether I agreed or not," Esther said. "I know you, my husband. I am smart enough to go along with what you have already decided. But it is right. Even if it may take away from our own children."

"How does it hurt our own children to save another child?" Max asked.

In the following months, Max sold the department store to the Belk's chain out of Charlotte, sold the food market to a retailer out of Charleston, and sold their house on Dolphin Street to a lieutenant general in the Marine Corps stationed on Pollock Island and nearing retirement age. He wired the fifty thousand dollars to Barnwell Middleton in Washington and received back a sobering telegram that stated how long the odds were and how improbable it was that this rescue could actually be consummated. But Barnwell Middleton pledged he would try his best.

Max had not sold the building of the small store that he had first opened in Waterford so many years before, and it was empty. The Rusoff family moved back into the top floor, and in no time, Max and Esther were back in business.

Nearly a year passed before Max received a telegram from Barnwell Middleton informing him that a merchant ship would arrive in the small port of Waterford on July 18, 1944. A girl named Ruth Graubart was listed among the passengers. Max called his wife and told her the good news, then called Silas McCall who told the news to Ginny Penn. The news moved from house to house in Waterford the way news travels in small towns, light and frisky and buoyant because the story brought such a sense of joy into a world too familiar with the news of hometown boys dying overseas.

When the boat arrived in Waterford, a pretty teenage girl walked down the gangplank accompanied, with grave formality, by the ship's captain. She looked shy and bewildered as she heard the noise begin in the crowd. Meeting Max and Esther, who greeted her in Yiddish, she curtsied. Max wept and opened his arms to her. When she rushed into them and buried her head in his great chest, the town roared out its greeting to her. It let her know that she was part of Waterford, South Carolina, from that day forward, that she had found her home. The town would take the girl, Ruth

Graubart, into their hearts and watch her finish high school and come of age to marry George Fox. The town would be there when she bore her first child, Shyla, and would be there when Ruth buried that same child.

But what the town remembered most and best was that first moment when the Jewish orphan, ransomed by strangers, touched down on Waterford soil for the first time and flew into the arms of the Great Jew.

Silas McCall would later tell his grandchildren that when he watched the girl's arrival, it marked the first time he was certain that America would win the war. No matter how many times he told the story to his grandchildren about Ruth's arrival, he always ended it the same way and it always gave the McCall children goose bumps when he got to the end.

The town roared, he would say, the town just roared.

But Ruth told her own story to no one in Waterford except to her husband and her daughter Shyla, until she told it to me in the spring of 1986 after we had reconciled and I had returned to the town with her granddaughter, Leah, to help my mother die.

It was only when Ruth had told me about her terrible history in Poland that I learned, at last, the identity of the lady of coins.

CHAPTER 25

I DROVE MY GRANDFATHER, SILAS MC-
Call, over to Waterford to pick up Ginny Penn
from the nursing home. I left my brothers at
my grandparents' house as they finished off a
ramp for Ginny Penn's wheelchair. My grandfather was a compact, cigarette-smoking Southerner, observant, but a man of few words.

"Be glad to get Ginny Penn home?" I
asked.

"Don't have much choice," Silas said. "She
likes to drive the nurses crazy."

"Dad all right?"

"Slept it off. Then caught a ride to town."

We put my grandmother in the backseat,

exhausted by the effort and emotion caused by the mechanics of checking out of the home. Bureaucracy always requires an expenditure of energy that is too much to ask, especially of the very old and very sick. Ginny Penn did not even wave back at the nurses who lined the porch to bid her farewell.

"Monsters," she said as Silas and I waved to them. "Leeches. Bed-pan emptiers. Disease-spreaders. Penicillin-fungi. They should not be allowed to touch genuine ladies or women of pure refinement."

"I thought they were nice," Silas said quietly, almost an aside.

"You never came to see me once," Ginny Penn hissed. "Better had I married Ulysses S. Grant than the traitorous wretch Silas Mc-Call."

"Could you stop off at the feed store?" my grandfather asked me. "I'd like to buy a muzzle."

"Grandpa came to see you every day, Ginny Penn," I said.

"My grandchildren deserted me. The whole town was on a death watch. It would've exploded with joy at the news of my demise."

"I'd have led the parade down Main Street," Silas muttered.

"Don't egg her on," I warned, touching his wrist. "Ginny Penn, my brothers are all down.

We spent the day building you a wheelchair ramp."

"That's what you call a homecoming gift? A wheelchair ramp?"

"I oversaw the preliminaries," I said. "It'll be great."

My four brothers were gathered at their grandparents' house when I drove up into the yard. The house had aged well and looked distinguished among the modern beach houses that had sprung up around it. Behind it, the fourteenth hole of a golf course designed by Robert Trent Jones made a dogleg away from the backyard. A golf cart bearing two sedate and dignified retirees drifted as soundlessly as a sailing ship toward the distant green. Four female white-tailed deer, beautiful in their streamlined thinness, fed on the high grasses in the rough. When I was a boy, I thought, the island was wild and you could look forever and never find a golf ball, but everything's different from when I was a boy.

Except, I thought, my grandparents were the same. Always they had seemed peculiar and unsuitable. They had also appeared conjoined by habit and not by love. It hurt Ginny Penn that we, her grandsons, preferred Silas to her and that we loved him with a fierce attachment that she would never know. But we would disagree with that assessment and tell her with clarity and accuracy that we loved her exactly as much as she would allow us to and that was always dependent on the ungovernable valences of her moods.

"The boys," I said.

"The best boys in the world," Silas added.

"They'll do in a pinch," Ginny Penn said, but I could tell she was both excited to be home and to have a reception committee waiting for her.

My brothers let out a cheer and ran down to greet her. They pounded on the side of the car and kept up their cheering until even the dour Ginny Penn had to smile. When she smiled, all four boys pretended to feel dizzy and fell onto their backs in a dead faint.

"They've always been goofy as puppies," she said, as Silas helped her out of the car and I retrieved the wheelchair from the porch.

Tee ran up the new ramp that lent the whole yard the smell of fresh lumber. He lay down at the top of the ramp and yelled to Ginny Penn, "Hey, old woman."

Ginny Penn flared and said, "Don't you call me 'old woman' or I'll switch you till it thunders."

"Look, Ginny Penn," Tee said happily. "Perfect angle."

Then, pretending he was a dead man in a B

movie, Tee let himself roll down the ramp and out onto the sidewalk.

"It needs some varnish," Ginny Penn said. "I detest raw wood. It offends my aesthetic."

"It's wonderful to see you too, Grandma," Dallas said.

"Thank you, boys, for building the ramp," Dupree added in a girlish voice.

"Not even a near-death experience changed her one iota, boys," Silas said, glumly pushing her up the ramp. "She'll be hell until she dies."

"That's my plan," she said.

In the middle of the ramp, my brothers stopped the wheelchair and began kissing her in welcome. They kissed her face and neck and tickled her ribs. They kissed her eyes and cheeks and forehead until she began to fend them off with her cane. They retreated from her, laughing, then pounced on her again when Silas maneuvered her near the front door. She seemed to both welcome and barely tolerate the kisses. It was their attention she craved, not their touch. She had always considered kissing to be the most overrated of human activities.

Outside we sat around the front porch as John Hardin sanded the ramp, smoothing down the rough spots. Of all of us, he was the only true carpenter and there was nothing he could not do with his hands. Though gifted, he was also unemployable since he could never take the pressure that even the most serene workplace made inevitable. We watched him sand the fresh lumber, admiring the economy of his labor.

Tee broke the silence by saying, "Let's face it. Ginny Penn's an asshole. Am I the only one that's noticed it?"

"Who?" Dupree said. "That sweet ol' thing?"

Leah walked out onto the back porch after having read Ginny Penn a poem she had written in honor of her homecoming.

"Did Ginny Penn like your poem, darling?" her uncle Dupree asked.

"I couldn't tell," Leah said. "She said she did."

"Don't worry about it," Tee said. "Being nice is out of character."

"Too much to ask," Dallas agreed.

"Did all of you know my mother?" Leah asked my brothers, who were surprised at the question. They gathered around her solicitously.

"Sure, Leah," Dupree said. "What do you want to know? What do you remember most about Shyla?"

"I don't remember much about having a mother, Uncle Dupree," Leah said.

"You sure had a nice one, darling," Dallas said.

"Pretty as a picture, just like you," Tee added.

"Did all of you like her?" Leah asked.

"Like her?" Dupree said. "We were all in love with your mama. Don't know if your daddy told you, but that was one sexy girl."

"Best dancer I ever saw," Tee said. "I never saw anyone who could do the shag as well as she could."

"What's the shag?"

"A girl born in South Carolina doesn't know what the shag is?" Dupree said. "That's a crime against humanity."

"Means your daddy ain't worth a damn," said Tee.

"They don't do the shag in Italy, boys," I defended myself. "I might as well teach her the hula."

"No excuses," Dupree said. "Let me pull my pickup truck close to the porch and I'll put on a tape. There's a tragic gap in my niece's education."

"Be better if the girl had been raised in a South Carolina orphanage," Dallas teased. "Makes me ashamed you're my brother, Jack."

"Look at Dupree with that pickup truck," John Hardin sneered. "He loves playin' dirtball better than anybody I've ever seen."

"Dupree's a redneck at heart," Tee said. "A redneck wannabee. It's the lowest form of life."

Dupree pulled his truck up to the porch, which was wind-burnt from exposure to the sea. He put in a tape and turned the volume up full blast.

"Carolina beach music," Dupree said, coming up on the porch. "The holiest sound on earth."

"Your uncles'll now make up for your father's negligence," Dallas said. "In fact, I may file a civil suit against him."

Dupree took Leah's hand and began showing her the steps. I grabbed Tee and began to dance and Leah watched with fascination, never having seen me dance before.

"The essence of the shag, Leah," I said, "is to put on a face of utter coolness. The shag is not about passion. It's about summer and secret desires and attitude. You have to have an utterly careless expression on your face."

"Who is this guy—Plato? We're just teaching the kid how to dance," Dupree said.

"The reason I can dance the girl's part," Tee said to Leah, "is because I'm younger and they used to force me to be the girl when they practiced the shag."

Dallas asked Leah to dance when the next song, "Double Shot of My Baby's Love," came blasting out of the truck.

"Your mother was the greatest shag dancer that ever lived," Dallas said.

"She could dance any dance there was," Dupree said.

"Hey, tell me Leah's not getting it fast," Dallas said in admiration.

"Got her mother's blood," Tee said. "This girl was born to shag. I got the dance after John Hardin. I'm gonna teach her the dirty shag."

"The dirty shag," Leah squealed. "Sounds like fun."

Leah became a lifelong lover of uncles on that day. She was consumed and enlarged by the joyous attention of her uncles and that pleasure shone in her face. Her body began to move in harmony with the rhythm and there seemed a ripening in the center of her girlhood as she spun in the full flood of her uncles' admiration. They lined up to dance with her and argued whose turn it was. They turned an afternoon on a porch into a promenade of bright strange glamour she would remember all her life. She had been selected, singled out, and was as powerful as a fairy tale queen surrounded by her cheering, high-spirited armies. By the end of that day, she could shag as well as any of her uncles.

I watched every single dance Leah danced with my brothers, whose sweetness moved me greatly. Then Dupree tapped me on the shoulder and said, "Next song's for you and Leah to dance to."

The song, "Save the Last Dance for Me" by the Drifters, filled the air and Leah noticed the change in me.

"What's wrong, Daddy?" she asked as I took her hand and asked for the privilege of this dance.

"Could you rewind so that I go back to the beginning, Dupree?" I asked. "I've got to explain the significance of this song." Then I turned to Leah. "Remember the story of me and Mama falling in love?" I asked.

"The night the house fell into the sea?" Leah asked.

"Same one. Well, when Mama and I danced in that room alone when everyone had run out of the house, we danced the shag."

"I didn't know that."

"I should've taught you how to do it. My brothers are right."

"It's okay, Daddy. You taught me lots of things."

"This was your Mama's and my favorite song. We fell in love dancing to it."

Leah had never danced with me, but she heard the humming of her uncles as they murmured with pleasure, watching us move to the words of the wonderful song. They clapped and stomped their feet and wolf-whistled at Leah as I spun her around on the weather-beaten porch. Her greatest surprise was that she couldn't shag as well as I did. And she said so. And as we danced I saw her slowly turning into a mirror image of Shyla, and then the tears came; they came, at last.

She didn't notice that I was weeping until my brothers grew quiet. We stopped dancing and I sat down on the porch steps. My child held me as the song her mother and I had loved best in the world completely undid me. I could bear the memory, but I could not bear the music that made the memory such a killing thing.

CHAPTER 26

IN EARLY MAY, A MONTH AFTER OUR return, at Lucy's insistence, I drove her up Highway 17 toward Charleston and the Trappist monastery out at Mepkin Abbey. Though she was vague about the reasons for her visit, she did mention she wanted to have Father Jude hear her confession. Ever since I had brought Father Jude to my mother's hospital bed, where he gave her Extreme Unction, I suspected there was more to this relationship than penitent and confessor, but I no longer thought, as we had when we were younger, that they were lovers. I had questioned Lucy, but she was a master of indirection. There was no query she could not succeed at not answering. The English language on her tongue became a smokescreen without her eyes changing expression in the least. As we drove to Charleston, I looked over at her. She looked calm and pretty.

For a long time I had wanted to get her off by herself to ask her all the unanswered questions I had stored up from childhood and had thought of again with my eyes bandaged in Rome. Though I lacked a clear strategy for milking her of this concealed trove of knowledge, I wanted to initiate the inquiry without arousing suspicion.

"I've had some wonderful news," she said suddenly, stretching her arms in the sunlight. Only since she developed leukemia could Lucy be talked into using her seat belt. She had always made it a point of honor not to wear one and it was odd for me to see her safely buckled up. "I want to share it with you, but I want you to promise not to tell another living soul."

"I promise to tell only one other person," I said. "Otherwise, I find myself untrustworthy. Secrets are too much of a burden to me."

"The Pope just annulled my marriage to your father. I can receive the sacraments again. Dr. Pitts and I got remarried in the church yesterday."

"Thanks for inviting your children."

"We didn't want to make a fuss," she said. "I wrote the Pope a thank-you note."

"You had five kids with Dad," I said.

"It was all a terrible mistake. I feel like I've awakened from a bad dream."

"Does that mean we're all bastards?" I asked, adjusting the rearview mirror.

Lucy giggled and said, "It never occurred to me. Oh dear. How comical. Yes, I imagine it does. I didn't even think to ask. Jude'll know."

"So the marriage never happened. All that pain and grief and suffering. None of it happened," I said.

"Everything happened," Lucy explained, "but the Church wiped the slate clean. There's no record of it happening."

"I'm a record of it happening," I insisted.

"No," Lucy said. "You're annulled."

"If I'm nothing, I can't be driving this car," I shouted. "I don't exist. I'm not here. My parents were never married and I was never born. Grab the wheel, Mama, because I'm one annulled son of a bitch."

I threw my hands up in the air and Lucy leaned over and gained control of the wheel.

Lucy said, "I think not being born might be the nicest gift I could ever bestow on my children. It wasn't a happy home I raised you up in."

"*Au contraire*. It was a dream come true," I

said. "Starring the bastard McCall children, their virgin mother, and their pickled father who would later be cuckolded and emasculated by the Pope himself."

"When your father gets the news I want to know every single word that comes out of his mouth. I'll cherish every syllable of his pain."

"You shouldn't have hard feelings about Dad," I said, taking control of the wheel again. "After all, you were never married to him."

"I don't have to be bitter anymore. It's like it never happened. Perhaps we could even be friends."

"I could introduce you," I offered. "Judge McCall, I'd like you to meet Mrs. Pitts. The Pope has quashed all rumors that you were once husband and wife and that you produced five children during your long and ghastly marriage."

"Now, you're making fun," Lucy cautioned.

"The Roman Catholic Church," I said, shaking my head. "Why did you raise me in such a ridiculous, brain-dead, dimwitted, sexually perverse, odd-duck, know-nothing, silly-assed church? We're Southern, for God's sake, Mama. I could've been an Anglican and had a nice golf stroke. Presbyterian and I could've had a puckered asshole and been able to clear my throat with authority. Methodist and not gagged when someone melted marshmallows on sweet potatoes. Baptist and I could've drunk in secret with great pleasure. Church of God and I could've spoken in unknown tongues. But no, you condemn me to weirdness and freakdom and solitude by raising me in the only church that could mark me as a loser in paradise among my peers."

"I raised my children in the Cadillac of religions," said Lucy.

"We're not your real children," I said. "The marriage was annulled. You can forget about morning sickness, the pain of childbirth, messy placentas, two o'clock feedings, measles, chicken pox . . . none of it happened. Your kids are five little nightmares you never had."

"The Cadillac," she said. "The top of the line." And she leaned her head back and closed her eyes.

Lucy said, after miles of silence, "I want Father Jude to hear my confession. Nothing else will quite do."

"Tell me why Father Jude is so important to you."

I could tell I had asked a question my mother didn't like and she paused for a long moment before answering.

"Later. I'm not going to let you ruin my day," Lucy said. "You always try to make me feel bad about the way I raised you. Well, here's the bottom line. You got a college education, a pretty child, and you have written a bunch of books with your name and picture on each one. And you try and make me feel like I did a bad job. You had a great childhood."

"Yeh, I sure lucked out."

"You don't even know what bad luck looks like."

"Tell me about my luck," I said, trying to sound ironic, not bitter, but bitterness leaked out all over the irony.

"When you were hit, you bled just like me," Lucy said. "But you did your bleeding in a warm bed . . . with a full stomach and with your mama coming in to press a cold washcloth to your face."

"When I was a little boy, you used to tell me you grew up in Atlanta."

"I spent some time in Atlanta," Lucy said defensively.

"You had a photograph of your parents on your bedside table."

"It was a good story," Lucy said. "It fooled your father."

I looked over at her and said, "But not Ginny Penn."

"Heavens no. Not Ginny Penn. She knew I came from nothing the moment she laid eyes on me."

"What's the deal?" I said.

Lucy didn't say anything for a few moments.

"It took Ginny Penn a while to check out my story. But she got round to it by and by. By the time she discovered the truth, I'd already dropped three of her grandchildren and had another on the way. By then, your daddy was personally trying to make a success out of that Jack Daniel's distillery operation up in Tennessee. Ginny Penn realized, no matter who was my kin, I was good enough to clean up her boy's vomit. I paid dearly for that little white lie."

"Who were your parents?"

"You don't want to know," she said. "They were less than nothing, beyond sorry. When the South does sorry, there's nothing sorrier on earth. That's how it was with my parents. Mama was sweet-natured, but pathetic and broken down the middle. Daddy was mean, but like Mama used to say, only when he was awake . . . ha ha!"

Her laugh chilled me.

"Mountain mean's different than other kinds of mean. A harder kind of man develops in a place where the light don't get in till late morning. Daddy never saw enough light."

"Did you love them?"

"Him, never. Wasn't much to love. Couldn't get a grip on something worthwhile . . ." she said. "He didn't allow himself any soft places. I never saw him smile once."

"Are they alive?"

"No, thank God," she said. "Jude and I wouldn't be here to tell the tale if they were."

"Jude and you? What do you mean?"

"I didn't say that," said Lucy.

"Did your father drink?"

"Ha!" Lucy snorted. "He was a worse drinker than your father ever was."

"No one's that bad," I said.

"That's what I thought too. You're too close to the middle line. Inch over. That's right. You think you know what to look out for in life, Jack. You think your childhood teaches you all the traps you need to worry about. But that's not how it works. Pain doesn't travel in straight lines. It circles back around and comes up behind you. It's the circles that kill you."

We came to the road leading to the abbey. The car moved through pools of undisturbed shade, giving me a lost feeling. The earth itself seemed to grow quiet as we approached the kneeling, tonsured nation of Mepkin; the forest unfurled itself in all the proud wildness of forbidden flags springing up in the outback. Hundred-year-old vines, like rigging, hung from the branches of river birch and bent oaks. As we turned into the long drive leading to the monastery, Lucy and I grew silent, as though we both were listening to secret commands. The weather itself lent a caved-in, hushed col-lusion to it all. I parked the car and walked over and rang the visitors' bell in the incensed air. Far off, we could hear the singing of monks. The buildings were new and looked like they were built for hillsides in California, not the South.

Father Jude appeared at the end of a pathway, his hands folded and invisible under his sleeves, walking with his head bent slightly forward. He and Lucy embraced and held each other for a long time.

Jude looked insubstantial and vegetal, his pale flesh like the white asparagus famous in the Argenteuil region of France. The priest had a lived-in, tortured face, yet I knew the man had almost no experience in the outside world. And I wondered at the withheld intimacy between them as I watched Father Jude lead Lucy into the chapel where Mass was being said.

After the service, I excused myself and went to the library where I spent the afternoon writing letters and glancing through the odd selection of magazines that passed muster with the censorious monk responsible for ordering periodicals for the abbey. Lucy explored the grounds of the abbey with Jude and even though they had asked me to join them, I felt they preferred to spend the time alone with each other.

I envied the private, cut-off quality of con-

templative life. I admired the intransigence of
their discipline, and in a century that seemed
more ridiculous to me with each passing year, I
thought that solitude and prayer and poverty
might be the most eloquent and defensible response to these absurd times where alienation
was both posture and philosophy.

I loved the simplicity of monks and longed
to emulate their all-consuming, uncomplicated
love of God. I liked the idea of denial and silence, but doubted I could take gracefully to
their practice.

On the ride back to Waterford, night moved
slowly into the lowlands and Lucy's weariness
was obvious as we drove between the light-infused trees that crowded the highway. Her exhaustion worried me and I imagined the approach of the white cells massing along the
contested borders of her bloodstream. Once I
had nested within her, fed on the warm river
that bloomed inside her, learned to love the
safety of the darkness of women, come to know
the serenity in the music of heartbeats, and that
mother love begins in the temple of the womb,
a stained-glass window that celebrates the origins and elixirs of blood-born life. The blood
that fed me, I thought, is killing her. This is
why people believe in gods and need them during the black hours beneath the cold light of
stars, I said to myself. Nothing else could touch

the lordly indifference of the world. My mother, there, I thought; it was in her I first knew of Eden and the planet I was about to enter naked and afraid.

"Quit thinking about my funeral," Lucy said, her eyes still shut. "I'm not dead yet. Just bone-tired."

"I was thinking how odd it was to live in a state where you can't even get decent Chinese food."

"You're lying," she said. "You had me dead and buried."

"Why don't I murder Dad?" I said. "We can all have a dry run to see what a parent's death feels like. But because it's just Dad, none of us have to be emotionally involved."

"Don't talk about your father like that," my mother ordered.

"He's not my father," I said. "Don't forget the annulment and the shame that is ours now that we're bastards."

"What do you know about shame, son?" Lucy asked, sitting up and smoothing out the wrinkles in her dress. Opening her purse, she took out an atomizer and sprayed White Shoulders cologne on her wrist and the car carried the full story of my childhood into the airstreams of the highway.

"A lot. I know a lot about shame."

She shook her head and rubbed the perfume into her throat and face.

"It hurts Jude that you left the Church," she said.

"It's none of his business," I said.

"He baptized all my boys. Gave you First Communion," she said.

"We used to think you two were lovers," I said. "I told him that when he gave you the last rites."

She laughed and said, "What did he say?"

"Not much. Personality's not his long suit."

"Jude told me it was time," my mother said, closing her eyes.

"Time for what?"

"To put the cards on the table," she said.

"Back to shame again, huh?" I said.

"Yeh. It always leads back there," Lucy said. "Father Jude's my brother, Jack. Your uncle."

"Odd," I said, after driving another mile of Carolina highway in silence. "Even for you, odd."

"I got caught up in my own lie. Never could figure out how to backtrack and start again. I could face anything but Ginny Penn's contempt. Know what I mean?"

"No," I said honestly. "I've no idea. It's traditional in most Southern families to introduce worthy young nephews to their blood uncles long before their thirty-seventh birthdays."

Lucy laughed, then said, "You're so old-fashioned."

"Even for us, Mama, this is too screwed up. Frankly, I wish Father Jude had just been your lover. It'd be so much easier to swallow."

"It made perfect sense to me," she said, "once upon a time."

"I can't wait to hear the details," I said, driving, then I shouted out the window, "the ghastly, fucking unbelievable details."

"Compose yourself," Lucy said, and she began to tell the story.

I listened.

CHAPTER 27

THE TRUTH IS THAT LUCY MCCALL was born a Dillard on dirty sheets in a three-room shotgun house within earshot of the Horsepasture River in the county of Pelzer, in the mountains of North Carolina. There was not a dentist or a doctor within a hundred miles of where she was born and few people over forty in the valley who still had their own teeth. Her father, A. J. Dillard, said he was a farmer, but he was neither an industrious nor a successful one. He drank when he should have been sowing and he drank all the way through harvesttime and through the first snow. His daughter never learned what the initials A.J. stood for and no one ever mentioned her mother's maiden name. Her mother's first name was Margaret.

Her brother, Jude, was born two years after she was on the same dirty sheets. Again, the father was passed out drunk and Margaret delivered the child by herself in silence, without making a single sound that might rouse her husband from his drunken slumber. She was always proud that she never asked for help nor asked to be beaten, the latter was something he always thought up for himself. Wife beating was both an itch and a pastime with A. J. Dillard, one that he had learned at the knee of his own father. No one in the family on either side could read or write. One had to travel to Ashville to find a copy of any book except the Bible. It was common for children to die in infancy in those parts, and broken-down women such as Margaret prayed for those merciful deaths. Later Margaret used to dream that her children were taken to see Jesus right after their deaths and fitted out with the prettiest angel's wings made out of lace and snow. Margaret was twelve years old when Lucy was born, fourteen when Jude arrived. In her portion of Appalachia, Pelzer County, she was not looked upon as a particularly young mother. But neighbors did pity her as an unlucky one. No one ever wasted breath by saying a good word about A. J. Dillard. A Dillard was the lowest form a white man could take in that part of the world, an all-white county with an unwritten sunshine law forbidding black people inside the county line after the sun went down. When the Depression finally struck America, no one in Pelzer County noticed anything different in their economy at all.

Lucy was born hungry and Margaret's milk flow was thin and weak and Lucy would stay hungry through most of her childhood.

Lucy never could pin down the exact moment when she understood that her father was dangerous. She grew up seeing blood and bruises on her mother's face, and thought that it was natural for a husband and wife to beat each other with fists. The beatings altered the way her mother looked, and as the years passed, Margaret's eyes would grow more troubled and the shape of her jaw and cheekbones would set into different angles as the bones were broken and rebroken. But Lucy always remembered her mother's sweetness.

When she was five and Jude three, her father went down from the mountains and hired himself out as a laborer on a tobacco farm outside of Raleigh. Sometimes, he would come back for the winter and sometimes he would send back money by mail, but he became less and less a part of their lives in the next five years. Margaret blossomed in his absence and discovered that she could coax more crops from the rock-strewn field than her husband ever could. She raised chickens and quail and bees in the yard around her unpainted house. Lucy and Jude learned how to fish with cane poles and worms along the bank of the Horsepasture River and caught trout for dinner much of the year. Margaret could use a shotgun as well as any man in the valley and she traded deer and bear she had shot for supplies she needed for the farm. By the time she was ten, Lucy could use a shotgun as well as her mother and took pride in the sore place on her shoulder when she went to bed after a successful hunt. She had cut her teeth on her father's .22 rifle and no squirrel or rabbit or possum was safe when she entered the forest. That .22 became a part of her and she would handle it as smoothly as she did a rolling pin when she was flattening out a batch of biscuit batter.

Once she killed a wild turkey after stalking it all day. It was a full-grown gobbler, a beast of such grandeur and wildness that she found herself admiring its cunning as it fled through thickets of blackberry and wild rose, moving swiftly as a racehorse as she followed its prints, large as a boy's hand when it crossed through giveaway patches of earth.

The churches of Appalachia during Lucy's

years worshiped a severe and unforgiving God. Though illiterate, both Margaret's and A.J.'s families were God-besotted and extreme in their beliefs. Their faith was hard-core, uncompromising, and single-minded in its intensity. At the height of their ecstasy, communion with the Lord, the Church of the Primitive God and His Saints passed poisonous snakes back and forth among the pale-throated righteous congregation who believed that the serpents would not harm them if their faith in God was sincere. Lucy could remember the Sabbath when two men failed the test and lay writhing on the floor, felled by an Eastern diamondback that was making his debut appearance. One of the men, struck in the eyeball, died within minutes. When they buried Oakie Shivers, the preacher exhorted his flock to try to live better lives and promised all of them that he had received a divine vision of Oakie writhing in hellfire for all eternity, the fangs of that serpent still attached to his eyeball. The preacher was named Boy Tommie Green and the Lord had appeared to him in a burning chariot near a field below Chimney Rock and called him in a voice like thunder to the ministry of snakes. He screamed out his sermons, which he never wrote down, nor did he ever purr out the name of Jesus. The word Jesus scissored through the air when Boy Tommie spoke and he wielded that name like a sound to frighten the mountain-broken sinners who came to his church for relief and succor. Eternal life seemed especially sweet to folk who had eaten songbirds and stray dogs for dinner and who tried to coax measly crops from fields more granite than loam.

Like most mountain men in that region, A.J. made his own liquor high above the Horsepasture River whenever the tobacco season ended and he had worn out all his welcomes everywhere else. As the years passed his homecomings became dreaded events and Lucy could never remember her father gentle or sober. Everything about him was as hard as an outcropping of stone. The beating of his wife and children was sport to him, one he could indulge upon waking, half-drunk and hungover, when he could run his family down, slap them for sins of which they were completely innocent, then grow morose and sorrowful as the cycle began anew when he took his first sip of clear whiskey. In midwinter, Lucy and Jude would pray for tobacco to begin blooming in central North Carolina fields. They had learned that husbands were masters of their own houses and that men held dominion over women and children and all the beasts of the field, but it was Boy Tommie who was destined to deliver all of them from the wrath and natural meanness of their father.

Boy Tommie could speak in the unknown tongues and quote the Gospel of Luke from the beginning to the end without once glancing down at the Bible. He was a wonder when it came to the things of the Lord, but could not be considered a saintly man because his eye for women was as advanced as his biblical knowledge.

Boy Tommie made his visits to the Dillard farm always during the height of tobacco season when he was sure A.J. was gone. Before he would enter the house for a Bible reading with Margaret, he would drop a copperhead onto the bare dirt ground and give long sticks to Lucy and little Jude and teach them how to race a snake around the yard, making sure you didn't lose the snake to either the river or the woods. The snake bore the coloring of an October path, and as the children teased the snake, Boy Tommie gave spiritual encouragement to Margaret inside the three-room house.

A.J. returned in early September one year, unannounced, his arm broken and set badly, splinted by a self-taught doctor who patched up migrant workers who cut each other up in fights or were injured in the tobacco fields. A.J. possessed an illiterate's intuition and he took the scene in quickly, as he saw his children lifting a snake high into the sunlight with a stick, unattended to in the unearthly quiet of a late

afternoon. When he found Boy Tommie on top
of his wife, both naked as the day they were
born, he killed Boy Tommie with a single blow
from an ax. The ax cleaved the preacher's brain
in half and his blood splattered against two
walls and over Margaret's face. A.J. rubbed her
lover's blood over Margaret's face and neck,
smearing pieces of his brain all over her breasts
and stomach. He beat her face until her blood
and Boy Tommie's blood commingled into
something love-born and sacramental. He beat
her with his good hand until he knew he had
broken that hand and the bones in her face.
Then he dragged her and kicked her naked out
into the yard before the eyes of the yard fowl
and mule and two stricken, terrified children.
A.J. took her to the Horsepasture River, cursing God's name and his wife's name and the
both of them covered with a dead man's blood,
and he plunged Margaret's face into a deep
chute of water, which ran scarlet from her
wounds. He held her there for a moment, then
brought her up to air and light to tell her to
prepare to die in water as the Lord had commanded them to be reborn in the same waters
of life. The screams of his wife were nothing
compared to his fury and the righteousness of
his vengeance, but a mistake was made, a terrible unrecallable error that he lived long
enough and in enough agony to regret. A.J.

had not heeded the silence of his bitter, pretty daughter, the one who was moving toward the river with a copperhead turned around the end of a long pole, a snake she had learned to love and trust.

A.J. took Margaret by the throat and struck her head against a rock that had a sharp place to it, opening up the back of her head, and a new flag of blood unfurled in the waters. But underwater, she heard the faraway, subdued cry of her husband who did not see the girl place the serpent around his neck, making it a loose-fitting collar, mountain-hued and vibrant. The fangs hit his wing bone first, then sent a second dosage of venom near the coccyx. It was there that A.J. caught the snake and hurled it into the water where it was swept downstream toward a deep trout pool where the copperhead reached the far bank and slithered off into the forest after its long captivity among the saved.

When he let Margaret go, she too was taken by the river, tumbling down a short rapids. She would have drowned but she caught hold of the exposed roots of a sycamore tree and hung on until she regained both her breath and a sense of where she was. She watched Lucy and little Jude sprinting up a path that led straight up the side of a mountain with A.J. in pursuit, but his pace slowed with each step taken. His hand kept searching for marks on his back he could not seem to find, his good fingers groping to find whatever it was that was paining him. Once or twice, he howled, then turned back looking for his wife. The poisons burned inside his veins, but he could still function in his rage well enough to drag the corpse of Boy Tommie to the river and spit as he let the swift current take the body to the first falls where it stuck between two rocks. Margaret watched in horror as the corpse sat up in the current and Boy Tommie's mouth and dead eyes opened and white water poured over his shoulders. She held on to the roots, the cold water slowing her heartbeat and her blood flow, and she did not dare pull herself from the river until it was near darkness and she believed all the rage and pain of her husband had subsided.

Bringing some of the river with her, she trailed that same water into her house looking for her children, who watched the scene from a boulder that gave them an overview of the farm where their childhood had gone wrong. She knew by heart where everything in her house was placed and she went to a kerosene lamp and the drawer where she kept matches and lit a light that took a bite out of the gloom. Walking out in the yard, she lifted the lantern to her face so her children could see her if they were hidden away but keeping watch. She called for them in the owl's voice she could imitate perfectly. Later, both children would remember this haunting mimicry of owls more than the sound of her own voice. Quiet as algae, they hung on the rock waiting to see if their father would appear to strike down their mother. The whole mountain seemed endangered by his arrival. Sensing the quiet, Lucy gave a signal by squeezing her brother's arm and they moved toward their house down a stony path they knew by heart.

They met their mother bringing a great length of thick rope out of the barn and the nervousness of disturbed chickens made the night noisy, unsettled. The river's voice calmed them as they neared the hard, grassless yard.

"Harness the mule," their mother said to the night more than to Lucy or Jude, and both children moved toward the barn as Margaret entered the house with a length of rope so heavy she staggered while carrying it. The lantern light poured out into the yard, feral and yellow as a hawk's eye. There was great economy to her movement after she'd decided what she had to do. Drunk, on his back and snoring, A.J. lay on the bloody bed where he had killed Boy Tommie and where both their children had been conceived in all the sorrow of their cutoff circumscribed lives. His throat was swollen from the poison. A.J. did not feel the rope as Margaret threw it over his chest and tied it tightly against the bed's steel frame. She then wound the rope around him, going under the bed and crawling to the other side, and pulling the rope tight against his body. As patiently as a garden spider, she wrapped him in a rope thick enough to tether a full-grown bull. Over his body and under the bed, she pulled the rope tight against him until he looked like a moth enfolded in deadly silk. She wanted there to be no chance of escape because she now knew what the stakes were and what hatred tasted like on the tongue and in the pit of the stomach. Margaret did not own a mirror and would have chosen not to look at herself as she felt the rough, hurt places on her face, traced them with an index finger that had been hurt on the rocks. Every time she moved she could feel the broken places catch on fire in her central nervous system. But she worked slowly, methodically, and she had a plan. She helped her children load all the food in the house in the wagon, and all their clothes and blankets and provisions. The children followed her commands to the letter and did not speak. She had become spectral to them, a strange woman holy enough to sleep with the man beloved by serpents and married to a man frenzied enough to try to kill them both.

Margaret went to the river and picked up a rock the size of a child's shoe. She liked the feel of it, its heft and weight and shape. She told her children to get into the wagon and try to fall asleep amid the bed linen and clothing. Jude fell asleep immediately, but Lucy only pretended to sleep and watched her mother go back into the house where the light was and where much of the knowledge she would take through her life about the relationship of men and women was about to reveal itself.

A. J. Dillard awoke to the terrible pain of the snakebite on his back and shoulders, which was serious enough to torture but not to kill him. The whiskey had dulled its sharpness before he had passed out unconscious on his bed. His mouth was dry and he needed a drink of water when he woke from a dreamless, restless sleep. His mouth tasted of cotton and sand and he began weeping as he felt his wounds burning and tried to turn over but felt the rope roughly cut into the veins of his throat. He screamed out Margaret's name and was sorry when she answered his call.

"Untie me, woman," he ordered as he saw her shadow enter the room, but he was in far too much pain to notice details. It was the detail of the stone in her hand that he failed to notice. "Then I'm gonna finish killing you. Then the girl what put a snake on me."

"You won't be leaving that bed," the woman said, moving toward him.

"A drink of water then if you're meaning to kill me."

"No water needed where you be going," Margaret said, climbing into the bed and straddling him between her legs, sitting on his chest staring into his eyes.

"I beat you ugly," he said, laughing through his pain.

"You beat me for the last time," his wife said and struck him in the head with the stone. He screamed once and the second blow caved in the upper bridge of his teeth. She kept striking his head and face until she could not recognize it as his face at all. It was covered over with blood and snot and tears. Lucy took it for as long as she could, then could no longer stand the sound of her father's begging. He kept saying he was sorry for all he had done and wasn't ready to leave this life yet and face the wrath of eternal judgment. The more blood he lost the more religious he became and the more he began to sound like Boy Tommie.

Lucy ran to her mother and tried to pull her off her father, but the woman was unloosed in her fury and would not tolerate restraining. She hit her husband's face again and again until her arm grew tired. Then she went to a bucket of water and washed her hands and face clean of all traces of his blood.

Finally her mother began to pour kerosene on the pine floorboards, spilling it over the curtains and makeshift furniture without any concern for waste or the future. Though Lucy did not understand why her mother was spreading kerosene all over the table and wallboard, her father did and he began to try to break the knots of the great rope by straining against them. He managed to lift the bed off the floor and it moved slowly, inch by inch, across the room, but then Margaret poured the last of the kerosene all over him.

"You don't have the guts," her husband said, but he knew little of the depths and the capacity for outrage his wife harbored in the secret caves and nests of her womanhood.

From the doorway, Margaret Dillard said good-bye to her husband. "Kiss Satan for me, A.J." And she hurled the lantern toward the bedroom and ran for the wagon.

The noise of her father dying took Lucy out of the Horsepasture Valley, and stayed with her down the long, treacherous dirt road that led out of those mountains toward Seneca, South Carolina. No one lived near enough to them to see the fire or heed A.J.'s agonized entreaties. Their mother never gave her house or mate another thought and concentrated on keeping the mule centered in the road.

They encountered unasked-for kindness on that journey out of the mountains where Margaret had spent every hour of her hill-encircled life. Farmers' wives, keen with the expertise of their own solitude, recognized the daring, unspeakable impulse that had brought the broken-cheeked woman to their door begging for food. They fed her eggs and milk and cheese because she was a woman and because she had two children. None would have been so generous to a man traveling alone.

For a solid month they roamed the back roads and visited the small towns of South Carolina as Margaret tried to come up with a plan. She caught sight of her own face in a mirror at a farm she stayed in outside of Clinton, South Carolina, and she wept when she saw the damage A.J. had inflicted. Once, she had been proud of her prettiness, but now felt the peculiar shame that ugliness grants a woman at no extra charge. She did not believe a young man could ever fall in love with such a disfigured, undermined face. If she herself was repulsed by her own image in a mirror, she could not hope to attract the attention of any decent or kindly disposed man. Because she had no clear idea of what to do or where to settle, she kept on pushing her mule from town to town hoping for a miracle. No miracle was in the making for Margaret Dillard and her children and outside Newberry her mule died.

In the next town, she walked her children to the front gate of a Protestant-affiliated institution called the Orphanage of the Ministry of the Lamb, which was run by missionaries who had spent time preaching the word of God to sub-Saharan tribes in Africa. It was located on the road between Newberry and Prosperity in the town of Duffordville. It was built along a railroad track and its houses had that anonymous blankness that small towns assume will keep disaster at bay. There was not a single note of vainglory in the architecture or setting of the town. At the entrance to the orphanage, Margaret pointed out the main building, a two-story wooden structure with shutterless windows and two unpainted Doric columns that looked like crutches holding up the house.

"They take orphans," Margaret said to her children. "That's where you'll live."

"But we have you," Lucy cried out. "We've got a mother."

"I know that," her mother said, but dreamily, absently.

That night they camped beneath a trestle and built a fire that warmed them and Margaret fed her children the last scraps of food she had saved. Indecision had defeated her and her eyes had given up on all thought of deliverance. She had prayed as hard as a being could pray and the only thing she got out of it was a dead mule and a tired, overworked heart. Margaret Dillard sang a lullaby to her children and whispered to them that their faces looked beautiful in the firelight. While they slept, she kissed them and covered them with her own blanket, and hung herself with a short piece of rope on the trestle above them. She looked upon her death as the last and only gift she could ever give to her children. The children woke to that gift.

In the years that followed, Lucy could never say the word "orphan" aloud without the word quivering with a terrible resonance. To her, an orphan was a child where evil could come sweetly home to rest, an innocent surrendered as a sacrifice to harm's way. At age ten, Lucy Dillard had seen her father murdered and her mother hang by her neck from a train trestle and she had every right to think that she had seen the worst the world had to offer a young girl. Then she met the Reverend Willis Bedenbaugh.

Very early, Lucy learned that for ordinary people an orphan was a hard thing to love. An orphan was something discarded, abandoned, and put out on the side of the road, completely dependent on the charity and sufferance of

strangers. In stories and movies it would later
infuriate her to see orphans always taken in by
generous, warmhearted families who would
treat them as though they had arrived in their
midst the normal way. She learned that there
were too many Willis Bedenbaughs in the
world and that they cut their teeth by preying
on the orphans of the world.

The Reverend Bedenbaugh was a softer
version of the man of God than the ones the
mountains of North Carolina made. He was
proud of his milky complexion and his burnt-
blond hair, which gave him the appearance of a
large, self-satisfied peach. His shoes were expensive and immaculately shined by an eigh-
teen-year-old orphan, brain-damaged and violent, who could never be placed with a
Christian family. His name was Enoch and he
lived in a stall at the back of the barn.

Since there was no school, the eighteen orphans attended chapel twice a day where they
endured sermons by the reverend that he read
to them verbatim out of a book entitled *The Art
of the Sermon*. His voice carried over the small
chapel and it had a brushed, soothing quality
that Lucy found attractive. The Reverend
Bedenbaugh was the first person she had ever
known who had been to college. For the first
couple of meetings, she and Jude wondered to
themselves where the snakes were. They could

not figure how a Christian would measure his love of Jesus if he didn't pass along a snake that could bite and kill him in the process. But they kept their own theology private and grew accustomed to the more rotund, constrained oratory of the South Carolina midlands.

The Reverend Bedenbaugh did not rape Lucy until she had been there a month. After he raped her, he dried her tears, and read to her a long passage from Ephesians and warned her about the wantonness of every woman and how women's bodies drew out the lust in godly men. He rewarded her with a piece of licorice candy and she hated the taste of licorice from that day forward.

Lucy discovered that he did not rape all the orphan girls, but had his favorites who received extra portions at dinner and were spared the more laborious chores on the orphan-run farm that supported them. When he drank he would come to the large room where the orphans slept in bunk beds. He usually came at three in the morning to make his selection. All the girls he favored had to sleep on the bottom bunks and none could wear panties. Soon, Lucy became his favorite prey and she learned to hate the smell of scotch as much as she loathed the taste of licorice.

One night when the reverend was inside her, Lucy opened her eyes and saw her brother,

Jude, staring down at her in pity and fury and with the helplessness of all boys who witness such a scene. She lifted her hand up toward him in the darkness and Jude reached down and held her hand until the reverend finished his business and rolled off her. Afterward, he would retire to his office on the same floor, read his Bible, and smoke his pipe. The smell of tobacco leaf would enter the lightless dormitory and the children would drift off to sleep knowing they were safe that night from further attacks. Then he would turn his kerosene lamp off and sleep on a small cot beside his desk.

In November, he had raped a new girl the first night she slept in the orphanage. The others had heard her struggling and screaming in the darkness and heard Reverend Bedenbaugh order her to shut her mouth and submit to the will of the Lord. They had also heard the moment he broke her neck. Before morning, Enoch had removed the girl and buried her next to Margaret Dillard in the paupers' graveyard that adjoined the orphanage. The drinking got worse after that and it was then that Bedenbaugh began to favor Lucy because she did not struggle and she made no sound. Her brother, Jude, made no sound either, but he held his sister's hand as she was violated on the bunk bed beneath him.

After the attacks on his sister, Jude would

watch every single movement Bedenbaugh made when he returned to his office. A large, unpaned window gave the preacher a view of the children's sleeping quarters, but it also enabled Jude to study him. When the reverend sat in his chair, he made an elaborate ceremony out of smoking his pipe. He would clean the bowl carefully with his pocketknife, then ream out the stem with a clean, white pipe cleaner. He smoked Prince Albert's tobacco, which he kept in large tins on his desk. He would inhale the robust smell of the raw tobacco, then grab a large pinch with his thumb and forefinger, tamping it down tightly with a flat-headed tool that looked like a nail to Jude. Then Bedenbaugh would take out a silver cigarette lighter, admire it in the lamplight, flick its small wheel with his thumb, and put the flame to the tobacco, whose smell would soon drift into the room and put Jude to sleep. The Reverend Bedenbaugh would then finish a pint bottle of scotch before he fell into a heavy sleep, punctuated by deep, comical snoring.

It took Jude over a month to come up with the plan he was praying for in chapel twice a day. That night after the reverend had returned to his office and he could hear Lucy weeping quietly, Jude watched the postcoital ceremonies and ablutions take place through the lit window. Even Lucy was asleep when the young boy moved like a cat from his upper bunk and made his way to the office door of Willis Bedenbaugh. He wanted to make Reverend Bedenbaugh deeply regret the fact that he had chosen to violate the sister of Jude Dillard, who was mountain-born and carried some of the rage of the mountain folk as his birthright. He waited for the snoring to begin and once it began, Jude entered the office.

The soft form slept and snored beneath a feather comforter. Jude went to the desk and saw the flaming eye of the pipe still lit in the ashtray, smoldering and angry. He opened the first drawer on the right as he had often seen Bedenbaugh do and he reached in and felt the tin can filled with fluid for the silver cigarette lighter. He found the cigarette lighter beside the pipe and he took that in his left hand and kept the lighter fluid in his right. His mother had done it differently, but his idea was much the same. Her strength had been in her resolution, in the fact that she had formed a plan. He wished he were older so he could understand more, but he was old enough to realize that he could not hold his sister's hand another time without dying of shame.

He removed the tiny red top of the lighter fluid and he began to apply it to the feather comforter that covered the reverend. The can made a squeaky sound, so he tried to time it with the man's snoring. Jude was patient and thorough and though it took him almost a half-hour, he managed to empty the tin can without spilling a drop on himself.

For another ten minutes, he tried to summon the courage to light the lighter. He had never lit a cigarette lighter and had only watched Reverend Bedenbaugh do it. He felt the rough wheel with his thumb. In his imagination, he spun it and it leapt with a flame that jumped to the roof of the orphanage. He flicked it once, but nothing happened except a small scratching noise like a rodent loose in a box. The sound changed the rhythm of the minister's snoring and Jude waited a full minute before daring to try again. The second time was no better and again the minister stirred in his sleep. On the third time, Bedenbaugh woke up and smelled the lighter fluid that had leaked onto his nightshirt, soaking it. It took Jude four times to learn how to work a cigarette lighter.

"What are you doing out of bed?" the man demanded, slurring the words.

The lighter ignited and before the boy touched it to the comforter, he sang in a clear voice, " 'Jesus loves me this I know, for the Bible tells me so.' "

Then he set the man afire and Bedenbaugh exploded into light, rising out of his bed and running with his bedclothes on fire. He ran through the dormitory screaming, and with each step he became more of a torch and less of a man. He burned increasingly brighter and his tongue, untouched by fire, could only make noise, not words. At the end of the room, his hair ignited the dark cotton drapes, as his body, crisped and blackened, sank to the floor on his knees and he died full of the smell of his own ruined, black-dappled flesh.

Jude Dillard watched the man on fire drop on the other side of the room, noticed the sleeve of fire climbing up the drapery, and realized that, at the age of eight, he had just killed his first man and felt that cleanliness of the spirit that justice always leaves as its signature. In his mind's eye, the burning shape of that man would stay with him always. Every confession or act of contrition he ever made included his remorse over the death of Willis Bedenbaugh. In nightmare after nightmare, Bedenbaugh would blend with his father in a terrible twinship and their mutual screams would teach the sleeping priest again and again about the penalties of fire. His contemplative, buried life began as he watched his enemy fall to the pinewood floor and heard the voices of orphans screaming out the word "fire." It also marked the beginnings of his life of silence and Jude could not utter a word for a full two years after the burning of the orphanage. Lucy led him out of the fire by the hand and he followed as obedient as prey toward whatever fate awaited him after his only murder.

The frame building burned all night and took over half the jobs of the village into the air with it. The general consensus was that Bedenbaugh had fallen asleep after finishing his half-pint of scotch and the ashes of his pipe had set his bedclothes on fire. He was the only fatality in a disaster that he himself had caused and the villagers saw some glimmer of justice in the incident. Bedenbaugh's remains were quickly buried and quickly forgotten, for little more than teeth and bones were raked out of the charred ruins.

A temporary home was set up in the girls' dormitory of Newberry College and a quick dispersal of the orphans began as a call for help went out among the farm families of the Piedmont. A tobacco farmer near Florence selected Jude from a lineup, but was dissuaded from taking him by Lucy who insisted that no one would separate brother and sister and split up what little family still existed for both of them. When the college students returned to Newberry College after their summer break, Lucy and Jude were the only two survivors of the orphanage fire who had not found homes.

Lucy longed for softness and deliverance in the eyes of people who came to look at her and her brother with the same appraising eyes with which they judged livestock.

But she knew that nothing was more unplaced or expendable than an orphan. By aligning herself with a speechless, damaged brother, she made herself unadoptable, unplaceable. Each day in Newberry her eyes hardened and she gained a source of interior strength as she began to understand the burden of being judged worthless. Her character formed that summer. Lucy would be living proof that you get in the way of a child savaged by fate at your own risk. By watching over her brother's interests she transformed herself.

In September, Lucy overheard a conversation in which the chaplain of the college spoke with the proctor of the girls' dorm about the possibility of committing Jude to the state mental hospital on Bull Street in Columbia. She had heard of peculiar children being sent to Bull Street and never being allowed to leave that institution again. But Lucy decided that she and her brother had been born to enough sorrow. She alone knew that her brother had reduced himself to a state of contrition that overwhelmed and hamstrung his every waking moment. He was a soft boy, a songbird who had lost its music to the fear of hawks. Jude needed a strong sister and strong she became. He had made her rapist pay a horrific price for her deflowering and she would protect him from the cells that muffled the cries of the insane. For two days she stole food from the college kitchen, stockpiling it beneath her cot. From a poor box in the Anglican chapel, Lucy stuck a piece of chewing gum tossed away by a Newberry coed to a long stick and raised up eighty-six cents as if by magic. She absolved herself of all guilt by explaining to her unobjectioning brother that they were as poor as anyone who would receive comfort from the coins in that poor box.

That night, they slipped away from the dormitory. Leading her brother by the hand, Lucy walked him through the sleeping, indrawn town to the outbound street she had heard called the Columbia highway. For eight hours, she forced-marched them both, putting miles between themselves and the town. They wandered the back roads of South Carolina for a month, sleeping in clearings in the forests, in fields of corn, in haylofts and stables. At night they moved from place to place, distrustful as all nocturnal creatures are, and they learned to relish the taste of raw eggs and warm milk fresh from a cow. They gleaned and foraged where they could around the outskirts of farms. By accident, they made their way toward the coast, avoiding Columbia because they dreaded the connotation of Bull Street and the asylum.

Since they started out only after sunset, they grew comfortable with starlight and they moved down dirt roads sided by deep fields of ripening crops and under a night sky ablaze with constellations they could not name. Because neither child had spent a day in school, the world held very few names for them.

Hand in hand, they traversed the state of South Carolina unnoticed. They left broken eggshells to mark their trail and gorged themselves on wild fruit and crabapples. They watched a drunken farmer club a dog to death that had killed a chicken and that night, over a fire that could be seen for miles, they ate the chicken and Lucy laughed for years over the thought that Jude had also wanted to take and eat the dog. She learned on that queer odyssey through darkness that hunger expands the horizons of one's recognized cuisines. The love they felt for each other sustained them and both would look back upon this long, adult-free journey as the happiest days of their scarred, ill-fated childhood.

Without plan, they drifted in an aimless, sleepwalking fashion beneath trees now embroidered with long scarves of moss and palms, bringing news of the coast. The earth itself changed perceptibly beneath their feet, becoming sandier and more acidic. Invisibly, the water table rose and cypress swamps began to echo with the night colloquies of owls and the territorial cry of a bull gator alarmed by the approach of a rival on the waters inky with silt and seed and algae. They passed through the forests unnoticed by the thousands of eyes that scanned the sunless, foreclosed world where most were hunters and all were prey.

As citizens of the night there was a fairy-land quality to their sense of movement. Since Jude could still not talk, Lucy made all decisions, such as where they would hide during the daylight hours. They roamed until they started to weaken, and once they started to weaken, they quickly began to die. When she could not waken Jude from his starved-out sleep, Lucy walked directly toward the smoke rising from an unpainted farmhouse. Without hesitation, she knocked on the door and the first black woman she ever would speak to answered the door. The black woman's name was Lotus and it was a day of deliverance for Lucy and her unconscious brother. Lucy could not have brought her brother to a home of poorer people or one more enlivened by a natural generosity of spirit.

When Jude awoke he was sucking on the little finger of a huge black woman who had dipped it into a jar of molasses her husband had milled himself. She had spread the molasses along Jude's gums and teeth. As a small girl

Lotus had known great deprivation herself and so she set to the task of fattening up the two white children who appeared out of nowhere at her front door on the edge of the Congaree swamp.

For three weeks, Lotus fattened her foundling white children, watching the color rise in their cheeks as she fed them with biscuits slathered with butter, bacon cooked crisp in a steel frying pan, and all the eggs she could get them to eat. At lunch and dinner, she cooked every kind of bean and vegetable she could coax from her garden and they feasted on cabbage and field peas and okra and pickled beets. Lotus made their bloodstreams electric with fat and iron and vitamins.

But a farmer moving a load of hay toward Orangeburg saw the two white children playing in the yard of a black family and reported it to a magistrate he struck up a conversation with in a crossroads feed store four miles away. His duty done, the farmer continued with his hay toward Orangeburg and his anonymous life, but not before the lives of Lucy and Jude Dillard were once more about to be altered.

Since it was against the law for black and white people to cohabitate, Sheriff Whittier simply took possession of Lucy and Jude, put them in the backseat of his car, and drove them to the county jail where he put the two children up for the night.

Again, they found themselves unwanted and without value and they were moved from jail to parish house until they were put on a train to Charleston with a circuit judge who turned them over to a terrifying woman dressed in a black, hooded robe who welcomed them to St. Ursula's Catholic Orphanage in Charleston. On a quiet street, tree-lined and moss-dappled, the children landed in a bizarre world of golden chalices and incense and splendidly cassocked priests who murmured in Latin. But they came to Catholicism without prejudice, since they had never seen a Catholic or heard of that religion in their entire lives. At first, they were amazed by its rituals and exoticism. The effigies of Jesus and the saints frightened them with their silent domination of niches and corners of the church and it seemed to Lucy one could go nowhere to escape the disapproving gazes of those lidless, all-seeing icons. The nuns and priests seemed otherworldly and were the first adults Lucy had encountered who dressed unlike the rest of humanity, but rather in imitation of the plaster of Paris statues they worshiped with folded hands and strings of black stone.

From the beginning, Jude flowered in the greenhouse environment he encountered in the good-hearted discipline of the nuns. He loved their strictness and passion for order. His silence they took as a sign of both saintliness and discipline and they favored him from the first day. One nun, Sister John Appassionata, took a special interest in Jude and under her devoted care he found his voice again. She taught him the alphabet and before long had him reading first-grade textbooks from beginning to end and doing subtraction problems. His mind was quick and he learned things in a hurry.

Lucy's experience at the orphanage was not as successful. After the soft ministrations of Lotus, Lucy felt more like an inmate at St. Ursula's than welcomed guest. The sister in charge of the girls' ward was a tight-lipped, straight-backed woman who tolerated neither laxness nor levity among the sixteen girls assigned to her dormitory. The world frightened her and she made sure she transferred that fear to all those girls in her charge. She taught them to hate their bodies because they had committed the unforgivable crime of being born female. In the Bible, there was proof that God hated women when he highlighted their subordination and created them second from a useless rib of Adam. The menstrual cycle gave testimony to woman's crime and her uncleanliness. Bernadine did not enjoy being a girl.

So, the city of Charleston, a stain-windowed greenhouse of ferny richness and wall-eyed, leering perversion, became the vessel of rescue for the two wandering children who had been born unlucky in the mean South. Charleston broke its poor in the same way the mountains did, but the city camouflaged the soft emanations of evil.

Charleston would prove to be a lucky city for Jude and a very unlucky one for Lucy. Their lives divided here and they would lose touch with each other for years. Jude would bloom under the tender gazes of nuns and priests who would glow in the presence of his natural goodness, which began to take on an otherworldly quality as he grew older. The rituals of Catholicism would nurture him from his first days in St. Ursula's. He withdrew into a country of prayer and, for him, that withdrawal contained the seeds of vocation. The Common of the Mass was rich in both silence and language and his spirit ripened in the luxury of its forms. Under the tutelage of John Appassionata, he asked that he and his sister be baptized in the Catholic cathedral as Roman Catholics. Thoroughly battle-hardened and cynical, Lucy saw the wisdom in this move and memorized the answers to catechism texts she heard the other girls reciting in class. Already, the nuns had noticed that Lucy could not read or write a word and she was openly referred to as "retarded" by Sister Bernadine. The word seemed to fix Lucy in time and made her invisible.

Soon she ran away from St. Ursula's for the first time. She knew what it was like to be a runaway, but she was new at doing it alone or in a city. Lucy was thirteen years old when she crossed East Bay Street and headed for the docks. Fast lessons would accrue to her and she would learn that there was nothing more dangerous in the world than a young girl trying to make it on her own in the sad part of a city. A man bought her a train ticket to Atlanta, where she led a wanton, luckless existence until my father walked into her life. That's what passed for a lucky day in my mother's life.

CHAPTER 28

SINCE THE FIRST DAY WE HAD ARRIVED in Waterford, Leah felt enormous pressure from all sides to be happy. It became almost a civic duty for her to look as though she were having a good time. People remarked about her happiness as often as they commented on the possibility of rain or the barometric pressure. Many times, she felt as closely watched as a prisoner on parole for good behavior. She did not mind being noticed, but resented being studied. The town made her far more aware of being motherless than Rome ever had. Wherever she turned, Leah was bumping into Shyla's past. Suddenly, her mother seemed everywhere, yet for Leah she remained elusive, untouchable in both her consciousness and life. The more Leah learned about her mother the less she was certain she knew anything about Shyla at all. In synagogue, one Saturday, Elsie Rosengarten, an elderly Jewish woman who had taught Shyla in the second grade, burst into tears when she was introduced to Leah.

I explained later, holding my child's hand. "It shocks people because you look so much like your mother."

"I look something like you too."

"Not enough for anyone to notice," I said, catching a sideways glimpse of Leah, wondering if the beauty of their children humbled all parents. Since our return there was rarely a night when I didn't get up at three in the morning to make sure Leah was still breathing.

"Do people think I'm going to do something to myself just because Mama did?" Leah said. "Is that why they're looking at me?"

"No, not at all," I said.

"It is so," she said. "You're just protecting me."

"No, I'm not. People can't believe I could raise a girl all by myself who'd seem so normal and well adjusted," I explained. "Your mother was all over you when you were a baby. Nuts for you. She wouldn't let me or anyone else near you for the first year. She made it seem as though it was a great sacrifice to let me change your diaper."

"How disgusting," Leah said.

"You'd think so," I said. "But it's nice when it's your kid and it's part of the job to be done. I liked changing your diaper."

"You're worried about your mother dying, aren't you?" Leah said, putting her cheek on my forearm. "I can tell."

For a moment I hesitated, but I could hear the call for intimacy in her voice, the desire for me to let her enter those grottoes where I tended my own fear of my mother's illness.

"You don't know what a bad son I've been to her, Leah," I said. "You don't know the things I've said to her. Unforgivable things. I've looked at her with pure hate in my eyes so many times. I never understood her and I punished her for that ignorance. I'm afraid she's going to die before I'm ever able to apologize enough times."

"She knows you love her, Daddy," Leah said. "I heard her tell Dr. Peyton the other night that she doesn't know any other son in the world who would move all the way from Italy just to be with his mama when she needed him."

"Did you make that up?"

"She said something like that," Leah said. "That's what she meant anyhow."

Early that night we walked on the beach again and felt the sea underfoot as we waded through the reflections of the evening star endlessly repeating itself in the pools created by the withdrawing tide. The coming of summer was announcing itself as the water temperature grew warmer every day. The cells of each wave began to light up with the approach of June, and each field on the way to town was covered with tomato vines and green fruit pulling sunlight out of the air. The days were already beginning to be hot long before the sea got the word. An ocean was a hard thing to warm up, but Leah and I felt it happening as we splashed along the beach waiting for the moon to rise. A mist rose off the cooling sand and gulls flew north above them in the last light. A gull cried and it always made me think of heartbreak and a solitude that had no name. I hoped my own loneliness was not contagious and that it would not pass through my bloodstream and enter the pale wrist of my daughter. I loved Southern nights like these, and I wished I were a brighter, less-brooding figure as we walked hand in hand along the beach and I steered her beneath the great sisterhood of stars unfurling in the night sky.

For an hour we walked along the shore until the night had taken hold completely as we started back toward Lucy's house. The stars

were brilliant now and the air smelled of sargassum, mollusks, and pine. Up ahead, we
heard a sudden commotion. The moon threw
off a reluctant, crescent-shaped light, and in it
Leah spotted the huge turtle ahead of us and
let out a cry of distress when she saw a young
man jump on the loggerhead's broad-backed
shell and begin slapping against the turtle's
shell and front flippers screaming like a buck-
eroo. We ran forward.

"Get off the turtle, son," I said, trying not
to lose my temper.

"Fuck you, mister," the boy spat out and
then I saw that he was showing off for his girlfriend.

"Please get off the turtle, son," I said.
"That's about as nice as I can say it, kid."

"Maybe you don't hear too well," the col-
lege-aged boy said. "Fuck you."

I grabbed the boy's shirt and he somersaulted backward off the turtle. He was older
and larger than I had first judged and he rose
up ready to fight.

"Relax. This is a female loggerhead who's
coming ashore to lay her eggs," I said.

"I hope you got a good lawyer, asshole,"
the boy said, "because there's a big lawsuit in
all this."

"Daddy, she's going back to the ocean,"
Leah cried out.

The loggerhead had slanted off to the right and was in the midst of a great heavy turn navigating her ponderous way back to the water. The boy tried to cut her off but stepped aside when I warned, "Her jaws can take your leg off, son. She can kill a full-grown shark with those jaws."

The boy skittered out of the way as the great beast rushed forward hissing, her breath rank and fishlike, polluting the air with an otherworldly smell. As soon as she reached deep enough water to displace her enormous weight, she transformed herself into something swift and angelic and disappeared like a seabird into the enfolding sea.

"You let it get away," the boy shouted.

"What were you going to do with it, kid," I asked, "paint its back and sell it to a five and dime?"

"I was going to cut its throat."

I had not noticed the approach of a flashlight coming down the beach, but Leah had and was already running toward the approaching figure. The next thing I knew the young man held up his knife threateningly close to my face.

"Loggerheads are on the endangered species list. It's a crime to interfere with their nesting," I said.

"Put the knife down, Oggie," the girlfriend pleaded.

"I've been fishing and hunting my whole life, partner," Oggie said, "and my father always told me how good turtle steaks tasted cooked over a driftwood fire."

"Your daddy's an old-timer," I said. "That could get you jail time now. There's easier ways to eat seafood."

"Can I see the bill of sale where it says you own this beach, asshole?" Oggie said.

"I used to swagger the same way when I was your age," I said, "but I didn't used to cuss. That's what MTV does to your sorry generation, don't you think?"

"Who climbed on the turtle's back?" I heard my mother say as the flashlight blinded Oggie, who turned his head away.

"I did," Oggie said. "I rode it for about ten yards before this jerk-off knocked me off it."

"What's the knife for, son?" Lucy demanded.

"This guy attacked me," Oggie said. "It's for self-defense."

The flashlight cracked down on the boy's wrist bone and the knife fell to the sand. I picked it up, walked to the water's edge where the surf was breaking cleanly, and hurled the knife as far as I could out to sea.

"That knife's private property," Oggie said, massaging his wrist.

"It still is," I said.

"My mother'll report you to the cops," he said, walking back toward the line of houses glowing with electric light.

"Who're your people?" Lucy asked. "Who do you belong to?"

"I'm a Jeter. My grandfather's Leonard Jeter."

"Tell Len I said hi. I'm Lucy Pitts," she said. "Keep off the turtles, son. We want them to put their eggs in the sand."

"I don't see you wearing no badge, lady."

"Shut up, Oggie," his girlfriend said as they disappeared out of the flashlight beam and into the paler light of houses.

"What'll the turtle do now?" Leah asked her grandmother.

"She might just dump her eggs in the ocean, darling girl," my mother responded, directing a beam of light out toward the waves. "But the urge is pretty strong for her to put them in the sand. Maybe she'll wait us out and come in when there's not a soul on the beach."

"Especially Oggie," Leah said.

"He's a Jeter," Lucy said. "His people are nothing but trash."

"Mother, please," I said.

"I'm just stating the facts," she said. "The whole family's got dirty fingernails. It runs with 'em, like freckles."

"Daddy doesn't like people to put labels on other people, Grandma," Leah explained.

"He doesn't?" Lucy said. "You can call a loggerhead a two-headed chicken, but that don't make it so. Same as a Jeter. You can dress that boy up in a tux, teach him the manners of a queen, and you still ain't got no Huguenot. Call a Jeter Rockefeller and you still got a Jeter striding up your backyard. Right, Jack?"

"Shut up, Mama," I said. "I'm trying to raise her to think differently."

Lucy laughed and said, "Too bad, son. You brought her South. That's the way the South thinks and she might as well get used to local custom."

The next morning Leah woke me before sunrise, telling me to hurry. She had fixed me a cup of coffee to take to the beach for the morning patrol. We rode our bicycles to Lucy's house and parked them near the outdoor shower before removing our Docksiders and joining Lucy who was already on the beach. Lucy handed Leah three seashells, which she had gathered along the tide line.

"Those are perfect for your collection. We'll fill up a jar of them and make you a lamp to take back to Rome," Lucy instructed, placing three lady slippers into Leah's hand. Leah admired them, then put them carefully into my pocket, and warned me not to forget they were there.

"Did the mother turtle come back?" Leah asked.

"It's your job to find out," Lucy said. "You and your father are responsible for this next mile of beach. I'm responsible for the whole program."

"We're the first people out," Leah said, surveying the island from north to south.

A squadron of brown pelicans flew overhead, their shape and wingspan so effortless in the morning air that their appearance seemed a quiet psalm in praise of flight itself. They passed over us like shadows stolen from the souls of other shadows.

"Let's go swimming," I suggested.

But Leah shook her head. "Not before we check the beach for loggerheads."

"I trust Leah with this job," Lucy said. "I don't trust you, Jack."

"A few minutes wouldn't make any difference."

For three hundred yards we walked in the wet sand, our footprints of different size but related in shape and with precisely the same arch. Leah kept her eyes on the ground ahead of her and she screamed when she saw the heavy markings of the loggerhead, cutting a swathe through the sand ahead of us.

"She came back," Leah shouted. "She came back."

Leah followed the deep cut the flippers had made when the turtle had returned from the sea. Lucy and I held back, letting Leah survey the scene where the tracks ended and the turtle had dug her nest.

I was carrying the bucket and the long silver probe, which was a nine-iron with its club face broken off during a match. Leah took the damaged club and approached the mound the loggerhead had thumped down like tobacco in a pipe before she had returned to the Atlantic.

"She lays her eggs while facing the sea. Study her shape. The turtle fills in the hole with the same hind flippers she digs it with," my mother said.

Leah probed the sand as my mother had taught her to during a training season that had gone on for over two months. Leaning on the ruined club, she stuck it into the sand and looked up at Lucy when it did not give. Pulling it out, Leah tried another spot in the great round indentation where the turtle's shape was imprinted. With quick, sound thrusts, she kept stabbing into the well-packed sand until she hit a spot where the shank of the golf club sank.

Leah knelt down and probed the sand cautiously with her index finger.

"It's here, Grandma," she cried out. "It feels like flour that's been sifted. The rest of the sand is hard-packed."

"That mother turtle fooled a lot of raccoons," Lucy said, "but she didn't fool Leah McCall one minute."

"Should I dig them up?" Leah said, looking up at her grandmother.

"We're taking them all up this year," Lucy said. "We're going to rebury them up by my house where it's safe."

"What does the South Carolina Wildlife Department say about that?" I asked.

"They don't like it worth a damn," Lucy admitted. "Dig, Leah. Dig, darling."

For several minutes, I watched as Leah lifted handfuls of sand from a carefully crafted, hourglass-shaped hole. Her eyes were fiercely concentrated on the job as she went deeper and deeper, relying totally on her sense of touch, letting her hand follow the soft and giving sand. Then she recoiled and froze.

"Something's there," Leah said.

"Lift it carefully," Lucy said. "Everything you bring out is precious."

Leah's arm moved slowly, bringing up a round white egg slightly larger than a baby's fist. It was ivory-colored, and leather soft. It was a capable-looking egg; it looked big enough to hatch ospreys or vultures, but not quite big enough to create something so beastly and magnificent as a loggerhead.

"Place the egg in the bucket carefully, Leah," Lucy said. "Make sure the egg is facing the exact same direction as it was when you took it out of the nest. Nature's got her reason for everything. Put some sand into the bottom of the bucket first. That's it."

Time after time, Leah reached into the darkness up to her shoulder and brought up from the nest a single egg like a jewel. Her movements were all reverential. Never did she hurry in her excitement and the introduction of each egg seemed like part of some elaborate dance of the seasons.

"Forty-eight, forty-nine, fifty . . ." Leah counted as she placed them one on top of the other and Lucy made notations in a small notebook.

"Look, the turtle tried to climb over these rocks and didn't make it," Lucy said, pointing to tracks that led up to the large granite boulders that the owners had imported for erosion control. Sand was a preeminent force in the low country and no rocks were indigenous to the area. "Our houses on the beach kill more loggerheads than ghost crabs or raccoons ever thought about killing. They should never've allowed houses to be built in front of the sand dunes."

"Seventy-one,   seventy-two,   seventy-three . . ." Leah kept counting.

"Was this a good place to nest?" I asked.

"A good spring tide would've flooded this hole for sure," she said. "This nest didn't have a chance. But you can't blame the loggerhead. What can she do about those damn rocks? She'd need a grappling hook and a long rope to get over them. Then how would the babies get back to the sea? The whole thing's a bad business."

Carefully, Lucy recorded the location of the nest, the day and time of its discovery, the number of eggs laid, and the approximate time the turtle had come ashore to hollow out her nest and lay her eggs. Leah placed one hundred twenty-two eggs in the bucket, then carefully filled the hole back up and packed it down neatly with her feet.

"Now, let's get these babies to a safe place," Lucy announced, handing the heavy bucket to me.

Leah walked ahead of us at a quick pace, taking the bucket to the area my mother had staked out for the birthing ground of this year's crop of loggerheads. My mother stopped to collect a row of clam shells that had washed up the night before. They were as prettily strewn as candy. When I turned back to the business at hand, I saw Leah being approached by a uniformed woman.

"Who's that?" I asked. "Up by your house?"

Lucy groaned and said, "Trouble, with a master's degree. Let me do the talking. She gets confused when someone's kind to her."

The young woman was uniformed and pretty and was talking to Leah in quick, animated conversation about the gathering of turtle eggs. Leah gestured toward them and then bent to the sand to demonstrate how she had found and procured the pail of eggs I was carrying.

"I've always loathed women named Jane," Lucy said, preparing for battle. "It predisposes them toward mischief and indigestion."

"You conducted a study?"

"A lifetime of observation, son," she whispered, but her voice turned voluble and cheerful as they approached the straight-backed woman. "Hello, Jane, I was just telling my son what a pretty name you've got. Jack, meet Jane Hartley. You've already met my granddaughter, Leah."

"You allowed her to dig up a whole nest of loggerheads," Jane said in a voice official and distant. She was wearing the uniform of the South Carolina Wildlife Department. "I bet you didn't tell Leah it was against state law and that you spent a day in jail last summer for doing the same thing."

"That's not true, is it, Grandma?" Leah said.

"It's technically true," Lucy admitted, "but nothing is so unconvincing as mere technical truth. Hand me the shovel, Jack. I'm going to dig a fresh hole."

"I'm confiscating these eggs," Jane said, getting up and taking a step toward me. But Lucy moved between us with resolve and intent.

"This year I'm not losing one egg to the stupidity of you idiots in the Wildlife Department. Not one," said Lucy.

"You love playing God, don't you, Lucy?" Jane said.

"For a long time," Lucy said, flipping through her salt-splashed notebook, "I played it by the book. Admit it, Jane. I didn't touch one turtle's nest. I followed all the directives of your department to the letter. Nature knows best, Jane Hartley and the State Wildlife Department said. Let the eggs lie where the mother buries them. Let nature take its course, you ordered. Nature's cruel but nature has its reasons."

"Those rules still apply," Jane said. "We

find it more logical to follow God's way of doing things than Lucy's way."

"My way gets a hell of a lot more baby loggerheads in the water than God's way and this notebook proves it," Lucy said, waving her notebook over her head like a weapon.

"My grandma loves the turtles," Leah said.

"She does love the turtles," Jane agreed. "It's the law she doesn't give a damn about."

"My son is a world-renowned writer and author of cookbooks," said Lucy with egregious ill-timing. "He'll remember every slanderous word you utter. He's got a mind like a steel trap."

"You are impervious to my mother's charms, Officer Hartley," I said.

"Your mother's a pain in the ass, Mr. Mc-Call," the woman stated. "My job is difficult enough without having to fight with someone who claims to be on the side of ecology."

"Listen to what her side did, Jack and Leah. They sent out a memorandum to all the turtle projects on the South Carolina coast. There's one on every island from here to the North Carolina coast. Every island's having erosion problems. Half the nesting habitat of the loggerheads've been destroyed in the past ten years. Everybody in the program's worried sick. Those geniuses put out a new set of rules that say we can't touch an egg or a nest once the turtle has laid. We can't protect a nest, move a nest, guard a nest—nothing. They've all got nice offices in Columbia. They're all drawing big salaries. They're all feeding off the life-blood of taxpayers like me."

"Someone's got to pay for my Maserati," Jane deadpanned to me.

"Could we compromise?" I suggested. "We've already gone a little far according to the law."

"If I had my way you'd get a year in jail for each egg in that bucket," she said briskly, but was startled when Leah began screaming.

"We could go to jail for one hundred twenty-two years, Daddy," Leah said, running to my side and encircling my waist with her arms. "Just for helping Grandma."

"I knew being exposed to that woman would come to no good," I said. "Relax, Leah. We're not going to jail."

"Lucy might this time," Jane said. "Looks like I caught you red-handed."

Lucy reached out and took the bucket out of my hand, then said, "I've tried to be reasonable with you people. I really have. You don't live with the problem every day, Jane. It's not fair and it's not right and it's sure as hell not good for the survival of these turtles."

"If man keeps interfering with the nests,

then these turtles have no chance of surviving," Jane countered.

"It's a theory, Jane. Something you write down on a piece of paper. Something that looks good and sounds good and reads pretty. But it doesn't work."

"It's worked for millions of years, Lucy. It's proven effective since the age of dinosaurs."

"Listen, Jack and Leah. Listen to what happened. We did what Jane here said. Down to the letter, we followed her directions. Because they had statistics and charts and their damn degrees. Because they had badges and guns and the weight of law behind them. Tell Leah what happened, Jane. Tell the child how well your theories worked."

"Our theories worked perfectly," the woman said, tightening her gun belt. "Nature allowed a certain number of nests to yield a certain number of loggerheads. Some nests were destroyed by predators. That has to be expected."

"Sounds reasonable, Mother," I said.

"Son, I acknowledge your expertise when it comes to ziti or pepperoni pizza. But you're in your rookie year with the turtle ladies," Lucy said, staring hard at Jane Hartley and being stared at in return.

"Lucy considers herself above the laws of nature," Jane said.

"The laws of nature are now killing me, Jane," Lucy shot back. "I'm painfully aware how subject I am to those laws. You won't be having this argument with me next year, but I pray to God one of the other turtle ladies'll take my place."

"Give me those eggs, Lucy."

"No," Lucy said, "I most certainly will not. What would you do with the eggs?"

"Take them back to my office," Jane answered. "Photograph them for evidence. Examine them for damage. Then bring them back to the island and rebury them as close to the original nesting site as possible."

"We need to get these eggs in the ground right this minute," said Lucy, walking over and picking up a shovel that she had leaned against the supports of her deck. "I'm moving all turtle nests on this island to the dry sand right in front of my house, Jane. That way, I can protect them myself because they won't be but twenty yards away from the pillow where I'm sleeping."

"And that way, you get to break the law every time a turtle comes up on this beach."

"What happened to the nests last year?" I asked.

"Nothing happened to them," Jane said.

"Only twenty percent of them produced any

hatchling turtles at all!" Lucy said, starting to dig her hole.

"The laws of nature prevailed," said Jane, addressing herself to me now. "Lucy's made the mistake of personalizing her relationship to all those eggs and loggerheads."

"Last year there were a hundred-twenty nests," Lucy countered. "But the erosion on the south side of the beach was terrible. A lot of beachfront was lost due to a bad nor'easter in February. Everybody on the beach started putting loads of granite in front of their houses. Bulldozers moved tons of sand over the rocks. The place crawled with dump trucks. When the turtles came in that May, it was like someone had built the great wall of China over their nesting grounds. Two of them laid their eggs in a sandbar twenty yards out into the ocean. That's how desperate they were. We moved those nests."

"With our permission," Jane said.

"Yes, but you refused permission to move any of the nests laid at the foot of the rocks for two miles along the south beach," Lucy said, attacking the sand with her shovel. "The spring tides were extraordinary last year. The whole ocean seemed to rise up and try to reach out toward dry land. Some tides covered the tops of the marsh grass. Fifty-six nests were wiped out by those tides. That's a possible six thousand turtles who didn't make it to the water because Jane and her colleagues are stupid."

"We made a mistake, Lucy. We admitted it."

"They wouldn't let me lay wire fencing to protect the nests from raccoons and dogs. Lost twenty-seven more nests that way. The goddamn coons are common as roaches on this island because they love to tip over garbage cans of fat tourists from Ohio. I found seventeen coons fighting and squalling over a nest of turtle eggs that they'd spread up and down the beach."

"We're on the same side in this battle," Jane said. "You've never understood that, Lucy."

"Then help me teach my granddaughter how to dig a turtle hole that'll make these eggs feel like Mama dug it."

"I want you to know, Mr. McCall, that your mother was like this before she got sick," Jane said, throwing up her hands in exasperation.

"I know," I said. "She raised me."

Lucy handled the shovel with economy and expertise and as she lifted the sand out in small spadefuls, a rounded hole that reproduced the hourglass-shaped nest excavated by the back flippers of the loggerhead began to emerge. It was a lovely, strange sort of mimicry and it made me realize the long patient hours of observation that she had spent studying the habits of those ungainly turtles.

"Come here, child," Lucy said to Leah. "Round it out on both sides now. Pretend you're the mother and you want to dig the loveliest and safest nest in the world for your babies. The shovel is your back flipper and you want your eggs to drop in a beautiful round room where the only sound they'll hear is the surf."

"Like this," Leah said, concentrating hard, as she slid the blade of the shovel along the side of the hole and brought up barely more than a half pound of sand.

"Perfect. Round that other side off. You think it's deep enough, Jane?"

Jane came over and inspected the hole. She went down on her knees and put her arm into the hole almost up to the shoulder.

"I'd go another six inches," she said, and Lucy nodded in agreement.

Leah dug out another six inches of sand and placed it on the small dune that rose up on one side of the nest. "What if it's not just right, Grandma? What'll happen?"

"Probably nothing. But since we're flying blind here, we might as well be as careful as we can. We've got a hundred twenty-two baby turtles counting on us to get it right."

"See what I mean about being too personal?" Jane said.

"Now comes the fun part," Lucy said, instructing Leah with unusual patience. "I think this is the greatest Easter egg hunt in the world. We find the eggs, dig them up, walk them to a safe place, and now we get to bury them again."

"You do it, Grandma," Leah asked. "I'll watch the first time."

"No. I want this whole nest to be yours. You'll help me watch over this one and all the rest. But I want you to put each one of these eggs down in the hole. So when they hatch, I'll have you dig them up and they'll know your smell."

"It doesn't happen that way, Lucy," Jane said archly.

"How the hell do you know?" Lucy shot back.

Leah took out the first egg and studied it as it gleamed in the May sunshine. She handled it with great delicacy and made sure the egg was facing in the same direction as it was when she removed it from its original nest. Her head almost disappeared from sight as she set the egg in its place as seriously as a priest laying a consecrated host on an altar cloth. When the first egg was put in, Leah looked to the adults for approval and received it from all three of us.

It took Leah almost a half-hour to fill up that hole with turtle eggs and the job went more quickly as she gained confidence in her handling and placement of them. When she began each egg was precious and by the time she finished the eggs felt familiar and comfortable in her hand.

Then Lucy taught her how to cover the eggs with the same sand they had taken from the hole and pack it down with the same firmness a three-hundred-pound mother would exert in her desire to camouflage the nest from the eyes of predators. They were smoothing out the sand above the nest and Jane was moving the wire cage over toward the nest when the sound of a male voice on the deck startled them all.

"Is that bitch bothering you again, Mama?" the voice said and I looked up to see my brother John Hardin staring out over the scene, shirtless behind a gate.

"I forgot to tell you, Jack. Your brother got in from Columbia late last night."

"Hey, John Hardin," Jane said, putting the wire fencing in place above the nest. "The bitch is only bothering your mama a little bit. Nothing to write home about."

"Should I beat her up, Mama?" John Hardin asked.

"Hush up. They'll be hauling you back up

to Bull Street if you can't put a brake on your tongue," Lucy said.

"Thanks a lot for visiting me in the hospital, Jack," John Hardin said, spotting me for the first time. "Every visiting hour I kept waiting for you to come and bring me some boiled peanuts and Heath Bars the way you used to. But no, you've gotten too big for John Hardin. You're much too busy shitting on French restaurants and writing whoopey-doo pieces on sun-dried tomatoes and balsamic vinegar to ever come visit your little brother on the crazy ward."

"Shut up, John Hardin. Your brother's still recuperating from getting himself shot up in Rome."

"I forgot about that, Jack," John Hardin said. "I'm so sorry. I read all about your being hurt and I wanted to fly straight to Rome to take care of you. Isn't that right, Mama?"

"That's certainly right, honey," she said, checking Jane's handiwork in placing the wire screen over the nest. Then in a lower voice she whispered to me. "In the condition he was in, he could've flown all the way there and not even bothered to call Delta."

"Who is that pretty thing?" John Hardin said, spotting Leah. "Is that the lovely Miss Leah McCall?"

"Hello, Uncle John Hardin."

"Run up here and give your uncle a big kiss," John Hardin said as Leah looked pleadingly at me. Then John Hardin opened the gate and I saw for the first time that he was wearing no clothes at all.

I shook my head and said, "Why don't you put on some clothes, John Hardin? Leah's never hugged a totally naked man before."

"Thanks, Daddy," Leah whispered.

Both Jane and Lucy turned away from the fencing and looked at John Hardin who stood proudly unclad and unapologetic above them.

"I became a nudist while at the state hospital, Mother," John Hardin said. "It's a matter of principle with me and I know you'll support my decision. It's an act of faith, not of folly. Of that, I assure you."

"Get your goddamn clothes on, boy," Lucy said, murderously. "Or I'm going to knock your unmentionables into the Atlantic with this shovel. Cover yourself up before this innocent young woman. I never heard of such carrying on in broad daylight."

She took off Jane Hartley's hat and shielded the young woman's eyes from the sight of her son's pale genitalia.

"I'm a scientist, Lucy. This doesn't shock me."

"I'm a mother, Jane, and this shocks the living hell out of me," Lucy said. "Call the crazy house, Jack, and tell them they didn't come close to fixin' what ails the nudist here."

"This is the way God made me, Leah," John Hardin said. "Do you see anything revolting or disgusting in God's work? I admit my dick's kind of ugly, but who are we to criticize the Lord's handiwork. Don't you agree?"

"What's 'a dick,' Daddy?" Leah asked me.

"American slang for penis," I said.

"Thank you, Daddy."

"You're very welcome, sweetheart."

"I think your dick is very pretty, John Hardin," Leah said kindly.

"See, Mama, you uptight puritan asshole," John Hardin screamed. "Beauty's in the eye of the pretender."

"You mean beholder," Lucy corrected.

"I mean exactly what I say I mean and nothing more," insisted John Hardin.

"Good, say anything you want. Just go put something over your elementals."

"Elementals," John Hardin said. "This ain't Plymouth Rock, Mother dear. It won't hurt you to say the word dick or hairy banana or cock or pecker . . ."

"Those are the words I was talking about the other day, Daddy," Leah said. "Those are the ones I hear on the playground."

"Once you know them all, then you're well on your way to being an American girl."

"I came into the world buck naked . . ." John Hardin said.

"I seem to remember that," Lucy said to Jane. "Would you like a cup of coffee?"

"Love one," Jane said.

"And naked shall I return to my true mother, the earth, not that woman that claims to have brought me forth in vileness and unholy jeopardy.

"That dog there walking on the beach is naked. That seagull, that pelican, that porpoise offshore—all, all naked and natural as they were on the day when they first saw their mothers and sunlight. I saw sunlight, then I saw this unfeeling bitch who raised me, Jane, and turned me into a lunatic to walk the earth unloved and uninvited into any home."

"Put your pants on and join us for coffee, son," Lucy said, washing her feet and hands of sand.

"You spoke nicely to me, Mama," John Hardin said. "I will join you. You catch more snakes with honey than Caesar did in Gaul."

"What did John Hardin mean about the honey, Daddy?" asked Leah.

"He wants me to speak nicely to him," Lucy answered. "He's got an odd relationship with the English language."

"Did you know that nudists commit fewer

murders than any other group, Jane?" John Hardin asked.

"I never knew that," Jane said. "But it doesn't surprise me."

"I scare you don't I?" John Hardin said to Jane Hartley. "You've never met a full-fledged, bona-fide schizophrenic in your life and I can see the fear in your eyes."

"Shut up, son," Lucy said, handing him a beach towel that he wrapped around himself as she crossed the deck and walked through the sliding glass door into her living room. "You don't have to present your credentials. Being stark naked's all the clue anyone needs."

"My sister's schizophrenic, John Hardin," Jane said, following Lucy into the house. "Your act's old to me."

John Hardin watched the young woman as she crossed the deck and disappeared inside the house.

"She's very pretty, isn't she, Jack?"

"Very pretty."

"Do you think she liked me, Leah?" John Hardin asked, and his voice was tender.

"She'd like you better with clothes," Leah said.

"That's prejudice," he said, his voice darkening an octave.

"She's used to boys wearing clothes, that's all," Leah said.

"Oh." John Hardin seemed mollified. "I've never known how to talk to pretty girls. Maybe you could help me, Leah. You're pretty. In fact, I bet you'll be elected Miss Italy some day. Unless you come back here where you'll be Miss America."

"Talk to her like that, John Hardin," Leah said. "Maybe she'd like that."

"I know you're supposed to say 'hi' to girls. I always do that. Then I know you're supposed to say something like 'Isn't this a beautiful day?' I say that when the day's nice. But what do you say when it's rainy or cold and what do you say after that? I mean, there's a million things you could say. But what does a pretty girl want to hear after a weather report? It's a mystery to me, Leah. Does she want to know that there was an earthquake in Pakistan last night? That's pretty important. Or would she rather know how a Jerry Lewis movie ended that I saw the other night in the hospital? Or makeup? Maybe she'd like to talk about makeup, but see, I don't use it. I'd be glad to talk about anything, but too many things come to my mind and I end up saying nothing. Pretty girls hate me, Leah."

"No they don't," Leah said. "They know just how you feel. Tell them what you just told us. Tell Miss Hartley. She'll understand."

"Now? Go in right now?"

"No, let everything come up naturally. Wait till it feels right," Leah said.

"Ah, I can't," John Hardin said. "Nothing ever feels right to me."

The next day, I drove Leah to the southwest tangent of the Isle of Orion to visit John Hardin in the tree house he had built for himself so he had a place to go whenever he felt the need to withdraw from society. The tree house was much discussed on both the island and Waterford, but seldom seen. John Hardin had built his pied-à-terre in a two-hundred-year-old live oak that hung over the tidal creek that cut a necklace of deep water through the great salt marsh. Since he was good with his hands and had enormous amounts of free time, the tree house had expanded over the years, gone through several renovations, and had five separate rooms plus a screened-in porch when I drove up beneath it and blew the horn to alert my brother. At the extreme end of the road, I pointed out to Leah the unpainted wooden building that my brothers and I had built and used as a fish camp all throughout our childhood days. It surprised me that the floating deck was in such good shape until I remembered that John Hardin lived here almost full-time when he was not locked up in the state hospital. The tree house was made from heart of pine and stained a natural color. There was both charm and eccentricity in its architecture and the rooms grew smaller and more turret-like as they spiraled up the tree, accommodating themselves to the higher and frailer branches. Everywhere the eye looked there were bird feeders and bird baths and wind chimes. The air could not move without music moving through every leaf and acorn on the tree. Most of the wind chimes were handmade and their music was slightly off-key and eccentric. But the house seemed spacious and congruent and Leah screamed with delight.

From above, we heard John Hardin call down to us and he lowered a wooden ladder from his living area. The house had three decks ingeniously constructed. On the top deck, John Hardin had built a small bedroom for himself with a hammock and a library filled with paperback books. He lit his uncommon house with candles and kerosene lanterns and cooked his meals with a small hibachi. The ocean breeze was his only air-conditioning and John Hardin freely admitted that his tree house was unusable during the winter. But historically, the cold months had almost always coincided with his breakdowns and he had availed himself of the free lodging that always awaited him on Bull Street in Columbia. In the creek, he caught most of his own food with his cast net and his rod and reel. Proud of his self-sufficiency, he pointed out his outhouse camouflaged in a thick clump of sea myrtle.

"It's illegal to have an outhouse on this stupid island," John Hardin said to Leah. "Zoning laws. There's a conspiracy afoot in America to make human beings ashamed of their waste products. I'm proud of my waste products."

"I've never thought much about mine," Leah said, smiling at me and following John Hardin into a small, bizarrely shaped room almost completely dominated by a Pawley's Island hammock.

"This is the guest bedroom. I haven't had any guests yet, but when I do this'll be where they sleep. You can come here anytime you want, Leah. You don't even need an invitation."

"Thank you so much, John Hardin. You're so sweet."

"It's strictly off-limits to the rest of my family. I better never catch your ass sneaking around my property, Jack."

"Wouldn't think of it," I said, feeling overgrown and claustrophobic as I made my way from one small enclosure to another. There were tricks to getting from room to room and very little appeared solid underfoot, and I had the feeling that I was on a yacht anchored in an open bay on a windy afternoon. John Hardin had decorated the walls of his sitting room with art given to him by fellow inmates of the state hospital. The paintings looked like stamps minted in a country where nightmares were used to lure a strange breed of tourist. It was a desperate cousin of art, disturbing in all its forms and images.

"All artists are schizophrenics," John Hardin said to Leah. "Did you know that Leah?"

"I don't think so."

"They all see the world with a skewed perspective. They paint what they know best—distortion."

"Are these friends of yours?" Leah asked.

"The only friends worth knowing. The ones who've been on Thorazine for at least a year. Thorazine keeps you so far away from yourself that your art becomes the only clue that lets you know you're still around."

"That's nice," Leah said, but nervously, aware she might be saying the wrong thing to her taut, thin-skinned uncle. "I'll paint some pictures for the guest room. Would you like that?"

John Hardin's face grew soft and he said, "I'd treasure them forever. You can bet on that."

"I'll paint a picture of the Piazza Farnese in

Rome," she promised. "I miss it so much that I can see the whole piazza when I shut my eyes."

"You miss it that much, darling?" I asked.

"Of course, Daddy. That's home."

"Waterford's home," John Hardin said. "Everything else is just local color."

"But Rome's where I grew up," Leah said. "You'd love it there."

"I've never liked people who can't speak English," John Hardin said. "I always think they've got something to hide."

"How ridiculous," I said. "How Southern."

"No matter," John Hardin said as he led us to the largest room, which had three lawn chairs, a hammock, and a screened porch to keep out the insects. John Hardin showed real talent for carpentry and, despite the hazardous footing, the rooms seemed to flow together with an unplanned naturalness as if the house were the result of a dream the tree had. A breeze lifted off the ocean and several hundred notes from the wind chimes tinkled like ice shaken in silver cups. They altered the mood of the forest the way an orchestra does a theater when it begins tuning up its instruments. The sound seemed discordant to me but had a calming effect on John Hardin.

John Hardin took a piece of paper out of his pocket and read it to himself silently before saying to Leah: "I wrote something out that I'd love your help with. I could see that you were kind of an expert on how men and women interact yesterday."

"No," she said. "I've never even had a boyfriend."

"But you know how I should talk to Jane Hartley if I want to impress her."

"You should be yourself, John Hardin. She'd like that."

"Listen to this," he asked. "You play the role of Jane. I'll play myself."

"Jesus Christ!" I said.

"It's fine, Daddy," Leah said, before I could continue. "Read it to me and I'll try to play Miss Hartley."

"She's a naturalist. A scientist. So I should try to carry on a conversation that interests her. Let her know right up front that we share mutual concerns. So we've sat down to dinner and ordered our meal. I ordered all vegetables. What if she's a vegetarian or hates people that don't mind eating the animals she's taken a vow to protect? That'd start the evening off wrong."

"I'd order whatever you feel like eating, John Hardin," Leah suggested.

"Good idea," he said, writing something down on his sheet of paper. "I'll order fish. Even if she's a vegetarian, I happen to know that some vegetarians don't mind eating seafood. And I love fish. Now you say something. Pretend you're Jane."

Leah hesitated, then said, "What a beautiful tie you're wearing tonight, John Hardin. It goes so well with your suit. It's nice that you're not a nudist anymore."

John Hardin looked confused, then looked down at his notes and said, "Did you know, Jane, that the male night moth emits a cry so powerful that its sound creates waves that can actually kill other insects in flight?"

He looked up at Leah, who was puzzled, but game. She said, "No I didn't know that. How interesting."

"The male night moth is the terror of the insect world," John Hardin read again from his notes. "Did you know that recent research proves that alligators like the taste of Labrador retrievers better than the taste of French poodles? Researchers believe that alligators are so accustomed to living near golf resorts and residential homes, they've actually added domestic dogs to the preferred meals on their food chain."

"Those poor dogs," said Leah in genuine horror.

"Isn't the weather lovely, Jane?" John Hardin read on.

"Yes, it's getting warmer every day, John Hardin," Leah said, glancing at me to see if she was performing up to par. I nodded and Leah went on. "Do you think it might rain tomorrow?"

"Funny you should mention rain. It reminds me of snow. Do you know that a female polar bear will cover her nose with her paw when she's hunting a seal near an air hole? That's because her nose is black and the snow around her is all white. The bear becomes invisible as she creeps up on the seal to make her kill."

"How do you know so much about nature?" Leah asked.

John Hardin smiled and began to read from his written text. "Because it is my conviction that man himself is part of nature and that to study nature is to study one's own self. A spider must eat a fly just as a man must eat a cheeseburger. It is all related and one and the same."

"I'd cut the fly and the cheeseburger line," I said, my nerves becoming frayed by the wind chimes.

"Food is food. In nature it don't make a damn. Jane's intelligent enough to get my drift."

"Maybe you could say a horse eats oats," Leah said. "A fly's sort of disgusting."

"Great idea, Leah. You're sensitive the way Jane's sensitive," John Hardin said. "You aren't sensitive for shit, Jack."

"Thanks," I said, then caught sight of a

boat rounding the bend of Sawgrass Creek. "That's Ledare. Want to go for a boat ride with us, John Hardin? She says she's got a surprise for us."

"No," he said. "I'm going to stay here and work on my imaginary conversation with Jane Hartley. Do you have any suggestions for me, Leah? Any inside stuff that might let me know how pretty girls think?"

Leah took her uncle's hand and kissed him on the cheek. "Everybody wants a friend. Just let Jane know how much you like her and everything else will be fine."

"I'm going to the library tomorrow to read all their books on nature. By the time I take her to dinner, I'll know more about animals than anyone she ever met."

"When're you thinking about taking her, John Hardin?" I asked.

"It'll be years," he said. "It'll take two or three years just studying before I could even think about asking her out."

"But she could meet someone else," Leah said.

"That's the chance I'll have to take," John Hardin said as Leah and I went down the wooden ladder.

"Don't tell anyone about my tree house," he warned as he joined us on the ground. "My enemies are everywhere and it drives them crazy when they hear that I'm a free man."

"Your secrets are safe with us," I said and turned to watch the powerboat approaching us from a mile away. Its drone was comforting, so familiar was it to this low country boy that it could not wake me even from a fitful sleep.

As we walked past the old fish camp, John Hardin unlocked its door and invited us inside. I was glad to see that he had fixed the place up, repaired the broken windows, and even painted it on the inside. The wood-burning stove was still in its corner and the same mildewed cots hugged the far wall, but John Hardin was using it for a workshop now and his tools were well ordered and in immaculate condition. There was a pile of fresh lumber, clean-smelling and newly cut.

"Do you know why I bought the wood?" he asked.

"No idea."

"I'm going to build a coffin for Mama."

"What a ghastly idea," I said. "Does she know?"

"Of course she doesn't know, it's going to be a surprise," John Hardin said, clearly hurt by my tone of voice. "It's one less thing she'll have to worry about. I'll build it strong. It'll be beautiful."

"She'll like that very much," Leah said.

"I'm not so sure," I said.

Leah cast her eyes disapprovingly at me and said, "My father's wrong. It's a wonderful thing."

"It'll be a work of art, Jack, you'll see. It'll be the most beautiful coffin ever seen in this county," John Hardin said, looking around as though intruders were listening to him. "This county is so full of drunkards and perjurers and scoundrels, whoremongers, Satanists, and tax evaders."

"Tax evaders?" I said.

"I don't have to pay taxes because of my status as a schizophrenic, but there are people who don't fill out any forms for the Internal Revenue Service. They're lower than fungi, mushrooms that grow on logs."

"Why don't you go on the boat with us?" Leah asked.

John Hardin watched the boat as it slowed down to make its approach to the dock.

"No, you go on," he said and like an animal he ran back to the tree, went swiftly up the ladder, drew it in, and shut the hard world out from under him again.

Ledare watched us as we peeled off shirts and pants, revealing our bathing suits underneath. As we stepped aboard, she motioned for Leah to come sit between her legs and take the wheel.

"You're not a low country girl until you can handle a boat," Ledare said. "Pull the gear back to reverse and let's head out toward Waterford Sound."

Leah did as she was told and the boat began to move slowly back into the middle of the creek.

"Turn the wheel to the right and straighten out the rudder," Ledare said. I watched as Leah followed the instructions closely; her dark intensity burned brightly in contrast to Ledare's generous blondness. Leah seemed inked by the sun while Ledare looked as though the sun had left no sign of its passage in the hue of her skin.

"The tide's still coming in and is almost high," Ledare said. "Don't worry about sandbars."

"How fast can we go?" Leah asked.

"Let her rip, child," Ledare said. "When you're a kid, you've got to get speed out of your system."

Leah opened up the throttle and the boat, a sixteen-foot Renken, Charleston-made, lifted up out of the displaced water and cut through the main channel between the Isle of Orion and the uninhabited Barnwell Island. Ledare pointed the way as we navigated the backwaters behind the barrier islands and the spartina

spread out in a vast green coverlet from horizon to horizon.

When we reached the Waterford River,
Ledare gave a sign for Leah to slow down and
put the boat in idle. I worked my way between
them, opened a beer, and sat down heavily,
taking the wheel. I adjusted my Atlanta Braves
baseball cap and put more sunscreen on my
face and neck as Ledare untangled rope in the
stern of the boat. Then she fed the rope out
behind the boat a little at a time, handling it
expertly like a trapeze artist testing equipment
under the Big Top.

"What're you doing, Ledare?" Leah asked.

"See that look in her eye?" I said. "She was
the four-time winner of the Sea Island Water
Festival Skiing Tournament."

"Five-time," Ledare corrected. "And that's
boys and girls, darling. I can ski better than any
boy who ever grew up in this town."

"Better than Daddy?"

Ledare laughed and looked fondly at me.
"Your daddy's a nice boy, Leah, but he can't
hold the top part of my bikini when it comes to
water skiing. Tell her, Jack. Swallow your male
pride and give it to her straight."

"She's arrogant beyond belief," I said. "But
the girl ain't human when she gets on skis.
Then she's poetry in motion. A goddess of the
sea."

Ledare jumped into the water feet first and Leah followed her example as I put the boat into forward gear and inched ahead, pulling the tow rope toward the two swimming figures behind me. Suddenly, it was as though I was transported into a thousand afternoons of my childhood when the smell of the river and the sound of motors purring overwhelmed me with a sense of deeply entered and deeply lived-out time. I could remember a hundred images of Ledare cutting through the water on her slalom, leaning into a turn so steep that she looked as though she were lying down against the surface of the water. All the laws of physics and all the beauty of geometry seemed to come into play when Ledare took to the water behind a fast boat. I watched as she coached and encouraged Leah and remembered how for most of my growing up I had assumed that Ledare would become the mother of my children. I watched as Ledare positioned Leah's hands on the tow bar and placed her feet in the skis and adjusted them tightly.

There was nothing that Ledare did in the water that did not seem graceful. She appeared water-bred and water-happy and she swam in a circle around a slightly frightened yet fiercely excited Leah, who had inherited an unquenchable competitive spirit from me. She hated failure and hated especially to have witnesses to that failure. But Ledare calmed her, instructed her to keep her skis together and her arms straight, and to let the boat do all the work. After putting on her own skis, she positioned herself behind Leah and placed Leah between her legs, with her skis outside of Leah's; she put her hands outside of Leah's hands on the tow bar, and gave me the signal to gun the motor.

Looking back, I saw that Leah had let go of the tow bar as soon as she heard the roar of the engine and that Ledare had dropped her handhold at the same time. She was gently talking to Leah as I circled the boat and brought the bar floating on top of the surface directly into Ledare's hands as she repositioned both of them for another try.

"A tight grip. Then arms straight out. You can't bend the arms. Get the skis on either side of the rope. Perfect, Leah. Now, I'm going to signal your daddy and we're gonna ski through town."

Leah held on the second time and she rose up on her skis, her weight leaning against Ledare's legs. They came out of the water together, Ledare's legs spread wide as she nursed her young skier along and they went for two hundred yards before Leah lost a ski and fell. Ledare fell simultaneously and swam to retrieve Leah's ski in the wake of the boat.

Again, Ledare gave the signal, Leah got up, and this time they passed together through town with Leah not daring to move a muscle and Ledare waving to passersby along the waterfront park. They went under the bridge and Leah caught a quick glimpse of cars passing above them.

Touching Leah on the shoulder, Ledare pointed toward the wake on the starboard side of the boat and using the pressure of her left hand urged Leah away from the boat. The two of them pointed their skis at the marina down Oyster Creek and, twinned in motion, they moved as one skier riding over the wake then racing along outside the boat, swift and lovely and graceful in their strange but buoyant pas de deux. I heard Leah squeal with joy and watched as Ledare coached her; and then the rope slackened and they waited for that precise moment when they felt its tension again and they let the power of the boat take control, bringing them swiftly back across the wake and then over the opposite one in two perfect leaps. I could hear Ledare talking above the noise of the motor, but could not make out the words. But I saw Leah relax and gain confidence under Ledare's patient tutelage. One can do anything, anything at all, I thought, if provided with a passionate and gifted teacher.

I made a circular motion with my index fin-

ger but Leah fell again as I turned the boat in a
slow   one-hundred-and-eighty-degree   curve.
When I came back around, Ledare insisted I
throw another ski rope from the back of the
boat so that she and Leah could ski separately
behind the boat.

"Is Leah ready for that?" I asked.

"She's a natural," Ledare said, nodding
toward Leah.

And natural she was as I gunned the motor
once more and woman and girl rose out of the
Waterford River in tandem, both screaming
with pleasure as I pulled them again through
the center of town past the many-columned
mansions set between the live oaks of Water
Street. I thought of Venice, that city lifted out
of the Adriatic, each palace sensual and removed as though designed by architects in love
with the shape of orchids and wedding cakes.
But I could not deny the fact that the simplicity
and spacing and proportion of the houses of
Waterford stirred my sense of aesthetics as
much as any canal ride in Venice.

For over a half-hour, I pulled them up and
down the Waterford River, then heeding a signal from Ledare that Leah was tiring, I anchored the boat on the sandbar directly across
from the town. After they climbed up into the
boat, and toweled themselves dry, Ledare
passed out tomato sandwiches, made with to-

matoes from her mother's garden, lettuce, mayonnaise, and Vidalia onions. I moaned with pleasure as I bit into the sandwich and the rich juice spilled out of the sandwich and down my face and arms. I opened the sandwich to inspect the slice of tomato I had just tasted. It was large and fire-engine red and glistened with juice and health. I remembered long ago, when I had gone out into a field with my grandfather, who had leaned down and cut a ripe tomato from a vine heavy with fruit. Silas had peeled the tomato with his pocketknife, then salted slices and handed them to me. I could not imagine that nectar in Paradise could have tasted any better than that freshly picked tomato. And for me that taste has always been and will be the taste of Waterford and summer.

The day was ending when we started back for the Isle of Orion, the sun playing along the surface of the water, turning a bank of cumulus clouds red in the west. On the way, we called out the buoys and channel markers and I could feel my sunburn start to tighten my face as the air cooled. As we passed Ladyface Island, Ledare suddenly pointed to a creek that I had fished when I was a boy. It was on an isolated, back side of the island that had escaped most of the overdevelopment that was changing the composition and feel of all the low country.

"Go by Henry Thomas' place," Ledare said.

"I haven't seen Henry since high school," I said. "He still have his welding business?"

"Went broke welding. He's in construction over on Hilton Head. The whole known world's in construction on Hilton Head. I saw him in the Piggly-Wiggly the other day. He asked about you."

"Henry and I played football together," I explained to Leah. "He was a player."

Leah asked through glazed, exhausted eyes, "What's that supposed to mean?"

"The boy was tough. He'd tear your head off if he got the chance."

"A redneck," Leah ventured. "Like my uncles talk about?"

"Of the purest variety," Ledare said. "The Grade-A, high-test kind. He could hide forever at the Darlington 500. That's a car race, darling."

"Henry's simple. But a real good citizen," I said.

"I went by his place last week. He wanted me to meet his youngest son," Ledare said. "He has Down's syndrome, but he's a sweetheart. Let's go see him."

"Leah's tired," I complained.

"I want Leah to see this," she said.

As the tide went out, the boat rode lower in the marshes and I made my way down long corridors of the marsh grass we had ridden above just hours ago. There was a time in my life I knew all these creeks well enough to navigate at night without ever consulting a chart, but now I consulted a map twice to check for bars and low water before I brought the boat in sight of Henry Thomas' house. It was an old wooden farmhouse with a screened-in porch that ran along the front. Four vehicles were parked around the yard, one permanently. A cock crowed somewhere in a field beyond the house and an egret hunted beneath the pilings of Henry's dock until he flushed when our boat drew too near his hunting grounds. Ledare pointed to a spot twenty yards across the creek where the water was shallower and whispered for me to cut the motor and drop anchor.

"Aren't we going to go on to the dock and say hello to Henry?"

"Shh," Ledare said, putting her finger to her lips. "He knows we're here. I told him we were coming."

The sunset turned the marsh gold and the western sky transformed itself into a window of rose and violet as its edges flowered and dimpled in its final burning haze. The water around us caught fire and the boat rested in a pool of cold flame. In silence, we watched the water shimmer like a peacock's feather in that shining foil of soft tide in retreat. Leah put her hand down and touched the lemony surface of the water.

A little boy ran out of Henry Thomas' house followed, at a distance, by his mother and father and two older sisters. The boy wore a tee shirt and shorts, a pair of black high-top sneakers, and a tiny life preserver. Yet he was fearless as he ran, slowing only when he inched his way down the ramp to the floating dock.

"His name is Oliver," Ledare whispered as Leah and I watched the boy thrust out his arms toward the sunset on the marsh and begin to spin in graceful circles. His thin, high-pitched voice broke out in song, and though the words were difficult to make out, I recognized the tune of "Mary Had a Little Lamb." Oliver looked toward the water expectantly, but saw nothing and cried out in surprise or frustration. Going down on his knees, he began to beat his hands against the warped, unpainted boards, singing another song, the words again un-recognizable, but the tune haunting and famil-iar.

"Rock of Ages," Ledare whispered to Leah.

Looking toward his family, Oliver, bewil-dered and hurt, threw his hands up, then began stamping his feet hard against the dock and his incessant tattoo echoed through the marsh. He began a third song and then a fourth. His fam-ily watched in motionless silence, although

Henry waved once to welcome the visitors in the boat.

"Here it comes," Ledare said.

A dorsal fin, curved as beautifully as a gondola, broke the still waters two hundred yards away coming out of much deeper water. The porpoise came swiftly, its green body jonquil-colored in the last light, then the color of straw, then a touch of ecru, until it rose out of the water when it approached the dock where Oliver sang. It lifted its head and Leah stood up and leaned forward when she heard the porpoise emit high-pitched sounds of its own.

The boy spun in delirious circles and began to speak or scream or croak out sounds too excited to have the discipline of language. If it was speech, it was dissonant and inhuman and strange. Oliver's face was lit with ecstasy and he put his arms out toward the porpoise and sang the tune to "Jesus Loves Me" to the bottle-nosed creature and all the long-legged wading birds who paused to listen to this strange outcry, this primitive interlude between sunset and night. As the boy grew more excited his voice grew shriller and less distinct. The voice seemed to calm the porpoise, which swam in slow circles, rising out of the water to make quieter noises of its own. Oliver's song had an eerie, unworldly harmony to it, but the porpoise's voice seemed half-human and more familiar. The rapture of the boy increased and he danced and pointed toward the porpoise and looked back toward his family. At the very end, Oliver was grunting and squeaking unintelligible sounds and every so often, the porpoise would answer with a faraway and much sadder sound.

When the porpoise turned back toward the sea, Oliver screamed out in protest, then waved furious and petulant good-byes, then sank to his knees, motionless, exhausted. Henry came down to the dock in half-light and lifted Oliver up in his arms. He waved to all of us in the boat, then walked the boy back to his family. For a full minute, the three of us in the boat were quiet, still in the scene we had witnessed. We could not name what we had just seen, but we knew it was a rare form of communion and dialogue.

"What was Oliver saying to that porpoise, Daddy?" Leah asked at last.

"Something wonderful, I think," I said. "But I don't know."

"Guess," she said.

"I know what they were saying," Ledare said as I started the motor.

"Tell me," Leah said.

"Oliver's saying to the porpoise, 'Does Jack love Ledare? Does Jack love Ledare?' And the porpoise is answering, 'He should. He should.' "

Leah rode in Ledare's lap as we followed in the wake of the porpoise as it headed out the sea lanes for the Atlantic, and the stars shone on us with a brightness of complete indifference.

CHAPTER 29

FOR ME MEMORY WAS THE COUNTRY
of the usable past but now I began to wonder if
there was not also a danger to unremembrance.
I had recently become acutely aware that mis-
translation, mistakes of emphasis, and the inev-
itability of a flawed interpretation of an experience could lead to an imperfect view of things.
I had thought that Shyla was fairly happy in our
marriage. Though I knew well the history of
her moods and depressions and migraines, I
began to think I had underestimated the battalion strength of those malignant, subterranean
demons that took her in despair to that bridge.
I had always thought her sadness was part of

Shyla's depth, for there was nothing I distrusted in people more than sunniness, personalities whose optimism seemed unearned. Shyla was full of so many deep places that I often felt she was exploring some newly discovered country of glaciers and ice fields whenever her black indwelling spirits took possession of her. Part of her allure was also her buoyancy and unpredictability. Shyla could not be kept down long, but I now knew I had failed to recognize the flip side to this virtue, that her time in the sunshine was limited because her truest self lay in her most inaccessible places.

As I told Leah stories of her mother, I kept coming upon images that had failed to speak their importance at the time. Following the music of her interior, Shyla had gone straight to a rendezvous with her own hangman. When I began the hard work of trying to figure out the course that had led to Shyla's destruction, I recalled strong images that I had carried intact without knowing what they really meant. Now I realized that Shyla had seemed embarrassed by her parents from the time I had any memory of the Foxes at all. Their accents embarrassed her. Their foreignness caused her shame.

Very early, Shyla used to spend afternoons at our house soaking up the rowdy atmosphere of an American home that seemed normal to her. Whenever she smelled hamburgers or popcorn or fried chicken being prepared in my mother's kitchen, Shyla would appear at the back door with her timid knock and Lucy would invite her in to feast on whatever was cooking.

I remembered well the first birthday party the Foxes gave Shyla.

My mother had taken Shyla and me to a movie matinee at the Breeze Theater, where we saw *Come Back Little Sheba* with Shirley Booth. The film was an odd choice for children our age but it was the only movie in town and my mother had no choice but to sit through the entire film as Shyla and I wandered the aisles and even ventured upstairs to the "Colored Section," which we found completely empty. The discovery thrilled us and my mother had to come looking for us in the middle of the film and found us taking turns drawing tattoos on each other's arms in ball-point pen. Before we left the movie house, Lucy scrubbed both tattoos off with Kleenex and her own saliva.

The party was to be a surprise and when Shyla came through the front door, her father played a baroque and spirited rendition of "Happy Birthday" that intimidated the Waterford children into an uneasy silence. Ruth and George and Lucy were the only ones who sang and Shyla had her face in her hands as she saw some of the neighborhood boys snickering at her father's guttural accent. Then George Fox announced, as though he were talking to a sophisticated audience at Carnegie Hall, that he had prepared a very special concert in honor of his daughter's birthday. The ten children invited to Shyla's party then had to sit still as George Fox played Liszt's Hungarian Rhapsody Number 2.

After the concert had mercifully ended, the awestruck but very restless children were herded into a dining room that was formally set and lit by silver candelabra. Shyla wore a bewildered expression that could have been disbelief or fear, but her face looked as though it had been flash-frozen. She knew what was coming, but felt helpless to interfere with the course of events.

"So," her mother said as her classmates sat in formal misery around the table, "now we eat like pigs. A feast for my sweet Shyla who was born, as you know it, on this day. She is an American girl and she should have an American birthday, no?"

Ruth pronounced the word "girl" like "gull" and the children at the table did not understand a single word she said. Several of the boys went under the table to hide their laughter. Only my mother's presence kept any semblance of order and she circled the table three times quelling the outbursts of silliness by the boys.

But even my mother could not control the amazement that broke spontaneously from the children's mouths when Ruth uncovered the numerous bowls which contained the feast she had been days secretly preparing for her daughter. There was borscht and sour cream, which none of us had ever seen, a Russian salad composed of mayonnaise, peas, and flakes of salmon, and something called cheese kreplach. One boy, Samuel Burbage, threw up in his own lap when he tasted pickled herring in sour cream. Hot tea was served in glass cups with handles and a plate of handmade Kaiser rolls was passed around the entire table without a single taker. Gefilte fish brought cries of amazement and several of the boys discovered happily a bowl of hard-boiled eggs that they identified and quickly passed around as the one food recognizably American.

Shyla endured her trial without commentary, but I remember the relief on her face when Ruth Fox returned to the dining room, followed by my mother, carrying a frosted birthday cake decked out with lighted candles. My mother led the children in a spirited rendition of "Happy Birthday," then took the cake out to the front porch to get all the children away from the scene of Mrs. Fox's crime. Outside, Shyla blew out the candles, and then the presents were brought out to be opened. Lucy then organized a game of hide-and-seek for all the boys and girls. But as Lucy was organizing the games in the front yard, Ruth was weeping while she cleaned the table of dishes full of untouched food.

My mother had saved Shyla's party by making the children forget about what they could not bring themselves to eat, but not for long.

When Samuel Burbage's mother came to retrieve her son, he screamed out as he ran to her, "They gave us raw fish in whipped cream, Mama. I puked when I ate it."

Harper Price's mother heard that her daughter had burned her tongue on the tea and that the doughnuts were hard as rocks.

"They're called 'bagels,' " Shyla tried to explain. "My mother bought them at Gottlieb's in Savannah."

Capers Middleton had never seen red soup and Ledare had never eaten cold fish or sweetened noodles and Elmer Bazemore, a shrimper's son, took only one taste of gefilte fish before he spit it out on his napkin. He swore to his parents that he had no idea where they found such a fish in American waters and that the flesh of that Jewish fish had actually burned his tongue and caused him to ask Mrs. Fox for several glasses of water. Later, Ruth

Fox explained that she had probably served the gefilte fish with too much horseradish.

The utter foreignness of Shyla's household became a minor obsession of her friends and classmates in Waterford. Children are born with a herd instinct, and nothing causes them to suffer more than habits of their parents that single out the child for censure and ridicule. Shyla spent her childhood aching to be an American. Yet it was deeper and more extraordinary than that: Shyla Fox yearned for another unreachable level of Americanism—she tried to turn herself into a Southerner, the most elusive and evasive American of all. Her whole life became a quiet devotional to mimicry. Each year her accent differed and thickened as she listened to the collective voices of the women in her town. The idioms of Southern speech delighted her as much as her parents' use of Yiddish appalled her. She became tyrannical and refused to let them converse in Yiddish when she was present. Their Yiddish was out of place and discordant in a land of azaleas, hominy, plantation tours, onion rings, buttered popcorn, Necco wafers, and 3 Musketeers candy bars "big enough to share with a pal."

"She thinks she is a Yankee Doodle Dandy," her father would often scoff.

"She wants a normal life," her mother

would argue. "Show me the great sin. It's the same thing I want for her."

It was more intuition than knowledge that led me to believe the atmosphere in the house across the yard was off-kilter and bizarre. That they celebrated holidays I had never heard of and could not pronounce seemed exotic enough, and I used to try to get Ruth Fox to teach me dirty words in Yiddish so I could torment my brothers when they got on my nerves. But there was something deeply disturbing and unsettled in the House of Fox that no one in my small town could begin to fathom. It was not merely foreignness that set their house apart, but a sadness so profound that it settled like a killing dust in every square inch of those immaculate, spacious rooms.

George and Ruth Fox were afraid of dogs and cats and their own shadows. I could see them peeking out at me from behind closed curtains whenever I would come knocking at the back door. They jumped whenever there was an unexpected knock at the door. Their hands trembled when they answered a ringing telephone. When Ruth Fox hung laundry to dry in the sun, she kept looking around for the movement of enemies on her flank. For years and years, I tried to decipher what was wrong. I spied and eavesdropped and watched the quiet motion of their family as I monitored their activities from the branches of the oak tree after dark. The only thing I could ever come up with was that Shyla's parents seemed to grow darker, not older. Mr. Fox would often wake up screaming in the middle of the night during nightmares he had brought with him to this country. When I asked Shyla what made her father scream at night, she told me that I must be dreaming myself, that she had never heard a thing. Once I heard him scream out the name of a woman, but it was no one I had ever heard of nor anyone who had ever lived in our neighborhood. After he awoke with this strange woman's name on his lips and as I moved along the branches of the moonlit oak that gave me access to such secrets, I heard Ruth comforting her husband. Listening to this sorrowful and intimate scene, I pinched myself hard, for Shyla's sake, to make sure I was not dreaming. I tried to overhear their conversation, but they were speaking to each other in another language. Though I could not understand that langugage, I knew enough about words to know that Ruth loved George Fox beyond all measure and time.

In the years that followed Shyla's party the sense of darkness and unhappiness in the Fox household seemed to deepen. I often thought perhaps it came from George Fox's fanatical absorption with his music. All of us were afraid

of Mr. Fox, with his impeccable Old World
manners, his disfigured hand, his suffering, and
his reticence that seemed unnatural when accompanied by his baleful glare. Though his music students adored him, they were gathered up
from the most sensitive and highly strung children. At night, as I tried to go to sleep, I listened to Mr. Fox play the piano, and I learned
from those evening recitals that music could
ache and hurt, that beautiful music was a place
a suffering man could hide.

I remember when I first told my mother
that I thought something was wrong with Shyla.
I had noticed that Ruth talked differently to
Shyla when she did not know I was around.
One day I had gone over to Shyla's bedroom
through the oak tree and was about to go
search for her in the house when I heard her
mother speaking to her downstairs. Before I
tiptoed back to the window and made my way
back through the secret avenue that connected
our houses, I heard Ruth's voice again. What
she said made me stop to make sure I had
heard it correctly.

"Close that door when you talk to me,"
Ruth shouted, "or we'll all be dead of pneumonia. That's what you want. For all of us to be
dead. Go and wash your hands. Don't play in
the dirt anymore. God didn't make you an ant.
My God. Those hands. Come here. Turn off

that stove. Are you crazy or what? Do you want the fire department to get a raise?"

I did not recognize the woman who was speaking, this off-center, nerve-damaged version of Ruth Fox. It was my first occluded view of the childhood Shyla was living through because the Germans had overrun and destroyed her parents' world. It would be much later that I would learn that the Nazis were frequent visitors to that house, that they sat with their blue-eyed stares through meals, belched at the lighting of the candles on every Sabbath eve, and that Shyla grew up believing that germs were simply lowercase Germans who fed on the souls of Jews.

As I passed through the thick branches of oak, I heard Ruth say, "Get away from that window, Shyla. The Angel of Death could be passing by."

I turned back and saw Shyla's small, fearful face. She waved at me and I waved back. I realize now that the Foxes' house on the Point in Waterford was simply an annex of Bergen-Belsen, a rest stop on the way to the crematoriums. Neither of Shyla's parents could leave the country of their hideous past. George Fox played his music to console those who went up in smoke and joined the airstreams over Poland. Each black note celebrated the loss of a soul who entered the river of death without the consolation of music. The house floated with tears and terror and uncontainable fury and music that made children dream of the jackbooted intruders who lit their way with torches made of Jewish hair.

After we were married, Shyla would tell me about her Southern childhood. She thought that at any moment German soldiers could surround her house in a rapid flanking movement in which every vine and redbud and azalea would perish. But these were offhand and unusual confessions for Shyla. Mostly she was silent to the point of obsession about her parents' war experiences. The subject became *verboten*, especially after Leah was born. Shyla could not bear thinking about a world that could put a child as affectionate and helpless as Leah inside a gas chamber. That world became the building material of her nightmares, but she rarely allowed it to make an appearance in her daily life.

I had no idea of the depth of her morbid obsession until I saw the freshly minted number of her father's tattoo on her forearm in the Charleston morgue after she killed herself. The presence of that raw angry number was an eloquent annotation binding her to the great blood-letting of her people.

After her death, it was I who became Holocaust-obsessed, I who studied those broken-open years with a passion and completeness I could not believe possible. That number on Shyla's arm haunted me because it hinted at a tortured life she had lived without my knowledge. I am sure I could have helped her had I known the depth of her preoccupation with the destruction of the Jews. She had spent her life hiding her Jewishness, wrapping it in a cocoon of secret, precious silks. Her spirituality bore fruit in darkness and a grotesque moth with skull marks on its powdery wings tried to take flight in the museum where she kept her soul chloroformed and pinned to velvet. Only when Leah was born did she seem interested in coming to terms with her Jewish roots. Shyla Fox had been raised in the dead center of Southern Christendom, accepted by her Christian playmates, happy in the changeless backwaters of small-town life where her Jewishness made her slightly bizarre and out of step. But at least her parents were considered churchgoing and God-fearing people, and Shyla used her small synagogue as escape hatch, theater, masquerade ball, and oasis. By the time she was a senior in high school, fifty Jewish families met for Sabbath ceremonies each week, and in a riot of light and noise and gossip Shyla felt she was in the center of a world that both cherished and was proud of her.

Her mother had not told Shyla anything

about puberty or issued a mother's warning about the changes that were going to take place in her body. When she first bled she thought she had cancer, thought she had displeased God in the most desperate, unspeakable manner. She entered her womanhood innocent and unprepared, and this marked her, at least to herself, as singular, chosen, and strange. She grew dreamier and more withdrawn. Her mother had protected her fiercely, and mother and daughter grew closer that year before the breakdowns began. It was then that Ruth Fox began to tell her daughter about the stories of the war. They began to spill out of Ruth in an undiluted manner she could not stem or help. Stories of both Ruth's and George's terrifying experiences entered the imagination of their precocious, exquisitely intense daughter, stories so lit with anguish that they would return with all their excessive power intact over and over again; and often when she began to bleed. So in Shyla's mind, the suffering of her parents during the war would be associated with her own shedding of blood. Ruth had always intended to tell Shyla all that happened to her, her husband, and their families in Eastern Europe, but had been waiting for the proper time, for Shyla to reach a certain point of maturity. Though she thought it was important that Shyla understand the world as a dangerous, unscrupulous place, she did not wish to imprint this information too early, nor did she wish Shyla to be filled with fear at the untrustworthiness and savagery of mankind. Somewhat arbitrarily, Ruth chose Shyla's puberty as the time to begin sharing these stories.

Inevitably, Ruth would look into the eyes of her Waterford neighbors and wonder what conditions would be required for them to take to the streets, wild and unappeasable, in their collective lust for Jewish blood. All through my childhood, unbeknownst to me, Ruth would study my face and try to place it under the visor of a Nazi cap. In every Christian she met, Ruth looked for the Nazi who lived just below the surface. But all of this I would learn later.

Shyla was a good listener and she took these stories and made them part of herself. They built libraries along the ridges of her brain where the weight of them turned to migraine and nightmare. It had relieved Ruth to share a portion of the agony she had held inside her for so long, but it was a while before she understood the depth of agony she had delivered to her oldest child.

From the age of ten to thirteen, Shyla retreated into the interior, became distant from her family and friends, and went through several bizarre episodes that led her to the offices of several child psychiatrists in the South.

Though she did well in school, she withdrew from almost all association with her friends and playmates. These were the years she made the most progress at the piano and the ones that gave her father hope that she might become a great teacher of music even if she lacked the virtuosity and passion that marked all of the best concert pianists. Shyla practiced for hours, and, like her father, she found respite in the black notes, escape in the dark, mysterious arrangement of music. Her discipline at the piano turned from a virtue into a form of dementia.

Soon she began to skip meals in order to master a new piece. Her love of her art made her fast, her parents said, and there was pride in their voices. The music seemed to play on forever: It lifted off her fingers in a ceaseless flood of notes, a river of noise and plainsong and elegy, that a dutiful daughter played out of a misspent, indirect love of a father who distrusted words and cherished only the harmonies of a keyboard. As a teacher, George was severe with Shyla because he believed that she was trying to reach a realm of competency that he thought she was not talented enough to reach. He pushed her hard, and each time she passed imaginary barriers he set for her. She mastered concertos he declared beyond her competence. As she dared him to set limits on her talent, he raised the ante higher and higher, knowing that she did not possess the range and the fluency that greatness in art required. He was right, and George Fox pushed his daughter until he broke her. When she finally snapped, she had lost ten pounds that she could barely afford to lose and the doctors in Waterford could not get her to eat. In the hospital they fed her glucose intravenously while her fingers played noiseless sonatas against her blanket.

When they let her out of the hospital, Shyla began what she would later call her "dark year," the year of masks, hallucinations, and grieving for the dead whose names she did not know. Without telling either of them, she took the stories that her mother had secretly told her and she took her parents' place, walking every step that they had walked, and suffering what they had suffered. Shyla starved herself, she refused water, her hands made music wherever her fingers touched down, and she spent that year grieving for parents who had not had the time to grieve, nor the resources, and certainly not the permission.

One day I found Shyla weeping on the garden bench against the brick wall that separated our two houses. I lifted myself up onto the wall and with both arms extended balanced myself expertly and ran along the wall until I spoke from above her and asked what was wrong. Then I saw the blood on her legs. Taking her by the hand, I led her a back way through a neighbor's gate and overgrown yard toward a portion of marsh that led to the dock behind our house. The jasmine was blooming and the bees looked as though they were stitching flowers together with invisible silken thread. I made her take off her shoes and socks and then both of us dove in our light summer clothes into the incoming tide.

"Saltwater cures everything," I assured her.

"I'm dying. I want to die I'm so embarrassed."

"It's probably something you ate," I said, using my mother's stock reply for everything.

"My mother will kill me when she sees I went swimming in this dress."

"We'll sneak into my house. We'll use the tree," I suggested.

The tides of Waterford washed Shyla clean and she and I sneaked into the yard of my house and scrambled up the back side of the live oak where I had hammered two-by-fours to make a ladder. Shyla undressed in my room and put on a tee shirt and old pair of my shorts; then she handed me her wet dress and underpants and asked me to throw them away. Afraid for her and worried about their discovery, I dug a deep hole beside the marsh in a place hidden by fences and placed the bag within. While I was completing my task, Shyla went to inform her mother she was bleeding to death.

Yet it was not that bleeding that was killing her slowly, but Shyla's inability to incorporate the wounds of her parents into a world that made any sense to her. Though she was being raised in a quiet backwater Southern town where almost any child could find a sense of safety, cohesion, and composure, she was born a child who could pull every electron of anguish from the aura surrounding a loved one and take it gladly into her own system. She consumed the pain of others because that was her food of choice, the one fruit she would always choose to smuggle out of Eden. Her disease was Auschwitz, but that was a difficult diagnosis for anyone to make in the low country of South Carolina in 1960.

For over a year she managed to hold herself together. Then her mother followed her after dinner one night, a meal that Shyla had barely touched, up the stairs to the attic, where she heard Shyla talking in whispers to a group of girls who were not answering back. For fifteen minutes she listened to this fearful monologue of instructions and encouragement, then opened the door suddenly and found Shyla surrounded by all the dolls of her girlhood, shrouded in black like nuns. Shyla was smuggling food to them every night and warning the dolls not to make noise when the Germans were patrolling outside.

Horrified, Ruth took her daughter in her arms and apologized for telling her anything about the terrible past. She had underestimated the extraordinary power of her own story and the fabulous sensitivity that Shyla brought to the taking in of that story.

The next day, my mother watched in disbelief as Shyla walked into our backyard and buried all her dolls in a mass grave she had dug the night before. That August was one of the hottest on record and it marked the first time that Shyla was sent to the Children's Division of the South Carolina State Mental Hospital. She was committed to Bull Street, where she remained for six weeks and was treated for extreme depression.

Shyla returned from Columbia unchanged, except that she seemed more inward and self-contained. Her fragility made her special, but we remained comfortable with each other and often did our homework together at the kitchen table at my house where the noise in that overpopulated household seemed to have a calming effect on her. I thought she was getting back to be the Shyla I had always known, and then one night that winter it snowed in

Waterford for the third time in the twentieth century. The snow triggered some clear but inexplicable image in Shyla that had nothing to do with the weather itself. The strange chemistry of snow and memory took possession of her and she learned again that madness wore many masks, could change addresses at will, was master of disguise, guile, and the cheap shot. This time it came to her in human form, in the shape of a beautiful, sorrowing woman.

When the woman appeared she brought with her an imaginary country that only Shyla could enter.

She subtracted the real world, erased it completely as she showed herself to Shyla and comforted her with wordless majesty. She was exceedingly kind.

Though Shyla always knew these visitations were born within her own mind, she never lost the sense of excitement the coming of the lady inspired within her. She could not summon her at will: The lady planned the visits with foresight and cunning. Each month, she followed the laws of menses and came only after Shyla's period had begun.

Once I found Shyla on her knees in a trancelike state in her garden. It was beginning to snow.

"Something's wrong with Shyla," I said when I found Mrs. Fox.

"What has happened?" she said, drying her hands on her apron and running out into the yard. She saw Shyla kneeling by the brick wall, moving her lips, but with no words coming forth from her slightly opened mouth, staring, transfixed, at something invisible.

"Shyla, it is your mother. Listen to me, Shyla. You cannot do this to me. Not to me or your father. You are a happy girl. You have everything. Everything, you hear? There's nothing to be afraid of. There's nothing to hurt you. You must be happy. It is your duty to be happy. What did he do to you? Did Jack hurt you? Did he touch you?"

"Jack would never do anything to hurt Shyla, Ruth," I heard my mother's voice say. "You know that better than anyone. How dare you accuse Jack of such a thing!"

Ruth turned her sad eyes toward my mother and put both hands up in the air in a pathetic, supplicating gesture. "I cannot bear it if something is wrong with my Shyla. I simply could not stand it, Lucy. You do not understand, but this is my hope and my husband's hope and every dream we have or ever had is contained in this girl and her sister. How could there be anything wrong? There is plenty of food and nice people and no bombs blowing up people in their sleep. Everything is good and I find her like this. For what, Lucy? You tell me for what."

My mother approached the kneeling girl from behind as the snow continued to fall. She knelt beside Shyla and put her arm around her shoulder.

"You all right, good-looking?" Lucy asked after a minute.

"What's that?" Shyla said, as she noticed the white buildup on her sweater.

"It's snow. I grew up with it in the mountains. But it's rare down here. You scared us, honey. It was like you went off to the moon for a visit."

"No, Mrs. McCall. I was here. Could you see it too?"

"See what, Shyla?" Lucy asked, looking back at Ruth.

"The lady," Shyla said.

"Oh my God, she is crazy for sure," Ruth said, walking around in circles until my mother stopped her with a withering look.

"How nice. Are you sure it was a lady?" Lucy asked.

"Oh yes, such a beautiful lady."

"I have dreams like that sometimes, too, Shyla," Lucy whispered. "Sometimes I think I see my poor dead mother and we have the nicest talk together and she seems so real I could reach out and brush the hair out of her eyes, but then I realize she's not really there at all. Maybe it's your imagination. Maybe you're just dreaming."

"No, Mrs. McCall. She's still there. She's on the fence."

"What else does the lady look like?" Lucy asked. "Describe her more carefully."

"Her hands are folded in prayer. A light around her head."

"Don't ask her anything more, Lucy," Ruth said. "I beg of you. She is crazy enough without having to answer these questions."

Lucy looked over at me, ignoring Ruth, and said, "It's the Virgin Mary. The Mother of Jesus. We're privileged to be witnesses of a holy apparition."

"I don't think Mary appears to Jews, Mama," I said.

"Are you in charge of her appointment calendar?" my mother answered and I could tell her mind was made up in this matter. "Besides, Mary was Jewish. It makes perfect sense, if you look at it in a certain light."

"Mrs. Fox doesn't seem like she's on the same wavelength," I observed.

"Shyla," Lucy asked with gentleness. "Do you know the statue that I keep in the front hall of my house?"

Shyla nodded her head.

"Is that the lady you're seeing? Is it the

Blessed Virgin Mary? The Mother of Jesus of Nazareth?"

Shyla looked at Lucy and affirmed the fact. "I think so."

Lucy made the sign of the cross and began to say the Apostles' Creed. "Say a rosary with me, Jack. We are witnesses, like the shepherd children of Fatima or with Bernadette at Lourdes."

"Mrs. Fox is crying, Mama. I think we better get Shyla inside her house. We're all covered with snow."

"And leave poor Mary outside alone?" Lucy said. "I wouldn't think of such a thing."

"I don't see nothin', Mama," I said nervously.

"You and I were not chosen to see, Jack," Lucy explained. "But we were chosen to bear witness to what Shyla has seen."

"I haven't seen what Shyla's seen. She's shivering, Mama. Get her inside."

"Will you stay out here and keep Mary company?" Lucy asked.

"Yeh," I said. "I'll baby-sit with Mary."

"Don't you be flip, young man," Lucy warned, helping Shyla to her feet and walking her to the back door of her house. "Ask for her intercession. Ask her to get your father to stop drinking."

"Mary, make my father quit being a drunk," I said.

"You call that praying?" Lucy said, looking back at me. "How about a little sincerity? If I was the Mother of God I wouldn't give you a damn thing if you asked for something in that tone of voice."

"I never prayed to a wall before," I said, irritable and cold.

"No one likes a doubting Thomas, son. And they certainly don't go far in life."

"What if it's just a figment of Shyla's imagination?" I asked. "What if there's nothing but ivy on this wall? Then what exactly am I praying for?"

"Then we're just making Shyla feel better. We're supporting her and believing in her. If there's nothing on that wall, you're just praying to the same God you normally pray to."

"I can do that inside where it's warm."

"Keep *her* company," Lucy warned.

It was the first reported apparition of Mary in the history of the South Carolina diocese. The news did not please the Waterford rabbi nor did it amuse Father Marcellus Byrd, the passive, unsociable priest who had been bumped around backwater parishes of the diocese for twenty years. In fact, it pleased no one at all except for my mother.

In the following six months, Shyla lived out

her life among the hurt and insane at the
mental hospital on Bull Street. Here, she
learned the awful laws of electricity. Her vision
of the weeping lady was replaced with nothingness and confusion. They stunned her brain
and made it imageless. Her lady died by the
conveyance of a power surge through the soft
tissues of her brain. Shyla shuffled through the
girls' ward on slippers, untouchable and undis-
mayable, and the doctors nodded to each other
when after her therapy she could not tell them
the name of her hometown. Shock treatment
was a natural predator of memory and she did
not recognize who I was when I sent her a letter that first week.

I wrote her every week she was away and
the live oak that served as highway and hiding
place between us seemed bereft without her.
My letters were inevitably shy and stilted, but
in each one I told her I wished that she would
come home soon. I had spent my entire childhood in shouting distance of Shyla and I felt
uncentered without her in the middle of my
own life. No one in town mentioned Shyla
when she was away. The stigma of the asylum
made her unmentionable and even her parents
seemed to avoid me in shame whenever I saw
them in the streets. Her disappearance was
more of an erasure than a going-away.

On the last day of school that June I left a

note for my parents that Mike, Capers, and I were going fishing out at the fish camp on the Isle of Orion and not to expect me back for a couple of days. Now began that period of delicious freedom when my pals and I spent the entire summer on the river far from the gaze or worry of parents. If a Waterford boy did not want to spend all of his time on a boat or playing sports, it was a cause for real parental concern. My father found the note and felt a twinge of nostalgia as he thought of his own timeless, languorous hours spent cruising past the oyster banks in search of feeding bass or sheepshead so long ago in that faraway time when he was allowed to think of himself as a boy.

At five in the morning, I went out of my window to the branch of the oak tree that almost touched down on the roof of my house. I caught a ride with a sheriff's deputy who was transferring a prisoner to the Central Correction Center in Columbia who drove me to the main entrance of the state hospital on Bull Street after delivering a stern lecture on the dangers of hitchhiking.

The grounds were lonely and well kept and the buildings looked well wrought but crestfallen. I wandered through the bricked-in campus for an hour, trying hard to look nonchalant and clear-headed. By the time I saw Shyla at visitors' hours, I thought my own sanity was suspect and temporary.

Shyla seemed older, more womanly than I remembered. She had the run of the place and took me on visits to the library, the canteen, where she paid for my lunch by signing her name, and the nondenominational chapel.

"You ought to watch crazy people come here and pray. It's better than the circus. Some of them scream out, 'Amen,' others shout 'Mama,' others go crazy and have to be dragged off to solitary by their attendants. But most of them just sing, pretty as angels. Crazy people have good voices. That's been a big surprise."

As we circumnavigated the seventy-seven fenced acres, exploring every nook and cranny, I gave Shyla a summary of all that had occurred during her lost months away from school and Waterford.

When we walked in front of the main administration building, Babcock, Shyla suddenly took me by the hand and led me up the front steps. We ran quickly to the back hall where she hurried me up three flights of stairs, then to a cavernous attic room that led to the great dome that dominated the skyline for miles around. A small narrow stairway took us through the gloomy fretwork of support beams that held the dome aloft. The woodwork was elaborate and it seemed as though ten forests had died to provide all the timber that buttressed that graceful, silver dome, which floated lighter than air above the trees of Columbia. When we reached the highest point on the stairway there was still a huge open space to the top of the structure. Hundreds of bats hung like baseball gloves, their eyes adjusted to the darkness. I could hear pigeons cooing in the eaves below them and could smell mildew and guano and mold in the stagnant air.

"Look up. I wanted to surprise you," Shyla whispered. "Straight up to the very top of the dome."

I did as I was told and I felt my retinas enlarge as I stared into the upper darkness, into a void that permitted no light. Gradually, I saw the bowl of the dome reveal itself in its amplitude and beauty of form but I saw nothing else.

"Look harder," she said. "They're looking at you."

"What's looking at me?" I asked.

"The surprise," she said.

Then I saw them in all their shy but confident wildness. A nesting pair of barn owls, the shape of beer cans, looked down at us from an eave twenty feet above. The owls could not have chosen a more precarious spot for the raising of their young. They glowed slightly with an otherworldly light and we could hear the impatient noises of unseen owlets whose cries of hunger sounded like kids in soda shops sucking up the dregs of malteds from tall glasses. It seemed like a place where evil came to lick its wounds and plan its mischief, a place in fairy tales where the ogre made its appearance in the lives of lost children.

Breathless, I watched the owls watch me with their rufous wings folded down tightly. I could not figure out if they reminded me of penguins or monkeys. There was beauty in their wildness, in their eerie stillness. They were praiseworthy sentinels to the country of the insane.

"How many young?" I whispered.

"Three left. There were five," Shyla whispered back.

"Where are the other two?"

"They were eaten by their brothers and sisters. I watched. You can't believe the number of rats and mice it takes to feed young owls."

"How did you find them?"

"I have the run of the place," Shyla said softly. "They know I'm not crazy."

"Then why are you here?"

"Because I saw the lady," she said.

"Why'd you bring me up here?" I asked. "It's spooky."

"So we'd be alone."

"Why'd you want us to be alone?" I said, feeling shut-in and misplaced.

Shyla smiled at me and said, "Because of this."

Shyla kissed me on the lips. I pulled back at first as though she had slapped me.

"Hold still, silly," Shyla said.

She kissed me again and her lips and mouth felt sweet against mine and I was happy to be in that place of fear and owls.

We kissed each other several more times.

"Good," Shyla said, "we've got that out of the way."

"Why'd you do that?"

"All the girls in the ward talk about kissing and everything else," said Shyla. "I wanted to get started and I didn't think you'd mind."

Licking my lips, which still tasted like her, I said, "We didn't do bad, did we? For rookies, I mean."

"I was expecting a lot more," Shyla admitted.

"What were you expecting?" I asked.

"I don't know," she said. "Just more. But that one didn't count. It wasn't real. We weren't carried away by passion."

"You didn't like it?"

"I didn't say that. It wasn't bad. It just wasn't all it was cracked up to be."

"Maybe I need to practice," I said, yet I

would not kiss Shyla again until we danced in the foundering sea-endangered house many years later.

"I wouldn't know," Shyla said. "I love coming up to this dome. It makes me feel like the only person in the world. Do the kids at school know I'm at the Crazy House?"

"They think you're out sick. Like you caught a terrible disease or something," I told her. "Mrs. Pinckney has us pray for you every week. We say the Lord's Prayer for your quick recovery."

"The Lord's Prayer?" Shyla said. "But I'm Jewish."

"It doesn't hurt anything," I said. "She just wants you to get well. We all do."

"Your daddy still drinking?"

"Yeh," I answered.

In winter they had taken Shyla away and in summer they returned her to Waterford; her time away was barely noticed by her classmates, who found themselves totally absorbed by the marvelous details of their own growing up. Her reentry was seamless, uncommented upon, and her absence quickly forgotten. She resumed her life in the house of dark music and we once more took to the branches of the live oak, where we continued our commentary on the events of the town. Neither of us ever referred to the day we climbed up under the dome of the Babcock Building and exchanged shy kisses beneath the patronage of barn owls. But those kisses held great value for both of us and we each held the memory of that day inviolate.

The summer she was away Jordan came to Waterford and his arrival would change Shyla's life as much as the lives of the rest of us. Because he had lived all over the world, he had the courage to speak opinions that no other Waterford boy dared articulate for fear of ridicule. Though not a free thinker, he was an original one who had small talent for following the rumors of the herd.

It was after an afternoon baseball game when my mother was feeding hamburgers to Capers, Mike, Jordan, and myself in the garden of our backyard that Shyla first saw Jordan. My brothers were tumbling around the yard playing hide-and-seek as Lucy yelled out that her azaleas were off-limits. Other grills in the neighborhood were lit and the smell of charcoal and grease and flame-licked steaks coalesced to make a one-time scent that would always smell like summer days to whomever inhaled it—along with the lavender and horsemint trampled by the children rushing to conceal themselves. My father, who had not attended the game, had poured himself a bourbon in a silver loving cup in his book-lined office and would continue to drink until he lost consciousness sometime that evening. His absence always took up as much room as his presence, and I would periodically look to the back door, every nerve ending alert, dreading my father's sudden appearance.

My mother, pretty with her children around her, loved feeding me and my friends after our games, not minding the fragrant sweat that lifted off our uniforms, and loved her garden and her house and her neighborhood and the sight of the light-infused river that curved by our property and out past the town. When she flipped the first batch of hamburgers, she noticed Shyla looking over the gate from behind the ivy.

"Get in here, girl," she called out to Shyla. "I'll fix you a hamburger and Jack'll introduce you to Jordan. He's the new young stud who just moved here."

It was hard to tell who blushed harder, Jordan or Shyla, but she joined the picnic table and laughed as we told stories about the game while her father began to play the piano in the background. It was her father's favorite form of disapproval. He went to his piano whenever he discovered her laughing among her friends. He punished her with music.

"That's a Beethoven piano sonata," Jordan said, cocking his head toward the music. "Who's playing that?"

"It's Shyla's father," my mother said.

"He's wonderful, Shyla," said Jordan.

"I'll take Elvis any day," Capers said to laughter.

When Capers and Mike left on their bicycles, dusk had fallen on the garden and my mother had gone in to get the younger children ready for bed. The music of George Fox continued without a pause and the notes of a Bach sonata fell among us like flung coins. Jordan and Shyla were talking about the pieces of music they loved the best and I was growing touchy, feeling ignored. Then I noticed that Jordan had stopped talking and was studying Shyla's face in the ever-changing yet still diaphanous light.

"Jack, you guys are idiots," Jordan said. "You didn't see it, did you? It was right in front of you all the time. None of you had a clue."

"What are you talking about?" I asked.

Jordan rose off the bench and went over to a frightened-looking Shyla. Carefully, Jordan took off her glasses and set them down on the picnic table. He undid the braid that held Shyla's hair in place and let her luxuriant dark hair fall over her shoulders. Though she had stiffened, Shyla had not uttered a word of protest.

"I'm an only child, Shyla, and I do my mother's hair whenever my father isn't around. My God, your hair is marvelous."

Her hair was a black winding river flowing through the dying light. He stroked that hair with his fingernails and it was as though he were digging his hands into a vault of black jewels. Too late, I saw it. Too late, I discovered what Jordan had found on the first day he ever met Shyla Fox.

Sitting down beside her, Jordan reached up and touched Shyla's face and smoothed the skin near her eyes and traced the line of her jaw and her cheekbone. I knew what Jordan was going to say long before he said it. I wanted to shout it out, but I did not have the right since I had not seen what had always been in front of me.

"You missed it, Jack." Jordan said again. "All you guys missed it. Shyla doesn't even know it. Do you, Shyla?"

"Know what, Jordan?" she asked.

"You're so beautiful, Shyla," he said. "You're the prettiest girl in this town."

"No, no," Shyla said and she hid her face in her hands.

Jordan did not take his eyes off her. "You

might as well get used to it, Shyla. You're gorgeous. Not a girl in this two-bit town can hold a candle to you."

Shyla got up and ran toward the music of her house. But she had heard Jordan's words and could not sleep that night when she thought of them. Later, in the first year of our marriage, she told me that her life began at that moment.

"Your life didn't begin until Jordan," I said, as we lay in bed years later.

"I was in an insane asylum that year, Jack. The lady came that year."

"They never did figure out what that was all about," I said, breathing the smell of Shyla in as we talked in darkness.

"My mother knew who the lady was from the very beginning," Shyla said. "It was part of a story from the war that she told me."

"What's the story?"

"I don't remember. I've tried, but nothing's there."

"Who does your mother think the lady was?"

"It's not important, darling."

"It's important to me. I'm your husband."

"My mother told me who it was on the first day she came," Shyla said. "It terrified her."

"The name of the lady?" I insisted.

Shyla kissed me, then rolled over to go to sleep.

It would be many years before I would put the pieces together and realize that Shyla had seen the lady of coins.

CHAPTER 30

I FELT SHAKEN EVERY TIME I AP-
proached Shyla's front door. I could take no
comfort, nor sense any touch of homecoming,
when I brought my daughter to the house
where her mother had played out the days of
her childhood and had grown into the prettiest
suicide the town had ever known. Her body lay
between the Foxes and me and there seemed to
be nothing we could do about it. We kept our
meetings brief but cordial. Leah's sheer exuberance and goodness bound us in an alliance
that we all recognized as a valuable result of
my return to Waterford. Since Leah had a need
for us to love one another, we accommodated

her as best we could. Ruth and I kept our discussions businesslike and friendly, while George and I kept out of each other's way and acted as though we had an unspoken agreement to keep our contempt for each other under wraps. Our civility made the enmity between us seem less radical.

Ruth's house would always be a piece of Europe lost in the hallucinatory placement of days. The Foxes had carried the gravity of their nostalgia for a homeland in their trunks and valises. This new country had succeeded in turning the Fox children into Americans, yet had not laid a finger on the parents. The English language was slippery on their tongues, too miscellaneous for precision, yet too colloquial and inaccessible to lend any sense of mastery to the immigrant. English was a fourth language for George, a third for Ruth. George Fox still dreamed in Polish; Ruth, in Yiddish; and both found it miraculous that they still dreamed at all.

It was during the Spoleto Festival that Ruth Fox called me and asked if I would allow her husband to take Leah to a chamber music concert in Charleston. When I readily agreed, she asked me if I would come to lunch at her house and said that there were some things she wished to discuss with me. In the formal manner we had adopted with each other, I realized that Ruth was going to tell me about her childhood during the war in Europe. We had developed a shorthand code so information could be passed between us with very little being said. Because of Shyla we tried to be gentle with each other. Because of Leah we tried to find the diplomatic means of truce and detente that would one day enable us to love each other again.

The subject of Leah was our safe ground and we discussed her long after we waved good-bye to Leah and George as they pulled out of the Foxes' driveway to begin the ninety-minute car ride to Charleston. We ate lunch on a white wicker table and she poured us glasses of California chardonnay. A dog barked far off in the town and the drone of lawn mowers could be heard on unseen lawns. The air was full of summer smells and honeybees sang in the full glory of jasmine. In this loneliest and safest of Southern towns, Ruth began to speak of Poland after the German invasion. She gave almost no introduction to her subject matter, but began in a far-off voice that I barely recognized as hers. I only tried to stop her once, but she silenced me with an uplifted hand. She needed to tell me the events that had brought her out of Poland to this veranda in Waterford —how a Jewish girl's fate could be so complex as to bring her to such an afternoon when she would face her Christian son-in-law and tell him of what she knew about damage and terror and bedlam in a world set afire and turned upside down by cataclysmic events. By telling me what happened to her, I soon recognized that Ruth was handing over to me a gift of extraordinary value. By informing me of her history, she was demonstrating her own need to close the door on our embattled past. It was the most generous thing anyone had ever done for me: Ruth was providing me with some key to the mystery of Shyla's death.

Ruth Fox had grown up in the town of Kronilov in Poland, the daughter of an Orthodox rabbi named Ephraim Graubart whose love of the Talmud was famous in many towns. Her mother's name was Hannah Shem-Tov. Her grandfather was a merchant who sold vodka and brandy, a rough, outspoken man with a thousand opinions. Ruth's grandmother was named Martha, a pious woman loved by Jew and non-Jew alike.

Ruth's childhood was happy and uneventful until she was thirteen and the war broke out. She remembered it as her whole world catching fire from all the bombs dropped on the town and the roads that soon began filling up with terrified refugees.

After the first day of bombing, Ruth and her family slept with the smell of burnt horse-flesh raw in their nostrils. Her grandfather, Moshe Shem-Tov, argued with her father, the rabbi, that they should make a run toward the Russian border, where Moshe had friends who could smuggle them across. But Ephraim Graubart had his congregants and as a rabbi he had never felt so needed or appreciated by the poor Jews who flocked to his synagogue. Because his daughter would not desert her husband and because his wife would not leave her only daughter behind, Moshe's run to the border never materialized, though his urge toward flight never left him in the terrible days that followed. The Polish Army had already been defeated, and the Germans had turned their fury on the Jews, their most defenseless citizens. The Germans who occupied Kronilov seemed omnipresent, invincible.

From the day following the first bombing and strafing, Ruth's mother began busying herself with sewing clothes for her children. When she was almost finished making new dresses for Ruth and her sister Tonya, Hannah made her way to her father's house and took him by complete surprise by asking him for all the money he was planning to leave to her upon his death. Moshe was taken aback and questioned his daughter sharply. But Hannah had inherited some of her father's cunning and sense of self-preservation. She had listened to the Jews of Kronilov discuss the rise of the Nazis and Adolf Hitler, she knew that those who remained in the town would have a very short future. As Ruth poured out her story, I let her voice take me.

"My mother prepared for the coming of the Germans by sewing. She made herself ready by making a dress for my sister and me. My grandfather, Moshe, could never say no to his only daughter, and when she explained that she must stay with her husband, the rabbi, she said she had a plan for the escape of her children. And so Moshe gave her the sixteen gold coins that he kept in a special book, gold coins that carry the image of Tsar Nicholas II. And she takes the coins and covers them with cloth, and turns them into buttons, eight for my new dress and eight for my sister's.

"By the time the dresses are finished, the Germans have set up their own provisional system of government in the broken, paralyzed town, and have begun their amusement of humiliating the civilians who fear them. They break the spirits of unarmed men for the fun of it. They take pleasure in the bayoneting of Hasidic Jews, whose foreign looks they hate. They take pleasure in hearing the most God-fearing of men plead for their lives in a German the soldiers cannot quite understand.

"During all the shooting and torment my mother always goes out into the street to help the wounded, and one day she brings home a young Polish boy who is badly hurt when soldiers open fire on a crowd. His name is Stefan and my mother sits with him caring for him as if he were her own son. For several days Stefan looks as though he might die, but my mother's care will not let him die and she feeds him and watches over him. My mother Hannah is like this always and does not care who is Jew or Gentile if someone is hurting and in need of help. For days he is not conscious, he is delirious and does not even know he is in this world. Finally, he begins to recover. He is a peasant from outside of Kronilov, and when he is strong enough to leave my mother sends a message to a tin peddler named Fishman, who travels from village to village doing his work. Fishman tells Stefan's mother that her son is recovering in a rabbi's house. When Stefan's mother, Christine, arrives at our house and finds her son alive, she is overcome with joy and gratitude, and drops to her knees to kiss my mother's hands in thanks.

"As the war goes on, conditions become worse and worse for all the Jews in Poland. The Nazis set up a gallows near the headquarters of their commander, Landau, and they take pleasure in hanging Jews who they catch stealing bread or trying to smuggle valuables. Ghettos are formed and Jews are crowded into them, in the worst, poorest sections of town, where the filth is unimaginable and the water impure. After the first winter passes, there is almost no food and people are transported to slave labor camps, as families struggle desperately to stay together. Jews are cut down in the streets every day for the crime of being Jewish.

"My mother had a good friend, a Christian, when she was a child, who lived next to her family. The girl, whose name was Maria, had no mother all the time she was young because she had died of influenza. Then Maria's father marries a widow with five other children, and because there were so many to feed Maria is put into a convent where she becomes a nun. Her name as a nun is Sister Paulina and she writes to my mother several times each year giving news of her life and asking for letters in return. Maria always says in her letters that if she could ever be of service to my mother, she will do whatever she can though she has no money, only prayers and her God. So as well as sewing the coins of Tsar Nicholas II hidden as buttons, my mother puts in my dress the address of the convent where Sister Paulina lives in Warsaw. She hides it on the inside, near the hem, but writes it clearly so if we ever get to Warsaw, we can find Sister Paulina. She also makes us memorize the address and she tests our knowledge of it every day, like a school assignment.

"And then, after a time in the darkness of morning the town is awakened by cries of, 'Out, Jews. Out of your houses, scum. Vermin. *Juden. Juden.*' You cannot know how the word 'Jew' sounds coming from a mouth that hates you. The Germans said the word *Juden* like it is the vilest profanity.

"They called for all Jews to come outside in the square for a selection. By the number of trucks assembled my grandfather knew this would be a very large selection and he was certain that this time his family would be taken. Unknown to us, this grandfather of mine had secretly prepared a place for us in an attic hidden next door. As the Jews filed out into the streets, our grandfather orders us to sneak out the back door and follow him up a back staircase that leads to a secret attic that he and a friend have prepared. They had paid a large price for this place, which was hidden from view and only reached by a ladder. It is stocked with food from the black market. Together, they make strict rules about how many from each family will be saved.

"The Nazis round up all the Jews in the

ghetto while we—two families—go up the ladder that leads to safety. The attic is small and there is no ventilation and we hear the murderous cries of the Germans and the trucks in low gear leaving the square loaded with Jews. My grandmother is so fearful that she trembles as she hides her face in my sister's hair. Everyone is afraid, but all are quiet. A sound can mean death.

"Soon we hear the Germans searching the buildings looking for people who have hidden. There are screams in the distance, then the sound of machine-gun fire. My father, the rabbi, has a look on his face that I know he is far away in prayer, not of this world anymore. But the rest of us are in the here and now and our fear is such that you can touch it.

"Below us on the first floor, we hear the Germans begin to search our own building, the one where we are hiding. No one dares breathe. Then, as they come to the stairs on the first floor, the infant of the oldest Smithberg daughter begins to cry.

"I see the look pass between the Smithberg daughter and her husband. Between Smithberg and his wife. My grandmother is in despair when she listens to the baby. When she hears the Germans coming up the stairs, she says, 'You have killed us all, my husband.' The mother covers the baby's mouth with her hand, but it does no good. The baby gets angry as any baby would. She offers her breast but the baby won't take it. The crying gets louder until her husband takes the baby and puts his great hand over the baby's mouth. He pinches the baby's nostrils. He covers the mouth with his palm. The baby grows silent. Her flesh turns blue. No one says anything as the baby dies before all of our eyes with the Germans searching the second floor. Somebody is found in hiding because we hear the quick burst of machine-gun fire. We also hear something much worse. We hear the barking of a dog. A moment later, the Germans are below us and we hear the dog's barking become frenzied as it lunges in fury toward our secret place.

"They herded us out of that place, but there was so much screaming that I don't remember anything except a German knocking my grandfather to the floor with the butt of a rifle. I run to my grandfather and fall into his arms, trying to protect him from further blows. My mother screams my name aloud. My name was the last word she spoke. A soldier put a bullet through her brain. A huge blade passes in front of my eyes and my grandfather's throat explodes in a jet of blood that sprays out against a far wall. The dog tears at the genitalia of Smithberg, who tries to defend himself. Then two of the soldiers take my sister and the other girls and me down the stairs, where they rape us. My sister is raped beside me. When the soldier is finished with her, he draws his knife and cuts her throat. The other girls are shot and left there.

"This soldier who did me is very young. A German boy with frightened eyes. When he is done, he looks at me. We are alone in a room with the dead girls. He had torn my pants off and he could not look at me when he was done. He fixes his pants and wipes the dust off his uniform. He raises up his rifle to shoot me. Then he lowers it. He puts his fingers to his lips for me to remain quiet. Then he reaches down and with his hand he takes my sister's blood and smears it all over my face. My sister's blood is still warm as he covers me with it. Then he fires a bullet into my dead sister and motions for me to play dead. I lie there until the trucks are all gone and it is quiet again. I rise up and I walk to the sewer opening that leads down to the river. Now I have no fear at all. Like a dead person, I walk through the filth beneath the streets and when I reach the river I wait until nightfall. When night comes, I walk until I am away from the town. I bathe. I clean myself of blood and the filth of the town and the German boy that is inside me. Then I make my way to the last bridge into the town and I cross over it when I am sure there is no one coming. I walk in the dark beneath the stars to find the farm where the wounded Pole, Stefan, and his mother, Christina, live. I hear my mother's voice saying to me, 'Go find Christina. Find Stefan. They will take care of you for a while. But they are very poor. You cannot stay with them too long. Other Poles will betray you to the Germans. The Germans will come to kill all of you.'

"It is a black night without stars, the road is black and I can see nothing, but I walk. It is of them I dream as I walk and I pray for them all night as I walk toward this Stefan and Christina.

"In the morning I stop before a small farm and watch as a man walks out from a barn smoking a cigarette. I hope to ask directions to Stefan's farm. I look at his face, but I do not trust him. So I walk further, hiding myself always until there is another farm. Here I see a young girl a little older than myself. Out in the fields, I see men, but a long way off. Hungry, I walk up and call out to her. She is surprised but comes to me and stares at me as though something is wrong. There is blood running down my leg, just a little bit, from what happened the day before. She takes me inside to see her mother and two little brothers. I ask about Stefan and Christina and the mother tells her daughter that I am a Jew and to take me back where she has found me.

"So we leave. But the Polish girl takes me to a barn and she gives me a chicken egg. Then she takes my hand and walks me through the fields. When we pass farmers she waves to them and makes me wave as though nothing is wrong. Without any word between us, I know she is taking me to Christina's house. We pass by a stream and she makes me wash my leg. We walk what seems like a long way, but only because I am hungry. We arrive at Christina's and Stefan's house and they are happy to see me. Before the girl can go, I go into a room and unravel a button. When she leaves I go with her and thank her. The first gold coin goes to her. The first five-ruble coin with the picture of Tsar Nicholas II.

"I know I am a danger to Christina and Stefan. They hide me in a barn above the pigs. The stink of the pigs is so bad that even the German dogs could not smell a little Jewish girl. Both warn me that Christina's husband hates the Jews and cannot be trusted with knowing the hiding place. I understand but tell them that I did not see my father die and that I would like to find my father and share his fate no matter what that is. Christina and Stefan look at each other strangely and the mother tells Stefan to show me but be careful.

"They feed me lunch, then Stefan walks me through many fields and up a long hill where there are many trees. Long before we get to these trees, I hear shots. Stefan tells me to be careful and quiet and that we must stay hidden or the Germans will kill us. Way down in this valley, I see those trucks unloading hundreds and hundreds of Jews. Big pits have been opened and the Germans make the poor Jews take off all their clothes and line up at this ditch. Little children are crying and holding their mothers' hands. Old women. Old men. Babies. Everyone goes into that great ditch. Then other prisoners throw lime and shovel dirt on the murdered bodies. So many people are shot that you cannot even count. I look for my father, but who could choose a father from all these truckloads and we are so far away that these all look like ants. Finally, I turn my eyes away and weep myself until there are tears no more to cry. I am thirteen years old. Stefan watches everything and I cry until the sun goes down and all the trucks drive off.

"When Stefan starts to return home, I will not go. Instead, I leave the hiding place and run down the long hill. I run and run and it still seems like it is miles away. At first Stefan tries to stop me, then he understands and just runs behind me. He knows I am only trying to see if my father might be alive somewhere on that field. The moon is not full but close when I get to the field where the slaughter took place. It smells of blood and lime and excrement too. I hear something but I do not know what it is. I walk out into that field and I feel that Stefan is behind me like some kind of angel, some kind of messenger from God, watching me, keeping me safe. I begin calling for my father. I call out the names of all the members of my family as I walk on the freshly dug ground. I am hearing something. Then I feel something as the earth begins to move beneath me. What I hear are the screams of Jews beneath the earth. Their mouths find an air pocket and they beg for help before the air is gone. All beneath me, the living are writhing in agony, and the turned earth moves as I walk over them. In horror, every step I take I am walking on someone not yet dead. My movement causes them to move. I call for my father as I make my way over these half-dead Jews who are my neighbors from Kronilov. Stefan finally leads me back to the hiding place and he feeds me each day, until one day his father follows him and discovers me.

"The father is a powerful, strong man and he is very angry at Christina and Stefan. How dare they hide a Jew on his farm when he knows nothing about it? Both tell him of my mother saving Stefan's life, but nothing moves this man. He says that he will kill the Jew and feed her to the pigs if she is not gone the next day. That evening they take me out to the woods and hide me. Then one morning, Christina tells me her brother will take me to Sister Paulina. Her brother Josef is taking a wagonload of cattle hides into a market in Warsaw, and he will hide me between the skins. Before I leave them, I give Stefan and Christina each a coin to thank them for saving my life, and I give to Josef the address my mother sewed into my dress where Sister Paulina lives in the convent.

"For several days, I am buried beneath the skins of cows. We are often stopped by German patrols, but Josef is bringing a wagonload of hides to make shoes for German soldiers, so there is no problem. At night we come to the old part of Warsaw and I have never seen such a big, beautiful city. We cross the Vistula River and Josef tells me it is the largest river in the world. The river seems like it is miles below us. He points out things he likes in the city. He is very proud of the capital city of his country. He is very proud to be Polish, so when we pass Germans Josef tips his hat to them as he passes then mutters that he would shovel coal on the fires of hell to burn their souls for eternity. He is a funny man and very sweet to me.

"Finally we come to the street. Josef goes

to the door, and raps on the brass knocker. He winks at me.

"An old nun answers the door and she and Josef talk. He points to the wagon and the nun shakes her head no. The talk grows louder and the nun disappears. Then another sister comes to the door and she argues with Josef. No good. He is a stubborn man and he has come to talk to one sister and only she will do. Finally, a sister comes to the door and listens to Josef. Already, I know this will be different because she steps out of the shadows and walks toward me as she listens to Josef explain why we are there. 'It is Hannah's girl, no?' she says to me and I nod to her and I know it is Paulina. When I kiss Josef on both cheeks in farewell, I slip a coin of my mother's into his pocket. I do it secretly so he will find it later because I don't think he would accept a gift.

"Paulina takes me to the Mother Superior, who says I may stay, but this was not a popular decision with one of the nuns. One named Magdalena says that if the Jewess is allowed to remain in the convent, the sisters would all be tortured and murdered and raped and the Holy Eucharist would be defiled by the Nazis. This sister says a Jew has no place in a convent dedicated to prayer and hard work. But the other nuns do not listen to this Magdalena.

"Then Paulina says to my surprise that I

told her I wished to study to be a Catholic. The Mother Superior asks me if that is true and I say yes. Then Paulina says that if I become Catholic I think I might even want to become a nun. Again I say yes because I see that Magdalena hates Jews as much as any Nazi. I nod my head and smile at the Mother Superior and tell her I very much would like to become a nun.

"I tell Paulina that night about my family, about my mother. She weeps hard because she loved my mother. Immediately, Paulina cuts my hair very short and puts me into the uniform of a novice. I live in her room for a month and each day and night she drills me in prayers and catechism. All day I study and Paulina tells me I am studying to save my life. She teaches me to sign myself with the cross, to genuflect before the altar, to use the holy water when I enter the chapel. She tells me, 'Ruth, this can save your life if the Germans ever catch you.' Every morning I go with her to the Mass and I watch her every move carefully. I rise when she rises. I kneel when she kneels. I say the Latin prayers, learn to say the rosary and all the prayers I can, and I pray all the time.

"I stay in this convent for two years. Every day I go to Communion, I sing hymns, I go to confession. But I keep a secret from everybody. When I first came to this convent, I still had my dress with the gold coins hidden beneath the buttons, which Magdalena tells me must be given to the poor. I cannot just give this dress away, because I may need it if something happens. So one night when everyone is asleep I take it to the church that adjoins the convent and I find a side altar in the back of the church where there is a statue of the Virgin Mary. There is a hollow space beneath the statue, and it is there I hide the dress with the coins.

"I come to pray and say my rosary in front of this statue of Mary every day. Paulina and the Mother Superior notice this and think I have a special relationship to the Blessed Virgin, which they like and encourage. I cannot always touch my dress, but sometimes I do when no one else is around, and because I know this cloth was once held by my mother, that each stitch was sewn by this woman I love and will never see again. I am comforted most of the time when I pray to this Mary. I pray to her as Jewish girl to Jewish girl. I say, 'Mary, you are Jewish as I am Jewish and you raised your son to live according to the Jewish law, the same as I am raised. As a Jew, I ask for your help, Mary. I beg of you to help me survive all of this. If any of my family is still alive, please help them and watch over them. I am still a pious Jew and will remain a Jew because it is what I am. Just as it is what you once were. I ask you and your son to protect me. Tell him that I am just a poor Jewish child as you once were. As he was in Nazareth when he grew up the son of a poor carpenter. Please watch over me and Sister Paulina and the other good sisters. If you do anything to Sister Magdalena, I will not care at all, for she is a fearful anti-Semite and I am told she was named after a fallen woman."

"One night after the last prayers in the church, I was praying to Mary when I felt something cold come over me, something bad. Quickly, I bless myself, I rise to return to my tiny room when there is a noise in the corridor leading to the convent.

"Then I see Sister Regina and Sister Paulina with their arms folded just so, where you could not see their hands, coming into the church. Behind them is an SS officer. He is a trim, short man. His uniform strikes a terror in me that I can feel to this day. His face is bloodless and arrogant. I stop and bow my head in obeisance to the Mother Superior.

" '*Jude?*' the German asked me.

" 'No,' I shook my head.

" 'You are a liar like all Jews,' he said.

" 'She is one of us,' Sister Paulina said. 'I grew up with her mother. We were baptized in the same church. Her mother and I were in the same confirmation class.'

" 'Poles lie as frequently as Jews.'

" 'You asked to see the girl,' Sister Regina said. 'Now you have seen her and now you know she is a legitimate member of our order.'

" 'We have received a report that you are hiding Jews,' the man said. 'This girl was specifically denounced.'

" 'She is a Catholic,' Paulina said.

" 'Would you swear that she was born a Catholic?' the SS man asked.

" 'I would swear it,' Sister Paulina said.

" 'You would burn in hell for all eternity to save one Jew,' the man said.

" 'To save any life,' the nun answered, 'I would gladly burn in hell.'

" 'I no longer believe in God or fairy tales,' the German said.

" 'Yet you believe in Hitler,' Paulina observed.

" 'I believe in greater Germany,' he said, his voice and temper rising.

"Sister Regina said, 'There are no Jews here. Your business is elsewhere.'

" 'How long have you been coaching this Jewess?' he asked and he is walking around me now, observing me, sniffing the air as though I will give off some scent that will betray me. I do not think I have ever been so afraid in my life. I could hear my own blood rushing through my ears.

"Then he said to me, 'I once was a seminarian in Berlin. Who was the angel who appeared to Mary telling her she would be the mother of God?'

"The SS man smiles at the two sisters and turns his eyes to me.

" 'It is the angel Gabriel who appears to the Virgin,' I say and I see Paulina smile behind the German.

" 'This event is known as what in the Catholic world?'

" 'The Annunciation, Herr,' I say.

"He asks me to recite all the prayers of the rosary and I recite them word for word. The German asks me to name the twelve Apostles of Christ and I could only name eleven of them. I sing the Latin hymn '*O Salutaris Hostia*' praising the Eucharist for him. I say the Act of Contrition and tell the words I say to the priest when I am in the confessional.

"I am doing so well that I begin to enjoy this testing of my faith. He lulls me into a sense of security . . . of confidence. He becomes a friendly man almost and his eyes soften and I forget he is German or SS. I am concentrating on the questions, which are hard even for a Catholic girl.

"Then he surprises me by asking, 'What does your father do?'

"I do not notice that he asks his question in

Yiddish. Before I could think I hear myself saying, 'He is a rabbi.'

"Behind the man, I saw Sister Regina crossing herself, but Paulina held her hands together with the folds of her habit covering her hands and fingers. The only flesh one could see is her sweet face, which had gone pale. The German is smiling in a very satisfied way. I have been tricked and I know I have not only killed myself but all the nuns and novices in the convent.

" 'We did not know this child was a Jew,' Sister Regina said.

" 'You knew it perfectly well, Sister,' the SS man said. 'I knew it when I saw her. The Jew has a certain look that even a nun's veil cannot hide.'

" 'A Catholic man brought her here,' Regina said. 'Her parents had been killed.'

" 'A nun denounced you at SS headquarters this afternoon. She also told me you had a short-wave radio hidden in the bell tower of this church that is used by the Polish resistance. Is that correct? Do not lie to me again.'

" 'It is correct. We are nuns, but we are also Polish,' Regina said.

" 'The German took my chin in his hand and forced me to stare in his eyes. 'I have seen enough Jews die, so it no longer bothers me. Then why should it bother me if a Jew lives?'

" 'I want the radio removed by tomorrow

morning, Sisters,' the man said. 'The nun who betrayed you is called Magdalena. She told me about the Jew and the radio.'

" 'The radio will be gone,' Regina said. 'May we keep Ruth? She has converted and we think she will make a good nun.'

"As he turned to leave, he said, 'I am a good soldier but a better German. Pray for me, Sisters.'

" 'We will pray for you,' Sister Regina promised.

" 'Pray for me, Jewess,' he said, smiling.

" 'I will also pray for you,' I answered.

"We listened to the click of his heels along the corridor and for a long time we said nothing to each other. The fear had silenced us.

" 'What will we do about Sister Magdelena?' Sister Paulina asked.

" 'She needs to spend some time at the Mother House. Isolation will do her good.'

" 'What if she finds another German officer to tell her story . . . ' Paulina started to ask, but was silenced when Regina raised a hand in warning.

" 'There will be no radio by morning. The right people must be alerted.'

" 'You must forget that you ever knew Yiddish,' Sister Paulina said.

" 'I am sorry I could not name all twelve Apostles, Sister Paulina,' I said.

" 'You forgot Judas,' Paulina said. 'But I hope Magdalena will always remember him.'

"But already, the Polish underground had been searching for a young Jewish girl by my very name whose mother had once come from the Ukrainian town of Kironittska but had drifted across the border into Poland. Two months later a man came to the convent at night to ask me many questions about my past. He told me that an American Jew by the name of Rusoff had paid a great sum of money to smuggle me to safety. I tell him that I have no relatives in America. But Paulina tells me to be quiet, this Rusoff knows many American politicians and must be a very famous and influential man to reach this far into war-torn Poland. Paulina takes a letter the man is holding and says, very surprised, 'Thank God, it is your own uncle Max. He was the brother of your father.' On the back of the letter's envelope is written the address: Max Rusoff, General Delivery, Waterford, South Carolina. I have never heard of this South Carolina until this moment of my life.

"Some more months go by. It is time to leave, and there is a last Mass to celebrate my departure, a High Mass. It is after this Mass at night that I retrieve the dress my mother made for me. The tall Pole comes for me one night. I am ready and all the nuns and the novices are there at my departure. I am carrying a small piece of luggage. Already I have hidden a gold coin under the pillow of Sister Paulina. I hug Regina and the other nuns. I say good-bye to the other novices. They are sweet girls but I do not know them well. After the war, I learn the reason. Almost eighty percent of them are Jewish girls like me and the nuns think it is safer if none of us knows about the others.

"The last thing Paulina says to me is '*Siostra*.' It means 'Sister' in Polish.

"I tell her I love her very much and I say '*Siostra*' to her as I walk out into the wartime city following the tall Pole.

"For many days I travel hidden and underground and then one night I am taken to a fishing boat where I am hidden below the deck. Before he leaves me to my fate, the Pole turns to me and kisses me on both cheeks and wishes me well in America. I never learn his name because in times like this knowledge itself can be dangerous. But he salutes me and he says to me—and I never forget these words as long as I am alive—he says, 'Long live free Poland.'

"Max Rusoff and his good family have ransomed me from the hands of my enemies. Some time later, I get off a ship in this South Carolina and hundreds of strangers are here to greet me. One steps forward. It is Max Rusoff, who is called the Great Jew. Behind him is his wife, Esther. They, who do not know me, embrace me. They, who are not kin to me, raise me up as their daughter. They, who owe me nothing, give me back my life. For me there is no tattoo, no concentration camp. I come out of this not bitter like my husband. I come out thinking there are many good people in the world and that this poor Jewish girl was lucky enough to find them in the middle of a terrible war. That is all. I am done. Telling you this story has been very hard. But it is what happened to me. Every word as I remember it."

I asked in the silence that followed, "Were you wearing the dress your mother made for you when you arrived in America?"

"No," Ruth said. "I had grown too big for it. But I had brought it with me. It had brought me luck during my journey."

"Where is the dress now?"

"By my bedside table. In a drawer," Ruth said to me.

"How many coins were left when you arrived in America? You seemed to have left them with a lot of people."

"Three. There were only three left. The dress was very heavy when I first put it on. It was light when I arrived here in America," she said.

"Shyla's necklace . . ." I asked.

Ruth reached for a gold chain on her throat

and pulled out a necklace that shone in the light. She had made it from one of the remaining five-ruble coins.

"I never take it off. Ever," Ruth said.

"Neither did Shyla," I said. "Until the end."

"My daughter Martha wears the other one. She, too, never takes it off."

"The lady of the coins?" I asked.

"The statue of Mary in the church," Ruth said. "I made the mistake of telling my Shyla that I think it is this lady who saved me. This is what I think to myself. It is here I pray to this lady who hides the coins. I say to Shyla that I think this Mother of Jesus took pity on me. She saw one Jewish girl and I think I reminded Mary of herself as a young girl."

"You think that was the lady that appeared to Shyla?" I asked. "The one she saw in her hallucinations."

"That is what I think, Jack," Ruth said. "If I had not told Shyla this story, maybe my daughter would be with us now. For so long, I feel like I helped kill my Shyla by telling her this."

"I don't think so," I said. "It's kind of nice in a way."

"How? I do not understand."

"Wouldn't it be nice if Mary appeared to Shyla after all the horror of the war? It'd be sweet, Ruth. The Jewish mother of the Christian God apologizing for what happened to a

Jewish girl's parents during the terrible ordeal of the Polish Jews. What a nice thing for the Mother of God to do."

"Such a thing does not happen," Ruth said.

"Too bad," I said. "It should."

"My husband wishes to speak to you soon, Jack," she said.

"About this?"

"He does not tell me."

That night, after Leah and Goerge returned from the Spoleto Festival, we ate dinner with the Foxes. Since Leah was tired, I agreed that she could spend the night with her grandparents and I would pick her up the following morning. She fell asleep while I was reading her a story in Shyla's old bed surrounded by the stuffed animals and teddy bears her mother had once loved. I kissed my daughter softly on the cheek and considered the despair and fury I would feel if this house were filling up below with soldiers who did not mind murdering children. The Jupiter Symphony of Mozart was playing softly downstairs and it was the sound of this music that made me seek out the company of George Fox.

In his first-floor music room, I found George Fox listening to the music, drinking cognac, and lost in reverie. Even in his own house, sitting on his own furniture, George had the haunted, broken look of a fallen angel. He jumped when I approached, and it was only then that I realized that every stranger who approached George Fox was an SS man in disguise. I wanted to say something kind and transfiguring to my father-in-law, but I stood before him wordless.

"You look pale, Jack," George said at last. "Have a glass of cognac with me."

"Ruth lost her whole family. I always knew that. But I really didn't know it at all."

"The story you just heard," George said, looking straight into me, "Ruth blames that story for Shyla's death. But I disagree with her."

"Why?" I asked.

"Because I think what happened to me in Europe killed Shyla. And I never told the whole story to anyone, Jack. No one has heard what happened to me because I thought anyone who heard it would never be able to sleep again or have any peace. You know what I learned, Jack? I learned that a story untold could be the one that kills you. I think Shyla might have died because of what I did not tell her, not what Ruth did. I thought silence was the proper resolution and strategy for what happened to me. I did not think my poisons and hatreds and shame would leak out and poison everything I loved."

"Darkness," I said. "That's the word that comes to me when I hear your name."

"Could I tell you what happened to me, Jack?" George Fox asked, his eyes now looking out toward the river and stars. "Would you listen? Not tonight. But some time soon."

"No," I said. "I don't think I need to hear it. Ruth's story was bad enough."

"There is a reason I would like to tell it to you," he said. "We have never liked each other, Jack. That is the truest thing between us. No?"

"True," I said.

"But you are raising Leah as a Jew. That surprised me."

"I am fulfilling a promise to Shyla."

"But Shyla is dead," George said.

"She's alive enough for me to keep that promise," I said.

"Will you have a cognac?"

"Yes," I said, sitting down, facing my old enemy.

"Will you come back and listen to me?" George started, then said a word that I had never heard him use. "Please."

CHAPTER 31

I TRIED TO OBSERVE HOW THE LOW country worked on Leah's imagination. Since she was new to the territory, I wondered if the lowlands would strike the same notes of authentic magic in her as it had in me. I doubted it had the power to refashion a girl who had grown up subject to the fabulous riot and confusion of Rome, but I had not reckoned with Waterford's quiet stamina of insinuation, the muscular allure of spartina and azalea, storax and redbud. The town took you prisoner and never once considered amnesty or early parole. I witnessed the process as Waterford began to lay its delicate fingerprints on Leah, and I hoped it would place its fingers on her heart and not her throat.

But it was the Isle of Orion that was fixing Leah's destiny.

I used the lagoon in back of our rented house as playground and textbook. When the weather got hot, we crabbed for our dinner with fish heads and chicken necks. I taught Leah that the flesh of the Atlantic blue crab was one of the most extraordinary delicacies in the kingdom of food, and that it was better even than the taste of Maine lobsters. Together, we caught a tubful of crabs and cleaned them on a picnic table in the backyard, the white meat glistening and fragrant with sea water. I taught her to make sea crab soup with fish stock that we spent days reducing. I believe in great, not good, stocks. When we tired of soup, I taught her to make crab cakes using only lumpfin crabmeat bound together with flour and egg whites, then flavored with Chablis, capers, scallions, and cayenne. I did not desecrate my crab cakes with bread crumbs or broken-up crackers. The taste of crab was what I loved. As a cook, I passed all my prejudices on to Leah, and as a rapt student she accepted these opinions and made them her own. Every night we cooked together, creating a bank of memories we would treasure all our lives.

I also taught Leah to roast the perfect

chicken, fry things the Southern way and the Italian way, bake a loaf of bread, compose a salad, put on a barbecue, shuck an oyster in under five seconds, make the best chocolate chip cookies in that part of the world, cook fish in parchment with fresh garlic, ginger, white wine, and soy sauce, and make biscuits that were better than Lucy's. When I was in a kitchen I could no longer feel the pressure of the world on my shoulders; for me cooking has always been a high form of play, and teaching someone how to make a meal memorable was a combination of thrill and gift that I never tired of giving.

On some low tides, I would take Leah to the small creeks at the back of the island and teach her to throw a cast net. I bought her a small net of her own and taught her to wrap the cord around her left wrist, to spread the net with her hands balanced between the weights, and to put the net between her teeth prior to the toss. I told her that the unfolding of a net is like the action of a woman's hoop skirt during the course of a waltz. It was a slow but satisfying way to catch a shrimp dinner. It was a fast way to trap bait.

I showed Leah that there was no inch of land or water without carnage or ambush: everything that lived in the tides was a hunter of some kind. The smallest minnow loomed like a barracuda in the world view of midges and the larvae of blue crabs and mussels.

When we had filled up our buckets with bait, we baited the hooks of our casting rods and fished for spottail bass, flounder, and sheepshead in the incoming tide.

"There's no animal you can't eat," I said one morning as Leah pulled a spottail bass on to the shore. "You can eat this fish raw if you need to."

"I don't need to," she said. "I'll never need to."

"How do you know?"

"I'll be like you when I grow up," she said. "I'll have credit cards."

I laughed.

"Listen to me. I'm very serious. You can eat insects, turtle eggs. You could eat a loggerhead turtle if you had to. Frogs, raccoons, possums. The world of protein's a large and varied one."

"It makes me want to throw up," she said.

"You never know what's going to happen," I said.

I thought about this for a moment before I went on. "Something terrible happens in everybody's life. Something out of the ordinary. I'm trying to raise you to be light on your feet. To be on your toes at all times, ready for the unexpected. You won't be able to prepare for it. It'll always take you by surprise. Like my mother:

she finally divorces my drunken, worthless father, marries a nice man, then gets rabbit-punched from behind with leukemia. It comes at night, when you're sleeping, when your guard is down."

"You shouldn't call your father worthless," Leah admonished. "It's not nice."

"You're the first kid I ever met who could make me feel immature," I said.

"You're mean to your daddy," she said, not looking at me. "All of you are."

"He's also drunk all the time."

"Maybe that's what happens to lonely people."

"You don't know what you're talking about."

"He visits me at school during lunchtime," Leah said. "He's always nice to me and he's never drunk. He's very sweet, Daddy, and I know he wishes you liked him better."

"I wish I liked him better too."

Leah said, "It's your job to like him. He's your daddy."

"You're awfully bossy for someone in elementary school."

"You taught me to be nice to everyone," she answered.

"Let me amend that slightly," I said. "Be nice to everyone except my father."

Leah shook her head sadly. "You're a bad

son. All my uncles are. Except John Hardin. He loves everybody."

"John Hardin doesn't count," I said.

"You don't understand John Hardin," she said. "Just like you don't understand your daddy."

"You're getting awfully big for your britches."

"Why? I'm glad I'm grown-up. Don't you like it?" she asked.

"Not at all. If the truth be known, I'd like to keep you exactly at this age for the rest of your life. I adore you at this exact time of your life. I like being around you ten times as much as I like being around any other person on earth. Though it might seem strange to you, I like you better than anyone else I've met on the planet earth. But like's not strong enough a word. How about 'adore,' 'worship,' 'plumb nuts about,' 'insane over' . . . nothing quite cuts it."

One should never underestimate the power of good teaching, but even bad teaching can have a strong effect. Delia Seignious taught South Carolina history for over forty years to the ninth-graders of Waterford and squelched any passion for history that was budding in the imaginations of her students. There was no area of the subject that she could not render paralyzingly dull. The text was as dry as a logarithm chart and her high-pitched, one-toned voice could induce stupor in the most hardened insomniac. It was one of the town's rites of passage to fall asleep in Mrs. Seignious' history class. Her week-long lecture on the siege of Charleston was so tedious that some students left her class never realizing the siege had ended.

Mrs. Seignious almost grew faint with delight on the first full day of classes in 1962 when she announced to her class that two descendants of some of the most distinguished names in South Carolina history were on her roll of students. She had Capers Middleton and Jordan Elliott stand up to be admired for the good taste they had displayed by being born into such notable families. Capers stood up tall and proud. His face had a chiseled beauty even in ninth grade. But Jordan arose scowling and disoriented in those new surroundings with the other kids regarding him with suspicion as a transfer student with strange ties to royalty.

On the following day, Jordan was tossed from class when he was caught placing wads of Juicy Fruit, to which Delia Seignious was famously "allergic," behind the map of colonial South Carolina. Mrs. Seignious explained to the class that Jordan was high-spirited and mischievous, but he was only following the immutable laws of genetics, since even a fool would know (Mrs. Seignious said this breathlessly) that it took a great deal of high spirits to break away from Mother England. And both Capers and Jordan were related to three South Carolinians who signed the Declaration of Independence. She herself, she added with becoming modesty, was related only to *one* signer of the Declaration.

"Both Mr. Middleton and Mr. Elliott come from fine, old, distinguished South Carolina families. One might ask what difference it could possibly make, but experience teaches it makes all the difference in the world. You can tell by the line of the jaw of both these young men that they descend from men and women who placed righteousness above mere glitter, justice above mere retribution, and elegance above the showy or the meretricious. You know what you're getting when you do business with a Middleton or an Elliott. Their character is set. Their breeding impeccable. Have sons, Capers. Have sons, Jordan. You must not allow these splendid South Carolina names to die out and be relegated into the boneyards of history. We will be studying the writings and exploits of your distinguished ancestors this year and both of you will walk taller when you apprehend the value of the fine stock from which you issue.

Every daughter you have will be a great name lost and cause for sorrow. Every son will be a name-carrier."

Mike made gagging sounds behind Jordan and whispered, "Hey, name-carrier. Can I borrow some Juicy Fruit after I puke?"

Jordan passed him a stick of Juicy Fruit, then shot Mike the finger. Mike said after class, "One can tell from the line of my dick that I'm descended from one of the most distinguished bagel makers on the Upper West Side."

"Have sons, Mike. Have sons," I cried out happily.

"I'd rather watch a jockstrap mildew than listen to that woman's voice," Jordan said. But Mrs. Seignious had found her champion in Capers and he defended both her pedagogy and the content of her course to all comers.

"It's important to know where you've come from," Capers said.

"Why?" I asked. "What possible difference could it make? America's a democracy. Everyone gets a fair shake."

"Nonsense," Jordan said. "Half this town's black. Tell me the color of your skin doesn't make a difference in this stupid part of the country."

"Their time will come," Capers predicted. "They haven't earned it yet."

"You sound like such an idiot, Capers," Jordan said. "You're talking like you're a hundred years old and you're only in ninth grade. You believe everything your parents believe."

"I have more respect for my parents than any two people on earth," Capers said. "I owe everything to them."

"You're the unhippest, uncoolest kid I've ever met, man," Jordan said, appraising his cousin with a clear, unstinting California eye. "You're lucky you were born so deep in the sticks. Your show would close in a week out on the West Coast."

"You're calling me a square, aren't you?" Capers demanded.

"It's far worse than that," said Jordan. "You're square root, man. You're the kind of guy that likes to wear socks at the beach."

"Maybe I'm just proud of who I am."

"Maybe you're just a Southern asshole," Jordan shot back.

"Have sons, Capers. Have sons, Jordan," I said, trying to cut the tension between them.

Mike said, "This course'll help me when I write my memoirs, *Jewboy in the Confederacy*. Do you think Mrs. Seignious ever heard of Ellis Island? It's just a hop, skip, and a jump down from Plymouth Rock."

"South Carolina history," Jordan said, shaking his head. "What a contradiction in terms. I've lived all over the world and I've never heard one person ever mention this state's name. It's nowhere, man. A loser state if there ever was one. Nothing's ever happened here."

"The state of South Carolina seceded from the Union first," Capers bristled. "We fired on Fort Sumter and were the first to answer the call to arms."

"Then the North came down and kicked your Confederate asses from Richmond to Vicksburg."

"We gave as good as we got. Our generalship was superb," said Capers, moving toward a relaxed Jordan with clenched fists.

"One never reads about Lee's March on New York, but one does come across Sherman's March to the Sea. I've studied Civil War battlefields with my father, Capers. I know a lot more about this subject than you do."

"You're not a true Southerner," Capers announced.

"I'm an American, pal, and proud of it."

"Your family arrived in the New World in seventeen- ought-nine. Mine came here in seventeen-ought-six. What went wrong with you?" Capers asked.

"When did your family get here, Jack?" Mike asked facetiously.

"Nineteen-ought-eight. Something like that," I said, laughing, and Capers thought the laughter was directed at him. "How about your family, Mike?"

"Very early, my family," Mike said. "They arrived on these virgin shores the same year the Edsel was introduced in Detroit."

"Have sons. Have sons," Mike and I sang together, laughing in each other's arms.

For another class, Delia Seignious read a chapter from William Elliott's 1859 book, *Carolina Sports by Land and Water.* Her reading voice was as monotonous as the sound of a running toilet. Half the class was asleep and the other half daydreaming while Delia labored to bring life to the serviceable prose of Jordan's great-grandfather and Capers' great-great-uncle on his mother's side. Delia read the first chapter, the showcase feature of the book that had once dazzled Yankee fishermen, in which the Honorable Mr. Elliott describes the pursuit of the great manta ray, or devilfish, through the waters of Waterford Sound. Only Delia Seignious, with her genius for monotony, could have rendered the hunt for the two-ton manta ray with its great black-backed wings and bat-shaped body to a colorless tale whose words settled over her class like a sleeping powder. She could make the "Charge of the Light Brigade" sound like the directions for folding a napkin in a debutante's handbook. When Mr. Elliott placed a harpoon near the spine of a devilfish and the enormous creature towed his slave-powered boat through the choppy waters off Hilton Head, the soft snoring of cheerleaders and football players intermingled and I felt the sweat soak through the back of my shirt. Great heat and mediocre teaching have done much to lower the collective IQ of the South over the centuries.

But one of her students listened to her with breathless attention and drank in every word she uttered. For Capers Middleton, what Delia Seignious offered up from the dusty granary of her knowledge played a central part in his image of himself and his world. He not only felt a close personal connection to South Carolina history, he thought of his own life as an enhancement and extension of it. From the day of his birth, he had enjoyed a highly developed sense of entitlement and privilege that had accrued to him through the accomplishments of his ancestors.

That Christmas, Capers received from his parents a first-edition copy of *Carolina Sports by Land and Water.* The book thrilled Capers with its spirited accounts of fishing and hunting expeditions that had taken place in a less-populated, pre–Civil War low country. The land Elliott described was a green paradise teeming with game and fish. Capers made a spiritual connection with William Elliott and hunted the same animals his ancestor had hunted and fished for the same fish at the exact same locations so lovingly described by this energetic forebear.

Capers' father commissioned a black metalworker from Charleston, who was expert in the repair of wrought-iron fences, to fashion a harpoon for Capers exactly like the one wielded by William Elliott when he took to the channel and sounds in search of the great manta rays. Capers held this weapon and imagined the wild, dangerous rides that ensued after one of the enormous beasts was harpooned and turned in agony toward the high seas. He called upon the spirits of his ancestors when he tracked bobcat or white-tailed deer through the vast acreage of old rice plantations. He designed a secret task for himself: he wanted to kill every fish and animal that William Elliott had named in his book.

In 1964, Jordan's father, now a full colonel, would be sent to a top-secret assignment overseas in a country called Vietnam. At that time none of us had ever heard of Vietnam.

Celestine Elliott took a home on the Point three blocks away from my house and a block away from both Capers and Mike. That summer we were inseparable. It was also the sum-

mer that Mike, Jordan, and I wished we had
paid more attention in Delia Seignious' South
Carolina history course.

In April, on every Sunday, Capers had been
borrowing his father's eighteen-foot Renken
fishing boat and taking to the river for an all-
day fishing trip. All of us were competitive fishermen who took great pride in our gear and
tackle; we changed baits and lures frequently as
conditions changed and teased each other re-
lentlessly as we went from oyster bank to deep
drop in our pursuit of game fish. We baited our
hooks with iced-down eels, then cast them in
front of the great swishing forms of cobia hunting along the surface. The cobia were torpedo-
shaped and powerful and they were my favorite
fish to cook and eat at a campfire.

Capers' harpoon had proved a symbolic but
useless gift. During a flounder gigging trip on a
moonless night, he had tried to use the harpoon to gig the flounder exposed in the soft
mud flats and sandbars by the light of a lantern
on a johnboat. We would let the boat drift over
shallow water and take turns gigging flounder
that had buried themselves in sand to await
prey passing overhead. The flounder's silhouette was as distinctive as a pretty woman's profile in a cameo. A three-pronged gig brought
the flounder into the boat cleanly. Capers' harpoon was so large that the fish was mutilated

and its flesh ruined by the blow. Once Capers
used the harpoon to land a fifty-pound sand
shark, but even then it proved too much
weapon for not enough fish. And so it lay unused that summer in the gunwale of the boat
tied to a hundred feet of thick marine rope.
From time to time Capers would justify its remaining there by reminding Jordan that the descendants of William Elliott never went to sea
unprepared for any emergency. But there were
too many fish to catch with regular tackle and
we even landed a cobia weighing over forty
pounds. I cooked those cobia steaks over a
campfire with corn oil, butter, and lemon juice,
and that became the first recipe I ever sold to a
newspaper.

In the first week of August, Mike hit a triple
off the wall at College Park in Charleston, driving in three runs and winning the Lower State
Championship for the Waterford American Legion Team. Capers had been on third, I was on
second, and Jordan on first when Mike teed off
on the first pitch by the Conway relief pitcher.
The four of us were growing strong together,
coming into our season as athletes at the same
time. When Jordan pitched, nothing was safe if
the ball went to the outfield where Mike played
a swift left field and Capers covered an amazing amount of ground in center and no one
dared test my now-legendary throwing arm in

right. Jordan knew we played a cunning outfield; little got by us, nothing through us, and
we always hit the cutoff man.

After the baseball season was over, we
moved into my family's fishing camp on the
southwest side of the Isle of Orion for the rest
of the summer.

During the first week, we loaded the Middletons' eighteen-foot Renken with extra tanks
of gas, chose a day of superb calm and a
weather report that called for nothing but clear
skies, then struck out with our seventy-five
horsepower motor for the Gulf Stream. The
older fishermen spoke of the Gulf Stream in
reverential tones as a great secret indigo river
born in the South bringing a warm current and
the traffic of marlin and whales toward the
North Star and England. Out there the waters
were silver or cobalt blue and the fish weighed
as much as automobiles. All fishermen who returned from the Gulf Stream told stories of
wonder and exhaustion about the strength of
the great fish coaxed up from the depths.

It took us an hour to get to the open sea
and we had told no one of our plans because
no adult would have allowed such a long trip in
such a small boat. Before sunrise, we had
passed the last buoy marking the channel opening. The sea was lakelike as the first light hit it
and the bow of our boat was pointed in the

direction of Africa. We felt as adventurous as though our destination actually was Cameroon or the Ivory Coast. In a cooler, we had packed enough food and drink to last for two days. We were averaging twenty knots as we got farther and farther away from the sight of land.

"My mama would kill my Jewish ass if she knew where I was right this minute," Mike said, as he scanned the horizon and saw only an endless circle of water. "She thinks that I'm crabbing for my dinner with chicken necks as we speak."

"We should've brought a radio," Jordan said.

"Low country boys don't need no radios," Capers said, keeping his eye on the compass and the boat pointed due east. "We were born in the pluff mud with gills and flippers. Man, I was born to go out to the Gulf Stream."

"We don't need radios, California boy," I teased, "because we've got gonads big as Goodyear blimps."

"You've got brains the size of houseflies," said Jordan, surveying the ocean around him. "Lucky this is such a pussy ocean. You wouldn't stick your big toe in the Pacific without a radio."

"They didn't have any radios on the *Mayflower*," Capers said. "Columbus couldn't call back to chat with Ferdinand. Nothing to fear, the master mariner's here."

"Nobody knows we're out here," Jordan said.

"The guy at the marina knows we're going on a trip," I said. "We filled up six tankfuls of fuel."

"We couldn't go if we told our parents," Capers said.

"My folks would have a cow if they knew I was out here," I said.

Capers called over the sound of the engine, "It might drive your father to drink."

I ignored the remark and looked back at where land was supposed to be.

"I could never be wild enough for my father," Jordan said. "I could drive up to Spartanburg, impregnate every girl at Converse College, and my father would still think I was a faggot."

Before we reached the Gulf Stream, we arrived at a vast acreage of sargassum, the grasslands of the North Atlantic that formed a drifting archipelago of brown seaweed, which was more chlorophyll-rich than Kansas. It was the first sign that we were nearing the Gulf Stream itself. In earth science class, our teacher, Walter Gnann, had drawn a chart of the Gulf Stream as it flowed out of the Gulf of Mexico and went up the coast of Florida. Mr. Gnann was one of those introspective scientists who believed that nature simply proved the amplitude and mathematical genius of God. With the Gulf Stream, Mr. Gnann could talk about weather patterns, the movement of fish and plant life from the Caribbean to the coast of South Carolina, and a natural application of the Coriolis force, the curved angle of lines drawn straight across a spinning surface. The earth spun on its axis, the moon pulled the waters with its puppeteer hands, and the Gulf Stream moved like a secret, warm-water Nile through the heart of the Atlantic keeping England from being a snow-bound kingdom. The Gulf Stream brought good news from the South to the cold, inhospitable countries of Europe, a love letter sent out of Southern waters to melt icebergs in the shipping lanes near Greenland.

The water changed when we entered the Gulf Stream itself, becoming a jewel-like blue that looked as if it flowed out of the heart of some stone not native to the region. The water was clean-looking and moving swiftly as a mountain river. As low country boys we found clear water to be deeply disturbing. As soon as the Renken entered the stream itself the color of the water went from dark to light blue. Once Capers looked down to see we were floating in two hundred feet of water. Glancing down at the depth-finder a few minutes later, Capers was stunned to find the ocean's depth had plummeted to a thousand feet. He reported this fact to the rest of us and we whistled in disbelief.

"You can drown in three feet of water as easy as a thousand," said Jordan, trying to relieve the sense of awe that had seized everyone on the boat. All of us hovered around the depth-finder, thumping it with our fingers to see if it were giving a false reading.

Mike said, "Yeh, but they've got a better chance of finding you in three feet of water. What kind of fish grows in water that deep?"

"Big mothers," Capers said.

"Anything that wants to," Jordan added. "You've got to be able to kick some ass when you hitch a ride north on the Gulf Stream."

"We might see some whales," I said.

Jordan said, "We should've brought a radio."

Capers laughed and said, "Radios are for pussies. Let's bait up."

I took over the wheel and turned the bow of the boat northward, adjusting it to trolling speed after taking the flow of the current into account. I loved the business of fishing, the beauty and efficiency of the tackle, the tying of elegant knots, the testing of the line, and the selection of the proper bait for the right conditions. It pleased me to watch my friends as they studied the contents of their well-organized tackle boxes before they made their choices for the moment they would cast their lines into these fabled waters. A half-moon rested in the western sky, a pale watermark left by the night before. I thought I saw birds skimming low across the water and then realized I was seeing my first flying fish. Their faces were doglike, earnest, and they had the wings of bad angels. Though I knew nothing of their habits, I guessed these fish flew because they were being pursued by something huge and deadly beneath them.

"Hell, let's get some baitfish," Mike said. "I'm not sure these artificial lures will attract the big fish out here worth a damn."

"Good idea," I said and turned the boat back toward shore, going a couple of miles before we found a spot near a great expanse of sargassum that looked promising. We anchored the boat, then dropped our lines deep, baited with cut mullet and shrimp. Floating in that perfectly still ocean, it was as though we were trapped in the reflection of the earth's image of itself. The gardens of sargassum were alive with fish and we used our smaller rods with twenty-pound test lines. Within twenty minutes Capers had put a hook through a small dolphin fish, while Mike and Jordan caught the more pedestrian mullet. In low voices we talked about the depth each one of us would fish once we returned to deep waters. It was agreed that Capers would fish deepest and that Jordan and Mike would troll from the side of the boat, one at fifty feet, the other at the surface. We checked the gaffe, the resiliency of our bigger rods, and discussed protocol if someone tied into a fish. I gave them the word when we entered the Gulf Stream once again and began calling out the depth as we entered deeper and deeper water.

"You've got too much line there," Mike said to Capers, who always came with more expensive equipment than the rest of us. His Plano tackle box overflowed with hooks and lures he had never used, but Capers was a flamboyant, competitive fisherman. He measured success by size and number. Since he was on his first trip to the Gulf Stream, he wanted to come back with a game fish and nothing less would do.

"Fifty-pound test line," Capers announced proudly.

"You could pull up an alligator with that," I yelled back to him.

"I'm putting my peanut dolphin down deep."

"What're we fishing for?" Mike asked. "I don't even know what I'm supposed to catch."

"We're trading up," said Jordan.

"Trophies," Capers said. "Things to put on our walls."

For a half-hour I cruised along, mesmerized by the circle of water around me and the circle of sky above that seemed made of one color and one substance. Only the sound of the boat seemed incongruent and unwelcome. I felt the wordless ingathering of harmony that comes when you strike out alone and enter into the cathedral-like silence of nature far removed from cities. For a brief moment, the noise of the motor had disappeared, expunged by the vastness and silkiness of an Atlantic that was initiating us to its depths with a perfect stillness. My three friends disappeared from my consciousness as I was sure I had disappeared from theirs.

Then, something took the dolphin, something large, something running far below. Jordan and Mike reeled in their lines, I cut the motor, and the three of us took up positions to watch Capers test his inland water skills as a fisherman of the Gulf Stream. Though Capers was always accused of using too much rod, he was not using too much for this fish. The fish had taken the hook and almost took the rod away from him as it made its first run, but Capers played it beautifully. The line sang off his reel and Capers let it go, enjoying the fact that he was onstage performing for his friends. We all watched the line playing out at an alarming rate as Capers began applying the slightest, most delicate bit of drag.

"What does it feel like?" Mike asked.

"Like I've hooked a locomotive," Capers answered.

He played the fish well, but it was a fish of great strength and heart and fighting spirit.

"I want to see this fish," Jordan said, after fifteen minutes of the contest had passed by without bringing it near the surface. By now the sweat glistened on Capers' face and chest and on the hairs on his legs.

"You'll have plenty of time to see it," Capers said. "I'm going to catch the son of a bitch."

"It might be too big to bring into the boat," I said. "Who knows what it is. It could be a mako or a great white."

"You forgot about my harpoon," Capers said, his voice strained as he fought the fish standing straight up. "Get it ready."

I pulled the harpoon out from under the bow of the boat and lifted the leather protective cover from the blade. Taking a whetstone from Capers' tackle box I sharpened its edges until I saw a wicked smile of new silver running the length of the blade. I touched the blade and drew a line of blood on my thumb. Mike brought out a rope and tied one end to the harpoon and the other to a stanchion in the boat.

Then we saw the fish. All of us had caught large fish during our careers on the water. But none of us were prepared for the size of the blue marlin that came leaping out of the water fifty yards behind the boat. I felt a sudden rush of joy and clarity as the marlin, in the full extension of its soaring leap into sunshine, took us into new realms. It was our first encounter with fish as myth, as nightmare, as beast.

We whooped in amazement, but Capers was too exhausted to make any noise at all. He felt a surge of adrenaline course through his body, easing the terrible aching of the muscles in his back, shoulders, and arms. His whole body fought the fish with all the cunning of a low country boy who had spent a lifetime landing spottail bass, king mackerel, and migrating blues. But I doubt whether all the fish Capers had ever caught would equal the astonishing weight of this one fierce and acrobatic marlin. It leapt again and danced across the still water on its great forked tail, agile as a ballerina, then fell into the sea like a small plane crashing near our boat.

We all whistled in awe.

"We can't bring him on the boat," I said.

"Bullshit," Capers cried out in a voice that did not sound like his own.

"It's bigger than the boat," I explained.

"We'll kill it with the harpoon," Mike said.

"Jack's right," Jordan said. "It could sink us."

"We'll tie it to the boat," Capers whispered.

"I've already read that book, man," Mike said. "That's *Old Man and the Sea* shit. We'll be fighting off the sharks all night."

"We've got a motor," I said. "We could make it back okay, I guess."

"Capers ain't caught it yet," said Jordan. "That fish isn't looking tired. It's just warming up."

"Want one of us to take over, pal?" Mike asked.

"It's my fish," Capers said. "I'm bringing it in by myself."

"That's the spirit that made our country great," I said sarcastically.

"You look like you're dying," Jordan said. "Mike was just trying to help."

"This could be a record," Capers gasped. "It won't count if anyone helps land the fish."

"We'll lie," I suggested. "We'll all swear on a stack of Bibles that you brought it in yourself."

"I believe in rules," Capers said, his shirt

drenched in sweat. "Rules are a form of discipline. They have their own reason for existing."

The three of us broke out in mock applause for Capers' speech.

"Laugh now, losers," Capers said. "But you'll read my name in *Sports Illustrated* after they weigh this baby back at the marina."

"Because you were so nasty about it," Mike said, "I'm gonna claim I helped reel in this fish."

"Me too."

"Same here," I agreed.

"You can all kiss my ass," Capers said. "My word's good in Waterford. I've got three hundred years of Middleton honesty backing me up."

Then the marlin made another long, deep run and the line sang off the reel again. It suddenly went slack and Capers began reeling in madly, his right hand moving in a blur as the fish shot up out of the depths for what would be another spectacular leap into the air. I could see the pain lining Capers' face and how he had lost his concentration because of it. The muscles in his hands and fingers were cramping and Capers shook one hand into the air, trying to get the circulation flowing again to put out the fiery spasms that were spreading along the nerves and muscles leading up his arm. As he once more frantically reeled in the line the marlin reversed its course and dove with all its mighty strength toward the bottom of the sea. When the line broke, the four of us groaned in one voice.

"Son of a bitch. Son of a bitch," Capers cried out feebly, as he reeled in the weightless line. His voice was despairing and he screamed out at the calm ocean, then hurled his rod and reel as far as he could throw it into the sea. It landed with a splash that seemed meaningless after the marlin's spectacular reentry into the water.

Watching Capers' bereft expression I waited breathlessly for him to break down and weep in sheer frustration, but instead he dove straight down off the stern of the boat into the water. He was underwater for a full twenty seconds before he emerged, took a breath, then plunged downward toward the bottom again.

When he returned to the surface, Jordan said, "I don't think you can catch him that way, Capers. He's probably halfway to Africa by now."

"I'll never hook another fish like that again in my life," Capers said as he treaded water. "A man only gets one chance in his life to catch a fish that big."

"What fish?" Mike said. "I didn't see a fish."

"You sorry son of a bitch," Capers said.

"Why don't you get in the boat?" I asked.

Capers shook his head and said, "I can't lift my arms."

"No wonder that fish got away," Mike said, extending a hand to Capers in the water. But Capers was too tired to even reach up to Mike, who leaned way down to the water and grabbed him under the armpits and motioned to me for help. As Capers moaned in pain, we lifted him out of the Atlantic.

Capers slumped into a seat, spent, worn-out, limp.

"All my life I've gotten everything I've wanted," he said. "Everything. Great parents, perfect grades. I'm the one who gets the hit in the ninth inning, scores the winning touchdown, takes the last shot. The prettiest girls write me notes in school. I've been elected class president every year since the third grade. Now this. Lost. Defeated. Fucked. I never wanted anything more than I did to catch that fish."

"Maybe the fish didn't know who you were," Jordan offered. "Hell, if that fish knew about the grades and the pretty girls, he'd have just jumped on into this boat."

"That was the biggest fish I ever saw," I said. "How much you think it weighed? I bet a thousand pounds."

"Naw," Mike said. "More like a hundred."

"Not an ounce more than fifty," Jordan

said. "Fish look bigger out here in the Gulf Stream."

"Sons of bitches," Capers said, his eyes closed. "The only thing I need in life is a better set of friends."

For another half-hour we trolled the Gulf Stream before we began to worry about the amount of fuel we were consuming and the small chance we had of making another strike. We decided to head back toward shore, stopping to bottom-fish near some of the heavier concentration of sargassum. Where there was seaweed, there was bound to be a profusion of sea life. When we came to a drop near what appeared to be a canyon wall of sargassum, Jordan threw out the anchor into the seaweed itself and its flanges hooked into the dense undersea jungle. While the rest of us changed tackle and baited hooks, Capers crawled up under the gunwale away from the heat of the sun and instantly fell asleep. His disappointment was still so bitter and recent that we thought it wiser to let Capers sleep off the marlin's fabulous memory than to coax him into fishing for red snapper.

We took turns rubbing each others' shoulders and backs with a combination of baby oil and Mercurochrome. Stripping down to our bathing suits, we glistened with sweat and oil as we let our lines out and fished the bottom with cut bait. Before we broke for lunch we had caught a string of fifteen grouper, the largest of which we estimated was twenty pounds.

For lunch we opened bags of potato chips, peanut M&M's, Hostess cupcakes, and cans of Vienna sausages. We snapped off the tops of Coca-Colas and root beers and talked quietly so as not to disturb the deep sleep of Capers, who had not moved a single muscle of his body. Our lunch was an infallible combination of the worst foods produced in America and it all tasted great. Jordan talked about trolling an artificial lure on the trip home that he heard had drawn the spirited attention of king mackerel near an artificial reef off the coast of Charleston. We spoke dreamily about fish, sports, girls, yet later could not remember a single specific of that conversation.

Taking our time, we gathered up all the trash and put it into a single bag. Capers was still sleeping too soundly to wake. I was sharpening my hook and Jordan was getting ready to cast when Mike said, "Let's fish here for just an hour, then head back to shore. We'll make sure we've got plenty of daylight when we head back."

"We've got plenty of time," I said, now tying the hook on to my lure.

"We're on a sandbar," Jordan said, looking down at his line.

"No way, José," Mike said. "This is the middle of the Atlantic. Sandbars won't be a problem until we get back to the sound."

I cast my line out near Jordan's and instantly saw that something was wrong. My bait had landed on a sandy bottom.

"I can see my bait," I said.

"I can see my bait on the bottom too," Jordan said.

"We're over sixty feet at least," Mike said, checking the depth-meter.

"Then how come we're both looking at our bait?" Jordan asked.

"We're in three feet of water, Mike," I said.

"I still read sixty feet."

"Read what you want," Jordan said. "Come look."

Mike walked to the back of the boat, shaking his head and swaggering as he pulled the bill of his baseball cap low over his forehead. He adjusted his sunglasses, then lifted them off so he could see into the water with less distortion.

"I see your baits," he said. "They are on the bottom . . ."

Then Jordan and I both heard Mike's voice freeze and we could feel his fear spreading like a fatal toxin in the air between us.

"Jesus Christ. Reel your lines in slow, boys. So slow that it can't feel a thing. Don't move.

Don't breathe. Don't do shit but slowly get your hooks away from that big son of a bitch."

"What is it?" Jordan whispered. "The marlin?"

"I don't know what the hell it is, but it could eat that marlin. My God, it just keeps on going. I've never seen anything so big in my whole life. Never."

We reeled our lines in slowly, with imperceptible movements of the wrists, and the light off the water made the water diamond-backed and opaque. Whatever Mike saw we could not yet see. When we set our rods down, we sank to our knees beside Mike and peered into the depths. Yet again, it looked as though we had drifted above a sandbar composed of the blackest parts of the sea and the earth. The black bottom we were over was alien and strange, but I still could not see what had alarmed Mike so much. Then Jordan spotted it and gasped in amazement.

"My God in heaven," he said. "Don't move a muscle, Jack. I see it, Mike. I see it. It's huge."

"I don't see nothing at all," I said, frustrated that I was looking at the exact same area that Jordan was. It was like one of those children's puzzles with the animals hidden in the foliated shapes of the forests—and then my eyes adjusted to what I was actually seeing.

Slowly, it became clear that what I thought was land was alive. Not only was it alive, I was staring at the largest sea creature I had ever seen. It wasn't swimming, it was hovering the way ospreys and kingfishers hover over lagoons before diving down for mullet. To my left I saw the delicate movement of a wing that must have weighed a ton. To my right, I saw a black fin break the surface of the water, then slide back beneath the water's barely ruffled surface.

"I've seen one of these things before," I said. "It's a manta ray. A devilfish. The biggest one in the world. They're harmless, just don't move a muscle. Call Delia Seignious."

When I was eight years old I had been taken out to fish the wreck of the *Brunswick Moon,* which had sunk off the Isle of Orion during the hurricane of 1893. My father and grandfather had brought me as a rite of passage; I was being initiated in the habits and folkways of men. My grandfather Silas taught me how to find the wreck by placing our boat in the center of six palmettos that sat to the right of a bent live oak on shore. I remembered that day not so much for the fish we had caught, but for the stories I heard the two men tell and the feeling that adulthood was a club and an entitlement. While we were coming back from that fishing trip we encountered a school of manta rays playing in the channel that led to the small port in Waterford.

Whether the manta rays were engaged in a mating ritual or frolicked for the sheer joy of play was never clear, but I knew that my father and grandfather felt as awed by this gathering of giants that day as I was. The rays frolicked with such enthusiasm that they made the water around them seem storm-tossed. It was like watching dark fields suddenly spring to life, new acreage at play. The shape of the mantas was bestial, demon-winged and massive. The school could have been mistaken for a feeding frenzy among tiger sharks lost in a maze of chum and blood. But what I remembered was how frisky they were, like spaniels, with each other, capable of great horseplay and affection. They leapt out of the water and played tag like overactive children released from a strict day-care center. The ocean was turbulent with their size and exuberance, and for an hour we had followed the manta rays as they performed their great and inexplicable dance along the coastal waters of South Carolina. Though huge, none of the mantas that day approached the immensity of the creature that hovered like a black, birdlike chimera three feet below us. It could have been asleep; it could have been watching us out of curiosity. The manta ray's mouth looked large enough to swallow our eighteen-foot Renken whole. The boat that had always seemed solid and seaworthy to me now seemed as fragile as a balsa raft.

"I'm going to try to hook this baby," I said, recovering my composure. "I hear they love shrimp."

I reached for my pole, but Jordan grabbed my wrist hard and held it. "I was joking," I said. "Do you think I'm an idiot?"

"You don't joke about something that big," Jordan said.

Then we heard Mike scream and turned around just in time to see Capers Middleton, the great-great nephew of William Elliott, raising his harpoon into the sunlight and throwing it powerfully toward the spine of the great manta ray. Neither Jordan nor I had time to utter a single word of alarm or caution—we saw the blade of the harpoon slashing through the air, then we were pitched forward as the manta ray came hurtling out of the water and over our boat. Looking up after my head hit the boat's railing, I saw the creature's white underbelly pass over the boat like some biblical angel of death after the expulsion from Paradise. A terrible breaking of metal interlocked with our terrified screams as the harpoon rope tangled with the motor and tore it off as though it were made of wax. We almost capsized as the rope swept along the length of the boat, and if any of us had been standing, it would have decapitated us in an instant. It tore the windshield off as though it were made of bread. The next thing we knew the boat was being dragged through the water at a speed that seemed enormous.

For several minutes, Jordan and I lay shaken next to each other, disoriented among the debris in the bottom of the boat. My left eyebrow was cut open and blood was streaming down my face. A hook had pierced Jordan's cheek and, in agony, he was trying to work it out. Mike and Capers lay still and blood was pooling beneath Capers' head. The sun was still high and I estimated that it must be nearing three o'clock in the afternoon. I could not believe how fast we were hurtling through the ocean without a motor. Before I rose, I tried to figure in my mind how large the fish was that passed over us in the agony of its first leap. Its shadow had cut the sun like an eclipse, and its shape was unearthly. I moved toward Mike and realized he was seriously hurt. A piece of broken bone was sticking out of an ugly wound on his forearm.

"Mike, you, oh, God," I cried out.

Then I heard a strangled sound and saw Jordan pointing to his mouth and the hook. I struggled toward Jordan and worked the hook until I saw it come out of the bloody soft tissue near Jordan's lower molars. Taking the hook I pulled it out the front of his mouth. Then reaching into my own tackle box, I took out a first-aid kit and rubbed the wounded cheek down with raw alcohol and again heard Jordan scream out in pain.

"We're in deep shit," I said.

"Help me throw Capers overboard," Jordan said, holding his cheek. "We're in this pickle because he's a dumb-ass."

"He didn't know," I said, trying to clean Jordan's face and keep my eyes away from Mike's broken arm.

"That thing could have killed all of us."

"Give it time," I said.

"Why did he throw that harpoon?"

"Because he lost the marlin," I guessed.

Jordan shook his head and said, "No. I bet he thought he was being true to the aristocratic spirit of our Elliott ancestors. Those family ties've screwed our boy up. He'd rather kill a Yankee at Antietam, but spearing a devilfish is the next best thing. He might've just killed all four of us."

"They'll come looking for us," I said, trying to be reassuring. "Waterford's got a great Marine Rescue Squad."

"They don't know where in the hell to look," Jordan said. "They think we're crabbing in one of the creeks, reading back issues of

Playboy magazine. It's gonna be a leap for them to know we're being towed out to sea by a two-ton manta ray."

We then placed life preservers beneath Mike's and Caper's heads; both were still unconscious. We climbed to the bow of the boat and studied the taut rope that disappeared into the sea thirty yards in front of us. The harpoon must have driven itself deep into that black-muscled wing and it occurred to me that the beast was simply fleeing like any grazing animal surprised by hunters and enduring unimaginable pain. The manta ray was trying to escape from our boat. That much was clear as the wind blew through our hair and the sun bore down on our faces and wounds, which stung every time the bow broke through a wave of a now-rising sea.

Later, we would talk about the things we should have done in those first minutes, but both Jordan and I were still in shock at the violence and suddenness of what had overtaken our fishing trip. We took no pleasure in the joyride by the great fish, but simply rode it out passively in a Zen-like state, subsumed by the awesome power of the unseen and the ineffable. One moment of sheer recklessness had placed us in great peril and we watched, witnesses to our own executions, as our fate played itself out in the water beneath us. But we could also feel the terror and the panic of the immense manta as it tore through the ocean with the blade driven into its flanks. We thought that we might soon die, and though we sat shoulder to shoulder on the boat, I felt as though I were taking that ruined, wild ride alone. We offered each other no sense of companionship or fraternity.

For twenty miles the manta ray dragged the boat through surf that grew increasingly rough. As a wind arose from the east, the animal began to slow down, no doubt from exhaustion and loss of blood. I wondered if we would be dragged down to the bottom of the sea when the giant manta died, and it was only then that I said, "Should we untie the rope?" to no one in particular.

"We'll have to cut it loose from that front cleat," Jordan said, still holding his hand over his cheek.

Then suddenly the rope slackened in the water and I thought that the manta ray had managed to free itself from the harpoon. But within seconds the manta came roaring out of the water in its full monstrous glory like some forgotten behemoth from the mythology of a lost continent. It was winged and titanic as it took to the air and flapped its wings like some fierce prehistoric bird. Its leap took us by surprise and we nearly fell off the side of the boat when it hit the water with a thunderous clap that could have been heard for miles. Frightened, we eased down into the seats of the boat and held on tightly as the manta ray executed a series of leaps. It rose out of the water again, then again, like some new species of death and darkness that fear had fashioned for its leisure.

Then the manta ray reversed its course and began coming toward the boat. Mike screamed in pain as he awoke, but we were so transfixed watching the rope go slack again, suspended in an agony of anticipation as we awaited the sounding of the great fish, that we did not respond. Mike was still screaming when the manta ray left the water, coming out toward and over us, the white belly passing over and blocking the sun once more, eradicating all hope of our deliverance and eventual safety. The boat seemed puny in the shadow of the wounded beast, and if the manta ray had landed on top of it, it would have crushed all four of us as easily as if we had been the larvae of eels. But the manta twisted away, somersaulted in midair, and loosed itself from the harpoon, snapping the rope at the same instant. Its left wing smashed down on the starboard side of the boat, and as the craft dipped into the sea we took in water before it suddenly righted itself.

Jordan and I began bailing with the Dixie

cups that lay scattered all over the boat. Bailing with two hands and cups, it seemed forever before the boat was mostly clear of water. Only then could we turn to Mike, whose moaning was dreadful to hear.

Jordan set Mike's broken arm as best he could, wrapping it tightly with rags torn from a tee shirt and waterproof tape from one of the tackle boxes. He checked on Capers and washed out the deep wound at the back of his head, guessing out loud that Capers had a concussion. He even offered to sew up the ugly gash that ran across my eyebrow, but I demurred.

We drifted that night, heavy with sun and exhaustion, into a dreamless sleep that resembled unconsciousness. It felt as deep as the sea itself.

I was already up when Capers awoke and the first light seeped out of the eastern horizon. Though still dazed and unsteady, he took in the sleeping figures around him, touched his head wound several times, and surveyed the condition of the boat.

"What in the hell did you boys do to my father's boat?" he said in a loud voice.

"Go back to sleep, Capers," I said.

"What'd you do to the motor?" Capers said. "Oh my God, my father's gonna kill you guys when he sees what you've done."

"You don't remember?" I asked.

"Remember what?"

"The manta ray?"

"You mean the marlin?" he said. "I hooked a marlin that got away. Then I went to sleep and I woke up and you guys have ruined my daddy's boat."

"Save your strength, Ahab," Jordan said, sitting up and looking out at the ocean spread out around us.

"You guys are going to have to help me pay for the damage," Capers said, his voice growing more shrill. "The motor alone cost over two thousand bucks."

Jordan went over to Mike and checked his arm. Mike, too, was awake, but his broken arm hurt too much for him to either speak or move. His eyes looked unnaturally bright and Jordan put his hand to his forehead and felt the fever.

"I demand to know what happened," Capers said. "I'm the captain of the vessel and I'll be goddamned if we're going to go another inch without someone telling me what went wrong. How do you expect us to go anywhere without a motor?" Capers asked no one in particular.

"Jack and I took a vote while you were asleep," Jordan said. "We thought it'd be fun to float back to Waterford."

I laughed, then explained to Capers and

Mike what had transpired after Capers had thrown the harpoon at the manta ray. Mike remembered seeing Capers lifting the harpoon, but Capers never regained a single memory of the incident. He sat and listened to the story with utter astonishment.

"You shouldn't've let me do that," Capers said, touching the sore place on the back of his head. "One of you should've stopped me."

"It was our fault, okay," Mike said. "Good thinking, Capers."

"Help me think of something to tell Dad," Capers said. "A whale. We got caught in a school of humpback whales and one of their tails knocked the engine loose. I'll work out some of the specifics."

"You'll have plenty of time," I said looking out where land was supposed to be.

Mike struggled to stand up, but the pain almost brought him to his knees. Jordan sat him down and tried to make him comfortable, propping up his arm with seat cushions and life preservers.

"Later on, I want to get you in the water, Mike. Let's make sure that wound is good and clean."

"No way. I'm not getting in no water that got shit in it big as that manta ray."

"I wish I could've seen it," Capers said.

Jordan answered, "You saw it well enough to get us here."

"We're lost at sea," Capers said.

"Thanks for that bulletin," Jordan said.

Mike laughed and said, "No, baby. We're just fucked. As fucked as any four humans have a right to be."

"I'll get us out of this," Capers said. "I'll think of something."

Capers stepped up and stood looking out toward the endless expanse of water. Putting his hands on his hips, he struck a pose of deeply aggrieved authority. For a full five minutes he stood there until Mike said, "You think of anything yet?"

Capers' voice was grave, subdued as he said, "Do you know we have a good chance of dying out here?"

"He's a thinker," Mike said, nodding. "He's got all the angles covered."

"Thanks for shedding more light on the subject," I said.

"We're not going to die," Jordan announced.

"What's going to stop us?" Mike asked.

"My father," Jordan said. "My asshole father."

"He's not here," Capers said.

"When I was a little boy, my old man would take me out on maneuvers with him on weekends. He told my mother we were going camping. He'd take me deep into the woods of Camp Lejeune or Quantico, force-march me fifteen or twenty miles, then make me pretend we were at war. We lived off the land. We ate mushrooms and crawdads and wild asparagus. I ate frog legs and flower petals and insects. Do you know that an insect is almost pure protein?"

"I hope you never open a restaurant, man," Mike said.

But Jordan continued: "I hated those weekends with my father and I was always afraid. He loved to test himself when there was nothing between him and nature. If one of America's enemies landed on these shores, he would tell me, men like him would take to the forests for years. They would hunt the enemy only at night using knives and sticks and razor blades. Once he killed a baby deer and we ate it for three straight nights. All of it . . . liver, kidneys, heart."

"Puke," said Mike.

"That won't help us out here," Capers said.

"Yes, it will. Just do whatever I tell you," said Jordan. "I know a lot about hunger and thirst. Before long we're all going to know a lot about both of them. But for now I can keep us all alive."

"Then do it," I said.

"But I'm the president of our class," Capers said.

The three of us studied him, suddenly dumbfounded, but Capers explained himself by saying, "What I mean is that I'm accustomed to leadership. Tell Jordan I've always been the class president. Tell him, Mike. Jack."

"We're not talking about who's going to set up tables for the sock hop," Mike said.

"His father taught him survival skills, Capers," I explained. "He's going to use those same skills to keep us alive out here on the ocean."

"But there's nothing to eat or drink out here," Capers said.

"Our first enemy is right there," Jordan said, pointing out toward the east. "If we're in this boat long enough, the sun's gonna kill us."

"Hey," said Capers. "Fort Lauderdale at Eastertime. This'll give us a chance to work on our tans."

"No time for jokes, son," Mike said. "Mike laughs less when Mike might die."

"Get us out of this, Jordan," I said. "You want to play leader of the pack, play leader of the pack."

"What do we do, Jordan?" Mike asked.

"You and Capers get under the gunwale, out of the sun. Take off all your clothes. Jack and I'll cover ourselves best we can. We've got a little bit of water left in the ice chest. We'll ration it out, but only at night. Jack and I'll spend all day fishing. Don't move around. Conserve energy."

"They'll find us sometime today," Capers said.

"Maybe. But we're going to act like they're never going to find us," Jordan said.

"You're just trying to scare us," Capers said.

"He's doing a damn good job too," I said.

"Yeh, that's exactly what I'm trying to do."

Mike asked, "Why, Jordan? What's the use of scaring us half to death?"

"Because no one knows where we are," said Jordan. "No one knows where to begin to look. We don't have a radio, flares, or emergency equipment of any kind. We've got enough water to last us for two or three days. If it doesn't rain after that, then we'll die of thirst in five days—maybe we'll last a week."

"What a pretty picture," I said.

"I'm going to be dead because Capers Middleton is an asshole," Mike said, shaking his head.

"There's no proof that I threw that harpoon," Capers said, as the three of us stared at him. "For all I know, the three of you might have plotted this tale while I was unconscious."

"Trust us, Capers," I said. "It wasn't no

flounder or mermaid that dragged us out this far and tore our motor off."

"My daddy's gonna kill me when he sees what we did to this boat," said Capers.

"We, paleface?" Mike asked. "I personally do not see where the first-person plural has any part in this conversation. You didn't ask anyone's permission to spear that fish. You gave in to an impulse, Capers. It was definitely freelance."

"Look, we went fishing," Capers said. "I was just trying to catch a fish. No one can blame me for that."

"The fish was as big as a building," I said. "You should've seen it."

Our submission to Jordan's discipline was complete. We followed every order he issued without argument. For a boy accustomed to solitude, he adjusted himself well to a life of scheduling and forced companionship, and command came surprisingly easily to him. We floated through still, airless days, and on the second evening at sea Jordan gave the order that each of us must jump into the ocean and wash ourselves and our clothing well. "Jack, you go in first. Capers and I'll lower Mike into the water. Mike, you've got to let the salt water clean out your wound. All of us need to soak our cuts and wounds. One man'll always stay in the boat while the others are in the water. Keep near the boat. Always, in reach."

I dropped over the side of the boat and entered an ocean that was cold and deep and frightening. The salt stung the wound that ran along my eyebrow, but I stifled a cry of pain and waited as Capers and Jordan carefully let Mike down without causing further injury to his arm. I took his weight and guided him gently into the water. None of us liked the way Mike looked; his complexion seemed ashy and waxen below his tan. But he made not a sound as his arm entered the water and he allowed Jordan to massage and manipulate the tightly bound splint. He moaned softly every time Jordan touched his broken arm, but he submitted to the tender ministrations because Jordan maintained his air of authority even while naked and dog-paddling in the Atlantic.

"Don't drink any salt water," Jordan said, "no matter how thirsty you get. The salt dehydrates you. It takes three times more urine to wash the salt out of your system than normal."

"Who're you?" Capers said from the boat. "My doctor?"

At night, we talked and fished and dried our clothes in the cool, clean air. We moved around freely, each of us assigned to his own separate duties. With lures and one of the baitfish that had survived the encounter with the manta ray, we began to fish in earnest knowing that what we caught was the only thing that would keep us alive. Jordan had checked the level of water in the ice chest and realized it would not last another day, and there had been no clouds in the sky for days.

When the sun was high, Jordan made Mike and Capers get beneath the gunwale of the boat, tightly packed and uncomfortable, but away from the strongest rays of the sun. He and I would pull the boat's tarpaulin cover over ourselves. High noon was a time of complete hibernation and stillness on the boat and we adapted our rhythms to a strict but altogether new cycle that was the exact opposite of our usual daily lives. We trained ourselves to be on the alert for any sounds of airplanes or boat engines that might be searching for us. Once we spotted a search plane flying to the north and we arose screaming and shouting as the aircraft drifted out of sight. That glimpse of possible rescue filled us with sudden, unearned hope, then plunged us downward into a sharp despair made keener by a growing hunger and thirst. Our talk of water became obsessional, then delusional, until Jordan forbade any of us to mention the subject again. Miraculously Mike's arm, though set hastily, showed no signs of infection where the broken bone had punctured his flesh.

As we floated we learned that thirst sharpened the edge of nightmare and that hunger was the perfect entree before hallucination. The heat and sunlight made our dreaming fireglazed and brittle. At dusk, we awoke drenched in sweat and plunged gratefully into the evening sea, naked alongside the drifting boat. The salt water teased us as we rinsed our mouths out again and again as we swam, spitting the water back into the ocean.

As soon as we were back on board, Jordan would give the order to get all the hooks in the water, despite the rancid condition of the bait. Our patience was rewarded on the fifth night when Capers hooked a small amberjack and brought it on board with a shout. Jordan immediately killed the fish, cut it into fresh bait, insisted that all the hooks be rebaited at once.

"Five days at sea and one shitty little amberjack," Mike said, disgusted as I pulled up his hand lines and baited them with the amberjack.

"I don't see why we're fishing anyway," Capers added. "We can't eat the fish even if we catch them."

"Yeh, we can," Jordan said. "And we will."

"You can't eat raw fish," I said.

"We're going to eat all the raw fish we catch and we're going to learn to love it," Jordan said, casting his line again and fishing deep.

"It makes me want to throw up just thinking about it," said Capers. "I can't do it, Jordan. No matter what you say."

"You'll do it when you get hungry enough. Or thirsty enough," Jordan assured us.

"I've never been able to eat a raw oyster," Mike admitted.

"Could you eat one now?" Jordan asked.

Mike thought for a moment, then said, "Yeh, I could eat a hundred of the bastards."

"When we were stationed in Japan with my father, my parents were fanatics about raw fish. It's Japan's greatest delicacy; they treat their fish with utter respect, and the man who cuts the fish is considered an artist."

But Capers would have no part of it: "You can do a lot of things, Jordan, but you can't make a Jap out of a Middleton."

"I bet I can," Jordan said, "because after you chew on the raw fish, it's going to quench your thirst. It's the water in the fish that's going to save our lives."

"Sucking water out of fish kidneys," I said. "Just what I've always wanted to do."

"Get your minds ready for it. We've been without water for over three whole days. We've already started to die."

"Could you phrase it a bit differently?" Mike asked.

"We're already weakening," Jordan said.

"Much better," I said. "Be careful how you use the language out here."

"I'll be careful about the language," Jordan said, "but you boys prepare yourself for a banquet of raw fish."

We put our freshly baited lines over and I was in mid-reverie when a shout came from Jordan. He had a serious bite on his line, and for ten minutes, he fought and finally landed a twenty-pound grouper in the boat. Jordan cut it up carefully and out of view of the rest of us. He waited until it was total darkness before he handed out the glistening strips of grouper to his three most reluctant diners. The flesh of the fish was translucent and held its ivory hue even under starlight.

As Jordan ate, relishing each drop of moisture before swallowing, Capers and Mike threw up twice, and I once, before we managed to keep any part of the meal down. The hurdle was psychological, but it was severe. Before the night was over, however, each of us had consumed over a pound of raw fish. Jordan was patient and kept his head. Even when we regurgitated our first pieces of fish: He saved that vomited-up fish for bait.

That night we caught fourteen other fish and the mood on the boat changed from resignation to resolve. We slept through the hot sun of the next day in the full knowledge that we had placed our trust in a captain who seemed to know what he was doing.

The next day a freighter passed within two thousand feet of our boat, but none of us heard anything until Jordan woke up when the wake of the larger ship hit us broadside and we screamed ourselves hoarse as we watched the ship disappear over the horizon. Still, we drifted south, borne by currents and winds. We talked constantly of rescue, of conversations we would have with our parents, of wrongs we would right back home, and of secrets we had always held close to the chest. Time seemed to lose all meaning as the countless waves slapped against the side of our boat. In one another's haunted faces, we could mark the toll our drifting was taking as we became more and more sunburned and hollow-cheeked, looking for deliverance upon an ocean whose indifference was magisterial, ineffaceable.

We gave up a hundred times each day and then discovered secret deposits of courage that we had not dared imagine. We told jokes, we despaired, we completed each day as we began it and our discipline held. One day after Capers had washed Mike carefully and Jordan made him take a few awkward sidestroke laps around the boat for exercise Mike screamed as I was lifting him into the boat. I thought I had hurt him accidentally, but what had caused the scream was a movement in a sea that had not moved all day. Then I saw it and Jordan, who was still in the water, saw it too. Capers' back was turned to the fin that was coming swiftly at him from fifty yards away. That fin stood far higher in the water than either Jordan's or Capers' head.

"Whale," Mike said and I wished he had been right.

Jordan reached for Capers as Capers spun around to see what Mike was pointing at.

The dark water was clear enough in the still, sun-suffused sea for Mike to make the first clear identification of the hammerhead. I remember to this day the terrible left eye of the great fish as it swooped by the boat. Mike saw the jaws open, as Capers and Jordan both came thrashing toward us screaming and absolutely frantic.

"A fucking shark," Mike said, and even with a broken arm, he leaned over to help Capers into the boat. But Jordan suddenly stopped; he seemed unable to move or make a decision. Slowly, he began swimming away from the boat with the three of us screaming at him.

Mike was the first to spot the fin again and it was heading toward Jordan with amazing speed. The shark shot through that water like lightning slicing through a night sky and this time Mike glanced down and saw that terrible eye as it passed Jordan's helpless, naked form.

Finally Jordan swam close enough for me to grab him by the wrist. Capers got his other arm and together we lifted him straight out of that ocean and certain horrible death in which we would have listened to Jordan's screams as he was torn apart in the water beneath us. The fin disappeared and then came around again, charging in full fury, and we watched in awe and terror. All of us saw the great right eye of the hammerhead count us as we cringed in what safety the boat could provide. That night, all of us wept, even Jordan, and it was good for the rest of us to see Jordan show fear at last.

We hardly moved all night. We listened to the hammerhead circle the boat and bump up against it in frustration. The stillness of the water and the brilliance of a nearly full moon turned that fin coppery as it stalked us. The shark would disappear for an hour or two, then return unbidden and without warning to see if we had made the mistake of entering the water again.

"My ass isn't touching water again unless it's a pool full of chlorine or a bathtub with my mother holding my pajamas standing right next to it," Mike said.

"What were you thinking when you were swimming toward that fin?" I asked Jordan, who shivered involuntarily before he said, "My body went numb with fear. It was like paralysis, like polio. I think my body was preparing for me to die. I don't know if I'd have felt anything if the shark had torn my leg off."

"You'd have felt something," Capers said. "Jesus, when I think of the teeth on that thing. I close my eyes and all I can think of is that mouth coming up to get you, Jordan."

"It had a set of dentures," I agreed.

"Boys, I want you to look over here at your buddy, Mike Hess," said Mike. "Take a good look, because you're never going to see him on a fishing trip again. You're never going to see him eating a fish again, you're never ever going to see him on a boat again."

We laughed together, then the shark swept past the boat once more and its tail slapped against the side of the boat as though the fish were trying to deliver some dread message to the humans on board. We held our breaths and listened for the fish to make another pass. In our imaginations, a thousand hammerheads infested the moonlit waters beneath us. The shark was omniscient, omnipresent, insatiable. It hunted us, and only us, in all the cunning of its despised species. It had smelled our bloodstreams as it moved through the bridal veils of Portuguese man-of-wars and the ink clouds of octopuses in full flight.

For three days the hammerhead bird-dogged our boat, sometimes disappearing for a half day at a time, but always reappearing just when we thought we had seen the last of it. Then suddenly it disappeared for good as a storm rose over the Atlantic. We cheered out loud when we saw the black furious clouds forming. Our thirst was so acute by that time we had placed the subject of water off-limits again. Our tongues felt black and swollen, as though we had been staked out to dry and packed in salt, and so we obsessively watched every cloud that passed overhead praying for a thunderhead to form.

When the shark disappeared for the last time, heading north, there was lightning in the eastern sky. Normally, we would have feared lightning in an open boat, but now there were cries of joy at the rain it portended. We unfolded the tarp that had been stowed under a seat and took the lid off the pathetically dried-out ice chest. None of us took our eyes off the clouds as the storm gathered slowly. We watched the clouds begin to spiral upward in great cumulus bursts as though shaped by magnificent, unseen hands, and we waited, our mouths dry, praying for the abundance of water they would bring to save us.

The wind rose, then the waves began to rise as the tide began its surge and run. Thunder that was miles away was suddenly upon us, and lightning carved its name above us before the rain came in sheets that stung our sunburned faces. Great drops moistened our lips and tongues and we wept in sheer relief.

Jordan screamed for us to keep our discipline and we held the tarpaulin loosely as rain filled its sagging middle with gallons of water. Together, we moved as one and made a funnel, then poured the streaming water into the ice chest. Again, Jordan called for us to catch more rainwater but the three of us had thrown ourselves at the ice chest and were filling Dixie cups and drinking ravenously. Then Jordan, too, lost control and joined us in that feast of fresh water. Its bright elixir brought our voices back as we drank our fill and rejoiced with the thunder. When we had drunk all we had collected, once more we spread the tarp to catch the precious water, filling the ice chest again to its capacity. As the storm worsened and the winds rose, a new fear began to fray the edges of our consciousness. Though we had prayed for rain and storm, we had said nothing of wind, nor even thought of it.

There was no moon or stars and as waves began to crash over the sides of the boat, we secured the ice chest and went to our appointed places. The waves began to build, looming above us, then dropping out from under the boat like hills dropped into the sea. Though the craft was seaworthy, we could not steer it into the waves and had to ride out the storm bobbing like a pelican between the enormous troughs. As the weight of one wave crashed over us I was almost carried overboard. It caught me holding tightly to the stern of the boat and carried me choking on seawater into the gunwale.

Another wave broke the ice chest loose and sent it overboard with a tackle box that had not been tied down after its last use. At Jordan's command we tightened the circles of our life jackets as he handed each of us lengths of rope so we could tie ourselves into the boat. We heard Mike get tossed head over heels and Jordan reached out and grabbed his bathing suit as Mike somersaulted backward and broke his arm again against the steering wheel.

The water of the great waves broke over us and lightning flashed to the west now as the storm moved on. Nature could answer one's prayer far too well as our boat, fragile as a leaf, floated in the utter blackness of thirty-foot seas and the night made us afraid to pray for rain with too much conviction.

In the morning, we woke to a foundering boat more than half-filled with water. Jordan and I spent that morning bailing out water with our hands—almost everything else had been washed overboard. Mike was moaning and barely conscious and we were afraid to touch the newly broken arm. Soon infection would begin to set in and there was nothing any of us could do about it. Capers had endured another blow to his head and a flap of his scalp opened up to reveal the whiteness of his skull. He was unconscious. Jordan and I had broken ribs during the night and it hurt both of us to breathe.

We cleared the boat of water until exhaustion overtook us, and we slept a deep sleep of both pain and despair. Another night passed and another day, then another night. Then day again and the sun began its work in earnest and we were too weak to hide from it. Now, the terrible burning started and somewhere in the middle of the next day we began to die. Our feet swelled and blisters began to form on our hands and faces.

We lost all sense of time or space or sense of where we might be on the planet, and the thought of death was not unpleasant to me. Jordan had become feverish and one night reached out his hand to me.

"Hey, Tonto," Jordan said. "It looks like the bad guys win."

"We gave it a hell of a run, kemo sabe," I whispered.

"To tell the truth," said Jordan, "I wish I hadn't come on this fishing trip."

I laughed, but even laughter hurt.

"Jack, can you hear me?"

"Yeh."

"Are we the only ones alive?"

"We're the only ones conscious," I said. "I envy those guys."

"The two Catholic boys," said Jordan.

"Yeh, lucky us."

"Let's say the rosary," Jordan said. "Let's put our lives in the hands of the Virgin Mary."

"I'll put my life in the hands of Zeus if it'll help."

"If it works, Jack, we'll owe our whole lives to her."

"I'm the only one in this boat who isn't crazy," I whispered to myself.

"Promise you'll dedicate your life to the Virgin Mary and to her son, Jesus, if we survive this?" Jordan asked.

"Have you lost your mind?" I asked.

I remember hearing Jordan begin the Apostles' Creed, then the sun again, then stars, then nothing, then stars again, then nothing, then nothing . . .

Then fog and movement.

I woke up having no idea if I was alive or dead.

"Get up, Jack," I heard Jordan say, "I need you. Get up now."

I rose, staggering. In the back of the boat I

saw Jordan with a broken paddle digging at the water, grimacing every time the boat moved even a little bit.

"Do you hear something?"

I stepped over the bodies of our two friends. They were still breathing but both looked dead. The fog was another form of blindness. I felt submerged in a river of milk. It was bright with false morning light and I could see nothing except my hand in front of me.

"Get on the bow," Jordan urged. "Do you hear it? Tell me if you hear it too."

I closed my eyes and concentrated on the sheer astonishment of being alive and being asked to listen. For a moment, I wondered if we were all dead and fog was the natural landscape when the last breath had been drawn.

"I hear it," I said suddenly. "I hear it. It's surf. The sound of waves crashing on the beach."

"Not that," Jordan said, "There's something in the water. Something alive."

Then I heard the other sound, the unworldly sound that had no connection to where we were or to the ocean. It sounded like an engine or a bellows or something hissing and exhausted somewhere near us in the fog. The sound grew closer until I thought it was a man dying in the water just beyond my reach. But then I realized it was not human and I drew back thinking of the migration of humpback whales along the coast, feeling vulnerable as I lay on the bow, my arms extended over it. My ribs were afire and the thing in the water made me afraid, yet I was more fearful of letting Jordan down . . . The sound of surf I suddenly realized was the sound of rescue and salvation.

Then I saw it coming directly toward me, as disoriented as I myself was, as displaced, as drawn away from his own element as I, but I reached out toward him and touched something that connected me solidly and completely to my own history, to my boyhood in the marshes and fields of the Carolinas. A white-tailed buck, as large and powerful as any I had ever seen, was swimming to a new home between islands. I had seen a buck do it once before in my life, and I grabbed hold of the left antler and felt my fingers lock around it. The buck's great muscled neck tried to loose itself from my grip, but I held that spiked bone tightly and I felt the boat turn with the rhythm of the swimming deer. The buck was in the deep water of a channel and the tide was going in. The deer finally gave up its own direction and just swam to save itself and took us with him.

From the stern, Jordan paddled as hard as he could trying to help the deer. I was crying with pain as I held my grip on the antler. The deer's breathing was labored and angry, yet the boat moved with him and the fog. Jordan was still saying a rosary that had no beginning or end when the boat hit land and the deer dragged me off the bow of the boat and deposited me into the black earth of the marsh, and spartina.

We had landed on Cumberland Island, Georgia, after fifteen days at sea. Jordan Elliott dragged himself out of the marsh and flagged down a forest ranger in a Jeep who called the Coast Guard; and we were flown by helicopter to Savannah, Georgia. The doctors said that both Capers and Mike would have died sometime in the next twenty-four hours and that it was a miracle that any of us survived the ordeal.

On the second night in the hospital, Jordan walked over to my bed, carrying his IV with him.

"A riddle, Jack?"

"I don't feel like playing any more games," I said.

"This one has great implications. Cosmic ones," said Jordan.

"Is it a joke?"

"No, it's the most serious thing in the world," Jordan said.

"Go ahead. I can't stop you."

"Where did we encounter God out there, Jack? Which one was God?"

"I don't know what you're talking about," I said. "Get away from me."

"Was it the blue marlin? Or the manta ray? Or was he in the fish we caught to survive like the loaves and the fishes? Or was it the hammerhead? The storm? Or the white-tailed buck?"

"Do I get to choose 'none of the above'?" I asked, disturbed.

"God was all of them," Jordan explained. "He came to us in different forms. He loved us and wanted to look out for us."

"He did a piss-poor job," I said.

"A great job," Jordan said. "We're all alive."

"How do you know this? About God, I mean. Appearing as those animals."

"I asked Mary, his mother," Jordan said. "You always have to go to the source."

PART V

CHAPTER 32

THROUGH NO PREFERENCE OR SELEC-
tion of our own, the graduating class of 1966, in
high schools all over America, found ourselves
cast like dice across the velvet-covered gam-
bling tables of history. There were no signposts
or catechisms or rules of the road to help us
navigate through the weary mazes of the sixties. We were shot out indiscriminately into the
trickery of the slippery, rampaging decade, and
the best we could do was cover our eyes and
ears and genitalia like pangolins or armadillos
and make sure that our soft underbellies were
not exposed for either inspection or slaughter.

The Class of 1966 was entering an America

that was newly hallucinatory and disfigured. The whole country seemed to have turned inward upon itself and all the old certainties seemed marginal and hollow, and that tangy confidence of a nation accustomed to strutting turned hesitant almost overnight. As our footsteps echoed across the stage, this class entered a country that was traveling incognito even to itself. We would become part of the first American generation of this century to wage war on each other. The Vietnam War would be the only foreign war ever fought on American soil. All were free to choose sides. Bystanders were ridiculed and not tolerated. There were no survivors in the sixties, only casualties and prisoners of war and veterans who cried out in the dark.

Though I still consider the sixties the silliest and stupidest of times, I will admit, under pressure, that some of it was wonderful, even magnificent. I felt acutely, transcendentally alive then, while none of the succeeding decades has made me feel a single thing. But I did not think I would have ever recognized the boy I had turned into back then. I was not even certain that the college boy, Jack McCall, would slow down to shake hands with the man he was required to turn into after all the smoke had cleared.

I had loved the University of South Carolina: my escape from my father's house seemed an emancipation of spirit beyond any price or measure. My father could no longer humiliate me because I simply was unavailable, no longer inhabiting the same house. Each day my teachers forced me to pay attention to the written works of writers I had not yet heard of. I discovered to my joy that these anonymous men and women who had practiced their secret wizardry with the English language long before I was born wrote exquisitely. It surprised me when I read Chaucer in Old English and found him to be a most hilarious writer. I had not even imagined that people laughed and kidded around in medieval England. In my innocence, I assumed that laughter itself was a modern innovation and held no place in the destinies of charwomen and longbowmen of years past. Drifting through books, I found the pleasures of discovery to be an almost daily occurrence.

My first two years of college were quiescent, exhilarating, busy. The immensity of the university, the anonymity of that unruly, self-governing city-state operating in full view of the state capitol provided me a bright glimpse of a world as rife with possibility and those prodigal chances, open-ended and acute, that a boy with nerve could run away with to the end of the earth. Ideas refreshed and overwhelmed

me as though some moon within me was perpetually full and the tide always high.

While other colleges in America seethed
and boiled during the nationwide debate on the
Vietnam War, we students of the University of
South Carolina drank. We drank bathtubs full
of a ghastly concoction called "purple Jesus,"
composed of unfermented grape juice and
cheap vodka. Silver kegs of beer enthroned in
melting pools of ice sat in royal attendance at
every student event. Drunkenness was a condition of choice among a high percentage of the
student body; and a studied, self-conscious
sense of irony and cool was the most highly
prized attitude among the males preening and
fanning their tail feathers for the edification of
the highly selective coeds.

The Greek system was paramount and un-
challenged in its authority over all aspects of
campus life when our freshman class arrived at
Carolina. The only Greek that I have ever
learned was in that first year, when I tried to
distinguish among the bewildering array of fraternities and sororities whose names caused
confusion and dissension among the ranks of
freshmen. Capers confided in me during the
first month that one's choice of a fraternity was
the most significant selection a man would
make before his engagement to a proper young
woman. He told me that five former KA's and

six former SAE's had written flattering letters of reference for him which both chapters had received the previous summer. From Ledare, I learned that three of her mother's sorority sisters had written letters on her behalf, but the fact that her mother herself was a Tri Delt from Carolina took much of the guesswork out of her fate. As a legacy, Ledare confessed, she was practically a shoo-in through no achievement of her own.

I attended most of the parties the fraternities gave and caught an infinitesimal glimpse of a social milieu I had heard rumor of but had never quite understood because of its subtlety. Ledare had broken up with me after high school graduation because she was coming upon her debutante season and my family and I did not quite cut the mustard among those committees that passed judgment on the desirability and entitlement of both the debutantes and their beaux. Since my father was a judge and a member of the bar and his mother was a Sinkler from Charleston, I had always assumed that my bloodline was passable, if not sublime. I never fully understood the depth of the mismatch my father had made when he had married my raw, unlettered mother. Nor could my mother help me navigate those perilous shallows. I understood neither the code nor the uniform of fraternity life and both were something that a young man needed drilled into his psyche long before rush week. Everything that was right about me in high school was wrong for the best fraternities. I was a quick study and could take the temperature of a room like a column of mercury, so I felt my otherness instantly as I watched the painfully cordial brothers assess me from head to foot.

In early August, I had received another surprising lesson in the mysterious social ethic that my friends seemed so at ease with. I had accompanied Capers and the imperious Mrs. Middleton on a shopping expedition to Berlin's in Charleston to purchase the proper clothing for Capers during that all-important first year.

"Remember," Eulalia Middleton said, "the first impression is the only impression that counts *and,*" she said, stretching the word out for emphasis, "the only one that lasts."

"So true. So true," said Mr. Berlin, helping Capers into a blue blazer.

"Wrapping is what turns a common present into a treasure," she intoned, as Capers studied himself in a black pin-striped suit.

"You should write a book, Mrs. Middleton," Mr. Berlin said, making chalk marks on the cuffs of the rolled-up pants. "Though these things seem obvious to us, you'd be appalled by some of the things I hear in this store."

"It's all just common sense *and,*" she said,

arching her eyebrows and catching my eye in the mirror, "good taste is just something one is born with or *not*."

When Capers bought a tuxedo that afternoon, I learned that one could actually purchase a tuxedo and not merely rent one for the night. When Capers' bill was added up, it came to over three thousand dollars and I whistled in amazement, then realized I had committed an unrecallable social gaffe as I saw Capers, Mrs. Middleton, and Mr. Berlin go to great pains to pretend they had not heard it. Making up figures in my head, I wondered if my parents had spent three thousand dollars on me during my entire life, and that counted food. But I was dazzled by the care that Capers and his mother took in the well-considered selection of his college wardrobe.

When Capers was trying on a beautifully cut London Fog raincoat, I had gasped at the price and said, "What'll you need that for, Capers?"

Mrs. Middleton looked quizzical, then said, "Do you think that it doesn't rain in the upper portions of the state?"

"Sure," I said. "But you can always duck inside somewhere. Run home."

"A gentleman doesn't *duck* anywhere," Mrs. Middleton explained. "*And* a gentleman is prepared for all exigencies of weather. You'll need a black umbrella to walk young ladies back to their sorority houses in the rain, Capers. What on earth will you do about those young ladies, Jack?"

"Guess I'll grab their hand and tell 'em to run for it with me."

"Indeed," said Mrs. Middleton, but I saw Mr. Berlin suppressing a smile.

Though I tried to assimilate all the protocols of college life in my off-key first semester, there was too much detail to process in such a short time. I was too self-conscious and disheveled to make a perfect fit into the complex pecking order of the best fraternities. I watched the stir that followed Capers' entrance into a fraternity mixer and realized that it was something far more mysterious than London Fog that made these potential brothers lukewarm and noncommittal when I trailed like a pilot fish behind Capers from party to party. The courtesies were all observed to the letter, yet I could feel my appearance creating almost no disturbances as I drifted from house to house in search of that perfect comfort zone that would tell me subliminally that I had come, at last, to the right place. Though no one told me straight-out, I became aware that I was not even remotely desirable to the top-rank fraternities on campus and was at best a low to midlist candidate in the second-rate fraternities.

Their surgery was done wordlessly and without anesthesia. Long before the fraternities made their final choices, I knew I was not in the running and I told all my friends from high school that I had decided to be an Independent.

Many years later, I would admit to myself that my fierce championing of the antiwar movement would have been unnecessary if SAE could have gotten beyond my mail-order catalog attire and the towering, unsettling rawness of my entrance into parties. The aura of the small town still clung to me; the cheap scent of the backwater followed my silent wanderings as I tried my best to find my own niche on the Carolina campus. I had expected to still spend most of my time with my best friends from Waterford and simply add dazzling names to that list as we entered into each and every phase of campus life. It troubled me, then displeased me that Capers and Ledare were taken out of circulation with friends like me as soon as they arrived on campus. While fraternities were courting Capers with an internecine ferocity, the sororities had practically gone to war to win Ledare's approval.

Mike had joined forces with the ZBT's, the Jewish fraternity, from the day he entered Carolina on the run and on the move. He was foresighted and clear-thinking and he knew where he was going. He had wanted to work in the movie industry since he was in high school, but he had to make his way toward filmdom. Though he majored in Business Administration, Mike immediately began to take every course the English department offered that had anything at all to do with film. He also went to the movies every day and made careful notes about what he thought about each and every film he saw. Whenever the lights went out in a movie theater and the credits began to roll on a huge screen, Mike was a perfectly happy man. College life fully engaged him with its extraordinarily busy social life, the seriousness of its academic course work, and the opportunity that it provided an ambitious boy like Mike to extend his horizons as far as his wit and depth could take him. Since he had come from a family that deeply loved him, Mike assumed that everyone he met would surrender to his basic good nature, and almost everyone did. His smile was infectious and sprang out of his generous yet inquisitional nature. He wanted to know the life story of everyone he passed and he had time to talk to anyone. He had a small genius for drawing out shy people and bringing them along as observers and cheerleaders in his fast-talking, pixilated world. On campus, he became famous for carrying an 8-millimeter camera everywhere he went. His skill with a camera slowly turned to a kind of artistry.

At the university, only Shyla seemed to remain unchanged in the heady atmospherics of college life. None of the vainglory and maneuvering among the coeds seemed of any interest to her at all. Since she was the prettiest Jewish girl on campus, and seemed to grow prettier every day, from the moment she set foot into her room in Capstone House she dated a whole series of the most desirable and attractive Jewish boys on campus, including the president of ZBT. She joined the newspaper staff of the *Gamecock* her first week and won a minor part in the first theatrical production of the young season in *Timon of Athens.* Nothing about her seemed changed or forced or derivative, and whenever I saw her I could turn a page backward in my life and see where I had once been by merely gauging her reaction to me. Though Shyla had dared me to fall in love with her the summer before when we danced in the Middletons' doomed beach house, she knew that I was not yet ready. She was patient and serene and confident that our history in the oak tree would eventually bring me to her. We often met for lunch in the Russell House and continued our childhood habit of telling each other everything. The one thing both of us agreed on was how much we missed Jordan and wished he had matriculated at the university instead of following in his father's footsteps to the Citadel. Neither of us thought the free-spirited Jordan would blossom in the Citadel's brutal trial by fire for its six hundred plebes.

Jordan's first letters began to arrive soon after the ordeal of plebe week was over and classes began. Under the cover of taking notes for his American history class, he wrote long diatribes about the indignities he and the other freshmen were forced to endure under the ungoverned rule of young sadists. "I wrote my mother a letter and thanked her for sending me to this wonderful hellhole. I reminded her that this is the same school that produced that wonderful sport she married and that some of these guys were actually making me miss my father. I've got this first sergeant, named Bell, who has taken a particular dislike to yours truly because he thinks the expression on my face reflects a bad attitude. Bell has the IQ of a Tater Tot and has no idea how bad my attitude is nor how bad I plan for it to become. I came here because my old man hates the fact that I'm alive and going around claiming to be his natural-born son. This whole thing's a bad idea. My roommate loves all this and his ambition's to be a sniper in Vietnam. It's like rooming with Heinrich Himmler. Ask Shyla and Ledare if they'll put hickeys all over my neck when they see me. Oh, but I neglected to tell you about the rich intellectual life at the Citadel. They showed the freshmen a stag movie last night where a woman makes love to a donkey. Believe me, both of us would've chosen the donkey. And my roommate, bless his fascist heart, is very proud of his ability to fart on command. He has shared this prized piece of information with his squad sergeant and he now farts loudly and happily whenever called upon to strut his stuff. If I thought about how much I miss all of you, I couldn't last another fifteen minutes here. Can you drive down to see me on my first leave? Yours truly, in torture and pain, Jordan."

When Jordan marched in his first dress parade, Shyla and I drove down on a Friday afternoon to take him to dinner at the Colony House. Before the upperclassmen let Jordan and his classmates leave the barracks, they conducted an impromptu sweat party where Jordan was required to perform over a hundred pushups before he could sign out at the main sally port.

When he came out to meet us, his head shaved, we saw that he had lost a great deal of weight.

"Why are you so skinny?" Shyla demanded to know.

"My first sergeant doesn't believe that animals and plants should die just to let a dumbhead live," Jordan said. "His mother taught him not to waste food and feeding a knob is, by definition, wasting food."

"Is this school teaching you anything?" I asked. "What're you majoring in?"

"Spit shine."

"No, really," Shyla said, laughing. "What's your field of study?"

"Hand grenades. With a minor in flame throwers."

We spent the night teasing and joking, but Jordan could not hide the deep sadness that provided both text and color for every story he told about life in the barracks. Another boy's face was so disfigured by acne they forced him to wear a paper bag over his head at mess. A freshman from Waycross, Georgia, who had grown up poaching alligators in the black silences of the Okefenokee Swamp, had a nervous breakdown in physics class.

What was getting to Jordan was the suffering of others; long ago he had grown accustomed to his own suffering. The cruelty he faced from the upperclassmen seemed buoyant and lightweight compared to his father's far more studied tyranny. Almost alone among the freshmen, Jordan found the meanspiritedness of boys almost comical. What he did find disheartening was that the Citadel seemed to represent an institutional mimicry of his father's dark spirit.

Before we even ordered, Jordan had eaten the whole loaf of freshly baked bread and a whole stick of butter that the waiter had brought with our menus. He also put four lumps of sugar into his iced tea and apologized profusely to his dinner companions.

"I'm hungry enough to eat the crotch out of a rag doll," Jordan said.

"Jordan!" Shyla warned.

"Sorry, Shyla. I heard that at mess. No cadet can finish a sentence without using the word 'fuck' at least once."

"I thought I liked Carolina," I admitted, "until I saw your place. Now I know I'm ecstatic."

"Jack's having a little trouble adjusting," Shyla said, "but the rest of us are in hog heaven. You ought to quit this dump and go to a real college."

"I'd love to find an honorable way out," Jordan said. "If I just quit, my father'd never pay my way to another college. The problem is that there's no real honorable way out of the Citadel except with a diploma."

"Think of something," Shyla said. "Jack needs a friend. Who'd've thought the big fella would be lonely on a campus chock-full of ten thousand people?"

"Jack's shy," Jordan said. "It'll take him a while to get his feet on the ground."

A voice above us said, "Cadet Elliott."

The three of us looked up to see a Citadel upperclassman standing above Jordan. Jordan immediately stood up at strict attention and entered into a semi-brace much to the consternation of the cadet.

"Not here, Elliott. At ease, mister. I'm eating dinner with my parents and I couldn't help but notice you unfastened the zipper on your dress blouse when you sat down. That's an upper-class privilege."

"I wasn't aware of that, sir."

"Report to my room ten minutes before taps, smackhead," the cadet whispered, then smiled as he looked down at Shyla. He was about to introduce himself when I grabbed him hard by the ear and jerked his head down toward me.

"Hey, acne breath," I said into the boy's ear. "I'm a patient in the state mental hospital on Bull Street. I killed my mother by stabbing her in the eye with a butcher knife. I never have to want to come looking for you, but if my cousin Jordan ever tells me to . . ." I lifted a steak knife off the tablecloth.

"Let him alone, Jack," Jordan said. "I'm very sorry, sir. My cousin doesn't get out of the hospital very often."

"I'm his nurse, Cadet," Shyla said. "I hope

he didn't frighten you. We'll have to increase his medication."

I released the frightened sergeant who said, "Thanks, Elliott. Forget about reporting to me. Enjoy your evening."

"Thank you, sir," Jordan said. "Are you sure you wouldn't like to join us, sir?"

"My mother didn't suffer," I said. "She died instantly."

As the cadet hurried back across the darkened room, Jordan said, giggling, "His name is Manson Summey and he's the meanest son of a bitch in the corps. He eats knobs for breakfast and brags about how many he's run out of the corps this year."

"Let him run you out. Come to Carolina," Shyla said. "We've got dormitories full of girls who'd just lap you up like cream. There's liquor, parties galore, big band music . . ."

"Then why's Jack so lonely?" Jordan asked, reaching across through the candlelit gloom and squeezing my wrist.

"Because he's Jack," Shyla said. "He thought we'd all grow up and you, me, Capers, Mike, Ledare, and him would all live in one great big house."

"What's wrong with that?" I said.

"Sounds like heaven to me," Jordan said, inhaling deeply as his steak arrived from the kitchen.

"It's impractical," Shyla said. "It shows no imagination."

"It shows good taste, Shyla," I said. "I know who my friends are."

It took Jordan Elliott another month of the plebe system before he decided he had a solution fantastic enough to get himself expelled from the Citadel, but in such a way that he could leave with both his dignity intact and his father's blessing. His father had believed that the Citadel would harden his son in those places that his mother had made soft in her husband's absences. What the general demanded was that the school do what he failed to do—make Jordan unlike his mother in every way.

The plan Jordan devised required the help of his friends at the University of South Carolina and made clear that Jordan had already developed his natural gift for strategic planning. Clear vision was an old habit of his and the stress of the plebe system only strengthened his proficiency at making correct decisions on the spur of the moment.

Two weeks before the annual Citadel-Furman football game, ten Citadel cadets had taken a weekend leave and kidnapped the sleek Arabian horse that served as Furman's mascot. The horse was a docile animal, beautifully proportioned and easily handled, but in the cadets' haste to make off with the Furman paladin, the horse was accidentally blinded by two cadets far too drunk to be loading a strange horse properly. When the cadets realized how serious the injuries to the mascot really were, they did what they considered the humane thing and put the horse down with a single pistol shot to the brain. One cadet made an error of judgment by spray painting the word "Citadel" on the dead animal's body.

Before this incident, Furman and the Citadel had been bitter rivals indeed. Afterward, the Citadel represented and embodied everything demonic and unspeakable in the modern world to this pretty, Baptist-governed college, which sat in the rolling hills outside of Greenville. The once placid and genteel student body of Furman rose up in sheer, barbaric fury when the news of the atrocity spread across campus. A photograph of the slain horse was on the front page of every newspaper in the state, and, fearing reprisals, the president of the Citadel, General Nugent, restricted all cadets to the campus until after the Furman game was over. Several Furman fraternities pledged to hang the Citadel bulldog at half-mast on the state capitol flagpole in honor of the slain paladin.

Jordan Elliott's first sergeant, Manson Summey, was visiting his girlfriend at Furman on the Sunday morning when the dead paladin's picture appeared in the *Greenville Morning News*. After kissing his girl good-bye at the entrance to her dormitory, fifty Furman boys, including half the football team, met Manson at his car.

When they returned Manson Summey to the Citadel campus two days later, they had shaved Manson's head and genitalia, dressed him in girl's panties, and covered him with chicken shit and chicken feathers they had gathered from a local farm in Greenville. They painted the word "Furman" on six buildings on the Citadel campus, including the chapel. The cadets vowed revenge when Manson was found chained and badly beaten up, lying in the middle of the parade ground. But General Nugent, after a conference call with the governor and the president of Furman, restricted all of his cadets to their rooms and stationed guards around the campus to prevent further incursions by Furman students. Tensions between the schools heated up to dangerous levels, and both football teams vowed to win the game that would take place in Charleston the following Saturday. Great male energy, undirected and captious, was loose in the air and the Citadel campus felt like a small warlike principality that was under siege. The word "Furman" had become an expletive among the aroused cadets for whom the beating and humiliation of Manson Summey had erased all memory of the death of Furman's horse.

Then freshman Jordan Elliott went to his company commander, Pinner Worrell, with a brilliant plan that combined military strategy with a biblical sensibility for vengeance. The plan was simple but cunning, and Cadet Captain Worrell agreed to sponsor it and even participate in it if Jordan could convince three non-Citadel people to drive the getaway cars. Jordan assured his commander that he had lined up the three drivers perfect for an operation that combined a love of fast driving and a passion for taking risks.

"Can they keep their mouths shut, Elliott?" Cadet Worrell asked.

"I'd trust them with my life, sir," Cadet Elliott assured him.

"But you're a knob, Elliott. The lowest form of waste product. A wet dream. A used Kotex. An ass-wipe. There will mostly be upperclassmen on this project. The crème de la crème. Veritable gods, Elliott, veritable gods."

"Sir, I'd trust the lives of veritable gods with these three friends. Even a used Kotex like me."

"I'll be responsible for all military and strategic aspects of this top-secret mission, dumbhead. Next year, I'll be in Vietnam killing gooks, plundering villages, pacifying the countryside, and generally kicking quite a bit of Asian ass. You, Elliott, will be responsible for transportation only. You're only a knobule, a sperm cell of a true Citadel man. I'll teach you everything you need to know about the subtleties of military genius."

"Sir, leave the transportation up to me."

On the Wednesday night before the Furman game, fifteen cadets from G Company dressed in fatigues gathered to hear last-minute instructions from Pinner Worrell. For the fifth time, he walked them through each step of their commando raid on the campus of Furman University. Each squad was required to paint at least three buildings before hustling to the rendezvous point for the rapid trip back to Charleston before reveille sounded. Timing was essential in this mission, he repeated over and over. The fifteen cadets synchronized their watches as Pinner went through their assignments once more. They had already loaded paint cans, brushes, wire cutters, and liquor into the three cars now parked and waiting in Hampton Park just off the Citadel campus. When the bugles echoed through the barracks at ten-thirty, the fifteen of them were standing at a side gate. They sprinted out the gate together and as they passed a junior sergeant they shouted "All in," running past him into the darkness, and raced for the railroad tracks behind the military science building. The cadets had to be back at the Citadel for morning reveille at six-fifteen. The city of Greenville lay two hundred and ten miles away.

With our three cars running, Capers, Mike, and I checked our watches, revved our engines, and waited for the cadets to charge through the azalea bushes that lined the railroad tracks. None of us had hesitated when Jordan had called and asked for help. For the sake of friendship, each of us loved the idea of racing our cars at full throttle from one end of the state to the other.

I revved my engine as Jordan climbed into the car beside me and his company commander, Pinner Worrell, rode shotgun. Three seniors leapt into the backseat yelling, "Go, go, go." Capers' Pontiac GTO took off first, burning rubber, followed by Mike's '57 red Chevrolet, which Mike kept in perfect condition. My car was more pedestrian, a gray '59 Chevrolet with odd tail fins that made it look grandmotherly. But it was my first car and I loved it precisely because of its homeliness and lack of style. It was not the swiftest of the three cars, but once it hit the highway it could cruise at high speeds with the best of them.

We flew through the residential streets of Charleston at seventy-five miles per hour and shot up the ramp to I-26 with our radios blasting out rock music and the cadets pouring shots of liquor to give themselves courage for the task at hand. Because he was a freshman, Jordan could not utter a word and I listened to the nervous talk of upperclassmen as I followed Mike's taillights and settled in for a hell-bent two-hour ride in which we planned to average one hundred five miles per hour.

In less than one hour we passed Columbia, a good hundred miles from Charleston and saw the city lights in the distance to the right. As we came up upon Newberry, I saw the blue lights of a highway patrolman's car in my rearview mirror and put my foot on the brake until Worrell told me that the patrolman was a Citadel alumnus who was privy to the plan. The patrol car raced by our three cars, and with his blue light leading the way we burst through the Carolina pinelands as the state began its slow climb into the mountains north of Greenville. I could feel the earth itself begin to rise and turn its energies toward the coming hills. Never had I traveled at such a speed or covered so much ground as we did rocketing through the state of South Carolina escorted by a highway patrolman wearing a Citadel ring.

When we passed by the exit to Clinton, I caught a brief glimpse of a flashlight blinking on and off quickly above us on the overpass. Far ahead on the overpass in front of us, I saw a single flickering answering light that was so swift I was not even certain I saw it. It registered on me dimly that this was a signal of some sort, but I was concentrating so hard on my driving I did not even remember it until later the next day. As we neared Greenville, Pinner Worrell took the cadets through their paces again, step by step, making sure that each member of his team knew his role perfectly.

"Wig, you've got the library. Just paint the words 'Bulldog' and 'The Citadel' on the front. Don't bother about the back. The same goes for all of you. Everybody be back here at exactly 0300 hours. Do you read me, gentlemen? Dumbhead, do I make myself understood?"

"Sir, yes sir," Jordan said.

"You get the girl's dorm, waste wad," Worrell said to Jordan. "No sniffing underwear hanging on the clothesline."

"I'll try to control myself, sir," Jordan said and the upperclassmen in the backseat laughed.

"Gauldy knob," Worrell said, but with brotherly affection as we turned off the interstate when we saw the road sign for Furman University.

"What's your job, Pinner?" one of the faceless cadets in the backseat asked.

"The commander of the team always takes the toughest job for himself," Worrell said.

"I'm spray-painting on the church the words 'Fuck Furman's Dead Paladin. The Citadel's Glad We Killed It.' "

"You're nuts, Worrell," a voice said admiringly. "Pure psycho."

"Thanks," Worrell said. "Thanks so much. That's what's gonna give me the edge in Nam. It's guys like you who paint the dorms. But only Worrell would think to paint the church on a Southern Baptist campus."

"But you're a Baptist, Worrell."

"I'm a pure fighting machine, Dobbins," Worrell corrected. "And this is a fucking war."

As I pulled up behind Mike's car beside the nine-foot chain-link fence that surrounded the Furman campus, Worrell said, "You'd've made a hell of a Citadel man, McCall. What a shame to lose a man like you to a pussy school like Carolina. Let's go, men. Absolute precision now. Military precision. Our plan's flawless. Only human error can fuck this up. And, gentlemen, in Worrell's army, there's no such thing as human error."

The cadet team in Capers' car had already cut a large hole through the fence with wire cutters and the first of the camouflaged cadets carrying backpacks full of cans of spray paint were already sprinting toward the Furman buildings three quarters of a mile away. The cadets were in splendid shape, their bodies honed and conditioned by long hours of running obstacle courses and quick-timing with chanting platoons.

When I threw the trunk open, I marveled at the speed and economy of the cadets as they slid into their backpacks, then sprinted toward the hole in the fence where they low-crawled through the opening. The moon, which had been behind a covering of clouds, sprang suddenly free and bathed the cadets in light as they raced. across the low hills silent and swift as brook trout. I watched Pinner Worrell disappear over one of the hills and was surprised to find Jordan Elliott coming out of the shadows behind me, laughing.

"You're gonna get in big trouble, Jordan," Capers said.

"Not as much as they are," Jordan said. "At least not yet."

Jordan pointed to his right and a flashlight clicked on twice, then was answered by a light to the left.

"Who's awake at this time of the morning?" Mike asked.

"The whole Furman campus. You remember Fergis Swanger?"

"Pulling guard for Hanahan High. Hell of a football player," Mike said.

Jordan pointed toward another flash of

light off to the east. "Fergis plays for Furman now. I called him the other night."

"What for?" Capers said. "You don't even know the poor son of a bitch."

"I told him every detail of the plan to paint the Furman campus."

"You rotten, lousy bastard," Mike said. "That's brilliant."

"But it's so two-faced," Capers said. "I really got to like those guys I drove up here."

"Then transfer," Jordan said. "Now you get out of here fast. If they find out you drove us, there won't be anything left of your cars except the aerials and the ashtrays."

"Why?" Capers asked. "Why'd you do this?"

"I had a classmate who sat at the same mess with me. We were lucky enough to get to eat with Mr. Pinner Worrell. Except Mr. Worrell didn't want to waste any of the Citadel's good money by feeding a knob. So he starved us. But he had this game he played. He found out what foods we hated. I hate brussels sprouts, so when he asked if I would like a serving of brussels sprouts, I said, 'No Sir.' He made me eat every brussels sprout on the table. This kid Gerald Minshew declined to drink tomato juice. So Worrell made him drink twelve glasses of tomato juice. What Minshew neglected to mention was that he was allergic to tomato juice. He almost died in the emergency room."

"What's the real reason for all this, Jordan?" Mike asked. "I'm not buying this hatred for brussels sprouts and love for poor Minshew."

"I got to get out of this school. It's not for me. I hate everything about the place except for going to sleep, then I dream about the place."

"Just leave," I suggested.

Jordan laughed bitterly. "I told you, Jack, I've begged my father to let me resign, but he won't hear of it. Mom tells me I've got to find an honorable way out of the Citadel or I have to stay here for four years."

"You call this honorable?" Capers said. "Those guys are going to get the shit kicked out of them."

"So am I," Jordan said, slipping down and crawling through the hole in the fence, only he headed west around the fence instead of following the path of the other cadets.

"Just come back with us," I said. "These Furman people'll kill you."

"If they don't, then everyone'll know I made the call," Jordan said. "Hey, thanks, guys. I'll never forget what you did for me tonight. Now take off before they catch you."

As Jordan disappeared over a hill a huge

roar went up a hundred yards in front of us as five hundred Furman boys executed a perfect double envelopment movement that cut the Citadel cadets off from their escape route. Some signal had been given and the campus bloomed suddenly with light, and what seemed like thousands of Furman men hidden in strategic points around the campus closed in and overwhelmed the surprised and desperately outnumbered cadets.

I found myself so mesmerized by the fierce virility of this howling mob that I nearly did not make it back to my car as a contingent of Furman baseball players armed with bats ran toward the parked cars. We leapt behind the driver's wheels and gunned the cars down the dirt road as Louisville sluggers flew over the fence in a deadly volley, caving in my hood and breaking Mike's rear window.

At an all-night gas station on I-26, we stopped for gas and to regroup.

"What was all that shit about?" I asked.

"We should be ashamed of ourselves for leaving those cadets behind," Capers said.

"You're right, Capers," I said. "Go back and pick yours up, as scheduled."

"You don't know what brotherhood is," Capers said. "You're not joining a fraternity."

"Teach me all about brotherhood, fraternity boy," I said. "Go back for those cadets."

"Jordan used us," Capers said.

I shook my head and said, "Jordan's our friend and we stand by him."

"My God," Mike said, "he does things no one would ever think of."

"He's dangerous," Capers said.

"So far," Mike said, laughing, "only to Citadel cadets."

And dangerous he was to those valiant, rough-and-ready cadets who made the journey to Furman that autumn night. Sixteen cadets slipped onto the Furman campus that night and none walked off campus on his own power. One cadet was lassoed out of an oak tree and pulled down to the ground, where he was stomped half to death by a Furman mob. Pinner Worrell's jaw was broken and three ribs cracked as he tried to spray-paint the line of attackers who felled him. His was one of three broken jaws recorded by the emergency room at the Greenville County Hospital. Seven of the cadets came to that hospital unconscious, including Jordan Elliott.

Jordan was also the only cadet to reach a single Furman building to desecrate it with the words "The Citadel." He was spray-painting those words on the gymnasium when he was sighted by a roving patrol of paladins who gave the alarm. Soon Jordan was in a footrace with Furman boys that he was destined to lose. He ran toward the tranquil lake that he had noticed on the map that Worrell had marked when they planned the mission. Feeling the mob almost upon him, he did a speed dive into the cold November waters and began stroking the Australian crawl as hard as he could toward the distant shore. Behind him, he heard five or six of the Furman boys enter the water and howl with displeasure as the cold bit into them. Since he could swim like an otter, Jordan had several fleeting moments of hope when he thought he might elude his pursuers.

Then he heard the sound of four canoes launched simultaneously in the water and looked back to see the canoes loaded with four beefy paddlers each, stroking in unison toward him. Laughing, Jordan turned to face them in the water. When the first canoe closed on him, he dove underwater and managed to tip it over, but an oar struck him in the back of the head, drawing blood. Before he felt himself sinking beneath the black water, he saw the shadows of the paddles coming from everywhere, in slow motion, again and again and again.

Jordan's concussion was severe and he was the last cadet to be released from the Greenville County Hospital and returned, under guard, to the Citadel. Like the others before him he was expelled for Conduct Unbecoming a Cadet, and while he was escorted to his room to pack his belongings, the cadets of Padgett-Thomas barracks gathered along the railings and cheered so loudly and for so long at Jordan's departure that even the fury of General Elliott was appeased by the final triumphant hurrah the corps extended to his son.

For the rest of the semester, Jordan lived with his parents at Camp Lejeune. In January, he matriculated at the University of South Carolina, where I had spray-painted the words "Go Furman" on the doorway leading into our dormitory.

CHAPTER 33

ON THE FIRST DAY OF JUNE, LUCY telephoned and asked if I would come over and visit with her alone. Her voice alarmed me and I had a sudden premonition of bad news. When I arrived she told me that the night before, she had awakened in darkness and felt a slight, an almost imperceptible change in her body, like the tiny rustle of cylinders shifting in a combination lock. She had always been able to read the signals her body gave off and had known each time she was pregnant long before her doctors confirmed her intuition. Last night, lying drenched in her own sweat, she knew that the cells that would kill her had returned. The leukemia was on the move again, she said, and this time it had come to stay.

Though I had seen my mother weep before, I had never seen her cry over her own mortality. She had done everything the doctor said for her to do, yet a death sentence had been passed on her. I do not think that her tears were out of self-pity, although that was my first thought as I sat there in my role of dumbstruck witness. As she cried, I began to understand. You weep at the loss of so beautiful a world and all those parts you will never be able to play again. The dark takes on different meaning. Your body has begun to prepare you for the last completion, for the peace and generosity of silence itself. I watched closely as my mother tried to imagine a world without Lucy Pitts. At first, it was beyond imagination, but her tears helped water the path. The idea of it tempted her at the center of where she lived. By weeping in front of me, Lucy was taking the first step toward dying well.

A better son would have embraced his mother and comforted her. But my body was shy when it came to all the common intimacies of touch. I put my hand out toward her shoulder, then withdrew it as soon as I came in range of her body. Her grief seemed to make her dangerous, electric. But behind it, an ancient code sounded its own venture of resignation.

Again, I reached out toward my mother, but my hand did not travel the distances that had suddenly grown up between us. In the heat of this morning, I felt a film of ice form over my own heart. Wordless, I tried to find the words that would bring peace to my mother. Knowing that I should take her up into my arms, I sat there paralyzed, thinking far too much about everything. Thus, I lost that most precious and life-defining of all moments forever. I could not think of touch without conjuring up visions of strangulation, the breathlessness that led to the deepest realms of terror. Where other men took comfort in the arms of their women, I brought visions of the pythoness, all the swiftness and airless panic of constriction.

As we sat out on her deck and listened to the waves come in, one by one, Lucy reiterated to me that she was living out the last months of her life. She said it was time to get her affairs straight, to tell the truths that needed to be told, to explain to her children that she had not abandoned us in the reeds on the day we were born, although she knew we thought she had. We had judged her unfairly and had declared her on the secret ballots we had counted behind her back to be our tenderest executioner. Because she had protected us from the horrors of her own childhood, she had not prepared us for the more commonplace suffering of our own. She had lied about who she was and where she came from because she wanted us to have a fresh start in a world that had manhandled her from the very beginning. She thought that love was the fiercest, most authentic part of her, yet feared she had never allowed it to air out properly, had kept it too tightly clenched and close to her chest. As she felt herself dying, she wanted me to know that she had loved her sons so much that it had frightened her. To contain that fear, Lucy had loved us in secret, had turned that love into an eccentric form of counterintelligence that had its own passwords and codes of silence. She had covered her feeling for us with thorns and barbed wire and had placed land mines in all the rose gardens leading to it. With outstretched arms her children had crossed those blown-out fields again and again to reach out for her. If she had known that love had to be earned and fought for, she would have imparted that lesson to us.

Only when the cancer had begun to eat away at her life did she remember the little girl she once had been. It was that same girl who brought trouble and misery to the art of loving. Love had to cross the threshold of a burning house where her father died in a fire set by her mother. Love had to tiptoe beneath the corpse of her inconsolable mother, who had hanged herself from a railroad trestle. What did love feel like when its hands were bloodstained in the strands of time? I could feel my mother try to explain all this and she struggled to find the proper words. But the language failed her and I heard just the waves again. She was breathing hard. It was time to put her house in order and she would try to repair the damage before she died. That was her pledge to me on the morning she told me that the leukemia had come back to take up residence in her body again, this time as a permanent guest.

Dr. Pitts joined us on the deck and I could tell that my mother had already shared the news with him. He walked over to her, fresh-shaven, dapper, and I could smell the sharp scent of his cologne in the air as he lifted my mother out of her chair and she collapsed into him. Her husband held her and I learned something about the quiet strength of men as he whispered something to her I could not hear. Enveloped in his arms, I saw the comfort that he conferred upon my mother by merely opening himself up to her. Not one of the men in my family could have performed this vital yet very simple function. My mother buried her face against his chest and I turned my own face away, realizing how much of an intruder I was at this moment of bittersweet intimacy.

"I think we should call off the party for

Lucy," Dr. Pitts said. "You can break the news to your brothers, Jack."

"No," my mother said, drawing back from him. "That's *my* party. It's still going to go on."

"They wanted to celebrate your remission," Dr. Pitts said.

"No one has to know I'm out of remission," she said. "It'll be our secret. No law that you have to tell your brothers everything. Is there, son?"

"No law," I agreed.

"I'll buy the prettiest dress in Atlanta," she said, kissing Dr. Pitts on the cheek. Then chilled me by saying, "It'll be the one I'm buried in."

And so my brothers and I began planning the party in honor of our mother that would take place on Labor Day and that we had announced to the world would celebrate the fact that her leukemia had stayed in remission for over a year. As we meted out each of our assigned tasks I was strangely comforted by the fact that none of my brothers yet knew that the white cells in her blood were on the march again. Her bloodstream had frightened all of us with its capacity for jeopardy and betrayal, and although we knew about mortality and accepted it on both an intellectual and primitive level, we had never focused on the fact that our mother might die, that she might one day leave us. Because she was so young when we were born, our mother seemed more like an older sister and confidante than she did a parent. Her complexity continued to surprise us all as we grew older, and it would have been impossible for any of us to describe her in a couple of glib, tossed-off sentences. If each of us had been compelled to do so, no doubt descriptions of five different women from various latitudes, or even solar systems, would have been the result. Lucy took pride in being mysterious, unplaceable, night-shaped. She had wept when we had told her about the party we planned to give her. While my brothers interpreted these tears as tears of gratitude, I knew she was weeping at her sons' fierce refusal to acknowledge that she was dying. Mike Hess offered to host the party and provide all the liquor at his plantation house. Dallas, Dupree, Tee, and I spent the week before gathering the food. What we had in mind was a day of ecstasy and jubilee celebrating Lucy's triumph over insurmountable odds.

When Dr. Peyton had called from the hospital with the results of her recent blood tests, he confirmed that she had gone out of remission. He told her she must come in to start more chemotherapy treatments the very next day.

"No way, little doctor," she said. "I know

my chemo now. It put a lot bigger hurting on me than leukemia ever did. My boys are planning a party for me and I wouldn't miss it for the world."

"Your choice. But while you're eating fried shrimp, those white cells are going to have an open season."

"I looked up my kind of leukemia in my husband's medical textbooks. According to them, my cancer is particularly ornery and I don't have a chance in hell of surviving, whether I get that chemo or not."

"There's always a chance, Lucy," the young doctor said.

"That same chance'll still be there after my party," Lucy said. "My boys have been planning this all summer."

"Why is this party so important to you?"

"Because it'll be the last party I'll ever attend on this good earth," she said. "And I plan to enjoy every minute of it. Please come; my boys know how to feed a crowd."

Tee had come up with the idea of throwing a huge, unforgettable party in praise of Lucy. Once he fastened his attention to this party in the abstract, he drove us to distraction to attend to the details that would make it a reality.

"I'm the idea man in this outfit," Tee told us. "It's up to you guys to bring the party favors and buy the swizzle sticks."

"How many people you thinking about inviting, idea man?" Dallas asked.

"The sky's the limit," Tee said.

We then told Lucy that there were no limits to the number of the people she could invite, and she took us at our word. Her heart softened even toward her enemies and her eyes would grow dim as she told us about why she had quit speaking to certain women in the town. She pitied anyone who had not gotten to know her since she finally summoned up the courage to kick the judge out of her life. She was a harder version of herself when she spent every waking moment trying to cover up for the havoc he left in the trail of his binges and blackouts. It was not fair that her life was ending just when she had it all figured out and was moving in a straight line, at last. She loved it that we had insisted on giving her the party and was moved that so many people had called to say they were coming.

In the last week of August my brothers and I got up early and went fishing for the party. Tee and Dupree went out on a boat in Lake Moultrie and caught the landlocked bass that grew to be huge in those chilly, man-made depths of the lake near Columbia. Silas McCall and Max Rusoff bought a license and spent the week trolling for shrimp even though both men had passed their eightieth birthdays. They headed the shrimp themselves and iced them in seawater in quart containers. The gathering of food for Lucy's party was ceremonious, valedictory. Only Dr. Pitts and I were weighted down by the awful knowledge that the cancer would soon steal the vitality and bloom from Lucy's famously rosy complexion. We knew that she was drying up from the inside.

The night before the party, on the Isle of Orion, Lucy led us down to the designated nesting grounds in front of her beach house. Here, marked with flat rectangular stakes, and rimmed with wire fencing, she and her volunteers had reburied the eggs of the mother loggerheads that had begun to lay their eggs in the warm, inert sand on May 15. The beach erosion had been furious, with great storms devouring the sand. Four nests had washed away before Lucy informed the South Carolina Wildlife Department that she was ignoring their directive to let the nests stay where the loggerheads had laid them in the sand. The sight of turtles' eggs soaked with seawater and torn open by crabs and sea birds sickened Lucy. Each gold yolk she found drying out against the shells represented another notch on the belt of extinction to her. There had been thirty-seven nests that summer and she and her co-workers had removed two thousand seventy-four eggs to the nursery that she could watch over from her front porch on the beach.

The incubation period in the hot sands was two months and even in the release of the baby loggerheads, Lucy did not see fit to obey the law to its letter. According to department rulings, if someone was granted permission to move a loggerhead's nest (which Lucy had not been granted), that individual could not touch that nest once the eggs had been reburied. The department agreed with Darwin that the laws of natural selection were paramount and should be allowed to make their own severe covenants of choice when the turtles burst from their nests and made their race for the sea.

But over the years Lucy had seen too much attrition among the ranks of the baby loggerheads that she considered wasteful and unnecessary. Once she had found ten baby turtles stacked like tin cans in the den of a ghost crab, most of them still alive and helpless, waiting for the crab to decapitate them and dine on their heads. She had watched as raccoons moved among the turtles, fighting with the seagulls who swept down on the babies from above, biting off their small heads and dropping their shells into the shallow breakwaters. Lucy had also witnessed the turtles making it to the waterline only to be snatched up by the wickedly swift blue crabs that waited for them in the surf or to be devoured by small sharks and blues who waited in deeper water.

Though she could do nothing about the enemies they encountered in the ocean, she devised a plan that at least gave them all a chance to make it into the sea. Every time that Lucy Pitts moved an egg that summer, she broke a South Carolina law. But almost every baby loggerhead under her protection knew the taste of seawater before it began on its journey out toward the Sargasso Sea.

At sunset, the night before her party, my mother marched out of her house holding Leah's hand and my brothers and I lined up behind her in single file. She carried a bucket and a large clam shell to dig into the undermined nest. Betty and Al Sobol, her chief assistants, were already waiting with the usual congregation of tourists and their overexcited children. The news of the turtle release program had already made it the leading tourist attraction on the island after golf. Lucy had a strict code of rules and instilled discipline into the tourists, who were careful to stay behind the demarcated area that Lucy had fenced off.

"Is the nest ripe?" Lucy asked Betty Sobol.

"See for yourself," Betty answered. "They're ready to go."

Lucy waited for us to gather around her and for the tourists to arrange themselves comfortably within earshot. She took her role of teacher with great seriousness and she had no comic side when it came to her turtles.

She brought the same sense of style to the turtle program that she had brought to the story of Sherman and Elizabeth during the Spring Tour of homes. What she said could not be written on placards, but there was a sincerity in her voice that was authentic, bankable. Before the development of the Isle of Orion, hundreds of loggerheads once made their nests on this same beach. The story was the same for many species of animal all over the world before the great, slow-footed dance of extinction gathered speed as man continued to poison and lay waste to everything he loved the best. She pointed to the nest they would uncover that night and told the children to note that the sand had fallen into a soft funnel, which meant the turtles had broken their shells and had begun to dig themselves out. They were interfering with this process, Lucy explained, because she wanted to give the most turtles the greatest possibility to survive the dangerous voyage ahead. The children groaned when Lucy told them that only one of these turtles would survive long enough to come back to this same beach to lay her eggs.

"Many of us will be dead when that lone turtle returns," Lucy said. "I want some of you children to promise me that you'll come back each summer to help make sure these turtles will continue to survive. Promise me. Raise your hands."

Leah's hand shot up first, followed by those of every child who stood attentive in that quasi-military semicircle. Noting the unanimity, Lucy nodded, then sank to her knees and studied the contours of the nest they would excavate that night.

"Dig with your hand tonight, darling," she said to Leah, who began to take handfuls of sand from the deepest point of the inverted V. When she took out her fourth handful of sand, she was holding a wriggling, electric body of a small turtle.

"Keep a strict count," Lucy warned. "One hundred nineteen eggs were in this nest." Lucy took the first turtle, examined it to see if it still had egg yolk attached to its abdomen, then placed it in her bucket.

"One," Leah said, and then she brought out two more turtles and handed them to her grandmother as children squealed and pressed forward.

Lucy studied each turtle for signs of the egg yolk which would drown them if it were still on their shells when they were placed in the ocean. A little blond girl broke lose from her mother and asked Lucy if she could hold one.

Lucy placed it in the five-year-old hand and asked, "What's your name, sweet roll?"

"Rachel," the child answered.

"Put it in the bucket. This turtle's named Rachel."

"Is it mine?" the girl asked.

"That's your turtle," Lucy answered. "Yours forever and ever."

Leah brought up ninety-six turtles that were ready to make their walks to the sea that evening. Twenty-three were still weighted down with yolk they would need to absorb before they tested their strength against the Atlantic. Leah buried those turtles again in the same sand she had removed. She smoothed it flat with the palm of her hand and covered it with wire to prevent the raccoons from making a mid-morning raid.

The crowd followed Lucy and Leah down to the beach fifty yards away. With the shaft of a damaged, headless five-iron, Lucy drew a large semicircle in the sand that she told the crowd they could not pass beyond. The tourists spread out along that drawn perimeter and watched closely as Leah tipped over the bucket and those ninety-six turtles boiled out and made their first struggling efforts to reach the sea. The tide was coming in and running strong to the north as those tiny loggerheads, afire with sudden life, each the size of a silver dollar and the color of unshined military shoes, fanned out in careless disorder, each one enclosed in the sudden responsibility of its own destiny. The crowd began to cheer, urging the turtles onward as they made their halting, unskilled way toward the roaring surf. One turtle led the way, breaking far ahead of the pack. But all of them moved in the same direction.

"How do they know to go toward the ocean?" a young mother asked.

"Scientists say the light," Lucy explained.

"What do you think?" the mother asked.

"These are South Carolina turtles like my boys here," Lucy said, smiling at us. "I think they listen to the waves. I think they just love beach music."

When the first turtle hit the first wave it tumbled upside down and righted itself quickly, undeterred. It had felt the element it was destined to join and when the second wave hit that turtle was swimming. Pure instinct drove those tiny turtles toward the surf as the topography and smell of that beachhead imprinted themselves forever in their newly hatched primitive brains. Once they had made this walk to the sea, you could take those loggerheads on a spaceflight to Mars, return them to the Lido of Venice, and they would still make their way back to the Isle of Orion to lay their eggs. In them, the homing instinct was a form of genius.

As each turtle reached the water, I could see the joy in Lucy's face. She never tired of watching the little creatures struggling over the sands until they reached the sea. Once in the water, they took off like young buntings in first flight. She watched as their tiny, snakelike heads appeared on the surface of the wind-driven sea, to take in a pinch of air, then resume their glorious and perilous journey. Her happiness was an earned pleasure that she could share with strangers.

"Leah," she said, reaching for Leah's hand again, "every time I see this, I feel like I've discovered God all over again."

A young mother who had red hair approached Lucy and said, "This is against the law, isn't it? I read an article recently that said that man should let nature work in its own way."

"Then nature wants the loggerhead turtle to die out," Lucy said.

"Then that is God's will," the woman said.

"It might be. But I sure as hell don't agree," Lucy said.

"You'd go against God's will?" the woman, who wore a gold cross on her necklace, said.

Lucy answered, "It won't be the first time the two of us've disagreed. This is the third night you've been with us for a turtle release."

"No, it's my fourth," the redheaded woman

said, looking away from the beach toward the line of houses.

"Stay for Labor Day," John Hardin said to the woman. "We're giving my mother a big party. Everyone's invited."

"I won't be here that long," the woman said, as Lucy saw revolving blue lights reflected in the woman's pupil. "In fact, I've got to leave now."

"You shouldn't've called the cops," Lucy said. "I try to help the turtles have a fighting chance."

"You break the law," the woman said. "I have a degree in biology. You're interfering with the natural process."

"Lady, you called the cops on my mother," John Hardin said, blocking the woman's escape route.

"Kill her, John Hardin," Tee said.

"Shut up, Tee," Dupree warned, moving between John Hardin and the woman. "Easy now. This can all be explained."

"My mother's got leukemia, lady," John Hardin said, his anger growing as the police drew closer. "You think going to jail's going to help my mother fight cancer?"

"No one's above the law," the woman said.

"How many years in prison'll I get after I kill this woman, Dallas?" John Hardin asked, and now some of the other tourists began to murmur among themselves and one woman shouted for the police to hurry.

"It wouldn't count as premeditated murder," Dallas said. "You went wild after the lady arrested your mama, who was dying of cancer. I think you'd probably serve three years with time off for good behavior."

"My boys are big pranksters, honey," Lucy said to the terrified woman.

"But I've spent half my life in the insane asylum up in Columbia," John Hardin said. "Surely, a jury'd have pity on a poor schizophrenic."

"Cut it out, John Hardin. Quit egging him on, Dallas. Relax, honey. Go on up to my house and fix yourself a drink," Lucy said, and she waved a finger of warning at the rest of us as the sheriff approached accompanied by the young woman who worked for the Wildlife Department.

"My, my, Sheriff," Lucy said. "What are you doing out here on a pretty night like this when hunters are out killing deer out of season and good ol' boys are staked out all over these creeks baiting for shrimp?"

"Got a complaint about you, Lucy," Sheriff Littlejohn said.

"I've got a drawerful of complaints about you, Lucy," the wildlife officer, Jane, said. "But

Lucy insists that she knows better than any law enforcement could."

"If you know so damn much, explain why the loggerhead's an endangered species," Lucy said.

"As your attorney of record, I advise you to remain silent, Mother," Dallas said.

"Mama, are they going to arrest the turtle lady?" a little girl cried out.

"I've been doing this same job for years. The same damn way," Lucy said. "They keep changing the rules on me."

"I've got a warrant for your arrest, Lucy," Sheriff Littlejohn said.

"Hey, Sheriff, Mom's sick. She's not going to spend the night in jail," I said.

"I went to school with you, Littlejohn," Dupree said. "You flunked English."

"I got a *D*," Littlejohn said.

"Who's got a tire iron?" John Hardin said to the crowd. "I'm gonna beat this redheaded woman down to crab bait."

"You heard him, Sheriff," the woman said. "He threatened me in earshot of the law itself."

"He's got more voices talking in his head than a TV set," the sheriff said. "Pay no mind."

"What law was broken, Sheriff?" Dallas asked.

"No one's allowed to go into a turtle nest," the sheriff said.

Jane from Wildlife said, "She helps them get to the ocean. That's against the rules."

"My mother didn't touch a nest tonight," I said. "You've got a beachful of witnesses. My daughter and I dug up that nest. Isn't that true?"

The crowd murmured its assent.

"Then I'll be pleased to arrest you, Jack."

"But she supervised the whole thing," the redheaded woman said. "She was definitely in command."

"Cuff me, Littlejohn," Lucy said, playing to the crowd. "It'll be front-page news across the state."

A man's voice rang out behind the sheriff. "Leave my wife alone, Littlejohn." It was Dr. Jim Pitts, who had run down from the screened-in porch to see what the disturbance was. "They were making pancakes and waffles from these turtle's eggs when we got to the island. Lucy changed all that."

"Get back to your houses, people," the sheriff called out to the crowd, but they refused to disassemble and remained clustered and aggravated, waiting to see how the confrontation would resolve itself.

"She sacrifices everything for these damn turtles," Dr. Pitts said. "Everything."

"We're not saying she hasn't done good work in the past . . ." Jane said.

"I dug up all the turtles, Sheriff," Leah said. "I put them in the bucket and I carried them down here near the beach. My grandmother didn't do one thing."

"That's right," people in the crowd said.

"If anyone touches you, Mama, I'll kill them with my bare hands," John Hardin said, moving between the sheriff and his mother.

"The arrest warrant's got your name on it, Lucy," Sheriff Littlejohn said.

"Let me just go down to the jailhouse," Lucy said. "Come with me, Dallas, and bail me out of there."

"Trust a goddamn lawyer in this country?" John Hardin said. "After Watergate I wouldn't trust one of you bastards to read out a phone number from the men's room."

"Shut up, John Hardin," Dupree said. "You sound like you need a shot."

"A man expresses a simple opinion, Dupree, and you call for Thorazine."

Sheriff Littlejohn ended the discussion by cuffing Lucy's hands together in a single, economical movement that caught everyone by surprise. Lucy took two steps toward the squad car, the sheriff firmly gripping her elbow. Then Lucy interfered with the arrest by fainting head first into the sand in front of her. Dr. Pitts lunged toward her and lifted her head out of the sand as John Hardin tackled the redheaded lady and wrestled her to the sand. My brothers pulled John Hardin off, but he punched Tee in the mouth and kicked Dallas squarely in the genitalia as the crowd began shouting so loudly that someone sitting on their deck up the beach went in and alerted Security at the Isle of Orion gate. When the sheriff fired a single shot in the air to restore calm, Dr. Pitts screamed loudly and commanded that everyone step back and allow Lucy room to breathe. Sheriff Littlejohn sighed, then bent down and un-locked the handcuffs that bound Lucy's wrists together. Lucy looked as frail as any shell that lay strewn and storm-tossed on the beach. Dr. Pitts had tears running down his face, but they were fierce tears of anger, not sorrow. Though he tried to speak, fury disbanded any words, and he stammered over the body of his wife. This stranger who had married my mother, I thought once more, loves her far more deeply than any of us realize.

"Rape, murder, pillage, drugs, and mayhem all over Waterford County," Tee screamed, "and the high sheriff of the low country boldly arrests our mother, an environmentalist with leukemia. Good work, Littlejohn, you silly-ass loser of the twentieth century."

The crowd slowly divested itself of a shape,

drifting like smoke into the gentle last light, a moon sneaking a forehead above the waterline to the east. I knelt down and lifted my mother up into my arms and began walking back to her house. Still trying to find words, Dr. Pitts trailed behind us and Dallas picked up Leah and rode her on his back, following our lead.

In the house Dr. Pitts exploded after I had taken Lucy to her bedroom and she had recovered strength enough to take a sip of water and change into her nightclothes before she fell asleep.

"I have something to say to you boys," Dr. Pitts began as he poured himself a tumbler full of scotch. "I know you love your mother and I know she loves you. But you'll kill her faster if you don't get control of yourselves. All of you need to learn to be part of a room without filling it up. You need to learn to be in a scene without being the whole scene. You don't need to be the funniest, the wildest, the craziest, the weirdest, or the loudest person on earth to get Lucy's attention. She loves all of you. But there's too much commotion around you boys. I demand that you quit turning every single thing into an event. Everything is over the top when you guys are around. Learn to relax. To muse things over. To look at things calmly and at a normal pace. Why is that impossible with you McCalls? Why must every day seem like a

home movie from the Apocalypse? Your
mother needs rest from all this. She needs
quiet. And tomorrow, you're giving her a party
and the whole town's invited. Everybody. I
haven't met a single soul who isn't invited to
Lucy's party. Black, white, everybody in town
has called to RSVP for tomorrow and even
Lucy doesn't know half of them. Things move
from an event, then a spectacle, then an extrav-
aganza. You attract noise and disorder. You're
all in love with what's bad for Lucy. You're killing her. You boys are killing what you can't
stand to say good-bye to . . ."

"I agree with Dr. Pitts," John Hardin said.
"You guys are just scumbugs and shouldn't be
allowed near Mama."

"Why don't you write a 'Dear Abby' column for fruitcakes, John Hardin?" Dupree
said.

"You had the worst grades of any of the
brothers, by far," John Hardin lashed back.
"The only job you could hold down was locking
up crazy people."

"No harm in that," Dupree said. "I get to
spend all my time round wonderful guys like
you."

"What a low-life, criminal-type loser you
are," John Hardin said to Dupree. "Making a
mockery of the mentally ill."

"You two are scaring Leah," Dallas suggested quietly. "Jack's raised her to think that life is full of teddy bears, free pizza, and photos of the tooth fairy. She's been vaccinated to fight off the full horror of being a McCall."

"Listen to you, here it goes," Dr. Pitts said. "Each one of you takes it to a higher and higher pitch. Can you shut up? Can you shut your mouths now and let my poor wife sleep?"

"Shall we call off the party?" Tee asked Dr. Pitts.

"Your mother would never speak to me again if I called off her party," Dr. Pitts said, rising and moving toward his bedroom. "Help me make it go smoothly, boys. Please. I beg of you."

"Hey, Doc," Dupree said seriously. "Thanks for loving our mom. It's nice of you and we appreciate it."

"She's had a hard life," I said, "and she hardly got a single break. But Mom's said that you are the best thing that ever happened to her."

When Lucy rose the next morning, refreshed and vibrant, she referred with delicious irony to our party for her as "The Last Supper." She put on a pretty dress that she had bought at Saks Fifth Avenue in Atlanta and a broad-brimmed hat that came from a boutique on the

Via del Corso in Rome. She radiated the natural prettiness she had brought with her out of
the North Carolina mountains, as she watched
Dr. Pitts make her breakfast and fret over her.
His sweetness clearly tickled her, even though
there was something schoolmarmish and fastidious about it. His mouth was pursed constantly
as though he had just said "harrumph" and his
face looked like the old maid on the dog-eared
pack of cards that we used to play with on
those days that we stayed home from school
with fevers. It seemed to me that their love was
based on their common need for order and
mannerliness in their lives. Both had endured
lives of chaos and incivility in their first marriages, and they provided each other with safe
harbor at last.

The town of Waterford had finally, after
forty years, grown accustomed to Lucy's way of
doing things. It knew the tenderhearted, deferential Lucy as well as it knew the vulgar, unac-
commodating one. Five hundred townspeople
came to her "Last Supper," two hundred more
than were invited. Lucy never stood on ceremony, and everyone in Waterford knew that
her door was always open. And she always
smiled in public. They all came to say good-bye
to her famous smile.

Mike Hess had suggested the whole affair
be catered and done up right but we had in-

sisted on doing all the cooking ourselves. Like all of my close friends, he had fallen in love with my mother long before he ever got around to falling in love with girls his own age. When Mike gave his first interview in *Premiere* magazine, he told his interrogator that he first knew that small towns were the residences of goddesses when he went to his best friend's fifth birthday party and caught a glimpse of Lucy McCall. Mike had spent so much time at my house as much because of Lucy's good-natured flirtatiousness with young boys as his closeness to me, and I always knew it. Lucy was one of those charismatic mothers who took the time to listen and counsel her children's friends and by so doing influenced all of us, for better or worse, who were lucky enough to be around her.

The Red Clay Ramblers set up on the riverbank and played their sweet music for hours at a time. Senator Ernest Hollings held court on one side of the huge expanse of grassy yard that led from the back of the house to the water, and his Republican counterpart, Strom Thurmond, kissed the hands of every lady in sight as the air filled up with the smell of a feast bad for the arteries and good for the soul. Dupree had a pot of Frogmore stew simmering near the line of picnic tables and I could smell the pork sausage, mingling with the fresh corn and shrimp, cutting the air with its special tang of barnyard, field, and saltwater creek. Opposite me stood Dallas, dressed in jeans and shirt, shoveling oysters onto tin sheets spread over cinder blocks and heated by a fierce wood fire. He would place the oysters with great precision, evening up their exposure to the heat, until they would pop open from the force of their own interior steam and spill their fragrant juices onto the tin. Then Dallas would shovel the opened oysters onto picnic tables covered with newspapers and the perfume of those washed-down mollusks gave off a silvery, slightly metallic musk of a rained-on acre of spartina. Tee and the sisters-in-law served platefuls of barbecue, which glistened in a mustard-based sauce that made the pork look like it had been painted with gold leaf. Three open bars had the crowd garrulous and ice chests full of beer were packed down and there for the taking. The women had come gussied up because they knew from experience that Lucy did not know the meaning of the word "casual" and would come dressed to kill no matter how hard they tried to wrestle the secret of the dress code for the party from her.

Mike had been standing beside Lucy and Dr. Pitts on the veranda to form an informal receiving line that marched up the front steps, shook hands with the guest of honor beneath the shade of eight Ionic columns, then passed through to the center of the house and down the outside staircase following the music and the smell of good food. I had given Leah the job of recording the entire event for posterity on a camcorder.

"You're the producer, the director, the soundman, and the gaffer all rolled into one. Make like Fellini. Make us all famous," I had told Leah.

For the rest of the afternoon Leah wandered, in her white dress, through the immense, good-natured crowd. She was now as much a part of Waterford as anyone there and each time she aimed her camera at a strange cluster of people, someone would notice her, step back, and introduce the entire group to her. More than once I heard some man or woman she had never met say, "Lawd, child, if you aren't the spitting image of your pretty mama. Shyla took ballet lessons with my grandchild, Bailey, and if those two just didn't have a time. She was graceful as a lily on stage. I know, child. I was there."

Leah seemed relieved to have her camera between her and the lost country of memory these people claimed to see with such clarity when they stared at her features. Every time I overheard the name Shyla, I felt again the cold solitude of being motherless that was being pressed on Leah. And I was glad she had the camera as a fence to protect herself, an excuse to be invisible. Cameras are a lifesaver for very shy people who have nowhere else to hide. Behind a lens they can disguise the fact that they have nothing to say to strangers.

As I kept eight pots of salted water turning out perfectly cooked pasta, it seemed as though the drama of my whole life paraded by. Mrs. Lipsitz, who had fitted my shoes during my entire boyhood, ordered spaghetti with pesto sauce from me as she stood chatting with Mr. Edwards, who sold me my first suit. He had come with Coach Small, who had taught me to throw a curve ball, and Coach Singleton, who had shared the secrets of downfield blocking with me. He stood near Miss Economy, who once made me sing "God Rest Ye Merry Gentlemen" solo on New Year's Eve when the ice storm hit Colleton and killed an oak tree that had been growing along the river when Columbus discovered America. Over fifty black people mingled through the crowd and I thought again how lucky I was to have been raised by Southern parents who not only were not racists, but who worked with uncommon zeal to ensure that we were uninfected by the South's virulent portable virus. Our parents represented something very fine and dangerous at a time when Southern whites stood shoulder to shoulder to demonstrate their attention to ideas both insupportable and un-American.

In 1956, when I was just eight years old, my father, Johnson Hagood McCall, was a brilliant, if irascible, jurist. At that time, in the early apprenticeship of his drinking, lawyers dreaded his court because he did not tolerate lack of preparation or the wasting of his time. His tongue lashings of counsel were famous and withering. His court sessions were orderly and his judgments fair. Though Johnson Hagood was neither a good father nor an admirable husband, the law ennobled him and brought out aspects of character that surprised even him. But it was not a good time in South Carolina history to combine valor with a judge's gavel.

He was a circuit judge of the Fourteenth Judicial District, and was away from Waterford for long periods of time in that position. The case that brought him to grief was simple but controversial in the rural county where it came to trial. A high school English teacher by the name of Tony Calabrese had been fired from his job for advocating openly in his classroom the integration of the public schools. Mr. Calabrese was employed by the Reese County School Board and Reese County was known all over South Carolina for the backwardness of its citizens. My father referred to Reese County as the "incest capital of the world" and he held its lawyers in utter contempt. Tony Calabrese admitted that he had advocated the integration of schools, but only as a teaching tool and only to stimulate class discussion among students who he felt were brain-dead and bereft of all ideas. It did not help that Tony Calabrese, who had been born in Haddonfield, New Jersey, to immigrants from Naples, was a practicing Roman Catholic and an open Republican.

As the trial unfolded, it became apparent to my father that the school board had not followed a single one of the procedures for due process when it fired Mr. Calabrese. On the witness stand, the teacher himself was fiery and unrepentant and gave the counsel for the school board all he could handle. Mr. Calabrese bristled with outrage and stated that the world of ideas would not be eclipsed in any classroom over which he presided and he would not be bullied by anyone for thinking whatever he saw fit to believe. As my father listened, he thought that the trial of Tony Calabrese was a good thing for every small town to go through and he found himself silently cheering for the embattled teacher as the mood of the courtroom grew testier and more hostile. He began to identify with this incandescent plaintiff who had brought suit against an ill-prepared school board.

Toward the end of the trial my father asked Calabrese, "How did you get down here to Reese County, sir?"

Calabrese looked up and smiled at him, then said, "Just beginner's luck, Your Honor."

My father laughed, but his was the only smile in that grim-faced court. He ruled in favor of Calabrese, reinstated him with pay, then made the mistake of lecturing both the school board and the citizenry of Reese County.

"You cannot fire a teacher for discussing in class what is contained in the daily headlines of our newspapers. One may disagree with the concept of integration, but anyone who reads can see it is inevitable. You can fire a hundred Calabreses today, but integration will still be coming tomorrow. Calabrese was simply preparing your children for the future. His firing was an act of frustration, because you want so much to hold on to the past. I've read *Brown v. the Board of Education* over and over again. It's bad public policy, but it's good law. You cannot fire a man for teaching about a constitutional right. Integration's coming to South Carolina, Calabrese or not."

That night in Reese County ten men in masks came for Tony Calabrese, and though he struggled, they beat him half to death with fists and ax handles. They burnt his car and his house and they drove him to the state line of New Jersey, where they dumped him bound up in an oyster sack and blind in one eye. The ten men who assaulted Calabrese were never caught but were well known among their fellow citizens, who believed in their hearts that Calabrese had received a well-deserved civics lesson in the Southern way of doing things.

The evening after the trial my father presided over a formal dinner of local officials and their wives who were meeting at our house to plan a political fund-raiser for a young politician by the name of Ernest F. Hollings, who was planning to run for governor. News of Calabrese's disappearance had reached Waterford and the sheriff had sent word that it might be wise to post a deputy at our house for the next week or so. Since my father felt no sense of danger in his hometown, he was not disturbed at all. But my mother was alarmed a great deal and as she prepared the meal that night, she checked all the approaches that led to the house and secretly put in a call to the sheriff to see if there was any late-arriving news about the abducted teacher. She was six months pregnant with my youngest brother, John Hardin, and she thought she knew much more intuitively than her husband how rural white people felt about the topic of integration. Dallas, Dupree, Tee, and I were put to bed early and all the locks were checked on the windows. The four of us had watched her break jelly glasses in the sink that afternoon and place the jagged fragments on the railing going around the veranda. As my mother took inventory of the situation, my father drank. The bourbon made him both self-righteous and less worried about the disappearance of Calabrese.

Because of Jack Daniel's, my father faced the evening unafraid; because of Jim Crow, Lucy put my brothers and me all in my room for safekeeping with the dog, Chippie, guarding the door.

Lucy had set her dining room table with great care, and she watched the languorous, confident guests as they slowly drifted into the dining room toward the aromas of baked Cornish hens and wild rice and turnip greens. She watched Becky Trask and Julia Randel take their seats as elegantly as monarch butterflies settling on peonies, while their husbands held their chairs and the candelabra glowed.

I was sound asleep when I heard Chippie rouse herself from my bed and walk over to stare out of the window into darkness. The hair on her spine stood out, erect, and there was a steady growl in her throat. Getting up and going to her, I stared out of the window and saw nothing in the moonless night. But I could not calm Chippie.

"It's nothing, Chippie," I said, but the hair on Chippie's neck said otherwise and there was a fierce humming in her throat that my words could not stifle.

Suddenly a brick crashed through the downstairs window and landed squarely on the dinner table. Other bricks followed and I heard Becky Trask scream when one of them struck her on the shoulder and every chair was overturned in the frantic scramble to avoid that shower of bricks. The half-burned candles were strewn around the room and my father found himself pressed face to face with the town's mayor, as a voice screamed out in the darkness, "We'll kill you, you nigger-lovin' judge. We'll kill you dead."

Then a fusillade of rifle fire burst through the window and I heard the women screaming and the men shouting for each other to do something. Then I heard a shotgun go off just beneath my window and it seemed as though someone was on the porch firing at short range below me.

"They're gonna shoot us down like dogs right here on the floor," I heard the mayor shout at my father and the shotgun rang out again as the attackers seemed to be running away into the night. Far off I heard a siren sound, which was answered by the steady, hysterical barking of Chippie, locked upstairs with my brothers and me.

In silence, the guests were lying on the floor when they saw a shadow cross the threshold of the front door, and in the dim, sputtering light of candles, they watched as Lucy returned her still-smoking shotgun to its rightful place in the closet by the front door. My mother understood the nature of the white people of Reese County far better than my father did with all his degrees and all the finesse he brought to bear in arcane areas of legal dissent.

She had prepared the meal and loaded her shotgun just in case there were unwanted visitors who had come to do her family harm. She was firing from the hip when she first opened that front door and she would have killed any man she had encountered on that blacked-out veranda.

The incident marked the first of many times that the town of Waterford would have to revise their opinion about my mother.

My brothers and I heard the story of those night riders over and over again during our childhood. The bullet holes were never repaired in the dining room plaster or in the mantel over the fireplace. Those bullet holes served as sacred reminders that our father had the courage of his convictions and it was important to stand for something of great value in a society that had debased itself with the fury of its own worst instincts. They also reminded us of a father we could take pride in, even though it was a father we hardly remembered. The shotgun pellets from Lucy's surprising fusillade remain embedded in three columns of the veranda as both mementos and lessons for us, her children, and a warning to those who would approach our house with malice and treachery in their hearts. They did so only at their own peril. The Calabrese trial was my father's finest hour.

I thought of those valiant days as I watched Governor Dick Riley take Lucy by the hand and escort her down the back steps to the applause of the crowd. Not bad for a redneck girl, Mama, I thought, as I watched Strom Thurmond kiss her hand and Ernest Hollings try to outrun Bishop Unterkoefler to get into the photographs that were being taken by newspapers from as far away as Charlotte. The Red Clay Ramblers broke into the "Tennessee Waltz" and Joe Riley, mayor of Charleston, danced with Lucy as other couples joined them. Tee made Leah put down the camcorder and dance with her "favorite" uncle. Before the day was out, Leah had danced with half the men in Waterford, growing dizzy trying to place the array of faces with her parents' history in this small, two-steepled town that she could see

through the arms of her ever-changing partners. I watched with a secret smile as she was
spun across the lawn by the sweet-natured men
who had grown up beside this river walking in
and out of my life and Shyla's.

When the Ramblers began a set of beach
music songs from the glory days of those long-
ago Myrtle Beach summers, I put my chef's
toque down amid the plates of steaming pasta
and ran out, with my apron flapping madly
around my legs, and asked my mother for a
dance. The song was "Green Eyes" by Jimmy
Ricks and the Ravens and it took me back to
the pier at Folly Beach in the summer of 1969
when I had joined all my high school friends on
a night ride up the cypress-columned Highway
17 in Capers' new Impala convertible, eight of
us drinking and singing along with a radio
turned up full-blast as the air, scented with the
black-water lilies of the Edisto River, rushed
over us.

I spun my mother into the applause and
sunlight and watched Leah recording our
dance with the camera as I sang the words of
"Green Eyes" to my pretty mother. I closed my
eyes and heard the rhythm of the song, and my
mother's hand transfigured itself into Shyla's
hand and my feet moved along the grass as
they had along the wooden floor of the Middletons' house with the Atlantic moving to the

music beneath us so many years ago. That was
a time when our love was an outline and a con-
cordance yet to be agreed on and Shyla's laughter as she danced while our classmates
screamed their fear at us was an invoice of col-
lusion and promise of things to come. Shyla
wrote a love song that night with her eyes every
time she looked at me. She made my bloodstream feel like the place that the gods had to
find before they could discover fire. My love for
Shyla was different from the love I felt as I
danced with my mother, yet there was a relationship that burned with a clear, rough energy
within me. The connection felt absolutely sacred to me between the woman who had given
birth to me and the woman who had given birth
to my sweet-faced Leah who was now filming
this dance. Is there anything on earth more
lovely than a son dancing with his mother famous for her small-town beauty? I thought,
and I tried to take the thought even further. I
felt lucky that I could love Lucy with a pure,
uncorrupted love because she was the sole possessor of the only mother's face I would ever
know. The word "mother" applied to a single
woman on earth and it hurt me deeply that I
had become a fugitive from this woman's confusion about how to love a son. Because of
Lucy's extraordinarily tangled character, I
knew that mothers could come in a dazzling

assortment of disguises . . . I felt a tap on my shoulder and Dallas asked to cut in on this dance and then I saw Tee and Dupree getting in line to follow suit. After she danced with each of us she could dance with the rest of the menfolk in town, but then I looked around and noticed that my father seemed everywhere in his unsolicited but welcome role of gray eminence. He roamed through the crowd with the bearing and discipline of a ringmaster. Because of his sodden history, his sons kept a close watch on his every movement and traded hand signals with one another when he moved out of one brother's quadrant of vision and into another's purview. After a lifetime observing my father get drunk and the inestimable horror he could wreak on all the lives he staggered into, I had come to understand why the military shot their guards who fell asleep on duty during wartime. I had seen my father ruin a dozen parties as nice as this one.

But he was managing to gain perfect control over himself for Lucy's party, even though his sons had suggested the wisdom of leaving off our father's name from the guest list. But Lucy had stopped by the law office and issued the invitation in person. Privately she told me they had talked together for over an hour, and that meeting had thrilled the judge because of

its intimacy and its validation of their years together.

"Your mother's quite a package, son," my
father said to me.

Lovingly, I answered him by saying, "Get
drunk and I'll kill you."

"I wouldn't think of getting drunk at my
own wife's party," he said with maddening
piety.

But my father was making good on his
word, and he moved from group to group with
the dignity of a minister of protocol. He was
dressed in an immaculate white summer suit.
Carefully, he avoided the central action where
Lucy and Dr. Pitts held court, but he conducted
himself with impeccable charm and grace.

"What a handsome man," I heard someone
say to Ledare, and I noticed that Leah kept the
camera on her grandfather whenever he glided
into view.

When the Red Clay Ramblers broke into
their rendition of Bert Kaempfert's "Wonderful by Night," my brothers looked quickly
toward the band, each of them sharing the
same thought I had, that money had exchanged
hands. It was my parents' favorite song to slow-
dance to, and I held my breath as I watched the
judge approach my mother from across the
yard.

He bowed deeply at my mother, who stood

beside Dr. Pitts; she curtsied in return. My father asked the doctor if he could have permission to dance with his pretty wife, and the doctor made a sweet, accommodating gesture with his arm. They spun out toward the lawn, my father swinging my mother in the broad, show-offy rendition of what had once been a simple waltz. Every other dancer moved to the side, and I could not bring myself to look at my brothers while our parents danced. I could not have spoken to another human being during their two minutes spinning on that well-manicured grass. That they danced so beautifully together moved me greatly; that their lives together had been such a perfect disaster shook me more; that these were my parents almost brought me to my knees. I followed them with my eyes and knew that the dance meant as much to both of them as it did to their sons.

At the end of the dance, my father led her back to Dr. Pitts and the two men embraced and Lucy led the crowd in its applause.

Mike and Ledare came up beside me and we stood together, our arms draped over each other's shoulders as the Red Clay Ramblers went classic with the beach music and moved right into "Sixty Minute Man" as the crowd roared its approval.

"My song. My song," Mike said, shimmying out and motioning for Ledare to join him.

Ledare moved out to meet him with the confidence of a cat measuring the distance between the floor and a tabletop.

"What a good-looking woman," I shouted at her.

"Damn right," she said. "Glad you noticed."

"Who sang this song? This holy, holy song that should be written down and placed in the Talmud?" Mike asked.

"I know. Give me a minute," Ledare said.

"It was Billy Ward and the Dominoes," I said.

"Jack's my main man," Mike said. "The past is as sacred to Jack as it is to me. Marry me, Ledare. You're the only woman I know that I haven't been married to."

"Could I make you happy, Mike?" Ledare asked.

"Of course not. Because I'd still be me. Trapped with the mind and soul of Mike Hess, who is satisfied with nothing. Who looks all over the world trying to be as happy as he was growing up here as a kid."

"I want to make someone happy," Ledare said. "I might even have a gift for it."

"Good line. Put it in the script. Nah. I like you far too much to marry you. My ex-wives hate me. They're all millionaires living better lives than Louis Quatorze and they all hate my guts. Go figure. Then call my accountant. He's the one it really bothers. Hey, Grandma, let's trip the light fantastic, darling."

Mike moved over with Ledare in tow and lifted Esther Rusoff out of her seat as she protested every step of the way. Ledare reached out and took Max Rusoff by the hand and all of them moved among the low country dancers.

"Make sure you film this, Leah," I said. "Ledare dancing with the Great Jew. Mike dancing with Esther, wife of the Great Jew."

I spotted Capers and his child-bride Betsy, making political hay as they worked the crowd together. Their smiles were congruent as though the same orthodontist had set their teeth using the same wiring. They moved like a pair of lions on the hunt, all concentration and feral grace. They sprang in tandem toward the flanks of voters. Periodically, I would see their eyes meet and a flash of recognition pass over them, acknowledging to each other that they made a good team.

"Betsy," I said, when they approached my table. "Does your insecurity come from long practice? Or was it just a natural gift?"

Betsy's eyes flashed with anger, but she was far too polished to rise to my bait.

"Oh, Jack. I was just talking about you. I do hope you've already purchased your ticket back to Italy."

"You're good, Betsy," I said. "What a shame this beautiful friendship'll wither from neglect."

"It will if I've got anything to do with it," she said.

"I like it when you're mean, Betsy," I said. "It excites me."

"Don't let my old friend Jack get a rise out of you, darling," Capers said. "It's me he's got a problem with."

"Glad that's straight," I said.

"I hear that my ex has her eye on you, Jack," Capers said.

"I sure hope so."

"That would make us related, in a way," he continued.

"Yes of course it would," I said. "We plan to name our first kid after you."

"How flattering," he said.

"I just don't think Enema's a very pretty name. Do you, Betsy?"

"Jack, Jack," Capers said. "Your manners."

"Excuse me, Betsy," I said. "What got into me?"

"I can't believe you once actually liked this guy," Betsy said to Capers.

"You misjudge me," I said in mock horror. "Once I reminded all the world of the Christ Child. Then I read *Das Kapital.*"

"I'm trying to think of where I've met a bigger asshole," Betsy said.

"In church. Waiting at the altar. Your wedding day, sweetie," I said.

Betsy seemed ready to explode, but instead she spotted a friend across the crowded yard and moved toward her, a huge smile lighting her way.

"Betsy's perfect for you, Capers," I said. "I think that's the worst thing I've ever said about anyone."

Both of us stopped when we saw Mike Hess beaming down on us.

"Your mother's having the time of her life," Mike said.

I looked out where my mother stood in a crowd of admirers and old friends. "She's having a ball. Thanks for doing this, Mike."

"I used to get a hard-on thinking about Lucy," Mike told Capers. "But hell, who didn't?"

"Mike says the sweetest things," I said.

"It's easy to be pretty," Capers said. "But being sexy's an art."

"You should know, Capers. You're both," Mike said.

"A gene pool's the highest-priced waterfront property," Capers laughed, then asked me, "You hear about Thursday?"

I shook my head and Mike said, "I told

Ledare to tell you to keep Thursday evening open."

"What's up?" I said.

"A sound-and-light show," Capers explained, walking toward Strom Thurmond's limousine as it pulled up to the senator.

"I can't tell you," Mike said. "Capers doesn't even know the specifics. But it's going to be big. Maybe one of the biggest nights in all our lives."

"Tell me more."

"Jordan called," Mike said. "He wants us all together one more time."

"I thought he was in Europe," I said, shaken by this information.

Mike laughed and said, "I bet you're lying, Jack. But don't worry about it. Jordan got in touch with me. I didn't have any luck at all trying to hunt him down."

"Where are we going to meet?"

"I can't tell you that," Mike said. "We're still in negotiations. He's like trying to pin down the Holy Ghost. But I think this is the breakthrough for our little film. He wants a confrontation with Capers."

"Why did he get in touch with you?" I asked.

"He finally agreed to let me buy his life story," Mike explained. "I think he wants to turn himself in. If you ask me, I bet he needs the money for his legal defense."

"Mike," I said, catching my friend by the wrist, "if you or Capers try to have Jordan arrested, they're going to find you both floating face down in the lobster tank at Harris Teeter."

"I'm on your side in this, man," Mike said. "Capers wouldn't think about crossing me."

"Be careful with this," I warned. "Half this party attended Jordan's memorial service in 1971. They still think he's dead."

"These are good Christian people," Mike said, his eyes surveying the party. "Resurrection should be an easy concept for them to swallow."

"Who else is going to be there?"

"Negotiations are still ongoing," Mike said. "I've told you more than I've told anyone. Keep Thursday open."

"I can't. I'm going to Fordham's Hardware to buy fertilizer for my African violets."

"You and Ledare come together," said Mike, ignoring me. "I'll call with the details."

"Do people in Hollywood ever tell you to get laid, Mike?" I asked.

"People are terrified of me in Hollywood," Mike said and his tone was informational, not hostile. "The maggotry can offer no higher compliment."

"I'll see you Thursday," I said.

"I was a nice kid, wasn't I, Jack?"

"You were wonderful. There's never been a nicer boy," I said.

"You don't like what I've become, do you?" Mike asked.

"I sure don't."

"Not even gravity can stop a free fall, Jack," Mike said, his voice odd with its slight furor of regret. "I once saw myself differently. A young man on the move. A man of distinction and accomplishment. Then I started watching the movie of my own life and was horror-stricken by what I saw. I embarrass my own mother."

"Be nicer, Mike. We're Southerners. There's a lot wrong with that, but nice comes easy to all of us. It's who we are."

"Ah!" Mike said, his attention drawn to a 1968 Volkswagen convertible that was once yellow, but was now unwashed and sun-bleached. "Look what's coming down the Avenue of Oaks. Didn't you drive that car in college?"

"It's been passed down to all my brothers. John Hardin's got it now. He's been making a present for Mom," I said.

A piece of furniture covered with blankets hung out of the convertible as John Hardin navigated the vehicle between parked cars until he reached the center table, where Lucy was holding court. The crowd was smaller now, but her dearest friends were still in attendance and the bartenders were still busy mixing drinks on two sides of the plantation house. Leah was sitting beside Lucy as she entertained the folks at her table with a series of stories that charmed with their wit, yet contained not a trace of rancor. Leah watched Lucy mesmerize her audience by halting in mid-sentence and raising a single, quizzical eyebrow in abbreviation before delivering her punch line. At home, Leah tried this technique on me, but could not arch one eyebrow without the other following suit. As Leah watched, Lucy's athletic eyebrow rose, aimed at John Hardin's car as her son made his way to her. John Hardin had the power to unnerve my mother, but her love for him, her wounded baby, was incontestable. She tried not to let her agitation show as he greeted her and her friends with his suspicious but palmy effusions. He had finished his gift and timed it perfectly to present it to her at her party. The crowd applauded as she rose and walked over to the car, her arm holding his. John Hardin still glistened from the sweat of his labors.

He possessed a theatrical side to his nature that could come off sometimes as bizarre and other times larger-than-life. With a showman's sense of timing, he made Lucy cover her eyes and one of the Ramblers, catching the spirit of the moment, accompanied the unveiling with a drum roll. Showing enormous flair, John Hardin pulled off a series of tarpaulins and blankets that were tied around his gift, then hesitated when he was about to take off the final layer. He gave it a yank, then lifted his present out of the backseat and laid it at his mother's feet, not noticing, at first, the gasp of surprise that exploded from the crowd.

John Hardin had made a coffin for Lucy from an oak tree that lightning had killed on the back side of the Isle of Orion. He laid the coffin out on the grass and demonstrated the workmanship to Lucy, moving her hand across the deeply polished grain of wood as though he had made her a violin from the most delicate, sweetest-smelling woods. The coffin shone and you could see the grain of the oak where the saw had cut and left its mark. I saw that she, too, had received a shock when John Hardin had lifted the last blanket covering his gift, but she had recovered faster than anyone else and knew that in John Hardin's proscribed and shaken world, this coffin was the love note of a schizophrenic son who could never tailor his inarticulate, stumbling gestures of ardor to the mainstream.

Dallas shook his head and said, "He also brought her three gallons of embalming fluid."

"Look at the workmanship," Dupree said

admiringly. "It's perfect. John Hardin ought to be building yachts."

"I'd like to say something witty," Tee said, moving over to be with us, "but I'm the slow-witted brother. I'll think of something hilarious I could've said, but it'll be two months from now when I'm getting off an interchange on I-26 or trying to get money from an instant banker when I know my account's overdrawn. I know you boys've already said six or seven lines that are drop-dead funny and you're waiting for me to weigh in with just one. I can't. Dad's sperm weakened as he aged. Mom's eggs were old and cracked when John Hardin and I came along. Let me just say, I think it's weird to give your mother a coffin when she's got cancer. Yeh, that's my statement to the press. Give it to any wire service you'd like."

"He saw a real need," Dupree said. "It may be a bit odd. But it sure saved Dr. Pitts a lot of cash."

"Poor Mom. What a trooper," Dallas said. "Now she's got to thank John Hardin like he just bought a wing of a college and had it named after her."

Lucy stood on her tiptoes and kissed John Hardin on the cheek and pulled him tightly against her. She put his forehead against hers and smiled at him until he blushed. Then Lucy stepped back, looked at the coffin, and played to the crowd. "Who gave my secret away? It's just what I wanted and I can't wait to try it on."

The laughter of the crowd was relieved and grateful. They cheered Lucy's quickness, her deftness at diffusing the situation.

John Hardin surprised us by responding. "I wanted to give my mother something that few sons have ever given their moms. Most of ya'll know that I've caused my mother great worries because I've suffered from things beyond my control. I worried that my mama would think I made this because I thought she was going to die soon. That's not it at all. Mama always taught her children that words were pretty, but anyone could talk. She said, pay attention to that man or woman who *acted,* who *did,* who *performed.* She taught us to trust in things we could see, not that we heard. I almost die myself when I think of my mother not being here. I can't stand it. I can barely speak about it. But when your time comes, Mama, I want you to know that I made this coffin loving you every minute. I cut the tree down and took it to the sawmill, and sanded down every inch of wood. I polished it until I could see my face in its reflection. My brothers put this party together and I didn't help them a bit. I was doing this. I was afraid it would upset you and your friends. But I pretended that I was building the house you would live in forever, the house you'd be in when God came to get you."

Lucy hugged her son again and John Hardin wept against her shoulder as the crowd cheered even louder. Then, he broke away from her and with his enormous strength, he lifted the coffin as easily as if it were a surfboard, returned it to the backseat of the convertible, and drove out of the vast backyard without even tasting the barbecue.

"Upstaged by a schizophrenic," Dallas said. "The story of my life."

"No," I said. "What we just saw was more. The party just had a perfect ending."

CHAPTER 34

''So, Jack.

"You think you want to know what happened to me during the war? In your innocence you believe it will provide answers, the hidden clue, the reasons why poor Shyla went off that bridge in Charleston. You think the bridge that took Shyla is connected to the gates of Auschwitz, don't you, Jack? In your life everything's a recipe. Just follow the directions in order, be careful with the measurements, do not experiment, time everything, and all can enjoy a perfect meal in a safe American home. But you think *I* left an ingredient out. Once you have it, you can hold it in your hands, weigh it, smell it, catalog it, add it to the recipe, and *voilà*, throw it in the stockpot, the recipe for the death of Shyla Fox will be complete.

"Got some time for hell, Jack? Let me give you a brief biography of worms. The worms of Europe were the fattest in the world during those years. I will walk you into the corridors of hell and I believe you will find my tour memorable and complete. I was there once, given an all-expense-paid trip by the unsmiling travel agents of the Third Reich. You like jokes, Jack, you always have and I expected you to smile when I said that, but no, you remained grim. No sense to be so serious. You and Shyla always told me that. The past is past. Let bygones be bygones. Okay. So you will not laugh. One promise though. You must sit through the whole story. No time out for vomiting. No tears. I will try to strangle you myself if you dare shed one Christian crocodile tear over the deaths of the ones I loved. Agree?"

"Agree," I said.

"So, Jack.

"We come together at last. You and I with our years of contempt for each other; no one else knows how deep it is or how long it has existed between us. I hated you for reasons you could not help, reasons unknown to you. How could you know you look like the son of an SS man, a panzer man, some pilot from the Luftwaffe? Blue eyes sing to me only a song of death. Blue eyes met my family on the platform of Auschwitz. Your blue eyes grew up next door to my house in Waterford. With blue eyes, Mengele pointed left and sent my whole family to the gas chamber. Shyla, too, went to the left when she walked into your arms.

"You have never met an artist like me. No, an artist as I once was. I rose out of the long traditions of Europe where artistry runs deep in the marrow of the selected few. Early, I indentured myself to the five horizontal lines where black notes were written on a sheet of music. It is a world of signs and notations that speaks to me with perfect clarity. It is a place of time signatures, fermatas, ledger lines, grace notes, and demisemiquavers that are the common tongue and heritage of musicians all over the world. It is something you know nothing about. As for music, you and your whole family are perfect idiots. It is something I cannot imagine being without. For without music, life is a journey through a desert that has not ever heard the rumor of God. In music's sweet harmony, I had all the proof I needed of a God who held the earth together between the staffs, where the heavens lay. Here, he marked all the lines and spaces with notes so perfect that they praised all of his creation with their beauty. Once I thought I was good enough to play even the music that God had written and coded secretly in the alignment of stars. At least, this is how I was taught to think. Look at the stars sometimes. They are only notes. They are music.

"Ah! The Holocaust, Jack. Yes, that word again. That stupid word, that empty vessel. I am so sick of that word. It is an exhausted word that means nothing, and we Jews have shoved it down the world's throat and dared anyone to use it improperly. One poor word cannot bear that much weight, yet this poor word must stagger under the load forever. The tracks of all the cattle cars, the moans of all the old people as they felt their own shit run down their legs in the befouled darkness, the screams of young mothers who watched as their infants died in their arms, the terrible thirst of children during the endless transits, the killing thirst, the thirst unforgettable until the millions rushed toward the ceilings of gas chambers ripping off their bloody fingernails as the gas killed them like insects . . . Holocaust. One English word should not be required to carry so many human hearts.

"We are not survivors. None of us. We were dice. We were thrown, hurled into the mouth of hell, and we learned that a human life was as worthless as a horsefly. Maggots hatching in excrement had a better chance of survival than a

Jew caught up in the machinery of the Third Reich. The Nazis had a genius for death. When the war began I had never seen a man die. Before it was over, I had come to terms with death, begging him to deliver me from a world beyond nightmare. I learned that nothing is worse than death's refusal to come. But death does not heed the wishes of mere dice. Dice just roll and come up with a number according to chance. But dice cannot feel. Dice are simply thrown, cast into the abyss. I can tell you how to find your way around in nothingness. I have the map in my possession, Jack. All the street names are covered with blood and the streets are all cobbled with the skulls of Jews. You are a Christian, Jack, and should feel right at home in this place. I hate your Christian face. I am sorry. I always have and I always will.

"The killing of the Jews, the roundups, the unimaginable savagery, the unimaginable made commonplace. The Holocaust was a Christian production from first to last. Sometimes, it was strictly a Catholic one. It all began with an observant Jew, this Christ. This same Jewish Christ has seen millions of his brothers and sisters killed in his name. This Christ who was circumcised, who kept faith with Jewish law to the letter, whose followers hunt down Jews like microbes or vermin. Even the cries of our children cannot move the Christian heart. The crying of our babies enraged the German soldiers. Babies. Their lack of control was an affront to the Reich. They were lucky when they made it as far as the gas chamber doors.

"You hate my eyes, Jack. Everyone hates my eyes. Because they are cold. Dead. You think I do not know this? I have a mirror. I avoid my eyes even when I shave. These eyes died in my head a long time ago and were forced to go on living because my body was alive. I can force myself to remember nothing. But my eyes saw, and there are bodies hung on meat hooks just behind my retina. My eyes became tinny and opaque from overexposure to horror. My eyes are repellent, not because they long for rest, but because they long for oblivion.

"It is all cliché now. Who has not heard this story a thousand times before? Jews cry out 'we must never forget' and then proceed to tell the same tale over and over again so repetitively, so desperately, that the words unravel around the edges, grow indistinct, and even I want to cover my ears and say 'shut up' to whoever is speaking. I am afraid that a time will come when our story cannot be heard because it has been told too often. It is a cliché because of German exactitude. Once they settled on the machinery of death, the Nazis did not deviate in their methodology. They entered every city, town, and shtetl with a careful blueprint for the destruction of Jews. All of us tell the same story. Only small details change.

"I was not born among Jews like you know here in Waterford. My father was a Berliner who fought for the Kaiser and who was wounded and decorated for his courage at the Somme. My mother's people were musicians and factory owners famous throughout Poland. These were people of the world, Jack, who had tasted the very best Europe had to offer. The Jews of Waterford are descendant from the dregs of Russian and Polish Jewry, the ones who lived out their lives unlettered and unschooled and smelling of raw potatoes and herring going bad. Why do you raise your eyebrows at me? You must understand this or you will understand nothing about me.

"Ruth is a descendant of such people. They were peasants who were peddlers and woodcutters who spoke Yiddish by day and searched their body hair for lice at night. In America, they would be like the black ones, the *Schwarzen*. I make no judgment. But this is who Ruth is and who I am. These are the origins. The history of Europe and my family conspired to make me a musician. I composed my first sonata when I was seven. At fourteen, I wrote a symphony in honor of my mother's fortieth birthday. There is not a family in South

Carolina as cultivated as the one into which I was born. I say this for definition's sake. There is no arrogance in my claim, just fact. Europe marked my family in its depths. It enfolded us in a culture that was a thousand years in the making. America has no culture. She is still in diapers.

"I had four sisters, all older than me. Their names were Beatrice, Tosca, Tonya, and Cordelia, not Jewish names you will note, but names chosen with discrimination from the worlds of literature and opera. Laughter followed them wherever they went. All married well, brilliantly. They seemed like young lionesses to me, strong, willful, and they refused to let my mother say a single harsh word to me. Whenever my poor mother would try to scold me, these sisters would surround me in a protective circle, their silk dresses brushing up against me, their tiny waists eye level, their hands caressing me and stroking my hair, their four voices arguing with my poor outnumbered mama. My father would read the paper, amused, as though he were watching the latest comedy from Paris.

"We were not good Jews; we were good Europeans. My father's library was breathtaking to behold with its leather sets of Dickens, Tolstoy, Balzac, and Zola. He was well schooled and brilliantly polished. As a factory owner, he was beloved. He avoided crassness, authoritarianism, and from his vast reading he knew that the happiness of workers would come back to him a thousand times in the riches that contentment always brings.

"My family attended synagogue on the High Holidays only. They were humanists, rationalists. My father was something of a freethinker, a man with his head in the clouds when he was not adding columns of numbers or ordering supplies for his factory.

"In our house in Warsaw, my mother was the center of the universe, and she wanted her children to have everything in the world. I was her only son and she worshiped me as few children have ever been worshiped. Her smile was like the sun to me. She was my first piano teacher. From the beginning, she told me I would be a master. She had no enemies. Except, of course, the entire Christian world, but I did not know this as a boy.

"At eighteen, I won an important competition for young pianists in Paris. My main competition was from a Dutchman by the name of Shoemaker. He was a true artist, but did not love the spotlight. Another pianist was Jeffrey Stoppard of London. Very strong. He had beautiful touch, but no sense of drama. The critics said I moved like the Prince of Darkness when I approached the piano. They nicknamed me *Le Loup Noir,* 'the Black Wolf.'

"There was a German pianist I remember best. His name was Heinrich Baumann and he was of the second tier in ability. He was passionate about music, but lacked the true gift, which he knew, even then. For years we wrote each other letters, discussing music, careers, everything. The night after the competition, we walked through Paris all night, and we were sitting on the steps of Sacré-Coeur when the sun rose over the city and turned the old buildings rose-colored and breathtaking. A city looks more beautiful after you have won a competition. Heinrich had finished third, his best finish ever. His letters stopped in 1938. Then it had become dangerous to write to a Jew. Even the Black Wolf.

"Single-mindedness is something I was born with. It is a necessary ingredient of all the great musicians. The pursuit of greatness means that laziness has no place in your life. In the morning, I would work on my scales. I am a great believer in the scales. Master the grammar of scales and the secrets of the best composers will reveal themselves to you in slow increments. My gift made harsh requirements of me. It made me aloof to all courtesies. I was neither kind nor cordial and dreamed only of black notes pouring off a scale like water over rocks. When I turned to new symphonies, I felt as happy as those astronauts who first stepped on the moon.

"But why do I waste my time telling you this story, Jack? You could not play 'Chopsticks' on the piano with the great Horowitz holding your hand. One of Shyla's most unforgivable betrayals was marrying a man who was an ignoramus when it came to music.

"I had a first wife, Jack. I also had three sons. You did not know I had a wife before Ruth?"

"No."

"You did not know I had children before Shyla and Martha?"

"No."

"It makes no difference. There is nothing in it to talk about the dead. Do you agree?"

"No."

"You do not know what it is like to lose a wife."

"Yes, I do," I said.

"Sonia and I were destined to meet. She was beautiful, as beautiful as the music I played to praise her. She, too, played the piano uncommonly well, especially for a woman of that time and place. I played in Warsaw soon after my triumph in Paris. The concert was sold out weeks in advance. My name was on the lips of every aficionado in Poland. That night was my coming out in my own birthplace. I tell you I was utterly brilliant that night. Flawless. I closed the performance with the Third Hungarian Rhapsody by Liszt because it is showy and crowd-pleasing. Sonia sat in the second row and I saw her when I walked onto the stage to begin my performance. She was like a pure flame burning out of control in that theater. Now, at this moment, I can close my eyes and see her as though time could not manage to extricate itself from that distinguished moment. She was the kind of woman accustomed to being noticed and she saw me see her, saw the exact moment of my surrender and her conquest, when I let myself be stolen away by her. I lost myself forever in that first glance. Though I played before an audience of over five hundred that night, I actually played only for her. When I rose to acknowledge the standing ovation, I noticed that she alone had refused to stand. Later, when I met her, I asked her why she had remained seated. She told me, 'Because I wanted to make sure you would seek me out to ask that very question.'

"Our marriage was one of the largest and most jubilant ever among the Jews of Warsaw. Both of our families were rich and cultured and hers was even famous for producing a line of distinguished rabbis on her mother's side that could be traced back to the eighteenth century.

We took our wedding trip to Paris where we stayed at the Hôtel George V and we wandered hand in hand through all the streets of Paris. In France we spoke to each other only in French. We made love whispering French to each other and I lost my shyness with her when I whispered French into her ear at night. Later, she would claim I made her pregnant on our first night together. Our bodies burned when we were together. I do not have any other way of saying it. I think it happens but once and only to the very young when it feels like your skin could ignite at the mere touch of another person. I could not satisfy myself with her or get enough of the endless feast her body provided. You get to love like that but once.

"Sonia knew music almost as well as I knew it. She would sit in the room as I practiced and I played for her approval. Never have I had an audience as spontaneous and knowledgeable as Sonia was. Her pregnancy was a source of great joy to us both and I poured out my soul at the keyboard so my sleeping, developing child could hear the most beautiful music in the world as it grew bones and lived in the womb of its mother. At that time, I had moments when I was sentimental as the next man, but you have not known this side of me. Long ago I buried that part of me. I never looked back upon it or sang kaddish or offered it a word of praise.

"Sonia loved it more than I did. My twin boys, Joseph and Aram, were born on your July 4. I played a song I wrote for that occasion all during Sonia's labor, because that was the wish of my Sonia.

"So, Jack.

"Not so many years pass, but it was a time that now seems like perfect happiness. Beneath the approving gaze of pretty Sonia and the sound of my growing boys in the nursery, I began to outreach even the talent I was born with. I reached that point where I could make the piano mourn or cry out or exult by laying my fingers just so.

"But the Nazi beast was growing. As a Jew, one felt hunted in the great cities as the voice of Hitler poisoned the airways. As a musician, I thought I was immune to the fury of armies and the faith of my fathers made little difference when I sat down before the music sheets and interpreted those passionate notes that Brahms, Chopin, Schumann—that all the great ones had left the world. Hitler meant nothing to me because of music and Sonia and my beautiful twin boys. When the newspapers disturbed me, I simply stopped reading the newspaper. When rumors flew wildly in the streets, I stayed indoors and commanded that Sonia do the same. When the radio made Sonia weep with fear, I turned off the radio and forbade its use. I refused to listen to the baying of the Nazi hound. Politics sickened and bored me.

"Then I heard scratching at my door, unprepared and in innocence, and saw the Nazi beast. So I played my music to calm the blood lust of the Nazi beast. This beast loved my music, came to my concerts, called for encores, threw roses on the stages, and bellowed out my name. It loved music so much, Jack, that I almost did not see the moment that it wiped the blood of my family from its fangs and claws. Jew-hating Poland was attacked by Jew-hating Germany. It was not until later that I learned that World War II had begun and I and my family were in the middle of it all.

"I learned in the first days of the war that I was not a man of action. How is a musician supposed to respond to dive-bombers? I found myself paralyzed with fright and I remained at the piano during the first bombing raid because I discovered I could not move. The piano seemed safer to me, friendlier than the basement where my wife and neighbors had fled. I heard the approach of the planes and the air raid sirens go off and I knew what I should do, but I could not make myself run. Instead, I found myself playing from the second movement of Beethoven's Piano Sonata No. 32 in C Minor, Op. 111. The very last movement of his last sonata of the complete set of thirty-two.

"You have never been in a country invaded. You cannot understand the chaos, the despair, the panic in the streets. I think it is why modern music and modern art are so ugly. My wife, Sonia, found me, after the bombers had returned to their bases, sitting on the piano bench, still playing, as though possessed. I had urinated in my pants. Such was my fear during that first raid. I think I thought my music would save me, form a protective barrier that would hover over me like some impregnable umbrella. Sonia was very kind and gentle with me. 'It is all right, my husband. Here, let me help you. Let me assist you. Please lean against me.' I do not remember having a single thought about Sonia or my sons during the bombing. Not one. Until that moment, it had never occurred to me that I was a coward of the most despicable kind. Now, even Sonia knew it.

"Sonia's father, Saul Youngerman, was a man of action. He could think clearly under pressure. Already, he had read Hitler's *Mein Kampf* and had watched his rise in Germany with a distrustful eye. He was a rich manufacturer who possessed fortunes in four countries and he told us he knew what Hitler had in mind. He commanded that we run east as fast as we could, keeping well ahead of the German Army. His two sons, Marek and Stefan, refused to leave Warsaw because their wives were city girls, born and bred to expect the comforts of Warsaw life. They had school-age children and even if the Germans won, they could not prevent their children from going to school. It is easy to mock their stupidity now, but remember, this was a time when the words Treblinka, Auschwitz, and Mauthausen had no meaning to the world. Not a single member of Sonia's family who stayed in Warsaw survived the war. Not one.

"With all the madness in the streets, with Warsaw itself wounded and bleeding, Saul Youngerman arranged for us to leave by boat, down the Vistula by barge, and then by oxen and wagons, which drove us twenty kilometers to a farm where two touring cars were waiting with uniformed chauffeurs. It was not the fact that Sonia's father was rich that made the difference. Many were the rich men who perished from starvation in the Warsaw Ghetto. It was that he had formed a plan in his head if something happened and he was not bashful in putting it into effect. By daytime we slept, and by night we moved. When we came to a border after the fourth night of very hard travel we crossed into a territory controlled by the Red Army. Saul figured that his family would be safe there since Ribbentrop and Molotov had signed the Nazi-Soviet Nonaggression Pact. His wife's brother runs a factory there and knows we are coming. On 5 September, we are taken in by the family Spiegel. We are put up in a beautiful house with a very fine piano that had recently been tuned in preparation for my arrival. The city that offers us deliverance is in the Ukraine. It is called Kironittska.

"The wheel of fate comes round to touch you unawares. This is the place from which your Great Jew, Max Rusoff, and his wife, Esther, are from. But fate reveals itself only slowly and in its own good time. So, we are there and every day I play the piano and crowds of people gather outside on the street to listen to my music. Everything is good for us in Kironittska from the beginning. Many people there are Jews, some twenty thousand, so we are well taken care of. News from Warsaw is worse each day, but we know this only from the radio. On 17 September, the Soviet Union attacks Poland from the east.

"I take on music students and some of them are very good, but it is not the life I would choose. My father-in-law takes several trips fraught with terrible danger back to Warsaw. He takes food and medicine to our family, then sneaks back after terrifying adventures to Kironittska. I have never known a braver man. The stories he brought back from Warsaw were each worse than the time before. By November, the main Jewish areas are enclosed in barbed wire. Jews are ordered to wear the Star of David. Saul Youngerman cannot be persuaded from still another trip back to Poland. He considers himself a Polish patriot, more than a Jew.

"Though we do not know this, my Sonia is pregnant with our third child when we arrive in Kironittska. But the child does not know the world it is coming into and continues to grow inside her. Though we are sick with worry about our loved ones in Poland, we are thankful that we have escaped. My third son, Jonathan, is born in June. If I could have seen the future, I would have beaten Jonathan's brains out on a rock beside the river. I would have fed rat poison to my twins, to Sonia, then myself.

"In June 1941, the Germans declare war on the Soviet Union. On June 22, there is the first massive air strike on the civilian population of Kironittska. Three weeks later, after being occupied by Hungarian troops for a brief period, I hear spoken in the streets the four most fearful words I ever heard: the Germans are here.

"The Germans are here. At this very instant, things change for the Jews. Because the Soviet Union is an ally of Germany we have relaxed our guard and consider ourselves safe. Rumors have come to us from Warsaw and then parts of Poland about the fate of Jews, but we discount them. After all, the Germans are human as we are. That year, I begin to go to the synagogue for morning prayers. And then one day the Germans burn the synagogue to the ground, with one hundred Jews inside it. If Sonia had not been sick that morning, I would have perished along with the rest. I consider those Jews that burned to death that morning to be the lucky ones.

"And then the Gestapo comes, inhuman, but handsome in a way that makes your blood run cold. The genius of the Gestapo is in their pride that they have graduated far beyond mercy. You cannot appeal to them on a human level because they are superhuman. A Ukrainian businessman owns the largest mansion in the city and this house is taken over by the Hauptsturmführer Rudolf Krüger for his headquarters. Kuzak is the name of the businessman and he protests that his family is one of the most distinguished in the Ukraine and that he demands the respect the name Kuzak merits in the city. Krüger obliges and hangs poor Kuzak from a timber protruding from his own house. The body is allowed to hang there for weeks as a sign to the citizens of Kironittska. Not until it begins to smell does Krüger order it cut down and thrown into a sewer.

"Of course, the Germans incur many unfortunate and necessary expenses in their war against the Jews. They are forced to levy heavy taxes on the Jewish population. They enlist the help of the Ukrainians in this. If the Ukrainians ever live down this ugly chapter of their history, then it means that God was asleep for the whole war. Instead of wearing the usual yellow armband, the Jews of Kironittska are required to wear a white one with a blue Jewish star that measures ten centimeters wide. Those Jews deliver all gold and silver articles to the offices of the Judenrat. My wedding ring and Sonia's are lost in this order. All electrical appliances and shoe leather are gathered up. All German books are confiscated. We are in the hands of criminals, murderers, and thieves. God's chosen people.

"Some poor misguided Jews hear that if they convert to Christianity they will be spared the horrible fate of their compatriots. One Friday there is a mass baptism where twenty entire Jewish families, with but a few exceptions among older members, are baptized. The Gestapo has a baptismal present ready and waiting for these new Gentiles. They are marched into the Christian cemetery and gunned down with machine gun fire. Children and women no exception. Later a member of the Judenrat, when he had gotten to know Krüger somewhat better, asks him why. Krüger makes it a joke. He says, 'If you take a pig inside a cathedral, you still have ham and bacon and the cathedral has not changed at all.' That member of the Judenrat is me.

"Judenrat. You do not know the word, Jack. It is my shame that I live with it. I have never admitted to anyone that I held such a position until this night when I tell you everything.

"Krüger selects a committee of Jews to administrate the Jewish affairs of this new ghetto. Failure to join means swift and certain death. By joining, it means I get to collaborate with the Germans in the torture and destruction of my own people. When the Germans need a work brigade to repair a bridge, a list of Jews is turned over to Krüger by the Judenrat. Whenever the Germans decide to reduce the size of the ghetto during an *Aktion*, we decide which Jews will be rounded up in the ghetto's main plaza, loaded on trucks, and driven away never to be seen again. By doing this, I think I am saving the lives of Sonia and my boys. And I am. But saving them for what?

"The leader of the Judenrat is a surgeon named Isaac Weinberger. He is a contemplative, patient man who assumes that the Nazis can be reasoned with like all other men. He is the one who insists that my father-in-law, Saul Youngerman, be in the Judenrat. Immediately, Saul sees all the dangers inherent in such a position, but also sees the wisdom in serving with such a group for the sake of his family. It is

Saul who insists on my participation. Very early he scares me by telling me in confidence that the Nazis plan to kill every Jew on the face of the earth. I laugh when he tells me this. I tell him that wartime brings out in each man the capacity for the grossest exaggeration. Taking off his glasses and wiping them, Saul tells me that he has always admired my genius, but that it does not protect me from thinking like a fool. We are in our quarters in the ghetto, my children are playing around us and my wife and mother-in-law are gossiping at the stove while fixing dinner. 'They are all corpses,' Saul Youngerman whispers to me. 'They are all corpses.'

"On 30 August, the Judenrat is required to provide the Germans with a list of all the Jewish intellectuals. In this list are 270 teachers, 34 pharmacists, 126 physicians, 35 engineers. I am also included in this list as a musician. The next day, one hundred men are selected from this list. They assemble together at daybreak, mount trucks, wave good-bye to their weeping families, and disappear from the face of the earth. Except for one man.

"His name is Lauber and he is one of the thirty-four pharmacists on the list. He comes back to the ghetto, at night, sneaking in as though this is deliverance. What he longs for is the comforting arms of his wife and the sounds of his children's voices. This he finds. He tells his story to the other wives whose husbands left in those trucks. They are driven fifty kilometers to a bean field where they are given shovels and ordered to dig. They dig a great hole, then strip naked, and kneel beside their handiwork. Then the machine guns of the Nazis relieve them of the burdens of this war. The chosen people return to the God who chose them.

"No one believes this man Lauber. The Gestapo discovers him. They take him, his wife, his children, his parents, and two other families in his house to the Jewish cemetery where all of them are shot. Only then does poor Lauber not look like a liar. Lauber's wife dies screaming at him that he should not have come back.

"Hauptsturmführer Krüger is a cruel Philistine and a pig who tries to assume airs of breeding and sophistication that he has not earned. To Dr. Weinberger he talks of his love of Wagner, yet cannot name one of the arias he loves to whistle. Weinberger tells him about me and I am ordered to play the piano for a group of a German war staff who are on their way forward to the front lines. While they eat I play and I listen to the Germans talk about the war effort and their many successes on the Russian front. They talk like normal men until they get drunk when they begin to talk like Nazi soldiers. At this feast, they consume more meat than the Jews of the ghetto have seen since the walls of the ghetto went up. Then they go to the library for cigars and cognac. All except one officer, who comes beside the piano and listens to me play. 'You still play like an angel. Even in times like this.' I look up and see my friend Heinrich Baumann. He sits down beside me on the bench and we take turns playing music for each other. He plays Mozart and I answer him with Chopin. As we play, Baumann asks about my situation and that of my family. He tells me that I have much to worry about because I am a Jew. After that dinner, he drives me to my house in the ghetto in his jeep. Soldiers salute him. He is a fighting man, not SS. At my home, he comes in and meets Sonia and kisses my children in their sleep. He bows when he meets Saul Youngerman and my mother-in-law. In a sack, he leaves a wonderful supply of flour and cans of meat and sacks of cornmeal. When he leaves, Herr Baumann kisses me and apologizes for the entire German nation. We are still part of the brotherhood of music, he tells me. He is killed leading his men against the Soviet troops at Stalingrad.

"A good German? No. Herr Baumann fought for Hitler's armies. At best, he was a member of the Judenrat like me. There are few Germans who could not forgive my participation in the Judenrat. They know me. I am one of them in some profound way that ties us together in all our sad humanity. We dance with the enemy and let him lead.

"Do you think you could throw your daughter Leah into a crematorium, Jack? Of course you do not. Your love for her is too great, correct? Let me starve you for a year. Let me beat you into submission. Let me kill everyone you love around you and work you until you drop. Let me humiliate you and fill your hair with lice and your bread with maggots. Let me test you to the limit and find out where civilization ends and depravity begins along the edges of your soul. Here's what they did to me, Jack. At the end of the war, I could have thrown the Messiah himself into the fires of the crematorium and I would have done it for an extra cup of soup. I could throw Ruth, Shyla, Martha, Sonia, my sons, Leah, and everyone else into those fires and never think of it again. Here is the trick, Jack. You have to break a man down completely and then you own him. Let me break you like they broke me and I promise you would throw Leah into a fire, hang her by her neck, see her raped by a hundred men, then have her throat cut, and her bodily parts thrown to starving dogs in the street. I upset you. I am sorry. I tell you what I know. But know this: it is possible for you to kill Leah with your own hands because the world has come apart and God has hidden his face in his hands and you will think, by killing her, you are proving your love of Leah like never before. I would kill Leah, myself, tonight, before I would let her go through what I did, Jack. And I love your daughter more than I love any person on this earth.

"No, she does not remind me of the sons I mourn. Nor does she remind me of Shyla. She is much calmer and more composed than Shyla ever was. No, your Leah strikes me in a place I thought was dead. She reminds me of Sonia, my sweet, lost wife.

"Krüger seems to grow fond of me and it agrees with his pretensions about himself and his culture to have me play the piano while he dines. He gets drunk easily and he cries. His only son, Wilhelm, comes back from the Russian front to celebrate his nineteenth birthday. Both father and son get drunk and they make me play German folk songs over and over. Then they chase me out when two Ukrainian whores arrive for their appointment. The next day, ten Jewish young men are selected and driven fifteen kilometers to a field leading to a river. These Jews are told they can make a run for the river and if they reach the water they will be free men. Krüger and his son are in the middle of the field fifty meters away with high-powered hunting rifles. As the Jews run, father and son take turns shooting down the running Jews. They are excellent marksmen. No matter how they dodge or how fast they run, no Jew makes it to the river. Krüger tells me the story later one evening when he demands that I play nothing but Haydn.

"An old Orthodox rabbi named Nebenstall is caught praying and is publicly humiliated by the Gestapo. They make him spit on the sacred Torah until he can no longer spit. Then they make him urinate on the Torah. Then they want him to shit on the Torah, which he cannot do because he has not eaten. They bring him bread. Loaf after loaf, they stuff down his throat. But they are too vigorous in making him eat bread and they strangle him on the bread and leave him in the street. Jews fight over the bread they leave sticking out of the mouth of the dead rabbi. Another rabbi retrieves the defiled Torah and buries it with great solemnity and secrecy in the Jewish cemetery.

"In October the Judenrat is required by Krüger to make another selection, this time of one thousand Jews. The ghetto is shrinking still again. We choose the lowest Jews among us, the poorest and the most despised; the sick and the hungry are easy targets, and so are the very old who have produced no families of distinction. We protect our families and those of our friends. Each time we waltz with the enemy, we cheapen and degrade ourselves. After the selection is over and the trucks depart, the Nazis give us extra food for our families. For a loaf of extra bread, we sell the children of Israel into something far worse than slavery.

"My father-in-law takes me almost by force to his factory one day. The head of his clothing factory has followed the Russians out of the city and Saul has to take over its operation. It is a clothing factory that the Germans turn into an operation for the making of winter coats for the military. Saul puts me next to a master tailor and orders the man to teach me to sew a coat. I am furious and scream at him that I am a pianist and that this is a place where peasants work. Saul grabs me and shakes me. He is old but strong. Learn how to sew, he screams at me. Learn how to do something the Germans can use. That they need. So the master tailor shows me how to sew along a seam. He makes me do it until I do it right. There is a whole different set of things to know about zippers and collars. Saul comes by to check on me and we argue again. But he makes me come each day. I sew when I should be practicing scales. I sew when I should be mastering the great composers. I sew and I hate my father-in-law. I tell you now, over forty years later, that this man I hate, Saul Youngerman, wants to save my life by teaching me to be a tailor. The Nazis would have sent Beethoven himself to the gas chamber, unless he could have sewn a shirt for a soldier on the Eastern Front. He made me a musician *and* a tailor.

"A young Gestapo man named Schmidt causes great fear among the Jews. He has a habit of slapping down Jewish men in the street when he passes them by. Schmidt loves it because some of the older men begin falling to their knees at the sight of him. Once, I see this with my own eyes. Schmidt is walking down a street in the ghetto and every man is kneeling before him. I am one of those men.

"Schmidt looks like an albino and is a notorious rapist. He would rape Ukrainian or Polish girls as soon as he would rape Jewish ones. There is only one difference. The Jewish girls he defiles as their parents listen in the next room, and then he shoots them. Some of them are no more than children. Jews hide their daughters when word spreads that Schmidt is approaching the ghetto.

"Soon, you know that a Jewish life is worth less than nothing. This is the only sure thing in the ghetto. Starvation becomes the daily lot. The search for food becomes a desperate thing. The fourteen entrances of the ghetto are all guarded by Ukrainian police. Some of the Ukrainians are kind and they suffer the same horrors as the fate of the Jews they try to help. Low-life Jewish informers testify about the kindness of the Ukrainians and they are removed from these barriers, never to be seen again. The Ordnungsdienst wear a military-like uniform designed by their own members. They are Jewish police and they earn favors by acting as informants to the Gestapo. They are stooges of the Gestapo. But I must tell you they are no worse than I am. The ghetto is an abattoir and all of us are beasts marked for slaughter. The only way a Jew can prove his innocence in such a nightmare is to turn up dead. People begin to die of starvation and their bodies are stacked like firewood outside of apartment buildings. Envy of the dead is common.

"There are Jews worse off than other Jews. I watch the men in charge of removing fecal matter to the river. These are starved, horrible-looking men who pull the wagons as though they are broken-down horses. The work is degrading, agonizing. A smell hangs over them. Yet their work saves us all from epidemic. Most of them end up dying of typhus.

"Gisela is the name of Sonia's mother. She is sweet and kind and beloved. But her husband, Saul Youngerman, drives her crazy by taking terrible chances. Saul bribes the Ukrainians and Jewish police. He finds ways to bribe even the Gestapo. He organizes a smug-

gling ring to bring food inside the ghetto. Even
though he knows the consequences of his foolish acts, Saul Youngerman makes secret contact with the partisans who skirmish with German patrols in the countryside. A Jewish
informant, a criminal by the name of Feldman,
reports to the Gestapo that Saul has smuggled
a gun into the ghetto. This is not true, but it is a
death warrant for Saul Youngerman. His wife,
Gisela, is taken to Gestapo Headquarters with
him. Sonia and my sons would have been taken
in also, but they are out in the streets with
Sonia looking for extra milk. I find them after a
frantic search through the ghetto—standing in
the sewers hiding.

"That same night I play the piano at Krüger's house for dinner. He gives no sign that he
knows my father-in-law is in his hands. Before I
can summon up the words or the courage to
ask about them, he dismisses me for the night.
When Sonia discovers I have not even asked
him about the fate of her parents, she turns her
face from me. Again and again, she turns away
as I try to explain myself.

"Other members of the Judenrat come to
see me about the fate of Saul and Gisela. We
agree to go as one body to the office of Krüger
to find out where they are so that at least we
will have strength in numbers. Dr. Isaac Weinberger leads our delegation as the head of the

Judenrat. Even the Nazis respect him because he treats and cures some members of the Gestapo when they break some bones after their truck goes into a ditch. When we see Krüger in his office, he strikes Weinberger with a swagger stick and beats the poor man while the others plead with him. Screaming, he tells us that there will be a special *Aktion* for the Judenrat and our Jew families if we do not learn to respect his position. Then he comes up to me and screams that he knows I am behind this visit. So, he says, you wish to see your father-in-law? I do not speak because fear renders me mute. But I nod my head. He tells me that he knows what to do with swine, that his grandfather raises swine, and that swine always end up the same way. Then he takes me to the slaughterhouse outside the ghetto and takes me inside. Here is where the Gestapo have set up their jail and interrogation center. I hear people screaming and moaning, but I see no one. Krüger walks fast and I follow him. The smell of blood and offal is everywhere, but I cannot tell if it is human or animal. We come to a guard at the door. Are the Youngermans *up* for a visit? he asks the German guard in colloquial German that he thinks I cannot understand. The guard smirks and says yes, they are *up* for a visit from anyone. I walk into the darkness and Krüger lights a lamp. They have hung Saul

Youngerman on a meat hook. The spike has pierced him through the shoulder blades. I do not recognize his face because it has been beaten so badly. But he is still alive and his swollen eyes are fixed on something across the room. Following his eyes, I see Gisela hanging by her feet, naked, and eviscerated with a long slit from her throat to her pubic area. Her intestines hang out of her almost obscuring her face. Krüger walks out as I watch. I hear him vomit in the passageway.

"That night he has me play Vivaldi's *The Four Seasons* for him at dinner.

"Even though she asks over and over, I never tell Sonia what I have seen at the slaughterhouse. I tell her that her parents have been taken away on a convoy. Nor do I tell the other members of the Judenrat. I do not feel that I should add any more to the common fear. By then, all of us know that we are at the mercy of lunatics and butchers. Sonia tries to hearten herself by thinking that her parents have been sent to work camps. I encourage this kind of thinking. Despair is a daily bread and there is plenty enough to go around.

"In July, one more *Aktion* and another five hundred Jews are taken out to the slaughter. The Jewish fire brigade is brought out in the countryside and forced to dig a mass grave. Then the poor Jews have to strip naked so their clothes can be used to make uniforms for the Reich. One young Jewish man named Wolinski lunges at a Gestapo guard as he stands in line ready to face the machine guns. He has hidden a six-inch knife taped to his thigh. The knife goes into the throat of the Gestapo man, who strangling on his own blood, runs after Wolinski and stabs him with a bayonet. It does not take long. Wolinski is half dead when he plays his own special rendition of 'Taps' for the Nazis. To honor Wolinski, the Germans round up another five hundred Jews the next day for annihilation. I know. Along with other members of the Judenrat, I stay up all night to see which Jewish names are placed on the list. Always, we choose the poorest and most helpless Jews among us. Always, we choose the Jews we do not know or who are not related to us.

"All my life I have been a fanatic about cleanliness. But forget about hygiene in the ghetto. Like any other Jew, I have to survive in a landscape of utter filth. At night, the rats are emperors of the dark and we hear them rattling the pots and pans and desperately looking for scraps of food. The best place for rats is by the cemetery where they can grow fat on what meat they find on the bones of starved Jews. The bedbugs are so bad and so numerous that often we must rouse our children and go sleep out in the streets beneath the stars. In winter, we have no choice but to do war with the bed-bugs, the roaches, and the lice. Water is precious. Even filthy it is precious. One night, an old Jew takes time to close his eyes and bless the piece of bread he is about to eat, when a rat leaps out of a closet and snatches the bread from the old Jew's hands. The Jew goes berserk and kills the rat with his shoe, butchers it, and cooks it over an open fire, then devours it ravenously. A rabbi comes to him, not to chastise the old Jew for eating unkosher food, but to find out how the animal tastes. Such is the desperation of the Jews of Kironittska.

"A criminal named Berger is put in charge of the Ordnungsdienst after its first boss is shot down in the street by the Oberscharführer for not carrying out an order quickly enough. This Berger is built strong as a bull and is a common laborer carrying freight at the railroad station. He is a drunkard, a lout, and dumb as a goy, Jack, if you will excuse the expression. Jews like this Berger are sickening to other Jews, but they are circumcised according to the covenant so what is one to do? The Nazis don't care if it's an Einstein or a Horowitz once they find the mezuzah on the doorpost and the foreskin cut. Berger is armed with a club and a uniform and he loves to beat educated Jews into submission. Some fear him more than they fear the average German soldier.

"Some Jewish girls become whores for the Nazis or for anyone else who can feed them. If a German soldier sleeps with a Jewish girl, it is death for both of them because of the racial laws. But men will be men and women, women, and for food, one will do anything. Because I am a member of the Judenrat, we have more food than the others, so I do not worry as much.

"One day in the main street of the ghetto I am walking home from the factory after a day of reconditioning fur coats into warm uniforms for German soldiers on the Eastern Front. I am exhausted by the work and so little hope. I am walking slowly home, head down, trying to attract the attention of no one, which is the best method of survival always. A commotion is suddenly around me like a storm. Many shouts, people yelling and crying. I look up and two members of the Gestapo have caught two young Jewish boys smuggling food into the ghetto. One boy is ten and the other is nine. They are brothers and they are crying as the soldiers slap their faces hard again and again. It is a square where they take these boys and there are nooses hanging from a scaffold where they hang Jews and Poles and Ukrainians who displease the Nazis. The Nazis love to hang people to make examples to others. Krüger drives up at this very moment in a jeep.

"Both boys are crying hard as they are forced toward the scaffold, but since they are obviously just boys I think that they will be all right. They have been trying to smuggle tins of fish and a bottle of vodka into the ghetto, things that now fetch an unbelievable price. Like a charade, the boys are lifted up on stools and their hands are tied behind their backs and nooses are put around their necks. The scene is so ghastly and I hear Jews moaning because they know it will do no good to lift their voices in protest. I myself feel like I am walking through some unimaginable landscape that would make sense only if I am in a nightmare. I cannot take my eyes off the boys, who under ordinary circumstances would be playing soccer in some school yard. Then I hear my name being called and it is Krüger who sees me and orders me to come out of the crowd that has gathered. They are only boys I say with my head bowed and he strikes me with a riding crop on the face and I taste blood in my mouth. Then there is another outbreak of noise and a man fights his way to the front of the crowd. It is Berger, the pompous ruffian who leads the Ordnungsdienst. He cries out, 'These are my sons. The sons of your obedient servant Berger, who will punish these sons within an inch of their lives. I so swear to my Maker.'

" 'These are not boys or sons,' Krüger says

to the crowd. 'These are enemies of the Reich who must be punished by the harshest measures.' Krüger reaches up and he makes sure that the nooses are tight. Both boys begin screaming for their father, who tries to fight his way to them but is felled by a blow to the back of the head from a rifle butt. But Berger is ox-like and maddened with fear and the screams of his sons bring him staggering to his feet as he calls out to his boys not to worry. In Yiddish, he keeps telling his sons that Yahweh will protect them. But Yahweh is taking a long vacation, far away from his chosen people in those years. He was not in Eastern Europe, Jack, of that I am certain.

"Again, I hear my name called out by Krüger. He says it softly, in an almost friendly way, so the crowd does not hear. 'You are a member of the Judenrat, a leader of your people,' he whispers to me. 'Let me see you make the hard decisions, perform the action that wartime requires of all the servants of the Reich. For so long Jews have been parasites and leeches. You perform an act that will help rid the Reich of such vermin. You hang those two pieces of shit, piano player.'

"Berger begins pleading for his children's lives and I hear German soldiers trying to beat him into silence, but he is strong and like an animal. He is clawing his way forward until restrained by three members of the Gestapo who appear from nowhere. Then Krüger says to me —and these are the words that change something in me, Jack—he says, 'If you do not hang them now, I will hang your pretty Sonia and all your pretty children on these same gallows tomorrow.' With these words, I do not hesitate to act for a second. I walk up to those boys and with their father watching me in hatred I kick those stools from under those boys. Krüger holds my neck as I try to turn away. He makes me watch the boys twitch and struggle and die in agony. It takes much longer for the younger boy to die than it does for the older one.

"Berger howls out in pain and I think I have never heard pain like that. It is so pure. They drag him off and I later hear that they take him to Gestapo Headquarters. Only the whores come back from there alive. When I get home, I tell my Sonia what I have done and she holds me tightly and kisses my face again and again. She tells me not to worry or to suffer, that we are being tested as Jews, and we will survive as Jews, and that we will show them all that we come from people who have been persecuted for three thousand years. They can do anything to our bodies, she tells me, kissing me, holding me tight to her breast, they can starve us and torture us and slaughter us by the tens of thousands, but our souls remain our own.

'They cannot rob us, my husband, of who we truly are.' Sonia was right about herself. She was wrong about George Fox.

"That night Krüger asks me to play something by Haydn and I play something instead by Telemann and the poor idiot has no idea of my deception. It is no sin not to have culture. It is a sin to pretend. That night as I play Telemann I pretend that I am playing before a royal audience in London and that I play so brilliantly that even the taciturn British rise to give me a standing ovation. I even pretend that on this day I have not participated in the hanging of two innocent Jewish boys. Their blood is on my hands as I play Telemann.

"The monster, Krüger, begins showing signs of intense nervousness as the fall weather grows colder. Some days he does not leave the house. On others, he is tempestuous and brutal and everywhere at once. A Jewish family is discovered to have hidden gold and diamonds beneath a stone of a Christian church and Krüger beats the entire family to death with a statue of St. Joseph he commandeered from the church. One of his victims is a two-year-old girl. The Jewish fire brigade is ordered to always have burial pits already dug for at least five hundred other bodies.

"On one of his more manic days, Krüger comes to the factory where I am sewing coats.

Every Jewish tailor who sees Krüger walk into the workplace almost has an instant heart attack. He has come to represent the Angel of Death himself in the ghetto. The administration of horror was taking a toll on even Krüger's face. His flesh is caving in on itself, as though he is rotting from the inside out. With his finger, he motions for me to come with him. What can I do? I am his slave and, of course, I follow him.

"In the back of the jeep he puts me. He spits on my Star of David as though to remind me what he thinks of all Jews. It is almost comical to me—for I should need any reminding? He drives me through the streets of Kironittska and stops outside of an orphanage that is filled with small children. It is the month a huge shipment of Hungarian Jews arrives in the ghetto, which does not want them and has no use for them. The Jews of Kironittska treat the Hungarian Jews abominably except for a few notable exceptions. Always, among humans, it is the notable exceptions that make God's creation of mankind seem like a good idea. But at the orphanage this day, the very idea of mankind is turned on its head.

"In trucks they have loaded over one hundred children, the smallest ones, the most helpless. Twelve of them are not even Jewish. Four have committed the crime of being Polish.

Eight are guilty of being Ukrainian. There are many infants. Some are crying. Most are too weak to cry. Krüger's jeep leads a small caravan out of town. I must tell you that I am fearing for my own life more than for anything on this trip. Not once can I remember thinking of any of these poor children. For one hour we drive until we get to the high country, the mountains barely visible from Kironittska on a clear day. We come to a bridge overlooking a gorge with a raging river three hundred feet below. It is such a height as not to be believed. The soldiers begin with the toddlers. Taking them by the feet, they put each child into a burlap bag. Most children cry, others struggle, some are already half-dead and protest not at all. Krüger takes out a beautiful hunting rifle that he tells me he used to hunt stag and wild hogs in Bavaria. It has carvings on the stock.

"On the drive to the bridge, the German soldiers have gotten drunk on brandy. One by one, they pick up these packages of unwanted children and throw them over the bridge into the river far below. The bridge seems to come apart with the special terror of children. The ones who are not packaged go into a panic. Some cry out for their mothers. None really know what is happening and that is the only humane thing about this indescribable scene. Krüger loads his rifle and takes aim. He takes shots at about every third child or infant as it is tossed off the bridge. He is a marksman famed even in the SS. He attempts to spin each bundle he fires at. One baby he spins three times before it hits the river and the German soldiers cheer Krüger for his accuracy. He has one run of hitting fifteen children in a row, before missing a baby he does not fire at until it almost hits the river. Before long, he grows impatient with the game and carefully replaces his rifle in its case. He yells at the soldiers to hurry up their work and they begin throwing the last twenty or thirty children into the gorge without even bothering to package them up. I see five naked babies plunging toward their deaths at varying heights above the gorge. Those babies are flying and innocent and doomed. Soon the work is finished and we drive back to the city. Krüger never directs a single word toward me. And I know that if I speak, he will put a bullet through my brain.

"That night he asks that I play something beautiful for him, something that will ease the great agony that comes with his command. I play the Concerto Number 21 of Mozart because it has a kind of secret beauty. In the middle of my playing, he begins to weep and I understand he is drunk again. He begins to talk but he does not talk about those slaughtered children. He talks of duty, stern duty. To be a good soldier, he must carry out each and every order of the Führer with all the ferocity he can muster. It would be easy for him to be soft, because as a civilian he is known for his softness and kindness and good cheer. Everyone tells him he spoils his children, especially his daughter, Bridget. He is a banker in his other life and his only problem is he wants to lend everyone money. It hurts him to say no even to the drunkards and the wastrels. For an hour he tells me in a monotone voice what a softie he is, how he loves to pick basketfuls of wild flowers for his Bridget, how he loves to play goalie against his two sons, and always makes sure he allows them to score before they return home for dinner. I play Mozart and I try to mind my own business. He weeps and drinks, weeps and drinks. Then he passes out and I tiptoe out of his house and walk back through the ghetto on the night that Krüger has ordered over a hundred orphans thrown to their deaths from a bridge in the Ukraine. If there is a God, Jack, those orphans are to have met Krüger on a bridge overlooking hell. God should then turn his back, as he did on his chosen people in the years I describe, and not turn around no matter how piteous the screams of Krüger become, no matter how long they last, and I pray it is eternity.

"Every day, I pass more and more starving

people. Their legs swell up and change colors. They move oddly as though they are under water and you begin to recognize those people who will be dead in just a few days. They have an aura and a stench and you learn to avoid them by walking far around them. Because I am a member of the Judenrat, a tailor at the factory, and the piano player of Krüger my family is well fed, considering. We live in filth and squalor, but we are as well fed as any Jews in the ghetto. For this I am grateful and my beautiful Sonia and my children are all alive.

"Then a Jew named Sklar, young, fiery, athletic, meets a Nazi who has come to arrest his mother and father with a jar of hydrochloric acid. This Sklar hurls the acid into the face of the Nazi beast, who screams as the acid burns out his eyeballs and half his face. This Sklar is killed immediately by other Germans and his parents are both shot in the head. Krüger orders that the body be publicly hanged and set on fire. But the blood lust of Krüger is not satisfied with such tame retribution. The Nazi without eyes or half a face is sent to his home in Düsseldorf and Krüger calls the Judenrat together for a night meeting in which he demands three hundred Jews to be hanged on the lampposts of Kironittska in reprisal for the attack on a soldier of the Reich. The Judenrat puts out a call for volunteers, but it is a rare man who volunteers for his own execution.

"The members of the Judenrat nearly go mad with anguish. Then the very old men are snatched up for the gallows and the reasoning is that they have tasted enough of life. Then the hospital is raided and the very sick are driven out of their beds. The insane are grabbed and we tell ourselves we are doing them a favor since they don't know the difference between life or death. Krüger is a black God whom we must obey as we select our fellow Jews for the slaughter. When we come up short with numbers, Krüger screams that he will hang every member of the Judenrat along with our families if we do not provide him with these souls. Then, to our great luck, we think then and suffer later, a shipment of Hungarian Jews arrives at the station. From lampposts, from rafters, from newly constructed gallows, three hundred Jews are sacrificed for one blind Nazi. Krüger lets them hang there until their bodies begin to decompose.

"On the night he lynchs those Jews, Krüger has me play Wagner for him. Wagner, the anti-Semite. But Krüger is a stupid man and his musical wishes this night do not reflect any sense of irony on his part. Again, he gets drunk and begins to mutter, 'You do not know the cost. You do not know the cost.' I play the piano as though I do not hear him. I play Wagner as this night three hundred Jewish men cross the Red Sea into the Promised Land. Three hundred men, men who have kept the covenant with their creator, swing in the cold winds that come down from the frozen mountains around Kironittska. I know the cost, Herr Krüger, I know the exact cost, because you make me help select each one of them.

"Judenrat. I can barely speak this name out loud. The shame I feel when I speak this word causes such despair that I have trouble breathing after I say it. In the Warsaw Ghetto, the head of the Judenrat kills himself. This is the only proper response, I think. But it requires a courage I walked into this war without. What will Sonia and my sons do if I slit my wrists or eat rat poison. I know four families who took rat poison all together. So they could die on their own terms. I wait until the Nazi beast grows hungry and looks around to feed. Who would think that the Nazi beast would one day turn toward pretty Sonia?

"Single-mindedly, I make up my mind that my wife and children will survive and the whole rest of the world be damned. Yet one day they close down the factory for suspected sabotage of a machine, but it is nothing and they send us all home with threats and no extra food ration for that day. I come to the crowded apartment where my family is housed among many families, including new arrivals from Hungary. My children are there being taken care of by an old Jewish farm woman from the country. I ask about my wife as I take the baby and my two older sons come to my lap and search my pockets for food. It is difficult to utter the sounds of my sons' names. When Sonia returns she is surprised to see me. Then very ashamed. I ask her where she has been, for it is dangerous for any attractive woman to be walking the streets with the Ukrainian police and the German soldiers always on patrol. She puts a finger to my lips, looks down at the floor, and says, 'Please do not ask, my husband.'

"That same night, the city sleeping, the snoring of strangers, a blanket separating us from the others, I reach over to bring my wife to me. I want to take comfort in her body. I wish to forget everything as I make love to her. She kisses me as always, then tells me that we can never make love ever again, that she has shamed me and shamed our families and that she can never be held by me again. She cries very hard in the darkness and asks my forgiveness. Over a month ago the monster, Krüger, comes to her and orders her to come to his house because he has decided that she will make a suitable whore. He goes to great lengths to tell her that he does not believe in the laws of racial purity espoused by the Nazis, but pays lip service to them for the sake of his career. Before him, she trembles and begs him not to make her do this. But because this Krüger is king of this portion of hell, he laughs at her and tells her he will be happy to shoot her husband and children down in the streets, then bring her to live in his house as a servant. Then he quits his explanation, his moment of seduction begins to bore him, and he rapes her on the couch near the piano. Each day he requires her to report to his house. Sonia begs Krüger not to let me know about her degradation. In his kindness, Krüger agrees to this. Each time it is a rape, dear husband, good Sonia says to me. Then she explains that she cannot love me because Krüger has given her syphilis. Sweet Sonia. Her suffering and shame that night in my arms are almost too much for either of us to bear. But toward morning we pledge our love to each other anew. They can take everything away from us, but our love for each other is forever.

"You think you have heard and imagined the worst that can happen to the ghetto Jews. Then something else happens so horrible that you shut down completely. You pray that you can imagine nothing. Your prayers are answered. You learn that evil is bottomless. The despair I feel in my stomach is like a paralysis.

"As I tell you this, Jack, I worry now about how I am telling it. Does he think I am exaggerating, I ask myself? Am I leaving out important details that would convince him of the authenticity of these events? Should I hide details that seem too lurid or unbelievable? Do I sound sincere enough? What do you think, Jack? Say something. Your eyes. I have always hated your eyes. Krüger eyes. The eyes of Germany. Ha! The eyes of my son-in-law.

"Typhoid comes. Then cholera. As it begins to grow colder the end of the ghetto comes nearer. Things are not going well for the German army on the Russian front. Mother Russia is beginning to eat the armies of its invaders as it always does. The looks on German faces begin to change.

"The dead begin to be put out on the streets like morning garbage.

"Krüger begins to talk to me as though we were old friends. He has a need to talk, so he chooses me. He does not like for me to answer out loud, so I nod as my fingers move along the keyboard. I learn to look sympathetic to his plight, to the agony of his command. He tells me something interesting. The monster, Krüger, tells me that I will never understand what it is like to have an entire city under my control. He knows that the city is ruled by pure terror, but he has learned that terror has its limits. I am playing Dvořák as he is telling me this. He spills his cognac as he contemplates this dilemma. Every life in Kironittska is there for the taking. He, Krüger, can order everyone killed. In Gestapo Headquarters, men and women are tortured to death frequently. He knows about nails under the fingernails and the pain it causes. Every place on the body can be used for torture. Scissors can be forced up nostrils, down eardrums, up anuses. Scrotums can be removed brutally. Every orifice can be turned into a tunnel of what he calls 'exquisite pain.' Every tongue can be made to talk, then ripped out. He realizes that human suffering no longer touches him at all. He can order ten thousand people killed and will think more about killing a fly with the heel of his boot. His daughter has come down with pneumonia and his son is making bad grades in school. He tells me he wishes his wife were a better cook. He had once played goalie on an elementary school soccer team. It will not be long now, he says, but he does not explain. Tonight, he would like to hear Mozart, instead of Beethoven. The idiot does not know I was playing Dvořák.

"The next day two thousand people are gathered together in an *Aktion*, taken out to a mass grave dug by the Jewish fire brigade, and machine-gunned in the snow. This time there is a surprise. This time they also kill all the members of the fire brigade.

"That night I am playing and Krüger is drunk when he arrives. I am playing Brahms. He comes and stands beside me as I play. He has never done this. He touches my shoulder in a fraternal way as if we are good friends. Then he puts his fingers under my nose. It is rough. It is sudden. 'That smell,' he says. 'That is your Sonia. Do you recognize that smell? It belongs to me. Forever. I own that smell. Do you hear me, Jew? I own that smell. That is what my whore smells like.' He seems almost ashamed after he says this. Then he gets angry at me. He slaps me hard and I fall off the stool. I rise and get back on the stool and resume my playing. He throws the cognac in my face. He screams that he hates Jews worse than Hitler does, that he will help his Führer kill all of them. He then says that I am the only one who understands him. That I am his friend. That he loves Sonia more than he loves his disgusting wife. He is worried about his daughter. He fears falling into the hands of the Russians. He grows sick. He vomits beside the piano. But it will be over soon. Very soon. He vomits again. He passes out in his own vomit. I call the Ukrainian housekeeper and together we carry him to his bedroom. I walk out into the night. I have never played Brahms again. I cannot. Brahms died for me and I cherished Brahms.

"There is something I must tell you about Sonia and me. After I learn about Krüger, I think it will poison the love between me and Sonia. She thinks the sight of her may repulse me. I think I may never be able to meet her gaze again. But that does not happen. Our love grows stronger and we cling to each other as though we are the last two people on earth who have not lost the capacity for love. We promise each other that Krüger cannot pollute the thing that is most beautiful between us. Our bodies and our fates belong to him. But we belong to each other.

"Sonia, Sonia. Sonia.

"There is not so much left now. In February in the dead of winter, the ghetto of Kironittska is eliminated. Fewer than a thousand Jews are left to be loaded into trains. Krüger comes to bid Sonia and me farewell. Though he cannot say it, I can see he is sorry we are leaving. He is in love with my Sonia. I can see this and it hurts him that Sonia looks at him with eyes that despise him. This monster, Krüger, is a lonely man. I have been lonely for forty years and I know about Krüger's loneliness. The train goes for two days, then stops in the freezing darkness. Our baby, Jonathan, dies on this night and it breaks something in Sonia. Other people, mostly old, freeze to death. The train moves off again. There is no water or facilities. Men and women must excrete. The smell shames us. The smell causes us despair. The sound of the children begging for water. Well, you can imagine what it is like. Except you cannot. I carry that journey on the train with me. The train breaks Sonia. It breaks her. All that we have endured and it is the train. My pretty Sonia dies before the Germans are kind enough to put her in the gas chamber. When they open the doors at Auschwitz, Sonia has lost her mind. She has gone on ahead. They have to pry her hands from around our baby, Jonathan.

"Here is my tattoo, Jack. The Germans love lists, catalogs, everything has its place. Because of my gift as a musician, they know I am coming. I am directed toward the line of life. Sonia and my twin sons go toward the line of death. The boys stand on either side of their mother, protecting her. They know that their mother is no longer there and even though they are only boys, both seem to grow into manhood in that line. They have to lead their mother to her death. Both wave good-bye to me. Secretly, so the Germans will not see. They are marched away into eternity. I try to catch Sonia's eye, but she is no longer there. I see her walk out of my life and I can still see after all these terrible years, these things that have happened, I can see why she was once called the most beautiful woman in Europe.

"I am putting on the camp uniform when I am hit by a blow from behind that knocks me to the floor. Then I am kicked in the stomach, then the face. There is commotion and I think a German guard is going to kill me in the changing room. It is Berger, the Jewish ruffian from Kironittska. The one whose boys stole food and were hanged for the crime. All Berger remembers is that I kicked the stools out from beneath his sons. 'This Jew is mine.'

"Berger is a Sonderkommando, one of the accursed Jews who is forced to remove the corpses from the gas chambers and take them to the crematoriums. Each day, he comes to find me to beat me some more. He is like some king among the damned. Some Krüger. Finally, he comes to take me away and slaps me and cuffs me on the back of the head. He passes easily through the barracks. Guards in the towers see him and he walks as though he were the concierge in this place. He brings me to a place and I hear Jewish voices singing a Hebrew song in praise of the Almighty. It is dark and the air is filled with black smoke. Then a screaming begins that is like no other sound on earth. Then there is silence. Berger knocks me to the ground again. He yanks me to my feet and pushes me ahead of him where other Jews are gathered and one of them is turning a wheel. Inside a door I am pushed and told to do what he does. There is a stack of dead Jews, hundreds of them. Mostly women and children and old people. I work hard to help remove them. I work beneath the blows of Berger. I drag bodies by the feet. Some are almost weightless. I am dragging one body when Berger stops me and makes me look down. It is Sonia. Then he makes me dig through the pile until I find my sons. I find them and bring them to Berger. He hands me pliers and tells me to pull all the gold teeth from Sonia's mouth. He yanks her mouth open and pulls out the first one in the most brutal manner. I cannot move, but he hits me in the face with the pliers. I open Sonia's mouth. I remove a tooth. Berger takes the pliers and begins to pull all the teeth out of her head. This Berger, too, is insane and he is also innocent. Later, there is a Jew who works in administration who has seen me in concert in the old days. He is a great lover of music. He finds out that Berger has me working night and day with the Sonderkommando. This unknown Jew is king of his realm and he puts Berger's number in a section marked for death. They come to get Berger and I am there when he is taken from a pile in the gas chamber.

"The rest of Auschwitz is just Auschwitz.

You can read about it. My experience is the same. I work. I suffer. I starve. Once I nearly die of dysentery. To survive, I play the music I love in my head all my working hours. I ask that the great composers assemble in my head to play their finest works for me. In squalor, I dine each night in my tuxedo with Beethoven, Bach, Mozart, Chopin, Liszt, Haydn, Puccini, Rimsky-Korsakov, Mahler, Strauss, Tchaikovsky, and all the others. Each evening, I dress slowly, taking care with my cuff links and studs and tying and retying my black tie until I get it just right. Before we play, I go to the great restaurants of Europe and I order the finest meals cooked by the finest chefs. I eat escargots glistening with butter and flecks of garlic and parsley, order roast duck with crisp brown skin and pods of fat just beneath the wing bones, eat baguettes dipped in olive oil, and crème brûlées with burnt crusts of brown sugar followed by layers of sweet cream that make the mouth pucker with pleasure. We would eat, not gorge, these great composers and I. Because I live in my head I survive by concentrating on the great silos of beauty I have stored up. I hear music amid the squalor. And I do what I promised myself I will not do under any circumstance: I survive. I disgrace myself by surviving.

"In the winter of 1945, I join one of the

forced marches when the Russians were nearing Auschwitz. We march through snow and
without food or rest. Many men fall by the way-
side and receive bullets. These bullets must
have felt like gifts. I am in Dachau when the
Americans liberate the camp. I remember none
of this. Later I am shown a pile of naked bodies. You know those photographs. Piles and
piles of dead scarecrows. The person showing
me the photograph is a doctor who has taken
the picture. After snapping the picture, he
thinks he sees my chest move. He checks my
pulse and races me to the hospital tent. My left
hand is frostbitten and gangrene has set in. He
removes the little finger of my left hand. I can
move the ring finger once I awake but it never
regains feeling. I have always regretted that this
doctor took that picture. He should have left
me on that pile. I was going back to Sonia.

"Ruth finds me in a DP camp, where she is
searching for survivors of her family. She hears
about a Jew looking for survivors from
Kironittska. We get married and because of
this I ruin the life of this very good woman. I
kiss her and I know she sees in my eye that I
am wishing for Sonia. I make love to her and I
sometimes whisper Sonia's name. Shyla and
Martha are born and I am also disappointed
because they are not the sons that I lost. I love
none of them. They disappoint me because

they are not my dead family. I cannot love
Ruth, Jack. I try and I cannot do it. I cannot
love Shyla or Martha. I can only love phan-
toms. I go to sleep loving all my ghosts and do
not wake up until my Shyla leaps from the
bridge.

"So, Jack."

PART VI

CHAPTER 35

I HATED THE SIXTIES AND I ESPE-
cially hate the memories I carry from the noise
and bedlam and discourtesy of those cacopho-
nous years. The shouting is what I recall most
clearly, then the posturing, then the lack of hygiene. It is the only decade I have lived through
that did not have the decency to call it quits
when its time had run out—1970, for me, was
the worst year of the sixties, by far.

It made me hate folk music and piety and
facial hair and tie-dyed shirts and political rhetoric of any kind. My idea of hell is to be caught
in an airport lounge during a snowstorm, listening to an aging hippie songstress whacking

away at her scratched-up Martin guitar as she plays "Blowin' in the Wind," "Puff the Magic Dragon," "I Gave My Love a Cherry," "Lemon Tree," and "We Shall Overcome," in that order. Once I was a wide-eyed captive of those times and there was no twelve-point program to wean me off the addiction to drivel I succumbed to during that dreary era of the Vietnam War. The greatest tragedy of that war was not the senseless death of young men on strangely named battlefields, but that it turned the whole country stupid overnight. It also made enemies of the closest group of friends I had ever known. We accidentally let ourselves be caught up in the zeitgeist and we were never the same again, any of us.

After the smoke had cleared, I promised myself I would never lose a friend because of something as subjective and slippery as political belief. "I'm an American," I announced to all around me. "And I get to think anything I want to and so do you, by God, so do you." It became my credo, the central theme of my life, but if it had not been for the intolerance and pigheadedness I exhibited with such grandiosity in those years and the weird sideburns and holier-than-thou attitude that I paraded around with, I would have entered into my maturity as uninterested in the world of ideas as any other Southerner. My whole character formed around the issue of Vietnam and it nearly brings me to my knees to admit it.

The Thursday after Lucy's party I drove up Highway 17 to Charleston with Ledare riding shotgun. We drove with the windows open and the smells of harvested crops and leaf-brandied rivers filled up the car and the wind slid through Ledare's honey-colored hair. Mike had sent invitations to both of us, requesting our presence at the Dock Street Theater in Charleston at precisely 2 P.M. No response was requested, but he phrased the invitation in a way that left no room for excuses for not showing up.

"What's Mike up to?" I asked.

"No good," she said.

"You know, don't you?"

"He's got something up his sleeve," she said, casting me a quizzical glance. "But he's kept it secret."

"Why?"

"He thinks we wouldn't show up if we knew what this was all about."

No theater in America can match the Dock Street Theater for both its intimacy and understated majesty. It has the hushed feeling of a building holding its breath, and its serenity grants comfort to both actors and audiences. It has the spare look of a Shaker church, and just being there makes you want to rush home to write a play. The stage is the size of a small dance floor; and as we entered I saw Mike watching a camera crew and soundman whom Ledare said he had flown in from the West Coast. I remembered that Mike had told me it was at the Dock Street Theater he had seen his first play as a child, a performance of Arthur Miller's *The Crucible*. It was so powerful that it had changed the course of his life forever. He grew up loving to watch actors pretending they were someone else, and speaking the made-up lines of strangers in love with the energy and passion of language. Though Mike had started out in the theater, he soon gravitated toward the world of film. In the theater, he said, he could create a sense of vibrancy, tension, and style, but in a movie he could make a whole world by allowing light to imprint shapes on moving rivers of film. One of the first things he did after the success of his first film was to join the board of the Dock Street Theater. Mike never forgot where he came from.

"Let's wrap it up in about ten minutes," Mike said to the crew, who were working with precision and speed. "Everybody knows the drill. Once we get started, my guests are not to be aware you boys are in the building. *Comprende?* You're neither to be seen nor heard. We're not after art here. I just want this recorded." he said as Ledare and I moved down the front aisle.

"What union rules apply here?" the man setting up camera angles asked and his voice was teasing.

"None, mousedick," Mike said, smiling. "South Carolina's a right-to-work state. Ever since Fort Sumter they've hated everything that even reminded them of the word 'union.'"

"What's this for?" a cameraman shouted from a rear balcony.

"Just a home movie," Mike said, clapping his hands.

As we approached Mike, he clapped his hands again and his crew disappeared and we did not see them again. His preparation was exacting and precise. We were the first to arrive.

"You're early," Mike said. "Early makes me nervous."

"Then we'll leave," Ledare said.

"No, I've staggered the time of arrival for everyone. Capers and Betsy were supposed to get here first, but they're late. Go up and take your seats. You're on stage left. The food's to die for and there's plenty to drink."

"What're our roles?" Ledare asked.

"Today, we improvise. Anything goes. Everything out on the table," Mike said. "It'll become clear to you when everyone shows up."

A movement caught my eye in the back of the theater and I turned to see the straight-backed silhouette of General Rembert Elliott standing at attention beside the back rows. He was joined by a taller gray-haired man and it surprised me when I saw my own father walking down the aisle dressed in his judicial robes. Together, they had driven up from Waterford. A woman cleared her throat behind me on-stage and I turned to see Celestine Elliott, who must have entered by the stage door, watching her husband approach with a look that could have shattered chrome.

When he saw his wife, General Elliott halted in his tracks and watched as she took her seat on the left side of the stage. I knew that they had not seen each other since the disastrous visit to Rome and had only communicated through the offices of their attorneys. The general bowed to me and Ledare with exaggerated formality.

"It scares me, Jack," Ledare said as we watched them make their way to their places.

"What?" I asked.

"When I'm seventy, I want all my mistakes behind me. I want thirty years of good and brilliant living behind me. Look at them. The judge, the general, Celestine. They're all in agony. I couldn't bear it if I thought the rest of my life would be as painful as my past."

"Introspection's a mistake," I said. "Be happy drifting along the shallows."

"That's no answer," she said.

"I agree," I said. "But at least it's a game plan."

Capers Middleton gave a shout of greeting to everyone as he and Betsy made their bold, confident entrance from the rear. Everything about them seemed exaggerated to me as if their metabolism was burning a bit brighter than the rest of ours. Their smiles seemed like grimaces to me. Like every politician I had ever seen, Capers' eyes took in all the players in the room at a single glance. I saw him nod at Ledare, but the gesture was condescending, dismissive. When Capers left someone behind, it was permanent and he granted no right of appeal, unless, of course, he found he needed a favor from that person along the way. With businesslike economy, he steered Betsy to their seats on the stage, wasting no time on small talk with Mike or us. Though it was vitally important to Capers that he seem in command of every situation, I could tell that he was nervous in the midst of this gathering from our mutual pasts.

Mike checked his watch and looked toward the side door of the Dock Street. My father had taken his place behind a desk on a raised platform with a judge's gavel on the desk. He hit the hammer twice on the oak desk, more to break the extraordinary tension than anything else. He looked more broken than old, and I realized how much I had neglected him since my return to Waterford and my clumsy attempts at caring for my mother. I tried to make myself feel about him the way I thought a son should about his father, but I could not fake an emotion that was not there. Pity surged through me unbidden when it was love I was after. My father stood up, smoothed out his robes, and adjusted his tie and collar. Then he sat down and resumed his seat like the rest of us.

Mike had arranged the seating brilliantly. At the back of stage center was the judge's chair and table and directly to the right was a handsome high-backed chair. Flowing from this centerpiece were comfortable plush chairs, set in big semicircles and facing each other. They were color-coordinated, lending an atmosphere that was both convivial and homey. On the left sat Ledare, Celestine, and I; next to me was a chair as yet unoccupied. Across from us were Capers, Betsy, General Elliott, and another unoccupied chair. Behind each of our chairs had been placed several taller wooden chairs. High above me on the left, I caught the barely perceptible movement of a cameraman adjusting a lens.

Mike stood at center stage, next to the judge, near the high-backed chair, where he could see all of us easily. "Welcome, my friends, and thank you for joining me today. I want all of you to know that you're being filmed and recorded. If you feel like speaking out, just raise your hand and Judge McCall will grant you permission to speak. When I take my seat, this will become like a court of law. The judge will preside. He is the only paid participant tonight. The rest of you are here because you've all been important to me in some way. I'm bound by my love and admiration for you. I've known most of you my whole life."

"Why here?" Mike asked rhetorically. "Because I thought in this theater, we could come together as though we were in a play, a drama that we will write together, tonight. I have brought two mystery guests to the Dock Street. This play will have surprises, but it will also have resolution. All of us will vote at the end of this performance. The man on trial has given me his permission to allow each of you to cast a vote deciding his fate.

"Ah! I see you're interested. Intrigued, perhaps. Hooked. I would give you the rules, but there are no rules. You are going to be asked to do nothing more or less than sit in judgment on the past. All of you except Betsy were either participants in the events we are about to describe together or witnesses. Some of you are the stars of this production, but all of you helped move the action in some way. *Hamlet* would not be *Hamlet* without Rosencrantz and Guildenstern, and this story would be incomplete without each of you.

"Everyone knows that Capers, Jack, and I were inseparable growing up. When I think of friendship, these are the two names that come to me first. Jack and I have grown apart and this hurts me more than I can say. I think it is also safe to say that Jack hates Capers, or at least dislikes him very much."

I sat in my place across from Capers and looked directly into his eyes and said, "Hate's the word, Mike."

Capers' wife, Betsy, who was seated next to her husband, said, "I told you from the beginning, Mike, I don't like this at all. I won't sit here and let my husband be criticized by a fake sous-chef."

I smiled and said, "I like you for your mind, Betsy. I wept during that last beauty pageant when you played 'Ode to Joy' on the kazoo."

"Don't bully my poor wife, Jack," Capers said. "It doesn't become you."

My father rapped his gavel on his desk at center stage and said, "That'll be enough, son."

"You don't get it," Capers said. "I still love you, Jack. That's what this evening's all about."

"Then it's going to be a long evening, pal," I said.

The gavel came down again. "I want order here."

Again, the gavel hammered against the oak desk and this time I kept quiet before my father's red-faced fury.

General Elliott stood up from where he sat, every inch the military man, his bearing authoritarian, fractious. He still looked as though he could swim a river and cut the throat of every guard near an ammo depot.

"This evening's about my son, isn't it?" he asked Mike.

"What happened to Jordan is central to everything, General. All of us know that. If the Marine Corps hadn't stationed you on Pollock Island, none of this would've happened. Jack and Capers would still be best friends. You and Celestine wouldn't be getting a divorce. I think it's possible that even Shyla might be alive today, though that may be a stretch. But Jordan coming to town changed everything. He not only became our best friend, he became our destiny."

"If you know anything about the whereabouts of my son, then you are required to report it to federal authorities. If you know where he is, you could be accused of harboring a fugitive. I'll turn you in myself, Mike, and you know I'm as good as my word."

"Shut up," Celestine said.

The judge rapped the gavel once more, a single, echoing note of order. The general turned again toward Mike. His voice was so pained it was as if he were addressing the commander of a firing squad.

"If you know the whereabouts of my son, you have a moral obligation to report that information to the authorities," he said.

From behind the curtain at stage left there was a slight movement and Jordan Elliott, immaculate in his Trappist robes, walked to center stage. Another monk and Father Jude accompanied him partway, then took their seats at the side of the stage in the shadows.

"Hello, Dad," Jordan said to the general. "You never did know what happened. You know all parts of the story except mine."

"Two innocent people died because of you," the general said, his astonishment at the sight of his son removing some of the edge in his voice. "Instead of a soldier, I raised a fugitive and a weakling."

"None of us knew it then, Dad," Jordan said, "but you had raised a priest."

"My Church would not accept a murderer at the altar," said the general, staring at the other two priests on the stage.

The abbot rose and went to stand beside Jordan, then said, "I met your son in Rome when he was a novice. I became both his sponsor and confessor. The forgiveness of sins is central to the profession of the Roman Catholic faith. Among the Trappists who have come to know him, your son is considered a good man by all and a saintly man by some."

"He's a disgrace to his country and his faith," the general said. "Who considers him a saint?"

"His confessor does," the abbot said, bowing and returning to his seat.

"I did not give you permission to sit down," the general said.

The abbot wiped his brow with his sleeve and said, "I don't need your permission to sit, thank you, General. You, sir, have retired and your rank is merely decorative. I am presently the abbot of Mepkin Abbey and my authority bears the weight and imprimatur of an unbroken two-thousand-year spiritual reign. And do not raise your voice to me again, sir. Your son is here at my suggestion and forbearance and I can take him away from here and hide him in places you've not dreamed of on this globe."

"Vatican II," the general sneered. "That's when the Church went wrong. That fat Pope who couldn't do a chin-up if his life depended on it got every liberal-thinking dildo and dandy he could dig up, got them together at Vatican II to dismantle everything that was true and unreplaceable in the Catholic Church. When the Church was stern the Church was good. I loathe this new, limp-wristed, feel-good, touchy-feely Church where the priests and nuns screw like mink and play the guitar at High Mass singing 'Kumbaya.' "

My father hit his desk again and said, "You're wasting time, General. You're rambling. It's time to move forward."

"There's one more mystery guest to present," Mike said. "Many of you won't know this guest except as legend. If you read the papers during our college years at Carolina, you'd recognize his name. Ladies and gentlemen, I introduce you all to 'Radical Bob' Merrill, the leader of the Students for a Democratic Society at Carolina from 1969 to 1971."

As I turned to watch Bob Merrill walk onto the stage behind me, I had a terrible realization that this night was going to be harder and more destructive on everyone than Mike had ever dreamt. I thought I hated Capers Middleton more than anyone in the world, but I had forgotten all about Radical Bob Merrill. Radical Bob had made a cameo appearance in all our lives, did incalculable damage, then dropped out of sight.

Merrill walked over to Capers and the two

men embraced. Bob then came across to Jordan and he embraced the priest. Turning to me, he extended his hand warily.

"If I take your hand," I said, "then the next stop's your throat."

"You should really try to grow up, Jack," Bob said. "It's time to let bygones be bygones."

"When you accepted this invitation tonight, Bob," I said, "did you figure out how you were going to get out of this theater without me kicking the shit out of you?"

The hammer sounded again, the judge cleared his throat, and Mike moved between the two of us.

"Who is Radical Bob?" my father asked.

"Radical Bob was the original leader of the antiwar movement on campus that swept us all up in its activities," Mike explained.

"Where is all this leading, Mike?" my father asked.

"Judge," Mike said, delighted at his cue. "I can't answer that question until we come to the very end of this production."

Ledare stood up and faced Mike. "What do you get out of this, Mike? You've always been generous, but you've never been generous to a fault."

"Thanks for that sterling recommendation, darling," Mike said. "But Ledare is right. I get the rights to Jordan's story for arranging this evening. If we decide that Jordan is guilty, then he'll turn himself in to the proper authorities on Pollock Island. Capers has offered his services as an attorney if Jordan is prosecuted for his crimes. Free of charge."

"So Capers will look heroic to the voters of South Carolina," Ledare said. " 'Middleton to Defend Killer Priest, Boyhood Friend.' "

"Cynicism makes you less pretty, dear," Capers said, smiling.

Ledare asked Jordan, "You agreed to let Capers be your lawyer?"

Jordan shook his head. "It's a nice offer, but it's the first I've heard of it."

"If he defends you, I hope you get the electric chair," I said.

"Jack, Jack," Capers said. "People'll get the idea we've had a falling out."

"Mike," I said, rising out of my seat. "You get a movie out of this. Capers gets to be governor. Jordan, maybe, gets to go to jail. Tell me, why this stage? This setting? With friends and enemies gathered together in the same room? This could be settled privately. If Jordan is happy as a priest, then let him be happy. Leave him in peace. Let him walk off this stage and return to wherever he's come from. You've put Jordan in great jeopardy. And why? For one of your movies? For Capers' election?"

"No, Jack," Mike said. "I've noticed over

the years how few times I've actually felt a part of a moment, electric, with every cell dazzled and tingling, with my whole body burning as though I were about to burst into flames. Listen to all of us breathing here. Feel the tension. This promises to be a night that none of us ever forgets. Our history surrounds us and tortures us. Yet there was once love that traveled among us, lighting us up and lighting our way. Tonight, I want us to find out together what happened to that love and why hatred can take the place of love with such ease."

"How do we start?" Capers asked.

My father hammered his gavel and said, "Whoever wants to speak must come to this witness chair. Whoever speaks must tell his or her truth, just as if this were a real court."

"Our stories are all so different," Ledare said. "I'm not the same person I was in college. I hate the girl I was."

"Then tell us about that hatred," Mike said. "All of us will tell our stories. There will be no order to the telling. Our stories will form some kind of truth that none of us at this moment grasps. All of our voices will form one story line. None of us can be hurt in any way by what is said here . . . except Jordan Elliott. But if we come to some truth about Jordan, I think we can come to the truth about each of us, about what we did during that time."

Mike snapped his fingers and the lights went out in the theater, leaving only the stage bathed in bright illumination. For a moment there was complete silence until the gavel rapped and Mike said, "We return now to the Vietnam War. President Nixon is in the White House. The country is at war with itself. The campuses around the nation are temples of rage. In Columbia, South Carolina, we are in the middle of our college lives. We are Southern. We are basically apolitical. The war is popular in our state, because South Carolina is conservative. Yet something is taking place at the university. The antiwar movement is taking hold and growing day by day. But we are still preoccupied with having dates for the football games and getting jobs after graduation.

"Ladies and gentlemen, I suggest to all of you that we walked into the history of our times without guile or preparation. We were sweet-natured, fun-loving, hard-drinking, fast-driving, quick-talking kids from Waterford. We could dance all night and often drove down to Myrtle Beach to do just that. The boys were all handsome and the girls were all pretty. We played hard, we laughed loud, and we were all in love with ourselves and our world. Then the larger world tapped us on the shoulder and introduced itself. Tapped hard. Made its presence known.

"Let us begin. Please don't stop until we listen to everyone."

Through a chorus of different voices and unique perspectives the story began to unfold. My father called on people to speak and at first he was strict about allowing no interruptions. The footlights bathed him in a mother-of-pearl corona as he listened, dressed in the black robes of justice, his authority unquestioned. He looked handsome and fine; authority became him.

He nodded first to Ledare, who understood his intent and took the witness chair. She had survived the battle we were about to relive by being a dispassionate witness, and it seemed fitting that it was she who would introduce the scene we were about to reenter.

As I listened to her sketch the background of those times, I realized that I never thought that Ledare had been paying any attention back then. It seemed to me that she had drifted along the fringes of cataclysm, impervious to outrage and untouched by any of the fevers or seizures that shook the rest of us. Her choice was to watch and not participate, and as she spoke I realized that she had become invisible to me back then as she slipped into the role of observer while the rest of us were pulled toward the epicenter.

"Who knew anything about Vietnam at

first?" Ledare said, looking at my father. "I mean, it had finally become a real war by the time we went to college. Sure, I watched all the demonstrations on TV, but South Carolina was different. I was far more interested in my sorority and good parties than anything else. All of us were like that. I thought more about makeup than the Mekong Delta. I was that kind of girl and there's no sense apologizing for it because that's how I was brought up. My parents wanted me to be serious about finding a mate and I had no responsibilities after that. College, for them, was a polishing off. The biggest deal on campus in my first two years was over the lack of student parking. I mean it. That was the real sore point among the students, what really got them riled up. Then things changed. Almost overnight. Everyone noticed it. It was in the air . . ."

Listening to her stirred my own memories and it took me back to those college years when I had never felt more a part of things as I made my way to classes in that comely and welcoming campus. In that first year the war was overwhelmingly popular and all of us went to hear Dean Rusk speak when the Secretary of State came to campus to defend his Democratic administration's policies. By this time, it had become dangerous for Dean Rusk to appear on an American campus, but as Carolina students we greeted him with enthusiasm and admiration. He warned against "communism," the most terrifying word in the English language at that time. As Southerners we could easily imagine working on a commune, but few of us could imagine living out the rest of our days as a godless people, bereft of our faith. And I thought quietly: the Vietnam War had another thing going for it in the South—we did not mind killing people or going to war against a nation we had never heard of. As Southerners we distrusted the federal government when it levied taxes or tried to interfere with the integrity of state laws, but we trusted it completely when it sent its soldiers into perilous, watery climes to kill yellow people who spoke in unknown tongues. No recruitment officer ever had trouble meeting his quota in South Carolina.

Then, in 1968, there was the Tet Offensive, the assassination of Martin Luther King, the murder of Robert Kennedy, the Chicago Convention, a whole coloratura of horror in transit along a time line.

As Ledare continued I remembered that our campus had been quiescent, indifferent, as students took over administration buildings at Columbia and Harvard. But hints and markings of change began to appear without the presence of any rhetoric or forethought. We started wearing our hair longer, grew mustaches, and the first beards began to appear. A gradual dressing down had begun subliminally and an SAE boy in a suit began to look odd, a museum piece drifting as flotsam along fraternity row. The daughters of small-town insurance adjusters and Baptist ministers began to dress like hippies and stopped wearing makeup except on weekend visits home. Except for Secession, no trend had ever had its birthplace in South Carolina. But the tumult on the other campuses and the antiauthoritarian tenor of the times could be measured by the length of the sideburns creeping down the faces of Carolina men.

Girls like Ledare had their lives already written for them long before they went to college. Her beauty was safe and homegrown, not exotic like Shyla's, not dangerous to the touch. The Tri Delts rushed her, feted her; she was practically crowned before she ever stepped onto the campus. The high school cheerleader simply changed the color of her pompons and skirt, and learned the new and much fancier routines of the college sidelines. Ledare was the kind of girl who dated the quarterback, but married the guy who edited the *Law Review*. During her sophomore year, she reigned as Miss Garnet and Black, and she was Homecoming Queen her junior year. Except for

Shyla, few noticed she was Phi Beta Kappa and was majoring in philosophy. Throughout their time there, Shyla tried to engage Ledare in political discussions, but Ledare felt safer in the libraries and in the blazing noise of autumn football crowds than locked in the malice of debate.

She was frightened of the times and she held back from them. Because she was so lovely, no one took the time to get to know her, including herself. And so it was in the Dock Street Theater that Ledare Ansley became the best person to describe the way we once were. She had seen the whole thing, observed it all from the top of homecoming floats. Only she could tell the point at which the everydayness of our college lives became inextricably bound up with the murderous urgencies of the war. Now, as I tuned back in to what she was saying, Ledare said it was Shyla who held the key. It was Shyla who changed the most, Shyla who turned herself into a dangerous and fascinating woman, and Shyla who brought Radical Bob into our close-knit group.

Onstage, Radical Bob Merrill laughed out loud when his name was mentioned for the first time.

" 'Radical Bob,' " he said. "Hearing that takes me back a long way."

"I agree with Ledare," Capers said, rising

from his chair and addressing the audience after he replaced Ledare in the witness stand. "It's hard to describe Shyla in those days. I don't remember Shyla ever talking much during elementary or junior high school. Remember how painfully shy she was back then? It seemed to hurt her physically just to be looked at. That fragility seemed to melt away in high school. She got prettier every year. Then sexier. Then you had that sheer intelligence, that brightness that could bully or tease or cajole. She could take over a room with her brain. In college, Shyla discovered she was a leader. She'd have made a great Republican."

Mike said, "She hated Republicans with her body and soul. She told me something during the McGovern campaign I've never forgotten. Shyla said, 'They used to call Southerners who hated black people racists. Now they call them Republicans.'"

"The Republicans haven't done a good job getting our message out to the black electorate," Capers agreed. "But we're working on it."

"If you get a single black vote, it means democracy ain't working," I said.

"Coming from you I take that as a compliment," Capers said.

The judge hammered his gavel and ordered, "That'll be enough from you, Jack. Settle down."

Capers began clapping, but the applause was mocking, increasing the tension: "A genius for exaggeration. A gift of Jack's as large as his overgrown body. He thinks his heart's as large as all outdoors. The pathetic fallacy of all American liberals. In theory, they love the black, the downtrodden, the crippled, and the poor, yet you never find any of these people at their dinner table."

The gavel again and the judge said, "Let's continue. You boys're like scorpions in a bottle."

General Elliott sat off to stage left, removed from everyone, his face a mask of disapproval. If he was listening he gave no sign of it. He stared directly at his son, who returned the stare without judgment. Jordan, the priest, was every bit as erect and gaunt, as righteous and as handsome as the general. Only one great difference was manifest between them: the darkness that Jordan brought to the theater was soft and lauds-polished, the general's darkness looked stolen from a firing range.

"Capers and I'll take up this part of the story," Mike said, "from the time when all of us boys grew our hair longer."

"I let my hair grow down to my shoulder blades," Capers remembered.

Ledare said, "Long hair's one thing but none of us lost a friend in the war. No matter what else happened none of our friends died in Vietnam."

"Some of mine did," General Elliott said loudly, his voice a sudden force onstage.

"But not Jordan. Not your son. Jordan's right in front of you," Celestine said. "He's here tonight facing you at last."

The general replied, "Jordan's deader than any soldier who fought and died honorably in Vietnam, Celestine. He's invisible to me. His cowardice blinds me to his reality. There's a fog between us so thick, so impassable. A river of blood stands between us. The blood of men I ordered into battle. Every time I try to see my son, their blood gets in my eyes. Their names blind me when I try to catch sight of Jordan. All the names on the wall of the Vietnam Memorial come toward me. Hundreds of thousands of letters, the names of all the dead boys who did their duty, who did right by America— their names march toward me in endless regiments when I try to catch sight of our cowardly son. Our Jordan."

There was silence, a breathtaking silence, and then I stood up and screamed at General Elliott, "With assholes like you leading us, I'm amazed one American boy ever came back in one piece from Vietnam. How can one, broken-down rigid old fart know everything in the world? Answer me that, General. That's your

son there. It's not a flag, or an M-1, or a gui-
don, or a hand grenade, or a parade ground, or
a foxhole—yet you've shown more love and de-
votion to all these things than you've ever
shown to your son. You knocked Jordan
around his whole childhood and everyone here
knows it. You knocked Celestine around too,
but only a couple of us know that. Oh, Brave
General of the Republic, who sits in judgment
of his son tonight . . . you're not half the man
your son is and you never were. You're a child-
beater and a wife-beater, a lightweight thinker,
a first-class bully, and the only reason you're
not a full-fledged Nazi is you can't speak German and we've got this Constitution that keeps
shitbirds like you in check."

The gavel. "Shut up, Jack. And sit down.
You're already too emotional and we have
hardly started."

"No, Judge," Mike said. "We're well into
our drama."

"I want to answer Jack," the general said,
rising to his feet and pointing his finger menacingly.

"Yours is the first generation that disgraced
America. When this country called out to its
sons, the lily-livered draft dodgers and mama's
boys of your era wore girls' panties to their
physicals, faked asthma attacks, poured sugar
into their urine samples, went on diets to get

below the weight limit, gorged themselves to exceed it, got girls pregnant to avoid the draft, joined the National Guard in droves to avoid combat. We needed men of iron in Vietnam and we had to choose them from a nation of pantywaists. We had to select warriors from a defiled pool of pretty boys who were more comfortable on a therapist's couch than walking point in the jungle. Our nation rots from the inside out. It's a republic without gonads, one that's grown fat, effeminate, and bloated with all the gross excesses of a society gone to seed. It sickens me. You sicken me, Jack."

"Well said, General," Capers said in the silence that followed.

Celestine Elliott stood up and said, "Talk to us about loyalty, dear. You raised Jordan to believe that loyalty was the most sterling quality in a soldier."

"I've not changed my mind," the general said, not looking at his estranged wife. "But Jack would know nothing of the kind of loyalty I was talking about."

"He could teach you some things about loyalty you've never dreamt of," she said. "Jack never once turned his back on our son. He's been absolutely loyal to the only child we ever brought forth on this earth. He's never wavered. He's never backed off. He's never asked for anything in return nor received a single thing in payment."

"That's not true," I said.

"What've you gotten from all this, Jack?" Celestine asked.

"Jordan's loved me. He's been an irreplaceable friend. He's made me less lonely in the world," I answered.

During this exchange, Jordan continued to keep his eyes fixed on his father. His expression hardly changed at all; it carried all the serenity of monastic life in its gaze.

Mike then took over the main story line of the narrative. All of us, he said, had been witnesses to the change in Shyla Fox once she met Radical Bob Merrill, who had transferred to Carolina from Columbia University during the summer of 1969. Bob had been with the radicals who had taken over Columbia's administration building and issued a series of demands so stringent that the New York police were called in to break the siege during a brutal, predawn raid that did great harm to Columbia's illustrious progressive reputation. Radical Bob himself had been asleep in Harlem when the raid took place because he was learning to make incendiary bombs from a black Muslim on probation, for use in disabling police units sent to interfere with political demonstrations. He came South to start a branch of the Students for a Democratic Society at the University of South Carolina. His first recruit on campus was Shyla Fox. Before he left the university, he had built the SDS chapter to a membership of just over fifty. He shaped them to his own will and educated them politically. So gifted was Radical Bob at organizing the somnolent students of the university that he received a special citation from national headquarters. But this was later, after Kent State, and the storm that had broken the lives of all of us gathered at the Dock Street Theater.

"I had never seen anybody like Radical Bob," Mike said. "He had long black hair like an Indian, spoke three languages, could quote entire pages of Walt Whitman, Karl Marx— nothing fazed him or bothered him. He wasn't a good public speaker, but what a judge of character, of leadership. He knew the South distrusted outsiders, so he set about the business of seducing Southerners to do his bidding. He stayed in the background, invisible, pulling the strings. He began our political education. No doubt about that. Except for Shyla, I don't think any of us had given two thoughts about the war. We were ripe for the picking. I'd been waiting my whole life for someone like Radical Bob. Cool. He wrote the script for cool. He made ideas come alive. All of us bought into his game plan. Except Jordan."

Radical Bob, dressed impeccably in a Brooks Brothers suit, his hair styled and his nails manicured, said, "Jordan was completely immune to the charms of revolutionary thought. He was far too emotional to be trusted in a political movement. His only danger to me was the allegiance he inspired in his friends. In their innocence, Shyla and Mike revered him. But I saw an alien. I discouraged Shyla and Mike from their friendship with Jordan. I did the same with Jack."

"But I was your real victory, Bob," Capers said. "I was your pièce de résistance."

"Ah yes," Bob said, smiling at Capers. "I set my sights on you in my first month on campus. Shyla and to a lesser extent Mike were great catches, but let's face it, they were Jewish and still could be discounted by the Southern dimwits I was trying to reach. I used my own Jewishness to hook them, but with you, I had to come up with a longer-range plan. So I drew up a strategy. When I found out about the Waterford connection among you, I suggested that Shyla start bringing all of you together at Yesterday's—a friendly gathering over a beer where we could eventually lead the conversation toward serious things. Toward the war. Toward a response to that war. And, of course, in the back of my mind, toward civil disobedience."

"The phrase of yours I remember best," Capers said, "was this one: 'If there's to be blood in the rice paddies of Vietnam, there must also be an equivalent amount of blood shed in the streets of South Carolina.' I learned a lot from you, Bob."

"You and Shyla were my best students. You could move a crowd like no one I ever saw, Capers."

"Vietnam made us all passionate, one way or the other," Capers said.

"The art of kissing did funny things to Judas too," I said, not bothering to look up at Capers. "Hit the hammer, Dad. Before these two love birds slide off the stage in their own slime."

Both Bob and Capers laughed, but the laughter was born of nervousness, and the tension in the theater tightened like a spring. Father Jude coughed. Celestine excused herself and made her way to the ladies' room. Ledare leaned forward in her seat. The gavel came down again and Mike continued the story that was bringing all of us into the sulfurous, exhausted past.

It was Mike who spoke but I felt myself remembering everything as I conjured up those gatherings in Yesterday's. From the start the Waterford crowd was central to the life of the university because, as a group, we were uncommonly active in student life. Ledare was swept up in cheerleading, sororities, and beauty pageants, carrying on the Southern traditions. She ran in place while the rest of us exhausted ourselves screaming epithets at each other, arguing late at night, trying to change everything by the force of our ideas. We liked being smart and we liked being loud, and Radical Bob picked up the tab for all the beer we drank at Yesterday's. Ledare broke up with Capers shortly after he met Radical Bob. A month later, Capers dropped out of his fraternity, Kappa Alpha, after delivering an antiwar speech to his KA brothers.

By the end of 1969, Capers Middleton, scion of one of the oldest and most distinguished families in South Carolina history, descendant of three signers of the Declaration of Independence, had become the acknowledged leader of the SDS and the radical student movement at South Carolina. In the background stood Bob Merrill, offering instruction, advice, and political direction. Second in command was Shyla, who now shared both Capers' bed and his commitment to stop the war in Southeast Asia and bring every American soldier home. To my own regret Capers and Shyla were inseparable figures on campus during those heady, unbridled days. In the mornings they drank espresso at the UFO coffeehouse on Gervais Street trying to talk young soldiers at Fort Jackson into declaring their opposition to the war. They traveled together all over the country attending demonstrations and conferences involving leaders in the peace movement. Shyla became famous for her beauty and eloquence, Capers for his courage in facing police lines and his ability to combine passion and practicality in the speeches he delivered every day to groups that ranged in number from five to a thousand. His oratory had a purring, hallucinatory quality that could spellbind a crowd within minutes.

"Shyla was the true revolutionary," Radical Bob said. "I knew as soon as I discovered her that she was a once-in-a-lifetime deal. I saw her cry when one of the other girls described the night her pet cat died ten years before. Shyla didn't know either the cat or the girl, but she had empathy for all God's creatures. It made her exciting and it made her naive. But you could take Shyla to the bank. She was the real thing. I think she was in love with Jack even then, but Jack wasn't political and he wouldn't change. Capers won her love by tossing off his past life and manning the barricades with her. Shyla felt that Capers was her own creation. Of course, I felt the exact same way about her.

"Shyla believed the Vietnam War was evil . . . but her vision was complicated by her parents' story. Her Jewishness was the key to all her antiwar activity. To her, the Vietnamese were Jews. The Americans were the invading army, so they became the Nazis in her mind. Every time I argued with Shyla about the war, she took me on a field trip to Auschwitz. Talk about the siege of Khe Sanh with the Marines and suddenly she had me riding in a cattle car across the Polish countryside. I learned that I was a different kind of Jew than Shyla. My mother and father had this extraordinary gratitude about America. I looked at the world through my parents' eyes. She looked at the world and her vision was obscured by her father's tattoo. I think she had a need to protest the war because no one said a word when her parents and their families were taken by the Nazis. Every picture of a dead Vietnamese reminded her of ditches piled with Jews. Her protest, her radicalism, everything was an extension of her family life. But Shyla's feelings were the realest thing about her. It was life and death with her."

"What was it for my son?" General Elliott asked. "I accept your description of Shyla's protest. Her sincerity I never doubted. Shyla was pure of spirit. By changing a few words of your description, you could've been describing the perfect infantryman. But tell me about Jordan. As far as I knew, he was as apolitical as

Jack. Yet both of them got caught up in this foolishness. I never understood it."

"Shyla wouldn't rest until she enlisted Jordan and Jack in SDS," Capers explained. "They'd laugh and tease her about her new-found radicalism. For a while they called her 'Jane Fonda.' But she got them to the rallies and the speeches. They were smart guys and if they hadn't been playing baseball I think they'd have gotten involved earlier."

"We were carried away by events," I said. "Things occurred beyond our control."

"You take it from here, Jack," Mike said, and I nodded and took the witness chair.

CHAPTER 36

I BEGAN MY PART OF THE TELLING slowly, but I tried to get my facts right. It would be a while before I was brought in to the main action, but I was certainly a witness to the startling changes among my friends. Once Shyla and Capers discovered the antiwar movement they were lost to us. Though they went to class only sporadically, they still maintained good grades. At twenty-one, Capers Middleton and Shyla Fox were the two most famous college students in the state who were not athletes. They were regulars on the evening news, and were widely quoted and photographed in the papers. Their first arrest took place when they protested a visit of Du Pont to the campus to recruit graduates for the corporation, which manufactured napalm. Their second arrest took place a week later when they tried to block an exit to the amphitheater when President Nixon was speaking in Charlotte. During this time, it seemed as if Capers and Shyla had passed into some twilight world of fanaticism. There were no questions about the war they could not answer. The two of them brimmed with the righteousness of their cause, and each week the antiwar movement grew stronger on campus because of their zeal and their remarkable skills of confrontation, organization, and debate.

But for most of us college was still the center of our lives.

Often after his classes, Jordan would walk over to the yearbook offices to meet me and sometimes Mike. I wrote almost all the copy for three straight yearbooks and Mike took more photographs than anyone who had ever worked for the *Garnet and Black*. In one photograph, Mike had caught the essence of the annual Miss Venus contest, where coeds from the sororities dressed in tight blouses, short shorts, and high heels, and paraded across a stage wearing paper bags over their heads. It was a traditional way to judge the Carolina woman who possessed the most desirable body; the

jury was a leering batch of fraternity boys famous for their testosterone level. Mike's photograph captured the bagged, anonymous
heads of this girls' lineup, their strained, pige-
onlike bosoms stuck out and shoved toward the
camera's lens, for the pleasure of one grotesque, ogling face of a fraternity boy, appreci-
ating breasts that seemed to stretch out into
infinity. I captioned it "The Teat Offensive."
When President Thomas Jones invited us to explain the play on words Mike and I both insisted it was a printer's error. Slowly, Mike succumbed to the call of Radical Bob, but he still
loved the yearbook; from the start we saw it as
our opportunity to record history with our own
signatures and slants on every page. For us, the
Garnet and Black was part epistle, part Rosetta
Stone, Hallmark card, Socratic dialogue, and
census report. It was a bright accumulation of
life assembled from the formlessness of ten
thousand lives thrown together in a great bouil-
labaisse and simmered for four years.

But when Capers and Shyla chalked up
their sixth arrest of the year in December of
1969, I said good-bye to all that. Mike and Jordan and I went down to bail them out. By this
time we were pros at bailing out our friends,
since Capers' and Shyla's parents had washed
their hands of any responsibility for their off-
springs' legal entanglements. The Foxes shared

the immigrant's dread of offending the authorities, while Capers' parents cut him off because he was destroying the reputation of a family name long celebrated in South Carolina history texts. Without parental support, the two of them often found themselves casualties of rough policework and were handcuffed and dragged by the hair into waiting paddy wagons. They learned that the police were blue-collar workers who had come out of marginal suburbs. They could easily hate the sight of long-haired, spoiled college kids who did not mind using the American flag to start up fires along the boulevards. A nightstick had put Capers in the hospital in November; Shyla received a punch with a closed fist by a highway patrolman later that month.

On this particular evening, a deputy named Willis Shealy took exception to the way I looked. Night had fallen and I knew this was a dangerous time in Southern jails, but my politeness was ingrained, even natural. The slack-jawed, hostile deputy sized me up in a way that told me I was in trouble.

"I got a sister with big tits whose hair isn't half as long as yours," Shealy said.

"The bondsman said the papers are all in order, sir," I said, avoiding eye contact.

"You hear what I said?" the deputy demanded.

"Yes, sir. I did."

"Your friend in there's got hair down to his ass. He got a dick or a pussy between his legs?"

"Sir," I said, "you'll have to ask Capers that."

"Get smart with me, boy, and you'll be spending the night with your buddy," Shealy said.

And just then, Jordan walked into the Columbia jail to see what was holding me up. Jordan had long ago returned to his California style and had one of the first ponytails among Carolina men.

"What's the problem?" Jordan asked.

"Another one," Shealy said, shaking his head in disgust. "If that college don't have a chicken coop full of faggots . . ."

But Jordan had no sense of restraint: "Look, loser, just let our friend out of jail and you can get back to counting your acne scars."

"My friend likes to joke around," I suggested.

Willis Shealy lifted his billy club from the metal desk in front of him and said, "He's joking with death. I played football in high school."

"Oh, God. Did you hear that, Jack?" Jordan said, lifting his hands in mock terror. "I wouldn't have dared open my mouth if I'd have known our superhero had played football. He must be one of those ass-kicking, take-no-prisoners sort of guys. My knees always get weak when I'm face-to-face with a fat-assed, pimple-faced dickhead who brags he played high school football."

Watching the billy club, I said, "Shut up, Jordan. Could you please release our friend, sir?"

"I don't like your faggot friend," the deputy said, taking a step closer to Jordan, who responded by moving a step toward Shealy.

"My friend hasn't been feeling well," I said.

The deputy laughed and said, "Can't cure diarrhea of the mouth."

"I puke every time I smell the body odor of the village redneck," Jordan said.

"Thanks for helping defuse the situation," I said.

"Hey, anytime I can lend a hand."

"I bet you love to suck dick, don't you, faggot?" Shealy said.

"Sir, if you could just hold your tongue, I think I can reason with my friend," I said. "Neither of you're helping me out."

"I happen to be an aficionado of sucking dick," Jordan said, enjoying himself now. The muscles in Shealy's clenched jaw tightened.

"Aficionado? Of course, that word's three syllables too long for you to handle, Shealy. But I've sucked some of the finest dicks in this country. I'm a master of the trade. My tongue is celebrated in queer bars around the country. I love fat dicks and skinny dicks. Some dicks taste like cheese, others like fresh pork, some like beef jerky, some like corn on the cob, but my favorite taste like sugarcane. Some guys' hygiene leaves something to be desired, you know, guys like you, Shealy, guys who bathe once a month whether they need it or not. Then a sardine taste comes to mind or maybe anchovies . . ." Jordan was on a roll and I had rarely seen him enjoying himself more.

"You're one sick son of a bitch," Shealy said. "I wouldn't let a pervert like you *in* my jail."

"Just release our friend Mr. Middleton," I said, "and I'll get this pervert out of your sight."

"I bet you're hung like a horse, Mr. Shealy," Jordan said, joking, moving another step forward as Shealy retreated. "I bet I couldn't even fit the whole thing in my mouth."

"If your friend moves a step closer," Shealy said to me, "I'll shoot both of you. Watch him now, while I get your friend inside."

As Shealy went back into the cell block, I said, "I got some problems with your technique."

"You were kissing ass," Jordan said cheerfully. "It didn't appear to be working."

"One should not scare a county deputy," I advised. "They're paid too little money and the only fun they have is killing someone brought in for a speeding violation."

"I thought you knew the South," Jordan said. "The only reason both of us aren't dead right now is because we're white."

"You need to be more cautious," I advised.

"Caution dulls me," said Jordan matter-of-factly. "I only begin to get interested when I throw caution to the wind."

"Do me a favor," I said. "Let me know when you do, so I can get out of your way."

Jordan said, "Don't be colorless, Jack. Promise me you won't be colorless."

"It's what I aspire to," I said as Capers was led out of the cell block by a still-shaken Shealy.

"What on earth did you say to poor Deputy Shealy?" Capers said on seeing us. "He's trembling like a leaf."

"Take your next demonstration outside the Richland County line, Middleton," Shealy warned. "And buy your squirrely friend there some mouthwash."

"Good line, Officer Shealy," Jordan said. "I love it when the hoi polloi come up with a clever comeback. It gives me renewed faith in the possibilities of public education for the masses."

"What the hell's he talking about?" Shealy asked me.

"Remember, Shealy," Jordan said, "the South's about story, not repartee."

"What an asshole," Shealy answered.

"You're a genius, sir," Jordan said. "You returned fire with both story and repartee."

Capers pulled his long hair back with both hands and asked, "What's Jordan been drinking?"

"He's high on life," I said. "Let's make like horse shit and hit the trail."

"That's a Boy Scout joke," said Capers. "If only my scoutmaster could see me now."

"Trying to destroy America," Jordan said. "And everything that made us great."

"Trying to save America," Capers said, his face growing serious.

"You've become something of a grump since you set out to save the planet and all its singing birds, Capers," Jordan said.

"Let's continue this discussion at Yesterday's," I suggested. "Mike has bailed out Jane Fonda. She'll want to yell at us too."

We all went off to Yesterday's, where Mike and Shyla were already nursing a drink at a table. Capers and Shyla kissed passionately as was their habit in those heady days of arrests and speeches shouted out of bullhorns. They held hands in public, were affectionate in ways that made me extremely uncomfortable and caused Jordan to avert his eyes. It was not enough that they were living together; their unvoiced message seemed to be that the fury of their beliefs had deepened the intensity of their sexual life. As we sat waiting for our beers in Yesterday's, their hands moved along each other's bodies as though the curves of their own pliant flesh were the only braille they could trust.

"Unglue yourselves," Mike said, "so we can order."

"You're just jealous," Capers said, staring deeply into Shyla's eyes. "I feel like I've lost my arms and legs when we're apart. It's like we've been one ever since the revolution took off."

"What revolution?" I asked.

"When're you gonna wake up, Jack?" Shyla said sharply. "How many bodies're going to have to pile up in Vietnam before it claims a share of your attention?"

"Seventy-two thousand three hundred and sixty-eight," I said, studying the menu.

"How can you make jokes when young American boys are dying in an immoral war?" Capers asked, grabbing my wrist.

Jordan was reading from his own menu and said, "I want a cheeseburger smothered with onions. And there's that fabulous hot dog also waiting to be eaten. Something in me also craves a salad. But then, I think of those boys dying in an immoral war, and I realize I don't want food at all. I want to carry a placard and march in an antiwar demonstration, and be morally superior to every human being I pass."

"I thought I was going to get a T-bone steak," I added. "But I can't think about red meat without thinking of Hué and body bags loaded up with young men who will never hear the words of the Gettysburg Address again. The T-bone seems immoral to me. Then I think about getting the red beans and rice, but the rice reminds me of the poor Viet Cong who are being killed while fighting a moral war against perfect shitheads like me. The rice is out. I want to order something that has no political message at all. So I think I'll get a raw carrot and a glass of water."

Mike warned, "Capers and Shyla don't think you boys are very funny."

"Too bad," I said.

"Tough titty," Jordan added.

"What's funny about Vietnam?" Shyla asked.

"It's made our whole country crazy," I said. "It's turned wonderful people like the two of you into fanatics. Look at you, Capers. From KA to Abbie Hoffman in a calendar year. And you, Shyla. You were more fun to be around than anyone I've ever met, but now I'd rather read back copies of the *Congressional Record* than be near your sorry ass. I don't understand why you can't be a liberal without turning into smug, pious assholes."

"We're trying to stop the war, Jack," Capers said. "I'm sorry our piety ruins your fun."

"Do you stand for anything?" Shyla asked.

" 'The Star-Spangled Banner,' " I said.

"Cheap patriotism," Capers sneered. "What I love about the American flag is one doesn't have to stand up for it. One can burn it, stomp on it, or throw it in the trash, and our Constitution grants us that precious right."

"There's a fascist in you, Jack, waiting to be born," Shyla said.

"If it's ever born, it'll be because I hung around you and Capers too long," I said. "Every time I'm with you, I want to drop an H-bomb on Hanoi."

"So you're for the war," Shyla shouted. "Admit it."

"We're in college," Jordan said. "No one's for this war. It's a stupid war, fought for stupid reasons, by stupid people."

"Then you're on our side," Shyla said.

"Yeh, we're on your side," Jordan said. "We're just a lot quieter about it."

"I can't be quiet about napalm and children on fire running down country roads," Capers said.

"Neither can I," said Shyla. "Nor can I sit with anyone who can."

As she and Capers rose to leave, I stood and said, "I'd like to make a toast to napalm. May it only strike innocent children, orphans clutching teddy bears, paraplegics, amputees waiting for prosthetic devices, beloved cartoon characters, nuns with rosaries and bad breath, cheerleaders from the Atlantic Coast Conference . . ."

I was still compiling my list when Capers and Shyla made their way out into the darkness.

"Humor's not their long suit these days," Mike said, snapping photographs of all of us as they retreated.

"It's all false," I said. "They've fallen in love with rhetoric and bullshit. They can talk for hours about free speech and then get pissed off when anyone says something they disagree with."

Mike said, "That's not why you're angry, Jack."

"Mike's right," Jordan said.

"Then why am I angry?" I asked. "It's good to have two friends who are all-wise and all-knowing and who can explain the ways of the world to their slow-witted friend."

"You're in love with Shyla," Mike said. "No

sin in that. But she only gets excited by the boys who run away from tear gas."

"I'm against the war," I said. "But I like America. So kill me."

"She's in a very radical stage," Mike explained.

"They're not serious about stopping this war," Jordan said, taking a long pull from his bottle.

"I think they are," Mike disagreed.

"No, they aren't. I don't agree with my old man very much," Jordan said, "but he said you could know how serious you were about something by how willing you were to risk everything for it. He told me last month that he wouldn't take Capers seriously until Capers gave him some sign that this wasn't just playacting."

"What would Capers have to do?" I asked.

Jordan laughed. "He said if Capers believed what he says he does, he'd blow up every barracks at Fort Jackson. My father doesn't mistake anyone for the real thing unless they're willing to lay down their lives for their beliefs. When Capers and Shyla kill their first MP, he'll start listening to them."

The war didn't come home to us until months later, the day Jordan was in my room reading Thomas Merton's *Seven Storey Mountain* and I was writing a letter to my mother. Mike appeared in the doorway.

"Hear the news?" he asked, carrying three cameras around his neck. "National Guardsmen killed some college students at an antiwar demonstration. Listen."

Jordan turned his head and said, "People're screaming."

I looked out the window and saw students emptying trash out the windows of the Education Building. Others were running down the streets, screaming and crying.

"Shyla and Capers have called for a rally," Mike exclaimed. "All this because Nixon bombed Cambodia. Wow, never underestimate the power of cause and effect."

From the second-story window, Mike began snapping the bizarre, sometimes violent reaction of students to the news of what we would soon learn were the Kent State killings.

It was one measure of President Nixon's innocence that he would have little idea how incendiary his incursion into Cambodia would prove to be among us, even the nation's most compliant students. A fearful discharge of energy was set off in the hearts of those of us who had long ago grown accustomed to our roles as wards of the state. We poured out of dormitories and fraternity and sorority houses and left our books untended in library carrels. We wan-

dered singly and in pairs until we gathered in a
group that was moving toward the Horseshoe,
past the open plaza outside of the Russell
House. Disoriented and without any sense of
purpose, we registered incomprehension, grief,
and betrayal over the senseless murder of four
of our own. If the deaths had occurred at the
already-radicalized Harvard or Columbia,
there would have been some context, some
force of mitigating circumstances. But the gun-
ning down of thirteen students in the idyllic
heartland town of Kent, Ohio, at Kent State, a
college far more deferential in its acquiescence
to authority than even the University of South
Carolina, was inconceivable. It was clear to us
that the government had declared open season
on anyone opposing the war. On that single
day, in the milling, insurgent coming together
of the students of America, all the dangers of
solidarity were set loose. Even the most docile
and passive of students felt the hot breath of
mutiny in the air as we walked toward the
Horseshoe. Grievance would soon turn to rage
and meekness turn mean, then majestic. What
was happening in this blind migration of students toward the open space between the library and the Russell House was taking place
on campuses all over America. Intellect and
reason had gone underground, civility hiber-

nated, and insurrection took the lead. Yet none of us knew where we were going.

Later, I thought that this moving without reason had been an unforgettable sensation that made me understand the comfort of herds, the safety that great numbers lend to religious pilgrimages. I had never been a part of something so much larger than myself. My hands trembled with fury and my mouth was dry; I felt irrational and murderous, yet curiously not angry as I walked with the students, many crying, around me.

By the time we reached the open space in front of the library, Capers and Shyla had already been arrested for unlawful assembly. News of their arrest spread angrily through the crowd along with the surprising fact that the president of the university himself had secured their releases. Like an overhang of mist from the Saluda River, the mob dissipated, almost shyly, breaking up as though a spell had been lifted by an unseen hand.

That night, Jordan, Mike, and I were at Yesterday's when Shyla and Capers walked in. They were welcomed by a thunderous ovation as they moved toward the bar with their fists raised and people reaching out to touch them. Capers wore a butterfly Band-Aid over his left eye where one of the arresting officers had banged his head against a wall. Shyla went to the front entrance of the restaurant and worked the crowd into a lather of self-righteousness, while Capers and Radical Bob worked the back door and the bar. Shouts echoed through the streets and a police car went up in flames near the stadium. The sound of sirens hovered over the city. It was not anarchy or even near it, but something had disturbed the sediments of dispassion in the loose boundaries of this college. You could feel the thrill of lethargy set afire. On this night, the pure fact of living seemed like a new branch of theology. There was wildness and disquiet along the tree-lined streets of a sleeping city. Over the televisions and the radios came the news that none of the slain students had been a radical and one had even belonged to a ROTC unit. The men in uniforms had turned their guns on college students. My generation cohered in outrage and parents everywhere were afraid.

The next afternoon, the gathering began again and I learned that the instinctual was far more fearful than the scheduled or the planned. The mob again made its way toward the end of the Horseshoe; and once more I felt the thrill of being part of something much larger than myself, as I was swept along by the movement of thousands. Jordan's hand held my elbow as we tried to see the speakers through the sunlight and the noise. Whispering in my ear, Jordan said he had never seen so many men with guns in his whole life, not even at Camp Pendleton. Hundreds of National Guardsmen had reinforced the highway patrol, and the air itself seemed gelatinous, unbreathable.

Shyla was speaking when we drew close enough to hear, but we were still fifty feet away from the speaker's platform. We heard Shyla saying, "They brought the war home for us yesterday. Because we did not want our soldiers buried in an unjust war, they decided to bury some of us instead. Because we came in peace, they tried to show us what the price of peace was going to be. Because we hate war, they decided to declare war on all of us. Let us answer their gunfire by rededicating ourselves to the cause of bringing our soldiers home. Let us bury our dead, then go about our business of burying the Vietnam War forever."

The applause that greeted her words was loud and insistent. Then Radical Bob moved toward the microphone. He had spoken but a few words when the head of the SLED—South Carolina Law Enforcement Division—agents, J. D. Strom, interrupted him and announced to the audience that no license to assemble had been granted by the city and that this demonstration was canceled by order of the mayor. Shoving Strom aside, Radical Bob tried to commandeer the microphone, but his actions were broken off by a slim, swift-moving team that handcuffed him with great efficiency. The crowd roared malignantly as Radical Bob was dragged off and thrown into the back of a squad car. Students on the edge of the crowd tried to break through the cordon of officers to free Bob, but were pushed back by a line of SLED agents.

Capers negotiated nose to nose with Colonel Strom, then was allowed to use the microphone to make an announcement.

"This meeting will reconvene in the theater of the Russell House. They may be able to stop us from talking to each other out here, but by God, we own the Student Union."

So, again, we moved, this time between the rifles, the pistols, and the batons of the forces of order, yet we were orderly and wondered at the necessity of this dark show of paranoia and force. The eyes of the police officers were filled with loathing as they watched the disorderly but unthreatening passage of the students between their ranks.

"They're worried about being killed," Jordan said. "The poor bastards are afraid of us."

"Why do so many fat people go into law enforcement?" I asked.

"Because they're wearing bulletproof vests.

Stay in the middle," Jordan warned. "If they start shooting, they'll thin out the edges first."

"They won't start shooting," I said. "These are just South Carolina country boys, like us."

"You think those National Guardsmen weren't just Ohio boys like those poor students?" Jordan said.

"Don't make me more nervous than I already am," I said. "Let's go back to our rooms. I personally don't give a gerbil's fart for the whole Vietnam War."

"Then that's a good reason to be here," Jordan said, but he did not explain what he meant.

On the ramp leading into the Russell House, I saw two attack helicopters hovering in the distance. One girl carrying a radio said it was reported that another thousand National Guardsmen were mobilizing in Charleston. I watched highway patrolmen passing canisters of tear gas through their ranks and heard the barking of Dobermans and German shepherds assembling behind the library. Already, the state had gathered enough firepower to eradicate a suburb of Hanoi, yet the enemy they faced were placing flowers and candy kisses into the holsters and cartridge belts of unsmiling patrolmen.

When we reached the Student Union, Jordan and I stood in one of the overflowing aisles as Capers Middleton walked out to center stage and to the podium. Applause went up like a fire among drought-stricken pines and grew in fury because our energy had been set off with no outlet. The cheering turned to screaming and the screaming turned to a roar, tribal and irresistible. So many students had crowded into the theater and spilled out into the hallways and corridors that the police and the guard had mostly been left outside. We were alone with one another again.

Capers surprisingly did not immediately start to speak. Instead, he enjoyed his first moment as a politician, as a man who had an instinctive appreciation for the ravenous needs of crowds. He watched the police and SLED agents force their way into the back of the auditorium and move through the students, whom they jostled and shoved out of their way, and he threw away the handwritten copy of the speech he had prepared. Once the phalanx of policemen had reached the front of the stage with their nightsticks at the ready, he began. "I'd like all of you to join me in singing a song most appropriate for this occasion. What we are doing truly is celebrating the greatness of this country. This is the country in which the British would not let us speak freely, assemble at will, or have a say in who would tax us. The British had thought of everything, except one thing: we were no longer English. The country had changed us and without knowing it, we had become Americans. As Americans, we taught the whole world about free speech. We invented it. And no one—I repeat, no one—is going to take it away from us."

Mike was up onstage photographing the crowd's reaction just as it erupted, electrified by the power of Capers' words. Jordan and I almost burst as we screamed until we were hoarse. "These poor cops're afraid of us. Let's show them there's no need to be afraid."

Then Capers stood before the microphone and sang in his merely serviceable tenor voice:

"O beautiful for spacious skies,
For amber waves of grain,
For purple mountain majesties
Above the fruited plain!

America! America! God shed his grace
on thee,
And crown thy good with brotherhood,
From sea to shining sea!"

We all wept during the singing of "America." Capers had managed to create a moment of great beauty. His instincts were accurate, his timing impeccable, and he seemed to exert leadership over the crowd by the authority of his presence alone. I had never seen a handsomer, more charismatic boy and I felt myself falling in love with this best of friends all over again.

Then law enforcement made their first strategic error. The city fire chief waddled out onstage, his saunter penguinesque and uncertain, and one could sense his unease before our crowd of long-haired students. He wrestled the microphone away from Capers. During their brief struggle, Capers was smiling and playing to the crowd, but the fire chief did not come to this moment of time in a playful mood. He thought that Capers was mocking him. He motioned with his left hand and the stage was suddenly filled with cops. One shot a small aerosol can of mace into Capers' eyes. Capers screamed, went down on his knees when a baton struck the back of his legs, and he fell to the floor face forward as a cop hit his head with a blackjack. Capers was unconscious as they carried him offstage to an ambulance waiting outside. We were so astonished by the sudden turn of events that there was not a sound in the auditorium and all I could actually hear was the shutter of Mike's camera opening and closing like the eyelids of some beast hidden from view.

The fire chief spoke up at last. "Mr. Middleton here didn't get a permit for this meeting. Y'all are busting every rule we got in the fire code. I'm authorized by the governor himself to issue a proclamation. Until further notice, no students'll be allowed in the Student Union. Understood? No students allowed in the Russell House. You've got five minutes to disperse."

A murmur went through the leaderless crowd and then I heard a voice beside me. It was Jordan speaking. "Hey, fatso. If the Student Union isn't for the students, then who in the hell is it for?"

"Arrest that boy," the fire chief said, turning away, but the PA system amplified his every word.

"I'm a student," Jordan yelled. "There's no law against a student being in his college's only Student Union. I want to know why all you damn cops and National Guardsmen are here. We built and paid for this house. We belong inside this house. You've come to our home and arrested and beaten our friends and interrupted our meeting and scared us in the place we feel safest. Then you've got the nerve to tell us we can't even be in the place that's got our name written on it."

"Do yourself a favor, son, and shut up," the fire chief said.

"Why should I shut up?" Jordan said. "I live here. My parents pay good money so I can attend classes here. I took tests so I could get into this college. All of us studied hard so we could get the chance to attend this university. You've no right to tell any of us to leave."

"You're creating a fire hazard," the chief said. "Only two thousand people are allowed in this theater at one time."

"Then take the cops and the soldiers and get your asses out of here. Then we'll have about the right number," Jordan said. Policemen had already started moving toward Jordan, but the crowd made it very difficult for anyone to get near him. The colonel in charge of the National Guard and the head of SLED took the fire chief's place at the microphone.

"Listen, people," the colonel said. His face had the soft, puffy texture of a woodland mushroom but he clearly hated the students. "I got me a little order here. An order granting me emergency powers issued by the governor's office. I just watched as you ignored an order to disperse by the fire marshal. I personally don't believe in the gentle, feel-good approach to mob rule. I want you to take your hippie-asses and get the hell out of here."

Jordan spoke again, growing calm as the fury of the crowd spread around him, volatile as wild fire.

"Please apologize for calling us hippie-asses, Colonel," Jordan asked. "I know my fellow students well and we are very sensitive to name-calling. We've been burdened with tender sensibilities and you just hurt our feelings."

"I gave an order to disperse, Betsy, or whatever your name is," the colonel said. "Sorry, I can't tell if you're a boy or a girl."

"Colonel," Jordan said. "Why don't you and I have a fistfight on that stage and you can find out if I'm a boy or not."

The roar from the students drowned out the colonel's next words.

". . . and I'd like to remind this crowd of draft dodgers and peaceniks that there are fine young American men fighting and dying in Vietnam right now, as we speak," the colonel said. "Do you know why these young men are dying?"

"Yeh, we sure do," Jordan screamed. "They weren't rich enough or lucky enough to be able to join the goddamn National Guard like you and these pussies with rifles you got us surrounded by . . ."

Again the rolling thunder of voices swept back and forth across that theater for several moments. The colonel tried several times to restore order, but his voice was puny, anemic.

"Our boys are dying in Vietnam for a cause they believe in," Jordan continued, finally, "and they've earned the love and respect of all of us. We now need to stop that war and bring them home. Our armed forces are out in the field killing the enemy, while you and your sorry National Guard, these chicken-shit, yellow-bellied bastards with their bayonets at ready, get to sit out the war pretending you've done your duty to our country. You aren't out in the jungle hunting Viet Cong. Your guns are locked and loaded and you've come on our campus to hunt your own American brothers and sisters. Yesterday you killed four of us in Ohio. How many of us you plan to kill today? Talk to me, National Guardsmen. I want one of you bastards to stand up and tell me that you aren't the biggest draft dodgers this country's ever seen. Tell me it wasn't the greatest day in your sorry lives when that piece of paper came in the mail saying you'd never catch malaria or clap in Vietnam."

"You're inciting to riot, young man," the colonel said after the noise died down.

"The students or the National Guard?" Jordan asked.

An exchange took place again at the podium and a slick, well-dressed young man from the governor's office took the colonel's place and got right down to business. "Any student found in the Russell House in five minutes will be suspended from the university for the rest of this semester. You will not be allowed to take exams or graduate with your class."

Shouts and curses again filled the air, yet there was movement in the crowd toward the doors and when all the shifting and maneuvering was over, five hundred students still remained rooted in their spots. I looked around and was surprised to see that I did not recognize most of them, nor did I spot a single member of the SDS.

The young man onstage presented a flawless style of no-nonsense leadership. His youth lent him an air of quiet fascist authority. His angelic face with his high coloring and good cheekbones made him look like a candidate for water commissioner or for leading a probe into ethical violations by union officials. More and more students began sneaking out, their heads down, running as soon as they reached the doors.

When five minutes had passed, the young man, who identified himself as Christopher Fisher, announced that the one hundred or so students still remaining, their eyes fierce in their loathing of him and the safety net he stood for in his buttoned-down propriety, were expelled from the university.

"Why am I here?" I said. "I should be back in the dorm studying for my Victorian Novel exam."

"Because you're a man of character," Jordan said, sitting easily beside me. "You've also never liked to cut and run just because an asshole told you to."

"We're not graduating," I said, letting the full weight of my impulsive decision wash over me. "No diplomas, no walk across the stage, no handshakes and hugs from the parents. I'm not even sure I'm against the Vietnam War and I'm not going to graduate because my friends are all fanatics and my roommate just had a nervous breakdown right before my eyes."

"They sent Capers to the hospital, unconscious," Jordan said. "They arrested Shyla for giving a speech."

"Oh yeh," I said. "I knew there was a high moral principal involved that I don't even believe in. I knew I was ruining my whole life for a perfectly stupid reason."

"Go on back to the room then," Jordan suggested.

"Then you'll think you're philosophically superior to me," I said.

"I already think that," replied Jordan, smiling.

"Shyla'd never talk to me again," I mused aloud.

Jordan nodded. "That's a given."

"Mike would take a photo of me sneaking out, cringing like a whipped dog."

"It'd be in all the papers," Jordan agreed.

"But I could move to Alaska where they've never heard of South Carolina," I said. "I could start a new life. Rumors of my cowardice would be dismissed. Or I could go to Vietnam. Volunteer. Become a Green Beret. Cut the throats of village chieftains soft on the Viet Cong. Win medals. Get laid in Bangkok on R&R. Parachute into the North and wreak havoc on supply lines. Make a necklace out of human ears. Step on a land mine. Lose both legs and watch a small pig run away with my balls in its mouth. Save up enough money to get an electric wheelchair. Set off metal detectors 'cause there's so much shrapnel in what's left of my dick. Nope. I'm staying."

"Good decision," Jordan said.

"But you were planning to join the Marines after graduation," I said.

"It was going to be a gift to my father," Jordan said, smiling. "I wanted to give him a single chance in our life together to be proud of me."

"I think you ought to see a career counselor to give you a few more options," I said as the circle of policemen and Guards tightened.

Jordan said, "This'll hurt my chance for Commandant."

"Our parents're going to kill us," I said.

"Oh, my God, my mother's going to hit the roof. She thinks she's earned my diploma."

"We can go to summer school."

Then Christopher Fisher's voice echoed through the theater again. "All those students who do not leave the Student Union in the next five minutes will be arrested. A state of emergency has been called. You now have exactly four minutes and forty seconds to return to your rooms."

Jordan stood up and said, "Yoo-hoo. Fellas, you're not getting the big picture. Let's go over this one more time. This *is* our room. This is the *Student* Union. *Student.* You see a pattern here?"

One of the students who had not said a word stood up at the far end of the dwindling circle. Though I did not recognize him, he looked far more warlike and menacing than the rest of us with his shaggy, unkempt hair, greasy headband, and torn jeans. His camouflage jacket lent authority to his rage and he began to scream orders to his fellow students.

"If the pigs want this building, let's burn the fucker down and let them keep the ashes. This peace shit isn't working with these assholes. They want to kick some ass, let's kick back. If they want to shoot a bunch of unarmed kids, let's go down while taking a few of them with us. I'm tired of talking, man. I want to kill me a pig."

Jordan shouted for everyone to keep their seats and he walked slowly over to the out-of-control student. He put his arm around the young man's shoulder, then grasped his neck with his hand. "Funny the way cops dress these days," Jordan said to the remaining demonstrators. "Anybody know this guy? I don't know a lot of you by name, but I've seen you around. I've been watching Mr. Radical here. He looks kind of overdressed, doesn't he? I mean he'd look natural at Berkeley, but he's gone Hollywood on us down here in Dixie. Now he wants us to charge the guys with the guns. Makes a lot of sense, huh!"

"Stool pigeon," some of the students started yelling.

"Get lost, pal," Jordan suggested. "These're nice kids. Don't get them shot."

"I hate this fucking war, man," the man shouted, appealing to the crowd. "Talk's bullshit. Action's what'll get their attention."

I moved in behind him and pulled a wallet out of his back pocket. His police badge was standard issue. I lifted it up high so the other students could see that Jordan had guessed right. The students, chastened already by their expulsion, hissed until the lead character actor of the afternoon drama skulked away into the ranks of his brethren.

"Everybody sure they want to be here?" Jordan said. "There's no shame in getting out of here now."

"They've no right to do this," a graduate student named Elayne Scott said. "How can they kick me out of my own school for sitting down in the Student Union?"

"I'm *for* the Vietnam War," a pretty girl named Laurel Lee said and I laughed when I recognized one of Ledare's Tri Delts. "But my mama and daddy taught me right from wrong and this is all wrong."

Then the order was given and the arrests were made.

CHAPTER 37

WHEN WE LEFT JAIL THE NEXT MORN-
ing, we had become emblematic of our times,
part of that troubling despoiled era when
Americans quit listening to one another.

Two hundred students and five television
cameras met us as we came out into the dazzling sunlight of a state where summer had
come early. Shyla and Capers hugged us in triumph, for the benefit of the cameras, then they
hustled us off to a quiet enclave on Blossom
Street where the SDS was planning its next
move. The radicals who had only tolerated Jordan and me before now treated us as if we had
had proven ourselves in some fearful test of

spite and venom. We were being cast as brothers in a circle we did not even like. But the night in jail had scared us and being lionized and fussed over felt good, providing the balms that calmed our jangled spirits. The marijuana was free and so was the Jack Daniel's.

I was high and happy when Shyla motioned to us to follow her. She led us to a backyard picnic table where Radical Bob had gathered a council of war for a meeting outside to ensure our conversations were not recorded. He was arguing that Jordan and I could not be trusted to attend this war council just because of a single arrest and a starring role in a demonstration that had spun out of everyone's control. He was afraid the movement had become the venue and training ground of amateurs who were freelancing without a revolutionary philosophy to ground them. Already that day, a hundred disheveled students had stormed the administration building in a spontaneous riot that had neither purpose nor leadership.

"Action without philosophy is anarchy," Radical Bob said.

"What?" I said. "Every time you open your mouth, Bob, it sounds like you learned your English at a Berlitz session."

"Who asked you?" Radical Bob shot back. "Just because you and Jordan went out and played heroes yesterday, it certainly didn't help make this war one day shorter."

"I noticed that none of you got arrested with us," Jordan said, looking around at the twenty-two veterans of SDS who sat in the yard around the picnic table. Many were passing joints back and forth, some so small it was as if they were trading pubic hairs pinched between thumbs and forefingers. On this day, except for Bob, the group was deferring to Jordan and me. By becoming front-page news, we had suddenly become valuable members of this very small South Carolina club.

"They risked everything, Bob," Shyla said. "And they lost everything. They got arrested along with all those other students. It's no surprise when people like you and me get arrested. It happens every day. But this was an uprising of anonymous students—no organization at all. Pure heroism, a battle cry of the common man. In one unplanned action, these students did more than the SDS has done in a year. Admittedly, they didn't know what they were doing. But it was brilliant."

"They shouldn't be a part of the action tonight," Bob said.

"I don't agree," Shyla said.

"You want to come with us?" Bob turned to me angrily. "Then come on, motherfucker."

"Is it nonviolent?" Jordan asked.

"Of course. We're trying to end a war, not start one."

Jordan looked over at me and said, "I'm too drunk to say no. Besides, I don't have any exams tomorrow."

"Or anywhere to go," I said. "They emptied our dorm room and chained it shut. We've got the rest of our lives to do what we want."

"Count us in," Jordan said.

At two the next morning, Capers Middleton, dressed in paramilitary regalia, broke a small window of a lavatory on the first floor of a Main Street building housing the Selective Service Office of South Carolina. He slipped through the darkness and came to the small door leading off an alleyway where a group of college students who would soon become known as the Columbia Twelve had gathered.

Forcing the door open, Capers put his fingers to his lips and led the rest of us into the interior of the building through the back staircase. The action had been planned for weeks and everyone performed their duties perfectly in the first minutes of the break-in. Keys stolen from the busy janitors opened the right locks. The boys carried heavy buckets of cow's blood and the girls brought all the incendiary material needed to burn the draft file of every boy in South Carolina.

Shyla went to the first file cabinet and with

not a single wasted moment pulled out the files and splayed them flat on the floor. Jordan and I followed her, covering each one with cow's blood. Capers led the group that was piling draft files into the center of a vast, colorless room. The pile grew higher and higher as Capers urged everyone to work faster. He checked his watch, nodded, and Radical Bob doused the files with gasoline. When Capers was exhorting everyone to superhuman effort I noticed an edge to his voice and stopped what I was doing. My nostrils were overwhelmed by gasoline, and I was exhausted from a lack of sleep. I looked over and saw Shyla's face, which looked like a nun's in ecstasy. In fact we all looked like a religious band about to ignite a heretic in some bizarre and surreally modern auto-da-fé. Alarms went off in me for no reason and I studied the faces of these friends and complete strangers, trying to fight off a sense of panic. Backing away from the long rows of files, I grabbed Jordan by the shoulders as I saw Radical Bob light a match and the others flick cigarette lighters and move toward the mountain of draft files.

"Let's burn the whole goddamn building down," Radical Bob said.

"No," Shyla said. "Just the files."

"Bob's right," Capers said. "If we're serious about the revolution, let's do the building. Let's do the whole town. Let's bring the war home. Show them what the Vietnamese people are going through."

"Shut up," Shyla said. "We're nonviolent. Nonviolent."

"Speak for yourself," Radical Bob said and the room erupted in flame and light and a hundred sirens went off outside as cops and firemen burst into the room. An army of cops swarmed over us, knocking us to the floor with billy clubs and fists. Two enormous men sat on me and handcuffed me, laughing when I howled in pain as they tightened the cuffs hard enough to cut the flow of blood into my wrists.

"Fucking pigs," Capers was screaming. "Fucking pigs. Who ratted?"

"I told you to keep your goddamn friends out of it," Radical Bob said. "Everything about this was amateur hour."

"We did nothing wrong," Shyla said. "We tried to strike a blow for peace. We didn't totally succeed, but they know we've been here."

"Oh shit," I heard Jordan moan.

"What's wrong?" I asked.

"We didn't think this one through," said Jordan. "This is a federal crime. We've stepped into some deep shit."

• • •

The day of our arraignment, we were taken in paddy wagons to the federal courthouse and had to run the gauntlet of news reporters and cameramen to enter the courthouse door. Mike was there and he knew exactly what to look for. His Nikon was set correctly when General Elliott, resplendent in his creased, perfectly fitting Marine uniform, broke out of the crowd and walked swiftly down the stairs to meet his son. A detective was leading Jordan up the stairs, pulling the handcuffs that bound him. When the general backhanded Jordan to his knees, Mike got the photo. The general, in his iconic fury, looked every inch the figure of indignant, long-suffering authority striking down the long-haired flouter of rules and law on the steps of a hall of justice. The photograph was a flawless cameo of almost biblical power of a father reestablishing authority in his own home. Stricken and on his knees, Jordan's agonized expression reflected the shame and humiliation of a childhood that had gone on too long. In the nation's mind, General Elliott represented America to adults, but to us he stood for everything that was tyrannical and immovable and dissembling in the American spirit turned leprous by Vietnam. Jordan on his knees carried all the power of deep symbol: his face registered the traces of betrayal that his generation felt. Mike's photo was the last ticket on a point of no return. Like a beaten Christ-figure, Jordan rose to face his father, walking up the step that separated them, staring into his father's eyes.

Then, General Elliott spit in his son's face and the world they had in common went into sudden, irrevocable eclipse. The war and what it did to the soul of America played itself out in that brief encounter between father and son. It was the undoing of Jordan Elliott. He crossed over into a borderland of hurt where no one could follow. In jail he forgot all about Vietnam and turned to what he could do that would most hurt his father. What could he do to break him? I had never before heard anyone pray with greater urgency, and Jordan was praying for the death of his father.

When I was released into the custody of my parents, my father rose to the occasion of my defense. The legal peril I had brought down on myself inspired him to sobriety, and he hand-picked the best criminal lawyers in the state to defend me. In private, he and my mother fought ferociously over our methods and tactics in protesting American involvement in Vietnam, but in public they were just as vehement in supporting my actions against all comers. The more they studied the Vietnam War, the softer their defense of those policies became. By the time my trial began, both Lucy and the judge had turned indefatigable and fierce in protecting me. Shyla's parents backed her with the same quiet zeal. Though Capers' parents disapproved of his every move, they too stood beside their radicalized, long-haired boy.

Among the students arrested at the Russell House, almost every parent showed up to support their children when the gathering of lawyers, prosecutors, and judges took place in the high-windowed courthouses. Every single parent, except for General Elliott.

To him, the matter was a simple one. We were all guilty of giving comfort and aid to the enemy; we were guilty of treason.

When Jordan walked out of jail, the general was waiting for him, but this time he did not strike Jordan in front of the cameras. Instead of driving home to Pollock Island, General Elliott drove Jordan directly to the grounds of the South Carolina State Mental Hospital on Bull Street. A military doctor, an associate justice of the State Supreme Court, and the general himself all signed a document declaring that Jordan Elliott was mentally incompetent to stand trial and was to be hospitalized for mental observation starting on that day. South Carolina had the simplest rules in America for locking up its incompetents and lunatics.

The trial took place in Columbia in early December. The passions loosed on America by the killings at Kent State had vanished and were replaced by an exhaustion that settled softly into the body politic. The whole country felt worn down and handicapped by years of force-fed tragedy.

Outside on the courthouse steps, the last great antiwar rally in South Carolina was in session as I drove up with my parents and brothers to face the consequences of my actions the previous May. No matter how hard I tried to re-create those events in my mind, I could not figure out what drove me to such egregious defiance of authority. I had been called an all-American boy for so long that it was part of my own secret self-image. I had never received a speeding ticket in my life, never flunked a pop quiz, and never given my parents a moment's worry about my grades. After leading an exemplary student life, I now faced a thirty-year prison sentence. I had thrown my diploma down the toilet because I had gotten angry at the deaths of four students I had never met, who went to a college I had never heard of, in a state I had never driven through in my life. The trial simply terrified me, and even Shyla's bravado could not dim the sense of indistinctness and flatness I saw when I looked to the future.

But under the harsh light of cameras again, outside the court with my father looking magisterial, my mother beautiful, and my brothers loyal, I whispered thanks to my family for sticking by me.

When the bailiff cried out for the court to rise, Judge Stanley Carswell walked out of his chambers with long, deliberate strides. He looked severe until he sat down and smiled. He studied us for a brief moment, shook his head sadly, then got down to the business at hand. He entertained several motions, then said, "Will the prosecution call its first witness."

The prosecutor was a veteran of the pure Southern textbook variety. He was portly, loquacious, and had one of those midland accents that conjured up salted hams hanging from dark rafters in a smokehouse. Sitting between Capers and me, Shyla elbowed both of us when the prosecutor's sweet tang lifted through the crowd. He began, "Your Honor, I would like to call as the first witness for the State of South Carolina, Mr. Capers Middleton."

In South Carolina, whatever infinitesimal, barely breathing, white-knuckled spirit of the sixties still existed died at that moment. Capers' turned state's evidence against us. He named every name, told every secret, turned over every file, revealed every conversation, noted every date and expenditure and phone call in his diary, sent dozens of people up and down the

East Coast to jail by the power of his testimony. The local chapter of the SDS folded during the first hour he spent in the witness chair. Carefully coached by the prosecutor, he described how J. D. Strom, the head agent of SLED, had recruited him to infiltrate the antiwar movement at the end of his junior year in college. Capers admitted that he had used his friendship with his childhood friend, Shyla Fox, to gain access to the inner circles of radical activity on campus. If it had not been for Shyla, Capers felt that he could never have won the trust of the true believers like Radical Bob Merrill. It was patriotism of the highest order and a fierce anticommunism that caused him to become an undercover agent for the state. His family had descended from one of the oldest and most distinguished in the South and his love of country was second to none. He believed that the radicals he met for the most part constituted no danger to the state whatsoever. In fact, he still loved his friends Shyla, Jordan, and me with all his heart and thought that we were simply immature dupes who were highly suggestible to inflammatory rhetoric we could not understand. During the course of his five-day testimony, Capers used the word "sheeplike" enough times that Shyla wrote a note to me saying Capers was making her feel like a rack of lamb. It was the one note of humor we managed during the course of the trial. And it was that same trial that changed everything about how we felt concerning friendship and politics and even love.

The counsels for the defense tore into Capers Middleton with all the scorn and contempt that the judge would allow. They scoffed at his sincerity when he claimed he acted as he did only because he felt his country was in grave jeopardy. They taunted Capers by reading back the words of his own speeches and by playing videotapes of Capers denouncing the war in the most cutting, withering phrases of mockery. By trying to make a laughingstock out of his masquerade, they only succeeded in bringing out the bristling patriot in Capers. He matched the defense lawyers in their disdain during the taunting sessions of his cross-examination. He refused to acknowledge that he had betrayed us in any way, but sadly would admit that we may very well have broken faith with America.

Then Capers spoke about Shyla without being able to look her in the eye. Above everyone he met in the antiwar movement, Shyla was the most passionate, articulate, and committed opponent of the war. Her idealism was unquestionable; she had served as his chief lieutenant and he depended on her for an innate genius for strategy and for her fearlessness. He told the court again and again that Shyla was the one person who acted from a deep sense of moral outrage against the Vietnam War. He attributed it to a longing for some earthly paradise that she had developed growing up with a father who had survived Auschwitz and a mother who had watched her family murdered by the Nazis.

Capers saved his most savage offensives for Radical Bob Merrill, the outsider from the great, yawning beast of New York City. Employing the ancient Southern fear of the carpetbagger and the scalawag, Capers wove a damning testimony about Merrill's subversiveness, his maladroit attempts to get them to move toward more and more radical acts. Bob's secret blueprint always called for violence. His voice was soft, but his ideas always ended with policemen dead and squad cars on fire. Radical Bob's most incantatory thought was thrilling and insurrect. His bottom line always was that the antiwar movement, if they were serious, should plan an incursion against the base at Fort Jackson itself.

"These antiwar people are all phonies," Capers told the court. "Even though I personally thought Radical Bob was crazy and out of his gourd, he did make a valid point. If people really are opposed to a war, they should be willing to give up their lives for that belief. All these folks wanted to do was march with signs, smoke dope, and get laid. My ancestors fought against Cornwallis and Grant. They fought against the Kaiser and Hitler. They fought, they didn't talk. They took up arms, they didn't write speeches or compose slogans. Though Radical Bob's dangerous, he showed me what was wrong with this whole antiwar movement. They have no guts. They lack the courage of their convictions and I'm happy to be the one to expose them for the cowards they really are."

The second witness for the prosecution did much to change the worldview of Capers Middleton. If a gasp of surprise went up among the shocked remnant of the Columbia Twelve when Capers revealed that he had worked as an agent for the South Carolina Law Enforcement Division, the earth itself seemed to open up when Radical Bob Merrill lifted out of his seat among the accused and took his place beside the judge as a witness for the government. The Federal Bureau of Investigation had recruited Bob as an informant during the troubles at Columbia University, and he had proven so valuable in his infiltration of that uprising that he was the natural choice when the local chapter of the FBI began to worry about subversive activities that arose when the UFO coffeehouse was founded to recruit young disaffected soldiers into the movement. Neither the FBI nor the state of South Carolina had any notion that both had insiders passing out information from the same feebly populated SDS chapter.

Though our defense proved that every illegal action we had participated in on the night of the break-in had been planned by either Capers or Radical Bob, we were found guilty of illegal trespass, breaking and entering, and malicious destruction of federal property. The judge sentenced us to a year in prison, but suspended that sentence due to our youth and obvious idealism. With quiet generosity, the judge gave us a real break.

When Capers came to the witness chair in the Dock Street Theater, all of us were silent as he picked up the story of his involvement with the trial. Though he told his side of the story well, I could still feel his uneasiness over his part in bringing down his friends. One minute would find him defensive, but in the next he would grow thoughtful as he tried to recall the passions and fears set loose during those harrowing days. With high-strung, nervous advocacy, Capers defended his actions as a form of patriotism and service to his country. When he signed up to work as a government agent, he had no way of knowing how Kent State would draw his closest friends into the trap he had set for the enemies of America.

"Shyla loved you, Capers," I heard Ledare say. "Why did you pretend to love her back?"

"I didn't pretend," Capers said, looking over at his ex-wife. "What I felt for Shyla was real. I never learned so much from anyone, never met anyone with such fine instincts for politics. She understood media, always made it work for us. I thought that later I would be able to explain to her what had happened. You know, on some occasion like this. My love for her was perfectly real—hell, we all loved Shyla —we grew up with her. But I was looking at a bigger picture. I thought our country was in trouble. I knew that Communists had infiltrated the antiwar movement. Unlike the rest of you, I had access to the agents."

"Your friends weren't Communists," Jordan Elliott said. "Jack and I weren't even political. Mike and Shyla were just against the war."

The general answered his son sharply. "You did your duty to your country, Capers. You've nothing to answer for."

"Capers has always been proud of what he did at Carolina," Ledare said. "We used to argue about it during our marriage."

"I wasn't proud," Capers corrected. "I was reconciled. There's a big difference."

"If it wasn't for you and Shyla, Jordan and I

wouldn't've even noticed Kent State," I said to Capers.

"I take full responsibility for what I did," Capers said. "I suggest you two do the same."

"You kept me out of the demonstrations," Mike said to Capers. "You made me the photographer. Said I should record history. Was that because you were protecting me?"

"You were too impressionable," Capers said. "I was protecting you from Shyla and your own worst instincts."

"So you were setting Shyla up?" Mike asked.

"She had set herself up. Shyla helped shape the form my radicalism would take. My main focus was Radical Bob."

"Ah, the irony," Bob said.

"It's what always happens in bureaucracy," Capers said.

"Were you paid a salary?" Jordan asked.

"Yes. Of course," said Capers as if surprised by the question. "And I earned it too."

As I listened to Capers and the others, it came back to me again how long it had taken me to recover the equilibrium I lost during that trial. I discovered that I did not have a revolutionary bone in my body and if the judge had sentenced me to the front lines of an in-country unit in Vietnam, I would have accepted my duty with gratitude. The prosecution had accused me, day after day, of not loving my country, and that left deep marks on me. My country was what I woke up to every day, what I saw and breathed in around me, it was what I knew and loved without putting a tag on it, and what I would die for if it were ever in jeopardy and I heard it call my name. In the stronghold of my realest self, I was forced by the trial to confront the man I was and the one I was on the way to becoming.

After the trial ended, Mike had met Capers Middleton outside the courtroom and had taken three photographs of Capers with his arm around Radical Bob. Then he had set his Nikons down carefully and had punched Capers in the jaw. Onlookers had needed to pull Mike off his old friend.

Throughout the long winter of 1971 that followed, I went through a period of self-inquiry and licking my wounds as I reviewed the damage I had done to my life. It was during this time that Shyla and I gravitated toward each other. As I look back on it I suppose our dance together was inevitable. We were like moons that gave off no light, attracted to the same illusory orbit. Shyla could barely recover her self-respect after having slept with Capers and having shared every secret with him for more than a year. It was not that he had lied about the war that most troubled her, it was that he had told her every night about his love for her, his undying admiration for all she stood for, his adoration of her body, and his ardent desire that they spend their entire lives together. That she could not sense such treachery and dissimulation in her own lover disturbed her far more than that he'd been secretly working for the state. It was not any residue of Capers and his bad faith she feared, but she did not know how to ever regain trust in herself and her own judgments again. Shyla had always considered herself reliable and incorruptible, but never had she thought of herself as an easy mark or gullible to the point of dishonor. She could easily accept the legal consequences of her own actions, but she could not bear being made a laughingstock or a fool for love. So she turned to me and I turned to her, neither of us knowing that we were both keeping a ruthless appointment with a bridge in Charleston.

CHAPTER 38

WHEN JORDAN TOOK THE SEAT ON THE Dock Street stage next to my father I realized that now all the pieces and small fragments of what happened to him would become a whole. I had always been hesitant to ask too many questions about a period of time both of us had found contaminated, and he had not volunteered any information. As Jordan spoke, I felt him relax under the steely gaze of his father for the first time. He spoke in a voice that was matter-of-fact, businesslike. His re-creation of events came easily to him and I suddenly remembered why my church taught that confession was good for the soul. As he talked, all of us leaned forward to hear each word articulated by this soft-spoken man. Even the general leaned forward in his chair.

"It was almost immediately after I arrived at Bull Street that I was thrown into solitary confinement in a room without furniture. The doctors had given me drugs to calm my fury over being committed, but I had continued to scream at the nurses, night attendants, and other patients, so they isolated me as much as possible. They also increased the dosage of my drugs, until I was barely coherent. When I was returned to the ward, no visitors were allowed, and I could receive letters from no one except my parents.

"I'm not sure when it was, but soon after, I received the first of four shock treatments, which calmed me almost to the point of insentience. I shuffled among the main populace of the most serious psychotics for months, wandering through a thick haze of cigarette smoke past men poleaxed by Thorazine. But what had looked like madness to the doctors and nurses was my inability to come to terms with my father's betrayal. The shock treatments made me forget, but eventually memory returned, slowly, and when it did it hurt. When I remembered my father's slap and his saliva running down my face, I tried to kill myself by hanging from a belt I had stolen from a sleeping guard. Later I tried to hang myself with bed sheets and was treated to another round of shock treatments. My mother came to visit me twice a week.

"I stayed at Bull Street until the following May. I had been there almost a year when they let me go. My release caught everyone by surprise. Especially me. In the middle of February, I had started cooperating with the staff completely. I turned on the charm. By the time I left, everyone loved me. I had gone on a campaign to get out of there. I even organized a blood drive for the Red Cross on my ward. I took out the blood of half the patients in the ward because they trusted me more than the nurses. After that, everyone trusted me, patients and doctors alike. I bided my time. I smiled at everyone. Then I secretly began to prepare for what I was going to do when I got out."

As we listened to Jordan we began to see the world as he saw it back then, after a long season of psychotic drugs and shock treatment.

It was during his stay in solitary, he said, that the attraction to monastic withdrawal began its pull on him. Back on the wards, he discovered the power of words to calm the terror of the meek and the distraught. He began to speak like a priest during this period and hid from everyone the terrible hatred that moved like a virus in his heart. The priest in him was born, but the warrior still seethed beneath. The only voices he heard in those long months in prison were those of his father and Capers. Their voices came to him nightly, taunting him.

When he left the hospital his plan was set. He wrote a postcard to his parents telling them that he was hitchhiking to California, where he wanted to take up surfing seriously again. Then he caught a ride with a policeman who was camping on the beach at St. Michael's Island with his girlfriend and who let him off at the gate on Pollock Island. There he introduced himself to the corporal on duty as General Elliott's son and caught a ride with the deputy provost marshal to the PX, and from there he walked to the general's quarters. The house was huge and mainly unoccupied and he spent the night in the unused servant's quarters. Noiselessly he hid among the man-sized azaleas and watched his parents eat dinner with no inkling that he was observing their every bite.

For the next two days, he said, he prepared his long answer to his father's humiliation of him on the courthouse steps. In his father's workshop, he made a small incendiary bomb with two flashlight batteries to power the small but effective detonator. He configured the architecture of the bomb carefully, borrowing freely from the supply of gunpowder his old man used to make musket balls for the Civil

War rifle used by one of their ancestors who rode with Wade Hampton. He wanted it light-weight and volatile, but safe enough for him to carry around by hand until he set the timer. He drew elaborate maps and worked out his plan in his mind again and again, making the necessary corrections until the proper time for action presented itself.

When his mother went out during the day and the maid was cleaning the upstairs, he moved quietly in the back door of the house and stole food from the pantry that looked forlorn and forgotten. When the maid had gone, he would sit at his mother's vanity and take in all her smells, the way he did as a boy. He even spent one night in his room because he wanted to capture again the feeling of being there. He could have forgiven his father every crime but one; he could not forgive him for stealing his entire childhood.

When his parents went away for a weekend at Highlands in the North Carolina mountains he made his final arrangements. He wrote a letter to them telling them every single thing he planned to do and why. He told them what he believed deeply in and everything he had come to feel about the world. He stated his opposition to the Vietnam War and admitted it had only grown stronger during his enforced imprisonment in Columbia. The only weakness that he acknowledged in his antiwar stance was his unwillingness to fight violence with violence of his own. To his mother, he left his undying love and gratitude. To his father, he left his corpse and his loathing and thanks for absolutely nothing. The letter, the rambling, embarrassingly rhetorical, half-cocked, egomaniacal relic of the sixties, he left in his mother's jewelry box.

On the Saturday night he chose to act, he walked the half-mile to the marina carrying his surfboard over his head. The night before he had placed the bomb beneath the front seat of the boat he had reserved for the weekend, by phone, in the name of his father's adjutant's son. He had checked out the engine by test-riding it the night before. He packed it with extra tanks of gas, junk food, and Coca-Cola, took a bottle of Wild Turkey from his father's liquor cabinet, then loaded bags of blood he had stolen from the donors at the state hospital. He packed the four pints of blood in newspaper and cotton gauze, then placed them in a small carry-on bag that he put in the fish locker. The blood was all type O, his own.

He described to us the care with which he dressed in his father's uniform, giving himself the rank of major, and placing all emblems of rank and all insignia in their proper places. He spit-shined his father's shoes. His hair was already cut in Marine Corps fashion thanks to the strict rules of his ward. Studying himself in his father's full-length mirror, he got a sudden glimpse of the life his father had wanted for him. He was a fine-looking Marine, but admitted that on this night, he was a dangerous, angry man who was thinking unclearly, his rage undercutting all undertones of reason.

In the general's staff car, he drove, erect in the rainy night. Several soldiers saluted when they saw the stars on the front fender and no one, he remarked wryly, returned a salute as sharply as Jordan Elliott, bred to the Corps. He drove the five miles to the Waterford Air Station, received the snappy salute of a PFC, then proceeded toward the airstrip and the hangars where the great warplanes were at rest. There were lights on in the guardhouses and officers on duty. But checking every squadron, looking for movement or signs of life, he saw that everything was hunkered down.

He said it took him a while to decide whether he wanted to blow up an A-4 or a Phantom jet. He loved the clean lines and beauty of both. Once, he explained, he had wanted to be a Marine aviator more than anything in the world. He wanted to be the flyboy who could come swiftly from the sky to rescue his father's beleaguered, pinned-down regiment. That was a lifetime ago but thinking about the past made him nostalgic, detoured him from concentrating on the mission at hand. But it bothered him, he explained to us, to blow up a plane he had once dreamt of flying, as though it would destroy that small part of his childhood that he still could return to without tears.

As he drove his father's car past the Bumblebee Squadron, the Shamrock Squadron, the shapes became grotesque and vaporous. And then, he saw it: a DC-3 parked at the end of the runway, a forlorn remnant of a past era of flight. Perfect for the point he wanted to make to his father. He pulled the car off the road behind some large shrubbery. He had packed the bomb carefully and now rewrapped the package with waterproof cloth before he moved out toward the plane. Only the lights of the runway lit his way and he felt invisible, he said, even to himself.

Swiftly and efficiently, he taped the package to the bottom of the DC-3's fuselage near the gas tank. He set the timer on the clock to go off at four o'clock that morning. He did not remember returning to Pollock Island nor did he remember parking his father's car in the garage and returning the extra key to its hiding place beneath a paint can.

In his parents' room again, he hung up his father's uniform in a closet. He went to a pho-

tograph album and took from it a favorite photograph of himself and his mother. Before he
replaced his father's shoes, he cleaned and spit-
shined them again.

Going to his father's bathroom, he stole a
fresh packet of Gillette blades from his medicine cabinet. With a tube of his mother's lipstick, he wrote the word *Jordan* on his father's
shaving kit.

Jordan turned to face the General: "I
wanted you to know I had used the house as
the base of operations."

Going to his mother's vanity, he read again
his suicide note which he thought sounded
rather shrill. He hoped he would have the courage to kill himself when the time came, but if
not, he had an alternate plan of action. Checking his watch, he went to his room and changed
into a bathing suit and his sweat clothes. Walking through the house for a last time, he took a
final inventory of the things that had accompanied him through childhood. "I was still running when I reached the marina and untied the
boat from its moorings and let it drift out with
the tide. I did not start the motor until I was
almost to the main channel in the sound. I was
past the three-mile limit when the DC-3 exploded." When he told us this, no one moved a
single muscle in the Dock Street Theater. It

looked as though all of us had forgotten how to breathe.

I knew all too well what else was going on that night. Just before midnight, Corporal Willet Egglesby met with the daughter of Colonel Harold Pruitt at a secret rendezvous in the breezeway of a vacant house located three houses away from the one where Bonnie Pruitt had escaped through her bedroom window. Their love affair had not gone over well with the rank-conscious Ellen Pruitt, who hounded her malleable husband to the point where he forbade his seventeen-year-old daughter to date her ardent corporal. Unbearable tension had become commonplace in the Pruitt household, until the corporal discovered the DC-3 on the runway near her house. Corporal Egglesby and the young Pruitt girl were making love when the bomb detonated and the two youngsters were buried side by side in the National Cemetery located down the road in Waterford.

Yet in the extraordinary mayhem caused by the plane's explosion, and in the reaction of the Marine Fire Brigade as well as of Waterford's Fire Station, much evidence was lost—there were so many firemen tracking through the scene of the fire, which no one suspected to be a crime. The bodies of Bonnie Pruitt and Corporal Egglesby were not found until late the next afternoon by naval experts flown in to examine the wreckage. When these same experts went to the house of Colonel Pruitt, the distraught and guilt-ridden Ellen Pruitt produced three suicide notes that Bonnie had written to her parents, declaring that she would kill herself if her parents insisted on keeping her apart from Willet Egglesby. Corporal Egglesby himself was the son of a highway construction engineer from West Virginia who was an expert with explosives. After a thorough investigation, the naval experts agreed that the two young lovers had made a suicide pact together and that the corporal had assembled a more-than-functional bomb to carry out their dark pledge to each other. In the experts' report, they lamented in the stiff-jointed language of career bureaucrats that the DC-3 gas tanks were full when the bomb went off. It was also noted that the couple was making love when the explosion occurred and that intercourse was not often linked to such obvious despair.

Celestine Elliott took up the narrative from there, slipping elegantly into the witness chair and speaking in the direction of Jordan, Ledare, and myself. She said that General Elliott had caught a hop back to the air station when he heard of the catastrophe. She drove directly from Highlands to their quarters on Pollock Island. By the time her husband arrived home after long hours of organizing the scene

and talking to news agencies, she had rid the
house of any sign of Jordan's presence. She had
scrubbed out his name, which he had written in
her lipstick on her husband's shaving kit. She
had followed her son's footsteps from the
maid's quarters to her husband's workshop to
the letter he had written and carefully hidden
in her jewel box. She had read Jordan's letter
confessing to the crime of blowing up the plane
in which he explained that he had done this to
show his father that he had inherited the general's fine, martial spirit, a spirit that understood the nature of military strategy, bold offensive, and the element of surprise. Jordan
wanted the destroyed plane to end his father's
career as a Marine officer. He wanted to bring
disgrace and ruin to his father's house. This act
was his reply to his father's humiliation of him
on the courthouse steps. His father's spit would
be answered with fire and his own blood.

In sentences that she had found almost unbearable to read, Celestine said, holding back
her tears, Jordan described how he'd reserved
the boat under another Marine's son's name
and stolen the packet of Gillette razors. He
wrote that he would head the boat out to sea at
night. He would cut his wrists and throat, and
when he felt weak would lower himself over the
sides of the boat after tying an anchor to his

waist. The last sentences were incoherent, she said, and far from characteristic of Jordan.

She burnt her son's last letter because she did not think her husband could survive it. She burnt it and washed the ashes down her kitchen drain. She fixed herself a drink and waited for her husband to come home. When the general arrived, a new wife awaited him, one far more broken and tamed than the one he had left on a golf course at Highlands.

Celestine began to drift into a twilight region where she seemed to be either sleepwalking or drinking far too much. Her husband thought the drinking was due to the death of Jordan. It had started after his boat was found drifting in the Atlantic with traces of his type-O blood soaking the seat cushions and staining the woodwork. The shrimper who found the boat said it looked as if someone had slaughtered a buck in the boat's gunwale.

It was then that the Elliotts consulted with the chaplain and planned the small private memorial service for Jordan. After the service, General Elliott confronted Shyla, Mike, and me outside the base church.

"I want you to know I think that his friends are responsible for my son's death," General Elliott said as Celestine tried to pull him away.

Shyla flashed with anger. "Funny, none of us raised him or hit him. We just loved Jordan.

We didn't spit on him or put him into an insane asylum."

"He was the best friend we ever had," I said, pulling Shyla out of harm's way. "We adored him."

"We know you did, Jack," Celestine said, and only when she spoke did we realize that Jordan's mother was drunk. For three years she stayed drunk and mourned her son and loathed her husband, yet hated herself for still loving the general. By her husband's side, Celestine did not feel a thing. Bourbon was a brown distraction and she drank until her husband was forced to retire out of embarrassment for her. On the day he retired at Pollock Island three years after Jordan's memorial service, she passed out on the reviewing stand and awoke in a detoxification center in Florida. Twice General Elliott had learned the hard way that enemies within a city's walls are ten times more dangerous than armies in the field and on the move. Many in the Corps had thought that the general would one day receive a presidential appointment as Commandant, but his troubles within his own family pointed to a lack of judgment and discipline on the home front.

Mike Hess stood up from his seat near my father and said, "So what is this day about? All this happened over fifteen years ago. It's terrible about the young girl and her Marine. No one denies that. But the important thing is to go on. Right or wrong? Those of us here all suffered because this war touched us in ways that we still don't know. Shyla never was the same after protesting that war. Jordan, we lost. He's been dead to most of us until now. We watched our generation turn against one another, hate one another, not speak to one another, and for what? Is this day about forgiveness?"

General Elliott stood and said, "No, it's about justice."

"Justice for whom, General?" The abbot of Mepkin Abbey stood on the stage, his cowl thrusting his face in shadow. "For you or for God? Are you seeking military justice or divine justice?"

"I am seeking both, Father," the general answered. "And I believe you and your entire order have stood in the way of justice of any kind."

"We know your son as a good priest and servant of God," Father Jude said quietly.

"He blew up two innocent people," the general said. "That's all that even God needs to know about my son."

Judge McCall tapped his gavel, and

checked his watch. "Let's figure out what we're doing. Let's bring this thing to a close."

"How did you get out of the country, son?" the general asked. "They found your boat out at sea."

"My surfboard," Jordan said. "It took me over two days to get back to land. I stayed a week on the Isle of Orion, at the McCalls' fish camp. I got my bearings. I fished and crabbed at night. When I felt rested and strong enough, I took Jack's johnboat and made my way to his house in the middle of the night."

I rose and said, "I can take the story from here."

Grief, that spring, lay immobile in me. After Jordan's memorial service I went to bed and stayed in my room, locking my door, and tried to figure out the exact moment when everything had gone wrong in my life.

Soon after the service Shyla left for an antiwar demonstration outside the UN building in New York, but I declined to join her. I had promised myself never again to lose all control over the circumstances that history might fling in my path. I planned to live a life of caution and restraint. I would grow my own herbs in a window box, raise a vegetable garden each year to remind myself that I was part of a grand cycle, improve my vocabulary by reading those authors happy to dance with the language, and choose my friends for their lack of oddness or flamboyance. No longer did I wish to suffer because of the furious energies of my best friends' passions for the high wire. Jordan had died because of his willfulness and his inability to either make peace with or avoid the orbit of his father. Shyla had rejected her parents' own passivity and thrown herself headlong into every new idea she encountered on the road that gave meaning to her life. Like some lost rabbi, her life was a constant search for a Torah yet to be written.

Mike's ambition burned with a bright flame, and already, he was working in the mail room of the William Morris Agency in Manhattan and had pitched his first film project to an agent he met in a steam room at the New York Athletic Club. Each night, he attended movies and off-Broadway plays that he wrote to me about, always appending his own notes and critiques, specifying how he would have improved the production had he been in charge. Mike did not suffer from the Southerner's burden of always looking back. I discovered that I had a shut-in's gift for paralysis.

And then one night I woke with a rough hand covering my mouth. I tried to scream, but I heard Jordan whispering for me to keep quiet. In the darkness, I went over the contours of Jordan's face to make sure it was him. Too surprised to speak, I put on a pair of Bermudas, old Docksiders, and a tee shirt and followed Jordan outside and down past the great oak, through the insect-shrill garden, and out to the floating dock, where we took off our shoes and let our feet dangle in the flooding tide.

"How's Jesus?" I asked. "I heard you'd gone to see him."

"The boy's fine. Asked about you," Jordan said, then he darkened. "I'm not right. Something's not right about me, Jack."

"You'll get no argument from me," I agreed. "Your blood was all over that boat."

"My type, but it belonged to other people," Jordan said. "I passed my time in the crazy house planning this. What did my father say about the plane?"

"What plane?" I asked.

"The one I blew up," said Jordan.

"You didn't do that, Jordan," I said, praying that I was right.

Jordan said in an eerie, disembodied voice, "I could field strip an M-1 blindfolded by the time I was eight years old. Want to know how to make a Molotov cocktail? A pipe bomb? Want me to show you how to set a punji stick dipped in human feces along a trail? I've walked half the sewer system in Waterford so I'd know how to escape if the Communists ever took over."

"Something far worse than that happened, Jordan," I said.

"I went too far with the plane, Jack," Jordan said. "I knew you'd hate that."

"You ever heard of Willet Egglesby or Bonnie Pruitt?" I asked.

"Naw. Who're they?"

"They were in the plane when it went up," I explained. "Folks think they blew themselves up. A lovers' pact."

I never understood why Jordan's scream of anguish did not wake every single sleeper in Waterford that night. The sound of horror erupted, unbidden and undefiled, from Jordan's throat. As he wept freely, I held him and tried to come up with a plan to hide him. Before daybreak, I managed to lead him back through the garden, up the tree, and into my bedroom. I pulled a chair under the trapdoor in my closet and led Jordan into the attic to sleep on a pile of old mattresses. The breakdown that General Elliott had manufactured now began to take hold of Jordan Elliott in earnest. He suffered grievously in the unbearable heat of that attic as the only other person in the world who knew he was alive plotted his escape in the bedroom below.

When Shyla arrived back in the low country the next day, I was waiting for her at the train station in Yemassee. She had developed a gift for functioning in the atmosphere of a war room, and prided herself on keeping a cool head when chaos was the order of the day, and I needed her for Jordan. I brought her to the attic, where the heat was oppressive and the three of us sweated as we tried to devise a way to remove Jordan from harm's way. We discussed going to our parents for help, but it was not the best time in the history of the republic for us to trust the counsel of our elders. We had all grown up too fast in the past few years and had experienced enough sedition among our own ranks to be able to trust anyone but ourselves. It was Shyla who came up with the cover story and I who devised the route of escape.

I got my car ready for a long journey, bought a used canoe from a Methodist girls' camp near Orangeburg and a tent from a hunting outfitter in Charleston. Shyla was in charge of food, which she packed in a picnic basket, placing the overflow in an ice chest. There were sausages and cheeses, bags of apples and oranges, dried fruits and cans of sardines, tuna fish, and enough bottles of wine to lend an air of festivity to every meal no matter how quickly we had to consume it during our time on the run.

Shyla went to her doctor, complained of sleeplessness and depression, and walked away with enough Valium and sleeping pills to put a small herd of bison asleep. Jordan slept for the first time under her careful dispensing of the medicine. I went for a blood test that next day and wrote a long letter to my parents in the periodical section of the town library. The letter was difficult to master because I was unaccustomed to the shy language of love. I had not started out to write a love letter, but that was what it turned into, even though I knew it would cause my parents enormous pain. I let Shyla read my letter as I was reading hers to George and Ruth Fox. Her letter was lovely; Shyla could express her love of her parents with a simplicity I could only envy. I leaned over and kissed her as she concentrated on what I had written. She looked up and I think it was at that moment that we gave our lives to each other.

The three of us left Waterford at two in the morning. We pushed my car far down the oak-lined street before starting the engine. Jordan lay beneath piles of blankets in the backseat. Both letters lay on the breakfast tables in the houses where Shyla and I had grown up. The letters explained that we had gone off to get married and would spend our honeymoon at Lake Lure in the North Carolina mountains. In fact we were moving toward the outskirts of Chicago less than twenty-four hours later, heading north.

We took turns driving and stopped only for gas and to use the rest rooms and we talked endlessly about the life we had shared together. We talked about everything except those dense, prodigious events that had precipitated our headlong journey into the unknown.

At one point, when I was studying a map, Jordan said, "It's hard to believe South Carolina and Minnesota're in the same country."

"It's all so weird," Shyla said. "They had to talk these people and all the people in South Carolina into going halfway across the world to shoot at Vietnamese peasants. That's some trick."

"If you never mention the Vietnam War again," I said, "I promise you'll never be included in any wife-beating statistics."

"You ever touch me," Shyla said, "you'll be reading about yourself when they interview eunuchs."

"Be happy. That's an order. You two owe me that much," Jordan said.

At the Gundersen Motel in Grand Marais, we spent the night under assumed names and went to the Bear Track Outfitters for a detailed map of an unpopulated borderland called the Boundary Waters. A guide worked out a route for us that would take us through pristine wilderness.

Early the next morning, we set off in a mist so soft it felt related to dandelion seed. We took down the canoe at a lake marked on the map, and as we moved our paddles through the waters, it was like entering into some cavern hollowed out of pure turquoise. At night, we camped on the banks of lakes and bathed naked in water still cold from the runoff of snow. We chilled our bottles of wine in the rocks that lined the edges of the water. We slept together in the same tent at night as we followed a string of lakes, strung like a rosary, through the thick, humming forests where black bears hustled their cubs away from the shoreline when our canoe appeared and moose observed us as calmly as philatelists when we moved past their quiet foraging in deep water.

On this voyage, our friendship, our unspoken love for one another, formed a mansion without pillars or supports. Drifting, we knew we were heading for a time when Jordan would disappear from our lives as precipitously as he had entered it on a skateboard, wild hair flying, so many years before. Shyla could feel the silence of glades healing Jordan of his most immediate agony. Wolves started to call to each other across the vast wilderness and we once heard a pack in full flight during a hunt. When we talked about God, we found it was easy to believe in him while moving through the medallionlike waters of these sun-swelled lakes. On pebbled beaches where we camped, Jordan would pull agates and fire opals from streambeds and present them to us as wedding gifts.

For ten days we drifted; and only when we came to a small lakeside town and saw a Canadian Mountie walking down a dock did we realize our journey was over. For three days, we had been in Canadian waters without knowing it. In Canada, Jordan could make his way among an entire people tolerant of war resisters.

When we ate dinner on our last night together, Shyla and I toasted Jordan, and drank to his future. We were sure we would never see him again and he told us that he would only put us in danger if he tried to communicate with us in any way.

"What you did for me goes beyond friendship," Jordan said, "because I know that you're both horrified by what I did. I'll try to make up for my actions. I'll try to find meaning in all this. I promise."

"We love you, Jordan," Shyla said. "That's meaning enough for anybody."

When we woke the next day, Jordan had slipped out into the Canadian countryside to begin his life on the run. Shyla and I started back, where the memory of Jordan was imprinted on every lake we crossed. We made love for the first time in Canada and found we liked it. It took us twice as long to retrace our steps back to Grand Marais. We told ourselves we had raised the art of a honeymoon to new plateaus. One night, we made love listening to a wolf pack gathering for the hunt. We both agreed we had started our married life off right. So we were married the next day by a justice of the peace in Grand Marais, Minnesota. It took us three weeks of camping before we finally made it back to South Carolina and the lives we were meant to lead.

The silence was passionate yet abstract in the theater when I stopped speaking and returned to my seat. We all needed to compose ourselves in the late Charleston afternoon. Like figures in a painting we looked as though we had lost ourselves in some barely glimpsed, stolen landscape where no one spoke our native tongue. Jordan had awakened a part of all of us that had long ago fallen prey to easy associations of misremembrance. The theater felt like a confessional underground. In the airlessness that

followed my account, I swallowed the dust of
time itself. I tried to consider the part I had
played in this excruciating drama of my college
years and realized I did not recognize the description of the boy I once was. Somewhere in
this story I found myself missing in action in a
tale of my own life. I waited for a summing up,
a gathering of all the disparate and contra-
dicting parts, a voice from the past to grant
benediction for a life I did not even realize I
was leading. In those heady days, I had let instinct rule my every move and thought nothing
through completely. The young man who spirited Jordan through the wolf-haunted country
of the Boundary Waters was dead and un-
mourned. I had lost the fiery, irreconcilable boy
I once was on a Charleston bridge, yet realized
that was the boy that everyone on this stage
remembered as me. It was the same boy I
feared had sent Shyla to her death, signed the
marching orders that directed her to the railing
overlooking Charleston and the home we
shared together. Looking at Ledare, I saw her
studying me and I knew that Ledare had bided
her time throughout this year and had made
the error of falling in love with me. She wore
this love in her eyes, all over her face, and
made no effort to hide it. I wanted to warn her,
to tell her that my love was all fury and sharp
edges. I made a sport of killing the women I

loved and I did it with a guile and a softness that had all the markings of a true vocation. But everywhere I looked on that stage, I found love peeling off from a dark squadron, making strafing runs against me. I had failed to live fully because I had not come to terms with the alliances and fates of this imbalanced gathering of souls. Our pain bound us in a terrible love knot. I wanted to speak, but so did everyone else.

We waited—wordless—and the cameras rolled unnoted all around us.

Something was keeping us from talking to one another. A presence had come onto that stage unbidden and invisible. As long as it lay there undetected there would be no armistice among us. I had not felt the presence of this ghost for so long it took me a while to recognize its demoralizing ascension. Then I saw it, and could recognize it as an old friend that had trailed us to this stage.

"Hello, Vietnam," I said to myself. "Long time no see." Yet it inked its shape in the tissues of the silence that held us in its tense concentric folds. As a country, Vietnam was not important; but as a wound, it was unbearable. We could not run far enough away from it; it followed us on stumps and crutches, prided itself on being omnipresent and inescapable. Though I had hated that war with my body and soul, I realized sitting there that Vietnam was still *my* war. I had blamed it for the great unraveling it had brought to America, the self-doubt, the breakdown of courtesy, the death of form, and the falling apart of all the old truths and the integrity of both law and institutions. Everything came up for grabs. Nothing survived the cut. The facile and the cheap became celebrated and the speech of idiots took on a benighted, kingly quality. Solidity was a concept found only in physics textbooks. Indifference took center stage and it was hard to believe anything. God pulled back. I had searched the whole world for something to believe in and I had come up empty-handed every time. "Hello, Vietnam," I said again to myself. "Time for us to make friends," as I waited for one of us to find our voice.

Finally, someone spoke and I was surprised to hear Capers Middleton's voice. "What was all this really about? I've heard everything and I still don't understand it. I need help with this. I truly do."

"That's how life goes," General Elliott said. "There are no guarantees."

"How convenient for you to say that," his wife, Celestine, said. "Avoid responsibility. Spread the blame. Like you've always done."

"What I'd like you to know . . ." Capers began.

"You're too hard on yourself . . ." Betsy said, taking her husband's arm.

"No, let me say this," Capers said and he looked as troubled as I have ever seen a man look. "I had no idea how this would turn out. I'd've done it all differently. I had no idea it could lead to all this. It hurt people I thought the world of. It won't let go of me. It's always there."

"I'm a lot easier on myself," Radical Bob Merrill said with an easy grin. Unlike the rest of us, Jordan's recitation had no emotional impact on him at all. "I did what I thought was right back then. Hindsight's groovy, but a total waste of time."

Mike Hess, the producer again, snapped his finger and said, "Bye-bye, Radical Bob. Go back to the hotel. Enjoy dinner and fly back into your life. You're dismissed."

Bob Merrill rose up and walked off, stage right, and out of our lives, forever. No one watched him go or even said good-bye.

"Okay," Mike said, facing the rest of us. "We need an ending to all this. Got to find an ending. Let's help each other out now."

"It got away from me, Dad," Jordan said to his father. "Nothing was clear to me."

"The times were folded wrong, odd. You couldn't hold them up and look at them. Things happened too fast," Ledare said.

"You weren't even alive then, Ledare," Mike said. "That was one spaceship you didn't ride."

"I was watching," Ledare said. "I inherited Capers, pulled him out of the wreckage. I think he suffered from all we've just listened to. I didn't think Capers could ever forgive me for loving him after what he did to his friends."

"I don't think you know the real Capers," Betsy said, rushing to her husband's defense.

"I'm guilty of a little insider trading there," Ledare said. "I've got more than a passing acquaintance of your boy there."

"That wasn't the real Capers," Betsy insisted. "Not the one I know."

"No, honey," Capers said. "They knew that was the real me. I'm asking them to accept that part of me. It was there all the time and all of them knew it. What I didn't know is that it had the power to hurt my friends. I ruined Jordan Elliott's life. Look what I did to his parents."

Betsy let the words settle, then said, "You've always been your own harshest critic."

"Shut up, Betsy," Mike Hess said. "Pretty please, but shut up."

"Can there be forgiveness?" Capers asked. "That's what I have to know."

"You? Asking forgiveness of them?" General Elliott said, in disbelief. "You're the only one on this stage who conducted yourself with honor in this whole affair."

"What would you know about honor?" Celestine asked her husband. "Tell us all you know about the subject, darling. Tell it to the wife and son you betrayed."

"Dad was true to his code, Mom," Jordan said. "He betrayed no one."

"Harsh code," I said.

"I didn't understand it either," Jordan admitted, "until I met a couple of Jesuits in Rome."

Father Jude and the abbott laughed, but the joke was too ecclesiastical for the rest of us.

"Jordan," Ledare said, "did you become a priest because it was the best place to hide from the past?"

"No," he said. "It was the best place to hide from the present. And from myself. But I grew into my vocation, Ledare. I was born to be a priest, but I had to kill two innocent people to find that out."

"Why didn't you just say an extra rosary, son?" the general asked sarcastically. "It would've saved two lives and the Marine Corps a plane."

"I wish it happened that way, Dad," said Jordan, his hands folded across his lap.

"What a shame you lacked character," General Elliott said to his son.

"It wasn't character I lacked," Jordan said. "It was moderation."

"Leave my son alone," Celestine said.

"He's my son too," the general said.

I said, "Then act like it. Look at him when he speaks, General."

"I can't help who I am," General Elliott said directly to me.

"Nor can I, Dad," Jordan said quietly.

Celestine rose to her feet and approached her husband fiercely. "Don't you see it, Rembert? It's so obvious now. No one could've acted in a different manner than they did. Fate's a maidservant of character. Hired help and nothing else. You haven't changed one degree since I met you. Look at you. Pure of spirit. Holier than thou. Watch your rigidity. I know what you're after today. I don't have to ask you. You don't have thoughts, only patterns. You'd charge an enemy's foxhole to save the lives of all of us here. But you'd charge it harder if you knew our son was hiding there. You want our boy in prison. You want him to rot in jail."

Jordan said, "I'm a monk, Mom. Cells hold no fear for me. It's another place to pray in."

"You were stolen out of my life, Jordan," she said. "I can never forgive him for doing that. And I never can forgive myself for letting it happen. I'm divorcing your father out of pure shame and exhaustion."

"You're wrong to do that, Celestine," the general said. "It's not that you loved Jordan more than I did. It's that you appeared to. That's all. The appearances of things formed you. I admit that . . ."

"Go on, General," said Mike Hess, and it came out as an order, not a request.

The general appeared surprised, then he went on. "I submit that I loved Jordan as much as my wife did. But within the restraints and limits of a man of my time. I was good at leading men into battle. Few men possess that gift. I could always connect with fighting men. A better father couldn't have been as good a soldier."

There was a rap on the gavel and I heard my father speak. "You're no longer a Marine, Rembert. That's all over. What are you going to do about Jordan now?"

"I'm going to hold him accountable," the general answered.

"I've seen something today that's surprised me," my father said, and suddenly I saw him look at me. "Jordan holds you in much higher regard than Jack holds me. Anyone can see that. Yet it seems to mean nothing to you."

"Jordan was raised to know right from

wrong," the general began, "but when his country called, he was absent."

"You mean the Vietnam thing?" Capers asked.

"Yeh, the Vietnam thing," the general answered. "You can't help the generation you were born in. I'm grateful I wasn't born in yours."

"Yeh, you came from great folks," I said, nearly exploding. "Thanks for presenting my generation with that fabulous little war. We'll die grateful that we tore into each other because you guys were stupid."

"It was too much war for you, Jack," General Elliott said.

I replied, "It was too *little* war for me, General. That's what you don't get."

"I was expecting more from you, Rembert," my father said to the general.

"You were expecting more of me?" the general asked, his voice stony.

"Jordan came here because he wanted to tell you his story," the judge said. "All the rest of us are superfluous."

"You fought the Germans in Europe, Judge. You were a decorated infantryman. What do you think about Jack and the others and how they responded when our nation needed them?"

"I wouldn't have done it their way," my father admitted.

"Indeed," the general said.

"But let's be truthful. We're holding them up to standards that no longer apply," the judge said. "My son Jack stood up for what he believed in. That's how he was raised."

I nodded my appreciation to my father and he returned it in kind. The general watched the acknowledgments pass between us.

"Let's be brutally honest," the general said. "He was raised by the town drunk, Judge. Standards, you say? I doubt if you were sober long enough to know if Jack was in the house."

"Stand at attention when you talk to my old man," I said to the general. "Ever talk to him like that again and I'll mop the fucking floor with your cheekbones."

The gavel hammered again and my father said, "You're out of order, Jack. The general made an excellent point."

"I'm very sorry for that, Johnson Hagood," General Elliott said.

"The heat of battle," my father said generously. "No harm done. Apologize to the general, Jack."

"Sorry, Rembert," I said, calling him by his first name for the first time in my life. "Got carried away."

"I like the thought of you wiping the floor

with Rembert," Celestine said, and Mike laughed out loud, cutting some of the tension that had built up.

"I've missed you, Jordan," Capers said, rising out of his seat and approaching the priest cautiously from the opposite side of the stage. "I can't get over that y'all think I betrayed my best friends. I can't think of myself like that. It goes against the grain. Shyla died without ever speaking to me again. I wrote her a letter once. Telling her I loved her, loved all of you. That none of us was responsible for what happened at Carolina. Shyla sent the letter back, unopened. Jack still can't look at me without hating my guts." Capers looked over at me and said, "Don't deny it, Jack."

"You hear anyone denying it?" I said.

"Shyla thought you loved her, Capers," Ledare said. "A couple of us made that mistake."

"I was bad news for you, Ledare," Capers said. "Every time I looked at you, it reminded me of how much I'd lost."

"Small potatoes, dear. All I gave up was my twenties and my belief in matrimony," Ledare said. "Otherwise I came out without a scratch."

"I'm sorry. Please forgive me," Capers said.

"That's enough, Capers," Betsy said. "Don't crawl. It doesn't become you, darling."

"Whoa!" Mike said. "Pure ice, Betsy. An

Eskimo girl couldn't have said it better or served it up chillier."

"I'm sorry, Ledare," Capers said. "When I left you I had started to notice that my life had gone wrong."

"Please save it, Capers," I said. "Hypocrisy makes me weepy."

The gavel again—Dad. "Jack, if you can't bring yourself to make peace with one of your best friends, then what hope does Jordan have with his father? How do we resolve this?"

"The film's running down. We need a wrap, people," Mike said.

I looked at my father and understood what was required of me this night, so I got up and faced Capers, who was still standing.

"I'm sorry, Jack. So sorry," he said to me. "I wish I could do it all again. I'd make everything right."

"When you're governor, I'm sending you all my parking tickets," I said.

We shook hands and when we both felt that we meant it, we embraced.

The general stood up and both Capers and I took our seats. He approached Jordan, who watched him come close without emotion.

"You said this was a mock trial," the general said to Mike. "I would like to cast my vote on the guilt or innocence of my son."

"Good," Mike said. "But I'm the producer

and the director. I'm casting mine first, General. But hell, you understand the chain of command better than anyone. Not guilty."

"Not guilty," Ledare said, followed by Celestine saying the same thing.

"Not guilty," the abbott and Father Jude said. "Not guilty," said Betsy and Capers.

"Not guilty," said my father, the judge.

"Now it's my vote," the general said, and I thought I heard his voice crack.

Celestine said to her son, who was meeting his father's stare, "It's not in him, Jordan. Love lies too deep for him. He can't get to it."

"I can get there for him, Mom," Jordan said. "It's easy for me."

"I'm sorry, son," the general said, but it was a father who was speaking now, not the general.

Jordan covered his father's mouth with his hand, with great gentleness. "No need for a vote, Dad. I know what it is. What it has to be. I came here to make it right with you. I've got to walk off this stage with a father in my life. I've proven that I can't live without one."

"I can't help who I am, son," the general said when Jordan's hand dropped.

"Nor I who I am," Jordan said.

"Tell me you were wrong."

"I was very wrong, Dad," the priest said. "My hatred of you got in the way. I should've followed the path you set for me. America's a good enough country to die for even when America's wrong. At least, for a boy like me. Raised the way you and Mom raised me."

"That's far enough, Jordan," I said. "It was a lousy war. Don't make him rub your nose in it anymore."

"What can I do, Dad?" Jordan said, waiting for his father's judgment.

"Turn yourself in," the general said. "If you do this, I'll back you all the way. I'll fight for you."

Jordan bowed before his father, assenting to his will. The two Trappists rose and walked toward him, both gaunt, prayer-weathered men. Jordan knelt and received both their blessings. The abbott then said, "Jordan had me call General Peatross at Pollock Island early this morning. I told him, General, that you'd be delivering your son to the provost marshal tomorrow at noon. General Peatross would like you to come by his office first. He says he knew Jordan as a child."

There was a muffled sob as Celestine Elliott left her seat and ran toward the darkness at the rear of the stage. Jordan followed her and we could hear him comforting his mother while the camera crew began to break up the set as the rest of us stood up in the middle of our actual lives. I watched my father walk over in his robes to comfort the general, who looked defeated and bereft after doing the only thing he could do.

That evening, we ate dinner at Betsy and Capers Middleton's beach house on Sullivan's Island. I set up shop on the deck looking out to the ocean and grilled onions and eggplant, hamburgers and steaks and shrimp until everyone was full and happy and Mike and Jordan had to run out for some more beer. The Trappists had made their way back to Mepkin Abbey and my father had driven the general back to Waterford. Celestine chose not to attend the party, but the rest of us felt great relief in the gathering at the Middleton household. Ledare's children, Sarah and young Capers, were glad to see their parents under the same roof, talking casually, and Betsy proved a good hostess as we gathered around the dining room table regaling each other with stories from the past. It was still strange for me to see Jordan out in public without looking over his shoulder or checking to see if someone had followed me to a secret rendezvous. A strange sense of freedom had come over him. He could not get enough of us. He drank us in, he fed on our spirits to the point of satiety. We gave ourselves to him and let him have this night completely.

After midnight, everyone had gone to bed somewhere in the sprawling house but Jordan, Capers, Mike, and me. We found ourselves walking along the beach of Sullivan's Island as a ship passed out of the harbor, Asia bound. The harbor pilot's boat met the ship when it reached the open sea and we walked in silence as we saw the smaller boat return toward the city.

"What now?" Mike asked. "I don't think I've ever been happier."

"What about Hollywood?" Capers said. "You have the pick of the starlets. You live like a king. That sounds better than eating burgers on a South Carolina beach with a bunch of high school assholes."

"Not to me," Mike said.

"Me neither," Jordan agreed.

"What about you?" Mike asked me.

"I hate to ruin the evening here," I said, "but I still think Capers is something of a scumbag."

"Oh that," Mike said. "You'll get over it."

"Time passing," Jordan said, his eyes casting upward toward the stars. "It's the big surprise in life. It might be the only one. It feels like we've been on this beach forever. Like we never lost each other."

"That reminds me," Capers said, snapping his fingers, and running suddenly back toward his house. When he returned he was carrying a surfboard over his head and we cheered when we saw it. We stripped down to our underwear and plunged into the warm-blooded, air-cooled Atlantic. The waves were calm and halfhearted as we swam out toward deep water.

"You call these waves?" Jordan said. "You call this an ocean?"

"The Jordan summer," Mike said, remembering.

"Never forgot it," I said.

"Remember my long hair?" the clean-cut monk said, laughing.

"Waterford's first hippie," Capers said. "My God. You were the first omen of the sixties. We should've tarred and feathered you and sent you back to where you belonged."

"Have sons, have sons," Mike cried happily.

"Where are the porpoises?" I asked. "We need porpoises, Mike."

"Get me special effects," Mike called out. "Call Warner Brothers."

"It comes back to this then," said Capers.

"Life doubles back. It takes you by surprise," Jordan said.

"Like a good movie," Mike said.

"Where were you going to send me, Capers?" Jordan asked. "Where is it you think I belonged?"

We were floating in the Atlantic, holding on

to the surfboard, with another summer ending and the warm wind soft against the surface and the taste of salt in our mouths. We drifted in the deep currents on a moonless night and because we were low country boys we were not afraid. Then Capers summed it up by reaching out and rumpling Jordan's hair, saying, "Here. You belong here. With us. Always."

CHAPTER 39

EVERY SON WILL HAVE HIS TIME IN A room like this, I thought, as I joined my brothers in our watch over our mother's bed. The smell of chemotherapy was familiar, the metallic scent leaving its trace on the membranes of my tongue. Its business was to slaughter the white blood cells that had multiplied in Lucy's bloodstream, those white cells that moved with the thrift of herds, crowding the red cells to the point of extinction. In my mind's eye, I saw my mother's blood turning into a deadly snow. And when I looked at her, I saw for the first time terror in her pretty blue eyes. Every cell in her body was lit up with the unnameable fear.

"If you really loved Mama, Jack," Dupree said, "you'd be out in your workshop finding a cure for cancer."

"That's what I hate about my brothers," John Hardin said, walking to Lucy's side. "You heard that, Mama. We should all be trying to make you feel like a million bucks and stupid Dupree starts in with his jokes."

"Tell us how we go about making Mom feel like a million bucks, " Dallas said. "We seem to lack your genius for bedside manners."

"Go ahead. Mock me, Dallas," John Hardin said. "I realize I'm an easy target. I know you laugh behind my back. Make fun of me. Write about me in the latrine while you're taking a piss. I see those things you write about me. I recognize your ugly, repulsive handwriting."

Dallas shook his head and answered, "I've never written a word on a bathroom wall in my whole life."

"You don't even have the guts to admit it," John Hardin said. "You and your kind are so despicable."

"I agree," Tee said. "Dallas and his kind're beneath contempt. What can you say about a man who won't own up to his own graffiti?"

"You write worse things about me than Dallas does," John Hardin said to Tee. "But I've got you boys back good. I told Mom all about it. I told her everything. Mom knows, assholes. Mom's gonna take care of business as soon as she's on her feet. Right, Mom?"

"That's right, John Hardin," Lucy said weakly.

"You're dreaming, John Hardin," Tee said, puzzled. "What did I write about you?"

"You wrote 'Call J. for the best blow job in town,' " he said. "Then you wrote down my telephone number."

"You don't have a phone," Dallas said. "You live in a tree, same as a sparrow."

"I'm too sharp for you guys," John Hardin said. "I'm always thinking way ahead of you guys."

"Quit picking on John Hardin," Lucy said. "I read about Jordan's arrest. It was in the morning paper, honey."

"He should've stayed put," I said.

"The past is the hardest thing to run from," Lucy said. "I think Jordan got tired of running from a person he never really was."

"Look, Mom still loves Jack the most," John Hardin observed. "It's not fair to prefer him just because of the stupid birth order."

"I was a child myself when Jack was born, John Hardin," said Lucy, touching my face with her left hand. "I never had a baby doll to play with as a girl. So I pretended that Jack was a doll baby some stranger had left under a

Christmas tree. I had no right to be raising up a child being so young myself, but Jack couldn't know that. When I breast-fed him for the first time, I didn't know the first thing about what I was doing. But Jack seemed to go along with everything I did. He made it easy for me. Jack and I grew up together. He was the first best friend I ever had and I knew he'd never leave me."

"I guess living in Italy was Jack's way of staying close," Dallas said.

"I wouldn't go to Italy if the Pope himself invited me to eat a Ragú dinner with him," John Hardin said. "Italians're the scariest people in the world. They're always taking blood oaths and selling drugs to black people and killing each other with shotguns. The men comb their hair with pig fat and the women all have big tits and say the rosary constantly and eat food that ends with vowels. The Mafia's been there so long it surprises me there's a single Italian left alive."

"I got an idea," Tee said. "John Hardin just proved what Hollywood has done to the image of Italians. Why doesn't the Mafia quit killing police informers and concentrate on murdering Hollywood directors and producers?"

"Mama's getting tired," Dupree said. "Why don't we come back into her room later."

"She's just tired of your sorry ass, Dupree," John Hardin said. "But who isn't?"

Dupree shook his head and whispered to no one in particular, "I can't believe I'm taking abuse from a psychotic."

"You hear that, Mom?" John Hardin said, pointing an accusatory finger at Dupree. "That should get you at least a month's restriction and no allowance at all. Ha! That'll teach you to make fun of a helpless schizophrenic. All my problems stem from a toxic gene pool that tadpoles couldn't grow in and a flock of shitbird brothers who've got no empathy for the disadvantaged among them. You assholes all picked on me when I was a little kid. Guess you hate me spilling the beans in front of Mom, huh, losers?"

"John Hardin," I said. "Did you notice that this is a hospital? That Mom's a bit under the weather?"

"Mr. Goddamn Big. Mr. I-live-in-Europe and fuck-anyone-who-lives-in-America. Mr. Chef Boyardee, don't-faggots-have-more-fun-wearing-aprons. Mr. Bullshit-on-rice trying to tell the little fella what to do. It's always open season on the mentally ill, Mom. You heard it from me first and now you're getting a live demonstration from your worthless sons."

"You're my sweetest boy, John Hardin," Lucy said, taking him by the hands and drawing him toward her. "They don't understand my baby boy, do they?"

"They don't know a thing," John Hardin said, his voice breaking. "They represent the normal world and that's so scary, Mom. It's always frightened me."

"I'll make them be nice to you, honey," Lucy said, winking at the rest of us, holding John Hardin close.

"We're the only kids in America punished for not being schizophrenics," Dallas said.

"The Dark One is jealous," Tee said.

"Green grows the Dark One," Dupree agreed.

"Let's clear out of here," I said. "Mom needs to rest."

"One of us'll be here at all times, Mama," Dupree said. "We're working out the shifts right now."

"They're leaving me out, Mom," John Hardin said. "Me, the one who loves you the most. I don't get to sit with you in your time of greatest need."

"The nurses're scared to death of John Hardin, Mama," Dallas said. "Everybody in town remembers the standoff at the bridge."

"I was hearing voices then," John Hardin explained. "That wasn't the real me."

"It sure looked like the real you, bro," Tee said. "Sounded like you too when you forced all your poor brothers to leap naked into the river."

"I'm a victim of a dysfunctional family," John Hardin said. "I'm not responsible for the actions I commit when the voices are in control."

"So, if you barbecue poor Mom one night," Dupree said, "carve her up like a Christmas hog, and serve her up at the homeless shelter in Savannah, we can't get pissed at you."

"I have a mental illness," John Hardin said proudly. "It's documented."

"Jesus Christ," I said. "Family life's too exhausting for any American to bear."

"Put John Hardin on the night shift," Tee suggested. "The boy has problems sleeping."

"Midnight to seven," Dupree said to John Hardin. "Think you can handle that, John Hardin, or do you want one of us to stay with you for company?"

"You guys aren't company," John Hardin said. "You're just birthmarks I've got to put up with."

"This won't be pretty twenty-four hours from now," Lucy said weakly. "This stuff may kill the cancer cells, but it'll come pretty close to killing me too."

John Hardin studied the ominous plastic bag filled with the foul-smelling liquid now being released into Lucy's bloodstream. "This shit don't work. It makes the doctors rich, the drug companies rich, and it'll kill our poor wonderful mother. Vitamin C is the only thing that'll cure leukemia. I read it in *Parade* magazine."

"Thank God, we've got Mr. Wizard on our side," Dallas said.

We gathered around Lucy's bed and the five of us kissed her until she begged us to leave. Tee began to cry and said, "I love you with my body and soul, Mom. Even though all of us recognize you did all you could to totally fuck my life up."

In the laughter that followed, Lucy sent us away before Tee took up the first watch. We had begun our vigil, and we timed our lives from that moment on around the cycles of her chemotherapy. I looked at my boisterous, free-spirited brothers and knew not one of us had done the hard work needed to face the next thirty or forty years without Lucy. In our own ways each of us had come to terms with life's impassivity and cruelty, but now we faced head-on the prospect of arising one morning to a sunrise not only impersonal, but one that was Lucy-less as well.

Outside in the waiting room, within its haze of tired cigarette smoke, we lingered for a final roundup of fears and thoughts. We all had seen the fear in Lucy's eyes.

"I'm the only one here who thinks Mom's

gonna be alive ten years from now," John Hardin said. "The rest of you boys have given up, haven't you?"

After a few minutes of forced banter and reassurance, Tee said, "I've got the first shift. Relieve me at midnight, John Hardin. The rest of you country boys get some sleep."

"Did you know that leukemia's the only cancer directly affected by the human emotions?" John Hardin asked us, his voice faintly disapproving. "I'm the only optimist in this dark bunch. Mom needs us to be sunny, not surly."

"If I go nuts and beat John Hardin's brains out with a tire tool, how long would I spend in the big house?" Dupree asked Dallas.

"First offender? You'd be iced for four years max with time off for good behavior."

"Can you do this?" I asked John Hardin, my arm across his shoulder. "We can't afford any screw-ups. You've got to earn our trust."

"Why? No one's ever trusted me before. With anything," John Hardin said. "That's why I've got such a bone to pick with the whole universe."

At midnight, while Waterford slept and the tide was moving out of the marshes and estuaries, John Hardin relieved Tee. Half-asleep himself, Tee gave John Hardin a quick hug then shuffled down the long shiny linoleum floor, forgetting to tie his shoelaces.

When a nurse came in at half past midnight to hook up a full bag of chemotherapy, she reported that John Hardin was tense but friendly as she checked Lucy's temperature and took her blood pressure. When Dupree arrived at the hospital at seven the next morning, he discovered that John Hardin and Lucy were missing. At a side entrance to the hospital, Dupree found the wheelchair that John Hardin had used to transport Lucy out of harm's way. He had left a note beneath her pillow that read, "I refuse to let them kill my poor mother with their poisons. This will also prove to my mother that I've always loved her a lot more than my asshole brothers. Some may call me a madman, but my mother will know, at last, that I put her *número uno* over all the mothers of the world."

When we heard the news, we gathered at the judge's to discuss strategies and apportion blame. Dallas scowled at Dupree and seemed more prickly than usual while Tee opened a beer and threw his cup of freshly brewed coffee down the sink.

"In a time of stress, alcohol is the drug of choice and caffeine is what you turn to when you've got to sober up," Tee said.

"Once again, I'm the laughingstock of this town because of my damn family," Dallas said.

"You guys don't get it. People seek legal advice from pillars of the community. I look like the fire hydrant where the neighborhood Chihuahuas mark their territory. I shouldn't've listened to you guys."

"Mom insisted that we include John Hardin," Tee said. "It was a slight error of calculation. Next time Mom's dying, we'll do it a bit differently."

"Her doctor went apeshit," Dupree reported. "He screamed at me for a half-hour. Dr. Pitts wasn't overjoyed either."

Dallas said, "She got enough chemotherapy in her to make her sick as hell, but not do her a single bit of good."

"He took Mom's car," I said. "When he calmed down, Dr. Pitts told me all the food's missing from Mom's pantry. No liquor in sight. Blankets, sheets, and towels gone from the linen closet. I checked the tree house when Dupree called this morning and they're not there."

Dupree said, "He doesn't have a credit card or much money to speak of. Everything was still in Mom's purse. There's no place for him to go. The highway patrol's been alerted and they should spot Mom's car soon enough and bring her back."

"John Hardin's got a few screws loose," Tee

said. "But he's smart as hell. The boy's got a plan. That I'll guarantee you."

"You know why we're in this mess," Dallas said. "Easy. Because our parents raised us up to be liberals in the South. They taught us to trust in our fellow man and to believe in his basic goodness. No one else in the world would let a psycho like John Hardin watch over their dying mother except us. If we'd been raised conservative like every other decent white Southerner, we'd never've let this nutbag near our mother."

"I would be a conservative if I'd never met any," I said. "They're selfish, mean-spirited, egocentric, reactionary, and boring."

"Yeh," Dallas nodded. "That's exactly what I aspire to."

"Guilt," Tee said. "I see Haiti, I feel guilty. Somalia, total guilt. El Salvador, bone-chilling guilt. Guatemala, guilt on the half-shell. The teeming streets of India, guilt."

"Losing Mom," Dupree said.

"Guilt," the four of us cried out as one.

"We should've seen it coming, bros," said Tee.

Dallas countered by saying, "How're you supposed to tell what a madman's gonna do?"

"He's not a madman," Dupree said. "He's our brother and we've got to find him before

Mom dies. We can't let her die out there with him. John Hardin couldn't handle that."

"I'll search the back roads," I said.

"I know he still hangs out at Yesterday's in Columbia," Dupree said. "Tee and I'll talk to them. Why don't you go to Charleston and see if he's been spotted up there, Dallas?"

"Yoo-hoo, boys. Real job here. Real clients who need me to be in the office. Secretary to pay. Overhead. This ring any bells for you folks?" Dallas asked.

"Mom's Cadillac is rose red," I said. "John Hardin'll look like a pimp on holiday rolling down a South Carolina back road."

"Bet you miss Italy, don't you, bro?" Tee asked.

"*Chi, io?*" I said.

"I wish I'd been born Italian," Dallas said. "Then I couldn't speak a word of English. I'd be completely in the dark. In this family, it's the only safe place to be."

"Call my house at six tonight," I suggested. "We can use Dallas' office as headquarters during the day. Where's Dad?"

"Drunk," Dupree said.

"Gee whiz. I'm shocked," Dallas said. "My papa overindulging. It's so unlike him."

"He drinks when there's pressure," Dupree explained.

"The only other time he drinks is when there's *no* pressure," I said.

Though much can be held against the smaller states like South Carolina, they provide a sense of intimacy and balance to their citizens. In less than twenty-four hours, the whole state was on the lookout for a 1985 red Cadillac Seville driven by a mental patient carrying a terribly weakened woman who had completed only two fifths of her latest chemotherapy treatments.

While Tee was checking hotel and motel reservations around the state and Dallas called all the sheriffs in the most rural counties, I sat in the newsroom of the *News and Courier* in Charleston making calls to editors trying to get front-page space describing Lucy's disappearance. When Dupree returned to Columbia he began searching out friends of John Hardin's in the scruffy speakeasies located on the fringe of the university. Alcohol was the first hermitage John Hardin sought when his mind grew disfigured and gauzy. In bars, he found nonjudgmental friends who listened to him patiently as he listed the forces arrayed against him. In those mirrored rooms, there was comfort in the vacancy of strangers adrift in the same fool's paradise John Hardin retreated to when panic-stricken or broken by the free-falling suffering that was his birthright.

Dupree knew about John Hardin's night circuit and had often answered calls from bartenders when his brother had drunk too much to walk home. Dupree was always moved that John Hardin had discovered a community of mislaid, churlish men and women who had also found life unbearable at times. When they heard about John Hardin's disappearance with his mother, they opened up to Dupree and gave him the telephone numbers and names of other friends. On the third day, Dupree found the one friend who could tell him where John Hardin had gone and how to find him.

Vernon Pellarin was wandering among a lineup of drugged depressives bumming cigarettes two hundred feet from Dupree's office on the grounds of the state hospital. Vernon was light-headed with his own drugs and he cheerfully told Dupree that he had given John Hardin the keys to his family's fishing lodge on the Edisto River. He thought it was about two weeks ago at Muldoon's bar near the capitol that he gave him the keys. The lodge belonged to Vernon and his brother, Casey, now that his father had died, but Casey lived in Spokane, Washington. John Hardin had revealed that he needed to find the most private, secluded spot in America because he wanted time to compose an essay that would change the course of contemporary society. Vernon was anxious to further a brave advance in American letters. The cabin was clean, simply furnished, and comfortable. However, it could only be reached by boat.

The following morning we put two bateaux into the Edisto River just downstream from Orangeburg. Tee and I were in one, Dupree and Dallas in the other. We needed to get Lucy back to the hospital, but we had to make sure that we did not hurt our most fragile brother in the process—or get hurt by him. When John Hardin turned to violence, he could terrorize an entire town, a fact that Waterford knew well and had experienced many times.

We let the current take us down the swift, rain-swollen Edisto. Oaks on the two shores leaned out over the water, touched branches, and exchanged birds and serpents, passing them almost hand to hand from one to the other. Water snakes eyed our two boats as we passed beneath the low-hanging trees. Dallas counted seven snakes wrapped around branches of one water oak we passed under.

"I hate snakes," Dallas said in a subdued voice. "What kind are they?"

"Cottonmouth moccasins," Tee said. "They're deadly poisonous. They bite you and you've got thirty seconds to make your peace with Jesus."

"They're water snakes," Dupree said. "They're all right."

"I don't like going under a tree and noticing fifty living creatures sizing me up for a meal," Dallas said.

"The snakes're fine," Dupree said. "John Hardin's our problem."

"Maybe we'll catch him in a good mood," I said. "Tell him we've got great tickets for the next Rolling Stones concert."

"I doubt it," Dupree said. "He's late for his shot. He's probably been drinking and he'll be agitated because he thinks the doctors're trying to kill Mom. We've got to be flexible when we see him. If we can talk him into letting us have Mom back, that's great. But we've got to get her back to the hospital one way or the other."

"You think he has a gun, bro?" Tee asked.

"Probably," Dupree said.

"You know who's the only crack shot in the family?" Tee asked me.

"Let me guess," I said. "John Hardin."

"He could trim a gnat's pubic hair at fifty feet," said Dallas. "The boy can handle a gun."

We passed four landings leading to small, nondescript houses before we rounded a curve of the river and saw a dock downriver fifty yards. John Hardin's boat was pulled up high into a weed-covered backyard. We tied our boats to the dock and, according to the plan we had devised the night before, made our way toward the cinder-block house in two groups, keeping well hidden by the deep woods on either side of the house. A plume of black smoke curled above the chimney in the windless morning. The air smelled of mildew and swamp cabbage. Deer tracks pocked the soft ground, scrolling an odd set of hieroglyphics on the forest floor.

Dupree remained the single legitimate outdoorsman among us. He raised bird dogs, kept the engine to his boat in repair, and made sure both his hunting and fishing licenses were current.

Tee and I watched Dupree as he moved with speed and quietness out of his hiding place to the side of the house, where he disappeared from our line of sight. Then we saw him low-crawling on his stomach to the front of the house, where he crouched on a makeshift porch, then peered into the bottom pane of a greasy window. Having trouble seeing, he moved on his hands and knees to the next window, rubbed it with his palm, and looked hard inside. He rubbed the window again and put one eye against the clean spot he made with a saliva-dampened finger. He did not hear the door open or see John Hardin until the deer rifle barrel touched his temple.

As Dupree raised his hands above his head,

John Hardin marched him out into the center of the grassless, weedy yard. He forced Dupree to kneel down with his hands behind his neck as John Hardin's eyes scanned the forest for signs of the rest of us.

"Come on out or I'm gonna shoot Dupree's dick off and feed it to the raccoons," John Hardin shouted, and his voice echoed off the walls of huge trees.

"He'll make us get naked again. Tease us about our little dicks. Make us swim for the bridge on Highway 17," Tee whispered, but I motioned for him to keep quiet.

Dallas broke first and emerged from the woods on the opposite side of the house trying to bluff his youngest brother with all the prestige of his profession.

"Just give it up, John Hardin," Dallas yelled authoritatively, waving a piece of paper. "This is a warrant for your arrest, little brother. It's been signed by three law enforcement officials in Waterford County and your own father. Dad wants you arrested and behind bars. He wants them to lock you up and melt down every key that fits your lock. I'm your only chance, John Hardin. With me as your lawyer, I promise I'll get you out on bail quicker than a trout farting in mountain water."

"A trout farting in mountain water?" I whispered. "Where'd he come up with that?"

"When he's scared, no metaphor's safe with Dallas," Tee explained. "Listen to his voice. He's terrified."

"You're wanted by the law in three states, John Hardin. There's a nationwide search on for you. An all-points bulletin. It's going to take brilliant legal work to keep you from doing hard time. A man who finished in the top ten in his law school class. A top-notch barrister who can charm a jury, reason with a judge, who can take a case that's an egg and turn it into an omelet."

"Get on your goddamn knees," John Hardin said, "before I blow your head clean off your neck."

"I hope your lawyer sucks," Dallas said, sinking to his knees. "I hope your roommate in prison's a huge, black gay rapist who's the captain of the prison basketball team."

"That was racist," Tee whispered.

"It sure was," I agreed.

"I could blow you guys apart. Right here. On your knees," John Hardin said. "And never serve a minute's time in prison. You know why? Because I'm crazy. I got the papers to prove it. Both you guys teased me when I was just a little kid. Who knows? That might be the whole key to my schizophrenia."

"Who knows?" Dupree said. "It might've been Mom's cooking."

"Shut up," John Hardin screamed. "Don't you say one word against our beautiful mother. Maybe she wasn't perfect. But look who she married—our horrible father, who didn't deserve to even know such a saint, much less to marry her. She had dreams, our mother did, big dreams, and you don't think she was disappointed having four asshole sons in a row? I admit I've disappointed Mom too. But she says that I was too sensitive to survive in this dog-eat-dog world. Her whole life was sacrificed to Dad and you smelly cocksuckers. Mom understands me like no one else."

"Then why are you killing her, John Hardin?" Dupree asked, matter-of-factly.

"Don't say that again. Don't you dare, horrible Dupree. Horrible, worthless, good-for-nothing Dupree."

"He's right," Dallas said. "Her only chance's the chemotherapy."

"You ought to see what it's doing to her," said John Hardin, and there was true horror in his voice. "She can't keep food down at all. Mom won't eat anything because she throws it right up. It's taking everything out of her. Killing her from the inside out."

And then Tee made his move toward the clearing. He entered in mid-scene talking wildly and with exaggerated hand motions like a sailor trying to flag down a passing ship. His

Southern accent deepened and grew shrill during crises, and when John Hardin pointed the rifle at him, Tee began to sound like a mule skinner in a Southern stock production.

"Bro, bro, bro, bro," Tee began barking at John Hardin, his voice rising in pitch like a lapdog. "Bro, bro, bro."

"What in the hell do you want, Tee?" John Hardin asked, leveling the rifle at his brother's heart. "I heard you the first time. How many times do you have to say 'bro' before you think I get it?"

"I was nervous, bro," Tee said.

"I hate being called 'bro,'" John Hardin said. "Say it one more time and I put a bullet in your heart. What've you got to be nervous about anyway?"

"My mama's dying. My brother's crazy. I got someone threatening to shoot my young ass," Tee wailed. "This ain't like lying in a hammock, bro."

"He said 'bro' again," Dupree said. "Shoot him, John Hardin."

"You shut up, Dupree," John Hardin warned.

"I've got an appointment back in town," Dupree said, looking at his watch. "I'll lose my job if I don't make it back."

"You, a job?" John Hardin laughed. "You

work at an insane asylum, locking up innocent crazy people like me."

"I'm meeting a client," Dallas said. "Big money's involved."

"You're nothing but a brown-shoe, two-bit lawyer who wears cheap ties and doesn't even own a fax machine," John Hardin said. "Dad may've been a drunk, but he had a great legal mind. He changed the world with his legal opinions while you fix traffic tickets for Puerto Ricans who get lost on I-95."

"That's a fairly accurate summation of my career," Dallas admitted and Dupree laughed.

"Always joking. Everything's a big laugh to you guys. But real humor is lost on you guys. What you love is humiliation, character assassination, ridicule . . ."

Tee said, "That's Dupree and Dallas, bro. My humor's just like yours, John Hardin."

"Thanks, Tee," Dallas said. "Nothing like a united front to get us all through this."

"We've got to take Mom back to the hospital," Dupree said, rising to his feet.

"Get back down on your knees," John Hardin demanded, striking the back of his brother's knees with the rifle butt.

By this time, I had seen and heard enough, and more out of sheer frustration than a moment of sudden valor, I charged out of the woods making as much noise as was humanly possible. I did not even cast a glance at John Hardin or the others, but ran directly up the unpainted steps of the cabin as John Hardin screamed at me from behind. I heard him yelling to halt as I entered the house and found my mother, frail and barely conscious, in a sweat-soaked sleeping bag by a wood-burning stove. I put my hand to her forehead; I don't think I have ever felt a higher fever on a human being. Lucy opened her eyes and tried to say a few words but she was delirious, lost to the voraciousness of her fever. Lifting her up, I was furious and unstoppable.

I walked out into the sunlight and went carefully down the ill-made stairs, moving toward John Hardin, whose rifle was pointed at my eyes. As I approached I prayed that John Hardin's basic sweetness would break through the disfigured latitudes of his madness. The death of my mother is driving me nuts, I thought, so why should it surprise any of us that John Hardin's having a hard time?

"Put my mother back where she belongs or I'm going to send you on an all-expense-paid trip to heaven."

"Then you can raise Leah for me, John Hardin," I shouted, nearing him. "You can tell her you shot her father down dead in the woods and you can tell her bedtime stories the rest of her childhood and put away money for her college education. Shyla's already killed herself, so Leah's used to not having a parent around. Of course, after killing Mom, leaving her in this condition, I don't care what you do to me. Just get out of my way, John Hardin. Mom must have a fever of a hundred and five and she's going to die in the next hour if we don't get her to a hospital. Are you trying to kill Mom?"

"No, Jack, I swear to God. I'm trying to save her, to help her. Ask Mom. Wake her up. She knows what I'm trying to do. I forgot to pack aspirin. That's all. I love her more than anyone. Much more than any of you guys. She knows that."

"Then help us get her to someone who can save her," I said.

"Please. Please," said Dallas, Dupree, and Tee, and John Hardin lowered the rifle.

Even after we got her to the hospital Lucy remained in the involuntary country of delirium. Again we hovered over her and whispered "I love you, Mama" a thousand times in a litany of endless valentines to ease her solitude and suffering. Beside her bed, the clear, foul-smelling chemotherapy once more dripped into the vein in her right arm. It burned as it entered and killed every blood cell it touched,

good and bad. It eased its way along the highways that connected her organs like distant cities. Down again it took her to the sacristies of
death. Her body turned inward on itself and
her vital signs wavered as her young doctor
monitored each step of her descent. He took
Lucy all the way down to the point of death,
then stopped the chemotherapy treatment forever and left her withered, tormented body for
Lucy herself to save.

Though Dr. Steve Payton thought Lucy
would die in the hospital on the first night of
her return, he underestimated the strength she
brought to the task of survival. Hers was a body
that had endured five hard labors and produced five baby boys who each weighed over
eight pounds. Twice, that first night, she almost
died, and twice she came back.

At the end of the second day, Lucy opened
her eyes and saw my brothers and me surrounding her. We cheered and screamed so
loudly that nurses came rushing in to quiet us.
Disoriented, she could not understand all the
commotion we made, but she winked at us.
Then she slept solidly for another five hours,
then awoke again to our shouts of encouragement.

After the second awakening, a distraught
Tee slipped out of the room. I followed him out
the back door of the hospital, into the clean air,

and joined him on the bank of the river, above the green fringe of spartina grass. Tee was crying softly when I reached him.

"I'm not ready for this, Jack, I swear I'm not. There should be classes in this shit. A book needs to be written to tell me how to act and feel now. Every move I make seems phony to me. Even these tears seem fake, like I'm pretending to care more than I do. She shouldn't have brought us in the world if she knew we were going to have to sit around and watch her die a little at a time. It's not that I love her ass so much either. I think you older boys got the best of Mom. I really do. Somewhere along the line, she quit being a mother to us. Okay, so she ran down. No big deal. But this is killing me and I don't know why. I even blame her for the way John Hardin is. I think she didn't raise the little bastard. Just watered him enough to grow. I'm sorry. I have no right to think any of this."

"Say anything you want," I said. "I think that's probably the best thing we can do while we're losing her."

"She loves John Hardin more than me for one lousy reason," Tee said. "Because he's mentally ill and I'm not. Is that fair? I'm jealous because I'm not a goddamn schizophrenic. I get psycho-envy every time I think about it."

"John Hardin needs Mom to love him most," I tried to explain. "He's a special case."

"He's a nut bag," Tee said. "He practically kills Mom and we pretend everything's fine just because John Hardin forgot to keep his date with the Thorazine clinic."

"He did what he could," I said. "I envy John Hardin. We sit around saying prayers to a God we know won't listen to us. But John Hardin kidnaps the woman he loves more than anyone on earth, takes her out of harm's way, and brings her to a make-believe castle in a hideaway that no one else knows about. Mom knows the rest of us love her in theory. But poor crazed, lunatic John Hardin steals away with her in the night and has the whole state on the alert looking for her. We hand our love of Mom over to the doctors. John Hardin takes her down the Edisto River, cooks her bass that he set a trot-line for, builds her fires, and feeds her by hand in a half-abandoned fish camp that you can't reach except by water. Like everything else, love's not worth much without some action to back it up."

"We went looking for her. We found her and brought her back," Tee said.

"Thank John Hardin for that," I said.

"When Mom dies that's going to leave just Dad," Tee continued.

"Let's go back inside," I suggested to Tee. "We can be there for her when she needs us."

Two nights later, at two in the morning, I was sleeping in a cot at the end of her bed when I heard her cry out and found her covered with vomit. Her hair was falling out in lifeless chunks again and her breath was ragged and coarse. Her hand squeezed my wrist as I wiped the vomit from her gown and cleaned it off her throat and arms. Even as I cleaned her up, she vomited again and again. I was covered with it when she began whispering that she had to get to the bathroom quickly.

"Everything's breaking up. It's coming apart," she whispered desperately, as I lifted her off the bed. She felt weightless and tiny, no larger than a loaf of bread. Her legs collapsed when her feet touched the cold linoleum floor and I lifted her from beneath her armpits and carried her like a rag doll to the bathroom. But as I placed her on the toilet, I saw and smelled the trail of diarrhea left in her path across the hospital room floor. Her insides seemed to fall out as she vomited and sprayed diarrhea everywhere. Tears flooded down her cheeks and she whimpered in humiliation and pain.

"Do the best you can, Mama, and I'll come back for you in a minute," I said, and I shut the bathroom door after clearing the vomit off her once again. I ripped the sheets and blankets off

her bed and changed them quickly. With another towel, I cleaned the trail of puddling excrement from the floor and disinfected it with
Lysol. I scrubbed the walls clean of vomit,
scrubbed myself, and then hurled a bundle of
foul laundry out into the hall. Then I knocked
softly on the door, got control of the panic and
the disgust in my voice, and said, "You okay,
Mama? Everything under control?"

"Could you bathe me, son?" she asked.

"It'd be a pleasure, Mama."

"I stink. I'm a mess."

"That's why they invented soap."

I got the hot water going and placed Lucy
beneath the showerhead. The water healed
something inside her and she moaned with
pleasure as I soaped her down from head to
foot, not feeling a bit odd that it was my
mother's own nakedness I was moving over
with my hands. As I washed her hair, small islands of it came out in my hands and I laid
them like linen on a towel rack just outside the
shower.

When I had dried her off, I put one of her
pink turbans over her head and placed a fresh
hospital gown on her body. I brushed her teeth
gently and let her wash her mouth out with
mouthwash again and again until the taste of
vomit was gone. I touched her cheeks and

throat with drops of White Shoulders perfume, the essence of Lucyhood to me.

When I returned her to her bed, she was already asleep. There were spots where I had not cleaned up completely and this time I went over the entire room from top to bottom and it sparkled when I finished. I arranged the flowers differently, bringing them closer to the bed. I wanted her to awake to the smell of roses and lilies and I even thought about sprinkling the last clear plastic bag of chemotherapy with her perfume.

An hour later, I was content at last that there was no trace of Lucy's violent sickness left in the room and I lay myself down, exhausted, on the cot. The moonlight on my face surprised me, and out the window the Southern stars that were written in the sky like the alphabet above a blackboard confronted me. Their light seemed familiar, comradely. I raised myself up on my elbow and looked out toward the river, which repeated the stars in perfect mimicry like a piece of backlit sheet music. I longed to be freed from all responsibility, to withdraw from all human connections, to hide out in that run-down cabin down the Edisto that could not be reached by postman or car, to live on what could be found in the forest or grown in the clearings or trapped in the river. Then I thought of Shyla. Her memory sharpened its knives against my heart, and there was only agony in its echo and encore. Within me, Shyla was sea sound and wind song. Staring at those stars, I made a constellation out of Shyla's pretty face. She haunted me with light.

Again and again, I sought the cool side of the pillowcase and tried vainly to find a comfort zone somewhere on that unfamiliar, lumpy cot. I tried to hear Lucy's breathing and could only make out the raw choir of insects calling to each other through the vast fields of grass. Finally, I sat up in the old despair of insomnia and saw the moonlight crossing over my mother's exhausted face. Her eyes were open and she was looking at the night sky too.

"I thought it was over last night," Lucy said, her lips chapped and feverish. "If I'd had a gun I'd have pulled the trigger myself."

"I'd've been happy to do it for you," I said. "I've never seen anybody so sick."

"I'll be grateful when it's just me and the cancer again," Lucy said. "This other stuff was made in factories. Leukemia might be killing me but at least it's my own recipe."

"You're going to be just fine, Mama," I said.

"I'm not," Lucy replied. "It's sweet how all my sons pretend I'm going to walk away from this. What's interesting is that I thought I'd be more afraid than I am. Oh, sometimes the fear nearly doubles me up. But mostly I feel a great sense of relief, of resignation. I feel a part of something vast. I was just looking at the moon. Look at it, Jack. It's almost full tonight and I've always known what the moon was doing and what phase it was in even if I wasn't paying attention. When I was a girl, I thought the moon was mountain born like me. I can barely remember what my mama's face looked like, Jack. But she was a sweet woman born to too much trouble. She once showed me and my brother the full moon. She told us about the man in the moon and how everyone claimed they could see a man's face if they stared hard enough. But she had never seen him. Her mother had told her that there was a lady in the moon that very few people ever got to see. It took patience to see her because she was shy about her beauty. She had a shining crown of hair and a perfect profile. The lady in the moon was seen from the side and she was as pretty as those women you see in cameos in jewelry shops in Asheville. You can only see her when the moon's coming up to full. She doesn't show herself to everyone. But once you see her, you never even think about the man in the moon again."

"Why didn't you ever tell us that story?" I asked.

"I just remembered it. Memories of my past

keep flooding in. I've no control over them. My poor brain seems to be in a hurry to think everything it can before the end," she said. "My mind feels like a museum that takes in every painting it's offered. I can't control the flow."

"It sounds kind of nice," I suggested.

"Help me with something, Jack."

"Be glad to, Mama. If I can."

"Since I've never died before, I don't know how to do it right," Lucy said. "I think I know what to say to Dr. Pitts, because he sees me through such a fog of love that he'll never know who I really am. But it's different with you boys. I put you through tests and made you jump through hoops that made your lives hard when they didn't have to be. I didn't know that my ignorance could hurt my kids like it did. Because I saw such awful things as a kid, I thought all I had to do was keep your bellies filled and enough clothes on your backs so you wouldn't hurt during the wintertime. I didn't know the first thing about psychology. Shoot, I was over forty before I knew the word started with a *p*. Psychology was the one animal in the forest I'd never heard tell of. I could track a deer or hunt bears with dogs or wait for a mountain lion to come back to its lair, but how do you set a trap for psychology, for something you can't see or know? I raised five pretty boys who all seem unhappy to me because something was cracked or missing in our family. Everyone seems mad at me. But my errors were made in the act of trying out the high wire. Every time I tried something it was the first time I ever did it. I was a girl who had to learn everything on the run. Trial and error was the only school I went to."

"You did great, Mama."

"I want to thank you for something else," she said.

"No need to," I assured her.

"I never thanked you for teaching me how to read," she said.

"I didn't know I did," I answered.

"When you came home from the first grade, you made me listen to everything you learned in school each day. You made me sit down with you while you did your homework."

"All kids do that," I said.

"See Spot run. Run, Spot. Run. Run," she remembered.

"The plot wasn't very good."

"I lived in terror that someone would find out," my mother said. "You were so patient with me, Jack. I was too embarrassed to even thank you."

"A pleasure, Mama. Just like everything else about you."

"Then why's everybody so mad?"

"Because we can't bear to think about you

dying," I said. "Not one of us can process that one piece of information without going absolutely berserk."

"Can I help you with it, Jack?" she asked.

"Don't do it. Stay here. Get off that train," I said.

"That train stops for everyone," Lucy said.

"Ginny Penn's been dying for twenty years," I said. "She's still around."

"Couldn't kill that girl with a stick," Lucy said, smiling. "Lord, me and Ginny Penn had some fights that Lee and Grant were glad they missed. Did you and Shyla fight much?"

"I don't think we fought much at all, Mama," I said. "We seemed to know what each other was thinking all the time. She seemed just like me in a lot of ways. Do you think Shyla killed herself because I made her unhappy, Mom?"

"No, of course I don't. You two were crazy about each other. She was hearing the voices that killed her when she was a little girl. John Hardin hears those same voices. There's a kind of songbird too pretty to fly with the crows and the starlings. The other birds attack it in flocks and tear it apart when it starts to sing. Nothing soft endures. Nature loathes meekness and goodness. Shyla got hurt early and deep. You kept her from the bridge as long as you could, son."

"You think she and John Hardin're alike?"

"Same tribe. Both of them so full of love it causes an imbalance. They fall over with the unbearable weight of it. The fall becomes what they do best. They grow accustomed to great odds. Love floods them, overwhelms them, and makes them impossible to be around. They need love in equal proportion to what they throw off. Everyone disappoints them. Eventually, they die of the cold. They can never find the right angel."

"I'm a cold man, Mama," I said. "There's something about me that chills anyone who tries to get close to me. I've known women who almost suffered from frostbite after we've spent a weekend together. I don't want it to be that way. But even when I'm most aware of it, I'm helpless to do anything about it. I've told Leah that I think that love is another thing that has to be taught. I think it can be divided into parts, numbered, and named to make its mastery easier. I don't think I was taught it, Mama. I think it might have bypassed you and Dad. Everyone talks about love all the time. It's like the weather. But how does a man like me learn to do it? How do I unlock those pipes and jets where it lies in the deepest part of me? If I knew how to do it, Mom, I'd let everybody have their fair share. I'd spread it around and I wouldn't skimp for anyone. But no one taught

me the steps to that dance. No one broke it
into parts. I think the only way I can love is in
secret. There's a deep, sourceless river I can
tap into when no one else is near. But because
it lies hidden and undiscovered, I can't lead expeditions to it. So I love strangely and
obliquely. My love becomes a kind of guesswork. It brings no refreshment nor eases any
pain."

"Leah. You adore Leah. Everyone knows
that. Especially the child."

"But I'm not sure she feels it. And is my
adoration the love that others talk about? The
danger will come when she tries to love a man
with a love that isn't real. If it isn't, then her
children will have to suffer from the same masquerade. But, except with Leah, I don't know
how to do it. I don't know what it is, Mama. I
don't know what it feels like or looks like or
where to find it."

"It's something that doesn't take to worry
very well. You can't handle it too much. You let
love be and it'll find its own way in its own
time."

"It doesn't work that way for me."

"Love any way you can, Jack," Lucy said. "I
don't think you're very good talking about it. It
comes easier to us girls. You get tongue-tied
and scared every time the subject comes up."

"It avoids me," I said. "I can never say what

I mean about it. I think about love all the time. Why can't there be a definition of it? Nine or ten words that sum it all up, that could be repeated over and over again until it became clear."

"You want to teach Leah about it?" Lucy whispered. "Is that it?"

"Yes—and I can't. I don't have a clue," I admitted.

"You don't need words, son. You've got all the equipment. Tell her love is cleaning vomit off your mother's gown and bed, cleaning diarrhea from a hospital floor. Flying five thousand miles when you hear your mother's sick. Tell her love is finding a very sick brother on the Edisto River and bringing him back without hurting him; bringing a drunk father home a hundred times during your teen years. Tell Leah it's raising a little girl alone. Love's action, Jack. It isn't talk and it never has been. You think these doctors and nurses won't know you love me when they see what you've done tonight? Think I don't know it, Jack?"

"I like it when I've got procedures to follow," I said. "When I'm moving around with something real to do."

"You'll have your hands full in the next few weeks," Lucy said. "I'm starting to run on empty. Time's short, Jack. The cancer's spread to my organs. It's everywhere now."

"Does believing in God help any?"

"Hell," she said. "Believe me when I tell you it's the only thing that helps at all."

Both of us laughed and I propped Lucy up on pillows so we could watch the dawn break together. "There it is again. Talk about dependable."

"Glad to see last night take off," I said.

"I'll be going home this weekend," Lucy said. "No, no. Don't try to talk me out of it. They've done what they can for me here. I'll hire nurses as I need them. I want to die listening to the ocean. I'd also like all my boys around me. All of them."

"John Hardin'll have to do some fast talking up at the state hospital," I said. "He's presently the most famous crazy person in the state."

"John Hardin isn't crazy," Lucy said, her head turned toward the light out of the east. "He's just his mama's boy. He thought if he hid me good enough, then death wouldn't know where to find me."

"Wish it worked that way," I said.

Lucy said, "Maybe it does. You boys didn't give it a chance."

So my mother returned to the Isle of Orion to live out the time allotted her. Though we all knew that Lucy was complicated, unknowable, and difficult, none of us knew exactly how cou-

rageous a woman she was until she began the
business of dying. Daily, she gave us lessons in
the art of dying well. Her house on the beach
filled up with friends who dropped by to make
their farewells and discovered, to their surprise, that they had come to a house of great
joy. Though she may have had many regrets
about her origins, Lucy had discovered most of
the secrets that the South sugarcoated its ladies
with and she charmed her visitors with her vi-
vaciousness. Mama had learned that being nice
summed up every book of etiquette ever written or every code of law passed down by word
of mouth.

On October 10, the last turtle nest of the
season was to be opened, and Lucy demanded
to be present. The cool weather had already
come to the low country of South Carolina, but
the ducks and geese had not yet made their
way this far south on the eastern flyway. We
still went swimming out in front of her house
twice a day and she liked to sit out on her deck
holding Dr. Pitts' hand as I walked out into
deep water with Leah standing on my shoulders or as Dallas swam out past the breakers.

Over a hundred people had gathered for
the release of the turtles when Lucy walked
with our help to the wire-protected nest harboring the turtle eggs that had been moved in
August. Lucy's volunteers had monitored the

emptying of forty-one nests on the Isle of Orion that season. Four thousand, six hundred, and thirty-three baby loggerheads had made it into the water.

Lucy stood before this final nest and asked Leah, "How many eggs were moved to this spot?"

Leah had her notebook and read out, "One hundred twenty-one eggs, Grandma."

"Who found the nest?"

"Betty Sobol, Grandma."

"Ah, Betty," Lucy said. "I've asked Betty to take over the program next year. I think it's time someone else took care of these turtles for a while. I'd like to sleep in with that good-look-ing husband of mine instead of traipsing all over these beaches at sunrise."

There was a brief outburst of applause when the task was passed to Betty Sobol, then the gravity of Lucy's condition quieted the crowd again.

"Does anyone object if Leah takes the tur-tles out of this nest? I'd do it myself, but I'm feeling a bit peaked. Can you do it once more, girl?"

"I was born to do it, Grandma," Leah said, and she knelt down in the sand and began dig-ging as a hundred people leaned forward to watch.

Leah dug down into the caved-in sand,

overcautious at first. Then she smiled, looked at her grandmother, and came up with a black, struggling miniature loggerhead. The crowd cheered when Leah handed it to Lucy. Lucy inspected it and put it in the sand-lined bucket. Leah came up with three turtles in the next scoop of her hand. Within the nest, the scrimmage of shells clicking made it sound like a hundred dice rolling across velvet. When Leah was done, she gathered all the eggshells and began to cover them with sand.

"Save one shell for yourself, Leah," Lucy ordered. "Now, you take these turtles down and release them twenty yards from the surf line. We want them to imprint this island's sand."

"Let's release them together, Grandma," Leah said, and she and Lucy began the slow walk down toward the breakers as the crowd parted to let them pass. It took all of Lucy's strength to make that walk, but no one could deter her, so Tee brought down a lawn chair for her to sit in at the spot where the turtles would begin their long, perilous voyage out into the Atlantic. Their claws scratched against the side of the bucket.

Lucy handed Leah the broken golf club, and Leah began to draw a vast semicircle in the sand that the observers could not cross. Inside this line was the free zone of the infant turtles.

The people on the beach toed the line with their bare feet and flip-flops, but did not cross it.

Setting the bucket on the ground, Lucy nodded to Leah, who turned the bucket gently on its side against the sand and the baby turtles began their four-flippered journey across their birthing ground to the sea. They rushed out toward the brightness of the water with all the fury of pure instinct ignited. Though their gait was comical, it was purposeful and resolute. Theirs was an ancient, frantic march. But these turtles would not meet an army of raccoons or an overflight of seagulls or the ominous gathering of ghost crabs, positioned like a tank battalion, waiting to cut off their dash to the waves. These turtles were cheered and urged on by those who had come to see them safely launched from the Isle of Orion.

The first turtle to reach the wet sand was five yards ahead of any of his competitors when the wave hit him and sent him somersaulting backward as it always did. But the small loggerhead recovered quickly, righted itself, and was a swimmer by the time the next wave hit. Each turtle tumbled when the first surf rushed over it, but each swam with great economy and beauty on the second wave. A single ghost crab moved out of its hole and seized one of the turtles by its neck, and moved in a flash to its lair beneath the sand. I noticed that Lucy too saw this encounter between hunter and prey, but she said not a word. The ghost crab was being true to its own nature and felt no animosity toward the turtle at all.

Soon the first waves were brimming with the shining backs of turtles, glinting like ebony among the snow-white spume. One turtle, confused, got turned around and started back toward the nest, but Leah took it and turned it in the right direction. She looked at her grandmother for approval and Lucy nodded her appreciation of a job well done. When all the turtles had reached the water, we tried to follow their trail by watching their tiny, eel-like heads come up for breath every six or seven strokes.

A seagull, scanning the beach, as it retired from the day's foraging, came up from the south, and the crowd moaned as it hung still as laundry over the surf line, then plunged down and came up with a loggerhead in its beak. The gull bit the head off the turtle, then dropped the rest of its body back into the ocean.

"I hate seagulls," Leah said.

"No, you don't. They do a good job at what they do," Lucy said. "You just love loggerheads."

• • •

In the week that followed I cooked fabulous meals for anyone who came to the house to say good-bye to my mother. Hundreds came and it moved us greatly that Lucy's life had not gone unnoticed by her townsmen. As her children, we knew all about Lucy's strangeness and insecurity, but we also knew about the unstinting nature of her sweetness. She had camouflaged the vinegar factory in her character with a great honeycomb along the sills and porches of her public self. The black leaders came, dressed in strict formality, to let her know that they remembered the extraordinary courage of the wife of the "Nigger Judge." I learned that week that my mother possessed a small genius for the right gesture. She had done thousands of things she did not have to do only because they felt comfortable to her. She had been prodigal with unnoticed, artless moments of making people happy to be alive.

Lucy could not eat a single thing that I cooked for her, yet she bragged that her friends had claimed they had never eaten so well, not even when they went to watch the Braves play in Atlanta. No one entered the house whom I did not feed, and I stayed at my command post in the kitchen because I was having difficulty controlling my helplessness. I could not get over the fact that I was facing a motherless world for the first time and it made me look at

Leah with new eyes as she played hostess, greeting people at the door and asking them to sign the guest book. Leah had informed me that school was not as important as helping her grandmother die and I wondered that such wisdom had issued forth in a girl so young.

One day, very late, Dr. Pitts picked up the telephone in the living room and dialed a number with all the rest of us present. We heard him say, "Hello, Judge," and I listened as he invited my father to come out. Still uncomfortable around the boisterousness of my brothers and me, Dr. Pitts had made certain that we understood that he needed our help in the days to come.

Those days came swiftly. I found that, though I had prepared myself for my mother's death, I had not readied myself for the details and what death would require of me. I watched the slow process of my mother becoming a complete stranger, a woman devoid of energy and animation who never left her bed, a hostess who could not rise to greet her guests. Her eyes grew dull with painkillers and she would ask Leah to lie down with her for a nap, then be asleep before Leah could even respond. Her bloodstream ripened its betrayal of her and grew dangerous as pitchblende to her health. Her decline steepened its angle hourly. What had been a slow, invisible process for so long began to show itself on the surface and accelerate the pace. Then the terrible galloping began.

There was the occasional evening when she seemed better, but they were rare. We swarmed about her, desperate for a task to perform, a heroic deed to pull off in exchange for Lucy's life. Our source was flickering out. We had grown out of this departing body. We were natives of the body now killing her. We poured each other drinks, clung to each other, and burst into tears while walking on the beach at night when the claustrophobia of death became too much for us. I thought my mother needed the ministrations and the laying on of hands that a daughter could do so much better than her roughhousing, excitable sons who waited around wishing Lucy would ask us to move a refrigerator or paint the garage. As a group, we were useless, disquieted, and in the way. The nurses were interchangeable, sweet, and efficient. We wanted to hold her in our collective arms, pass her around from son to son, but we were shy about touch, deficient in all displays of physical affection, and afraid we would break something as the withering began its work and her skin took on the pallor of writing paper.

Lucy seemed to rally one day and the spirits of the entire house rose with her like some flood tide cleansing the marshes after a hard winter. That morning when I brought in the breakfast that I knew she would not touch, I found Lucy sitting up with Leah, teaching her how to apply makeup. Leah had apparently made a mess of putting lipstick on her own and Lucy's lips, but she was doing better the second time around. I laid the tray down and watched as my mother passed on the mysterious rites of cosmetics to my daughter.

"Close your eye when you put the eyeshadow on. Then open it ever so slightly. You want the eyeshadow to coat both lids evenly. That's right. That's good. Now, let's go on to perfume. Remember, less is more when it comes to perfume. The reason a skunk's a skunk is he doesn't understand moderation. I'm leaving you all my makeup and perfume. I want you to think about me when you use it. Let's redo your foundation. What do you say?"

"Sure," Leah said. "But do you feel up to it?"

"Leah's too young to wear makeup," I said, aware of my echoing Lucy's criticism in Rome, and how prissy and parental I sounded.

"Maybe," Lucy agreed, "but not too young to learn how to put it on. Besides, I'm not going to be around to teach her the tricks of the trade. I'm ignorant about a lot of things, but I'm Leonardo da Vinci when it comes to makeup. Leah, this is part of my legacy to you. You're collecting your inheritance, honey."

Later in the morning I found Leah reading a children's book to Lucy in her clear, musical voice. I could hear Italy sneaking into Leah's pronunciation of English and it always pleased me. I sat down listening to Leah read *Charlotte's Web* aloud. I had read the book so many times to her that I could almost speak along with her, word for pretty word.

Lucy smiled at me and said, "No one ever told me these stories when I was little. What a nice way to go to sleep."

"Why didn't your parents read to you, Grandma?" Leah asked.

"They couldn't read, darling," she said. "Neither could I until your daddy taught me. He ever tell you that?"

"It was our secret, Mama," I said.

"But ain't it a sweet thing for Leah to know about her daddy? He wasn't just my boy. He was my teacher too," Lucy said, and fell into a deep sleep.

Father Jude arrived from the monastery that night and Dupree picked up John Hardin at the state hospital. Esther and the Great Jew were coming out of the bedroom with Silas and Ginny Penn when John Hardin entered the house where the fresh flowers were beginning to die in the vases and a low tide made the sea

riper and more aromatic as a wind blew in from
the east. Ledare was fixing drinks for the adults
and I was fixing enough pasta carbonara to
feed a rugby team. In a guest bedroom, Jude
went to prepare himself for the administration
of the last rites. For a solid week he had prayed
and fasted for his sister. His faith was unshak-
able and he believed that any of Lucy's sins
were lightweight to the God who had wept his
way through this unendurable century. The entire monastery had stockpiled prayers for Lucy.
She would enter paradise buoyed up on a field
of praise, well recommended, and extremely
well regarded by a small platoon of holy men in
the service of the Lord.

That night Father Jude said Mass and Lucy
asked that he say it in Latin and that Dupree
and I serve as altar boys. The French windows
were thrown wide open and the sea air entered
the room like an extra communicant. Lucy
asked her brother to add a prayer for all her
loggerheads now swimming toward the kelp-
draped sluices of the Sargasso Sea. After she
received Communion, we bowed our heads,
then each of us, her sons, took the hosts on our
tongues and I prayed for her with all the fierceness that had come to me in this moment. Tears
got in the way of my prayers. Now my prayers
did not float like wood smoke toward the
heights of the world, but were set adrift,

stained and waterlogged with tears. The air tasted like salt and so did the faces of friends and relatives when they kissed me.

Late that night, Lucy called for just me and my brothers to come to her alone. We went reluctantly as though the colonel in charge of a firing squad had just sent for us. The summons had come at last, the inexorable violation. It seemed as though these last days were the only moments I had ever lived life to its fullest, when we gathered in agony to say good-bye to our mother. But Tee hesitated on the threshold of her room and would not move.

"I can't do it," Tee said tearfully. "I don't have it in me."

When he finished weeping, he got control of himself and followed us into the room. By this time, we, too, were exhausted and knew that dying was a full-time job, more hard labor than some palmy, soft surrender to the night. It took enormous concentration for us to look toward our mother. Lesions had formed on her gums and lips as her body no longer fought infections. She had given death all it could handle but her hard, unyielding body had now been tested to its limits. Her rosy complexion had yellowed and something dark was moving close to her eyes. Her stillness began its silent walk as we waited for her to speak. Dallas handed her a glass of water and she grimaced in pain as she drank. The water glass was stained with blood when he set the glass down.

As she tried to speak, John Hardin, fidgety in the solemn atmosphere, started: "Mama, you wouldn't believe what just happened. The doctor came in and said, 'Lucy's gonna be her old self by tomorrow morning.' The doc was laughing and said he'd just run a few more tests and found out it wasn't leukemia after all. Hell, he screwed up the original diagnosis. It's just a head cold, or psoriasis at the very worst. Said you'll be playing thirty-six holes of golf a day by next week. Come on, you guys. Put smiles back on your faces."

Dupree shrugged and said, "I made a bad mistake springing him on a pass."

"Hush," Lucy whispered. "I got something to say to you."

We grew still as the ocean spoke to the night a single wave at a time.

"I did the best I could for you boys," she said. "I wish I had done better by you. You should've been born in the house of a queen."

"We were," Dupree said in a barely audible voice.

"Damn right we were," said Dallas.

"Shhh," Lucy said, and we had to lean forward to hear her. "I should've loved you more and needed you less. You were the only things I ever got for free."

"Mama, Mama, Mama," John Hardin said, sinking on his knees beside her, and sobbing, Lucy lapsed into her final coma hearing the first word that all of us spoke in the English language. Into that night, my mother slipped away from me.

It took Lucy forty hours to die and we hardly left her side. Doctors and nurses came and went, checking her vital signs and making her comfortable. Her breathing became an agonized, desperate noise. It was a ragged and hydraulic sound, and for me it became the only sound on earth.

We spent those last hours kissing her frequently and telling her how deeply we loved her. Then I began to read Leah's children's books out loud to her. She had lived a storyless childhood, so I read in the last day of her life the books she had missed. I told her about Winnie the Pooh and Yertle the Turtle, took her *Where the Wild Things Are,* introduced her to *Peter Rabbit* and *Alice in Wonderland.* Each of us took turns reading to her out of *Grimm's Fairy Tales,* and, at the very last, Leah insisted that I tell all the Great Dog Chippie stories I had told her during our years of exile from the family in Rome.

I told Leah's favorite Great Dog Chippie

stories to my brothers' amusement, but then I saw the moment they got hooked by the power of the stories themselves. I watched as Leah took turns sitting in my brothers' laps and I thought how wonderful it must be to have an excess of adoring uncles to choose from.

Then, an hour before Lucy died, I told one last story of that splendid dog who had died before John Hardin or Tee ever got to know her well.

"In a pretty house, on a pretty island, in the pretty state of South Carolina, a woman named Lucy was getting ready to make her last journey. She had already said her good-byes and gotten her affairs straight. She had kissed her granddaughter Leah farewell and had taught her how to do her nails and apply makeup to her face. Her sons had gathered around her and she had made all of them feel good by choosing the right words to make them remember her fondly forever. Even though her favorite son, by far, was Jack, she was equally nice to all of them at this moment of departure."

Even John Hardin laughed good-naturedly at this aside.

"It took her a long time to die because she loved the earth and her town and her family so much. But when she left she was amazed to lift out of her body and rise above the house and the ocean. She looked down on the moon and

the stars and the Milky Way, free of her body,
and she felt winged and floating and beautiful
as she spun around in the sweet light of stars
she passed.

"Then she came to the place she had heard
about. It was in a field of wildflowers surrounded by mountains, prettier than the Blue
Ridge, higher than the Alps. Lucy had never
felt as at home before. This was the place, she
knew that, but did not know it by name.

"Lucy heard a voice thunder out above her.
She knew it was the voice of God. It was stern,
but lovely. She awaited his judgment with confidence, with ardor. Her granddaughter Leah
had applied her makeup for this long trip home
and Lucy knew she was going to look pretty to
the God who had created her.

"But another voice sounded behind her and
it terrified her. Lucy turned to see Satan and
his armies of demons crossing the field to claim
her as their own. Satan was puce-colored and
hideous and he danced up behind Lucy where
she could feel his hot breath on her neck.

"Satan roared, 'She is mine. I claim her for
the underearth. She has earned her portion of
fire honestly. You have no business with this
one and I claim for hell what is mine.'

" 'Slowly, Satan,' the voice of the Lord rang
out. 'This is Lucy McCall from Waterford. You
have no claim on this woman at all. Though

you want every soul that comes this way, you did not earn this one.'

" 'I claim her anyway, Lord. She has suffered much on earth and she is well accustomed to pain. Pain is what she knows best. Without suffering, she would never feel at home.'

"Though Lucy struggled mightily, she felt Satan's hand tighten around her throat and when she tried to speak she could not form the words and found herself being dragged out of the field so fragrant with wildflowers. Lucy thought she was doomed to hell for all eternity when she heard something . . ."

"I know what she heard," Leah squealed.

"What's that?" her uncles asked.

"She heard, 'Grrrr-grrrr.' "

"Where was that sound coming from?" Dallas asked.

"It's the Great Dog Chippie," Leah said. "Just in the nick of time. She'll save the day. Even if God can't. Right, Daddy?"

"The fangs of the Great Dog Chippie were white and wolflike. Her lips were curled and her black, muscled body looked like a panther's walking toward Satan. The other demons shrank back in terror, but not Satan. But Chippie had never approached an enemy with such ferocity. Her eyes were yellow and she moved in for the kill. She crouched, ready to spring at the source of all evil. The dog had come to greet the woman who had found her as a stray, taken her into a house full of children, fed her, stroked her fur, loved her as a dog needed to be loved.

" 'Ha!' Satan cried out. 'You think I should fear a dog.'

"He was addressing God himself, still holding Lucy.

" 'No. You need not fear a dog,' God answered. 'Except for this one.'

" 'Why this one? Why this cur?'

" 'Because I sent the dog. The dog does my will,' God answered.

"And the Prince of Darkness released Lucy and returned to his house of fire.

"Lucy went to her knees and kissed the Great Dog Chippie and accepted her kisses in return. Then the dog led the way through flowers, toward the light."

That night Lucy died with my brothers and me around her. When the undertaker came to take her body the next morning, her nightgown was still wet from the tears of her five sons, two husbands, one brother, and her granddaughter Leah McCall. The world seemed to stop when she stopped breathing, but a high tide was on the way into the rivers and sounds, and the sun lit a fire on the horizon, the first sunrise Lucy had ever missed since she had slept in her seaside house.

At her funeral Mass, one could hear an entire town mourning. Her five sons and her ex-husband, the judge, served as her pallbearers and they carried the beautiful, polished coffin her son John Hardin had made for her to the front of the church. It was a gray overcast day and Dr. Pitts wept during the whole service as did Dallas, Dupree, Tee, John Hardin, my father, and I. There was not a stiff upper lip among us. Lucy's love had indentured and leveled us; her tenderness leaked out of us. She left us hurt and powerless, on our knees. At the cemetery, my brothers and I buried her, taking our time speaking with her as though she could hear us. I had lost the word "mother" forever, and I could not bear it.

After listening to the condolences of the town, which had gathered at the house on the Isle of Orion, tired of mourning and depleted from the effort of smiling, I put on my bathing suit and with Leah went out for a long swim in the ocean. The water felt warm and silken and Leah's hair glistened like a seal's as she dove off my shoulders and rode the huge breaking waves all the way to shore. I said little but took comfort and undiminishable pleasure in the physicality of swimming, the pull of the tide, the swell and rocking of the ocean itself. Leah

had learned to swim like an otter, throw a
shrimp net as well as I could, and could already
slalom behind a ski boat. She was becoming a
low country girl and I held her close to me as
we rested in the surf twenty yards from shore.

"Look, Daddy," Leah said. "Ledare's calling us in."

On the shore, still dressed from the funeral,
but barefoot now with her black dress and
pearls, Ledare waved to us and we both swam
toward her.

When we reached the shore, Ledare held
something in her hand. "Betty Sobol just
brought this by. Someone found it wandering
on the golf course. She thinks it's been lost for
days."

Ledare opened her hand and in it was a tiny
loggerhead turtle, but pure white, the first albino I had ever seen. It was motionless, and
Ledare said, "Betty thinks it might be dead.
She was wondering if you and Leah would take
it out to deep water. If it's alive, she doesn't
think it could survive this surf."

I took the turtle in my hand and held it like
a pocket watch in my palm. "No sign of life," I
said.

"Let's put him in the water, Daddy," said
Leah. "We'll go as deep as we can."

I put Leah on my shoulders and I began
walking toward the strong waves, bracing my-

self as they broke across my chest. I handed the turtle up to Leah and told her to keep it high above her head, away from the waves.

"Even if it's not alive, Leah, it can become part of the food chain," I said.

"Great, Daddy. Being part of the food chain."

The walk against the tide was a struggle, but when we were beyond the breakers, Leah handed the lifeless turtle to me. I checked it a last time, then took it and plunged it into the rich warm Atlantic waters. After a few moments, I felt the loggerhead stir once, then I felt the ignition as the turtle moved all four flippers and the life force of instinct burned through every cell in its body.

"It's alive," I cried out to Leah and I released the turtle at the surface. Both Leah and I then swam beside it as the albino got its bearings, drew in a breath, and disappeared from sight. Dog-paddling, we saw the tiny white head come up six feet away from us, then plunge again. We followed the turtle until we reached water over my head. Then we swam back to shore, where Ledare was waiting for us.

EPILOGUE

THE FOLLOWING SUMMER, LEDARE Ansley and I got married in the city of Rome and invited everyone we loved to the wedding. When we wrote the movie that Mike Hess had hired us to write, we discovered that we could not live without each other. When I finally got around to asking her to marry me, I found out that Ledare and Leah had recently picked out her wedding dress in Charleston; she had already made up a guest list and written out the announcement for the newspaper. The only person surprised by my falling in love with Ledare was me. But I had lived a long time knowing of the hardships and perils that eat around the edges of even the strongest loves. I wanted to be absolutely sure.

I popped the question to her at a party we gave for Jordon Elliott the day before he began serving his prison sentence at Fort Leavenworth. He had received a five-year prison term for manslaughter and malicious destruction of federal property. The lead prosecutor wanted to put Jordan behind bars for twenty years for murder, but Capers Middleton worked out a deal after convincing the federal authorities that a whole monastery would testify to Jordan's saintly attributes if the case ever came to trial. General Rembert Elliott moved to Kansas to be with his son for the entire period of his incarceration. Throughout the pretrial maneuverings, the general was fiercely protective of his son at every step. Each day, General Elliott visited Jordan in prison, and a deep affection grew between them. To their surprise and delight, they discovered how deeply a friendship between a father and son could cut through all the hurt and refuse of a troubled past. In the ruins of their lives, they had found each other and clung to each other and became reconciled even to their amazing differences.

On the night before the wedding, Ledare and I walked up to the Janiculum with the ancient, misted city spread beneath us in a secret hive of final, rushing motion before the sun's last light splashed along the fringes of the western hills. The last party we would ever attend without being man and wife was in preparation down there amid the pale lights that came on one by one in the many neighborhoods. I had decided that the Janiculum was the right place to give Shyla's letter to Ledare. The letter explained some things in a clear, exact way that I knew I could never manage to express. In a courtroom long ago, it had won me the right to raise Leah after the Foxes had sued me for custody of their grandchild. It had touched me deeply, blindingly. It had let me know that I had once known a passion that very few men or women would ever know or feel or even long for in their entire lives. It was the reason I could let Shyla go, but never tell her good-bye. Now, on the night before my wedding to Ledare, I needed to break off and to let the love of Ledare perform its gentle work on my damaged, Southern heart.

"So, here it is," Ledare said, as I handed it to her. "The famous letter."

"It deserves to be famous," I said. "You'll see."

"Who's read it?" she asked.

"The courts of South Carolina and now you," I said. "I won't give it to Leah soon. She's been through enough for a while."

"I'm already jealous enough of you and

Shyla, of all that I think you had together," Ledare said. "Will this make it worse?"

"It'll explain it. Part of it's written about you."

"About me?"

"You'll see."

Ledare took the letter out of the envelope carefully. It had been written quickly and it took her a while to grow accustomed to the idiosyncrasies of Shyla's troubled, hurried hand.

Dear Jack,

It shouldn't end this way, but it must, my love, I swear to you it must. Remember the night we first fell in love, the night the house fell into the sea and we learned we couldn't keep our hands off each other? We couldn't imagine then loving anyone else because of the fire we started that night. And remember the night we conceived Leah in the bed on the top floor of the Hotel Raphael in Rome? That was the best for me because we both wanted a child, the best because we were turning all the craziness and desperation of our lives into something that indicated hope between us. When you and I were right, Jack, we could set the whole world on fire with our bodies and make the world perfect.

I didn't tell you why I left you and Leah, Jack, but I'm telling you now. It's crazy again. And this time it's too much. The lady came back. The lady of the coins came back, the woman I told you about when we were kids. She only came to stare at me and have pity on me when I was a child, but this time she came back cruel. This time she talked in the voices of Germans and spat at me for being a Jew. As a girl, Jack, I couldn't bear what my parents had suffered. Their pain touched me as nothing else ever has. I woke up every morning to their unspoken grief, their war with the world that no words could ever explain. I carried their pain inside me like a child. I sucked on it, fed off it, let it ride in my blood in shards and crystals. Never have I been strong enough to measure up to my parents' terrible history. What they endured tortures me, moves me, makes me wild with helplessness.

The lady of the coins is calling for me now, Jack, and I can't resist her voice. I have no coins sewn into the buttons of my dress to buy my way out or pay anyone off. The camps call me, Jack. My tattoo is fresh and the long ride in the cattle cars is over. I dream of Zyklon B. I have to follow the voice and when I leap off the bridge, Jack, I am simply going to the pits of the starved and broken bodies of six million Jews and throwing myself among them because I can't stop their haunting of me. My mother's and father's bodies lie among these slaughtered Jews and they weren't ever lucky enough to get to die. In these pits, where I've always dreamed I belonged, I'll take my rightful place. I'll be the Jew who pulls the gold teeth from the dead, the Jew who offers her emaciated body for the making of soap to wash the bodies of the soldiers of the Reich as they battle on the Russian front. It is madness, Jack, but it is real. It's always been the truest thing about me and I beg your forgiveness.

But, Jack, Dear Jack, Good Jack—how can I leave you and Leah? How do I tell the lady of the coins about my love for you both? But it's not my love she's after, it's my life. Her voice is so seductive in its brutal sweetness and she knows her business well. She knows I can't love anyone when my country is the country of the altered, the obsessed, the weeping, and the broken.

It's for the best, Jack, the best for me. After I'm gone, please tell Leah all about me. Tell her all the good parts. Raise her well. Love her for the both of us. Cherish her as I would have. Find the mother in you, Jack. She's there and she's a good mother and I'm depending on you to find and honor her and raise Leah with that sweetest, softest part of you. Do the job I was supposed to, Jack, and don't let anyone stop you. Honor me and remember me by the adoration of our child.

And, Jack, dear Jack, you'll meet another woman someday. Already I love this woman and cherish her and respect her and envy her. She's got my sweet man and I'd have fought any woman in the world if she'd tried to take you away from me. Tell her that and tell her about me.

But tell her this and I'm telling you this, Jack, and I want you to listen to it.

I'm waiting for you, Jack. I'm waiting in that house that the sea took the first night we loved each other, when we knew that our destinies had touched. Love her well and be faithful to her, but

tell her I'm getting that house ready for
your arrival. I'm waiting for you there
now, Jack, while you're reading this letter. It's beneath the sea and angels float
in its corners and peek out behind the
cupboards. I'll listen for your knock and
I'll open the door and I'll drag you up to
that room where we danced to beach
music and kissed while lying on the carpet and I dared you to fall in love with
me.

Marry a nice woman, Jack, but not
one so nice that you won't want to get
back to me in our house beneath the
sea. I hope she's pretty and I hope she'll
love our daughter as much as I would
have. But tell her I won't give you up
completely, Jack. I'll let her borrow you
for a little while. I go now, but I'll be
waiting for you, darling, in that house
pulled into the sea.

I command you, Jack, as the last cry
of my soul and my undying love for you,
marry a fabulous woman, but tell her
that I'm the one who brought you to the
dance. Tell her that you have to save the
last dance for me.

Oh, darling
Shyla

Ledare read the letter three times before she folded it carefully and handed it back to me. For several moments she did not speak, trying to hold back her tears.

"I can't love you the way Shyla did, Jack," she said, at last. "I'm not built that way."

"It was a mistake to show you the letter," I said.

"No it wasn't," she said, taking my hand in hers and kissing it. "It's a beautiful letter and a heartbreaking one. As your bride-to-be, I find it a bit intimidating. I find it unanswerable."

"So do I," I said. "In some ways I've been a prisoner to that letter. I used to cry every time I read it. I quit crying a couple of years ago."

"Let's go down the hill and have a hell of a life, Jack," Ledare said. "Let's love each other as well as we can. But Shyla can have the last dance. She earned it."

Jordan had sent a long letter from his prison cell in Leavenworth blessing our marriage and promising to say a Mass for us that same day in the States. He had learned that cells held no fear for him and that the discipline of prisons seemed almost lax to him after following the strictures of the Trappist rule for so long. He had written to me about the prison ministry the authorities allowed him to run and the courses in both theology and philosophy he taught to the inmates. He said it made him ache for humanity to see so many men in such great and ceaseless pain and it alarmed him that so few of them knew how to pray for relief of their suffering. It was not that the other prisoners were godless men that disturbed Jordan, but the fact that their belief in God gave them so little comfort. They talked to him about the stultifying emptiness of their American lives. Their spirits were bereft and undeveloped. Dreamlessness made their eyes vacant and trapped. Jordan had never met so many men in desperate need of spiritual advice.

In one letter he had written that he was very happy. His time in prison had reintroduced him to the world and had made his commitment to the priesthood all the stronger. It had ratified and enhanced his vocation. He had turned Leavenworth into a wing of his monastery and he infused many of his fellow prisoners with the strange luminant beauty of a Trappist's willful solitude. Jordan wrote that he prayed often and did his best to atone for the crime he committed while being a hot-blooded young man when he, along with his country, split apart along some central seam. Daily, he prayed for the repose of the souls of the young man and woman he had killed by accident, but killed nonetheless. He also sent his love and blessings and asked that he be allowed to marry us again when he got out of prison.

I wired him that same day that Ledare and I would not really consider ourselves married until he personally blessed our union.

The next day, on the morning of the wedding, Leah and I left the Piazza Farnese for a walk through the brown dazzling alleyways of the city where she had lived most of her childhood. I wanted one last morning with my daughter alone and Ledare had understood perfectly. When it was right, I thought as I walked hand in hand with Leah, the love between us contained elements of tenderness and reliance and secret conveyance that made it different from all other forms of love.

Since hearing the stories of George and Ruth Fox, I often found myself looking at Leah and trying to imagine her being loaded onto a cattle car or her head being shaved before she stumbled toward the gas chambers or her small hands raised up in terror as she was being force-marched through a village to a freshly dug pit where the machine-gunners awaited her. I drank in the beauty of my daughter and knew I would kill every German in the world before I would let them hurt my child. I could not bear the thought that the world had once been demonic enough to hunt down and exterminate children as though they were insects or vermin. Leah McCall, daughter of a Jewish woman, would have been black ash hanging over the mountains of Poland had she been born fifty years before this day, I thought, tightening my grip.

But on this morning, I told Leah the story of Ruth Fox and her harrowing survival during World War II. I described the murder of Ruth's family, her escape into the world of the Catholic Resistance, and her hiding in a convent until the Great Jew miraculously ransomed her out of wartime Poland and brought her to Waterford, South Carolina. For the first time I told Leah about the dress her great-grandmother had sewn for her daughter Ruth, and how that long-dead woman had hidden eight cloth-covered gold coins as buttons which Ruth was to use to buy her way out of trouble.

As we drifted past the dark shops, I felt the power of the story grab me again as I told Leah how Ruth had concealed the coin-laden dress behind an altar where the Virgin Mary stood crowned as the Queen of the Angels and how her grandmother Ruth had prayed to this woman that she knew had been born a Jew in Palestine two thousand years ago. I told her that Ruth had believed her whole life that Mary had heard and answered the prayers of one Jewish girl who asked for her intercession in a church in war-torn Poland. Ruth had called the statue the lady of coins and it was a story that had marked Leah's mother Shyla deeply and for all time.

On Ponte Mazzini, overlooking the Tiber, I presented Leah with the coin necklace that Shyla had worn every day of her life, except her last one. In her will, Shyla specified that the necklace be given to Leah when she was old enough to hear the story. She trusted me to make the decision when that would be.

"When the war was over, Ruth had three coins left in her dress. She had necklaces made with each one of them. She wears one of them. Aunt Martha has another. This was your mother's necklace, Leah. It was her most beloved possession. I'd like you to remember her every time you wear it. And remember your grandmother's story."

Leah put on Shyla's necklace and her neck and shoulders were as lovely as her mother's. I was starting to notice the first shy ripening toward womanhood and it both touched and frightened me. I prayed that Leah would have the good fortune to fall in love with a man completely different from myself, a man less tortured and with a smaller stable of demons, one who loved laughter and language and possessed a small genius for sunniness and joy.

"I'll wear it every day of my life, Daddy," Leah said.

"Your mama'd love that," I said. "We better be getting back, kid. You've got to help me get married today."

Leah said, "I can't wait. It's about time you got me a mother, don't you agree?"

"Yeh," I said. "I agree. By the way, Leah. Thanks for being the kid you are. You are the sweetest, nicest, most adorable child I've ever seen in my life and you were that way from the day we brought you home from the hospital to right now. I didn't do a goddamn thing except watch you in utter admiration and fascination."

"Take a little bit of credit, Daddy," Leah said, studying the gold coin on the end of the necklace before looking back at me. "I didn't grow up by myself. You raised me."

"It was a pleasure, kid," I said.

Late that afternoon, our wedding party gathered on the Capitoline hill, in a piazza designed by Michelangelo. Storm clouds were gathering and a light breeze from the Apennines suddenly turned gusty, and sheets of newspaper winged across the paving stones. The banns of over fifty couples were posted in the glass-encased bulletin boards that lined the outer wall of an ancient building that was part art museum and part wedding chapel. It was to this spot that Romans came to have their marriages legalized by the city of Rome. The banns were written down in an Old World showy penmanship. All around us, in distinct and separate groups, lovely Roman brides with their dark, nervous fiancés stood uncomfortably among their jubilant families, waiting for their names to be called in the overcast piazza. Looking around, I thought the human species was in fine shape and tried to think of something more beautiful than women and couldn't come up with a thing. The propagation of the species was a dance of total joy.

When our names were finally called, a loud cheer went up from our friends and relatives who had come to Rome for the ceremony. A large, rowdy contingent from Waterford had arrived the week before the wedding and it reminded me that there was no wilder crowd on earth than a group of traveling Southerners. They whooped and hollered as they made their way into the grand hall which smelled of leather and old velvet and whose high-ceilinged stateliness silenced everyone as we moved toward the solemn men, elegant and impassive as llamas, who would conduct and record the ceremony forever in the annals of Rome. The South Carolinians gathered on the left side of the aisle and my Roman friends took their seats on the right. Leah's teacher, Suor Rosaria, was there, sitting beside Paris and Linda Shaw, and she blew me a kiss. I bowed to the Raskovic brothers, and waved to the waiter, Freddie, who had deserted Da Fortunato at noon to be at our ceremony. Several of the doctors who had cared for me after the airport massacre were there. Marcella Hazan and her husband had come down from Venice and Giuliano Bugialli drove down after his cooking class in Florence had finished for the week. Journalists and great cooks had come together to celebrate the marriage of one of their own. I took a quick, silent survey and figured that at least thirty cookbooks could be accounted for on this side of the chapel. If a bomb exploded during the wedding, I thought, the eating habits of half the world would change.

Ledare blew kisses to our smaller South Carolinian contingent. My brothers and their families had arrived two weeks early and had traveled all over Italy in a whirlwind tour I had arranged. Ledare's mother brought smiles to the Roman side when she waved one finger at them and drawled, "Ciao, y'all." She and her husband had brought Ledare and Capers' children with them. The Great Jew was there with his wife, Esther, accompanied by Silas and Ginny Penn, who had made a full and unexpected recovery from her broken hip. In Rome, she remained peevish because she thought the Italians spoke a foreign language just to be peculiar and irritate her. Dr. Pitts sat in the back with Celestine Elliott, who still had not spoken to her husband after his part in putting Jordan in jail. Three of Ledare's suitemates from the university were there with their husbands. Mike arrived late, bringing with him the achingly beautiful actress Saundra Scott, who would later become his fifth wife. Shyla's sister, Martha, sat in the front row with her fiancé from Atlanta.

My father was not present and had sent a brief note explaining ". . . that I'm still drunk and probably always will be. I can't make it, Jack and Ledare, and there's no excuse for it. I just can't. My wedding present to you is that I won't embarrass either of you at your wedding. It's the best I can do."

The magistrate performing the ceremony cleared his throat and motioned that the ceremony was about to begin. Leah moved up beside us holding a bouquet of flowers and wearing a white silk dress that made her long dark hair look like black flame against her shoulders. On her bare throat she wore Shyla's necklace and the profile of Tsar Nicholas was as sharp as the outline of Leah's collarbones.

I bent down to kiss her and was surprised when I felt tears on her face. "Why are you crying?"

"Because I'm happy, silly," Leah said.

Ledare and I took our places in two gilded, elaborately carved chairs. Beside us sat the best man and the matron of honor, the choice of whom had become the subject of some controversy.

We had chosen George and Ruth Fox, and when both families had begun to object we told them the decision was not discussable.

It had been Ledare's idea and tears came to my eyes when she told me. Ledare had a lifelong instinct for the proper gesture and the moment of grace, and she recognized in both our lives the terrible, ineffable need for reconciliation and healing. I had told Ledare what the Foxes had endured during the war and how it had pained me that I had learned it so late. By asking Shyla's mother to be her matron of honor, Ledare thought she was making a statement of pure love to Leah. My asking George Fox to be my best man would hopefully heal some of the old wounds and scars between us. It would also bring the spirit of Shyla into the proceedings and remind everyone of how much history and heartbreak had led to this wonderful moment when Ledare and I would pledge ourselves to each other for the rest of our lives.

Then Ledare and I stood and looked at each other and both liked what we saw.

When the magistrate pronounced us man and wife, our friends and families rose and gave us a standing ovation as I kissed Ledare.

We all returned to the Piazza Farnese and had the wedding reception on the terraces of my apartment, my brothers having brought tapes full of Carolina beach music. The South Carolinians taught the Romans how to shag that night and the party did not break up until two in the morning. In an amazing show of graceful diplomacy, Dallas, Dupree, and Tee knew better than to play "Save the Last Dance for Me." But they would tell everyone in South Carolina from that day forward that they had introduced beach music to Italy.

I was serving cognac to the last guests when Ledare came over to tell me that she was going with her two children to take her parents back to the Hassler Hotel. I told her to let me come with her, but she pointed to all the people still lingering in the living room and said that she wanted to tuck her parents into bed. Both had drunk too much Italian wine and my brother Dupree had offered to drive and John Hardin wanted to go along for the ride.

"But it's our wedding night," I said, and she stood on tiptoes to kiss me.

"I'll wake you up," she promised.

"I won't be asleep," I said. "I want to see the sunrise."

She smiled. "You made a good decision."

"Never made a better one."

"I'll hold you to that," she said.

"That's why I gave you that ring," I said, pointing to her gold band.

"And that's why I accepted it."

When the party was finally over, I went up to the terrace again and looked out on the tawny, many-alleyed city. At night it looked carved from brown sugar. The two fountains spoke to each other in the pretty speech of falling water on the piazza below. I wanted to thank the city of Rome for healing me and treating me with kid gloves when I was broken on the inside. Rome had taught me that beauty alone was sometimes enough; it had sheltered and nursed me and put me back on course. I tried to find the words to thank a whole city and I looked out into the rooftops at the bright lights burning on the street along the Tiber and told myself I would one day write a love letter to Rome that would contain all the praise and thanks I could summon for my time here. There was a noise behind me and I turned to see Leah coming up to be with me.

"I thought you'd gone to bed," I said.

"I was too excited to sleep," she said as she took my hand. We looked out onto the piazza together, my daughter and I, who had made our life here for so long, looking down onto this spacious and comely piazza. I owed so much to this child and this city and I realized that words were sometimes nothing more than notes you wrote to your deepest self as you fought to articulate the splendor and the magic and the ineluctable sense of loss that you felt in the swift, disturbing hours.

"It's been you and me alone for a long time, Leah," I said, as a single car passed below us in the night.

"Too long, Daddy," she said.

"We've been like the Lone Ranger and Tonto," I said.

"Better than that," she said.

"I think so too."

"Daddy."

"Yeh, kid."

"I couldn't help thinking about Mama," she said. "I felt bad because I was really happy for you and Ledare."

"Don't feel bad," I said. "I've thought about her all day too."

"Why?"

"Because I wanted to tell her everything about the wedding," I said. "We used to talk about everything. I wanted to let her know about you, me, and Ledare."

"What would you tell her, Daddy?"

"That I thought we were going to be all right," I said.

"Better than all right," Leah said. "We'll be great. We'll be a family."

"You've always wanted that, haven't you, kid?"

"Uh-huh. But I wanted it for you, more

than me. You were so lonely, Daddy. I couldn't stand it that you were so alone."

"I should've hidden it better."

"No one else knew it," she said. "But don't forget: I'm your girl. There's not much I don't know about you."

A car pulled up to our building and we watched Ledare and my brothers get out of it below us. Dupree and John Hardin stripped down to their underwear and climbed in the great fountain and began swimming, Dupree going underwater, and John Hardin doing the backstroke. Leah broke free from me and ran down to join Ledare, who held their clothes.

I laughed to myself as I watched my brothers enjoying their illegal swim. Tee and Dallas came out the front door with Leah, and Tee plunged into the deep fountain without even removing his suit. Leah joined him in her party dress and I watched it all unfold below me in a world that seemed far away, yet very dear.

I began to fade out in this dream of a world with the rest of my life spread before me. I was grateful for so many things that they seemed uncountable.

I wished my mother and father could have been here to share this evening with me. I tossed out a prayer to Lucy and I thanked her for loving me as well as she could. She had cherished me in her own way and she had made me feel kingly in a town where they had once laughed at her. I gave thanks to my brothers and my friends, my hometown and my home state, and my love of good food and travel and strange places. There was a fullness to my life now I was just recognizing. I had come to Rome a hurt and Shyla-haunted man and I knew now there were worse things to be.

I heard the voices of those I loved laughing in the piazza below. I thanked the world for bringing them to me. Then I gave myself for a last time to Shyla Fox and let her spirit wash over me and forgive me my happiness.

I thanked her to myself and apologized that I had to leave her now. Though I did not speak out loud, I told her that I had been as true to her as I knew how to be and that I would never have left her, no matter how grievous her suffering or permanent her scars. Closing my eyes, I filled up with my incurable need for Shyla again, my love for that girl who used to approach me through the secret, leafy avenues of an oak, who reconfigured my entire world by opening up the deposits of her soul for my inspection.

"Jack," I heard a voice call out from down below me, and it surprised me but there was my wife. Looking down, I saw that Ledare had joined her new family swimming in the dazzling fountain. She had always been a beautiful swimmer and she was side-stroking with Leah beside her. Her wedding dress clung to her, and my brothers and daughter waved for me to join them. I caught a glimpse of my left hand and was surprised to see it change forever with the ring that Ledare had bought and placed on my finger that day. I touched the new ring and it felt very much like new life.

Before I went down to join Ledare and the others, I remembered my appointment and I smiled, knowing that one day Shyla and I would be together again. Because she had promised it and because she had taught me to honor the eminence of magic in our frail human drama, I knew that Shyla was waiting for me, biding her time, looking forward to the dance that would last forever, in a house somewhere beneath the great bright sea.